REBIRTH

Necrotic Apocalypse Book Five

D. PETRIE

MOUNTAINDALE
PRESS

CHAPTER ONE

"Who the fuck are you?" Becca stood staring into the crimson eyes of a woman shrouded in darkness.

"You can call me Abby." She stepped forward out of the gloom and gestured to a name tag pinned to the lapel of a black vest.

Becca read the name over three times, having no idea if it should mean something to her or not. The last thing she remembered was being betrayed by Bancroft's men and trapped aboard a sinking cargo ship. Digby and Parker had found her, but she had been bitten by a revenant and the sun was setting. She'd been left with only one option to protect her friends.

"I killed myself."

Becca remembered plunging an icicle through her own heart.

There hadn't been time to think of anything else. Taking her own life had just seemed like the most reasonable thing to do given the circumstances. A memory passed through her head of Digby reaching toward her as the ocean dragged her away into the bowels of the ship. She forced the image away. She didn't want to remember the devastation on the zombie's face. It felt like it had happened only seconds ago.

Now, somehow, she was a long way from there.

The shadows filling the edges of her surroundings retreated little by little, revealing more until the entire space was visible. She was standing in the aisle of an old-style train, with wood paneling and brass covering nearly every surface.

Becca pressed a hand against her chest. Her body was as solid as she had been while she was alive, complete with a steady heartbeat. The rumbling of the tracks below matched the vibrations she felt in her feet. From the motion of the car she rode in, they were traveling in a circle along an incline. Becca glanced from left to right, finding a row of bench seats facing forward on either side, each upholstered with red velvet. Windows lined the walls but she couldn't see anything outside.

"We're going up?"

"Yes. Think of it as decompression. The essence that surrounded your spark before is not compatible with this realm, therefore you need to absorb more to be able to interact with anything here." The strange woman stood in the aisle facing her. Her hair was green to match her fingernails. She was dressed in a black vest and matching slacks, making her look like some kind of caterer or bartender.

"Okay, Abby? Where the hell am I?" Becca took the offensive.

"You're dead." The woman shrugged. "And you could stand to be a little more polite."

Becca hesitated, breathing in a lungful of air. It smelled earthy but somehow clean. "Why do I feel so real?"

"This realm is one of perception. Being real is all you have ever known, why wouldn't you perceive yourself the same here?" She placed a hand to her chest, displaying the flawless green polish that covered her nails. "I don't normally come to meet new arrivals, but considering that you showed up on the same day that another two Heretics somehow opened a passage to this realm, I thought I should check in."

Becca glanced to her HUD.

It was gone.

Obviously, the two Heretics that she mentioned had been Digby and Parker.

"How do you know I'm a Heretic?" Becca fished for more information, trying to get an understanding of who she was dealing with.

"You were a Heretic. You stopped being one when you passed," the woman corrected. "And it's one of the few things I am informed of when someone arrives here, along with how they died, of course. You seem to have passed when a curse pushed your spark from your body."

Becca caught a detail that didn't make sense in her words. Surprisingly, her mind hadn't tried to dispute the fact that she was dead, but instead, the manner in which her death had happened. "I didn't die from being bitten by a revenant, I died because I stabbed myself in the heart."

Abby clicked her tongue. "That's not what I was told."

"Well, that's what happened," Becca snapped back, unsure why she was even angry about it.

"What did you stab yourself with?" Abby folded her arms.

"An icicle." Becca gasped as soon as she said it, realizing the mistake she'd made in the last chaotic moments of her life.

The reason for the discrepancy was obvious now that she was able to look back on her actions. Icicles were great for killing revenants since they held the wound open to stop the creatures from healing. Then again, that only worked if the icicle stayed in position. In her case, she had been washed away by the ocean right after impaling herself. The combination of her body heat and the rushing water must have dislodged it. The passive healing that came with the curse would have handled the rest.

"Oh no." Becca leaned on the back of the seat next to her as the horror of her mistake sunk in. "There's still a revenant of me down there on Earth." She paused, looking back to Abby with a worried expression before adding, "Or, up there on Earth?"

"It's not quite as simple as being up or down." The red-eyed woman sucked air through her teeth.

Dread bubbled through Becca's stomach as she tried to convince herself that her mistake hadn't gotten anyone killed. That her revenant hadn't hurt anyone she cared about. "It's okay, it has to be. Digby is dead, I wouldn't have attacked him. And the seawater probably carried me far enough into the ship to give the others time to escape." She snapped her attention back to the woman waiting patiently for her to work through her trauma. "I didn't hurt anyone, right?" Becca spun, making sure the train she was on was empty beside her and the crimson-eyed woman. "They would be here if I had killed them, right?"

"I don't know." Abby shrugged.

"How can you not know? You're Death, aren't you?"

"Oh, no, I'm not." Abby suddenly looked embarrassed. "I was the Heretic Seed's original caretaker before it was shattered. I'm as dead as you are. I just have a few perks because I used to manage the Seed's connection to magic and the weirdness that comes up with it. I had thought my job was finished when I died, but with you Heretics showing up here, I guess I was mistaken."

"And where is here?" Becca let out a frustrated growl.

"We call it Dusk." The woman, who was apparently not Death, gestured to the train around them. "As in the fading light before the dark. And like I said, this place isn't that simple. You've hit somewhat of a speed bump on your way to the great beyond. Not everyone does. In fact, coming here is rare in the grand scheme of things. That is why I don't know anything about your companions."

Becca slapped a hand to her head and dragged it down her face, having trouble processing the information. "I'm so confused."

Dying was somehow the least of her trouble.

Becca had never been religious. Hell, she had always just assumed there was no such thing as an afterlife. Now, not only was she wrong, but apparently, the afterlife was different from what anyone had predicted. To make matters more confusing, she was talking to some random ass woman claiming to be the Heretic Seed's original caretaker, whatever that was. From Abby's description, a caretaker sounded a lot like some kind of system administrator.

Was that even possible? Could the Heretic Seed be that straightforward?

Becca let out a long sigh as she lowered herself into one of the train's bench seats. She dropped her head back, leaving her feet in the aisle as she stared up at the ceiling.

"You're confused? How do you think I feel?" The Seed's original caretaker scoffed before plopping down in the seat across from her. "I haven't seen a Heretic in centuries. And suddenly the world ends and you all start popping up again. It's great that there's someone to stand up against Autem back there in the world, but I'm not exactly caught up on the situation."

"Wait, you said not everyone comes here? That this is just a speed bump on the way to the great beyond?" Becca sat back up. "Could I go back?"

Abby's mouth fell open at the absurdity of the question. "That's not really how death works." Then she closed her mouth. "Wait, what did you just say a moment ago about someone being dead?"

Becca jabbed a thumb into her chest. "Yeah, I'm dead."

"No, not you." Abby waved a hand back and forth. "You said Digby is dead, so you wouldn't have attacked him as a revenant. What did you mean by that?"

"Oh yeah, Digby, he's probably one of the Heretics you met. He's a zombie." Becca shrugged, having nothing left to offer.

The woman's crimson eyes widened as she dug her green fingernails into the cushion of her seat. "Oh no. I knew there was something off about him."

"What do you mean by 'oh no'?" Becca arched an eyebrow.

Abby cringed a little. "Just, um, out of curiosity. How important to the fight with Autem is your zombie friend?"

"Very important, he's the leader of the Heretics. There wouldn't be anyone to fight back if it hadn't been for him." Becca narrowed her eyes at the woman. "Why, what did you do?"

"What did I do? Nothing." Abby raised a hand, holding her thumb and pointer finger an inch apart. "But I may have given your friend just a tiny bit of bad information about his spark."

"What?" Becca leaned forward, staring directly into the woman's otherworldly pupils.

From there, words began falling from Abby's mouth in a long sentence filled with assumptions and misunderstandings. "Well, you see, your friend told me he had a shard of the Seed lodged in his heart, which I assumed meant it was embedded in his chest next to his heart, not in his actual heart, because, well, you know, if it was in his heart, he'd be dead, and the idea that I was talking to a zombie wasn't exactly my first thought. I was more concerned with how two people from the mortal world had somehow opened a passage to the realm of the dead."

Becca shook her head. "But why is that important?"

"It's important because your zombie friend wanted to know how to access the Heretic Seed's full power, and I told him that to do that, he needed to remove the Seed's fragment from his chest and put it back. That doing so would allow the Seed to absorb his soul and convert it into a new caretaker."

"And you wouldn't have told him that if you had realized he was dead?" Becca tried to follow along.

Abby hissed air through her teeth. "I might have at least given him a warning."

"A warning about what?" Becca tapped a finger, her body tensing in anticipation of the answer.

"That depends." The Seed's original caretaker frowned. "How stable would you say your friend Digby is, you know, mentally speaking?"

Becca folded her arms, deciding not to sugarcoat things. "He's an impulsive narcissist, with delusions of grandeur, whose primary motivation is spite."

"That," Abby paused before adding, "is less than ideal."

"Why?"

"Because giving up his spark to create a caretaker would basically leave his body without a soul." She nodded as if still doing math in her head. "If I remember correctly from my time in the Seed, if your friend was human, that wouldn't be a big deal. Humans can exist fine without a soul for quite some time. Most will reach old age and die before it presents a problem. Obviously, having the lifespan of a Heretic complicates the issue. Over time, they may begin to lose things like empathy and self-awareness, but it is still quite manageable. The worst that can happen is that a soulless human might become somewhat of a jerk. And the world is already full of those."

"But," Becca added the word she knew was coming.

"But, for a zombie, things are a little trickier." The past caretaker tapped a finger on the back of the seat in front of her. "A zombie with a soul is not unheard of. After all, the heart is an important center for the mana system and as a part of that system, the spark flows through the heart continuously. By eating enough hearts in a short amount of time, a zombie can consume trace amounts of their victim's souls, and that can create a stable spark within them if done so fast enough."

Becca gasped, finally understanding how some of the other conscious zombies she'd met had been created. Zombies like Rufus back in California and Clint who had been produced by Henwick. They both had been zombie masters and had eaten plenty of hearts before becoming aware of their actions. After that, they had seemed downright human despite being walking corpses. She filed that bit of knowledge away as Abby continued.

"The problem is that in a normal human, the spark acts in tandem with their mind, with both reinforcing the other. Each part holds the same information to make sure the other remains balanced. The human brain is like a machine, one that needs to be maintained so that it continues to operate as a true representation of the person it belongs to. The spark monitors and updates itself with every new development so that when the person dies, it can carry them into the afterlife."

"Okay, so the soul is a backup system." Becca nodded along.

"Yes, and the reason a zombie that possesses one can continue to operate with a mostly normal human mind is because their spark is constantly restoring the information in their necrotic brain."

"Oh shit." Becca started to see where things were going. "And what happens if there's no spark to restore a conscious zombie's mind?"

The Seed's original caretaker cringed again, before quickly adding, "A rapid descent into madness, followed by a complete unraveling of their consciousness. After that, they would become nothing more than a mindless walking corpse. It would be a true death in that they would simply cease to exist. The only thing that would remain would be the soul that still exists within the Seed as its caretaker. Though, there is a limit to how that version of him can communicate with the outside world."

"Well, shit. Why the hell did you tell him to give up his soul?" Becca sprang up from her seat.

The caretaker jumped up as well. "I didn't know the whole situation. I told you already, it's hard to stay up to date with everything back on Earth when you've been dead for centuries."

"Why, then, didn't you ask questions before handing out life-altering advice to a couple of Heretics that had popped in for a visit from the mortal realm?" Becca's voice climbed with each word.

"I was trying to be mysterious." Abby stomped a foot. "Your friends aren't exactly the brightest, and I thought that maintaining an air of authority was the best way to make sure they took me seriously."

Becca groaned and walked to the rear of the train only to

pace back to Abby. "Okay, I get that you're some kind of age-old system admin, but with all due respect, what the hell?"

"It's alright." Abby stood up from her seat. "We can fix this."

"How?"

"The caretaker!" She brightened up.

"Isn't that you?" Becca eyed her.

"No, not me. The other one. The version of your zombie friend that has joined with the Seed. He should be able to…" She trailed off, only to add a disappointed, "Shit."

"Shit, what?" Becca was getting sick of asking for clarification.

"The Seed's caretaker is too new." She deflated. "When I took the job, it took weeks to learn how to fill the role. I'm sure the Heretic Seed's caretaker would be able to save the zombie version of itself if given the time, but time is not a luxury that we have."

"Of course not." Becca threw up both hands.

The caretaker perked up regardless. "It's okay. I'm sure there is a way to fix everything. We just have to do some research."

"We?" Becca placed a hand to her chest. "What am I going to do?"

"You're coming with me." Abby turned toward the front of the train. "We'll reach the city soon. Once we're there, we can try and figure out a way to help your friend repair his spark. I'll need you to carry a message back to tell him how to fix it."

"But you just said there was no way for me to go back? Which is it?"

"You can't go back, at least not permanently. That's not something I can do from this side. But there is a way to send someone back long enough to give a message, provided we have someone here that has a close personal connection to a person back on Earth. We just need to teach you how."

Becca's mouth fell open at the thought of going back, even

if it was only temporary. She'd left so much behind. So many people.

Would she get to see everyone?

What would she say to them?

Would she get to say goodbye this time?

That was when her mind circled back around to something else Abby had said. "Wait, we're heading toward a city?"

Abby chuckled, still facing the front of the train as the lights of a subway platform became visible up ahead. "Of course there's a city. This is the afterlife. And I can tell you one thing, it's far more than anyone has ever imagined."

Becca's heart began to beat faster as her mind started to accept what was happening.

"What do you say, Rebecca Alvarez, are you ready to learn the secrets of the afterlife?" The Heretic Seed's original caretaker turned back to give her an excited smile only for her face to drop a second later. "Hey, what is going on with you, there?"

"What?" Becca screwed up her eyes at the question.

"What's all this?" Abby raised a hand to gesture to Becca's general area.

"What?" She repeated, this time louder, as she looked down at her body. A startled yelp escaped from her mouth as soon as she did, finding her feet barely visible. Only the faintest of outlines of her shoes stood upon the carpeted aisle. A trail of color streamed behind her as if her physical body was somehow being drained away.

That was when she realized she couldn't feel her heart beating anymore.

"That's not good." Becca raised her head just as an unknown force yanked her backward.

"Wait!" Abby's hand snapped out to catch hold of her wrist, nearly falling over as soon as she did. She grabbed one of the nearby seats to brace herself.

"What's happening to me?" Becca's voice climbed into a shrill panic as she lost contact with the ground, her legs flying out behind her. It felt like something was pulling at everything that she was, stripping her away, little by little.

"I don't know what this is." Abby held on tight to her wrist. "It has never happened before. But I think something is summoning you. Something powerful!"

Becca glanced behind her as the door at the rear of the train suddenly swung open with nothing but darkness beyond. Wind filled the train like a giant vacuum was trying to suck her right out of it. She wasn't sure how she could tell, but somehow, something was beckoning her. No, that wasn't right. It wasn't asking.

It was demanding.

Becca snapped her head back to the caretaker struggling to hold on to her wrist. "Whatever happens to me, promise you will find a way to save Digby!"

Abby's eyes widened. "I can't! Not without you to help."

"Arg! What good are you?" Becca reached forward with her free hand to grab hold of one of the seats only to have it pass right through the cushion.

"I'm sorry, I don't—" the Seed's original caretaker started to say before a wild look entered her crimson eyes. "Wait, if I can't help, then you need to find another caretaker."

"But you said the Seed's caretaker couldn't help?" Becca's vision faded as her eyes lost form, leaving her to shout over the roaring wind. Abby's hand slipped through her own, the force behind her tearing her from the train as a fading voice shouted to her.

"There is another caretaker!"

Those were the last words Becca heard before her head ceased to exist. Everything was drained away until there was nothing left but a single point of shining light.

A spark, plummeting into the dark.

CHAPTER TWO

FIVE MINUTES EARLIER...

Alex stared down at his feet as he lay in a bed propped up by pillows in the medical area of the casino in Las Vegas. His toes hurt on account of being rammed into a pair of woman's red sequined shoes that were far too small to fit him. The slippers had been the first thing he'd asked for as soon as he came out of surgery to remove a magekiller bullet from his skull.

"Did it work?" Lana asked from the foot of the bed.

The nineteen-year-old student-turned-emergency-surgeon had dug the magekiller bullet from his brain with a pair of tweezers. The infirmary that they had set up in the casino was a far cry from a hospital, but it served their needs well enough. Lana's healing magic had taken care of the rest.

"I don't know, maybe." Alex stared at the shoes a little harder to compensate for the fact that he only had one eye left after the surgery. For a second, he thought he felt something tug on his mana, but there was no way to be sure if the enchantment on the shoes had worked.

Alex tried not to think of everything that had happened

during the night. He tried not to think about everything they'd lost.

A bandage was taped over the empty space where his left eye used to be. Now, it was just an empty socket. Apparently, too much of the organ had been lost for Lana's healing magic to repair it. His depth perception was going to be a problem, but at least he was alive. That was more than he could say for Becca.

"Still nothing?" Lana checked again.

"I can't tell." Alex sighed and dropped back into the pillows behind him. "Who knows if these shoes even have the power to bring back the dead."

There was no way to know all the spells that existed in the world, but according to the pair of slippers' description, they would let the wearer cast any spell once. Alex had hoped that there might be a spell that could bring Becca back to life, soul and all. But after trying nonstop for a few minutes, he was feeling less confident. Surely, a spell that powerful would draw enough mana from him that he would feel it something to know it was working.

"Have you tried clicking your heels together?" Parker sat up in a bed across from his. She hadn't been hurt, but she'd never been one to pass up a place to lie down. Plus, she hadn't exactly gotten much sleep after everything.

Alex sat back up and clicked his heels together. "I don't think that makes a difference."

"It might not work without a body." Lana sat down at the foot of Parker's bed.

"True, but there could also be a time limit to how long a person can be dead before bringing them back becomes impossible. And I don't have a clue how we would be able to get her body back anyway." Alex dropped back down and stared up at the ceiling, still getting used to how the world looked with one eye missing.

"It was worth a try." Parker shrugged. "I mean, it's Becca. If there is a way to bring her back then we gotta try."

Alex closed his remaining eye, cursing Bancroft and his mercenaries for putting the magekiller bullet in his head. If they hadn't, he wouldn't have been silenced. Then he could have just cleansed the curse that had taken his friend's life. Most of all, he cursed himself for falling into Bancroft's trap in the first place. Then again, they were bound to lose someone eventually. It had been a miracle that so few had died already.

Still, losing Becca hit different.

"I guess that's that." Alex sat back up and kicked off the shoes. "I'm going to need something to hide these in. As of now, only a few people even know the slippers exist and I'd like to keep it that way. They may not be able to bring back the dead, but they could still be capable of something dangerous."

"That's reasonable. I can take them down to the casino's vaults." Lana walked across the infirmary to grab a first aid kit, emptied it, and put the shoes in. "If these slippers really can cast every spell in the world, then having them around feels like leaving a loaded gun laying out in the open. Even a stray thought could smite a building."

"Well, at least we know there's no spell to bring someone back from the dead." Alex scratched at the bandage that covered his eye.

"Or someone has already used the shoes to cast a revival spell sometime before we got them," Parker added.

"I suppose that's possible." Alex nodded. "The description of the shoes says that they can cast any spell, but only once. Henwick could have already used that spell up." He pushed the subject aside and glanced back to Lana. "How's Mason doing?"

The soldier had also been shot with a magekiller round but unlike Alex, it had been lodged in his gut. Surprisingly, that had turned out to be worse since the positioning of the bullet continued to cause damage as time went on. In the end, he had been in worse shape.

"I got the bullet out of Mason before I came in to work on you. He recovered almost instantly after a couple heal spells. Took off as soon as he was able to walk again." Lana pointed to the ceiling. "He went upstairs, should still be there. I can't imagine what he's going through. He was closer to Becca than anyone."

"I know." Alex lowered his head.

Parker slid out of her bed and walked over to his. "How are you doing, though?"

Alex blew out a sigh. "I don't know. I always try not to think about this stuff. Everyone I ever knew died a month ago, but this…" He paused. "Losing Becca isn't something I can just block out."

"I get that." Parker nodded. "I try not to think about what happened to my…" She trailed off as she rubbed at her temples.

"You alright?" Lana's expression grew serious, clearly entering doctor mode. "Headache?"

"Yeah." Parker closed her eyes tight. "I've been getting them ever since I got back from my little adventure with Dig through the Seed's battle royal. I'm starting to worry that it has something to do with this weird messenger class that I've been given."

Lana began a short examination of the pink-haired woman. "I can't say that doesn't worry me too. But it could just be migraines or a side effect of being unconscious for so long. Why don't you come back for a thorough check-up later when I don't have another patient in the room?"

"You got it, doc." She gave her a thumbs up.

"Technically, I'm not a doctor." Lana deflated a little. "You know, 'cause I never went to med school."

"Yeah, but you did just take a bullet out of my brain an hour ago." Alex slid his legs out of bed. "And I still know my ABGs."

"You mean ABCs." Parker arched an eyebrow at him.

"I'm kidding." Alex chuckled as he stood up, only to stumble a few feet as soon as he put weight on his legs.

"Easy now." Lana caught him. "I get that you have magic

and all, but there is still a chance that you have some kind of brain damage left over."

"That's not good." Alex shuddered, realizing that he shouldn't have been stumbling with his heightened agility. He took a few seconds to steady himself, then he glanced to the info ring at the corner of his vision to open his stats. The little circle snapped front and center in response to show him what he feared.

STATUS
Name: Alex Sanders
Race: Human
Heretic Class: Artificer
Mana: 325 / 325
Mana Composition: Balanced
Current Level: 28 (6,078 experience to next level.)

ATTRIBUTES
Constitution: 46
Defense: 41
Strength: 42
Dexterity: 41
Agility: 18
Intelligence: 44
Perception: 41
Will: 67
AILMENTS
Brain Cloud, Demerit to Agility.

"I have a brain cloud." He stared at the status condition. "What the hell?"

"Hmm, apparently that's what the Seed calls brain damage." Lana furrowed her brow. "There must have been some tissue that was too far gone to repair, the same as your eye."

"Yeah, and it dropped my agility below the level for an

average non-magic person." He sat back down on his bed. "Fuck me. It's eighteen. That's twenty-five points less than I had!"

"Damn." Parker pointed to her head. "But you did get shot in the brain, so overall, that's not so bad if you think about it. Sure, you can't do a backflip, but beyond that, you'll live."

"I guess." He grumbled at the loss of his ninja skills. "I hate this."

"I know." Parker placed a hand to her chest. "But would you rather be a messenger and have no idea what that even means or how to learn more spells?"

"That's fair." Alex stood up again. "We should probably get out of here and make sure Digby is okay. He's been through a lot too, and I don't really want to leave him on his own for long. There's no telling what he might do to deal with everything."

"That's probably a good idea. He can be…" Parker hesitated before adding, "Unpredictable."

"That's putting it nicely." Alex turned to Lana. "Do you have an eye patch or something in the medical supplies?"

"Oh, I think so." She headed for a box that sat on a shelf and produced a plastic pouch. "Here you go."

"I guess it's a pirate's life for me from now on." Alex tore open the plastic, finding a simple black eye patch. He grimaced. "It looks like one you would get with a cheap Halloween costume."

"Did you think I would have something cooler?" Lana folded her arms.

"I don't know." He shrugged. "But it would have been badass if I could get one of those ones that you wear at an angle."

Lana frowned. "Sorry removing a bullet from your brain wasn't good enough. I'll run out and find you a cooler eye patch, right away."

"You're right." He inclined his head. "I love my new eye patch. Thank you for the brain surgery."

Lana glowered at him. "I'm sure."

With that, he peeled off his bandage and pulled the black elastic band around his head to secure the patch into place.

"Should I take you trick or treating?" Parker smirked.

"Probably not." He sighed. "Not really in the mood for candy."

"True, I'm not either." She frowned and turned toward the door.

Alex gave Lana a final thankful nod and followed. From there, they headed straight for Digby's room. It was empty.

"That's not a good sign." Alex exchanged a concerned glance with Parker.

"We should check on Bancroft," she added, sounding worried.

If Alex knew anything about the zombie, it was only a matter of time before he busted into the traitor's room and tore his head off. Granted, tearing Bancroft's head off probably wouldn't bother anyone at this point. Especially since the news of his betrayal had begun to spread throughout the casino's inhabitants. The sun would be rising soon and people were starting to wake up. It wouldn't be long before everyone knew the losses they'd suffered.

Ultimately, it was going to be a difficult task to keep everyone from demanding a public hanging, considering Bancroft's men had killed so many of their Heretics. They had been people. Some with families.

The whole situation was a mess.

To Alex's surprise, Digby wasn't down by Bancroft's room either. Two guards had been stationed by the door. Tavern would keep the man from escaping, but it seemed wise to keep him under watch regardless. According to the guards, Digby had stopped in to talk to their prisoner. There had been a considerable amount of yelling but Bancroft remained alive after the zombie had stormed off. Beyond that, they had no idea where Digby was.

Turning away from Bancroft's room to continue the search, Alex found Hawk walking into the hall at the other end.

"Hey…" Alex raised a hand toward him, only to trail off and lower it again when a pang of guilt hit him. He'd been so wrapped up in how he was feeling, that he'd forgotten how much worse losing Becca had to be for Hawk. After all, he had just lost the last family member he'd had. They may have only been connected by paperwork, but with the world ending, things like that had become even more important.

"I'm in a hurry," Hawk mumbled as he adjusted the strap of a backpack that he carried slung over one shoulder.

"Where are you going?" Parker gestured to the bag.

"I don't know. Dig wanted me to get a pack ready to leave. He didn't say anything else." Hawk kept walking.

"Hey." Alex reached out for him as two words slipped from his mouth. "I'm sorry."

Hawk slowed to a stop in front of him but avoided eye contact. "For what?"

"You know…" Alex struggled to say her name. "Becca."

"Yeah. It sucks." Hawk shrugged. At first, he didn't seem fazed, though the puffiness around his eyes betrayed him. Alex didn't call attention to it, not wanting to upset him. If he wanted to try to act tough, that was fine.

"Do you know where Dig is now?" Parker asked.

"He said he had to check on something and went down to the lobby. I could have done without seeing him cut that fragment of the Seed out of his heart, though."

Parker gasped. "He did that already?"

"Yeah, he ripped it out right in front of me."

"Shit." Alex took a step back. "I thought we'd at least talk about things first."

"Yeah, well, Dig doesn't seem like he wants to wait around for much anymore. Or at least he's got some plans that he's working on." Hawk glanced back to the door where Bancroft was being held. "I was kind of hoping he'd just eat that asshole already. I don't know what he's thinking, keeping him alive after…" He trailed off.

"I know." Alex sighed. "I'm not really sure what to do with Bancroft either. Not after what he did."

Hawk let out a frustrated growl. "If Dig doesn't kill him, I sure as hell will."

Alex flinched at the harshness of his tone. They weren't the words of a twelve-year-old. There was so much anger in them. More anger than a kid Hawk's age should ever have to bear. Fortunately, Parker chimed in with some sarcasm to defuse the tension.

"Yeah, I'm sure." She rolled her eyes. "That's what we need, a pre-teen executioner."

"I'm just saying," Hawk grumbled to himself.

"I know." Alex leaned to the side to try to get in his line of sight. "But that's not gonna happen. If you need anything else, non-murder-related. Like, if you just want to talk. let me know. Okay?"

"Yeah." Hawk pulled the bag he carried higher onto his shoulder and started walking again. "I gotta get going."

"Okay, but don't go leaving the city with Digby or anything without me. If he has a mission planned, then we need to stay together." Alex would have liked to think he had something more to offer. Some kind words to make the world feel a little less dark for the young rogue. In the end, all he could do was stare at Hawk's back as he disappeared into a room further down.

"Do you think he'll be okay?" Parker stared at the door as well, her eyes glossy.

"I hope so." Alex turned away. "He's a tough kid, and right now I'm more worried about Dig."

Parker sucked in a breath. "Let's get to the lobby."

On the way down the stairs, they ran into a number of people, most offering condolences while adding suggestions for what to do with Bancroft. None were particularly merciful. When they reached the lobby, the people got angrier. Many of the Heretics that had been killed had been volunteers who had already lost their loved ones in the apocalypse, but a few still had families. They wanted blood. Alex tried his best not to say anything concrete about Bancroft's fate.

Obviously, they couldn't just hold someone prisoner forever. Granted, they were still holding two men upstairs that had murdered people under the orders of Rivers, Vegas's previous leader. No one knew what to do with them, so they had just been keeping them up there. That was all well and good for them, but in Bancroft's case, the man was too dangerous to keep around like that.

The idea of holding a public execution, though, felt like taking the city in the wrong direction.

What sort of precedent would that set?

Alex understood the need for justice, and that he had killed people before, but still, executing a prisoner seemed barbaric. It certainly wouldn't lead to the type of society that Alex had envisioned for Vegas. He just hoped Digby might agree. Granted, they couldn't discuss any of it until they found the elusive zombie.

To cover more ground, Alex stopped by the supply counter in the lobby to pick up a pair of walkies before parting ways with Parker. That way they could let each other know if one of them came across Digby.

Alex started to worry when they still hadn't found a trace of him over an hour later. The fact that he had vanished without telling anyone where he was going made it clear that the necromancer was up to something he didn't want others to know about.

It wasn't until the sun began to rise that Parker reported the zombie's location.

"Hey, Alex? Can you come meet me outside on the strip? I found him." Her tone sounded concerned.

Alex raised his radio. "I'll be right there. What was he doing outside?"

A solid ten seconds of silence answered back before Parker spoke again.

"I think you're going to want to come see this for yourself."

CHAPTER THREE

Alex rushed out onto the strip as the few revenants that still stalked the city at night found shelter from the rising sun in the shadows of the surrounding buildings. The creatures weren't much of a threat during the day, provided there weren't any lightbreakers hidden among the stragglers.

It had been over a week since a swarm of the creatures had been released from one of the casinos on the other end of the strip. The survivors had made some progress after Alex had found a way to create new Heretics using the rings of dead Guardians, but Bancroft's betrayal was going to slow them down. Hopefully, the fact that Digby had finished reassembling the Heretic Seed would help them rebuild their Heretics and get the city on track.

Alex found the necromancer right where Parker had told him he was. She was already there, standing in the middle of the strip, looking uneasy. Digby stood a few feet away from her, near an abandoned van, with his back turned to Alex. Asher perched on his shoulder as the rising sun shined down on him to give him a peaceful feel.

"Oh thank god, he's not doing anything crazy." Alex blew out a relieved sigh and rushed toward them.

His relief proved more and more premature the closer he got. First, he noticed the severed limb that the zombie was carrying. It was pale, probably claimed from a revenant. Several large bites had been taken from the side. It wasn't like Digby to eat the old-fashioned way. Not when he could just open his maw.

As Alex approached, he noticed another figure standing behind the van.

An armored zombie, also eating a severed limb, was waiting patiently for new orders from its master. A row of fingers wrapped around its neck like a collar before running down the monster's chest like a zipper of interlocked digits. It was hard to tell with the slabs of necrotic muscle that covered its body and the horned bone mask that covered its face, but Alex was pretty sure it had once been one of Bancroft's men. One of the ones that had betrayed them back on the cargo ship.

He froze when he saw what was laying on the ground at the hulking zombie's feet.

The nuke.

For some reason, Alex had assumed that the warhead had been lost in the desert where Digby had fought Bancroft's men after they left the cargo ship. At least, he'd hoped it had been. Apparently, Digby had retrieved it somehow. He was shouting before he knew what he was doing.

"What the hell is that, Digby?"

The zombie casually turned toward him and glanced down at the severed limb he had been eating. "It's a revenant's hand. I got hungry and one just happened by, so I snatched it up for me and my minion here."

Asher cawed as if to back him up.

Alex nearly fell over at Digby's obvious omittance of the nuclear warhead on the ground beside him.

Parker looked equally shocked. "Dig, I don't think he was

talking about your snack." She whipped her finger out in the direction of the armored zombie and flicked it back and forth between the monster and the weapon on the ground by its feet. "He's talking about that."

"Oh," Digby glanced toward his minion. "That's Ducky, Bancroft's ex-illusionist. I reanimated him after I killed him in the desert. I'm thinking of keeping him around."

"And?" Alex folded his arms.

"Ah yes, you're probably referring to that." The necromancer used the severed hand he was eating to gesture toward the nuclear weapon.

"Ya think?" Parker walked over to the warhead and threw both hands toward it. "How did you even get this thing back here?"

"I ordered Ducky to retrieve it." Digby held his head high, as if proud that he'd thought of it.

"Okay, but why did you bring it here?" Alex deflated with an elongated sigh.

Digby dropped both hands to his sides and leaned his head toward Asher. "Go ahead and take to the sky. There are still some zombie stragglers out in the city and we need them for our horde."

Asher nodded and flapped into the air as Digby turned back to Alex.

"Alright, about this weapon, I couldn't rightly leave it where it was for anyone to find. What was I supposed to do? Bury it like a dog? Besides, if Bancroft wanted it badly enough to hurt so many people, then it must be worth something."

"Are you insane?" Alex slapped a hand to his forehead.

"Actually, he does have a point." Parker crouched next to the bomb. "Leaving a nuke in the desert isn't a great plan." She finished her statement by patting the warhead with one hand like it was a puppy.

Alex winced. "Don't touch it."

"It's not like it's armed." She stood back up.

"Alright, fine." Alex rolled his eyes. They were right. He

might not have liked the idea of using the thing, but at least having it in their possession meant that they knew where it was. "But we need to store it somewhere secure."

"Well obviously." Digby stomped a foot. "I'm not a bloody idiot. I know that this thing could blow all of Vegas off the map. I just want to keep it here until we can use it."

"Use it?" Alex eyed him sideways. "On what?"

"Autem, of course." Digby stared at him as if he was shocked that Alex hadn't come to the same conclusion. "I had a bit of a realization, not long ago. The way I see it, this weapon could even the odds against Henwick. All we have to do is find their settlement over on the other side of this land and blow it up. That'll show Henwick who he is dealing with. He'll probably go hide up on the moon once all his Guardians have been burnt out of existence." He punctuated his plan with a mirthless laugh.

Alex's jaw fell open before he shook off the shock of the zombie's words. "Digby, I know Autem's the literal evil empire, but from what we know, they have taken in hundreds, if not thousands of innocent survivors."

"Yeah." Parker stared at Digby in disbelief. "I'm pretty sure blowing up civilians is a war crime."

"Bah." Digby waved away the concern. "Serves them right for picking the wrong side."

Alex looked to Parker, unsure what to say. The Digby he knew would never have suggested killing innocent people so casually.

That was when Parker gestured to him with her head. "Hey, Alex? Can I talk to you for a second? You know, away from the nuclear warhead?"

Alex glanced at Digby who had returned to eating a severed limb, then back to her. "Yeah, sure."

"We'll be right back." She nodded to Digby before leading Alex far enough away from the necromancer that he couldn't hear them.

"Okay, that was messed up, right?" She looked back to

Digby, making it obvious that they were talking about him if it had not been already. "I get that he's angry about everything, and he tends to talk a lot of trash, but he sounded serious."

Alex avoided looking back at him in an attempt to be subtle. "I get being angry, and I can relate to wanting to hit someone back. But I think I would draw the line at war crimes. And I can't believe Digby would really do it. He might be kind of a jerk, but he's always cared about innocent people before."

"What if he's changed?" Parker made a face that said there was more to her question.

"Why, did something bad happen while you two were in the Seed?"

"Nothing horrible, but we did meet Henwick's spark." She leaned her head back and forth. "The guy's soul stayed with his fragment of the Seed when he removed it from his arm. So the body walking around out here is basically him but without a soul. The problem is that the person we met in the Seed was ultimately a good guy in the end. He sacrificed his existence to save us."

"Henwick saved you?" Alex furrowed his brow.

"Yeah, I got to know him pretty well and, any way you look at it, the man that is fighting against us is a completely different person."

"And you think it's because he has no soul." Alex followed her line of thinking.

"Maybe Digby's sudden change in morals might be related to the fact that he just gave up his spark when he removed that fragment from his heart. I know the original caretaker we spoke to said it should be alright, but he's definitely acting different."

That was when the zombie started shouting at them from across the strip. "You realize I know you are talking about me. You could at least have the decency to include me."

Alex exchanged a look with Parker before returning to Digby.

"Okay, we have a concern." Alex tried to break the ice only for Parker to throw herself right through it.

"We think you might be insane."

"What?" Digby staggered back in indignation.

"Parker told me about Henwick and how he has become a different person since losing his soul." Alex gestured to the nuke. "And we can't help but worry that maybe you needed yours after hearing your plan."

"Bah." Digby rolled his eyes. "I asked the Seed's original caretaker about that and she said I would be fine."

"She did say that." Parker stepped closer to him. "But we didn't have a lot of time and maybe we don't know the whole situation."

Digby glowered at her. "Well, what choice did I have? We needed the Seed's full power. Even if there were clear side effects, I would still have to remove the shard from my heart. We can't afford to pass up power, no matter the sacrifice. Not anymore. Not after…"

"I know." Alex filled the silence as the zombie trailed off. "But you might not be the same person that you were."

"Of course I am. Who else would I be?" Digby threw up his hands.

"A copy," Parker answered.

"No." Alex shook his head. "You're a simulacrum."

Digby's face went blank. "A what now?"

"It's a thing in D&D." Alex spoke faster, excited to be able to apply some gaming terms to the situation. "A simulacrum is basically a magical duplicate. The real you, meaning your soul, exists within the Seed, leaving a version of you out here with us. And it restores your brain whenever it's damaged. So you may feel like you, but the truth is you're a separate entity."

Digby frowned. "I don't love that explanation."

"I don't blame you; I think we all want to believe that we are the original." Alex shrugged. "But in the end, it doesn't matter. To everyone out here in the world, you are real."

"Indeed, I am." The zombie seemed to relax.

"But now that you have lost your soul, there is a chance that you are incomplete."

"I don't feel incomplete." Digby looked down at himself.

"Yes, but you remember what you were like before." Alex twirled a finger counterclockwise. "I want you to think back about everything you've done in the last month, and tell me if the person who did all that would have suggested killing innocent people, including children."

Digby raised a hand to wave the question away only to lower it back down. "Alright, you may have a point. But if my judgment is impaired, what do you suggest I do about it? I can't second guess every bloody thing I do."

"Maybe you could consult the rest of your friends before doing anything significant." Alex shrugged.

"Oh good, all my decisions will be decided by committee." Digby groaned before snapping his eyes to Parker. "How about this, then. Parker will be in charge of me."

"What?" The pink-haired soldier jumped back.

"Yes, that should do it." Digby stepped toward her. "Despite your shortcomings, you showed proper judgment while we were trapped in the Seed together. I can think of no one better to advise me. With you at my side, you can raise any concern about my actions that you might have and inform me if I am about to make the wrong choice." A crooked grin crept across his face. "You would guide me, like my conscience."

"Oh, no way." Parker swung her hands back and forth. "I don't want to play Jiminy Cricket to a zombie. My life is weird enough."

"I fail to see what insects have to do with this." Digby's grin faded.

Alex considered the proposal. It actually wasn't a bad idea. Parker did have a good sense of right and wrong, and he'd seen her stats. For starters, she was smarter than she seemed, and the fact that she had a huge amount of mana would make her a good partner for Digby. If he ever got low on MP and didn't have a minion around, he could always leach mana from her. Plus, having one person keep an eye on the zombie would probably work better than having to consult several.

Alex eyed Parker while scratching his chin.

She grimaced. "I don't like the way you're looking at me."

"It's actually a good idea," Alex admitted.

"Excellent. Then it's settled." Digby clapped his hands.

Parker groaned whilst letting her arms dangle limply at her sides. "I hate my life."

"Sorry, to change the subject, but we really should get that inside." Alex gestured to the nuke.

"Indeed." Digby opened his maw on the ground and tossed in the severed limb he'd been snacking on. Then he wiped his hands on his pants. His clothing was a mess after everything that had happened the night before, anyway. Once his snack was disposed of, he headed for the doors of the casino as Ducky, his armored minion, followed, dragging the warhead behind him.

"Hey." Alex jumped to block their path. "Don't just walk in through the front door."

"Yeah, maybe don't bring the nuclear weapon through the lobby where everyone is having their breakfast." Parker sighed. "I guess that's my first piece of advice."

"Ah yes." Digby pulled away from the door and headed for the parking garage entrance instead.

Alex nodded to Parker as she followed the zombie. She would let him know if Digby was going to do anything that would set the settlement on a dark path.

He watched them walk into the shadows of the parking structure. Something was definitely off about the zombie. Not that Digby had ever been a picture of sanity before. He just hoped things wouldn't get worse.

Then again, they could be wrong.

Becca had been the closest thing Digby had to a best friend, so it was completely reasonable that he was having trouble processing his grief. Lashing out wasn't healthy, but it was understandable.

Either way, Alex couldn't shake the feeling that things were about to get complicated.

He broke into a jog to catch up. "Hey! Wait up!"

For now, all he could do was wait and see.

CHAPTER FOUR

"You have a what?" Deuce's voice came from Alex's radio. The ex-bouncer turned city security chief sounded incredulous.

"We have a nuclear warhead." Alex stood in the garage next to the weapon as he reported the acquisition a second time. He'd made sure to switch to a private channel, not wanting to announce to everyone in the settlement what they had. "I'm going to need you to come get it and bring it down to the vaults."

Deuce had a few other questions as well as some choice comments, but he sent a team out to meet them regardless. While he waited for the nuclear warhead retrieval team, Alex turned back to Parker and Digby, who were standing by the Camaro that Alex had modified to run off mana rather than gas. He wasn't finished with it, but he had managed to get it to float a couple of feet off the ground using the runecraft that he had been able to learn from Autem's warding rods and the Guardian rings that he'd dismantled. All things considered, it was a giant leap forward in terms of the blend between magic and technology.

Of course, this was the first time he'd seen the floating car since they had returned.

"What did you do to my baby?" Alex grimaced at the state of his pride and joy after Parker had driven it across the desert and the ocean to rescue him and Mason from the sinking cargo ship.

"Ah…" Parker trailed off awkwardly.

Alex rushed to the vehicle. "Oh my god, I know it was dark and I was kind of out of it, but I had no idea the car was this bad off. And are these bullet holes?" He picked at the crusty layer of reddish-pink material that coated the hood. The wipers had smeared it all over the windshield. "What even is this stuff?"

"You remember Bancroft's man, Malcolm, right?" Digby hooked a thumb back at Parker. "She hit him at top speed."

"What?" Alex turned to her.

The pink-haired soldier simply held her hands together before pulling them apart to pantomime Malcolm exploding on impact.

"Oh gross." He promptly wiped his hand on his pants.

"Indeed." Digby chuckled. "It certainly was surprising."

"About that." Parker leaned closer to Digby while wrinkling her nose at a patch of gore that was dried on the shoulder of his coat. "I think you still have a piece of… Okay, I'm not even sure what it is, but you need a shower and a change of clothes."

Alex nodded in agreement, expecting the zombie to snap back with an argument.

Instead, Digby simply nodded. "I do need to bathe, don't I? It seems Malcolm got some distance when you splattered him all over the desert." He banged on the Camaro with the back of one hand. "Though, I am impressed that this cobbled-together heap continued to function afterward."

"Cobbled-together? It got us back to Vegas, didn't it?" Alex grumbled, not appreciating his creation being criticized. "And you realize I only built that thing to go about seventy-five miles per hour at the most. To be honest, I can't believe it didn't explode or something with what you two put it through."

"I am glad we didn't explode, then." Digby glanced to Alex. "Death trap aside, the progress you made with those runes is substantial."

"Oh, ah, thanks." Alex scratched at the back of his neck. "I have a lot more ideas, actually."

"Good." Digby picked a piece of Malcolm from his shirt. "Because we're going to need plenty more where that came from."

Alex felt a smile tug on the corner of his mouth. "I think I can do that. I'm really interested to see where these runes can take us. What their limits are. Eventually, I'd love to expand my workshop into a full building. Once I have the rest of the strip warded, we can take over one of the other casinos and turn it into a full-fledged research and development lab."

"You think we can ward the whole strip?" Parker looked back at him.

"Yeah, that part should be easy." Alex reached into his pocket and pulled out a set of warding rods. He had started carrying a few at all times. "These are easy to manufacture once you understand how. The only thing that slows the process down is that there's only one of me."

"That would be amazing." She stretched her arms out. "Imagine being able to walk around outside again without having to watch your back. I'm sure we'd need guard patrols to keep an eye out for lightbreakers, but other than that, life could start to get back to normal. And with the power we're getting from the Hoover Dam, maybe we can turn all the backlights on."

Alex allowed himself to indulge in the fantasy for a moment before returning to reality. "I'd probably keep the lights to a minimum. We don't want Autem figuring out that we're here."

"Indeed." Digby tapped a foot. "No sense advertising our location."

The conversation ended when Deuce's team showed up to

take the nuke. Digby sent Ducky, his oversized minion, with them to help take the warhead down to one of the vaults. The bomb would be safe enough there until they could come up with a better plan for it. Then again, they could just close the door and forget about the nuke altogether.

Either way, Alex didn't want to think about it.

After parting ways with Ducky and the nuke, he headed back upstairs with Digby and Parker to the floor where Bancroft was being held. The zombie passed their prisoner's door without looking at it. He ducked into a room further down the hall, the same one that Hawk had disappeared into earlier.

Following Digby in, Alex found it to be a basic hotel room just like most of the others. The backpack Hawk had been carrying lay on a bed, and the desk that sat against the wall was littered with a collection of seemingly random items.

Glancing down at the desk, a few items stuck out. A copy of Atlas Shrugged, a pair of gold cufflinks, a guardian ring, and a pocket watch. They all looked old but well cared for. The pocket watch still carried a flawless shine.

"Is this Bancroft's stuff?" Alex refrained from touching anything.

"Yes," Digby growled, as if hearing the man's name was all it took to frustrate him. "I cleaned out his room last night."

Parker flipped through the copy of Atlas Shrugged. "What are you gonna do with him?"

"I have been thinking about that all night, actually." Digby stood over the backpack, holding one of the straps taut like he was trying to choke it to death. "It has taken everything I have not to go in there and command Tavern to tear themselves free of their fleshy prison."

"Gross." Parker winced.

"Quite." Digby let go of the backpack's strap. "But as much as he would deserve it, there is much more at play than just finding an adequate punishment."

Alex relaxed a little. "That was my concern as well."

"Yes." Digby unzipped the backpack before looking to Parker. "Hand me that book, would you?"

"Sure." Parker tossed him the copy of Atlas Shrugged.

Digby shoved it in the bag. "The timepiece as well."

Parker grabbed the pocket watch and popped it open. "Oh, fancy."

"Yes, I'm sure." Digby held out his hand. "Sometime this century, Parker."

"Oh sorry." She snapped the watch shut and handed it over.

He shoved that in the bag as well.

"You want the cufflinks too?" She scooped them up.

"No, I can't imagine Charles will need them anymore." Digby zipped the backpack shut. "Besides, Alex can use the gold in his runecraft work."

"Okay." Alex picked up the cufflinks and dropped them into his pocket. "I'll try to make them into something worthwhile."

"Excellent." Digby tossed the bag aside and headed back toward the door. "I am going to do as Parker has suggested. A shower and a change of clothes. I'm afraid I look like a common corpse." The zombie gestured to the black stain that covered his shirt.

"About that." Alex stepped closer. "After you removed the Seed's fragment, were you able to get more access to the Seed?"

"Yes." Digby stood a little taller. "Allow me to show you."

With that, the zombie glanced to the side as if looking at his HUD. The instant he did, Alex noticed a second circle had appeared on the edge of his vision, in the center of the Seed's information ring that had already been there.

"There. That should give you the same control that I have. I can't give this power to anyone else, unfortunately. Only you, because your connection to the Seed was established by the black ring I gave you back when we met." Digby held up his hand to display the delicate pattern of runes that traced a line around his finger. "From what I learned from my time trapped in the Heretic Seed's realm, the rings were an attempt by Autem to control the Seed's power, much like the system that they eventually created as the Guardian Core. I only found the rings by chance all those centuries ago, but thanks to them, we have a special rank that sets us above the rest of Vegas's magic users. It allows us to take magic away from any that step out of line. Even block specific spells and abilities from individuals."

Alex frowned, not liking how that last part sounded. If they started giving and taking magic away from people, it would be easy to take things too far. That alone gave him and Digby a tremendous amount of power over the people.

Digby sighed a moment later. "I just wish I could have given this power to Rebecca. She would have known how to manage it."

Again, Alex noticed the pain in the zombie's gravelly voice.

"You okay?" Parker gave him a sympathetic look.

"I'll be alright." Digby gave a half-hearted shrug. "It just doesn't feel real. I keep expecting one of her projections to show up any minute."

"That would be nice." Alex let a sad smile show for a moment.

"Anyway." Digby turned toward the door, seeming a little more like himself. "I must get cleaned up. I'd like to meet back downstairs by the fountain in the settlement's center in one-half hour."

"Sure, and I'll familiarize myself with the changes to the Heretic Seed." Alex followed him to the door.

Parker motioned to follow Digby but hesitated. "Do I, like, go with you now?"

Digby narrowed his eyes at her. "I am going to take a shower."

"Hey, I've never been someone's conscience before. I don't know how this is supposed to work."

"Well, you don't have to follow me around every second." He sighed. "I'm sure checking on me once a day and accompanying me on missions will suffice."

"I ain't arguing." She held up her hands. "I didn't want to watch you shower, anyway."

"Good." He stomped out of the room in a huff.

Alex ignored them, too excited to see what new options the Seed offered. He glanced to the new circle in his vision, watching it snap to the space in front of him and expand into three separate windows. Each populated themselves with text while organizing into an overlapping system of menus. The layout shifted depending on which he was focused on, to keep that one on top of the others.

"Oh wow."

"Good for you." Parker folded her arms, clearly annoyed that she hadn't gotten any new options.

Most of the information was self-explanatory. In the first circular window, there was a list of names. Digby Graves, Charles Bancroft, Alex Sanders, Parker Earner, and so on. It was a list of every Heretic that had been created so far, in order of level. By focusing on any of them, he could re-sort the list by any descriptor he wanted. He focused on Parker's name, causing the display to fade away to make room for a new one that showed her basic stats and her two spells. There was also a log that showed each use of her spells so far, complete with time stamps. That part would be important if they were going to share magic with everyone. If there was no way to hide a spell's use, then there would be no way to misuse the power without being caught.

Alex willed the Seed to return to the menu with the three rings that had been displayed before. The list of Heretics wasn't particularly long, but he reordered it a few times and read each name to make sure Becca wasn't somehow still listed.

She wasn't.

Her absence in the readout made his stomach turn, his grief coiling through his insides.

The second circle in the menu held a list of every spell that had been unlocked collectively by all Heretics. By focusing on any one spell, the first list would reorganize itself to show only the Heretics that had the spell in question. So far, there was nothing that he hadn't already seen, except, of course, Parker's two messenger spells.

This will be useful.

The third window was even more important. At the top, the word Covens was listed. Digby's name sat below as leader, with Alex and Asher underneath it. He arched an eyebrow.

Hang on now, is that a party menu?

That would explain some of the problems they had been having with experience. The Seed hadn't been awarding him anything if a Heretic outside his coven dealt the killing blow. Because of that, he had barely gained any XP the entire time Digby had been stuck in the Seed. All the new Heretics, like Hawk, were listed as a single player, of sorts. The issue hadn't been a problem while the necromancer and Parker were off on their own, but that was probably due to them being in a separate world where they had no parties set up. When Digby had returned, the Seed must have added him back to their coven.

That's pretty cool.

He focused on the list and willed it to add a second coven. Nothing happened. Then he willed it to set Parker as the leader. That did the trick. A new line appeared that read, Earner. He looked at Parker, who was balancing one of her daggers on the tip of a finger. It was actually an impressive display, considering how effortlessly she kept the blade upright. He glanced back to his HUD and flicked his focus to her name on the first window. Her stats filled his view to tell him that she had been putting every extra point she had into dexterity.

That explains the newfound talent.

Before he closed her information window, he did a double take at her will stat, as well as her mana value. "Why is your will so high?"

She held both hands out beside her letting her dagger dangle from a finger. "I don't know."

"What do you mean, you don't know?" He squinted at her.

"I figure the Seed found some loophole to give me the stat along with my messenger class. The Seed was all glitching out and needed me to turn it off and on again to get things to work right, so who knows why my will is like that." She shoved her dagger back in its sheath as if putting a pin in the conversation so she didn't have to think about it anymore.

Alex let it go and glanced back to her information, catching something else. "Your last name is Earner?"

"Huh?"

"Your last name, I thought it was Parker."

"Why?" She cocked her head to one side.

"'Cause you were in the military. Sax and Mason call each other by their last names. I figured that pattern meant the same for you."

"Oh. Yeah." She stared blankly for a moment, then rubbed at her forehead. "I don't know, man. They just call me by my first name. Plus, I think Mason uses his last name because his first name is silly."

"What is it?" Alex asked, realizing he didn't know.

"Francis." She slid her dagger back into its sheath.

"Heh, classic." He nodded. "Anyway, I have access to a party menu now so I made you your own coven. I think I can put people in with you."

"Okay, so that makes me, what? The leader?" She frowned.

"Yeah, I think so."

"Hmm." She looked up and to the side. "Can you move me to Dig's party instead of giving me my own? If I'm gonna be his conscience, I should be in his coven."

"Sure." He focused on the list and moved her name to sit above his own.

"At least Dig can leach mana from me if I'm around. Not like I have any good spells to spend my MP on anyway," she grumbled.

"I wouldn't say your spells are bad." Alex closed the Seed's admin menu. "That Mirror Passage one is going to be important."

"Think so?" She stood a little taller.

"Definitely. It's basically fast travel." He took a step toward her letting his curiosity take over. "Are there any limitations?"

She flicked her eyes to the full-length mirror that hung near the door. "I need a reflective surface on my end and I need to have a clear image in my head of the mirror at the destination. So I need to have seen it as it appears now." She nodded to herself before adding. "Oh, and the passage can't take you from an immaterial realm to a material one and vice versa. We tried that."

"So if I showed you a postcard or something that had a picture of a reflective surface, like that big bean-shaped sculpture in Chicago, could you open a passage to there?" He gestured to the mirror.

"I think so." She raised her eyebrows.

His mind began to race with possibilities. "We need to start gathering some travel magazines and stuff. We could put together a binder for you with images of mirrors or windows all over the world."

"Maybe we should start a little smaller before opening a travel agency." She glowered at him.

"Okay, starting small. Can you open a passage to the lobby?" He hooked a thumb at the mirror on the wall. "We've got to head down there to meet Digby, anyway."

"I think I can do that." Parker walked across the room to stand in front of the reflective surface and raised a hand toward it. "Okay, I can take us to the front entrance of the casino if I used the glass doors there as the other end of the spell."

Alex held his breath in anticipation until the surface of the mirror began to ripple like water.

"That should do it." Parker dropped her hand to her side.

"Oh my god." Alex practically leapt toward the passage, stopping just before touching it. The fact that there was an actual portal in front of him was hard to wrap his head around. He had so many questions.

Before he had the chance to ask anything, a hand emerged from the rippling surface. The terrified and confused face of

Sax followed. He fell face first after catching his foot on the bottom of the mirror's frame. His hand grabbed hold of Alex's shirt.

He screamed.

Alex screamed.

Parker screamed in solidarity.

Sax toppled onto Alex, who was now realizing it had been a mistake to stand directly in front of the open passage. Together, they fell to the carpet with Sax on top, still screaming. Alex struggled to keep the flailing man from kneeing him anywhere sensitive, while simultaneously cursing his decreased agility. In the end, he found himself holding the confused man and patting him on the back whilst whispering the first thing that came to his mind.

"Shhh, it's okay, buddy."

The moment of chaos finally faded.

Sax pushed himself up and looked around the room with his mouth hanging open. "How did I get here? I… was just checking the warding rods at the entrance and tried to go back inside. All I did was reach out to push the door open."

"Oh shit, that's on me." Parker slapped her hand to her face. "I probably shouldn't have set a door that people use regularly as a destination for my passage."

"Did I just walk through a portal?" Sax got himself up to his knees.

"Yeah, we were experimenting," Alex explained from his place, laying on the floor with the soldier still straddling one leg.

Sax took a deep breath. "That scared the hell out of me. My heart is still racing. I had no idea what was happening."

"Sorry. But could you…?" Alex gestured for him to get up.

"Am I upstairs?" He disentangled himself and got to his feet.

"We're in a room on the floor where Bancroft is being held." Parker pointed to the wall. "He's in a room that way."

"At least that saves me a trip." Sax brushed himself off. "Digby wanted me to meet Deuce to get Bancroft and bring him down to the fountain area. Elenore is gathering all the survivors there now. I guess he plans to talk to everyone about what happened yesterday."

Alex's face fell. "And Digby wants Bancroft there for that?"

"I guess. Half the people downstairs want that guy's head." He sighed. "I can't say I disagree. Not after what he did."

"I realize that." Alex pushed himself off the floor. "But we also have to be careful about how we do things here."

Sax nodded. "I can't say I disagree with that either. But almost everyone in Vegas is already gathering downstairs. So whatever Graves has in mind is happening."

"Crap." Parker took a step toward the mirror passage. "I am not off to a good start with keeping an eye on him."

"We should get down there." Alex tensed. "Dig doesn't exactly seem like he's in the right mindset to make any major decisions, right now."

Parker glanced back to him. "Are any of us, really?"

CHAPTER FIVE

Alex held his breath as he emerged from the rippling surface of the casino's front doors, only exhaling when he was standing firmly on the ground again. He was still in shock that the ability to fast travel was real. He turned back just in time to see Parker appear through the door's window behind him. The glass shimmered like water. Then, it simply returned to normal as soon as she exited the surface.

"Woah." He shook off his astonishment and shifted his attention back to his surroundings.

A few people were milling about, but most were already gathered at the center of the casino.

"Let's head to the canals." Alex started walking.

Up until recently, they had only been using a tiny portion of the casino due to the electricity demands. Most of the activity had revolved around one of the restaurants near the check-in area that they had been using as a communal dining space. Things had certainly changed now that they were being supplied with power by the Hoover Dam.

As Alex walked into the casino's new gathering point, he couldn't help but gaze up at the mural of puffy clouds floating in a sky of blue that covered the ceiling. The room was so large that it gave the illusion of being outside. Instead of walls, he was surrounded by facades of buildings, each with a storefront or restaurant within. A canal filled with water looped around the space. There were even boats. The tile floor reminded him of a city street where tables had been placed for people to sit around a large fountain. The casino's residents had taken to calling the area the town square, which he kind of appreciated. It made him feel like he lived in some kind of fantasy village. Overall, it was a pleasant place to spend the apocalypse.

They still weren't using the guest floors where the penthouses were. Sure, it would give them more luxurious spaces, but that would only raise the question of who got to live there. Things like that had to be done fairly. Alex had struggled to afford rent enough in his life to understand that.

Bancroft had tried to introduce a system of currency to the people to varying degrees of success. In some ways, it worked. The fact that it used poker chips in combination with an enchantment system meant that it could never be counterfeited. It also helped to organize aspects of everyday survival in a way that felt familiar. That being said, Bancroft hadn't exactly been generous when assigning a basic income. Considering the fact that the man kept a copy of Atlas Shrugged in his room, it wasn't hard to see why. In the end, they would either need to do away with the currency system and try something else, or alter it in a way that worked better for everyone.

Alex added that to the list of things he was going to have to talk to Digby about.

Economics aside, the casino had come a long way, and not a moment too soon considering they now had over a thousand people to take care of. As he and Parker passed through the canal area and headed down one of many vaulted hallways, the sound of murmuring grew louder.

"Remind me to ask for Elenore's help more often." Alex stepped into the atrium on the second floor overlooking one of the casino's largest fountains. "I can't believe she gathered so many people so fast."

The atrium was a large octagonal space, where a pair of grand stairways bracketed a manufactured waterfall that flowed from where near Alex stood, down to a rectangular pool below. People filled the steps that curled along the walls to reach the floor. Narrow spurts of water sprayed a few feet into the air at regular intervals from the pool. A few hundred more people filled the space around the fountain, all looking up to where Alex and Parker stood at the top of the waterfall. Balconies surrounded them on all sides, wrapping the floor they were on as well as the one above. The sun shined in through the atrium's glass ceiling, bathing the room in a bright glow that shimmered on the water's surface.

Alex couldn't help but wonder if Parker's Mirror Passage spell could create a portal in the water below. In theory, it would work.

"Looks like almost everyone showed up." He commented on the crowd.

"I'm sure everyone wants to know what's going on." Parker pushed up on her toes to lean over the railing. "Losing people isn't something new, but they are still going to want to know what's going to happen from here on out."

"True." Alex turned around in search of Digby, catching sight of him as he entered the atrium.

The zombie was coming from the third floor dressed in a new vest and slacks. A new coat billowed behind him as he descended a flight of stairs. Hawk followed behind him, carrying the backpack that they had helped Digby with earlier.

The running water in the fountain below stopped flowing as the waterfall at the top ran dry. Digby must have had someone turn off the pumps so that he didn't have to talk over the sound of the falling water. It was practical, while also adding an element of theatrics to the necromancer's entrance. Alex wasn't sure if that part had been on purpose or not.

Stepping forward, he tried to get Digby's attention, hoping

to hear some of what he planned to say before he blurted out something disturbing in front of the thousand or so people watching.

"Digby?" He attempted to block the zombie's path.

"Not now, Alex." Digby sidestepped him. "This won't take long; we will speak after."

"Wait." He rushed to catch up. It was weird that Digby hadn't spoken to him first before addressing everyone in Vegas. It was almost as if the zombie was trying to get away with something. He immediately regretted letting him out of his sight. Maybe Parker did need to watch him shower, after all. "Hey, are you sure you're good for this? I mean, we should talk about what we're doing with Bancroft as a group first."

Digby stopped and sighed. "I know why you're worried, but I assure you I have put enough thought into this. Allow me to do this on my own. I think what I have to say will return some of the confidence you had in my mental state."

Alex's gut twisted. It was true that the zombie had made some odd choices in the past, but he had come a long way and that had to be worth something. Besides, everyone was watching; if he argued with Digby now, it would probably make them all look fractured.

"Okay, I trust you." Alex gave him a nod and stepped back.

"Thank you." Digby continued walking until he stood at the railing that separated the balcony from the now inactive waterfall. Then he gestured back to both of them, beckoning for Alex and Parker to stand with him.

"Oh." Alex glanced to Parker who shrugged and took a place at Digby's side. Alex followed, to bracket the zombie.

I just hope whatever he has to say is reasonable, Alex thought, realizing that the formation they stood in seemed to non-verbally endorse the zombie's plans, presenting a unified front. Digby didn't give him time to change his mind before speaking.

"By now, you have all heard about the tragedy that befell our settlement last night." Digby leaned forward on the railing and lowered his head. "We lost much. Nearly all of our Heretics perished on that accursed mission. And the ones that returned…" He glanced to Alex and his missing eye. "Well, we lost more than we ever thought we could." A long moment passed before he started again.

"We were betrayed. Plain and simple. I would like to think that something might have gone differently had I not been trapped within the Heretic Seed, but in truth, I don't know what I could have done. The situation here in Vegas with Bancroft and his men had never been ideal. Accepting them into our city had been a necessity to keep our location a secret, and to secure the fragments needed to restore the Heretic Seed. I wish there had been another way to gain the power we need for the fight to come." He sighed, sounding sincere. "I wish I could return your loved ones to you. Even with the power of the Heretic Seed, I cannot. All I can do… is have their names engraved here." He gestured to a blank section of wall behind him. "And make sure that nothing like this ever happens again."

The crowd around them gave a few slow claps.

"That's why I don't want to wait any longer to offer everyone here the power that they deserve. We may have paid a high price, but as much as I wish 'twas not the case, our fight is not over. Autem will not allow anyone to defy them and we cannot hide from them forever. So we must be ready." He gestured back to the casino's main floor, down the hallway behind him. "We will be moving the Heretic Seed's obelisk to the town square. There, anyone may touch it to gain its power."

A wave of gasps resonated through the crowd. Clearly, the people hadn't realized that he would offer magic to everyone without question.

"I will add that accepting this power does not mean that you are volunteering to go to war, only that you wish to live in this new world. We need just as many people working to build this city as we do soldiers, and magic will aid us in those efforts, as well as increase the level of safety and survivability for everyone. Never again do I want to be stuck in a situation where we don't have access to the right spell or class to save one of our own." He lowered his head again.

"That being said, war is coming, so I hope that I can count on enough of you to train and learn the skills it will take to stand against Autem when the time comes. And for my part, I will see to it that we acquire all the resources and advantages that this world has to offer. We will not be caught off guard again. When Autem darkens our door, I vow that we will be ready. I believe that, together, we can build a force that will make Autem regret the day they crossed us."

The zombie's declaration was met by applause, indicating that recruitment might not be on their list of problems. Alex caught the corner of Digby's mouth tug upward. It fell back down when a voice called out from the crowd below.

"What's going to happen to Bancroft?"

A woman from one of the balconies followed his lead. "Where is he now?"

"He should be hanged," a man called down from the third floor.

Several more shouted out after.

Alex tensed, afraid that they might end up with an angry mob on their hands if Digby couldn't come up with a good answer to their frustrations. To Alex's surprise, the crowd quieted down when Digby raised his hands. Not everyone had known one of the Heretics that they had lost, but there had been a growing sense of community in the city as time went on. This was especially true of the people that had been with them from the beginning.

"I understand how you all feel. And I can't deny that a desire for retribution sits at the forefront of my mind." Digby slapped a hand down on the railing. "Bancroft deserves death."

Alex flinched at his words.

That was when he noticed the crowd parting at the back of the room. He leaned forward on the railing and squinted as Bancroft walked into the space with his hands bound. Mason stood behind him with one hand holding tight to the back of his shirt collar and the other resting a sword on the man's shoulder. The blade pressed against the side of Bancroft's throat. The soldier wore a black cowboy hat on his head that Alex had seen in Becca's room a couple of days prior. A blank expression covered Mason's face and the brim of the Stetson cast a shadow over his eyes, making him hard to read.

Sax walked on the other side, also armed with a sword, but leaving it in its sheath

Oh no. Alex froze.

He wanted Bancroft dead as much as anyone else, but a public beheading was not what they needed right now. No matter how much the people called out for blood, giving it to them would only set a bad precedent. Without a better option, he leaned closer to Digby and whispered, "This isn't how we want to do things."

The necromancer leaned in his direction as well and offered two words. "Trust me."

Alex stared at the zombie for a long beat before forcing himself to relax.

Bancroft stopped in front of the fountain below.

Alex tried not to imagine Mason cutting off his head so that it toppled into the pool of water. There was a level of theatrics to the image that seemed to be Digby's style. He shook off the thought, hoping he was wrong. The crowd turned in the direction of the prisoner, looking like they might simply tear Bancroft apart right then and there.

"Charles," Digby started. "Do you deny the accusations that have been leveled against you?"

Bancroft glanced from side to side before looking up. "I was merely doing what was best for this city."

"By betraying and killing its people?" Digby leaned forward on the railing.

Bancroft struggled against Mason's grip. "This city needs stability. It needs order."

"Order?" Digby arched an eyebrow. "From where I stand, what you call order, most would call going hungry to serve the upper nobility. I will be the first to admit that I am not exactly cut out to lead, but I am fortunate enough to have people standing beside me that can fill in the gaps where I may be found lacking."

Bancroft remained quiet.

For once, Digby was actually making a good point. Of course, that was when Alex realized that the zombie was gesturing to him and Parker as the people that would help him lead. He nearly choked despite not eating anything. Digby continued before he had time to dwell on it.

"I'll tell you what I won't do, Charles." The zombie stood up straight. "I am not going to lord over you. There was a time when I would have taken immense joy in publicly chastising you here. But now, after so much fighting and so much loss, it all just leaves a bitter taste in my mouth. And that's coming from someone that eats people."

Alex cringed. Reminding the people that he was a man-eating monster was not the best look. To his surprise, not one person gasped. There were even a couple of chuckles at the zombie's overly dark sense of humor.

Digby grinned for a moment, letting the smile fall a second later.

"Bancroft." He looked the man dead in the eyes. "You killed my friend." Digby let that sink in, making it clear that he had lost just as much as anyone else in the room.

Alex's remaining eye began to tear up. He wiped his face on his shoulder without trying to hide it. There hadn't been much time for him to think, but Becca had been his friend too.

"I meant what I said." Digby extended a finger at the prisoner. "You, Charles Bancroft, deserve death. Hell, you deserve worse than that. I want you to regret your actions. I want you to understand what you took from this world." He dropped his hand to his side and shrugged. "Honestly, I racked my brain to think of something appropriate. But you know what?" He gestured toward Hawk who was standing behind them.

The young rogue stepped forward and passed Digby the

backpack he was carrying earlier. The zombie proceeded to toss it over the railing. Sax caught it.

"That's for you." Digby held both hands out. "Congratulations, Charles, you're banished."

A chorus of murmurs passed through the crowd.

Alex furrowed his brow. *Is he serious?*

"I know what you're all thinking." Digby raised a hand to quiet the room. "That seems a little too light of a punishment, not to mention it's dangerous to let someone that knows our location simply walk away. But have no fear, I will be leaving my minion, Tavern, right where they are. By maintaining control over this condemned man's skeleton, he will still have to follow our rules. If not, well, there will be consequences."

"Alright, Graves." Bancroft stared up at him. "What are your rules?"

"Simple." Digby thrust a finger toward the door. "You will leave this place and never return. Tavern will see to it that you don't. If you so much as take one step toward Vegas, you will be parting ways with your skeleton. The same goes for if you attempt to tell anyone of our location. Or if you speak to anyone at all, for that matter. In fact, if you see anyone out there, you will avoid all contact and keep walking. You have proven that you don't understand the value of having companions, so you will have none to comfort you from here on. I want you to be alone with nothing but your own thoughts."

"Anything else?" Bancroft asked, clearly suppressing a groan.

"Yes." Digby grinned. "No magic."

"You can't be serious." The man's eyes bulged. "I will be killed within days."

"Well, that really sounds like a you problem." Digby shrugged nonchalantly. "Besides, it is only fair, considering how many good people you killed." He glanced around the room. "I think everyone can agree with me on that."

Many in the crowd nodded along.

Alex glanced at the info ring at the edge of his vision and willed it to show him Bancroft's spells. All had been blocked.

"You may as well behead me right here, then." The prisoner glared up at Digby.

"Don't tempt me." The zombie glared right back. "At least this way, you will have a small chance. My only hope is that you live long enough to understand the weight of your crimes."

With that, Mason lowered his sword from Bancroft's neck and stepped around him to cut the rope that they had used to bind his hands. Sax shoved the backpack into his arms as soon as he was free. The man stood there for a moment looking confused as a room of a thousand people stared at him.

"Well, get going." Digby made a shooing motion with his hands.

"Now?" Bancroft took a sudden step back.

"No time like the present." The necromancer shrugged.

Bancroft's jaw dropped as Mason grabbed him by the back of the shirt again and turned him toward the door. The soldier gave the man a solid shove from there.

"And Tavern." Digby leaned over the railing as Bancroft's body stopped and turned with an uncomfortable stagger.

"Yeah, boss?" The skeleton's voice slithered from the man's throat.

"I took the liberty of adding a few flasks of spirits to your supplies, so enjoy your trip."

"Sweet."

Bancroft snapped his mouth shut as soon as the skeleton released control over his body. Then, he scurried out of the room.

The crowd turned back to Digby all at once, some looking a little skeptical.

Digby nodded. "I give him a ten percent chance of making it someplace safe. If he doesn't, then he will suffer the same as everyone that he's thrown to the wolves." Digby clapped his hands together. "Well, that settles that. I hope to see everyone back in the main square once we get the Heretic Seed relocated.

I will be available there if anyone has any questions or concerns. I thank you all for your time."

With that Digby stepped away from the railing and turned to Alex. "Did that quell your concerns?"

Alex relaxed. "You had me worried you were going to behead him."

"I had a good mind to."

"I'm glad you didn't." Alex glanced back toward the door that Bancroft had just exited through.

He couldn't help but notice he couldn't see Mason's new hat in the crowd anywhere. The soldier must have had something to do other than hang around. He was sure to be dealing with his own grief.

"I'm gonna go check on Mason," Parker spoke up, noticing his absence as well. Alex caught a concerned look on her face as she made for the stairs. Maybe she was worried he might do something he'd regret, like follow Bancroft. After all, he was sure to believe the man responsible for Becca's death.

Digby cleared his throat, pulling Alex's attention away from the crowd. "I should be going as well. Someone will need to oversee the process of connecting the people of this city to the Heretic Seed."

"Oh, sure." Alex nodded. "Let me know if you need any help."

"Nonsense." Digby waved away his offer as he began walking away. "I'm sure you have important things to do down in your workshop." He didn't wait for Alex to respond before rushing off toward the town square.

An uneasy feeling settled in Alex's chest. Digby had handled the situation well, but still, he couldn't shake the feeling that they should be worried. The necromancer had seemed so confident in the way he controlled the crowd. It was possible that Digby had just grown as a leader, but if that was true, why wasn't Alex happier about it?

He shook off the question, hoping that he was just overthinking things. Either way, the zombie had been right, he did have things to do down in his workshop. For one, he needed to make Digby a new staff after he'd smashed his last one across the face of one of Bancroft's men the day before.

"I may as well get to work." He shoved his hands in his pockets and headed down to the forge. Kristen was bound to be annoyed that he hadn't gone down to get her, anyway.

The workers wouldn't start filtering in until after breakfast, giving Alex just enough time to test out a new staff design that he'd been thinking about. He strolled into the forge a few minutes later and fired up the equipment. Walking back to his workshop at the far end of the space, he pushed through the door to grab a couple of ingredients he needed.

Alex found Kristen's skull staring at him as he entered the door and reached for the light switch.

He probably should have checked if anyone else was in the room.

"Behind you," Kristen commented as if she didn't really care if he heard her or not.

Alex tensed as a heavy hand grabbed the back of his collar and yanked him further into the shadows of the darkened workshop. He let out a yelp as his attacker growled one question in his face.

"Where are the shoes?"

CHAPTER SIX

"Hey! Wait! Shit!" Alex flailed as he found himself face to face with Mason, so close that the brim of the soldier's new hat brushed against his forehead. The darkened workshop cast his face in shadows.

"Where's the shoes?" Mason's voice came out gruff and desperate.

"I did try to warn you that someone was lurking in here," Kristen commented from her place on the workbench.

"Shoes?" Alex would have crossed his eyes in confusion, unsure what he had done to piss the guy off. Though the fact that he only had the one made that impossible.

"The slippers, damn it!" Mason shook him.

"Oh." Alex held up his hand, hoping to calm the soldier. He'd mentioned the shoes to Mason before the mission a day ago. Back before they'd lost Becca.

"Where are they? I need them." Mason tightened his grip on Alex's collar. "You should have used them as soon as we got back. I have been looking for them all morning."

"I had the slippers with me earlier, then I sent them down to the vaults with Lana." Alex grabbed hold of his wrists, squeezing to make it clear that he would fight back if the soldier didn't let him go. "And if you mean I should have used the slippers to bring back Becca, I already tried."

Mason released him immediately. "You did?"

"Of course I did." Alex pulled away, putting a few feet of space between them. "I tried to bring her back as soon as Lana got that bullet out of my brain."

"Oh." Mason started to calm down only to lunge toward him a moment later. "Did it work?"

"No." Alex stepped back to keep him at bay.

"How do you know it didn't?" Mason's eyes darted around the room.

Alex gestured to the space between them. "Because I don't see her here anywhere. Besides, I didn't feel any pull on my mana when I tried. The shoes don't seem to have access to a spell to revive the dead. Even if they did at one point, they will only cast each spell once. So someone must have used it before we got our hands on them."

"Damn." Mason deflated, looking small. Clearly, he was processing things in his own way and struggling to think straight. He had just lost his girlfriend less than twenty-four hours ago. "I'm… I'm sorry for grabbing you. I didn't know you had tried already. I thought that—"

"That I had forgotten about her?" Alex's voice grew a little louder at the absurdity of the assumption. "How could I?"

"I get it." Mason gave a weak nod. "Of course you tried already. She was your friend." He perked up a second later, shifting back into a manic desperation. "But we should try again. Something could have gone wrong."

Alex sighed. "I know how you feel, but I tried several times and I felt nothing."

That was when a chuckle came from the other side of the room.

"You have something to say?" Mason spun toward Kristen's skull.

"You Heretics never cease to surprise me." She paused. "That isn't a compliment, by the way."

Alex strode across the room to the workbench she sat on. "If you know something, just say so. You helped Digby with Bancroft before, so there has to be some part of you that understands how important things are."

"I didn't intend to help Graves. I just…" She trailed off.

"Fine. I don't care whose side you're on or how you feel about it." Alex picked her up. "I'm asking you to tell us what you know. If there's a way to save Becca, we have to try. I'll bring you up to Digby and have him ask if I have to."

"How could either of you possibly cast a revival spell?" She asked in a tone that sounded antagonistic.

"I'm not going to stand here while you mock us!" Mason shouted at the skull.

"I am serious," she shouted back. "A revival spell is beyond the reach of even Henwick's power. You would need thousands of years of experience to gain the attributes and cultivate the skills needed to unlock such a spell."

"But it is possible." Alex read between the lines of her answer. He lowered the skull back to the workbench.

"Now you're paying attention." She chuckled to herself.

"She's right." Alex spun around. "A spell like that would require too much from the caster. Probably more mana than I could ever have."

"But those slippers are supposed to grant wishes." Mason slapped the back of one hand into his other. "They are supposed to be able to cast any spell."

That was when Alex figured out the trick. "If we lack the stats to cast a revival spell, then the only way that description of those shoes could be true would be if they could make up the difference." Alex paced a few steps. "They have their own mana."

"What?" Mason stared at him with a blank expression.

"Finally," Kristen said with an annoyed tone in her voice.

Alex connected the dots. "The cloak of steel that I gave

Becca had its own mana system that absorbed life essence during the day to produce a barrier. The shoes must work the same way."

"Then the mana to cast the spell wouldn't come from you." Mason caught up to the conversation. "That's why you didn't feel anything pulling on your magic."

"Exactly." Alex nodded only to shake his head a moment later. "Wait, that doesn't mean that the spell hasn't already been used by someone else. Kristen just said not even Henwick has access to a revival spell. He could have used it years ago, for all we know."

"Or that was why he was holding them on the moon, to make sure he could bring someone back from the dead if he needed to," Mason added.

"Crap, we need to get the shoes." Alex turned toward the door. "I have to check something." He glanced back and gave Kristen a nod. "Thank you."

"I didn't do anything." She denied helping as usual.

Alex didn't argue. If she wanted to keep pretending that she didn't care about them, that was fine.

"Come on." He rushed out of the room with Mason close behind.

It wasn't long before they were staring at the door of the casino's vault. Alex hadn't actually been down there yet, but a pair of Deuce's men stood on either side of the massive rectangular door. Beyond that it was just a hallway in the sub-level. The guards opened the door without question.

"Woah." Alex staggered in the doorway at the sight of several worthless blocks of shrink-wrapped cash that were stacked along the wall. They sat beside the nuke that Digby had claimed.

"We should really find a way to seal that door magically." Alex stared at the nuke, wondering how easy it would be to rig it to explode. Surely someone in the city had the knowledge needed.

"Where are the shoes?" Mason ignored the bomb, rushing in with the same single-minded goal that had consumed him.

"Here." Alex walked in and found the first aid bag that Lana had brought down earlier. He glanced back at the open door to make sure the guards outside weren't watching. Then he gestured for Mason to close the door. The slippers were too dangerous to let their existence be known to everyone. Not only that, but they had lost more than just Becca; if it got out that there was even a chance to bring back the dead, people would never stop asking.

Mason closed the door, making sure not to lock them in by mistake. He thrust out a hand as soon as they were alone. "Alright, give them to me."

"No." Alex kicked his shoes off. "It has to be me."

"Why?" Mason sounded frustrated.

"Because I already tried." Alex pulled the slippers from the first aid bag and dropped them to the floor in front of him. "Basically, we have two possibilities. Either the spell has been cast already by someone else, or I cast it this morning without realizing it."

"How can we tell which?" Mason stepped closer.

"I just have to try to cast something else. A simple spell, but one that I don't have access to." He started to squeeze one foot into one of the tiny slippers. "The enchantment on the shoes will let the wearer cast any spell with two limitations. The first is that each spell may only be cast once. The second is that the enchantment is strictly one per customer. So if someone already used the slippers to revive a person, I should still be able to cast something else now. But if no one had used the spell and I cast it this morning without realizing, then I would have used up my one use and the shoes won't let me cast anything else."

"That makes sense." Mason knelt down as if to help him get the other shoe on. "Just hurry."

"I am hurrying." Alex forced his heel into the right slipper. "They aren't exactly my size, here."

A few seconds of Mason grabbing at his feet later, and

Alex's left foot slid into the other sequined slipper. He stared down at his feet, ignoring how ridiculous he looked, then he raised a hand to the space in front of him and tried to cast an illusion the way Becca used to.

Nothing happened.

His heart rose, daring to let him hope.

"What are you casting?" Mason stared at him while anxiously tapping a finger on his leg.

"Everything I can think of." Alex cycled through all the spells that he knew of that he didn't have access to. He even attempted a Mirror Passage, using a reflective portion of the vault door. When nothing happened, he dropped his hand back down.

Mason watched, holding his breath.

Alex locked eyes with him. "I can't cast anything."

"Then it worked." Mason sunk down to sit on a shrink-wrapped block of cash, his face a mix of relief and confusion.

"I think so." Alex stared at his feet, realizing that he may have just resurrected his friend through the unconventional use of footwear. "Holy crap, if this really worked, then we need to start looking for more artifacts like these shoes. If something like them exists, then there have to be more enchantments out there."

"We need to tell Graves." Mason started moving for the door.

Alex hesitated. "Maybe we should wait until we know more."

"Why?" Mason stared at him, looking agitated again.

Alex looked around the room while he thought of a reason. If he was honest, Mason was worrying him. It was understandable that he was a little unstable, but now wasn't the time to be jumping into action. Telling Digby wasn't the problem, but with the two of them, Alex could see Mason making demands of the zombie while he was also dealing with things of his own. Digby had seemed a little off and Mason could definitely take advantage of that fact. The only problem was that he couldn't just tell the soldier the truth.

"Last time I spoke to Digby, he was having a hard time dealing with things." It wasn't technically a lie. "I'd just give him a couple days to avoid giving him whiplash."

The soldier seemed to accept that, only to jump up a moment later with a horrified look on his face. "Wait! If the spell worked, then why is Becca not back here?"

Dread swept through Alex's mind as the question hung in the air.

Mason was right.

The spell had certainly worked by now. Becca should have been alive since the morning. For all they knew, she had revived at the bottom of the ocean only to drown again. He forced that thought out of his head, unwilling to consider the possibility. She had to have made it out.

That only raised an obvious question.

If she was alive, then where was she?

CHAPTER SEVEN

SEVERAL HOURS EARLIER...

There is another caretaker.

The words of Abby, the Heretic Seed's original caretaker, echoed through Becca's mind as darkness surrounded her.

Another caretaker? How could that be possible?

Becca pushed the question aside. It didn't matter. Something had summoned her from whatever afterlife the universe had in store for her. She wasn't sure why, but something told her that she was going back.

That, somehow, she was falling back to Earth.

If that was true, she was getting a second chance. If *that* was true, she could fix everything. She could live her life. Everything would be better!

The world exploded into existence an instant later, sending her senses into overload.

Darkness swirled around her, only letting through flashes of light as a cacophony of sound came from all sides. It was so much louder than anything she had heard before, even with the enhanced senses of a Heretic. It was as if someone had turned the volume knob up to a thousand.

Screams, gunfire, alarms, and her own pounding heartbeat mixed with a chorus of constant screeching, like the screams of a hundred bats. Details hit her eyes in an uncontrolled blur of information, far too much for her to take in. A gunshot boomed like a cannon as pain tore through her stomach before bursting out her back. For a second, she thought she'd been shot, but the pain was quickly drowned out by an intense vibration that faded to nothing. Still, her muscles were on fire, the burn of a hundred workouts all hitting her at once, in a cycle of damage and regeneration.

A guttural snarl came from someplace close by as the overpowering scent of sweat, urine, and blood filled her nose. Confusion invaded her mind as she realized the snarl had come from her.

It was chaos.

The chaos all stopped when the taste of copper flooded her mouth and warmth splashed down her front.

Becca's overloaded senses faded back down to normal as everything came into focus, leaving her standing there, her heart pounding as she clutched something tight against her body. The muscles in her jaw clenched, drawing her attention to the man's throat that she was currently biting.

Horror filled her mind at what she was doing, but she didn't stop. At least, not right away.

Finally, she dropped the corpse in her arms, realizing where she was.

Earth.

The familiar passenger compartment of a kestrel surrounded her. Nearly every inch of the aircraft's interior was spattered with blood. The bodies of five dead Guardians, including the one at her feet, lay strewn about the cabin as if they had been thrown about like rag dolls.

Hanging from her neck were four catch poles. Like the kind that animal control would use to capture a rabid dog. The wire loops of each were tight around her neck. So tight that they dug into her skin. The ends of each pole had been snapped like twigs. The other ends dangled from metal rings attached to the cabin's ceiling. It was as if a monster the Guardians had captured had broken free.

No, that wasn't right. It was as if *she* had broken free.

That was when she noticed the alarm sounding from the cockpit behind her.

Turning, Becca followed a trail of bullet holes that marred the wall of the passenger compartment. Someone had panic-fired an entire magazine. The path of destruction continued straight through the controls where a dead Guardian lay slumped across the console to complete a squad of six. A bullet hole in the back of his head, combined with the spray of gray matter on the windshield, explained what had happened. There had been a fight in the back and he had been hit by friendly fire along with the damaged controls.

Becca stood, observing the inside of the kestrel like a detective investigating the scene of a crime, putting clues together piece by piece only to find the culprit had never left. Her mind struggled to deny the obvious until she caught her reflection in a piece of polished plexi mounted to the wall of the cabin.

"Was I always that pale?"

Her tongue slid against a pair of pointed canines as she spoke, a trickle of blood running from her lips to join the pints that had spilled down her front. She closed her mouth and swallowed on instinct rather than let herself drool anymore on the floor.

"Oh no." Becca froze as she stared at her reflection in disbelief. Her eyes shined back at her like embers drifting from a roaring fire. That was when the facts finally sunk in.

"I'm a revenant."

Somehow, she had returned from the afterlife only to be dropped right back into her cursed body. Before she could dwell on the revelation, the kestrel began to drift to one side.

"Shit!" Becca frantically pulled the wire loops from around

her neck as the abrasions left behind healed almost instantly. She spun back to the cockpit as soon as she was done, catching a glimpse of a familiar cityscape through the gore-spattered windshield. Becca knew where she was in an instant.

"How did I get…?"

The view of the skyline shifted as the aircraft began to drift into an uncontrolled spin, a view of the Washington Monument whipping by. Somehow, she had been brought across the entire country from where she'd died. All the way to the East Coast.

Questions filled Becca's mind. All with no answers.

How did she get aboard a kestrel? Why had she been brought to Washington, D.C.? How long had she been gone? How was she going to find another caretaker? Would she be able to help Digby before his mind unraveled?

Then there was the question she was actively avoiding.

What had she become?

That last one was answered as the first rays of morning sunlight shined in through the cockpit window.

Becca let out a sudden and involuntary hiss as the aircraft spun into an uncontrolled spiral. She fell back into one of the seats that lined the passenger compartment. The bodies of dead Guardians tumbled across the floor until they were plastered to the walls by the motion of the spinning craft. The man that Becca had dropped moments ago landed in the seat next to her, his head hanging at an unnatural angle. Becca recoiled from the corpse, only for the cabin's movement to shove the gaping hole in his throat in her face, the unmistakable markings of her teeth marring his flesh.

The kestrel slammed into the side of a building before she had a chance to deny the obvious.

She had been given a second chance at life, and it was going to get weird.

That had been several hours ago.

Now, Becca stood in the employee bathroom of a small electronics store, staring into a mirror. Her filthy clothes lay on the floor in a pile, barely more than rags. Two dozen empty water bottles from a long dead vending machine littered the tile. Her face dripped with water, her skin raw from scrubbing. Finally, the blood that had covered her chin and neck were gone.

All Becca knew was that she had been dead.

Then, she wasn't.

She'd seen a glimpse of what awaited her beyond the veil, but something had summoned her spark from the great beyond. All the way back to her cursed body. She had the sneaking suspicion she had Alex and a certain pair of slippers to thank for her return. That was the only thing that made sense.

She wasn't sure if she should be grateful or not.

Returning to life had done nothing to reverse the curse that killed her. The fact that her body had become a revenant meant that some lifestyle changes were needed.

Becca couldn't remember much from the first few moments of her new monstrous existence. Just that everything had been overwhelming. Sight, sound, smell, touch, and even taste. It had all been punched up to a level where she could barely separate it all. From the blood and general state of the kestrel she'd woken up in, it was safe to say she had turned every Guardian on board into a juice box. As far as how she had gotten on board the aircraft, or how it had gotten her across the country to the East Coast, she had no idea.

The kestrel had slammed into a building before she could do any investigating.

Once the craft had come to a stop and the world stopped spinning, she'd unbuckled herself from the seat she'd strapped into, and ran. The squad she'd killed must have sent a distress call and now that she was on the East Coast, she had no idea how close she was to the settlement that Autem had started there. It was only a matter of time before more kestrels came looking for her and the missing Guardians. Sure enough, she had heard more aircraft in the distance as she fled the wreckage of the downed kestrel.

Becca wanted to keep running.

Hell, she wanted to run all the way back to Vegas. Unfortunately, becoming a revenant had come with a list of problems that made going home impossible. For starters, she felt like absolute trash.

Becca could remember bits and pieces from when she had first woken up aboard the kestrel. In that moment, she had been unbelievably strong and fast. Looking down at the filthy shirt that she had tossed on the floor of the bathroom, she counted seven bullet holes.

Brief flashes of pain echoed through her mind, bullets tearing straight through her chest and abdomen before exploding out her back. That hadn't even slowed her down. No, the wounds had healed within seconds, faster than any revenant she'd ever seen.

She had been unstoppable.

That had been just before dawn. Now, the morning sun shined down mercilessly, washing away all that power and leaving her weaker than she'd ever felt in her life.

Becca could feel her body attempting to heal the cuts and bruises she'd sustained during the crash as the sun rose, but something inside her felt wrong. She had been aware of the magic inside her since she'd become a Heretic, but now it was impossible to ignore. It was like a part of her mana system was poisoning the rest. It was probably because of the shift in the ambient mana balance that the daylight brought. It wasn't painful, but it completely cut off any of the supernatural abilities that had come along with her curse.

Even worse, it made her feel weak.

The fact that her body itself had never actually died, and only rejected her soul temporarily, meant that she should have retained the enhanced stats of a Heretic even if she was no longer connected to the Seed. Despite that, she felt like she was walking through mud. Physically, she seemed to be weaker than the average, unenhanced human. Even her senses had been dulled back down to where they had been before Digby had connected her to the Heretic Seed. Now, without her heightened perception, she felt like a sitting duck.

Then there was the exhaustion. If it wasn't for the fact that she was still so close to the kestrel's crash site, she would have curled up in the first closet she found and slept for days. She'd even got winded while walking the few blocks to reach the electronics store that she'd chosen as a temporary refuge.

Becca had seen revenants go dormant during the day before; now she knew why they were so lethargic. From here on out, she would need to take a cue from the creatures and wait until nightfall before becoming active. Even if the situation allowed her to run straight back to Vegas, she simply didn't have the physical strength to travel alone during the day.

Of course, that brought up the second problem stopping her from going home.

Digby.

With what Abby, the original caretaker, had told her during her brief visit to the afterlife, Digby, her friend, was doomed. Without his soul, all that awaited him was a spiral into madness before returning to the state of a mindless zombie. That was, if she couldn't find a way to save him.

Abby's words echoed again.

There is another caretaker.

If that was true, Becca had to find them and ask how to fix Digby. Fortunately for her, she had an idea of where this other caretaker might be.

The Guardian Core.

The Autem Empire had built their own version of the Heretic Seed to give magic to their forces. She was lacking in the details of how they did it, but from what she was beginning to piece together, a caretaker was an important part of the process. Meaning that if she was going to find one to help her, Autem's capital was the place to start.

Somehow, she needed to get access to the Guardian Core and make contact with its caretaker. As far as how she expected to convince an entity like that to help her, she had no idea, but she had to try. It was the only way to save Digby, and he didn't have time left for her to go home for help. His mind would be lost before she made it back.

She was on her own.

Just a lone revenant against an evil empire.

Becca pulled several paper towels from a dispenser on the bathroom wall and dried her body.

She had been starting to tan a little after leaving her apartment in Seattle and spending time outside, but now, her skin had become deathly pale. She could probably blind someone if the sun caught her at the right angle. Combined with the bleached blond hair that had been a part of her disguise for when she and Digby had infiltrated Skyline's base a couple weeks ago, she looked like a ghost.

Becca frowned.

She hadn't thought much about the transformation that revenants went through, but obviously some had darker skin than others. They were all just a few shades lighter than they had been during life. Now that it had happened to her, there was something uncomfortable about the shift in her complexion. It was like something had been stolen from her.

Her eyes had mostly returned to normal now that the sun was up. Apparently, the bright orange flecks that had been present in her irises before were a part of her nocturnal enhancements. Baring her teeth at the mirror, she let out a relieved sigh at the fact that only her canines had become elongated while the rest of her teeth had remained normal. Most of the revenants she'd seen had an entire mouth filled with jagged spikes, leaving her with some relief that she'd been spared.

That wasn't the only difference either. Becca wrinkled her nose, grateful that it hadn't transformed into the bat-like snout that most of the creatures had. She wasn't sure why she retained a human nose, but she was certainly glad she had.

Pushing back her wet hair, she turned her head to look at one of her ears. She traced the now-pointed lobe with her finger. They didn't stick out far like a fantasy elf or anything, but her ears were definitely longer and more angular than they had been.

With her hair down, she could pass for human. Well, that would be true if she still lived in the pre-apocalypse world. Now that revenants were more common than people, it was more likely that anyone she ran into would assume she was just another monster from the paleness of her skin, rather than accepting her as a regular person.

Checking her chest and stomach, Becca couldn't find any trace that she had been shot several times. Though, she was still covered in minor cuts and scratches from the crash. It had happened just as the sun was rising, which brought her healing to a halt. She made sure none of the injuries were severe enough to need additional attention before finishing up in the bathroom and heading back into the electronic store's backroom.

Grabbing an extra-large polo shirt from a shelf of employee uniforms, she pulled it on over her head. The clothes she'd been wearing had been torn, shot, and stained too many times to even be called clothes anymore. Not to mention everything had been practically soaked in blood. In the end, the apocalypse was a bad time to become a nudist, so she had to wear something.

Becca tugged on the back of her new polo shirt to make sure it was long enough to cover her ass and made a point to find a better alternative as soon as she could. Ultimately, it was just good to be clean again. Even if she was going commando.

The back room of the electronics store was as good a place as any to get her bearings. It was a small space, piled with boxes of stock. The power must have failed weeks ago, leaving it dark. Becca had claimed a flashlight and batteries on her way into the shop.

The window of the store front had already been broken, though she didn't find any revenants inside. Actually, she hadn't run into any of the creatures. It made sense that they were all in hiding during the day. Though, their absence made her worry about how close she was to the empire's capital. Autem had been in the area for over a month, and had probably cleared most of the creatures out. The fact that she hadn't seen any at all might have meant she was much closer to their capital than she wanted to be. Either way, there was bound to still be a few revenants left that hadn't been killed. Becca just hoped they wouldn't be hostile to her on account of their shared curse. She decided to stay in the back room just in case.

Turning to the boxes of stock, Becca pushed all thought of what she had become from her head and got to work. She had fled the downed kestrel in a hurry, but not before grabbing a few pieces of equipment. A pack of rations and the chest armor of a dead Guardian lay in a pile near the door where she'd dropped them earlier. She'd cleaned the blood off the armor already. A sword was still slotted into the armor's magnetic sheath.

Becca sat down at the desk where she'd placed the most important piece of equipment, a portable drone console. All kestrels had one. Before running for her life, she'd removed the drone from its housing in the passenger compartment of the aircraft. The unit was meant to be used as an access point to fly the kestrel remotely when needed. After pulling the drone out, she'd shoved it into its provided carrying case to take with her. If Autem's capital was really nearby, she was going to need the drone to find and investigate it.

Almost just as important was the plastic carry case itself. Not only did it have a space to hold the drone, but it also held a charging system complete with several ports, a full power bank, and a folding solar panel for when it ran dead. Becca fished through the shelves of stock that lined the store's back room, finding a decent laptop. Unwrapping it, she plugged it into the charging system. Once it had enough power to turn it on, she went back to the desk to grab the last thing she had taken from the crashed kestrel.

Its black box.

Technically, the aircraft's flight recorder was orange, but it did the same thing as a black box. Becca had deactivated the box's emergency beacon that had been broadcasting upon impact, so it couldn't be traced to her current location. Though, the fact that she took it made it obvious that she had survived and was on the run. Autem would look for it as soon as they found the crash site, and the fact that it was gone would bring search teams after her. It would have been better to leave it, but she had too many questions.

After looting the electronic shop for various parts and connectors, she was finally able to get some answers.

Listening to the kestrel's recorded communications told her everything. Bancroft had been right that Autem would be coming to investigate the sunken cargo ship where they had found the nuke. They had arrived not long after she had died and found that the ship had gone down. They didn't have the diving equipment or time to do a thorough search of the vessel, but they found something better.

Her.

According to the comms, Becca's revenant had been found swimming in the ocean near where the ship had sunk. They matched her face to images from the heist back on Skyline's base and immediately captured her. Becca furrowed her brow, unsure what they would want with a mindless creature. All she knew was that her revenant was being brought back for processing. As far as what that meant, she had no idea, but at least it explained how she had gotten aboard a kestrel flying over Washington, D.C.

Even more curious, there was mention of a second Heretic, though the communications lacked a name. The kestrels had stumbled across whoever it was on a beach on the way back to the East Coast. The second aircraft stayed behind to capture them for interrogation.

Becca tried not to panic.

If the flight recording was true, then a Heretic had survived the betrayal of Bancroft's men. They must have escaped the ship and swam the three miles back to California's shore. Becca tried to figure out who it might be, but there wasn't enough information. It couldn't have been Mason or Alex. They had left with Digby and there was no mention of them in the recordings. All she knew was that, whoever the Heretic was, they'd been captured.

Becca added that fact to the list of reasons why she couldn't go home to Vegas just yet. If Autem had captured a Heretic, it was only a matter of time before they found out where Digby and the others were hiding. Be it torture or some other means, Autem would make the prisoner talk. Somehow, she was going to need to find a way to keep things quiet.

The recordings continued from there. She skipped to the end, just before the crash. To the moment that her soul had returned from the dead.

Becca held her breath as she listened to the events that followed unfolded.

"She's getting agitated," a gruff voice said, sounding low as if picked up from the pilot's mic in the cockpit.

"We're almost there," another responded.

What followed sent an icy chill down Becca's spine. A snarl mixed with a hiss. She recognized her own voice in it. Then, things got weird.

"What the hell!" a Guardian shouted. "She changed!"

"What?" another voice questioned.

"Analyze her!" the first called back, sounding panicked.

"That's not possible," another cried.

Their voices faded as a vicious growl drowned them out. The sound of her restraints snapping came next. Then, there were only screams. The recording ended with a burst of gunfire.

Becca arched a concerned eyebrow as she looked down at herself.

"What had they seen?"

Her HUD had vanished after her death had disconnected her from the Seed, leaving her with no way to check her status. Though from the tone of the Guardian's voice, whatever her description was, it had scared the shit out of him.

"I must be a special type of revenant." Becca shrugged as she slouched into her chair. "Maybe that's why my nose looks normal."

After a minute of staring up at the ceiling in thought, she returned her attention to the laptop she'd looted. It was unlikely that she would be able to contact Vegas, but she had to try. After fifteen minutes, she gave up. The Internet had finally died, right down to its last vestiges. It was possible that she could log in to Autem's satellite network through the drone, but she wasn't a skilled enough hacker to do that without being noticed. Even if she did, nobody back in Vegas had a system that could receive a message.

"Shit." Becca closed the laptop.

She could only imagine how everyone back home was dealing with things. They had lost nearly all of their Heretics. Guilt clawed at her stomach at the thought of Hawk being left alone again. The kid had just found out she was his sister, only to have her torn away from him. Then there was Digby. If he really was in danger of losing his mind, there was no telling what he might do in search of revenge.

Hopefully none of that would happen. Hopefully, they all knew she was alive already. If she was right, and Alex had used the slippers they stole from Henwick to resurrect her, then they should be aware she'd returned. They had no way to find her and she had no way to contact them, but they should at least know she was alive.

Her thought's screeched to a halt as the sound of a vehicle came from someplace outside the storefront's broken window.

"Damn!"

They were patrolling the area already. It would only be a matter of time before there were boots on the ground searching for her.

"Time to go."

The broken window in the storefront almost guaranteed that a squad would check the shop. Not to mention she'd left too much evidence that she'd been there to clean fast enough. She needed someplace safe to wait out the search.

Becca jumped up from the desk and started gathering her things. The drone went back in its case, and the laptop got shoved into the pack she'd taken from the kestrel. There was no time to put on the chest armor she'd looted, so she just shoved an arm through a strap and tried her best to ignore her lack of pants. There wasn't time to care. She snatched an unopened smart phone from a shelf on her way out the back door, and rushed into the alley behind the store.

From there, she sprinted in the opposite direction of the sound she'd heard. She only made it a few strides before getting tired.

"Stupid sunlight." Becca panted as she rushed to the end of the alley.

Stopping to make sure the coast was clear, she nearly screamed when the familiar chittering of a revenant came from behind her. Becca spun to find a nightflyer huddled against a dumpster, trying to take advantage of what little shade it could find while using its wings for additional cover. It must have been caught out in the open when the sun rose and tried its best to get out of the light.

On instinct, Becca raised her hand to cast Icicle.

Nothing happened; her mana system felt like molasses flowing through her body. She started to reach for the sword that was attached to the back of her stolen armor, then she stopped herself. The creature didn't seem hostile or even interested in her beyond a slight curiosity.

"That's right." She let out a breath. "We're on the same team now."

Becca had seen revenants interact with each other. They never seemed to be as cooperative as zombies, but they did tend to move in swarms without attacking one another. Unfortunately, she didn't have time to find out for sure before she heard excited voices coming from the shop that she had just fled. The search team must have picked up her trail. They would reach the alley next.

"Shit." Becca's heart jumped into her throat as she spun in search of someplace to hide.

The only option was the dumpster the Revenant was using for shade. She shook her head. There was no way she could get inside in her condition without making too much noise. The only place left was...

Becca snapped her head to the revenant nightflyer as the voices in the shop behind her grew louder. It was male, with broad, muscular shoulders, just big enough to hide someone smaller behind.

"Okay, I am going to regret this." Becca stepped into biting range, hoping the creature really was friendly.

It made no motion to attack.

"Good enough for me." She shrugged.

Shoving herself against the dumpster, she slipped between it and the revenant. The creature hissed in protest as she pushed it out of the shade a few inches, then it shoved back, pressing its body against hers. Becca slid the drone case, black box, her pack, and her armor into the space beneath the dumpster, wishing it was large enough for her to fit as well.

The sound of a door being kicked open followed by boots on pavement announced the search team. They approached as she huddled in the corner where the wall of the alley and the dumpster met. She tucked her body as close together as possible. The revenant nightflyer handled the rest, huddling tight into the space with her to stay out of the sun, its wings draping over them both. Becca suppressed a panicked gasp as the creature pressed its face against her neck.

The boots of at least three Guardians rushed past them.

For a moment, Becca worried that they might grab the nightflyer to make sure it wasn't her, but the fact that it was clearly male and much larger than her should have shielded the creature from suspicion.

The boots stopped regardless.

"Hey, it's a flyer," a voice commented.

"Tag it," another ordered. "The night shift will come back for it after the area has been searched."

A sudden pop sounded as the nightflyer let out a cry. A barbed metal pin poked through the membrane of the creature's wing. The boots continued on from there, leaving Becca and her new revenant friend alone once again. She didn't dare move for several minutes in fear that the Guardians would come back. The nightflyer's hot breath wheezed against her neck, clearly feeling as weak as she did.

Eventually, she grew brave enough to run her hand down the creature's wing to the piece of metal that hung from it. It was some kind of tracker.

"What is Autem doing?" Becca moved her hand away before sliding herself out from under the revenant's wings and retrieving her things from beneath the dumpster.

She needed to move.

Heading back in the direction the search team had come from, she slipped back into the electronic store. They had already been past there so it was unlikely that they would come back before searching other places. She would be safer there than if she tried to find someplace new.

Once she was back inside, she moved some of the boxes of stock away from the wall so that there was enough room to slip behind them and placed boxes at either end of the narrow space. With a shelf above her, it wasn't obvious that a person was in there. It just looked like a stack of boxes.

After a half hour of hiding, she started to feel a little safer. Pushing back out of her hiding place, she opened the drone case and assembled the unit for flight. There wasn't time to hide forever. She was going to need an escape route, and taking to the sky would be the fastest way to get information.

Setting the drone up in the storefront, Becca returned to her hiding place behind the boxes in the back and launched. She'd taken the drone off Autem's satellite network, which decreased its range, but it could still get high enough to give a look at the area. She flicked on the unit's optical camouflage before flying it out of the broken window.

From there she went straight up.

She hadn't even had it in the air for more than a minute before finding exactly what she feared.

"My god." Her voice was barely audible.

She was closer to the empire's capital than she thought.

So much closer.

CHAPTER EIGHT

"Fucking hell…" Becca stared down at the screen of the stolen drone's console.

Autem had been busy.

Busy building.

A structure loomed over Washington, D.C. like a gravestone marking the death of the nation. It was hard to tell exactly what it was. All she knew was that it was big, several thousand feet wide and a few hundred tall. Even through the screen of the drone console, the structure was enormous.

Becca wanted to fly the drone closer. She wanted to investigate the monstrous thing. She wanted to gather intel for the task ahead of her. Instead, she brought the drone back down. Whatever Autem was building wasn't just big, it was close. Too close for her to risk staying where she was any longer.

Using the drone, she found the search team that had passed her before. Making a pass of the area, she located another three search teams in addition to the nearest. Making note of their positions, she scouted a destination and plotted a path through the next few city blocks to get there. At least with that, she could make a move without getting caught.

"I really wish I still had my Cartography spell right now," Becca grumbled at the loss of her magic.

Once she was ready to go, she gathered her things and headed out. Back in the alleyway, she decided to ditch the black box, but not before finding a new use for it. Using a set of USB cables from the electronic store, Becca tied the kestrel's flight recorder to the revenant nightflyer that she had hidden beneath earlier. The creature was surprisingly cooperative.

After securing the black box, she pulled a plastic water bottle from her pack of rations and stuck it to the top of the flight recorder using a roll of duct tape she'd looted from the store. Loosening the cap, she taped one end of a cable to it and the other to the revenant's wrist. That way, the creature would probably pull the cap the rest of the way off. It could be thirty seconds or ten minutes from now. She hoped for the latter.

If her idea worked, the water in the bottle would spill down the side of the black box to trigger a built-in moisture sensor and reactivate the location beacon. It was a feature that all flight recorders had so that an aircraft could be found if it had crashed in water. With the signal broadcasting again, the search teams would converge, giving her a clear window to make some distance.

Of course, there was also the chance that the revenant just wouldn't move in the right way to dislodge the bottle's cap and nothing would happen at all. The plan was worth a try regardless.

There were still aircraft in the distance, but with her drone set to follow, it would be able to alert her if any were coming close enough to see her. Leaving the alleyway, Becca stuck to the shadows as much as possible, partially to stay out of sight as well as to stay out of the sun. It was hard to believe how something as simple as daylight could make her feel so weak.

It wasn't long before she'd made it several blocks to the destination that she'd scouted with the drone earlier, a small thrift shop with a broken front door. There was still a lot of ground to cover to get away from whatever Autem was building, but the thrift shop was a good place as any to wait for that revenant to activate the black box's beacon.

Plus, the store was bound to have pants.

As much as Becca would have liked to have taken her time to do some shopping, a beep came from the drone case to indicate that the black box's beacon had just been activated.

"Shit!" Becca tore off the oversized polo shirt she'd been wearing as a dress and streaked her way down the aisles of the shop in a hurry.

If she wanted to take advantage of the distraction, there wasn't time to be picky. She had to get what she needed and get out of there.

The first item on her list was undergarments. Becca was surprised the store even had any, figuring no one would want to buy used underwear. Hell, it wouldn't have been her first choice either, but it had been a month since the world ended and finding something was better than going commando.

Passing over some lingerie—because ew—she grabbed a one-piece swimsuit off a rack, and suppressed a cringe as she stepped into it. Unable to take time to try anything on, she threw on a pair of red athletic pants with a stripe down one side that was part of a matching tracksuit. She grabbed the jacket too, pulling it on over a random t-shirt she'd snatched from a shelf. The words, 'It's me, I'm the problem,' were written across the chest.

Once she was clothed, she zipped up her track jacket, ignoring the fact that she looked like she belonged in the Russian mob, and slipped into the Guardian armor she'd stolen.

"That should be enough time to get the search teams out of the way." Becca grabbed her pack and drone case, then made for the door.

It wasn't for another three hours that she'd made it far enough from whatever Autem was building to finally find a place to rest. It probably would have been safer to keep going, but with the sun flooding the world with life essence, all Becca wanted to do was lay down.

Finding an office building with the front door intact and unlocked, she slipped inside. She made sure to lock it behind her before landing her drone on the roof and skulking her way to a stairwell. She only made it up a few flights before running out of breath.

"God damn curse." Becca dropped down and sat on the landing of the fourth floor, looking up at another ten flights above her. She groaned and let her pack slide off her back, opening it to retrieve a package of emergency rations. The blocky packaging read beef stew.

"Yeah, right." Becca tore it open.

She had been putting off eating ever since she'd woke up, not feeling hungry until now. Having a stomach full of blood probably had something to do with it. Plus, she was afraid that the curse had taken away her ability to eat regular food the way it had Digby in the beginning. After taking a few bites with a spork that came with the rations, she waited. A full minute later, she still hadn't thrown up or anything. With that, she shrugged and kept eating, grateful that she could still eat like a human.

Once her lunch was finished, Becca went in her pack to grab the smart phone she'd looted on her way out of the electronic store. It started up after a few minutes of charging. She kept it plugged in while she searched for a notepad app and created a new document.

At the top she wrote one word.

STATUS

Beneath that, she added all of the information that she had before being cursed, or at least what she could remember. She left some things blank and updated others that made sense.

Name: Rebecca Alvarez
Race: Revenant
Class: Unknown
Mana: 325 / 325

Mana Composition: Unbalanced
Current Level: Unknown

ATTRIBUTES
Constitution: 48
Defense: 43
Strength: 42
Dexterity: 46
Agility: 43
Intelligence: 48
Perception: 74
Will: 44

AILMENTS
Cursed

Adding that last word was a little over dramatic, but she left it there to indulge in a bit of self-pity. After that, she thought back to the moment she'd awoken to her new existence to figure out what her abilities might be. Considering she knew that zombies worked off a system, it stood to reason that revenants did as well. Even if she couldn't see her information.

She created a new note with another heading.

ABILITIES

When she had first become aware, it had felt like her body had gone into overdrive. Her senses were out of control and she was impossibly strong. Those seemed like the most obvious powers.

Enhanced Senses
Description: Jack all senses up to 11.
Enhanced Strength
Description: Become super strong.

There had also been a moment where the shadows seemed to come alive around her, as well as the sound of countless screeching cries. There was a good chance she had imagined both, but she typed them in anyway, making sure to leave a question mark at the end.

Dark Bending?
Description: Literally no idea, but does something with shadows. Might have been in my head.

Then there was the healing. She'd killed enough revenants to know how that worked.

Continuous Regeneration
Description: Heal any wound as long as you have enough mana to do so. This ability cannot be paused or canceled. This ability cannot heal a wound with a foreign object still inside.

That was all she could come up with for abilities. The problem was that she had no idea how to use any of her newfound powers. Instead, some kind of instinct had taken over to compel her to attack. She was sure that she had killed that squad of Guardians, but she had done so entirely on autopilot. She may not have remembered the moment well, but if there was one thing she was sure of, it was that she couldn't have stopped herself.

That brought her to the next section.

RACIAL TRAITS
Ravenous

Becca stared at the word, remembering how Digby had struggled with the affliction.

Description: Lose complete control of your actions in the single-minded pursuit of prey.

There was no way to know what had triggered it, but she hadn't been forced to attack the search team earlier so it wasn't anything as simple as being in the presence of prey. It had to be something else. She was going to have to find a way to manage the problem if she ever planned to be around people again, otherwise she could hurt someone, or worse.

The last thing she added was the weakness that had plagued her all day.

Sun Poisoning
Description: Lose all access to magic and enhanced physical capabilities while the sun shines. Become weaker than the average human when in direct sunlight.

Frowning at the screen, Becca's eyelids grew heavier. She hadn't actually realized how tired she'd been. The urge to sleep practically demanded that she lay down. Looking up at the ten floors above her, she reached up to the railing of the stairwell to hoist herself off the landing. She fell back down as soon as she did, lacking the strength to get herself upright. The day really had taken its toll.

"I'll rest for a few minutes, then I'll go up to get the drone." Becca let her head rest against the wall, afraid to actually lay down. The last thing she needed was to sleep the whole day away.

She snapped her eyes open almost as soon as she closed them.

At least, that was what she thought.

Grabbing her phone, the first thing she noticed was that it had been fully charged. Then she looked at the time.

"Shit!" Becca stared down at the tiny readout at the corner of the screen.

She'd slept for hours.

It would be dark soon.

"What the hell is wrong with me?"

Becca pulled herself up, still feeling weak. She left her pack where it was and started climbing. The ascent took longer than she would have liked, considering she'd needed to stop and catch her breath three times. She wasn't exactly sure when the sun would be setting, but from her condition, it hadn't gone down yet.

Reaching the roof of the building, she unlocked the door that led outside and pushed through it. She stopped as soon as she did.

The sun hung low in the sky, leaving just a few more minutes of daylight before finally retiring for the night. Its deep orange light silhouetted the structure that Autem was building. She still couldn't make out what it was, just that it was huge, like a sports stadium, but taller. They must have demolished a hundred city blocks. From where she stood a few miles away, it looked like a dark tooth protruding from the world. Aircraft buzzed around it as well as the surrounding area, each craft another dark speck on the horizon.

Becca cursed her hindered senses, unable to make out the details of the scene. The aircraft seemed to fly similar to a kestrel, but many were larger. Becca looked down at the drone that she'd landed on the roof. There wasn't a point in staying up there in the open. She grabbed the unit and turned to the door behind her.

Once she was back inside again, she started down to get her pack. She only made it one floor before she heard voices coming from below.

Becca slapped a hand over her mouth to suppress a gasp. They had found her already. Her mind flashed back to the pack that she'd left on the fourth floor landing. It was only a matter of time before they found it and called in more support.

"I need to hide." Becca reached for the nearest door and pulled it open.

Once inside the building's top floor hallway, she immediately found it under construction. The space must have been in the middle of a renovation when the world ended. Some of the walls were painted a sterile white, but others were still bare drywall. Becca rushed down the hall. None of the rooms had any doors, allowing the orange light of the setting sun to flood into the corridor. Only some of the windows had blinds installed.

Most of the rooms were empty, but a few had furniture. One even had a brand-new conference table, its surface still covered with protective foam. If she could find someplace to hide until the sun set, Becca could use her abilities again. As long as she went easy on her powers, she might not end up tearing anyone apart or popping them open like a Capri Sun. She had to hold back a little.

Becca stopped at a room further down the hall that faced Autem's construction site.

"What the…?" She trailed off as she noticed a desk had been dragged into the middle of the room.

On top of the desk sat a propane stove and several unopened beers. A few empty cans lay on the floor amidst a collection of empty bags of Cheetos and Top Ramen. Becca stepped inside the room, finding a stack of various supplies lining one side. Canned goods and packages of bottled water, enough to sustain her for a couple weeks.

The wall behind the supplies was covered with a few dozen games of Tic Tac Toe, as well as another couple rounds of hangman.

Beside that, was… well, there was a dick.

Someone had literally drawn a dick on the wall. A permanent marker sat on the floor beneath the illustration.

"Someone's been living here." At least two, judging from the Tic Tac Toe games. Becca flicked her eyes to the window. It had a clear view of Autem's construction. Whoever was staying there had been staking out the empire's activities.

"Wait…" Becca arched an eyebrow, stepping toward the desk.

Was it possible that whoever was coming up the stairs had the same goal as her? Becca took a breath, unsure if she should hide, draw her sword from its sheath, or stand where she was and wait for her company to arrive.

She flexed her fingers, still feeling weak. It wasn't quite as bad as before, but fighting was probably out of the question. Unless she could stall until the sun was completely gone.

Daylight still flooded the room with the same oppressive orange glow. Its one saving grace was that the light gave everything in the space a warm hue, including her. There was a strong possibility that no one would notice she was a revenant right away, giving her a chance. If she was careful, she could stall long enough to have some more options.

That was when she heard the door of the stairwell open down the hall. Footsteps followed. Taking a breath, she stepped back away from the entryway and turned to face it.

"Okay, just do like Digby would." She exhaled. "Just talk out of your ass and hope for the best."

That was when an enormous, overly muscled man walked in. He stopped in the doorway as soon as he saw her. The backpack she'd left on the stairs hung from his right hand. By her best guess, he was in his mid-twenties, with short hair and a scruffy face. A tank top and a pair of camouflage pants made him look like some kind of mercenary. A tattoo covered his left shoulder all the way down to his elbow to complete the look. It was just a bunch of crisscrossing black lines, making his skin look like the tread of a tire.

One thing was for sure, he wasn't one of Autem's Guardians.

Becca opened her mouth to speak, but he held up a hand. For a second, he looked like he was going to say something, but instead he just yawned. It continued for several seconds as if he had just woken up from a nap. Becca frowned. From the extra-large man's casual demeanor, she assumed he was the artist behind the penis on the wall.

Finishing his yawn, he leaned back into the hall. "Hey Leon, we have a Guardian in here."

Becca looked down at her armor, realizing that she was at least partially dressed in one of Autem's uniforms. Though, the track suit underneath didn't match.

A second man entered before she could argue, shoving at the first as he tried to get past him. The new arrival was much smaller, with a slender build. Becca felt her skin heat up for an instant when he looked into her eyes. He was pretty. Like some kind of cosplay model. The kind of guy that probably looked good in eyeliner. He was a little younger than the larger man, with black, shoulder length hair pushed back so the sides hung down to frame his face. All he wore was a loose t-shirt and a pair of pants tight enough to make the goblin king proud.

He clapped his hands together. "Okay, I'm pretty sure we didn't leave a sign down stairs that said Guardians welcome, come on in."

The sun began to fall just below the silhouette of Autem's fortress outside the window, dimming the blanket of orange that permeated every corner of the room. Becca felt some of the weakness inside her fade. Her mana still felt out of reach, but some of the strength seemed to be returning. At half strength, there was a chance she could win against a pair of normal humans, even if one was the size of a house.

"I'm not a Guardian." Becca tried to stall.

"Do ya really think we're gonna buy that?" The larger of the two men folded his arms in a way that flexed his biceps. "We're going to have to take that sword from you and tie you up."

The smaller one sighed. "Yes, you know how it is. Can't take too many chances."

Becca groaned, realizing that she wasn't going to talk her way out of things so easily. It was just as well. As the shadows outside grew, her mana started to shift. Honestly, it had been a hard day, and kicking these guys asses would probably help get out some of her stress. All she had to do was make sure she didn't kill them.

Becca grinned. "You can try tying me up if you want. But I can't guarantee that it will go well."

The big guy nodded at her challenge. "I don't like hitting women, but I'll make an exception for a Guardian."

"Well, you both have fun with it then." The smaller man shoved his hands in his pockets and walked off to lean against the wall near the stack of canned goods.

Becca raised a fist, feeling some of the natural limits of her body peel away along with the last shreds of sunlight. "I'll try not to go overboard."

The big guy laughed. "I won't."

With that, Becca kicked off into a run.

Her opponent charged at the same time. He may have been big, but he had no idea what kind of monster she was. Becca leapt into the air, knees first. The world around her almost seemed to slow as her heightened senses began to stretch out the moment, the sound of everything around her becoming crisp. She soared through the air, the intoxicating power of a revenant waking up after a day of lying dormant.

For that one instant, she felt like anything was possible.

Then she slammed into a brick wall. Or, at least, that was what it felt like. All of her momentum stopped at once as her knees impacted with the over-muscled chest of the man rushing toward her. He didn't even flinch. Instead, he wrapped his arms around her back and clasped his hands behind her to lock her into a position kneeling against his upper body. She tensed her legs in attempt to break free, but the lingering life essence around her was still disrupting her body.

"Wha—" She couldn't form a coherent word as the burly man continued to run through the room, carrying her in a vice-like embrace, like she was nothing.

Becca's mind raced as her enhanced senses began to throw a million different details at her at once. Staring back over the shoulder of her opponent, the attractive, slender man leaning against the wall simply waved as if to say, 'Bye-bye.'

She shifted her attention back to the man carrying her through the room. Her jaw dropped, practically in slow motion, when she finally realized her mistake. The setting sun had coated her opponent in the same warm glow that she had been depending on to hide her pale skin. Now, with the light fading from the sky, the telltale signs were hard to miss.

He was pale.

Even worse, his eyes shined with the same orange flicker of a dying fire. Her captor opened his mouth to let out a growl, revealing a pair of thick fangs.

He was a revenant.

CHAPTER NINE

"Shit!" Becca's back slammed into a wall.

Drywall cracked against her body, a cloud of plaster filling the air to flood her nose and throat. Wood splintered as something inside her snapped. She was pretty sure it was a rib.

The mana inside her burned as if struggling to push out the life essence within its balance. Her body began to stitch itself back together slowly, the healing speeding up with each heartbeat. Confusion layered on top of panic as the massive intelligent revenant that she had picked a fight with continued to run, their momentum carrying them straight through the wall that he had slammed her into.

Clouds of plaster dust billowed in their wake as a new room surrounded her. It was the conference room she had passed on her way down the hall. The beast of a man that held her charged straight past the long table in the center. A human-sized hole was left in the wall behind him. Becca's eyes nearly crossed at the absurdity of what had just happened.

Then she slammed into another wall, her body being used as a battering ram. Drywall crumbled and wood splintered, falling behind her unstoppable captor. A twinge of pain streaked through her back before her body's healing erased it.

"Next stop, break room." The man chuckled as they both plowed through another wall at full speed.

He skidded to a stop and let go as soon as they were through. Becca kicked off without looking at what was behind her, just trying to get away. She crashed into a refrigerator, cracking her head against the stainless steel surface before she hit the ground.

"Oh, break room," she repeated as she realized why there was a fridge behind her.

"I'm surprised you're still conscious." Her opponent stepped toward her. "Let me guess, you cast a heal."

She kicked herself away in a blind scramble. It was as if every time she tried to use the physical strength that came with being a revenant, her body just turned everything up all at once. The result made it nearly impossible to know what was happening. Without her ravenous trait active, she had no way to use any of her new powers to fight. It was all just a chaotic mess.

So why wasn't her opponent having the same problem?

It didn't seem to matter that they were both revenants. He just happened to have more experience. Also, he was bigger. Clearly, he hadn't realized what she was yet. Otherwise, he might have at least hesitated before ramming her through three walls.

Grabbing hold of the refrigerator handle behind her, Becca hoisted herself back to her feet. The break room she had been dropped in was narrow, with just a simple galley kitchen. The massive revenant cracked his neck and stalked toward her. Becca changed tactics. If she couldn't beat him with brute strength, she could at least try to outsmart him. Shutting down her revenant strength, she tried her best to look scared. All she needed was for him to get close.

Becca smiled as he stepped into range, then she yanked the refrigerator door open to slam it into his face. She let the revenant inside her lose for an instant to increase the impact.

Her wrist hurt for a second from the overexertion, but the pain vanished in seconds.

The burly revenant fell back, clearly not expecting to be hit that hard. Becca took the moment for what it was, grabbing the back of the refrigerator and pulling it over on top of him. She immediately hopped up and over the appliance.

"Oof!" The man underneath coughed out a lungful of air.

Becca was pretty sure the door handle had hit him some-place important.

"Good."

She jumped back down on the other side of the fridge and started for the hole in the wall that she had been carried through. She came to a sudden stop when a meaty hand grabbed her ankle with a vice-like grip. Falling back down to the floor, she snagged an empty coffee pot from the counter on the way and rotated her body to launch the empty glass container back at her captor. The coffee pot shattered against his forehead.

He let go.

Becca kicked him in the face as she scrambled through the narrow galley kitchen, her feet slipping on shards of broken glass. After a few feet, she found the traction to get back up and sprinted into the conference room that she had been carried through earlier. On her way, she grabbed the backs of two office chairs and yanked them over to slow down the man behind her.

As she looked back, the massive revenant stumbled through the hole in the wall, his face covered in small cuts. They healed in seconds, leaving him to wipe away the excess blood on his arm. It coated the tattooed skin of his bicep with a pink smear.

Becca snapped her head forward and kept running despite having no idea what she was going to do. The smaller man was waiting for her in the first room. He must have been a revenant too, and he could probably use his abilities without overloading his senses, unlike her. All that left her with was her magic base abilities, ventriloquism and her darkness bending. That is, if she hadn't imagined them before.

An office chair slammed into her back before she could try anything. Becca fell to the floor, the chair tumbling to the side. She hadn't slowed down the beast behind her at all. No, the only thing throwing furniture in his path had done was hand him something to toss at her. She had been thinking like a human, not like the monster that she had become.

That was going to have to change.

"Back off!" Becca threw caution to the wind and rolled over as the large man stalked toward her. She raised a hand and willed whatever magic she had to do its thing.

The shadows all around the room swam toward her, growing darker, until a torrent of twenty bats erupted from the darkness to swirl toward her opponent. He shielded his face as the tiny shadow creatures went for his eyes. The sound of screeching filled the room.

Becca stared up in disbelief as he swatted at the bats, occasionally hitting one. Each time, they burst into a smoky cloud of gloom.

"Why the hell do I shoot bats?"

"Since when do Guardians do shadecraft?" The oversized revenant swatted away the last of the flying shadow rodents and continued toward her.

"I told you I'm not a Guardian!" She scooted away from him before throwing herself through the hole in the wall where the long-haired man stood waiting.

"Well, who are you then?" The slender revenant stepped toward her as his larger partner ducked through the hole behind her. "And why are you wearing Guardian armor?"

Both men closed in on her as she got up and pulled her sword from its sheath. She swiped it back and forth to hold them at bay. They didn't stop. She wasn't a threat. The strength and senses that came with her curse were a liability. All she could do with her power was shoot a few stupid bats around. Clearly, when the curse was handing out revenant abilities, she had gotten the short end of the stick.

Both men stopped in their tracks when a voice with a British accent came from the hallway.

"Oi! The fuck are you two doing?"

Becca kept her sword pointed at the large revenant and her other hand aimed at the smaller one as she flicked her eyes to the hall. A short woman stood in the doorway with an annoyed expression on her face. She was older than the other two, mid to late thirties, with a mess of shoulder length hair tied back haphazardly. A simple black, canvas jacket was zipped up to her neck. Matching black pants covered her legs, and a combat knife peeked out from a sheath at her lower back. A plastic shopping bag full of cans hung from one hand.

Most importantly, her skin was a healthy shade of peach.

Both men stood down and backed off as soon as she arrived.

"Ah, we kind of caught this woman in here and things got out of hand." The slender revenant waved a finger in the direction of the hole in the wall. "Ozzie did most of that over there."

"Oh thanks, dude, just throw me under the bus, why don't you?" The larger man, apparently named Ozzie, complained before adding, "I thought she was a Guardian."

The short woman dropped the plastic bag of cans and slapped a hand over her face, looking like a tired mom that had been stuck with the kids for too long. "What Guardian do you know wears a tracksuit under their gear? Obviously, she nicked the armor. Which means she's not a Guardian."

"That's what I have been saying." Becca let the tip of her sword fall a few inches.

"Well, in my defense," the smaller revenant shoved his hand into his pockets, "I had worked that out before the fight started."

"I'm sure you did, Leon," the woman growled in his direction. "But that just raises the question, why did you not see fit to stop it?"

"Oh, I was bored." He glanced around before adding,

"Plus, she seemed to be looking for a fight, so who was I to stop her?"

"That's actually fair." Becca lowered her sword the rest of the way. She had been a little too aggressive, thinking the fight was going to be an easy win. That had been before she realized she was up against a revenant.

The guy with long hair, apparently named Leon, threw both hands out toward her as if her confession had just proved his innocence. "See, Harlow. It was mostly fun for everyone."

The woman tensed the instant he used her name. "Did you seriously just use my real name in front of some random person? We have code names for a reason."

"Are you really still worried about that, Har?" Ozzie gestured to the window. "The world did end and everything. There's no more cops and shit to care about your real name."

Becca flicked her eyes around the room at each of them, suddenly feeling like she had stumbled upon a group that was just as dysfunctional as her own back in Vegas.

"Fine, fine." The short woman, whose real name was apparently Harlow, waved her hand at Ozzie before looking back to Becca. "Just who are you, and why did you pick a fight with these idiots?"

Becca lowered her head, not wanting to actually explain her somewhat embarrassing reasoning. "Because I thought I could take them. I sort of didn't realize they were both revenants too."

Both of the pale men gasped as soon as the words left her mouth, as if she had just delivered the worst insult in the world.

"Why on Earth would you think we were revenants?" Leon placed a hand to his chest as if wounded.

"Yeah, 'cause last time I checked, we were capable of holding an intelligent conversation," Ozzie added.

"That's a bit of a stretch." Harlow glowered at him.

"Very funny." Leon brushed off the comment before locking eyes with Becca. "But again, I need to ask. Why would you think we're revenants?"

"Because that's what I am?" Becca let the tip of her sword rest on the floor unsure what they were talking about.

"Seriously?" Ozzie looked at her like she had two heads.

"You have no idea what you are." Leon stepped closer to her. "Do you?"

Becca stepped back, her mind urging her to run away before hearing any more. Instead, she stamped down the fear and asked, "What am I?"

A warm smile spread across Leon's face. The kind reserved for family.

"You're a vampire, obviously."

Becca staggered as the word washed over her, leaving her standing with her arms limp and mouth agape.

"I'm a what, now?"

"A vampire. That's why you don't have the bat face." Leon reached forward to tap a finger on her nose, adding a quiet, "Boop."

Becca's eyes crossed. "Did you seriously just boop my nose?"

"Oh, sorry." Leon shoved his hand behind his back.

Becca leaned on her sword. It felt like her whole world had fallen apart all over again, the rug pulled out from under her. Dropping her hand from her head she swept her eyes across the trio of strangers. "Who are you people?"

"We're—" Ozzie started to answer only for Harlow to immediately shush him.

Leon stepped toward the short woman. "Is there really a need for secrecy at this point?"

Harlow rolled her eyes before finally turning to Becca.

"Have you ever heard of the Fools?"

CHAPTER TEN

"Vampires and Fools."

Becca sat in a chair within a partially demolished conference room, unsure what to make of everything that had happened so far. It was only minutes earlier that she had been rammed through the room's wall like it had been nothing.

After dropping the bombshell that she was, in fact, a vampire, Leon had offered her some food. He had made a point to specify that it was normal human food. All Becca could do was nod, not knowing what else to say. After that, he closed the blinds and lit a few camping lanterns. Then he pulled his oversized friend, Ozzie, away with him, probably to give her a little space while she processed things. The effort was undermined by the fact that they kept looking over at her as obviously as possible.

"How could she not know what she is?" Ozzie held a hand up to hide his mouth, as if to stop her from reading his lips despite whispering loud enough for Becca to hear.

"I just want to know who turned her," Leon added.

Eventually, Harlow, the short woman with a British accent, shushed them both. She seemed to be in charge, even if the two vampires argued with most of her orders. For the moment, the mysterious woman was content to leave Becca be. She was starting to think Harlow's silence was simply because she didn't know what to do with her. Not that Becca knew what to do with herself either.

Instead, she focused on the three strangers, trying to learn what she could.

Ozzie, the over-muscled vampire that had thrown her through the wall, brushed plaster dust from his short, messy hair. Then he cracked open one of the beers that had been sitting on the desk and entered the conference room to sit down in a chair at the opposite end of the table from her. He put his feet up, like he was actively trying to look cool. The effort ended up making him appear awkward instead. Becca watched as he glanced back at Leon every few minutes. It was clear from the way they interacted that they had worked together for a while. Something about them reminded Becca of characters from a sitcom, like they were just a couple of roommates, always getting into shenanigans.

Tavern would probably like them.

If she had to guess, Leon was the older of the two. As far as how old, she had no idea. He could have been older than Digby for all she knew, despite him looking around twenty-one. What made her think he was older was how he moved. As he prepared the camping stove and opened a few cans of stew, all actions were purposeful and precise, with little hesitation. He was more confident than someone who had only lived one lifetime. If she listened closely, she could hear the hint of an accent when he spoke, though she couldn't place where it was from. It sounded like several European accents blending together.

Ozzie was a different story. Mostly he spoke without an accent, but every now and then, a few words came out with a level of Bostonian flair. It reminded her of one of Bancroft's men, who had a much thicker version of the accent. Though, Ozzie hadn't told anyone to fuck themselves yet, so that was a point in his favor. From the way he carried himself, he was almost certainly putting up a front, like a big kid playing grown up. He looked around her age, and she was pretty sure he wasn't much older, even if he was an immortal vampire. Granted, from the way he'd wiped the floor with her minutes before, he definitely had more experience with his powers than she did.

Strangely, the pair of bloodsucking monsters didn't strike her as suspicious. There was something simple and uncomplicated about them that had a way of setting her at ease. The fact that they were all vampires might have had something to do with it. A kind of kinship or whatever.

The same couldn't be said for the third member of their group who leaned against the far wall, watching her.

Harlow.

That was what the vampires had called her, and she seemed annoyed every time they did. She hadn't complained about them using her real name again, but Becca noticed the short woman's eye twitch every time they did. The fact that she had been going by a code name made it clear that she was more than she appeared. All Becca knew was that she worked for an organization called the Fools. She was going to have to find out more. Especially if these Fools were investigating Autem's imperial capital. They could be allies, but also competition.

Despite being the obvious person in charge, Harlow didn't give many orders. In fact, she didn't seem to say much if she could help it, as if she was afraid to let something important slip. Then again, the way she kept watch on Becca made it clear she was good at assessing threats. Maybe a little too good, to a point where she was getting paranoid. It reminded Becca of herself, when she'd been forced to take control of Vegas while Digby was trapped in the Seed.

From the look of Harlow's eyes, teeth, and ears, she wasn't a vampire. Ozzie and Leon could have easily killed her for food. The fact that they hadn't gave Becca more reason to relax. If they were able to stay in control while working with a human, then maybe there was hope for her.

"Breakfast is ready." Leon brought over a disposable bowl full of cheap canned stew. Becca started eating as soon as he handed her a spoon, only now realizing how hungry she was. "There's plenty more, and I'm guessing from your appetite that you just turned?"

She paused. "You can tell that?"

"Yep. Turning takes a lot out of you. Plus, you haven't seemed to have figured out how to use your abilities yet." He slid a bowl to Ozzie. "He was the same way when he turned."

"I couldn't throw bats at people, though." Ozzie started shoveling stew into his mouth before he was done talking. "Didn't know a newbie could do that."

"That is an important point, actually." Leon served Harlow, who continued to stare at Becca instead of eating. "How exactly did you turn?"

"I was bitten by a revenant. That's why I thought I was one." Becca decided to keep her little trip to the land of the dead a secret, adding only, "When I woke up, I was on board a kestrel, captured by a squad of Guardians. I killed them all before I really knew what was happening."

"The thirst do be like that." Leon ran his tongue across his left fang. "If you had just turned, your mana was probably too low to keep your system going. Your thirst would have forced you to feed. It's like a compulsion, so you want to avoid letting your mana fall that low in the future."

"How does drinking blood replenish my mana?" Becca tried to learn what she could about her new existence. "And how could I have become a vampire if I was bitten by a revenant?"

"Blood carries mana," Ozzie chimed in as he scraped strew from his bowl. "And the revs are just shitty vampires."

Leon glowered at his partner. "Technically, the curse that creates revenants is the same curse that creates us," Leon added. "The conditions are just different."

"How are there not more vampires running around, then?" Becca took another bite of stew as she tried to make sense of it.

"If a vampire bites a human." Leon turned to Harlow and

raised his right arm to hide his face in his elbow, mimicking a classic image of Dracula.

"I will stake you, you know?" Harlow eyed him sideways.

He responded with an exaggerated hiss before dropping his arm to his side and continuing the explanation. "Basically, you have three choices when dealing with prey. You can kill them, turn them, or let them live." He clicked his tongue. "Letting them live is considered bad form."

"Why?" Becca finished her stew.

"Because that's how you get revenants." Leon refilled her bowl and got himself one. "Once a person has been bitten, the curse will lay dormant until nightfall. After dark sets in, it goes to work fast. Historically, most vampires kill their prey after feeding. That way, there's no chance of a revenant being created. I don't think I need to explain why we don't want revenants running free out there." He gestured to the world outside.

"Yeah, that's pretty self-explanatory." Becca nodded.

"We can't go turning everyone into more vampires either. That would be too noticeable." Leon set his bowl down and patted the back of Ozzie's chair. "Plus, no one wants to be saddled with the responsibility of teaching a new vampire the ropes."

Becca raised her eyebrows, getting confirmation that Leon had been the one to turn Ozzie. "And how does a vampire turn someone?"

"You anchor their soul." Leon dropped into a chair and started to eat. "The transformation from human to vampire involves a reconfiguration of the mana system. The problem with that process is that it pushes out the soul, sending it off to wherever people go when they die despite the body still being alive. And since the soul is the core of the mana system, a person without one will become a failed vampire, or what we all know as revenants. So to stop your prey from failing, you have to anchor their soul long enough for the transformation to complete."

"So a rev is just a vampire without a soul." Ozzie leaned back in his chair and put his feet up again. "Like I said, a shitty vampire."

"Oh." Becca's eyes widened as she began to understand. "I think I know how I turned. Or at least I think I do."

The three of them looked at her expectantly.

"I think a friend of mine used an enchanted item to…" She trailed off for a moment, trying to think of a way to avoid raising more questions. "I think my soul was anchored without a vampire involved."

Both Ozzie and Harlow looked to Leon as if to confirm if that was possible.

"That would certainly explain things." He shrugged before turning a suspicious eye in her direction. "Though, one thing doesn't add up."

"And that is?" Becca narrowed her eyes, realizing that the whole explanation had doubled as an interrogation. He was using her inexperience to get information out of her.

"If you really are a new vampire, like you said, then how are you able to throw bats around like you did?" He placed both hands together and flapped them up and down before dropping them to the armrests of his chair. "That was shadecraft, and I'm pretty sure you used a banshee in combination to make the little things squeak. I'm not an expert with either ability, but I know they exist and I know that a newborn vampire shouldn't have them. Even if you did somehow access that level of ability, you would need experience with illusion magic to be able to use them like that."

Harlow adjusted her position in her chair, as if getting ready to pull her knife if need be. "Care to explain who you really are?"

Becca gave an exaggerated shrug, realizing she needed to come clean, at least about some things. "I was a Heretic Illusionist before I was bitten."

"A Heretic?" Harlow leaned forward immediately. "Are you

a part of the group that's been causing Autem so much trouble?" From the expression on her face, she was impressed.

Becca leaned into the confession, sitting a little taller. "Yes, my people have been fighting Henwick and his forces since the world ended."

"Where are the rest of the Heretics now?" Harlow's voice climbed, suddenly sounding more concerned.

Becca pushed her empty bowl away. "I don't know how comfortable I am answering that without knowing more about your side."

Harlow slapped a hand down on the table. "We don't have time for you to get comfortable. We've lost too much already."

She closed her mouth a second later, clearly realizing she'd said too much. From the look in her eyes, one thing was obvious.

They were desperate.

Whoever these Fools were, they had already lost.

"You said you were a part of an organization, one that fought against Autem." Becca looked Harlow in the face. "How many of you are left besides you three?"

"None." A quiver entered Harlow's voice. "I think it's just me."

"Just you?" Becca glanced to Leon and Ozzie wondering why she hadn't said us.

"We're mercenaries." Ozzie gestured to himself and Leon. "More like free agents."

"The Fools have been fighting a losing war with Autem for all of history." Leon gestured to himself. "They've frequently used vampires to help balance the scales. Though, the two of us have been contracted by the Fools for a few years now."

Becca furrowed her brow, wondering how Harlow was keeping a pair of vampire mercenaries in her service when money had lost all purpose. There must have been more to the situation. She needed to keep them talking.

"What happened to the rest of your organization?"

Harlow shook her head. "The Fools aren't an organization.

Just a loose network of people. They get together and form troupes whenever there's a need. The point is to only act if absolutely necessary. That way our actions impact as few people as possible and preserve the world's freedom to make its own choices. We tend to clash with Autem, because their goal is to protect humanity by removing choice all together."

"And you were the leader of your team, what did you call it? A troupe?" Becca tried to ask more without seeming too aggressive. Clearly, the woman had been through a lot and a little empathy would go a long way.

"It's a throwback to the Fools' roots. They started as jesters and the like so we call each cell a troupe." She lowered her head. "And no, I wasn't in charge. I was just a bodyguard. My troupe had been working on something important, though. Something that could have given us the power to stop all this from happening, or at least save as many people as possible when the end came."

"What was it?" Becca leaned forward.

"Magic," Leon answered as if trying to give Harlow a break from talking about her past. "Or at least a way to access magic. That has always been at the center of the fight. Autem has more resources, so they were able to tap into the world's mana on a small scale. That fact kept the Fools at a disadvantage and playing catch up. The only saving grace was that Autem hadn't fully unlocked magic yet, so they couldn't give it to just anyone. Instead, they found people like Henwick, who had established a connection to magic on their own and found ways to exploit or contain it. They've also had a few experimental systems over the years that had been able to connect to single users like Bancroft. Beyond that, they also used enchantments and runes to give themselves an edge. Their end goal, however, was always to create a Heretic Seed of their own, but with more control options. It was only a matter of time before they succeeded, so the Fools had to do the same to compete."

"It was an arms race." Harlow looked back up from the table. "Especially the last few decades, as modern technology advanced to create new possibilities. The only thing holding back both sides, until now, was the caretaker."

Becca nearly jumped up from her chair at the mention of the one thing that could save Digby and fix everything. "You created one?"

Harlow shook her head. "I didn't have anything to do with the technical stuff. I just know what I overheard. We were able to reverse engineer an artificial caretaker system using information gained by a troupe that came before us. They had obtained one of the Heretic Seed's fragments sometime in the seventies."

"So your caretaker is an A.I.?" Becca furrowed her brow.

"Something like that." Harlow held up one hand. "That's the part that handles the important stuff regarding magic, and Autem was able to get that far as well." Holding up her other hand, she added, "But there's a second part that's needed to unlock magic completely."

"A soul." Becca remembered what the Seed's original caretaker had told her back while she had been dead. Digby had given the Heretic Seed his spark.

"So you know?" Harlow arched an eyebrow clearly wondering how she was so well informed.

"I only know the basics." Becca decided to be honest.

Harlow kept her eye on her for another few seconds before continuing. "The caretaker system requires a person to become its interface to give it a human perspective of the world. Without that, you can't get full access to magic. Autem has never been able to find any willing candidates within their forces that were compatible with a caretaker."

"They're all control freaks," Ozzie added.

"When your entire goal is to force your world view on others, is anyone really surprised?" Leon picked at his stew.

"Yes." Harlow stood up from her chair. "Whoever created the Heretic Seed obviously knew a caretaker would be a powerful entity. Its system controls magic and how we interact with it, and the soul that tells that system what to do could abuse that power easily. Hence the need for compatibility. It's like a test. If a person clings to power and control, their soul simply rejects the caretaker. While someone with empathy and the ability to see the world through many lenses can bond with the system without much fuss. So basically—"

"They need to care," Becca finished her sentence.

Digby may have been a snarky jerk, but if there was one thing that she knew was true, it was that he always cared about others when it mattered. Not only that, but he never sought power for himself. No, he pursued it because he needed it to survive and to protect others. If it was up to him, he would much rather be left alone. It actually made sense why his soul was able to join with the Seed's caretaker. The Fools must have found someone similar if they had been able to create one. If so, that was probably the other caretaker that Abby had mentioned while Becca was dead. The one that could help her save Digby.

That was when an obvious detail stood out. Autem, clearly, had gained full access to magic, and Harlow hadn't. Becca winced as she asked another question, already knowing the answer.

"Let me guess, you found a candidate that was compatible with your artificial caretaker, but Autem stole it as soon as you merged them together?"

The look on Harlow's face said it all. "It happened a few months before they nuked Seattle. Before the world ended. The science team had just made a breakthrough after months of trying to get the caretaker to work right. Things started moving fast after that. There was a lot to do to get a magic system running, plus we had other irons in the fire, so my troupe was stretched thin. I was the only one available to guard the caretaker."

"And that was when Autem struck." Becca sunk into her chair.

"It was like Henwick was waiting for us to create the caretaker for him." Harlow held onto the back of the chair she had been sitting in, her fingers digging into the cushion. "He led the attack himself. I did everything I could, but Henwick was too strong to fight alone. In the end, I was left half-dead and Henwick walked off with our caretaker. A month later, the Guardian Core was up and running."

Becca ran over the timeline in her head to see if it synced up with what she knew. It certainly explained why Skyline had so few magic users back in Seattle and why most were low levels. She'd always wondered why, other than Bancroft, they hadn't had more than a handful of squads. However, if Autem had only gained full access to magic a few months earlier, the number of magic users in their mercenary force made sense. They were probably still in the process of rolling out the Guardian Core system when Digby returned and brought the curse back. Autem must have been scrambling to take advantage of it.

Becca placed both hands on the table and pushed herself up, feeling like she and her new friends could come to an understanding. "Am I correct in assuming that you are here to try to get the caretaker back? That's why you're watching Autem's capital, to find a way in?"

"Of course. It's my fault we lost the caretaker. I have to do this." Harlow let go of her chair and let her arm fall to her side. "Besides, I was just a grunt, not a tactician. I don't know what else to do, right now."

"Unfortunately, attacking them with just the three of us is out of the question." Leon gestured to the window, beyond which lay their target.

"It would be suicide." Ozzie scoffed.

"That's why we need to know where your Heretics are." Harlow leaned on the table with sincerity in her eyes. "We want the same thing. If we can put together a strike team of magic users, we might have a chance. Not to mention reclaiming the caretaker would take away the empire's ability to make more Guardians."

Becca folded her arms, considering it. Then she shook her head. "Things aren't that simple."

Harlow's face dropped. "What?"

"We are preparing for a fight with Autem." Becca deflated. "But there are a few obstacles. For one, our strongest magic user is dying and he doesn't know it. Well, technically he's already dead, but that has never been a problem before now. The real problem is his mind."

"So it's true." Leon cleared away the empty bowls on the table. "You have a zombie necromancer leading your side. That explains why you and your friends have been able to do as much damage as you have."

"Yes, his name is Digby, and the fact that he can raise a horde has been vital to nearly every win we've had." Becca took in a slow breath, working out how to explain things. "Not long ago, we stole back the Heretic Seed's fragments and reassembled the obelisk."

Harlow gasped in response. "Then you've done it. You've unlocked magic."

"Yes, but in doing so, Digby gave up his spark to make a new caretaker, leaving himself without a soul. Apparently, a human can live without one, but for a zombie like him, it's important. He'll lose his mind within a week without his soul, and we don't stand a chance without him. That's why I'm here. I have to find a way to save him before that happens."

"Then we need to get to him now." Harlow looked like she might start packing up that very second. "If your mate can raise a horde, we can attack the empire's capital and extract our caretaker. Maybe we can figure out how to trade out ours for the one that has his soul in the Seed. That way we can return it to your zombie friend."

"There's not enough time." Becca took one last look into each of their eyes before putting her trust in the trio. "Digby is in Las Vegas. That's where my people are hiding. I have no way to contact them, and they might not know I'm alive. It would take us days to travel there and more to get back here. We could try and steal a kestrel or something, but it would still take weeks to build up a force that would have a shot against Autem. Digby will have lost his mind by then, and we will lose our strongest piece on the board. We can make more Heretics now that the Seed is whole, but they will still need to train and we are limited by the number of survivors we can gather. Without Digby, Autem has the resources to build their army faster."

Harlow lowered herself back into her chair. "That's it then. It's impossible."

Becca turned to the window to avoid eye contact with anyone as silence fell across the room. She just needed time to think. Through the narrow spaces between the blinds, she could see lights shining in the distance from Autem's capital. The massive construction project loomed over the cityscape.

There was no way to get help.

Even with Harlow and her mercenary vampires, that only made four of them. No matter how she did the math, it wasn't enough for an assault. Not against whatever fortress Autem was building. That was when an insane thought passed through her mind.

"What would Digby do?" She turned around. "How much have you learned about that structure the empire is building out there?"

"We've scouted it, but haven't learned much. It seems to be a giant wall." Leon flicked his eyes to Harlow to add more.

"But we do have some information about what's inside." She reached into a pocket and pulled out a flash drive. "It's not much, just some building plans that we were able to get before the internet died, but it's something."

"I'm going to need to see everything you have." Becca glanced at Leon. "And I'm going to need you to give me a crash course in how to be a vampire."

"I can do that." He gave her a sideways look. "Why? What are you thinking?"

Becca channeled her inner Digby.

"How do you feel about heists?"

CHAPTER ELEVEN

"What do you want?" Digby opened the door of his room in Vegas to find Parker standing in the hallway. She held some kind of plastic book in her arms, clutching it close to her chest.

"The covens are getting ready to head out, so I thought I'd come on up and, um, get you." She glanced around, looking in almost every direction other than his eyes.

Digby glowered at her. "Here to check up on me, eh? Making sure I haven't gone insane, are you?"

"I would never." Parker shook her head a little too hard only to stop and add, "But, you haven't gone insane, right?"

Digby let a moment of silence pass before answering. "Not that I'm aware."

"Oh good." Parker swayed back and forth. "I was just checkin'."

"Shut up, Parker." He grabbed his coat and threw it on, making sure the Goblin King's pauldron was securely attached.

It had only been one day and he was already regretting his decision to let the pink-haired soldier monitor his behavior. Henwick may have gone mad after losing his soul, but that was him. Digby was relatively sure he didn't have anything to worry about. Hell, he felt more sane than he ever had in his life. The only reason he had suggested that Parker keep an eye on him was to put her and Alex's concerns at ease. He never actually expected the lazy soldier to take the job seriously. Now, the constant check-ins were beginning to get old. He was going to have to find a way to get her to back off if he was going to retain his sanity.

Parker fell in beside him as soon as he left his room.

He suppressed an annoyed sigh and continued walking in silence as he debated on if he could annoy her enough to get her to leave him be.

After his speech the day before, the entire casino had been buzzing with activity. It was a good thing too. With the setback of Bancroft's betrayal, they had a lot of ground to cover and little time to waste. Fortunately, it seemed that giving the people access to magic had proved surprisingly motivating.

In just a few hours after moving the Seed's obelisk to the town square at the center of the casino, nearly half of the people staying there had accepted its power and become Heretics. There was something unifying about seeing so many new names join their ranks, like they had all become a part of the same horde. On top of that, by freely sharing the Seed's power, while being upfront about his expectations, Digby had gained a new level of trust throughout the settlement. Obviously, he didn't mention the fact that he and Alex could take it all away just as easily. He just hoped he wouldn't have to do it.

There were people that had yet to accept the Seed's power, but Digby was sure they would come around when they saw the difference that magic made for everyone else. The Seed would help to ensure their survival in a way that was personally empowering. The immortality didn't hurt either.

With a thought, he brought up a list on his HUD to show the classes of everyone who had taken his offer. He made a point to sort it, placing the more advanced classes first.

Artificer: 1

Cleric: 1

Messenger: 1

Necromancer: 2

Rogue: 1

Tempestarii: 1

Enchanter: 33

Fighter: 336

Mage: 335

There were so many. They had only had a handful of magic users the night before. Now, they had an army. He just hoped he would be able to make use of them properly. Fortunately, he wasn't alone.

As soon as each new Heretic stepped away from the Seed's obelisk, Elenore and Deuce stepped in to organize them based on their previous experience and preferences. The pair had become Digby's go-to people for anything concerning the city's internal operations. Together, they began organizing Vegas's forces. Some of the people had accepted magic in order to increase their odds of survival in the apocalypse, while others had done so to fight for their new home. It had actually surprised Digby how many of the settlers wanted to join the fight. Though, he hoped more would be willing to stand against Henwick's empire as the war grew closer.

Training the Heretics came next.

Digby pulled out a small leatherbound notebook that Elenore had sent up to his room. Inside was a list of people organized into covens of six Heretics each. Every coven was labeled with a number as well as what role its members would play. About half were dedicated to building up the city. This included clearing the streets of revenants, warding the strip, working the forge, security patrols, and helping to manage Asher's horde.

The rest of the covens were devoted to the war effort and had been relegated to Digby's command. Reading over the names, he noticed a few that were missing. Alex and Mason were among the absent. He didn't question why, assuming that they would be joining his group along with Parker.

Willing the Seed to reorganize their forces into covens that matched the list, Digby found that most were made up of a mix between mages and fighters, with one enchanter to round things out. It was a good balance for safety, giving each coven an enchanter that could cleanse a curse as well as two or three mages that could heal.

On the last page of the notebook was his coven.

To his surprise, Mason and Alex weren't listed there either. Instead, it was just Parker and four random names. Even stranger, all four were enchanters. Digby arched an eyebrow, wondering whose idea that was. He made a note to ask Elenore as soon as he saw her. Then, he closed his notebook and shoved it in his pocket.

Turning his attention back to his HUD, he frowned at the numbers that labeled each coven. There was something about it that lacked flair. With that in mind, he willed the Seed to change each coven's designation. Instead of numbers, he assigned an animal to each group, making sure his choice matched their role. The squads that were tasked with jobs within the city were named after familiar critters. Rabbit, mouse, goose, and so on. The rest that were made up of Heretics that had chosen to fight against Autem got more mythical names. Griffin, Kraken, Chimera.

He named his own Goblin, after the king who had worn his pauldron before him. He glanced at Parker walking beside him as his coven's second in command. The pink-haired woman stared blankly at the ceiling. Digby shook his head, then searched his HUD for a coven led by Sax and named it Dragon, with the intent of keeping it close. If Mason wasn't going to lead one of the groups, he wanted at least one reliable soldier around.

He had a feeling that he was going to need the help, with everything they had planned. After all, a war was brewing, and they needed to be ready. Hence why he was heading down to the parking garage first thing in the morning. Magic wasn't the only thing they needed. No, they also needed weapons, equipment, and a way to transport Heretics and the horde. Fortunately, there was a whole world of abandoned military bases to loot, and with Parker's Mirror Passage spell, the only limit was of what places they could find pictures of. As such, the day would be spent exploring their options.

Parker broke away from him as soon as they reached the casino's garage, saying she still had things to check on concerning where she needed to open a passage first. Digby relaxed as soon as she was gone, finally getting some time to himself. Though, after a minute or so of being alone with his thoughts, he sent a call across his bond to Asher to keep from dwelling on everything that had gone wrong before.

The deceased raven answered his call, flapping into the garage a moment later, as if she had already been waiting for a chance to speak to him.

"Ah, there you are, girl." He scratched at her chin as she landed on his shoulder. "And how is our horde doing?"

He immediately sensed disappointment from his minion.

"That bad, hmm?"

She nodded, sending a thought back to him. "This place was picked clean. Less than one hundred dead to join us."

"You're right, that's not a very large horde. I'll have to use my Fingers of Death to turn some revenants to our side." Digby patted her wing. "I'll see what I can do to bring you some new friends while I'm away as well."

Asher cawed happily before settling into a position leaning against his neck.

Rows of cars had been lined up, running down one aisle of the garage, while members of Digby's mythic covens rushed this way and that, making last minute preparations. Most of them were geared up for battle. It was unlikely that they would face too much opposition during the day, but it was better to be safe than sorry.

It was good to see everyone working to move forward after

the losses that they had suffered. After all, sitting around and moping never solved anything. Digby had done enough of that, replaying Rebecca's death over and over in his mind. In a way, he was just glad to have something to take his mind off things. Ever since he'd accessed the power to build his army, he simply hadn't had time to think about anything else.

At least, that was what he told himself.

Following the row of cars down, he reached a large alcove in the parking garage on the bottom level near the casino's loading docks. Digby stopped to stare at the three enormous mirrors that had been fastened into place against the concrete within the alcove. Sparks fell from the ceiling as a few of Deuce's men welded some last-minute supports into place for the reflective surfaces. Asher cawed and flapped her wings in protest to the noise.

The mirrors had originally lined one of the grand hallways inside the casino to make the already large space seem even bigger. Now, they served a new purpose. At ten feet high and twelve wide, they were big enough to transport a variety of vehicles through one of Parker's passages. Provided the mirror at the other end was as large. If not, they had additional mirrors stored nearby. That way they could open the portal and carry one through with them if there wasn't anything large enough at their destination. Then all they had to do was temporarily install it at the other end and reopen a passage.

Digby swept his eyes across the area, finding Parker standing by a cement pillar. She was casually flipping through the plastic book that she had been carrying earlier without looking up. She still didn't look up when he approached, so he cleared his throat to announce his presence.

"Blar!" She jumped back, dropping her book. She kicked out a foot to catch it before it hit the ground. For a second it looked like she might be successful, but it toppled over and hit the concrete anyway.

"Looks like you need to drop a few more points into dexterity." Digby bent down to pick up the book, curious what was inside the thing.

"Yeah." Parker pulled one of her daggers out and tossed it in the air, catching it by the blade before flipping it again and catching the handle. "I thought I was getting better."

"Impressive. You'll be able to rival that Jack the Ripper fellow soon."

"Meh, it's not really a competition." She shrugged, then slid her dagger back in its sheath. "Can I have my binder back?"

Digby ignored her request and flipped through a selection of plastic sleeves inside. Each contained images of various mirrors in different locations that they could travel to. There was at least a few dozen. "How did you find this many pictures?"

"That was Elenore. She got a whole team of people to search the casino's magazines and post cards. I was surprised that we were able to find that many too. Though, to be honest, there's still a lot of places that we would like to reach that we haven't found anything for. We're still looking for some key locations. It would have been faster if the internet didn't shit itself, though." Parker shook her hand at him. "Now give me the binder. I know you don't wash your hands."

"Oh, please, I wash plenty." He hesitated, trying to remember the last time he'd done so before adding, "I showered yesterday."

She wrinkled her nose. "Yeah, only because you were covered in bits of one of Bancroft's men."

"Details, details." Digby rolled his eyes. "Do you have any locations in this book where we might find some equipment and supplies?"

She snatched the binder away and flipped to a page. "Yeah. Pictures of military bases have been hard to find, but we found one that I can use for a passage that will take us directly to a prime target. It's a naval base that's far enough from the mainland so that it should be off Autem's radar, to a degree. We just need to make sure we don't make it obvious that we're there in a way that can be seen by a satellite. We might even find some survivors to join us like we did at the Hoover Dam."

"It's as good a place as any to start." Digby put his hand in his pockets as Parker beckoned to one woman and three men standing not too far away.

They promptly rushed toward him, lined up, and stood at attention. Each was dressed in body armor and carried a rifle.

"Umm, yes?" Digby stared at them, unsure what they wanted.

Asher added a confused caw.

"This is the rest of our squad." Parker stood between them. "Alex wants you to power level some of the Enchanters to get them up to Artificer. That way, we can get a real research and development department working on the runes that he's been experimenting with." She gestured from left to right. "This is Mike, John, Thelma, and Kim."

"Thank you for taking us with you." Mike nodded. "I was an engineer before all this so I'm looking forward to getting back to work."

"We will try our best not to slow you down," Thelma added. "And I designed theme park rides, which I realize is not quite the same thing as magic runes."

John gestured to himself. "I was an architect."

"Rocket scientist." Kim finished the introductions looking proud of himself.

Digby ignored the man's grinning and leaned to Parker. "What do you mean by power level?"

She thought for a second. "It's when someone stronger does all the fighting for a group of lower-level people so they get easy experience. We can't risk sending our enchanters into danger since we don't have that many, but if they stay behind you and me, they can reach Artificer faster. Some of the experience will be lost because of your level, but Alex said there should be some overflow, provided you take on things like active revenants."

Digby frowned, not liking the sudden responsibility. "Why doesn't Alex do it then?"

"Because I'm not going with you." The Artificer in question pulled up in that death trap of a floating car that he'd constructed. Digby hadn't heard him approach on account of the fact that the vehicle was practically silent.

Digby spun around. "What do you mean you're not coming?"

Alex stopped the car in front of one of the mirrors and got out. "I had a thought yesterday."

Digby couldn't help but notice an excited look in the Artificer's eyes. "No doubt this thought of yours indulges your more immature interests."

Alex stopped with his mouth hanging open. "Okay, that's fair, but I think you'll agree with me anyway."

"Alright, what is this idea of yours?" Digby groaned.

"Well, I have been thinking about the items Henwick had in his vault on the moon, and the Goblin King's coat that you found in the pop museum back in Seattle." He stood a little taller, clearly feeling confident. "If movie props have gained such powerful enchantments just by being famous, then there has to be more items out there that have gained abilities as well. I took a trip to the mob museum here in Vegas yesterday, but I didn't find anything. So I'm thinking I need to broaden my search to find some artifacts that are more famous. I put in a request with Elenore's research team to find images of pop culture museums and they got me one in Hollywood. I want to check it out to see what's there."

Digby stared at him for a moment. It actually was a good idea.

"That could be really cool." Parker hopped toward him.

"Right?" Alex nodded excitedly, giving off a similar energy as a dog that had just been given a new bone to chew on. "Think about it, we could equip our best Heretics with gear that boosts their stats or gives them new abilities."

"Alright, I can't say I'm against it." Digby folded his arms. "But you're going to need a coven of your own. And at least one member will need the Mirror Link spell so that you can communicate with Parker to get a return passage opened."

"Way ahead of you." Alex hooked a thumb back over his shoulder. "I have a team in the car."

Digby leaned to one side so he could look past the Artificer to see the vehicle. In the passenger seat sat Lana. Considering she had just unlocked the cleric class, that satisfied their communications requirements. Behind her sat Hawk, holding the skull of Kristen, the deceased seer. Beside him was Lana's traitorous brother, Alvin.

"Are you mad?" Digby turned his attention back to Alex. "You intend to take an irritating skull and two children on this quest of yours, one of which has betrayed us in the past. Oh, and the skull has tried to get you killed as well."

"She's not that bad." Alex shrugged. "I re-engraved the runes on her that Bancroft's men sabotaged, so the spell that keeps her talking shouldn't wear off. Kristen knows a lot about Autem, so I'm hoping she'll come around to our side if we give her a chance. Provided she can look past the part where you arranged her murder." He looked back. "Besides, most of the revs are dormant during the day, and zombies are scarce out there. I don't intend on going anywhere too dangerous, and if we get a whiff of any serious threats, we'll get a passage back. Ultimately, I think an easy mission is kinda what Hawk needs right now. Or rather, leaving him home while we do everything is the worst thing for him."

Digby sighed. The boy had been doing his best to act like nothing had changed, but it was obvious that his efforts were a front. Maybe a quest really would be good for the child. It wasn't like Digby knew how to handle the situation, anyway. "Alright, Hawk will prove helpful on this venture, but Alvin is still a liability."

"Yeah, he kinda drank the Kool-Aid when he was with Autem, but he's been doing better and showing him a little trust might help." Alex looked back to the car. "I had him link with the Heretic Seed, so he has his magic back and can gain experience, but I immediately blocked his spells so he can't use them to contact Autem."

Digby considered it for a moment, then he willed the Seed to create a new coven and added each member of Alex's group to it. When he was done, he named the coven Unicorn. "Just make sure Alvin doesn't trick you into giving him access to his magic. All he needs to do is cast Mirror Link and he could tell Henwick exactly where we are."

"I won't." Alex handed Parker a card with a street on it. "You should be able to open a passage to the Walk of Fame in Hollywood. That was all I could find, but it's as good a place as any to start."

"Okay." She started for the mirror mounted to the wall only to stop and look back. "You guys should probably get out of the car and push it through the passage. I haven't sent anything that big yet, and I'd rather not test any theories with you inside."

"Good point." Alex slapped a hand on the roof of the car. "Everyone out."

"Yay, more child labor." Hawk crawled out of the back still holding Kristen's skull.

"Yes, make sure you put your backs into it," the deceased seer added. "I would help but, you know, I'm dead. Because you murdered me."

"I'm getting real sick of that joke, Kristen." Alex grabbed the skull and shoved it into a messenger bag. "And it's a flying car; it's easy to push. So stop complaining about child labor." He got behind the vehicle only to stop and hold up a finger. "Oh, before I forget."

The artificer walked around the car to reach in through a window to grab something long, pulling it out to present it to Digby. "Tada, new staff."

"Oh?" He approached the weapon, finding it different from his last one. Sure, it still had the hollow diamond shape at the top, adorned with a skull at its base, except now, it had been coated in gold, with more of the metal dripping down the shaft where it must have cooled. At the bottom, a human femur had been affixed to the end, also dipped in gold, though with less drips, as if the bone had been dipped separately from to the weapon. "Interesting."

"I changed up the design to see if we could get a different enchantment." Alex held the staff tight and closed his eyes. "Now let's get it imbued."

"Alright, then." Digby placed his hand on the weapon as well, Alex's spell requiring a donation of thirty mana to activate the enchantment. He felt the pull on his magic immediately. The Heretic Seed informed him of the item's creation a moment later.

Alex sighed when it failed to bestow any new abilities beyond the same twenty percent cost reduction to death magic. "Damn. I thought I really had something there."

"Well, failure or not, it will be good for something." Digby raised the staff up before dropping it back down, enjoying the metallic clank the golden femur made on the concrete.

"I'll keep trying." Alex shrugged before heading back to push the car.

"Come help." Lana exited the passenger seat to let her brother out behind her.

Alvin said nothing, but took a place beside her at the back of the car regardless.

"Hey," Digby called to Hawk.

"Yeah?" The boy turned around.

A quiet voice inside of Digby told him to say something nice, but all that came out was, "Don't do anything foolish."

"Yeah, don't you fuck anything up either." Hawk turned away and helped push the car.

Parker studied the picture Alex had given her for a few seconds, then raised her hand to the largest mirror. "Okay, I think I have it."

The reflective surface began to ripple and Alex shoved the vehicle forward. It vanished into the mirror seconds later. Everyone stood still as if waiting for a crash. None came. Eventually, Alex stepped through only to return with a report that the destination was clear of enemies. After that, he just waved goodbye and stepped through again. The others did the same.

Parker swiped a hand through the air the moment they were gone. The mirror's rippling ceased as soon as she did. Afterward, she pulled a small plastic case from her pocket and flipped it open to reveal a hand mirror. The tiny reflective surface changed as a Link spell filled it with a view of Lana's face as seen through a second mirror that she had carried through with her. She moved her end of the link to show the area where they had arrived. The car had made it to the other side without incident. Parker wished them luck and closed the case in her hand.

"That's handy." Digby eyed Parker as she shoved the little mirror into her pocket.

"It's a makeup compact. We got a bunch of them and distributed them to everyone that has the Link spell. It's not quite the same as having a radio, but we can stay in contact from anywhere in the world. Pretty cool, right?"

"Indeed." Digby spun around. "Now, where is Mason?"

Just as the question left his mouth, Digby caught a glimpse of that ridiculous hat that the soldier had been wearing since yesterday. Mason looked tired, but wore a hardened expression on his face. Behind him followed the last person Digby expected to see him with, Clint.

Digby furrowed his brow at the group, unsure why Vegas's only other zombie necromancer was carrying a staff of his own and dressed in full armor, as if ready to head out on a mission.

"What is this now?" He walked toward the group.

"Good, I haven't missed you." Mason slowed to a stop. "I had to get Clint ready to leave."

"I see that, and where were you intending on taking him?" Digby eyed the other zombie before flicking his eyes back to Mason.

"Sorry, I have something that I have to check out on the coast and I need Clint for it." Mason adjusted his hat.

"The coast?" Digby leaned to one side. "What would you want there?"

"Becca's alive."

"What?" Mason's words hit Digby like a swift kick to the head from an annoyed horse.

Parker gasped just as Mason added, "We think," to his statement.

"What do you mean, you think?" Digby closed the gap between them in one step. "Is she alive or not? It is a pretty damn big difference."

"I know." Mason stepped forward practically shoving his chest into Digby's. "That's why I am checking. Alex used the slippers to cast a spell that could revive the dead. That's why I need to find her body. We have no idea how the spell works, but if it called her soul back, I have to find her."

Digby struggled to wrap his mind around what he was hearing. Even harder was understanding why no one had mentioned the development to him. "Why didn't you say something sooner?"

"Alex didn't want to get anyone's hopes up until we heard from her." Mason glanced around. "And I know you're going through some stuff."

"No, I most certainly am not going through anything." Digby raised his staff and dropped it back down hard. "You both should have told me the moment you tried to revive her."

"Well, I'm telling you now." Mason didn't budge. "We were hoping Becca would show up in the Seed's list of Heretics, or that she would project herself to one of us to let us know she's alive, but it's been twenty-four hours and there's been no sign. I am not going to wait any more. That's why I'm going out to find her, and I need Clint to do that. He can swim down to that sunken ship without any gear and explore."

"I really don't mind." Clint moved to step between them.

"Not now, Clint." Digby snapped at the zombie while keeping his eyes focused on Mason. "What happens if you called her spark back to her body, and she woke up at the bottom of the ocean?"

"I have to believe she survived." Mason shook his head. "We couldn't wait. The spell might not have worked if we waited too long."

Digby's blood boiled at the thought of not being included in something so important. Even more so because Alex had kept him in the dark. Obviously, he'd done so because of his and Parker's ridiculous theory that he might become a monster like Henwick now that he didn't have a soul.

"Fine." Digby resisted the urge to explode at the man. Mason was sure to be dealing with his own grief and yelling at him would only make him look like the monster that everyone feared he would become. "Take Clint, but don't take any unnecessary risks. I need him to help manage the horde."

"Understood." Mason finally stepped back. "I'll take a coven with us." He glanced to Parker. "Do you have a location near the coast in your binder of photos?"

"No, but I can send you to the campsite where we all met." She looked up and to the side. "I remember enough mirrors and windows there to open a passage. There should be a few cars there still. You would just have to find somewhere with a boat to get out to the cargo ship."

"That's good enough." Mason gave her a nod.

"I want to hear about what you find the moment you know anything," Digby insisted before turning back to Clint. "What about the horde? Can Asher manage it while you're away?"

Clint hesitated, clearly not wanting to get snapped at again. "I have secured the building where the horde is being kept. They will be content there. If any of the teams that are clearing the strip have any recent revenant corpses, there is a side entrance that leads to a balcony where the bodies can be tossed in without issue. Asher should not be needed and is free to accompany you."

"Just make sure you are all back by nightfall." Digby willed the Seed to create a new coven and added Mason and Clint. He pointed out a coven named Pegasus and told them to bring them.

Mason gave a firm nod and headed out. Parker went with him to open a passage.

Digby watched them go, still shocked that they hadn't told him anything. Alex had literally just spoken to him and said nothing.

What kind of apprentice hides such important matters like that? Am I really so untrustworthy? Digby tightened his fingers around his staff. *Do they really think so little of me after all this time?*

"Bah!" He shook his head. "I don't have time for self-pity. And I'll give Alex a piece of my mind when he returns."

Digby turned to look at the Heretics that were ready to head out.

"Right now, I have work to do."

CHAPTER TWELVE

Disorientation flooded Digby's mind as he stepped into the rippling surface of the mirror in the casino's garage. It was like missing a step at the bottom of a flight of stairs. An instant later, his foot touched solid ground, only for a second detail to carry on his state of confusion.

"That's odd."

Digby stood, leaning on his staff and staring at the sky as a sunrise chased several revenants off the sidewalk where he had just emerged from the surface of a window. It had been mid-day in Vegas where he'd entered the passage, yet, here on the other side it was only dawn. The air was a bit warmer as well. The climate in Las Vegas had been beginning to cool off in recent weeks but here, it still felt like the peak of summer.

"How far did Parker send me?"

Digby swept his eyes across the area to make sure it was safe for the rest of the covens to come through. There were still a few revenants making their way into the cover of the buildings nearby. It would be best to wait until the sun was a little higher to make sure all of the threats were dormant before bringing any humans through the passage.

Finding a large sign not far away, the words Pearl Harbor Historic Sites were written across its surface in three-dimensional lettering. A row of palm trees lined a walkway that stretched toward a parking lot.

Digby turned to survey the area. "Where the devil am I?"

The naval base had been selected as a destination because it was large enough to have much of what his army needed. Plus, it was one of the few places that was easy to find a photo of. From what Digby understood, it was a place that held some kind of historic value, though he hadn't had time to look into things more than that.

Digby called to Asher across their bond to see how far away from her he was. There was no answer beyond a vague feeling of curiosity.

"Hmm…" Digby scratched his chin. "It seems I am further from my minion than I have ever been."

With that in mind, he decided to test a theory by giving her a command over the distance. He hoped she would still understand what he wanted as long as he didn't ask anything too complicated.

Digby focused on their bond. *Come to me.*

The deceased raven burst from the rippling window a moment later, landing on his shoulder.

"So you could hear me?" Digby gave her a pat.

She sent a few words across their bond.

Not hear. Feel.

"I see. Words are not necessary." He nodded before changing his focus to connect with his armored zombie, Ducky, and ordered him to join them as well.

Last he'd seen the oversized minion, he'd been standing in the corner of the casino's garage. Again, he only felt a vague presence over the distance. Despite that, Ducky lumbered through the passage not long after.

"Good, good." Digby grinned at his ability to command his minions over such distances.

Finally, he focused on his link to Tavern. By now, the

infernal spirit and their treacherous host, Bancroft, would be miles away from Vegas. The same vague feeling told him that the skeleton was still accessible, meaning Bancroft hadn't perished since his banishment. Digby sent a command to Tavern, telling them to slap the scoundrel in the face, just to remind him that he could.

A cackle rumbled through his chest at the thought of Bancroft hitting himself at random a thousand miles away.

That was when a voice came from behind him.

"Hey, ah, is it safe over here?"

Digby turned to find Sax, poking his head out from the passage. The surface of the window rippled around his face like water.

"Yes, it's safe enough." Digby gestured for him to come through.

"Oh, good." Sax emerged the rest of the way looking a bit unsteady.

Apparently, traveling across the world in one step was just as strange for him as it had been for Digby. The soldier carried a heavy rifle with a grenade launcher mounted on the underside of the barrel. Digby recognized the weapon from the zombie movies he'd watched a few weeks ago, though he hadn't seen one in use before. Sax adjusted a bandoleer of ammunition for the weapon that was slung across his chest. He must have been carrying ten grenades on him. Digby smiled, finding the image of such a slender man wielding so much firepower amusing, and that wasn't even counting his magic.

Digby checked the Seed's information, finding that the soldier had a healing spell as well as fireball. They were the same spells that he had started with.

Turning away from Sax, he faced the open passage as the rest of Dragon coven emerged from the window, each member moving to set up a perimeter around their entry point.

Despite having magic, each member of the coven carried the same rifle including the grenade launcher on the bottom. Hopefully they would become less reliant on the weapons, but for now, they needed experience. In time, they were sure to find confidence in their magic.

Once the perimeter was warded, a team of Deuce's men traversed the portal, carrying with them the largest mirror that the passage's exit could accommodate. After temporarily installing it nearby, Parker joined Digby on his end and recast her spell to connect the mirrors in Vegas with the larger one they had brought. The rest of the covens came through after that, pushing several vehicles to help them with their exploration of the area.

Digby waited patiently while the process was completed. Well, maybe not that patiently.

"Where the bloody hell are we?" He stomped his way toward Parker.

"We're in Hawaii," she answered matter-of-factly.

"Yes, but where is that? How far from home are we?" Digby threw a hand up toward the sky. "The sun has barely traveled far enough to bring light to this land."

"Yeah, that's how time zones work." Parker suddenly cocked her head to one side. "Wait a sec, what did you say about the sun?"

Digby furrowed his brow, unsure what detail he had gotten wrong. "I mean that your passage must have taken us far, because the sun has barely traveled to this part of the world."

She continued to stare at him for several seconds before finally speaking. "Dig, do you think the sun revolves around the earth?"

"Of course it does." Digby held his staff to the sky. "How else do you explain it being dawn here, yet mid-day in Vegas?"

Parker cringed. "Wow."

"Alright, out with it." Digby folded his arms. "From your reaction, I'm obviously wrong. So go ahead and have a good laugh at my expense and move on."

"I'm not going to laugh at you. It's not your fault you grew up in medieval times. It is a little funny, though." She shrugged.

"The earth orbits the sun while it spins on its axis. That's why we have day and night."

"That's ridiculous. Everyone would just fall off." Digby stared at the pink-haired soldier. It wasn't like she was the most reliable source of information. "You must be mistaken."

Parker turned and called to Sax. "Hey, does the earth revolve around the sun?"

"Yeah?" He looked at her, confused by the question. Then he glanced at Digby and nodded. "Oh, did you not know that?"

"Apparently not!" Digby ground his teeth, annoyed that he'd been wrong.

Sax held up both hands to make a circle. "You know the Earth is round, right?"

"Yes, I know the Earth is round!" Digby slammed the end of his staff on the pavement. "I have been to bloody space, damn it! Now come on, we have work to do."

Both Parker and Sax refrained from making further comments about his lack of a modern education as he stormed off toward the nearest building. There wasn't a need to search every structure, but they did need to find a place to set up a more secure camp to operate out of during their stay. Plus, it would be a good place for the new Heretics to gain some experience, considering how many revenants he'd seen when he'd arrived. The creatures weren't worth much in their dormant state, but the first few levels would come fast.

Glancing to his HUD, he brought up his information.

STATUS
Name: Digby Graves
Race: Zombie
Heretic Class: Necromancer
Mana: 325 / 325
Mana Composition: Unbalanced
Current Level: 38 (6,452 experience to next level.)

ATTRIBUTES

Constitution: 36
Defense: 42
Strength: 40
Dexterity: 40
Agility: 46
Intelligence: 64
Perception: 49
Will: 50

There was no way he was going to gain enough experience for a level during the daylight when all the revenants were dormant. Not unless there were a fair amount of lightbreakers in the mix that remained active. All was not lost however, he could gain resources. In some ways, they were more important than levels. After all, he was close to unlocking a new tier of mutations. All he had to do was claim one more.

Digby willed the Seed to show him the requirements for the last mutation in the Zombie Emissary Tier along with the current contents of his void.

BODY CRAFT
Description: By consuming the corpses of life forms other than human, you may gain a better understanding of biology and body structures. Once understood, you may use your gained knowledge to alter your physical body to adapt to any given situation. All alterations require the consumption of void resources.
Resource Requirements: 200 mind
Limitations: Once claimed, each use requires the consumption of void resources appropriate to the size and complexity of the alteration.

VOID RESOURCES
BONE: 43
FLESH: 30
HEART: 48

MIND: 42
SINEW: 46
VISCERA: 30

Digby frowned. He still had a way to go. Then again, this was the perfect opportunity to gain some ground. There was sure to be a few hundred dormant revenants around. All he needed to do was stand back while the new Heretics gained levels, and swoop in to claim the corpses when they were done. He chuckled to himself.

"This may work out in my favor, after all."

Asher gave a confident caw from her perch on his shoulder.

"Yes." He patted her. "Now how about you take to the skies and see if you can find any of the dead roaming about. We still need all we can find for our horde."

Asher gave him a nod and flapped into the air.

Digby watched her go, a feeling of pleasure drifting back to him across their bond. The little zombie master seemed to be enjoying the change in scenery.

With that, Digby stopped a few dozen feet from the entrance of one of the buildings to wait for the rest of the Heretics. Several of the structures in the area had been built with a large awning to provide shade for visitors. Now they were being used by a few small clusters of Revenants. Judging from the doors of the building, which were mostly broken, there were more revenants inside.

Digby made a point of removing himself from the coven he'd been assigned to, leaving Parker listed as leader. With so many Heretics present, there wasn't much need for him to guard the enchanters that he had been tasked with chaperoning. After that, he placed himself in a coven with Asher and Ducky. Technically, there was no reason to add his minions into a group, but it felt right for the dead to stick together.

"What's the plan, here?" Sax and the rest of Dragon coven stopped beside him. Parker and the four enchanters followed, along with another twenty groups of level one Heretics.

"Alright." Digby stepped in front of them. "This is going to be an eventful day. We shall start by clearing the revenants out of as many of these buildings as possible while exploring. Report back any supplies, weapons, or vehicles that we can make use of. In the process, everyone here should be able to get several levels. Once we're through clearing some of the buildings, we will choose one to set up a camp so we can travel back and forth between Vegas easily." He leaned to Sax and Parker. "Care to add anything?"

A flash of panic swept across their faces, but Sax stepped forward first. Parker looked relieved.

"Let's do this as safely as possible." Sax held his rifle close to his chest. "We have plenty of firepower, but prioritize the use of your magic whenever possible. We'll split up into groups of two covens each and spread out from here. Take things slow and eliminate targets one at a time. If you run into anything big, like a bloodstalker or a swarm, retreat back here. Once you're safe, Digby and Dragon coven will head back with you to deal with the situation." He tapped the tube on the bottom of his rifle. "That's why we have the grenade launchers."

"Indeed." Digby gave him an approving nod.

As much as he would have preferred Mason to have been there to lead his strongest coven, Sax was doing a decent job of filling the soldier's shoes.

"Alright, are we ready?" Digby turned and raised his staff toward the building's entrance.

Dragon coven fell in line behind him, each member with their rifles and magic at the ready. Parker drew her daggers and took a position in the back along with the enchanters.

"Let's go." Digby marched forward.

The rest of the covens broke off to head in different directions. Many took the vehicles they brought to investigate other parts of the base.

Before going inside any of the buildings, Digby headed for a group of five revenants that were huddled under an awning. They were pressed against the side of the building past the entrance. He stepped out of the way to let Sax and his coven handle them. As they approached the creatures, a sixth revenant emerged from the open door of the building to flank them from the side. Digby made a motion to handle the threat, but before he could, the entirety of Dragon coven turned.

Two icicles and a dozen bullets tore through the creature in seconds. Sax added to the effort by launching a fireball in the revenant's face. It didn't even have time to screech or flail. No, it just hit the floor in a bloody mess.

"I think you got it." Digby leaned on his staff as if taking it easy.

"I guess we probably should have planned that better." Sax looked back to the rest of his coven, adding a shrug.

They moved on after that, reaching the group of five revenants at the corner of the building. The creatures reached out and hissed at them but moved too slow to attack adequately. Sax ordered his Heretics to take their time, and one by one, each of them dispatched a foe.

The enchanters watched on, looking scared.

Digby checked the Seed's information to find that each member of Dragon coven had leveled up.

Not bad.

He followed up by opening his maw and taking in the corpses. His resources ticked up by one point for each body. After handling the cleanup, Digby headed for the building's entrance. He ordered Ducky to accompany him as well, just in case.

The four enchanters stared at the hulking zombie as it followed him. Beyond that, they continued to stand behind Parker while doing nothing.

That's going to have to change.

Digby eyed them for a moment before calling out. "Alright Mike, Thelma, Kim, and…" He trailed off, staring at the fourth member of the group, realizing he'd forgotten the man's name. He probably should have brought up the Seed's list of covens to find out, but his pause was beginning to get awkward, so he just guessed. "Paul."

"John," the man corrected.

"Yes, that's what I said." Digby ignored the correction and beckoned for them to follow. "Come along. We're going to get you some levels."

The four enchanters looked back and forth to each other, exchanging uneasy glances before following.

As soon as Digby entered the building, he picked up the trail of what must have been a large group of revenants. It would have been hard not to notice. There had been a queue set up within the space. It was similar to what they had back in the casino at the management counters. Just a series of poles positioned evenly across the floor with a strip of fabric connecting them.

At one point, the queue had been used to organize visitors, but now, most of the posts had been knocked down. The revenants that had passed through didn't have the same ability to follow the rules as humans it seemed. No, they had just walked through, knocking the posts over as they got in the way. There was even a lone revenant still tangled in the fabric strips that littered the floor. With the sun shining in through the entrance and windows, the creature seemed unable to untangle itself. Instead, it struggled to crawl whilst dragging several posts with it.

Obviously, a swarm had passed through here.

Digby looked for other signs to indicate which way they had gone, finding a few garbage receptacles laying on their side further down.

They must have moved further into the building to avoid the sun that shined in from the windows.

Digby pointed to the lone creature struggling on the floor. "Deal with that, would you."

The four enchanters immediately tensed.

"Sometime today." Digby leaned on his staff and waved his hand in a circle.

After about ten seconds of looking at each other, Thelma stepped forward and drew a pistol. It probably would have made more sense to have drawn a sword and cast Enchant Weapon, but from her expression, she didn't feel confident enough to get that close. She stopped at around twenty feet away.

"You can get closer." Digby gestured for her to continue on. "At that distance, you're likely to miss."

"Ah, okay." She inched her way closer.

Digby waited patiently as she approached the creature as it continued to crawl away from the sun. Once she was within ten feet, she looked back to Digby. He motioned for her to continue. She took a moment to convince herself, then forced herself to walk straight up to the revenant until she was standing over it. From there, she took aim at its head. Then she cast Enchant Weapon.

The pistol barked, followed by a geyser of gore that exploded into the air to coat her hand. From the look of the wound, she had enchanted the bullet rather than the gun, resulting in a much more volatile projectile.

"Ah gawd!" Thelma recoiled, gagging. A moment later, she relaxed, her eyes moving from side to side, clearly reading her first ever kill notification.

The other enchanters did the same, receiving the experience for being a part of Thelma's coven.

"Well done." Digby opened his maw with a chuckle and consumed the corpse. "Just a few hundred more to go."

From there, he walked on, following the signs of the swarm that had passed through. Various things had been knocked over, just like the trash cans near the entrance. The enchanters and Dragon coven fanned out behind him. They came across a few small clusters of five to ten revenants as they continued. The covens dealt with them one by one, gaining more confidence as they progressed. Eventually, even the enchanters had drawn their swords and moved in close.

The only incident occurred when a revenant lightbreaker

emerged from the center of one group of creatures to rush Sax. Parker stepped in to plant a dagger into its back but not before it got a bite in. Fortunately, having four enchanters at the ready to cleanse him, Sax's cursed status was short-lived. The soldier was back to killing revenants in less than a minute. Strangely, the moment of danger seemed to give the rest of the new Heretics even more confidence. It was as if seeing how easily something so dangerous could be handled by working together had helped them feel safer.

Digby listened as distant gunfire came from someplace else in the area. The other covens were encountering their own fights. He glanced at his HUD, willing the Seed to show him the levels of everyone that had come on the expedition with him. Even as he read over the information, levels ticked up here and there.

They were making slow but steady progress.

After clearing the building, they moved to another, then another, taking out any revenants that were on the way. Stopping to gaze out across the harbor, Digby grinned. It was an impressive place. There were several small war ships docked, as well as one drifting through the water in the middle. A crew had probably tried to set sail but been overrun before they could reach the sea.

Beyond that, there was a cargo ship of some kind. Digby ignored it in favor of staring at the largest vessel in the harbor. It was massive and had several cannons mounted along its length. Something like that would certainly make Henwick think twice about crossing him.

Too bad we can't face Autem on the ocean. Digby frowned. *Hopefully we can find something that will be useful on the land or in the air.*

Digby turned away from the harbor and continued on. It wasn't long before he found something just as important for the war to come. Stepping into one of the buildings, a mass of pale forms stood inside huddled together against the far wall where the sunlight couldn't reach. Digby held up a hand to keep any of the living humans from entering.

There must have been hundreds of the creatures.

The swarm was enough to overrun the Heretics that had accompanied him, even in their dormant state. The sunlight wouldn't be enough to keep them from attacking when their numbers were so high.

More importantly, there were enough of the creatures to claim his body craft mutation. Digby stared at the revenants. There was a good hundred feet from the entrance to where the swarm stood. A few of the creatures looked back in his direction but paid him no mind other than that. Though, the moment the humans entered the boarding area, that would change. The only question was, could his Heretics kill the swarm before any of the revenants could cross the space to reach them?

Digby slowly backed out of the room to rejoin Parker and the others.

"Aright, it looks like those creatures are dormant, so they shouldn't be able to move fast and they can't heal, but they have numbers in their favor." Digby glanced at the rifles that the members of Dragon coven carried. "I think a torrent of enchanted bullets should be able to do some damage before they reach all of you delicious humans."

"Don't call us delicious." Parker frowned at him.

"Fine. Edible humans, then." Digby waved away her complaint.

"That's not better." She glowered at him.

"Yes, yes. Anyway, I will handle any of the creatures that get too close and we can fall back if we begin to get overrun."

"That sounds like a plan." Sax patted a hand to the grenade launcher attached to the underside of his rifle. "Plus, I really want to fire this thing."

"Of course." Digby laughed. "By all means, fire away."

"That's all I needed to hear." Sax held out his rifle to be enchanted along with the rest of his coven.

A minute later, they were ready. Digby reentered the large room first, finding a good space on the floor to open his maw if things got too tense. That way he could just swallow some of the swarm whole to thin it out. The revenants slowly began to realize that there was fresh blood in the vicinity as the humans entered behind him. A chorus of chittering cries announced their aggression.

"Alright," Digby raised his staff toward the mass of enemies, "let them have it."

All at once, the room lit up with enchanted gunfire. The revenants cried out as heads, limbs, and viscera exploded from their bodies. The creatures tried to walk forward, only to trip over each other as corpses fell to the floor. Only a few were able to make it more than a dozen feet. The swarm was reduced by almost a third when the guns clicked empty one by one.

"Reload!" Digby shouted as the remaining sixty percent of revenants began pushing forward, making their way over the bodies of their fallen.

Empty magazines dropped to the floor as screeches filled the other side of the room. Each rifle reloaded in a sequence of hard click-clacks. Another wave of death erupted from the line of Heretics to tear through every revenant that made it halfway across the room.

Digby grinned.

The creatures never stood a chance. Not when he had an army behind him. Sax didn't even need to fire his grenade launcher. Digby willed the Seed to show him the names of everyone behind him and watched as their levels ticked up at a steady pace.

Foe after foe fell, a cackle rising in his throat with each one.

It was so easy.

Finally, things were falling into place. All he needed was a little time. Then even, Autem would be unable to stand against him.

Hell, with enough preparation, no one could.

CHAPTER THIRTEEN

"See, doesn't the car ride nice and smooth now that it's going an appropriate speed?" Alex slowed his floating Camaro to a stop in front of a rundown old museum in Las Angeles.

"True, the ride isn't that bad when I'm not struggling to keep my lunch down while spinning across the desert at two hundred miles per hour." Lana popped her door open to get out and pulled her seat forward to let Hawk exit behind her.

"That car smells like ass, though."

Alex glowered at Hawk as he exited the driver's seat. "Yeah, well, there's still bits of Malcolm's ass stuck in the grill."

"Gross." Alvin slipped out of the car behind him.

Alex turned away from the vehicle only to frown at the museum in front of him, having trouble hiding his disappointment with his quest so far. They had spent the afternoon searching through Hollywood's more reputable museums on a quest for famous pop culture artifacts. So far, they had come up with nothing. Everywhere they went, they found the front doors broken in. One held a swarm of revenants that they didn't dare disturb, while the rest had clearly been home to the creatures at some point in the last month.

The displays were all a mess, making it hard to even tell what movie props were there. There was probably a revenant running around out there with Doc Brown's lab coat wrapped around its arm or something. Either way, there was nothing there that carried a mass enchantment that could help.

Still, Alex didn't want to go home empty handed, so they loaded back into the Camaro.

Thanks to a map brochure that he'd picked up off the street, they were able to find the Get Reel action movie museum and gift shop. The place was a hole in the wall, with a weathered sign above the door that was badly in need of paint. The tag line, 'Where shit gets reel,' was written on the door itself.

"At least the door on this one is intact."

Alex pulled an iron key from his pocket to cast Detect Enemy. The key grew slightly cool to the touch, indicating that there were hostile creatures nearby, but not close enough to worry. Once he was sure they were clear, he pulled his seat forward to let Hawk out.

Hawk stood next to the car stretching his legs before reaching into the car to grab Kristen's skull. He immediately tossed her to Alex. "Don't forget your girlfriend."

"Oh please." The skull scoffed as she tumbled through the air. "I could do better."

"I'm sure." Alex caught her and stuffed her into his messenger bag, making a point to leave the flap open so she could still talk. Then he approached the museum's door, looking back to Hawk when he got there. "Hey, you wanna grab a crowbar?"

The young rogue popped the trunk and fetched the tool. He handed it over without another word. Alex started to shove the crowbar into the door but stopped to offer it back to Hawk. "Hey, do you want a crack at it, bud? I mean, I know you like breaking things."

Hawk let out a sigh. "You don't have to keep trying to make me feel better. I can handle my shit. And stop calling me bud. You sound like one of my old foster parents."

"Okay, noted." Alex went quiet, debating on if he should tell the kid that his sister might be alive. He sighed, deciding to keep it to himself. If he and Mason turned out to be wrong about bringing Becca back from the dead, getting Hawk's hopes up would be cruel. Instead, he just gave him a sympathetic smile. "I know you're a tough kid, but it's okay to be upset, you know. I'm an adult and I've barely been keeping myself together here."

"Sometimes letting yourself be vulnerable is the mature thing to do." Lana joined them with her brother in tow. "You have people in your life that care, so lean on them if you have to. There's nothing wrong with that."

"I know. I'm just… angry." Hawk rolled his eyes before adding, "At everyone."

"That's reasonable." Alex nodded.

"Why didn't you save her?" Hawk stared at the ground.

"Oh." Alex froze, realizing that he was one of the people that the rogue blamed. He was probably right to.

Hawk turned to Lana next. "And why didn't you? You were there, right? Shit, why didn't Dig?" He slapped a hand on his thigh. "Why wasn't Becca more careful? Every one of you just fucked it all up."

Alex's chest ached. "You're not wrong. I think we all share in the blame."

"No, you don't," Hawk said, barely above a whisper as he contradicted himself. "You got shot in the head, and your eyeball exploded. I know you couldn't have helped. No one could have. It was just shit luck."

"But you're still angry at us?" Alex leaned against the door of the museum.

Hawk nodded. "It's not fair."

Everyone fell silent, knowing what else to say. That was when Kristen decided to make everything worse.

"Oh, cry me a river. So that horrible woman got herself cursed. At least no one chopped her head off."

Alex clenched his jaw and yanked the skull from his bag.

"Okay, I get it, we killed you, and that sucks. But let's be honest, we are at war. And you were an enemy on the side that destroyed the whole damn world. You get that? Right? You were an enemy combatant that would have killed literal children if we hadn't killed you first. So at a certain point, I'm going to stop having sympathy for your situation and just tell you to shut up."

"I wasn't involved in Henwick's plans to end the world." She huffed back. "I mostly did paperwork."

"That doesn't make it better." Alex held her up to his face. "You could have spoken up or resisted. Hell, you could have left if you wanted to, but you didn't. You ignored the crap Henwick did because it wasn't aimed at you. You just let it all happen."

A ghostly silence came from the skull.

"That's what I thought." Alex set her down on the pavement next to the door. "I don't care if you're still mad at us for killing you. That doesn't give you the right to be an asshole to Hawk, who just lost the only person in the world who came close to being family." He finished the conversation by jamming the crowbar into the door and yanking back on it until a quiet voice spoke up from behind him.

"Can I?" Alvin held out a hand.

"Sure." Alex stepped aside, leaving the crowbar hanging from the door so that he could give it a go.

Alvin gripped the crowbar and yanked until the door bent enough for the lock to fail. Alex left Kristen's skull where it was and took the crowbar from Alvin before heading in.

"Hey, where are you going?" the seer called out as he disappeared inside. "You can't just leave me here."

The others followed him in, leaving her outside to think about that.

The museum inside was pretty run down. Display cases were placed against the wall labeled by dingy metal plates. A gift shop full of shot glasses and key chains filled a room to the right of the entryway. A row of vending machines stood at the back.

"At least we can loot some snacks." Lana walked into the space. "God knows Vegas needs everything it can get."

"I can do that." Alvin looked back and forth as if expecting someone to stop him.

"Hawk, go with him." Alex gestured toward the kitchen.

The young rogue nodded and did as he was told, still looking somber.

Alex waited until they were both out of earshot before saying anything. "It seems like Alvin is trying."

Lana folded her arms. "We'll see the next time he has the chance to abandon me in favor of rejoining Autem."

She approached a display case containing a mannequin of Arnold Schwarzenegger dressed like the Terminator. Alex joined her. According to the costume description, the only item that was authentic was the sunglasses. A brief moment of hope passed as Alex analyzed the eyewear. His heart sank when the Seed told him nothing. He debated taking the glasses anyway, but decided against it. Sunglasses wouldn't be practical, even if they did cover his missing eye.

Lana placed her hand on the glass. "I get it, though."

"Get what?" Alex turned to look for something else of interest.

"I get why Alvin betrayed us." She headed in the other direction. "I probably would have too if I had been in his position."

"You think so?" Alex looked back at her.

She shrugged. "We had literally just seen our dad get murdered by some random guys. And Autem told us our mom was in an area overrun by monsters. The empire took us in and offered us a place to live. After going through all that, having someone to take care of us would have meant a lot. Just having someplace to belong is pretty tempting. If I had been enrolled in Autem's little indoctrination school instead of forced to join Skyline, I probably would have fallen for it too."

"I can understand that." Alex nodded. "When you're lost at

sea, any life boat is better than none. Even if it's some kind of weird theocratic empire like Autem."

"I just hope it's not too late to repair the damage they did to him." She checked out another display. "I keep thinking about the way he looked at me when he left us behind. It was like he'd didn't even care."

"Well, it looks like he's beginning to come around." Alex trailed off as he stepped toward another glass case.

Focusing on the articles of clothing that adorned the mannequin inside, he took an inventory. First, there was a brown leather jacket. It was cool, but came up with no enchantments when analyzed. He checked the boots, pants, and shirt next. All nothing. Then, his gaze traveled up to an eye patch that sat at an angle on the figure's face. A lock of hair fell beside it from a dusty brown wig.

Patch of Rebellion
MASS ENCHANTMENT: Due to the belief and admiration
shared by a large number of people, this item has gained
a conditional power of its own.
Ability 1: Guiding Hand
The wearer of this item will gain an innate ability to target
an opponent's weak points with minimal training.
Ability 2: Will of the Rebel
The wearer of this item will gain +20 Will.

Alex didn't even hesitate before raising the crowbar and swinging it at the glass. Glittering shards fell as the display case shattered to give him access to the treasure inside. He nearly tripped over his own feet as he climbed up to snatch the eye patch, forgetting about the demerit he had to his agility.

"What did you find?" Lana rushed over.

He'd pulled the metal description plate off the wall and handed it to her.

She read it over, then looked up at him with an eyebrow raised. "Who's Snake Plissken?"

"A guy with a cooler eye patch than mine." He pulled off the one he'd been wearing and tossed it over his shoulder. Then he slipped the new one on, making a point to position it at an angle. He turned to Lana as soon as it was in place. "What do you think?"

She gave him a noncommittal shrug and handed him her compact so he could see himself in its mirror. At first glance, his new eye patch wasn't that much different. The movie that it had come from had been made back in the Eighties, way before the modern superhero movies that had redesigned eye patches to look more badass. However, his new one was made out of a better, more durable material. It was a little smaller too, allowing it to fit his face better. Overall, it was a big improvement. Not to mention the abilities it came with sounded powerful.

He glanced at his HUD to see if his overall mana capacity had gone up with his will.

MP 325/325

He furrowed his brow at the numbers.

"What?" Lana eyed him sideways.

Alex willed the Seed to show him his stats, finding them unchanged. "The eye patch was supposed to increase my will and give me an ability that would help in combat. But my stats haven't changed."

"Maybe you're not wearing it right," she offered.

"How can you wear an eye patch wrong?" Alex glanced through the rest of his stats finding nothing out of the ordinary other than his brain cloud and its massive demerit to his agility. He hoped the problem had nothing to do with his condition. Eventually, he willed the Seed to show him the item's description again.

MASS ENCHANTMENT: Due to the belief and admiration

shared by a large number of people, this item has gained a conditional power of its own.

That was when Alex noticed the word conditional in there. He must have been too excited by what he'd found to scroll all the way down the description, leaving a couple lines below what his HUD displayed. Looking down further, the text moved to show him the rest of the item's description.

CONDITIONS FOR USE
Condition 1: Impairment
The user of this item must be unable to use one eye through either injury or by birth.
Condition 2: Rebellion
To activate the abilities offered by this item, the wearer must commit an act of rebellion against an authoritative presence at least once every hour. *Time to annoy some authority figures.*

"The hell does that even mean?" Alex let his mouth hang open.

"What?" Lana leaned closer.

"Apparently there's two conditions to using this thing's abilities." He tapped the eye patch. "The first is that you have to be missing an eye."

"That part's convenient."

"Yeah, but the second part is that I have to rebel against authority at least once an hour."

At that Lana laughed. "You aren't exactly the most rebellious."

"I know." He groaned. "What am I supposed to do, just start flipping everyone off?"

"Works for me." Hawk emerged from the gift shop carrying a box of prepackaged snacks under one arm while holding up a middle finger with the other. He lowered it when he reached them. "Who are we flipping off?"

"Authority," Lana answered. "And where's Alvin?"

"Cool." Hawk hooked a thumb over his shoulder. "And he's right behind me."

Alex looked to the gift shop but there was no sign of Alvin. His forehead started to sweat, immediately regretting letting him out of his sight. He started walking toward the gift shop just as Alvin emerged, carrying another box of food.

Both Alex and Lana blew out a sigh of relief only to immediately pretend to look at one of the displays as if they hadn't suspected Alvin of trying to run away at the first chance he got.

"Cool eye patch." Hawk cut through the awkwardness before pulling a silver lighter from his pocket. A red apple with a green worm adorned the front. "Check it out." He flipped it open and closed. "Found it in the gift shop. There's more if you want one."

"Sure, grab one for me. You never know when you might need some fire." Alex looked back to the compact that Lana had handed him to check his eye patch again. He dropped it a second later when a Link spell replaced his image with a close up of Parker's face.

Scrambling for the mirror, he prayed that it wouldn't break. The plastic container hit the floor just in front of his foot. He cringed as his other leg moved, still in motion, his shoe kicking the compact across the floor.

Parker's voice followed it. "What's happening?"

"Shit, crap, damn." Alex scrambled across the floor, sliding on broken bits of the display case he'd smashed.

"I got it." Alvin dropped the box of snacks that he carried and crouched to slap a hand on top of the compact as it skidded by him.

Alex crashed into another display case as he tried and failed to stop himself. He bounced off the glass and came to rest laying on the floor where he cursed his impaired motor function. At least his defense and constitution were still solid. Otherwise, he could have gotten hurt.

Pushing himself up, he found Alvin holding out the compact toward him. Parker looked out from the mirror inside.

"You okay, there?"

"Yeah, I'm fine." Alex sighed.

"Good, because we're going to need your expertise. Dig has..." She let a long pause pass by before adding, "An idea."

"What kind of an idea?" He stood back up.

Parker looked away from him, as if checking to make sure she was alone, then she blew out a sigh and answered.

"The only kind of idea he has: an insane one."

CHAPTER FOURTEEN

"What do you mean by insane?" Digby stood with both hands held out at his sides.

"I don't even know where to begin." Thelma stood in front of him, scratching her head.

After killing a swarm of a couple hundred revenants, the woman had reached the artificer class along with Mike, Kim, and the other member of Parker's coven that Digby could remember.

So far several of the harbor's buildings had been secured. There was still more to explore, but the Heretics needed a break. After leveling up so many times, food had become a priority. Taking over an empty maintenance hangar that had originally been used for small aircraft, they set up a camp and installed a large mirror on the back wall.

Once the building was warded, he sent his Heretics back to Vegas through one of Parker's passages where Campbell already had dinner waiting. Digby had decided to stay behind with Asher and Ducky, after all, he had already consumed his fill. Parker had returned not long after.

She'd probably come back to keep an eye on him.

To get some time to himself, he'd gone for a walk along the harbor to look at the ships. That was where he'd gotten an idea that he needed an expert opinion on. Hence why Thelma was now standing in front of him and calling his plan insane.

"Do you have any idea what you're asking?" Thelma stepped forward as Mike wandered out of the hangar behind her, still eating from a container of food he must have brought through the passage from Vegas. Kim and the last member of the research and development coven followed behind Mike.

"I see no reason why what I'm asking would be impossible." Digby leaned to one side to look past Thelma and Mike, to ask the rest of the group, "What about you, are you with the naysayers or are you ready to step forward and do the impossible?"

"Ah…" Kim hesitated. "I've only had magic for a day."

"I've only had magic for a day." Digby repeated the excuse in his snarkiest tone. "Do you think that stopped me when I awoke in your time with necromantic power coursing through my corpse? No, I headed out into the world and gave it what for." He finished his statement by shaking his staff in the air triumphantly.

"Didn't you release the curse that ended the world when you woke up?" the last of the four artificers commented from the back of the group.

"No one asked you, Paul." Digby glowered at the man.

"My name's John," he corrected for the umpteenth time.

"Yes, yes, that's what I said." Digby lowered his staff.

"Look, Mr. Graves," Thelma spoke up. "We understand what you're saying, but we don't know the first thing about how to do what you ask. The runecraft required is not something we fully understand."

"How complicated could it be? You just slap a few symbols on some metal." He swept the head of his staff over the ground as if writing a few imaginary runes.

"It's a little more complicated than that, from what I under-stand." Thelma folded her arms.

"Oh please." Digby waved away her concerns with a hand. "If Alex can get that car of his to fly, then I see no reason why the four of you can't put your heads together and figure out a way to get one of these in the air." He threw a hand out in the direction of what he considered an entirely reasonable request.

The four artificers followed the path of his hand to the harbor and the USS Missouri that was docked there.

Mike blew out a frustrated sigh. "Mr. Graves, a battleship is way different than a Camaro."

"That's Lord Graves," he corrected. "And really, how different could it be? It's just bigger."

That was when Alex emerged from the aircraft hangar where they had set up camp.

Digby groaned. *Parker must have called him back from his little treasure hunt to talk some sense into me.*

Ultimately, Alex was the last person he wanted to see after the way he had hidden the fact that Rebecca might be alive from him. Then again, if someone was going to agree with him, his apprentice might be his best bet. Digby decided to put his annoyance with his apprentice aside for the moment.

"What's bigger?" Alex stopped, standing beside the four members of his R&D team.

"He wants us to do the same thing to the Missouri that you did to that car." Thelma shrugged as if she was sure the conversation would shift in her favor now that back up had arrived.

Digby grinned.

She had no idea how wrong she was.

If there was one thing Digby knew, it was that there was no way in hell his apprentice was going to pass up the chance to build an airship.

"It will never work." Alex frowned.

"Wait, what?" Digby's voice climbed as his anger flooded back. "You were supposed to agree with me!"

"Let me finish." Alex winced, clearly unaware how mad Digby really was at him. "Getting the Missouri to fly is out. The ship is just too big and it would be impossible to control without a large crew acting in sync. If we just wanted to use it for travel, then maybe that would be okay, but for combat it wouldn't be maneuverable. Plus, I think it's a museum now, so isn't it cemented to the bottom of the harbor or something?" He looked at the others getting a bunch of shrugs in return. "But if you want to use those smaller ships." He gestured to the other boats in the harbor. "Well, that's another story. And honestly, I'd kind of like to see it."

"Wait, seriously?" Thelma snapped her head to him.

Digby let his anger fade again, replacing it with a smug grin.

"That's why we have an R&D team. I'll just have to give everyone a rundown on how the runes work." Alex scratched at his eye patch. "Actually, that hangar you've secured will make a great place to set up our operation."

"Indeed." Digby nodded.

"I guess we have some catching up to do, then." Thelma sighed.

"Probably going to have to pull an all-nighter," Mike added before turning back to the hangar.

"Yes, you do that." Digby leaned on his staff as the artificers left together.

One member of the group rolled their eyes but none argued beyond that.

"And Alex?" Digby stopped his apprentice. "I heard from Mason what you two have been hiding from me and I just want to say, I wish you had included me."

"What we've been hiding?" Alex's eyes darted around for a moment before he added, "Oh, that."

"Yes, that." He tightened his grip on his staff.

Digby was debating saying nothing, but it didn't seem wise to keep his anger bottled up. Especially when everyone was worried about his sanity. If he held everything until he exploded, they would only misunderstand.

"Sorry." Alex walked up to him. "We're still figuring things out, and I wasn't sure how you would react to hearing I might have brought Becca back."

"Because I'm insane?" Digby gave him the coldest stare he could muster.

"No." Alex lowered his eyes to the ground. "Because Becca was your best friend."

His words cut straight through Digby's chest. He wasn't wrong.

Alex sighed as he continued. "Losing a friend sucks. And after seeing how well you handled things yesterday with Bancroft, I didn't want to throw a bunch of uncertainty on you. Especially when everyone in Vegas needs a leader."

"Then why did you tell Mason that you feared for my sanity?" Digby grimaced, catching his apprentice in a lie.

Alex leaned to one side. "You should have seen him. Mason practically attacked me the other day about using those shoes. I mean, I get it, but it still freaked me out. I was worried I might say the wrong thing and make everything worse. So I tried to make it seem like I was more worried about you than him."

Digby stared at him for a long moment, unsure if he could believe him.

"Fine." Digby clapped his hands, adding, "There's no sense dwelling on it."

Technically, he still intended on dwelling on it for the rest of the night, but he didn't want to talk about it anymore.

With that, they headed back to the hangar. Digby watched for a couple of hours as Alex taught a class to the new artificers and got them started on the path to unlocking the Engraving spell that would be needed. By the time it began to get dark, they had all gained most of the spells that Alex had so far, minus the combat spells that he'd gotten from the rings of dead Guardians.

Thanks to the hangar's wardings, they were able to continue working well into the night. A couple covens stood guard just in case they needed deal with the occasional ward breaker that decided to come in uninvited. With nothing better to do, Digby went to check out the battleship that was docked not far away.

He wasn't ready to give up on the idea of getting the enormous vessel in the air.

Besides, he hadn't gained a level all day and there was bound to be revenants on board.

Parker had offered to go with him but he turned her down, declaring that he didn't need a babysitter every second of the day. She'd tried to argue, but in the end, her magic was too important to risk her wandering around the place at night with him. He took Ducky with him instead. Asher flapped down to his shoulder as soon as he left.

"Ah, there you are." Digby took his time, relaxing for the first moment that day.

It was good to finally have some time to himself. Parker meant well, but he was getting very sick of being watched. Plus, with the resources he'd gained throughout the day, he'd reached the requirements for his last mutation and something told him she didn't have the stomach to watch him experiment with it.

Digby glanced toward his HUD at the message that had been popping up every hour since he'd absorbed that swarm of revenants into his maw earlier.

New mutation available, Body Craft.
Accept?

Digby stared at the text on his HUD as he walked toward the USS Missouri. He hadn't accepted the ability yet. Mostly because he wasn't entirely sure what it would do. According to the description, it would allow him to alter his body freely, provided he understood what he wanted to craft it into. It sounded powerful, but like Alex had said, the people of Vegas needed a leader, and transforming into something entirely inhuman in front of them would probably lose him a few supporters.

The curiosity had been killing him though. After all, many of his mutations seemed to go hand in hand with one another and his magic always interacted with them in interesting ways.

His Apex Predator ability allowed him to eat anything even if it wasn't human. The Dissection mutation allowed him to understand what he ate. The connection hadn't been spelled out, but both abilities seemed designed to support this new Body Craft mutation.

On top of that, there was his Mend Undead ability. That one had allowed him to not only heal his minions, but target them with his necrotic armor as well. The result gave his zombies access to the same enhancement to their physical prowess as he had. Following that logic, it was possible the same would be true with Body Craft. He glanced back at Ducky as the armored zombie plodded along behind him.

At least I have someone to test this theory on.

He patted Asher's side. "Might be able to give you a little more power as well."

She nuzzled his neck in response, clearly approving of the prospect.

Ultimately, he knew there was something important about the Body Craft ability. When he had first read the mutation's description, it had scared him. As if accepting it would drag him further from what little sense of humanity that he'd clung to. That was why he'd saved it for last. Now, though, the power it offered just seemed too valuable to ignore. If he was going to defeat Henwick, he had no choice.

The lives of everyone in Vegas depended on it.

He willed the Seed to accept the ability as soon as he reached the battleship's walkway. Then he collapsed, a surge of sensation flooding his body and sending him into spasms. Digby clung to one side of the walkway's railing with one hand, his other slapping down against the rough textured floor. He wasn't in pain. No, it was something else. It was like a seal had just been peeled off his body to unlock something new. The feeling passed a few moments later. He trembled. The sound of the water beneath the walkway sloshed against the bottom of the ship.

Digby looked at his hands.

They hadn't changed.

"Well, at least I didn't turn into a blob of necrotic flesh." He pulled himself up and checked his body over for any differences.

Finding himself unchanged, he frowned. A part of him was hoping for something impressive. Something like the bone gauntlet or crown he'd had back before his Sheep's Clothing mutation had erased them to return his human appearance. If he was honest, a part of him had missed having claws.

That was when his hand began to itch.

He scratched it absentmindedly, only stopping when he realized it felt strange.

Digby jerked his hand up to hold it in front of his face. He couldn't believe his eyes. His claws had returned. It wasn't the full gauntlet that he'd had before, but still, he had claws again. They were identical to that of a lurker type zombie.

"Well, I'll be damned." He willed his hand to return to normal, watching as it shifted and popped. The additional skin and bone cracked and peeled away, leaving his digits the same as they had been before. Even the letters that spelled out the word 'luck' on his knuckles had been restored. The excess flesh and bone simply crumbled to the floor of the walkway.

Glancing at his HUD, he checked his resources. None of them had fallen. Probably because claws didn't take much. He willed his hand to transform again. This time, he watched the appropriate resources fall by one. His mana fell by a few points as well. His mouth fell open. The ability was limited only by his resources, his MP, what kind of bodies he understood, and his imagination.

"I'm going to need to start eating more animals."

The possibilities were endless.

That was when he noticed another message running across the bottom of his HUD.

New Mutation Path Unlocked, Lord of the Dead.

"Well, now we're talking." He cackled to himself as he looked over the new path's options.

MUTATIONS:

SOUL EATER
Drag your prey into a temporary immaterial space. If devoured within this space, you will consume their spark. Consuming the spark of another may result in the advancement of other abilities or attributes. Consuming the spark of another may also result in the discovery of new abilities. Consumed sparks may also be saved to use later.
Resource Requirements: 5 Still-Beating Human Hearts

SPIRIT CALLER
Draw the echoes of the lingering dead toward you across great distances. Each use will consume 100MP.
Resource Requirements: 10 Sparks

CALL OF THE CONSUMED
Reform the body of a spark you have consumed from the resources available to you. This temporary entity will fight alongside you and will be capable of most abilities that it had in life. Each use will require a temporary mana donation of 150MP as well as the resources required to restore the called echo's original body.
Resource Requirements: 25 Sparks

CURSE BLAST
Unleash a blast capable of eroding a target's natural and supernatural defense. Once a target's defenses have been negated, your curse will spread to them. This version of the curse will take effect immediately. The time it takes to negate defenses may vary. This mutation will cost 10MP per second that it is active.

Resource Requirements: 50 Sparks

"Good lord." Digby staggered as he finished reading those last two. They were incredible.

He reread the requirements of each ability, unsure what to make of them. So far, every mutation he'd gained had only required body parts, but these were different. To start with, Soul Eater only needed five hearts, but they were specifically from living humans. There must have been some kind of difference between a revenant or the recently deceased and a live person. Looking at the rest of the mutations, they all required sparks. That could only mean that he needed to take the Soul Eater ability first and use it to reach the rest.

Checking his HUD, he found a new line listed under his resources.

Sparks: 0

He thought back to the time he'd spent trapped in the Heretic Seed's realm with Parker. Back then, he had devoured three sparks—Henwick, Sybil, and Jack the Ripper—despite not having the ability to do so. The fact that they were in an immaterial realm must have been a loophole.

"I guess I will need to start eating some more humans, soul and all." He let a cackle roll through his chest. "I hope Autem sends a few of their Guardians my way."

Asher cawed to join in his celebration as Ducky turned sideways to fit on the walkway that led to the battleship. Digby continued on toward the deck. His jaw dropped as soon as he reached it. The ship was huge. He could hardly believe that humanity had built something so large. The cannons alone were larger than Ducky, and there were several of them. His astonishment was immediately replaced by annoyance that Alex didn't think they could get it in the air. It seemed like such a waste.

"Oh well." He scratched Asher's chin. "I suppose we will have to settle for the smaller ships across the way."

Digby wandered to the side of the ship to stare out at his armada. The moon was nearly full, shining its light down across the harbor. Looking back at the hangar where the artificers were still hard at work, he could see a few revenants lingering just outside of the building's wards. The covens standing guard dealt with them easily from within their perimeter. It looked like they had it under control.

About the only thing that would be a problem would be bloodstalkers. The warding would only do so much against one considering the extra-large, evolved revenants could probably tear through the side of the building if given enough time. Granted, Digby hadn't seen any bloodstalkers since he'd arrived in Hawaii.

Of course, that was when one decided to climb out of the water directly beneath where Digby stood. It must have been hiding in down there to stay out of the sun during the day.

"Well hello there." Digby stepped away from the railing as the creature clawed its way up the side of the ship to the deck.

He checked his HUD.

Revenant Bloodstalker, Rare, Active, Neutral

The creature lacked the wings that some of the others had. It must have been less evolved. Digby hoped it didn't have that irritating conceal ability that he'd come across before. It reached up over the rail and pulled its dripping body up and over onto the deck. Every inch of the beast was wrinkled and pruned from spending so much time in the water.

Digby chuckled. It looked ridiculous.

The creature paid him no mind; instead, it gazed out at the hangar where the artificers worked. It gave a snort, ejecting water from its nostrils before shaking some of the seawater off.

"Thinking of heading over there to eat my Heretics? Ready

for a bit of dinner, are you?" He stepped toward the blood-stalker. "Sorry, but I can't have that."

Digby nudged Asher, telling her to get someplace safe, before raising his staff in preparation to summon Jack's echo. Asher flapped up to one of the railings on the battleship's upper deck. Then Digby lowered his staff.

"What am I doing?"

Killing the revenant outright, would be a waste. Sure, he was powerful enough now to eliminate the bloodstalker with a few summons of his wraith and crone, but that would negate the value of the creature itself. Instead, with his Fingers of Death spell, he could convert the giant revenant into a minion instead. All he had to do was hold it still and get close.

"Alright then, time to join the horde." Digby held his staff toward the beast and summoned his crone.

A dozen spectral hands reached from the deck of the ship to wrap around the bloodstalker's legs and abdomen. Digby drew back his clawed hand and prepared to lunge. Things went wrong the moment he kicked off, when something slammed into him from behind.

"What?" Digby fell over, dropping his staff to the deck. He landed in a roll a few feet away.

Sweeping his vision across the deck, he found nothing. A screech from above told him he was looking in the wrong place. He snapped his eyes up to find a winged figure flapping through the night.

Revenant Nightflyer, Uncommon, Hostile

The thing must have been on the ship's upper deck and turned hostile the instant he attacked the bloodstalker.

"Think you can hit me in the back and get away with it?" Digby thrust a finger in the creature's direction as he willed his other hand to shift into a claw as well.

Digby glanced back at the bloodstalker to make sure it was still bound by the crone's spectral hands. It was, but at the rate it was struggling, it wouldn't stay that way for long. He couldn't go after both. A caw from Asher set his priorities. The raven flapped through the sky with the nightflyer giving chase. Its hostile status must have transferred to her as a part of Digby's coven.

"No you don't." He opened his maw on the ship's deck and planted his foot over the opening.

Casting Forge, he launched himself into the air with a post of blood that surged from the shadowy void under his foot. He kicked off and spent the additional ten mana and reforged the post to throw himself further. The maneuver sent him flying straight for the nightflyer. He slammed into it, claws-first, to bury one hand in the creature's chest. He had half a mind to cast Fingers of Death, but held back. The revenant offered something more valuable than its service as a minion.

Wings.

Digby had never eaten one of the flying creatures before, and with his new Body Craft mutation, the more variety that he could consume, the better.

The revenant screeched and struggled to stay airborne as Digby hung from its ribcage. He cast Frost Touch, sending a wave of cold radiating out from his claws to freeze the creature's insides. The nightflyer cried out in protest just before going silent, unable to heal the excessive damage.

"That's right!" Digby gloated as Asher flew by to back him up with a victorious caw.

Of course, that was when Digby remembered that the revenant had been the only thing keeping him in the air.

He looked down. "This may have been a bad idea."

Digby plummeted back to the deck of the ship below along with his prey. He cast Necrotic Regeneration in anticipation of the damage that was coming and tried to shift his position so that at least his head would be cushioned by the body of the nightflyer. They slammed down a second later, cracking one of his arms and both knee caps.

"Well, that could have gone better." Digby struggled to straighten himself out as his body pieced itself back together.

A caw from Asher drew his attention back to the blood-stalker that he had restrained moments before, or at least, to the place where it had been.

"Gah!"

The beast was gone.

Digby spun just as the air beside him began to ripple, the bloodstalker stepping right out of thin air. It had evolved to use the conceal ability, after all. The beast grabbed one of Digby's nearly healed legs and whipped him across the deck. Wind rushed past his ears for a split second, followed by the crack of bone and the hollow gong of his body slamming into the base of the ship's frontmost cannons.

Digby cast another Necrotic Regeneration. The heavy foot-steps of the overgrown revenant stomped toward him. Unable to do anything to defend himself, he called to Ducky over the bond he shared with the armored minion. All he could see was a blurry image of the bloodstalker raising its claws above him. It stopped an instant before shredding him to pieces, a smaller form shoving into its side.

"Oh, thank god." Digby let himself slump against the base of the cannons to repair his broken body.

Ducky bought him time with a solid uppercut to the blood-stalker's jaw. The crunch of bone came from both the armored zombie as well as the revenant. The beast reeled back with a wet-sounding screech, blood spraying from its mouth. Ducky's arm fell limp at his side. It was a solid hit, yet it only took seconds for the bloodstalker to shrug it off, its jawbone snapping back into place with an audible pop.

Ducky tried to defend with his other hand, but even under the necrotic armor, he was just a common zombie. He wasn't fast enough.

The bloodstalker raked one of its massive clawed hands across the zombie's chest. His necrotic armor came away in meaty chunks to reveal the common dead within. There was nothing Ducky could do. The revenant was nearly three times his size, faster, and stronger. His minion never stood a chance.

At least, not unless something changed.

Digby raised his hand toward Ducky and willed his Body Craft ability to go to work. He may not have eaten the variety of creatures needed to understand the complexities of all that was possible, but he had eaten plenty of humans. Immediately, Digby felt a drain on his resources as they poured from his void into his minion. It wasn't much, but it was enough to repair the damage done by the curse, returning to Ducky the physical capabilities he'd possessed while alive. To enhance his minion further, he reapplied his necrotic armor.

The bloodstalker swiped another claw at his minion, only to have the zombie catch it mid-swing. A confused expression fell across the revenant's bat-like face.

Digby checked his mana.

MP: 299/369

The transformation had only cost ten points.

The bloodstalker swiped and clawed against the armored zombie, tearing away chunks. Digby mended it in seconds, letting a steady flow of resources empower his minion. Ducky pushed forward, slamming his shoulder into the creature's gut to nearly throw it off balance. The revenant shoved back. Ducky fell to the deck. The fight was still uneven, but Ducky had gained the strength needed to slow the bloodstalker down. Digby could handle the rest.

Standing back up, now that his body had healed, Digby rushed to get his staff and summoned an echo. The crimson form of a murderous wraith flickered into existence, its knife gleaming as it slashed up the side of the revenant's body. Blood sprayed the deck of the ship, coating Digby's boots. He summoned his wraith again, dropping his mana to half. The crimson echo struck a second time, Ducky holding the bloodstalker's legs as it tried to stomp him out of existence.

Blood poured down, the moon reflecting in the pool that gathered on the deck around Ducky. Still, as severe as the creature's wounds were, they began to close.

"Not yet you don't." Digby cast Blood Forge, sending a crimson spike shooting up from the pool on the deck to punch through the revenant's neck.

The revenant flailed, clawing at its throat to try and pull it out. A final gurgling screech came from the creature as its continuous healing failed. Then it fell silent, its corpse sliding down the crimson spike that impaled it. Digby stared at the body as Ducky dragged himself out from under it. Asher landed back on one of the railings above.

"Well done, both of you." Digby cast Leach to draw enough mana from them to return some of what he'd used.

It was clear that he probably should have brought a little more backup with him before running off to experiment with his new mutation, but he couldn't argue with its power. Even with what little he could do with it, Body Craft had the potential to become his most powerful ability.

Digby swept his eyes across the now blood-drenched ship. Then he raised them to the sky where a couple of revenants flapped in the distance. *I think I'm going to need to expand the menu.*

The corner of his mouth tugged upward into a crooked grin as he heard another revenant sneaking up behind him. Digby glanced to the deck, catching the creature's shadow stretching across the wood that covered it. He frowned, noticing that it didn't have any wings.

Digby held up a claw. "Sorry, but I've eaten enough common revenants. The only use I have for you is as a minion."

With that, he spun with a laugh and plunged his claws into the foe's chest up to his knuckles and cast Fingers of Death.

Then he saw their face.

"Wait, no!" Digby froze as the Heretic Seed analyzed his prey.

Human, Common

CHAPTER FIFTEEN

"God no!" Digby stared at the man in front of him, his eyes falling to the blood seeping from the wound in his chest.

The wound that his claws were currently buried in.

He could feel the man's heart beating against one of his fingers.

He wore a dingy uniform. The letters on the left side read Navy. The name Ames was spelled out on the other side. Digby's shadow stretched across the deck of the Missouri, the dark shape impaling another with its hand. The man must have been holed up inside the ship and came out when he heard Digby's voice.

"Who are...?" Ames choked out a couple words before his body began to convulse.

"No!" Digby looked down at his hand as the crimson stain spread from his claws. "I didn't know. I thought you were..."

The man, Ames, fell backward against the base of the battleship's cannons. Digby's claws came free of the wound with a fountain of blood.

"I'm sorry!" He dropped to his knees to press his hands against the wound.

Casting Forge, he caused a thin membrane of blood to harden at the opening of each of the five, claw-shaped holes. It didn't matter. It was already too late. Digby had cast Fingers of Death before he'd realized what he'd done.

The curse had already taken hold.

Not even summoning an echo could change that now. Henwick's spark had only given him the power to heal, not to cleanse a curse. Otherwise, he wouldn't have lost Rebecca the way he had. Veins of black stretched up the dying man's neck. Then, he went still.

Common human defeated. 24 experience awarded.

"No," Digby repeated, kneeling on the ship's deck while pressing his clawed hands to the sides of his head. His victim's blood dripped down his fingers to run down his cheek. "I didn't know, I didn't know!"

The horror of what he'd done set in.

He had killed innocent people before.

Hell, he was the origin of the curse that had ended the world. None of that had been his fault, though. He wasn't in control of himself back then. He couldn't have stopped himself.

As horrible as it was, none of that was truly his fault.

This time, it was.

He'd been feeling confident after killing that bloodstalker. Too confident. With his new Body Craft mutation, he felt unstoppable. So much so, that he didn't even look at what was behind him before attacking. He'd been so sure it was a revenant.

Ames's corpse twitched. Then his eyes blinked open. A hollow moan came next.

"What do I do? What do I do?" Digby knelt there, trembling.

There was nothing he could do.

He glanced back to the hangar where he had left Parker. The impulse to run to her crossed his mind. To tell her what he'd done. Obviously, she couldn't help, but maybe she would understand. After spending so much time together back in the Seed's realm, she had to know it was an accident. That it had just been a stupid mistake.

Right?

Digby's face fell.

What if she doesn't believe me?

He turned back to Ames, his new minion, as he pushed himself up.

"No, don't get up." Digby shoved the zombie back down. "Someone will see you."

His words hung in the air, taking him back to the day he'd awoken in Seattle when he'd realized he'd eaten two people. His first thought had been to cover up the crime. He'd thought he'd come a long way from back then. That the person he'd become was different.

Maybe old habits don't die so easily.

Digby shook his head. "Don't be stupid. Of course you have changed."

He reminded himself that his first thought had been to tell Parker what had happened. Despite everyone's theories about him and his missing soul, he was not, in fact, insane. Though, the problem was that not everyone was as sure about that as he was. Parker had always been understanding before, but now, with her role as his conscience, she was more likely to be suspicious.

"I never should have said anything about blowing up Autem's settlement. I should have kept the plan to myself. If I had just kept my mouth shut, Parker wouldn't be chaperoning me, and Alex would have trusted me enough to tell me what he's been up to."

Odds were, they would understand what had happened here. That it was a tragic accident. Though, with the way everyone had been suspicious of him, this incident would still be a strike against him. Parker would only worry about his sanity more, and Alex might hide more from him. It would hinder his ability to build his army. To fight against his enemies. With the Autem empire getting stronger every day, he couldn't afford to be slowed down.

The people of Vegas depended on it.

They depended on him.

If he let this accident disrupt his plans, they all could lose everything.

"I can't let that happen." He clenched his jaw and swallowed the guilt of what he'd done. Looking back to Ames, he had only one choice. "No one can find out."

He winced, hearing his own words. They made him sound like the common criminal that he used to be all those centuries ago.

"No. This is nothing like that." He shook his head.

Back then, everything had been about self-preservation. This was something different. This was for the good of his people. That was what mattered. If he could defeat Henwick and make sure everyone was safe, then he could tell them everything afterward. If he still needs to face punishment then, so be it, but for now, there was no time to waste.

"That settles it." Digby stood up, looking down at Ames. "Now, how do I hide the fact that I killed you?"

The first thing he had to do was mend the wound on the zombie's chest. Otherwise, the manner in which the man had died would be obvious. If Ames had been a revenant, then the wound would make sense, but on a zombie, the evidence left by his Fingers of Death was too incriminating.

Unfortunately, that was when a voice called up from the bottom of the walkway that led up to the ship's deck.

"Hey, Dig? You up there?"

Digby snapped his head to the other side of the ship where the top of the walkway was. The voice belonged to Sax.

Why the hell is he here?

He rushed to the other side of the deck, practically running into the railing. He relaxed when he saw that Sax was still on the ground and hadn't set foot on the walkway. The entirety of Dragon coven stood behind him.

"Ah, hello there." Digby stood up straight trying to act normal.

Sax waved. "Hey, the shifts are changing back at the hangar and Parker was going to head back to Vegas to get a nap. I thought I'd check and see if you needed anything before she goes."

"No, thank you." Digby glanced back over his shoulder at Ames as the zombie crawled around the deck, still obeying his order not to get up.

Of course, that was when the zombie decided to moan.

"What was that?"

"Nothing." Digby turned back and shushed his new minion. "I mean, it was Ducky. The damn zombie never shuts up."

"Oh." Sax nodded.

"Indeed, we were just handling a few enemies up here." Digby leaned one arm on the railing in an attempt to look casual.

"Is Ducky enough help?" Sax started for the walkway that led up to the deck, his coven following behind. "We can give you a hand."

"What?" Digby pulled away from the railing, looking back at Ames crawling out in the open. "No, I wouldn't want to trouble you and your coven."

The sound of Sax's boots on the walkway continued, getting closer. "Don't worry about it. We'd love to get another level. I'm almost to level fifteen, and I think I will get a new class then. I'm thinking pyromancer on account of how cool it sounds."

Digby wiped some of the blood from his claws. *Damn! There's no stopping him!*

Finally, he did the only thing he could. Thrusting a hand toward Ames's animated corpse, he opened his maw and swallowed the zombie whole. Sax strode up onto the deck a second later.

"I assure you, Ducky and I need no assistance." He turned to the armored zombie standing not far away. "Right, Ducky?"

The monster answered with a grunt.

"You sure?"

That was when a message popped up across his vision.

WARNING, you have consumed a body that contains an active void, into your own void. Doing so will destabilize both voids, resulting in the annihilation of both, as well as the destruction of the surrounding area. You have between thirty seconds and one minute to reverse this issue before the process becomes irrecoverable. *Good lord, how did we come from the same person? Spit out the zombie already!*

"Gah!" Digby recoiled from the message.

"Woah, you okay?" Sax stepped toward him with a handout.

"Yes, I'm fine." Digby swatted him away, while simultaneously looking for an excuse for his panicked outburst and a place to spit the body back out of his void where no one would see. "I, ah, just felt something from Asher across our bond." He snapped his head up to the upper deck. "What is it, girl? A revenant?"

The raven hopped along the railing above, offering an unhelpful caw that somehow sounded confused.

"Oh, yes, I know." Digby tried to calm down. "She just thought she saw something." He shook his head. "Birds, am I right?"

WARNING, you have anywhere between fifteen and forty-five seconds before your void is annihilated. *What is wrong with you? Spit it out already!*

"I should run up there to make sure there's nothing to worry about." Digby continued his farce, sprinting over to a narrow set of stairs that led to the upper deck. He nearly crashed into a chain that stretched across it. A sign hung from the metal links, that read 'No access, please use other stairs.' Digby grabbed the railings and hoisted himself over the chain before rushing up the steps.

WARNING, annihilation imminent. *I can't restore your existence if there is nobody left to house it.*

Digby opened his maw on the upper deck the moment he reached the top of the steps and called forth the offending zombie. Ames flopped back out onto the deck along with a viscous coating of necrotic blood. Though, now, the monster was nothing more than an inanimate corpse.

Digby stared at it in confusion, unsure why the zombie had perished. It must have had something to do with his void destabilizing. He shook off the question. There wasn't time to investigate it now. Instead, he went back to the railing and called to Ducky. "Could you come up here, please?"

The hulking zombie followed to the stairs, snapping the chain that barred the entrance and looking ridiculous as he hauled his giant body up the narrow steps. Sax and the rest of his coven waited down below for Ducky to climb up. Digby sent a mental command across his bond with the zombie.

Stall, but don't make it obvious.

He immediately regretted the command when Ducky stopped halfway up and stared into the distance. Digby cursed the monster. He may have restored Ducky's physical capabilities but mentally, he was not all there.

"Um, I guess we'll take the stairs on the other side of the ship." Sax turned and started heading the other way.

Blast! Digby beckoned frantically to Ducky. "Get up here."

The zombie resumed his climb, reaching the top a moment later. Digby immediately gave a mental command to move Ames's body. Ducky obliged, albeit slowly, as he grabbed the corpse by the legs and dragged it toward an open hatch that led into the ship.

Digby ran to help, taking the corpse's hands. Of course, it slipped through his fingers, leaving him two fistfuls of black goo. Ames's head fell back against the deck with a wet thud. Sax's footsteps coming up the step on the other side announced his arrival. Digby shoved his messy hands behind his back and spun to face the stairs.

"Ah, Sax, there you are." Digby stepped between the soldier and Ducky to block the line of sight just as the armored zombie dragged Ames's corpse the rest of the way into the ship. A trail of necrotic blood marked the direction that they had gone.

Sax glanced around. "We can start clearing the inside of the ship if that helps."

"Um." Digby struggled to come up with a way to get rid of him. Then it came to him. "It would actually be more helpful if you could focus on one of the smaller ships on the other side of the harbor."

"Really?" Sax looked out across the water.

"I should say so." Digby swept an arm out toward the vessels. "Alex has made it abundantly clear that we shan't be able to get this battleship out of the water with the level of magic that we currently possess. But those smaller ships are another story, and our artificers are going to need them clear of enemies so that they can get to work."

"Sure, we can help with that." Sax took a step back toward the steps he'd just climbed. "You sure you don't need anything, though?"

"No, I'll be alright." Digby glanced back at the open hatch to make sure Ducky had successfully moved the body. "Besides, I just unlocked a new mutation that I have been experimenting with. Without going into much detail, it's not for the faint of heart." He finished by holding out a messy clawed hand and willing it to return to normal. The excess flesh turned black and mixed with the necrotic blood that coated his fingers before falling away in wet chunks.

"Oh gross." Sax grimaced. "Sure, sure, say no more. We'll leave you to your experiments."

Digby forced a grin. "Yes, that would probably be best for all involved."

Sax stopped on his way down and held out a walkie-talkie. "Keep this on you just in case."

Digby took the radio and gave a nod. With that, he sent Sax and the rest of Dragon coven on their way. He practically collapsed against the railing once they were gone.

"How did I make such a mess of this?"

The guilt of hiding his crime from his allies clashed with the knowledge that it had been his only option. If he wanted to protect them from Autem, he had no choice. He pushed the conflict out of his mind and headed back into the ship where Ducky stood over the corpse.

"Well, now what do I do with it?" Digby stared down at the body covered in black goo.

The five claw-shaped wounds in the chest were still visible, and now that Ames had ceased to be a zombie, there was no way to mend the damage. He certainly didn't want to try eating it again after what had happened before. Digby glanced back at the open hatch behind him.

"I suppose we could toss the body in the sea." He frowned. "But then it might just float back up where someone might find it."

Digby walked further into the ship, finding description plates mounted to walls and roped-off rooms. The vessel truly was a museum. It was all very interesting, but he didn't have time to indulge in a history lesson.

"Alright." He walked back to where Ames's corpse lay in the middle of a narrow corridor. "Let's not overthink things."

Digby held up a hand and cast cremation. The body ignited instantly. He watched it burn. "At least cremation is somewhat of a proper way to lay this man to rest." He knelt down, feeling the heat of the flames in front of him. "I am sorry, Ames. Your end was a cruel twist of fate, but there is little more that I can do for you."

When the flames burnt out, he gathered the ashes and left-over bits of bone and opened his maw to cast Forge. Black blood seeped from his void to mix with the man's remains before forming a rectangular block. He gave it to Ducky with an order to throw it overboard and vowed to add the man's name to the wall of heroes back in Vegas when everything was all over.

After he was done, there was nothing left but a blackened section of floor in the corridor. Hopefully, no one would ask questions. Though, if they did, he could just say that the floor was like that when he'd got there. In the end, there was no evidence left to reveal what had happened.

Digby deflated, again, feeling the conflict inside him. That was when a whisper came from behind him.

"This is how it must be."

Digby spun to find no one there. He arched an eyebrow. "Hello?"

He waited a few seconds for someone to answer.

No one did.

"Who's there?" Digby flicked his eyes around the corridor, finding only Ducky. "You didn't say anything just now, did you?"

Ducky responded with a grunt.

"Right, of course not." Digby ran a claw through his hair. "Must have been my imagination." He forced an awkward chuckle. "Either that, or Parker's right and I really am losing my mind."

To put everything behind him, he headed back out onto the deck to search for another flying revenant so that he could continue his Body Craft experiments. The walkie-talkie that Sax had left him came alive as soon as he stepped back out onto the deck.

"Hey, Dig?"

Digby grabbed it and thumbed the button with a claw. "Yes?"

"Can you come join us back at the hangar? We just got some news." The soldier sounded uneasy.

"Very well, I shall be there momentarily." Digby lowered the radio, wondering if he should have been so agreeable. The last thing he wanted to do was look guilty by acting out of character. He shrugged off the worry and grabbed his staff before heading back.

He understood why Sax had sounded uneasy the moment he arrived, finding Mason and Clint standing within the hangar's warded perimeter. The soldier still wore his new hat while the zombie beside him held a bundle of black and red fabric.

"What have you learned?" Digby asked before he'd even reached them.

"I couldn't find Rebecca's body." Clint held up the bundle in his hands. "I searched as much of the sunken ship as I could, but all I found was her cloak."

Digby flicked his eyes to Mason. "What does this mean?"

"It means she got out." He smiled, standing taller like a massive weight had been lifted from his shoulders. "She's alive."

Digby leaned on his staff, feeling like he might fall over. The news was almost too good to be true. Then he frowned.

"But if she escaped the ship, where the devil is she?"

CHAPTER SIXTEEN

"Wait no!" Becca flew backward, her back hitting the wall of the office building hard enough to crack the drywall.

At least this time she didn't go through it.

"You starting to get the hang of this?" Ozzie stood over her.

"This is stupid." She started to get up, only to let herself fall back against the wall. She could already feel the bruises fade away as her body healed itself. The damage hadn't been severe, but there was no way to stop the vampiric healing ability. Instead, it was just a continuous reminder that she wasn't human anymore.

Becca frowned. She still didn't know much about what she had become.

All she knew was that she didn't like it.

After meeting the group of Fools and getting a lesson in the secret history of the war between them and the Autem Empire, she had been forced to turn in early. Apparently, fatigue was a common problem for newly turned vampires. She just couldn't take in enough mana to support her abilities.

As she was learning, vampires had a significantly lower absorption rate than Heretics. Especially while the sun was up.

Instead of her mana being replenished in minutes, it now took days. From what she could feel, she had blown through a little less than half her MP during her fight with Ozzie. During the day, she'd only gained ten percent back. Leon assured her that she'd get used to it as she learned to be more conservative with her mana.

Hence, her training.

Leon crouched down beside her, the glow of a camping lantern on the floor behind him. "I understand that this exercise seems dumb. But it does work."

"So getting the crap beat out of me is all part of the process?" She rolled her eyes.

"I had to do the same thing when I turned." Ozzie pranced around like a boxer. "And it's not like I hit you that hard."

"The wall would like to beg to differ." Becca swept her hands through the plaster dust that covered the floor. "What do you have against walls, anyway?" She gestured to the giant hole that he had rammed her through the night before.

"Not like we have to worry about getting the security deposit back on this place." He shrugged.

Leon held a hand out to help her up. "The most important part of learning to use your abilities as a vampire is learning how not to use them. It's more about subtlety. If you allow your body to tap into its full prowess every time you're threatened, you'll burn through your mana supply in under a minute. So yeah, you're going to have to learn to resist the instinct to let loose while in a fight until you absolutely need to. And even then, you need to keep it to controlled bursts."

Becca groaned in protest but took his hand regardless.

As stupid as her training was, she couldn't argue with the fact that the two vampires had more experience than her. Listening to their advice was her only choice. Especially if they intended to steal the Guardian Core's caretaker with only a few days of planning. In the end, it was the only way to save Digby from the fate he didn't even know was waiting for him.

That made her training more important, and there wasn't time to screw around.

"When are we going to get to the important stuff?" Becca folded her arms, getting sick of getting kicked around by Ozzie all night. "I get that I need to control myself, but I also need to learn how to get stronger."

"Okay. Fine." Leon walked in a little circle before sitting down on the floor in the middle of the room. "We should give your healing a break anyway."

"Guess my part's done then." Ozzie turned and headed out of the room, grabbing a beer on his way.

Leon patted the carpet in front of him. "Come sit. I won't bite."

Becca sighed and did as she was told. "You know, you are a vampire. You literally bite people all the time."

"Not all the time." He shook his head. "I'll have you know that I didn't kill anyone for nearly the entire last century." He paused. "Well, unless you count Nazis. I killed a few Nazis, you know, as a treat."

"Good to know." Becca filed that little detail away. She might not have trusted her new friends completely yet, but hey, no one liked Nazis, so that was probably a point in their favor.

"However, one thing to note is that because I attempted to live a normal life for a hundred years or so, I lost almost all of my power."

"That can happen?" Becca leaned away, suddenly worried about the abilities she'd gained and how many people she would have to kill to maintain them.

"Being a vampire is both similar to being a Heretic, and very different. Our abilities do increase in power and evolve the more we use them. But they also fade over time if we don't." He flexed an arm. "It's like a muscle; if you don't use it, you lose it."

"So how do I use it?" Becca leaned forward.

He held up a finger. "To start, I want you to think back to

what it felt like when you killed those Guardians back on that kestrel."

"It was chaos," she answered without needing to think. "I was impossibly strong and fast. The world seemed to vibrate around me."

"What do you mean by vibrate?" He grabbed hold of a detail.

Becca thought about her wording. "Everything was loud and bright, and it was hard to focus. To a point where I couldn't tell who I was even attacking or where I was until everyone was dead. I didn't even realize I'd been shot a half dozen times until after, when I saw the holes in my shirt."

"So you get why using your full power is a problem? It becomes as much of a liability as an asset." He chuckled. "A vampire in control of their power could have dodged those bullets."

"So teach me." She started to stand up.

"I am." Leon grabbed her hand to pull her back to the floor. As soon as she was sitting again, he placed her hand on his chest.

On reflex, Becca pulled away, uncomfortable with the sudden intimacy of the act. He hadn't done anything wrong, but the overall smoothness of his movements had thrown her off guard. Leon let go without argument, a knowing look in his eyes as if he'd just deduced every insecurity she had, of which, she had many. The realization made her feel far more vulnerable than if she had just let him hold her hand without protest.

He lowered his head. "Sorry, I was going to take you through some sensory exercises."

She took a deep breath, trying not to blush. "You're one of *those* vampires, aren't you?"

"What do you mean?" He raised his head, pushing his hair back in a practiced motion that left it in the optimal position to accent his youthful face.

"You know." She glanced away. "You're one of those

vampires that traveled through history, ravishing every young woman you came across."

He let out a laugh. "Don't be ridiculous. I have been around a long time; how could I limit myself to only ravishing women? But I see your point. I've certainly gone through a slut arc or two."

Becca arched an eyebrow at his wording. He had a way of slipping back and forth between speaking formally and modern slang. It was like he had been updating his vocabulary to match the times but hadn't quite gotten it all to sync up.

Eventually, she held out a hand. "Okay, let's get this sensory lesson going, then."

He smirked as he took her hand and placed it back against his chest. "To start, I want you to pay attention to my heart."

"Yeah, it's beating."

"Well, that's good." He feigned relief before becoming serious again. "Now, the key to being a vampire is subtlety. Your power isn't just an on-off sort of thing. It's not even one power. It's several that weave together; physical, mental, and magical. Your instincts will tell you to fire them all up at full blast, but it's about isolating them. Once you do that, you can push on each individually."

Becca adjusted her position to get more comfortable, getting the feeling that things were going to take a while. "So by sepa-rating my abilities, I'll be able to stretch my mana consumption?"

"Yes, but this way, you will also be able to develop your skills in a way that fits you. If you just go all out all the time, you'll end up splitting your attention across all your abilities and stunting your overall growth. If you focus on just a few, you'll get much more out of them in the end."

"That's what determines what class a vampire will become?"

He nodded. "Your class, from what I can tell, is nightmare. Though I don't know much about what you can do, other than your abilities are fear-based."

"That sounds aggressive." She frowned. "Probably because of my past as an illusionist."

"I assume so." He flattened his hand against hers. "Let's start by listening to my heartbeat while ignoring what your hand is feeling. Try to force your sense of touch out of the picture and isolate your hearing."

Becca focused on her hearing the way she had when she was a Heretic.

Unfortunately, the moment she did, she was hit with a sudden rush of sensations. Leon's heartbeat alone slammed against her like a drum pounding in her head while traces of plaster dust invaded her nose. Even the gentle light of the camping lantern crashed into her like a tsunami, casting shadows across the floor like razors as the world around her flooded with sound. Everything was so vivid, yet so tangled that she couldn't pick out the details. She winced and pushed it all away.

After a few deep breaths, everything faded back to normal.

Clearly, she was going to need more practice.

"Do you have any pointers?"

Leon inhaled and closed his eyes. "Picture your senses as something tangible. Like threads stretched taut in the air. Then, imagine pushing on one."

Becca attempted to picture the threads but found the image hard to connect with in a way that made sense. After a minute, she shook the image out of her head and pictured something else. With her appreciation for music and the significance it had played in her magic, something with a similar quality seemed like a good way to bridge the gap between her abilities as a Heretic and the power she'd gained.

Five strings stretched out in her mind. At first, she tried to picture them attached to a guitar due to the familiarity. Something about that felt too complicated, though. She stripped the strings away and stretched them across something simpler.

A harp.

As soon as she had the thought, everything else clicked into place. Pushing gently on one string, Leon's heartbeat grew from background noise to her main focus. At the same time, the feeling of his chest remained the same without overpowering her.

"Oh wow."

"Good. Finding a heartbeat is going to be your best method of locating prey." Leon gestured to the hallway with his head. "Now push harder, tell me which direction Ozzie and Harlow are in."

She ran her finger against the imaginary harp string in her head, pressing against it. Slowly, another rhythmic pumping reached her. A second followed.

"Ozzie is a couple doors down." She glanced to the other end of the room. "Harlow is on the other side of that wall."

An irregular thump thump accompanied the woman's heartbeat. At first, Becca thought there was another person in the room with her, but something about the pattern didn't feel right.

"There's something else."

Leon took her hand off his chest and placed it to the floor. "Try adding another sense to your search."

Becca reached out to press against the harp string in her mind. It wasn't long before she could feel everyone's heartbeats clearer. Not only did she know what direction they were coming from, but how far away each person was. Pushing their heartbeats away, she settled in on the strange irregular pattern she'd noticed before, its source suddenly becoming obvious.

"Is Harlow bouncing a tennis ball?"

Leon laughed. "She does that when she's nervous."

"Is she nervous a lot?" Becca let her senses fade back to normal.

"She's been through a lot." He looked Becca in the eyes. "I can tell you don't trust her—or us, for that matter—but Harlow means well. And she's trying her best. Though, putting up with Ozzie and me doesn't make things easier for her."

Becca couldn't help but notice a sympathetic tone in his voice, but before she could ask anything else, he stood up.

"Okay, that concludes your basic training. Now comes the fun part." He pushed the desk that sat in the room off to the side by the window. Then, he held up a hand in a 'come at me' gesture. "I want you to hit me. Provided you can."

Becca hopped up, feeling like she was finally getting the hang of things. Granted, it was obvious he had something up his sleeve. She paced back and forth to size him up, then without warning, she tried to kick him in the shin. Unsurprisingly, he moved his leg. Which was why she yanked hers back again to try and hook her foot around his other ankle.

The vampire simply hopped to avoid it.

"Nice one." His relaxed expression told her that she had little hope of landing a hit.

"Fine, let's see if I can level things out." Becca thought about the other aspects of her prowess and added five new strings to her imaginary harp. One to represent each of the physical stats she had as a Heretic; strength, constitution, defense, dexterity, and agility. She pushed on that last one alone. Her agility was already well above the normal human standard thanks to the levels she'd gained as a Heretic before losing her connection with the Seed, but adding even just a little of her mana into the stat changed everything.

All at once her limbs became impossibly light, while at the same time giving her a new awareness of her body. She slid her foot across the floor, feeling every stabilizer muscle in her leg adjust as her balance shifted. Leon arched an eyebrow, clearly understanding what she'd done.

Becca attacked without hesitation, rotating her hip to launch a kick at his head. She tugged on her strength for an instant to increase her momentum. Her foot moved with an inhuman quickness, giving her a strange awareness of the resistance the air itself held as she pushed through it.

Leon ducked like a boxer, dropping down only to bounce back up. She didn't stop there. Instead, she let the momentum of her kick carry her as she launched her other foot into the air with a bit of added strength. The result sent her other leg straight for his head. The vampire pulled back to avoid the kick, however, the sudden movement sent him falling backward.

Becca's foot tore through space as her momentum threw her entire body into a mid-air spiral. She let herself go, watching as the world spun around her. In the same second, Leon caught himself and kicked off the floor. Plaster dust trailed from the toe of his shoe as he executed a backflip that doubled as an attack. Becca responded in kind, her body's rotation placing her perpendicular to the floor. She separated her legs as Leon's foot sliced through the space between them.

Locking her eyes to a point on the floor, she twisted her body to meet the ground. She landed on all fours in a stable but uncoordinated stance. The amount of control she had was incredible. It was like night and day compared to the state she'd been in back when she had first woken up. On top of that, she was starting to sense something inside her. It had always been there, but now she was so much more aware of it.

Her mana system.

She may not have had a HUD to display her exact MP, but she knew the rough amount. That last little burst had only used one or two percent of her total. No doubt her time as a Heretic had helped, but Leon had been right. She could stretch her mana much farther using it more selectively rather than just blasting all of her stats and senses at once.

Leon crouched where he'd landed on the floor a few feet away. He looked like a cat ready to pounce with his hands out in front of him, his back arched, and his legs bent. Obviously, he had more skill than her. Still, she wanted to at least land a hit.

"Why can't I hit you?" She bared her fangs on instinct.

"No vampire is the same. We all have different abilities." He winked. "Some of us are just faster."

"So you can enhance your reaction speed. Good to know your specialty." She smirked as he gave away a detail about himself.

He held his pose, ready to launch in her direction. "Yes, I barely use my stats except for agility, dexterity, and perception. It's best to focus on three. But right now, I think you should be more worried about your own specialty instead of figuring out mine."

Becca's face fell as she realized she'd been so focused on her physical abilities she'd forgotten the rest. But what was her specialty? Agility and perception were a must. That left one more. That one was just as obvious, intelligence. More specifically, magic.

With that, she willed her ability into action. It wouldn't take much to distract him. Becca imagined Ozzie's voice calling to them.

Nothing happened.

"What?" Her mind crashed to a halt.

Of course, that was when Leon decided to pounce. The unreasonably attractive vampire launched in her direction, using the point of his elbow like a battering ram.

Becca tore her mind away from the confusion of her magic's failure as she pushed her agility and tapped her strength to throw herself straight up in the air. Leon streaked beneath her. She landed as he slid to a stop behind her. They both stood back up, now back to back. She spun on her heel to face him. He did the same.

"Why didn't it work?" She hopped back.

"You really need an inner monologue, you know." Leon pointed to his head.

"Shut up, I'm not used to having people around to listen," she groaned back at him.

"Are you used to vampires kicking your ass?" She let out a somewhat bubbly laugh. "Because you should know enough now to be able to hold your own if I get serious."

"Do I have a choice?" She raised her fists and got ready to push her stats.

He didn't even answer before darting forward. Becca threw up a hand to deflect whatever was coming but he simply closed his fingers around her wrist and yanked her forward. For an instant, he nearly launched her across the room, but she pressed her agility along with a slight burst of strength. The combination helped her find the traction to resist him, leaving them standing face to face. She smirked, feeling proud that he hadn't gotten his way.

Then, he simply vanished. Something slammed into her back in the same second. Pain radiated out from between her shoulder blades as a rib cracked.

"Fuck!" Becca staggered away, unsure how he'd even hit her.

The vampire had been in front of her one second then the next, he was ramming an elbow into her back. He wasn't lying about being faster. She'd barely even seen him move.

"Hey, watch the damage." She growled as her body repaired whatever he'd just broken. She could sense her mana falling. The blow had cost her another five percent. Overall, she was down to about forty percent, including what she'd spent wrestling with Ozzie earlier. "My mana won't last if I have to heal."

"Good point." He paced around her. "You should probably stop letting me hit you, then." With that, he threw a kick at her side. It came in high, toward her shoulder.

"Shit." She pushed her defense, knowing she couldn't dodge fast enough.

His foot slammed into her shoulder as a shimmer of blue light swept across her. The impact threw her sideways toward the window, but other than that, she was unharmed. The realization that she could still create a barrier by feeding mana into her defense gave her a new option. It wasn't the same as casting a spell, but it would give her an instant of protection if she timed it right.

Leon came at her again, his movements practically a blur. She leaned into her defense as well as her agility and strength to raise a barrier on impact and to stop her from being knocked to the side. At the same time, she raised her arms to protect her head. He brought a flurry of hits down upon her, but she held firm. She may not have been able to avoid getting kicked, but she could at least tank the blows to buy time to think. The effort still cost mana, but not as much as it would cost to heal the damage.

"Very good, but if you depend too much on your strength and defense like that, you'll end up like Ozzie and lose your class advantage." Leon kicked her square in the forearms.

"Oh yeah? So tanking is his specialty?" She tried to keep him talking if only to slow the next attack.

"Ozzie is the opposite of me. He mostly uses strength, defense, and constitution. It's simple but effective. He's near impossible to kill when he gets serious." Leon lunged forward only to weave to the side and slip behind her, close enough to whisper in her ear. "But what's your talent?"

Becca tried to think. Her specialty had been illusions, something that still seemed partially true. Granted, all she could do was manifest bats, and her ventriloquism ability had become unreliable since becoming a vampire.

That was when she realized her mistake.

She had lost all of her spells along with her connection with the Heretic Seed. So why did she think her ventriloquism spell remained the same when none of her other abilities had translated? The simple answer was that it hadn't. If that was true, what did the ability do?

Then the answer hit her.

Nightmares.

That was what Leon said her class was. He'd called her ventriloquism something else the night before. What was it?

Banshee.

It all started to make sense. It wasn't that the ability had failed a second ago, she had been using it wrong. It had more to do with her intent than the result. It wasn't enough to cause a distraction. No, she was a nightmare. If she wanted her magic to work, then it had to be scary. Her intent had to be to cause fear. That was why she could create bats. They were spooky, the kind of thing that went bump in the night. Good old psychological warfare.

Becca felt for her mana, finding around twenty-five percent left after tanking Leon's hits, then she fed some into her Banshee ability. A second later, their sparring was interrupted by a sudden scream from a room next door.

It was Harlow's voice.

Leon stopped mid-kick, his attention shifting to the door. A shout from Ozzie followed.

"Shit! Autem's here!"

Becca smirked as Leon fell for the ruse. Autem still had no idea where they were. The voices had just been an imitation. One meant to cause fear. She reached forward to curl her fingers through Leon's hair. She nearly gave herself away by opening her mouth to declare her victory. She forced the thought back inside, fighting her habit to say everything out loud.

You're not dodging this time.

She pushed on her agility with an instant of strength to plant a foot into the back of Leon's legs while yanking back on his hair. The combination forced him to the floor.

"Wait! We're—" Leon's knees hit the carpet as Becca pulled his head back. He went silent a second later, clearly realizing what had happened. "I guess you figured out what you're good at."

"I'm a nightmare." She leaned close to his ear as she let go of his hair. "I guess I'm best at causing fear."

That was when Ozzy and Harlow came running into the room.

"What's happening? I just heard..." Harlow cocked her head to the side like a confused dog, still holding a tennis ball in her hand. "I think that was my voice."

"Yeah, same," Ozzie added.

Leon stood back up. "We were sparring. And apparently, our new friend figured out how to use her magic."

"I worked it out." Becca pulled out her phone and opened

her notes app, deleting her ventriloquism ability, and replacing it.

Banshee

Mimic any sound, provided the intent of that sound is to frighten, scare, or cause psychological harm.

"That should do it." She scrolled back up to her stats, looking up when she realized she was missing an important detail. "Hey, how do I level up?"

"Umm, we don't have levels." Ozzie eyed her with confusion. "You just get stronger by feeding and using your abilities."

"I get that. But what about feeding?" She reached for her mana, feeling about half remaining. "Can I get someone to donate some blood? That way I don't bite anyone and end up cursing or killing them."

"Yes and no." Leon sat down on the desk that he'd pushed against the window. Moonlight slipped through the blinds behind him to bathe him in a gentle glow. "If you want to live a normal life and never use your abilities, a donor can keep your mana high enough to avoid losing control. But like I said, you won't have enough to use your abilities and they will fade over time."

"Sorry, murdering bad guys is the only way to power up." Ozzie bared his fangs. "Biting is the only way to really get at what we need."

"Why?" Becca let a hint of frustration enter her voice. "Why do we specifically have to bite people?"

"Because blood isn't what sustains us, mana does." Leon pulled grabbed a beer from a six-pack on the desk and popped the tab. "If all we did was drink the blood that spills from a wound, we would only get a fraction of the mana a person carries. It might be enough to keep you from succumbing to a ravenous thirst, but not enough to keep any of your abilities active." He took a sip, grimacing at the taste. Then he grabbed a second beer and tossed it to Ozzie.

The overgrown vampire caught it and immediately bit into the side near the bottom before pulling the tab at the top.

Harlow rolled her eyes as he shotgunned the beer.

Ozzie pulled the can away empty a few seconds later, then spiked it on the floor. He followed the act with a performative flex of his biceps.

"Thank you for the demonstration." Leon inclined his head to his friend before continuing. "When we bite a person and draw in their blood, it creates a link between our mana system and theirs. Once that connection is made, we can drain their essence across that link. Meaning we can take their entire mana system all at once. The reason that we get stronger that way is because, by doing that, we take in a small amount of their soul in the process."

"Wait, does that mean we literally eat people's souls?" Becca shuddered at the idea that she had already done it to a squad of Guardians.

"It's not like we take all of it." Ozzie held up two fingers close together. "Just, you know, a taste."

"Yes, that's all it takes," Leon added matter-of-factly. "The human soul has such a high mana content that even a taste is enough to replenish all of your mana in an instant." He shrugged. "And a soul is not that special. You lose a little of it every time you use magic, but it fills itself back in over time. Souls are resilient like that."

"Then why do we kill people? Couldn't we just take a little and let it heal?" Becca waved a hand toward the window and the dead world beyond.

"Because once you've established a link between mana systems, it's too late." Leon deflated. "Think of it like an STD."

"Ew, no." Becca grimaced.

Ozzie just laughed. "Yeah, 'cause Leon knows all about STDs."

"Oh please, I do not." He folded his arms to pout before giving Becca a wink. "Vampires are actually immune to most diseases and infections."

"Not everything, dude." Ozzie eyed him sideways.

"Oh, come on, I had a somewhat itchy situation, like, a hundred years ago." Leon groaned. "I can't believe I told you about that."

"How could I forget? You told me you set yourself on fire to deal with it." Ozzie continued to laugh.

"Well, when your body continuously regenerates, you have a few more treatment options available." Leon held his head high as if proud of himself for thinking of an unorthodox solution.

"Oi!" Harlow stomped a foot. "No one wants to hear 'bout your ye olde crabs."

"Yes, sorry. Where was I?" He placed a finger to his chin. "Oh yes. So, connecting your mana system to another's allows your curse to spread to them. Once that happens, it's only a matter of time before their soul is pushed from their body. The best thing we can do for our prey is to end it quickly and, in the process, take in what little of their soul we can hold. The rest just dissipates or passes on to where ever souls go."

"What about turning someone?" Becca held out a hand. "You said that to do that we have to anchor their soul in their body to stop them from becoming a revenant. That's how we complete the transformation, right?"

"That part's simple." Leon bared his fangs. "Once you have your mana system linked with someone else's, you just hold onto the connection without drawing any mana from them. As long as you can maintain the link while the curse takes hold, their soul will remain where it is rather than being pushed out."

"That's all well and nice," Harlow interrupted. "But if you're done sorting out your abilities, I need some vampires to do some recon out there if we are going to be ready to pull off a heist."

Becca swallowed hard, remembering that there wasn't time for any more training. The streets outside were full of threats, and she was going to have to deal with them one way or another.

"You ready to use your powers out there for real?" Leon gave her a supportive smile.

"I'm going to have to be." Becca gave a weak shrug.

"Good." Harlow turned to exit the room. "I'll be down in the lobby when you're ready for a briefing."

Becca took in a slow breath before letting it out.

"There's no turning back now."

CHAPTER SEVENTEEN

Down in the lobby of the office building, Becca slipped back into the armor she'd looted off a dead Guardian just after crash landing in Washington, D.C. The moon hung in the sky outside, filling the dark room with the same cool light that had become her new normal as a nocturnal predator.

Catching her reflection in the window, she frowned. Even without the bat nose and bad teeth, she looked more revenant than human. Especially in the pale light of the nearly full moon.

"Oi, gather 'round, there's a lot to go over." Harlow set Becca's laptop down on the lobby's reception desk and inserted a USB drive into the side.

"Yeah, gotta get the newbie up to speed." Ozzie fastened the straps of one of Autem's chest protectors as he joined her at the desk. He left a firefighter's ax leaning against the side and holstered a heavy revolver at his hip. The weapons suited his tank-like build.

Leon kept watch at the door, wearing a simple, black tactical vest. Unlike his partner, he wore no armor. Though, with his speed, he probably didn't need it. For weapons, he carried a narrow, curved sword like what a cavalryman or a pirate might use. A long dagger, with a wide cross hilt, was sheathed on his right hip, opposite his sword. They looked like weapons he'd picked up over the course of centuries, making her wonder again exactly how old he was.

Becca pushed the question out of her mind and focused on the situation at hand. "Okay, what do you know so far about Autem's base?"

Harlow turned the laptop around, showing a complex architectural drawing of some kind of fortress. "This is what the empire is building out there."

"Shit." Becca's eyes widened.

"Shit is right." Harlow pointed to the screen. "The fortress is made up of two parts. An outer wall and a central structure that we believe is housed within. We've only been able to get pictures of the outside, obviously." She brought up some grainy images that had been shot from various points throughout the surrounding area.

"The thing's massive." Ozzie held out both hands to indicate the size. "And it's got five sides, like that government building, what's it called?"

"The Pentagon." Leon helped him out, looking disappointed that his partner hadn't come up with it on his own.

"Yes." Harlow nodded, looking equally disappointed. "The wall has five equal sides, and it surrounds close to a square mile of land. The immediate area outside is well warded against revenants and has a heavy Guardian presence."

"That's where Autem has been housing the survivors that they have taken in as citizens of their empire. They're using the preexisting buildings in the area as a refugee camp, with kestrels flying in more people every day." Leon sighed. "They're growing fast."

"We'll have to find a way through the camp before we can even try to get into the fortress." Harlow continued. "According to these files, the wall is going to be the hard part. For starters, it's two hundred feet high and over a hundred feet thick. From the size, it's more than just a wall. We've observed aircraft entering it through various openings on its sides, so we assume it contains a number of facilities within."

"Any idea how many kestrels are in there?" Becca asked.

"Only a few are here in D.C. at a time since most are out in the world looking for survivors," Harlow responded in a defeated tone.

"That doesn't sound so bad?" Becca leaned to one side.

"That's because kestrels aren't the only thing to worry about," Leon commented.

"Since ending the world, the empire has begun rolling out new aircraft that, for obvious reasons, couldn't be used openly until now." Harlow tapped on the laptop to bring up a few more grainy images.

Becca understood why the new aircraft couldn't be used publicly as soon as she saw the first picture.

They were powered by magic.

At first glance, the craft looked somewhat like a kestrel, only larger. The difference was that there were no propellers. In their place were four cylinders housed within metal rings positioned on each corner. Each was covered in runes.

"Most of what we've seen have either been gunships or dropships." Harlow switched the image to another craft with a detachable compartment that could carry troops or supplies. "We don't have an exact count of how many of these craft they have, but it's in the several dozens."

"That's bad." Becca slapped a hand down to the desk. "They don't even know Autem has aircraft beyond kestrels back in Vegas. But if they have a whole fleet of them, Digby won't stand a chance if he decides to go to war."

"Then we need to make sure we pull this off before anything happens." A grave expression fell across Harlow's face. "A lot is riding on this mission. And we have very little time to prepare."

"Unlike Autem." Becca leaned on the desk, feeling the weight of the situation. "They must have had these magic-powered aircraft ready to go long before they ended the world.

Though, the thing I don't understand is how they built this wall so fast. Just transporting the materials would be hard to hide. Unless..."

Becca remembered the elevator that she had ridden in to reach Henwick's home on the moon. The thing hadn't actually traveled through space, meaning that Autem must have had a way to make some kind of portal.

"They have a gateway." Harlow pointed to the space within the wall.

"What's that?" Becca looked up from the screen.

"It's a complicated system of runes, hundreds of thousands of them," Leon added. "We've seen Autem use them before. It's a stationary structure that links to another matching one some-place else. They're large and extremely hard to build, but they work."

Becca nodded, understanding how Autem was moving so fast. "They must have had the materials for this fortress ready to go just like they did the aircraft. Once the world ended, all they did was plop down a new gateway in the middle of D.C. and start transporting everything from another location."

"Yes. From what we've seen, they even had sections of this wall pre-assembled." Leon put his hands together like he was connecting two Legos.

"What about the structure inside?" Becca moved on.

"That we know less about." Harlow brought up a new image of a building. It had five sides as well. "According to our files, once we get past the outer wall, we'll have to cross several hundred feet of open space, then find a way into the central building. We can access the caretaker from a room on the fifth floor."

Becca's mind got stuck on a detail. "How do you know that? For that matter, how do we even know the caretaker we need is stored in this building?"

"Who do you think sent the files?" Harlow gave her a knowing look.

"The caretaker?"

"Yes." Harlow nodded. "One thing that we have going in our favor is that the caretaker is on our side. Autem may be able to get what they want out of them, but the caretaker is unpredictable and near impossible to control completely. It will rebel. There's no way to know how much the caretaker will be able to help us, but at least someone inside Autem is looking out for us."

"The caretaker was able to send these files along with some intel just before the Internet kicked the bucket for good." Ozzie punted an empty beer can across the floor.

"One of the things we were sent was a schedule for when the caretaker was to be transferred to this location. That was a few days ago." Harlow gestured to the street outside. "The empire pulled all of their Guardians into the fortress inside for a couple of hours. They seem to have shut down the Guardian Core at that time. Unfortunately, we didn't have enough notice to be able to take advantage of that window in any meaningful way." She deflated. "I may have failed to protect the caretaker, but they have never stopped fighting to help us."

The guilt in Harlow's voice was palpable.

"We'll get it back." Becca tried to say something positive.

"Oh yeah, we just have to sneak through a well-guarded refugee camp, make it past a two-hundred-foot-high wall, pass through an open area with no cover, then make it to the fifth floor of the building at the center." Ozzie held both hands out. "Oh, and then we have to get out of there with the caretaker."

"You're not helping." Leon shot him a sharp look.

"Actually, some of that might not be as bad as it sounds." Becca walked through the lobby toward the doors at the front of the office building before turning back around. "Autem has been crazy busy this last month building all of this. They have to be stretching their resources thin, and I doubt that the fortress has been completed beyond the basic structure."

"You think it's an unfinished Death Star situation?" Leon nodded.

"Yes, and good to know age-old vampires have at least seen

Star Wars." Becca paced back and forth. "Getting through the camp outside will be easy enough. I've moved freely amongst them before. Guardians practically never analyze anyone. So as long as we blend in and don't do anything to stick out, we should be fine."

"Okay, so we're gonna need a spray tan," Ozzie joked.

She pointed in his direction. "That could work, actually. As for the wall, and everything else. The construction happening inside should create holes in their security, like Swiss cheese. There's no way to manage workers in a rapidly changing environment like that. We can probably use the work crews to slip through."

"That's quite a large probably." Harlow leaned on the reception desk.

"Yes, but we have another advantage." Becca's heart rate sped up along with her pacing as she channeled her inner Digby. "This plan is insane."

"Ah, yeah, it is." Ozzie looked confused.

Becca spun back to him. "And that's why it might work. Autem knows I'm alive, but by now, they must have assumed I kept running after slipping through their search area. The idea that I stayed so close, and that I'd be crazy enough to break into the literal heart of their empire to steal their most important asset—"

"Is bonkers." Harlow slowly nodded as she finished Becca's sentence. "So they'll never expect it."

"Exactly." Becca pointed in her direction. "Everyone inside that wall believes they are safe. They think they are untouchable."

"And we're going to exploit that." Leon started smiling.

"Okay, I'm here for it." An excited expression shined on Ozzie's face.

Becca stood tall before taking a few deep breaths and letting herself fall back to reality. Her excitement died almost immediately. "Oh my fucking god, this is insane. Digby always made this sort of thing look easy, but shit, we're all going to die."

Everyone in the lobby deflated, letting a long moment of silence pass.

"We're really doing this, aren't we?" Ozzie glanced around the room.

Harlow blew out a heavy sigh. "I don't think we have a choice."

Becca opened her mouth to say something hopeful, only to close it again after saying nothing. No matter how much she tried to channel Digby's carefree and somewhat arrogant attitude, she couldn't ignore the fact.

They were likely planning a suicide mission.

The heist they pulled off back on Skyline's base had been different. Sure, it had been Digby's resourcefulness that had saved them in the end, but they'd had more time and more information to get ready. Now, though, they were flying by the seat of their pants and operating off assumptions.

Looking around the room at her new allies, she couldn't shake the feeling of dread that had anchored itself deep within her gut.

There was no way all of them were going to make it out.

Maybe that was alright. Becca winced at the intrusive thought. Though, she couldn't deny it was the first time she'd had that thought since waking up as the bloodthirsty monster that she had become. What kind of life could she have at this point? Ozzie and Leon both seemed to be used to killing to survive, but she had trouble believing she could reach that point as well. Her only choice would be to never use her abilities once she got back to Vegas. That way, she wouldn't run the risk of having her mana drop too low, but in the apocalypse, was that even an option?

It would probably be better for everyone if she didn't make it back.

The thought gave her a strange sense of calm. As if accepting her fate made it easier to risk it all on a heist that was likely to fail.

All that mattered was someone got the caretaker and made it back to Vegas to save Digby. Even if it wasn't her.

Her thoughts were interrupted by a strange humming.

"Shit, hide!" Ozzie dove behind the reception desk just as a spotlight outside lit up the street.

Becca stepped away from the building's glass doors and threw herself against the wall just beside it. Leon did the same on the other side. Harlow ducked down, with Ozzie, her hand reaching up to grab the laptop.

The spotlight from the sky swept across the street outside, before returning to shine directly into the lobby. Becca shielded her eyes, resisting an instinctive urge to hiss as the space around her flooded with light.

"What's happening?" Becca asked over the growing hum from outside.

The familiar sound of boots on pavement came next, followed by voices.

Leon drew his dagger, ready to stab the first person to enter. "They've found us. It's all over."

CHAPTER EIGHTEEN

"It can't be over." Becca wrapped her hand around the handle of the sword that came with her stolen armor as light poured in through the lobby's front doors. She flattened herself against the wall next to them.

The sound of boots outside got closer as well as the hum of whatever aircraft hovered above. Becca assumed it was one of those new kestrels with the mana-powered flight systems.

It was definitely Autem.

After a few seconds, the spotlight pulled away, only to be replaced by individual flashlights from the Guardians approaching the door outside. Becca pulled on her sword, snapping it out of its magnetic sheath.

Leon pressed himself against the wall on the other side of the door, holding his dagger close to his chest. He glanced at her, silently agreeing to attack as soon as the Guardians entered. Flashlights swept back and forth across the lobby floor.

Harlow and Ozzie tried to peek out from behind the reception desk but ducked back into cover, unable to avoid being seen.

The only question in Becca's head was whether or not

anyone had locked the lobby door. If so, that could buy them a few seconds. That was when the handle shook. The rattle of the deadbolt told her it was secure.

A gruff voice from outside agreed. "It's locked."

"Should we bother searching it?" another asked.

Several flashlights shined in as Becca used the reflection in her sword's blade to catch a glimpse of the men outside. One of them held up a hand to block the window's glare and placed his face close to the glass. For a moment, the lights lingered on an empty beer can that Ozzie had kicked earlier, but they moved on a second later.

"No, check the back entrance first." The man pulled away from the window. "If the doors are still intact, there probably aren't any in there. We'll check the back entrance, but if that's locked too, then we'll find more somewhere else."

With that, the flashlights pulled away one by one, leaving them in the darkened lobby. The voices trailed off as did the sound of the mana fueled aircraft above.

"What the hell was that?" Becca tilted her head back to rest it against the wall.

"I don't know." Leon stepped away from the wall he'd been hiding against before moving away from the doors altogether. "It didn't seem like they were looking for any of us."

"Then what are they looking for?" Ozzie peeked up from behind the reception desk.

"No idea." Harlow stood up. "We've seen plenty of activity in the area, but we just assumed they were looking for any survivors that haven't already come to them for safety."

"But if they're looking for survivors, why would a locked door stop them? If anything, that would make it more likely that humans were hiding in here." Becca stepped away from the doors. "Plus, why would they be looking at night?"

"I haven't a clue how to answer any of that, either." Harlow shrugged.

That was when Becca got an idea. "Wait here."

Running back up to the top floor of the building, she gave

thanks to the night for returning her inhuman endurance. It wasn't long before she retrieved what she needed and returned to the lobby. She set her drone down on the floor and placed its control console down on the reception desk.

She activated the unit without hesitation. "Someone open the door."

Leon obliged, allowing the drone to fly straight out of the lobby. Becca hit the optical camouflage immediately and took off in the direction that the squad of Guardians went. She found them within a minute.

Overhead, an aircraft circled the area, its rune-covered cylindrical engines spinning in place within their housings. Its flat shape and the way it floated through the buildings made it look like some sort of alien spaceship. Eventually, it returned to the fortress a few miles away, leaving the squad of Guardians to search for whatever they were looking for.

The squad continued their way through the street, making no effort to be quiet, as if they had no fear from the revenants that might still dwell in the area. They must have already thinned the creatures' population out. That was why she had seen so few on her way through the city earlier.

Eventually, the drone reached the limit of its range a few blocks away from the Lincoln Memorial. There was something unsettling about seeing so many places of historical significance empty. Becca watched them for as long as she could, but eventually they disappeared into a building. She let the drone hang in the air at the edge of its range, watching the door for their exit. A half hour went by and there was still no sign of them.

"We need to get out there." Becca brought the drone back. "I want to know what they're doing."

"Are you sure?" Harlow questioned. "They almost found us just now. I'm not sure we should go kicking any hornet's nest when we have a heist to prepare for."

"That's true, but we know so little about the situation here already." Becca leaned on the reception desk where her drone equipment lay. "It would be dumb not to try to get more intel on the situation."

"She's right." Ozzie rested his ax on his shoulder.

Leon slid his dagger back into its sheath. "Depending on what that squad is doing, we could try to take them and make it look like revenants did it. That way we could at least interrogate one."

"That's quite risky." Harlow shook her head.

"True, but so is everything." Becca tapped a finger on the desk. "We don't really have a choice other than to move fast and to be aggressive."

"Alright." Harlow sighed. "I suppose there's no avoiding it, then."

With that, Becca gave her a crash course in drone operation so she could give them some surveillance support from a distance. Taking control over the drone, Harlow took it for a few laps around the lobby before stopping it in front of Ozzie. "Don't do anything stupid out there."

"Yeah, don't do anything dumb," Leon added.

Harlow flicked a thumb on the controls to turn the drone to face him. "You are no better."

Leon clutched a hand to his heart in a theatrical manner. "Ouch."

Becca smirked as she watched the three of them, being reminded of Digby, Alex, and Hawk. She frowned a second later, hoping that everyone back in Vegas had been doing well without her. Wiping a tear from her eye, she headed for the door.

The street outside was dead quiet.

Becca took a moment to listen, leaning on her hearing. Above, the street lights were dark. The power grid must have died weeks ago.

She took a moment to orient herself.

The fortress was a few miles away. In between stood the old buildings that had made up the government just a month earlier. Standing there in the streets of Washington, D.C., it was hard to believe so much had changed. For so long, it had stood as the nation's capital, now it was just another corpse.

A part of her wondered what had happened to everyone that worked in the city. All the congressmen and senators. Had they all died? Or did Autem cut some of them a deal? Maybe they were still holed up in a bunker a hundred feet below the streets. She frowned. Either way, the old world was gone and Autem was building a new one on its bones, now that the empire had snuffed the old world out.

All she knew was that a big part of her wanted to tear it all down.

Becca had never been patriotic, largely because she had seen firsthand how things ran behind the scenes. The fact that Autem had been able to operate under the guise of Skyline was a testament to how broken the system had been. Still, she couldn't help but feel a little empty, like she had lost the last shred of her home, even if that home had been a lie to begin with.

"You good?" Ozzie looked at her expectantly.

Becca realized she had been staring off into nothing for a while and shook off her melancholy. "I'm fine. Just contemplating the fall of the nation."

"It happens." Leon held the lobby's door so that the drone could exit. "Cities fall, civilizations crumble. Everyone thinks the world they live in is strong, but you would be surprised at how easy a society can be torn down. It doesn't always take a zombie apocalypse."

Becca eyed him. The way Leon spoke, one would think he had been there for the fall of Rome.

Crouching down, she powered on the drone and waved a hand in front of its camera. "Can you see alright, Harlow?"

"I, ah, yeah. I can see you." Her voice came from the drone. "I'll scout the area ahead to make sure you have a clear path. Call me on the radio if you need anything specific."

Becca took a radio from Ozzie and clipped it to her belt as she watched the drone activate its camouflage, becoming a blurry, transparent spot hovering in the air. She couldn't help but feel exposed, being on the other end of the situation after having piloted a drone from the safety of her apartment in Seattle for so long.

"What do we do if we run into any revenants?"

"Nothing." Ozzie shrugged. "They won't attack us as long as we don't attack first. Just give them a nod and keep walking like when you see someone you went to high school with in the grocery store."

"Just make sure to act fast if you do need to kill one for any reason." Leon swiped his cutlass through the air. "If you let them get all riled up, others will start to join in. Granted, I haven't seen any around, so it might be a moot point."

"Good to know regardless." Becca hoped it wouldn't come to that. "We should stick to the shadows, anyway."

They only made it a few blocks before the hum of one of Autem's new aircraft came from behind them.

"Quick! Hide." Leon dove for an alleyway, grabbing Ozzie by a strap on his gear. The oversized vampire snagged the shoulder of Becca's armor at the same time.

"Hey, wait!" She stumbled to the side of the street.

Leon poked his head out from behind a dumpster. "Come on and get out of sight."

Becca slipped behind him as Ozzie jumped in behind her, leaving her squished between them. All three of them stayed quiet to wait for the aircraft to pass. They couldn't see much from their hiding space, but Becca didn't dare get any closer. There was no telling what sort detection capabilities they had on board that craft. For now, it seemed focused on the street.

A spotlight shined down at the edge of her view. Getting a better look at the aircraft, she watched as it floated through the air. It had the same drone-like design as a kestrel, but it was around twice the size and bore a larger cockpit area. Extending from the back like a tail, a detachable compartment hung between the rear flight units. Its hull was painted white, with the Autem Empire's crest displayed on the bottom in gold.

Combined with the otherworldly sound of its mana engines, the craft felt more like a spaceship from some theocratic alien race.

We come in peace. If you will accept our nine angels as your lords and saviors, that is.

The spotlight swept along the ground as if ready to abduct a cow from the local farm. That was when Becca noticed there was something running through the street below.

"What?"

Squinting, she found a pair of revenants sprinting through the street, their panicked screeches filling her with confusion. She half expected the craft to open fire, but instead, all she heard was a mechanical click-clack followed by a pop. A projectile burst in the air just above the two fleeing revenants an instant later, sending bits of metal spinning through the space around them. The creatures skidded to a stop as six pieces of the projectile snapped into positions floating in the air surrounding them to create a perimeter that they couldn't cross.

"A ward?" Becca furrowed her brow.

The spotlight lingered on the pair of revenants for a moment before the craft above moved on. Leaving the two creatures behind, trapped within the wards that it had fired.

"What the hell are they doing?" Leon peeked out from behind the dumpster just above Becca, his chin a couple inches from the top of her head.

"They must have trapped the revs for their guys to kill later." Ozzie peeked out above Leon, shoving the slender vampire down so that his chin bonked Becca in the head.

"Excuse me." Becca shoved at them both. "I don't remember auditioning for the Three Stooges." She rubbed at her head. "And I don't think they intend to kill those revenants. They would have just shot them from above. Plus, that compartment on the back of that craft was weird."

"Why?" Ozzie stepped out from behind the dumpster.

"Because Autem already controls the area." Leon followed her line of thinking. "They have no need to transport troops or supplies around the city after occupying it for a month."

"Then what are they carrying?" Ozzie swung his ax back and forth casually.

"Revenants." Becca crept out of the alleyway, toward the creatures trapped in the street. "They were collecting monsters in California, and I saw some revs back on Skyline's base when I infiltrated it. They had them standing between warding rods like some kind of test subjects. They must be capturing them here too; that was why they didn't kill these ones. They just left them here to be picked up later."

"I don't like the sound of that." Leon grimaced. "There's a history of people poking around with revenants."

"Is that why you killed a bunch of Nazis in the past?" Becca eyed him.

He sighed. "Among other reasons."

Ozzie followed them into the street. "Okay, so if they are collecting revs, then the big question is, what do they want with them?"

"No idea." Becca examined the wards as the revenants inside ignored her. They were the same as the rods she'd seen before. "But I bet there's some answers in that building that we saw that squad disappear into."

"Let's go, then." Ozzie nodded to the two revenants as if they were high school classmates that he'd run into at the store, then he started walking.

From there, they stuck to the alleyways and made their way to the destination. They didn't run into anymore revenants on the way, but they made a point to be extra careful. Especially once they were out of the drone's range and no longer had eyes in the sky. As they approached the building that the squad had entered, they ducked into another alleyway. There was no telling when another aircraft might fly by.

"I wish the drone's range could reach us." Becca stared at the wall of the building. "We could slip it inside to get an idea of what's going on in there."

Leon gave her a knowing look, then placed a hand to the wall. "We don't need a drone for that."

Becca placed her hand to the wall beside him.

"Just let your senses do the work." Leon gave her a practical lesson. "Feed your hearing and your touch."

She let her mana flow, picking up dozens of heartbeats within the building. Tearing her hand away as if the wall had burnt her, she gasped.

"Shit." She stepped back. "There's at least five squads in there."

Leon didn't move his hand, instead he just eyed her and arched an eyebrow. "Are there?"

Becca hesitated, then she placed her hand to the wall to try again.

The heartbeats of the people inside answered her search, but this time she forced herself to stay calm so she could pay attention to the details. She had been right about the number of inhabitants, but their positioning was odd. There were two groups. The closest was just on the other side of the wall, around twenty-six hearts beating in a scattered array of noise. She pushed them out of her mind and focused on what was left.

Finding five heartbeats remaining, the facts became clear. There was no way to tell who was human and who wasn't, but their positioning was enough. They weren't all Guardians. No, the larger group was all revenants. Only the five on the other side of the building were there by choice.

"They're using this building to hold the revs they've collected. They must gather them into groups, then call in one of those aircraft to come pick them up once there's enough for a full shipment." Becca worked out the details. "Sometime in the next few hours, they will take this group back to the fortress."

That was when Ozzie slapped Leon on the shoulder. "Dude, I know how to get into that fortress."

"What the hell?" Leon raised a fist as if to punch him back.

"Hey, keep it down." Becca smacked them both. "And what's your idea?"

"Okay, so we do it like this." Ozzie held out both hands.

"We find ourselves a big group of common revs. Then we just hide amongst them and wait for Autem's guys to do the rest."

"That's a terrible idea." Leon stared at his partner while letting his arms hang limp. "We're not Wookies."

"No, but it might actually work." Becca tapped a finger on her forearm. "We don't look completely like revenants but we are pale enough to pass as long as no one looks too carefully. They probably won't bring us all the way to the inner structure, but they should bring us through the refugee camp and inside the outer wall. We'll just have to make sure we don't do anything that gets us analyzed."

"How do we get through the rest of their security?" Leon started to get on board.

"I think I know a way to get someone else inside." Becca prepared to launch into an explanation, only to stop when Leon held up a hand.

"What?" She furrowed her brow as he reached for his dagger and launched it in a blur of motion.

A gurgling croak came from a couple dozen feet away as a man dressed in Guardian armor appeared from thin air, the dagger lodged in his throat.

Becca realized the mistake she'd made as soon as she saw him. She had only picked up five Guardians inside the building, but there had been a sixth with the group. Leon must have been keeping his enhanced senses active, allowing him to notice the invisible threat.

"A Conceal spell." Becca didn't need a HUD to know that the man was either a rogue or an illusionist. Rogue was more likely, considering he'd just been standing there and not using some kind of decoy.

Leon darted toward the man, catching him just before he fell. A quick twist of his hand tore the dagger free from his throat in an arc that spattered the ground with blood. Becca's throat went dry the second the smell hit her senses. Leon opened his mouth to sink his teeth into the rogue, but stopped just before biting. Then, he turned to her.

"Quick, before he dies."

The implication was clear. It was time for her to feed.

Becca took a step forward, her instincts pulling her toward the meal, nearly taking control. She put her foot down as her stomach churned in conflict with the rest of her body. Her mana was still well below half, yet the sudden revulsion nearly made her throw up.

"Hurry." Leon clutched the man close, reminding her of how Digby held his victims just before tearing their throat out.

Becca recoiled as her instincts crashed against what little humanity she still had. Eventually, she just dropped to her knees, her mind telling her to throw up at the thought of feeding. Even worse was the fact that she didn't, her body urging her to attack. It was so much different from when she'd killed those Guardians on the kestrel two nights ago. Back then, there had been no thoughts, or guilt, or even shame. Now, it was like her mind was making up for lost time.

"Damn." Leon stopped waiting and plunged his fangs into the man.

Becca ducked her head and covered her ears, wishing she couldn't hear him swallowing. "Why am I like this?"

"Hey, it's okay." A heavy hand came to rest on her back as Ozzie crouched beside her. "It's not easy for everyone. I had trouble too."

"I'm sorry, I just…" Becca raised her head as Leon dropped the body to the pavement.

"It's fine." He shook his head. "I shouldn't have put so much pressure on you so soon."

Becca nodded, appreciating the understanding that both vampires showed. Nausea swam through her stomach as her throat begged for a drink. She forced the dueling sensations into the back of her mind and tried not to look at the blood.

"That rogue must have come out here. The rest of his squad will come looking for him." She refocused on the situation. "We can't let them find us."

"What do we do about this guy?" Ozzie stood over the dead rogue.

"Leave him." Becca waved away the concern. "The knife wound isn't obvious with the bite on top of it. It will look like a revenant caught him off guard."

"What do you want to do about the rest of the Guardians inside?" Leon asked.

Becca started to answer but hesitated when she realized that the two vampires were looking to her for orders. After her refusal to feed, she would have thought they might have lost confidence in her. Then again, maybe freaking out wasn't that uncommon.

"The other Guardians…" She turned toward the building, remembering Ozzie's idea to blend in with some revenants. With a hard swallow, she added, "I think we have to kill them. If they're gone, we can release the revs they've captured. Autem will need to send another squad out here tomorrow night to regather them. That will give us the opportunity we need to mix into the group."

"Okay." Ozzie nodded. "How do we do this?"

"I'd say this rogue was around level thirty." Leon nudged the corpse on the ground with his foot. "The rest of the team inside should be about the same."

Becca sucked in a breath. "Five level thirties? That's kind of a lot for us."

"You took out a whole squad a couple nights ago. They were probably a little lower level but not by much," Ozzie reminded her.

"Yes, but I was ravenous at the time, and I could have just as easily died in the process." She argued back, unsure why she was speaking against her own plan.

No, that was a lie.

She knew exactly why she was against it.

It was because, if they went inside, she would use her abilities and probably take some damage. When the dust settled, she would have to feed. There would be no avoiding it.

Her stomach still hadn't settled from before.

"I know how things seem. But I think we can do this," Leon tried to encourage her. "We just need the right plan."

"We can't hang around here all night, standing over this rogue that Leon murdered." Ozzie gestured to the alleyway around them. "You know, on account of this being a crime scene now."

Becca took a deep breath. "Fine. I will go in the front of the building while you both sneak in the back." She started to unbuckle her armor. "I'll pretend I'm a survivor and that I need help. That should give me a few seconds before one of them analyzes me. I'll get close, then hit them with bats. You two attack from behind in the chaos."

"Got it." Leon started for the back of the building.

Becca nodded.

"Don't worry, you got this." Ozzie gave her a double thumbs up before jogging to catch up to Leon.

"You heard the vampire mercenary," Becca merely blew out a sigh, "you got this."

CHAPTER NINETEEN

"I so don't have this." Becca hesitated just outside the front entrance of the building where a squad of five Guardians were holding a couple dozen revenants captive. Her feet refused to take another step despite the fact that lay before her.

The men inside had to die.

At this point, a few murders weren't a big deal, but the fact that she was going to need to drink their blood was something else altogether. She kept telling herself that it was the only way to get stronger, but that wasn't helping. A part of her wished she had her ravenous trait active to make things easier.

"How did Dig get over this in the beginning?" She'd seen the zombie chomp into enough enemies to know that it was possible to get over the initial revulsion that came with a bit of cannibalism. Though, it could also just mean that the instincts of a zombie were stronger than those of a vampire.

Becca growled at herself and raked her hands through her hair in frustration.

Of course, that was when her little freak-out was interrupted.

"We're in position." Leon's voice came across her radio in a whisper. "Waiting for your move."

"Shit." Becca forced herself to step into the doorway of the building before whispering, "I'm going in."

With that, she tried her best to focus on the next step. All she had to do was go in and create a distraction. There was no reason to think about what came after that.

Slipping out of her body armor, she placed it on the ground outside, not wanting to make it obvious that she'd looted a Guardian's corpse. If she wanted to convince the squad inside that she was just a person in need of help, even for a few seconds, she was going to have to go in without any gear. In addition, she pulled her hair out of her ponytail so that it covered her ears and made a point to keep her head down to hide her eyes.

Then, she pressed her palm against the cool glass of the door and gently cracked it open. The Guardians were in a room somewhere beyond the lobby. She didn't even need to push her senses to know that much. The group was talking loud enough that she could hear their voices from the entrance.

Becca took a moment to look over the space. It wasn't anything fancy, just a hotel. The no-frills kind of place that people traveling for business stayed at. A sign that read Function Hall A pointed in the direction that the revenants were being held. The check-in desk sat in the middle of the lobby, with a seating area off to the side for a continental breakfast. A rack of small cereal boxes and other non-perishable goods sat in the corner. Becca ignored them, forcing herself forward.

There was no going back now.

"Hello?" she called out as she approached a manager's office behind the check in counter. "Is someone there?" It seemed wise to say something to avoid being mistaken for a revenant.

The sound of boots squeaking on the tile floor answered her as a man wearing Autem's crest on his armor exited. He immediately held a flashlight in her face, practically blinding her.

Becca closed her eyes and pushed on her other senses. Even blind, she knew exactly where everyone was.

"I'm sorry, but I need help." She made sure to hold her hands up to look as non-threatening as possible.

The rest of the squad came out as well. From the sounds of their equipment, two of them carried rifles. Becca caught the thrum of a bow string, realizing that one of the weapons was a crossbow.

Probably a cleric and an artificer.

"Where'd you come from?" one of the men barked.

"I'm alone and saw the construction." Becca kept her hands up as a pair of heartbeats approached the group from behind.

Leon and Ozzie were right where they needed to be.

"Have you been bit by anything?" the man holding the light asked, finally lowering it from her face.

"No, I'm fine." She showed them her arms. She took a breath, trying to look scared while she checked the weapons of the other three Guardians. Two carried swords, while the last just held a pistol. The one with a crossbow aimed at her carried a sword on his back as well.

She did the math.

Two knights, a mage, an enchanter, and a cleric.

One of the men holding a sword stepped forward from the back of the group to speak for them, making it clear who was in charge. "You can relax. The construction you saw is our capital. We would be glad to take you there, miss."

"Thank you. Oh god, thank you." Becca let out a little sob as she crouched down, her leg muscles preparing to leap. Focusing on the goal, she reminded herself that none of the men could be allowed to call for help.

"It's okay." The leader of the squad approached her just as Leon and Ozzie crept out of the shadows behind the group. "You're safe now."

"Good, but you aren't." Becca flicked her eyes to him, giving him a good look at the embers that burned within.

"What?" The man hesitated for a second as his mind processed what he was seeing.

Becca didn't give him the chance to finish.

Feeding mana to her shadecraft ability, the room dimmed as darkness flooded toward them. Even the flashlights they held faded just before a swarm of bats erupted from the floor. She flicked a few points of mana to her Banshee to give each bat a screech to make their blood run cold. Her mana fell as the swarm filled the lobby, blocking out the moonlight that shined in from the windows.

The plan had progressed to the next step.

Becca launched herself forward, making a point to use her strength sparingly. Not only would it be bad to waste the mana, but it was clear that she wasn't going to be a tank like Ozzie. The last thing she wanted was to overdevelop her physical capabilities and end up stifling the rest.

She plowed into the knight in front of her just as he was pulling his sword from his sheath. Without a weapon of her own, she slammed her knee into his chin, feeling something shatter. A howl of pain came from the man as teeth flew from his mouth in a spray of crimson.

Two of the other Guardians cried out as Ozzie and Leon fell upon them in unison.

The knight swung his blade in an uncoordinated swipe, but she kicked off his chest, springing into the air. She pushed her agility to send herself flipping backward as the knight fell into another of his men. She landed in a somewhat planned crouch.

The bats continued to obscure the vision of everyone in the lobby. Becca kept the swarm going, letting her mana fall.

Her attention was pulled away a second later when the twang of a bowstring struck the air. A bolt fired off at an odd angle that sent it skidding across the floor. The projectile glowed, leaving an afterimage that traced its path through the swarm of shadows. The arrow hit a piece of furniture with a thunk just before it exploded. The chair was reduced to splinters in an instant.

Locking her eyes on the knight that she had just knocked down, she leapt forward to take advantage of the opening. A burst of bullets exploded into the air, the lobby lighting up in a flicker of muzzle fire. Silhouettes of bats covered the walls as several rounds punched into the check-in desk, sending fragments of laminated particleboard into the air.

Becca ducked as she landed on top of the knight, bringing her face close to his. It would have been so easy to take what she needed. Something inside her practically cried out to do it. She pulled away and slammed a fist down into his face, knocking another tooth free. Bringing her fist down again, a wave of shimmering light swept across his body as a barrier formed.

"Shit." She cursed herself for not taking the opportunity to kill him seconds before.

The squeak of a boot told her someone was coming from behind. The sound was followed by the snap of a sword being removed from a sheath. Pushing on her senses, she reached back and fed a few points of mana into her defense to manifest a barrier. A sword slammed down into her palm in a brief flash of blue light. She kept the barrier going long enough to wrench the sword free of its owner. Then she flicked a few points of mana into her dexterity, just enough to flip the sword in her hand and catch it by the handle.

The knight beneath her clutched a hand over his broken jaw as he swung his sword toward her. She met his blade. A burst of power exploded from his weapon as it met hers. He must have cast Kinetic Impact to strengthen the blow. Unprepared for the sudden force, Becca's hand flew back, nearly dropping her sword. She kept hold of it by throwing a couple of points of mana into dexterity and strength each.

Her blade sunk into something soft as the Guardian she had taken it from cried out. She caught the scent of blood as she glanced back. He clutched a hand over a wound on his side, a trickle of blood running through his fingers. Becca's mouth salivated as her continued use of her shadecraft brought her mana below ten percent. The urge to feed swelled as the repulsion in her mind grew quieter and quieter.

"Fuck it." Becca leapt up at the man as terror filled his face.

Her teeth sank in, spilling warmth into her mouth. Her mind retreated, letting her instincts take control as the blood flowed. Mana trickled across the bridge between his body and her own until she sensed something more. Her mana system reached out to grab hold of it. Yanking back on the essence inside her prey, something came loose in a surge of power.

She felt her mana system swell to take it all in.

In seconds, it was full.

No, it was more than that.

Something had changed. She wasn't sure how she could tell, but somehow her total mana had increased. Not much, just a few points overall, but still it was more than she had before.

Tearing her fangs free from the dying man's throat, she fed more mana into her shadecraft. Becca knelt as her bats circled her, a tornado of shrieking shadows, their tiny wings beating at the air.

Of course, that was when she realized her mana was plummeting.

"Becca, cool it with the bats!" Ozzie lay on his back trying to stay out of the swarm's path.

Leon pulled his fangs free of one of the Guardian's necks a few feet away. "Yeah, I think we won here."

Becca willed the swarm away, each of the bats disappearing into a cloudy blur of darkness as they vanished. The room's light level returned to normal.

Sweeping her eyes across the scene, all of the Guardians were dead except for the knight with a broken jaw. Leon and Ozzie had taken the rest out. The knight had pulled himself up and was now leaning on his sword with one hand while he covered his mouth with the other.

He stared daggers at her.

"He's all yours." Leon returned to biting the Guardian he held.

"What?" Becca looked back to him and Ozzie.

"I think you can handle it." Ozzie simply leaned against the wall. "Not like he can radio for help like that."

Becca turned back to the knight as he tightened his hand around the grip of his sword. His eyes narrowed as he stood up straight.

"Come on then." Becca got ready to defend as the knight kicked off.

He raised his sword with a gurgled cry that was probably supposed to be intimidating.

Becca felt for her mana; she still had half remaining. Her experience as a Heretic told her to be conservative with it. The vampire in her told her otherwise. There was no sense in saving mana when more was just a bite away.

Dropping her sword, she reached out to her sides as if grabbing hold of the shadows that filled the room. The gloom rushed toward her all at once to surround her in a shroud of darkness, then she simply threw it at him. A torrent of bats so dense that it was hard to tell where one of the creatures ended and the next started erupted from her body. It was just a flood of wings and teeth.

The darkness hit the knight square in the chest, flowing over him and throwing him back. He fell to a knee in a shimmer of blue light as his barrier fought to hold her shadows at bay. She stomped forward, yelling as she fed mana to her shadecraft.

The knight growled as he tried to stand against the force that battered his body. Then, his barrier broke. His growl shifted to a scream in seconds as the bats tore at his face. Becca immediately let go of the shadows and lunged forward.

His screams were cut off when her teeth sank into his throat. She felt for his spark, yanking as soon as she found it, her mana pool filling and expanding until it could stretch no further. For a moment, she could have sworn she felt everything that remained burst around her, the energy of his spark dissipating as it passed on to whatever was next.

She wished she had been able to find out more about the

afterlife that she was sending people to while she had been there herself. Though, maybe it was for the best. Maybe the living shouldn't know that much about such things.

Becca dropped the knight's corpse to the floor, his body crumpling at her feet as she began to realize what she'd done. Taking in the carnage around her, one thing had become abundantly clear. As a Heretic, she could never have won that fight, but with what she had become, it had been easy.

Hell, it had been fun.

Wiping blood away from her face with her wrist, she spat some on the floor. "Is this really normal?"

"It is for us." Ozzie pushed off the wall he leaned against.

"You'll get used to it," Leon added. "You just need to stop listening to that voice in your head telling you it's wrong."

Becca stared at the bodies on the floor. "We're monsters."

"Maybe." Ozzie shrugged. "But you never have to fear what goes bump in the night if that bump is you."

"I know it seems wrong." Leon walked up to her without bothering to clean the blood off his face. "But we need this power to help the people that remain in this world. So I'd say your humanity is a small price to pay." Leon shook his head. "But regardless, we need to get moving. Someone is going to come looking for these guys when they don't report in."

"Shit, yeah." Becca forced her worries down, swallowing them along with the traces of blood in her mouth. "We can leave the bodies here. They look enough like a swarm of revenants killed them."

Being careful not to leave anything incriminating behind, they headed for the function room where the creatures were being held. Sure enough, there were warding rods bolted to the door frame. They were much larger than the little floating ones that they had stolen from Autem before. They must have been planning to use this room for at least a few nights to merit a more permanent installation.

Opening the doors, Becca found a swarm of revenants. It was hard to get a full count with the way they were standing.

She relaxed a little. That meant it would be easier to mix into the group the next night without anyone noticing.

"Okay, we need to set these revs free in a way that looks like they got out on their own." She stepped into the room as both Leon and Ozzie reached out to stop her.

"Wait!"

Becca turned as she passed through the wards, her body immediately filling with pain. An unintelligible scream poured from her mouth as her legs buckled to drop her forward into the room. The revenants inside just looked at her as she writhed on the floor. The agony was worse than anything she had ever felt, like every cell in her body was on fire.

"Grab my legs!" Leon shouted back to Ozzie as he dove into the room behind her, landing on her feet with his body still sticking halfway out of the threshold. He winced in pain, gritting his teeth as if suddenly afflicted by the same invisible force that was attacking her.

"I got you." Ozzie grabbed hold of Leon's shoes and dragged them both out of the room.

The pain vanished as soon as Becca passed the threshold again, leaving her painting on the floor with smoke wafting from her body.

"What the fuck was that?"

"A hearth ward." Leon gasped for air as he pushed up from the floor. "We can't enter without being invited."

Ozzie pointed to the warding rods that were bolted to the door frame. "These things have a bunch of crap that keeps us out."

Becca pushed up onto her elbows, smelling like a burnt Hot Pocket. "Are you fucking kidding me?"

"The wards are based on a mass enchantment. Basically, enough people believe vampires can't enter a home without being invited, so the ambient mana inside reacts when we try." Leon stood up and offered her a hand. "Churches have a similar thing, but the invitation part doesn't work. We just can't enter unless we cultivate the ability to break wards."

"How do we do that?" She took his hand and pulled herself up. "I know there's a type of revenant that can."

"A revenant wardbreaker is a rare evolution and has a high will value, unlike the rest that have none. You, on the other hand, would have to focus on your will stat for a few decades to cross a ward without triggering it." He let go of her hand once she was stable. "But there isn't much else you can do with your will stat, so most of us don't bother."

"Yeah." Ozzie shrugged. "I don't want to go places I'm not wanted, anyway."

Becca threw a hand out at the revenants inside. "How are they in there? Aren't revs affected by the same shit as us?"

"My guess is, they were invited." Leon pantomimed pushing something. "Invitations are subjective. If a human shoves one of us or a revenant through the threshold, that would count."

Becca pulled on the neck of the bathing suit she was wearing under her tracksuit to let out some of the burnt smell. "Doesn't someone have to live there for a mass enchantment to work?"

"Normally, yes. A hearth ward works on any structure where one or more people are living permanently." Leon tapped the side of one of the warding rods. "But Autem can still set up artificial wards. These ones were designed to keep things in while keeping others out. Most of the bigger ones will carry additional defenses."

Becca furrowed her brow. "Wait, so why were revenants able to kill people in their homes when the world ended?"

"Depends on the people inside." Ozzie gestured to the door-way. "When the news of zombies and revenants spread, most people left their homes to find someplace safe, and the ones that stayed figured they would have to run eventually. The mojo behind the magic stops seeing their house as permanent. It's like, you can enter a person's hotel room fine, but that changes if they plan to stay there forever."

"Great, so everyone I know who lives in Vegas in hotel rooms will need to invite me in." Becca deflated.

"Yep." Ozzie patted her on the shoulder to welcome her to the club.

"Awesome." Becca groaned. "What do we do about these revenants then? We can't drag them out if we can't go through the door."

"Nah, it's a fake hearth ward. Not a big deal." Ozzie walked back to where the dead Guardians were and picked up one of their rifles. Then, without warning, he shouldered the weapon.

"Wait, don't—" Becca threw a hand out to stop him but he was already firing before she could do anything.

The rifle barked as splinters exploded from the doorframe.

The revenants all turned toward the door the instant he began firing. For a second, Becca thought they might have perceived the act as an attack. Then Ozzie lowered the rifle.

"Okay, everybody out. You guys are free." The oversized vampire waved the revenants out of the room.

Most of the creatures chittered and screeched but presented no hostile intentions, many passing by Becca and Leon to leave the room. She took a closer look at the door frame, finding the warding rod damaged along with the wood around it.

"I figure with the rogue dead outside and these guys in here, the likely story of what happened is a rev entered the building and attacked the group." Ozzie put the rifle back in the hands of one of the dead Guardians. "This jackass fired his gun and accidentally hit the warding rod. The swarm did the rest."

"It's believable enough." Leon pointed to the revenants as they began to investigate the bodies, many taking a bite to get at whatever blood might have remained. "Our accomplices are already helping out."

"That should be enough. I doubt Autem is going to send a forensics team out here to investigate." Becca walked past the creatures on her way back to the lobby, feeling strange that they were no longer a threat. Especially considering that she'd been killed by one not too long ago. "Autem's patrols will need to regather these revs now that they've escaped. It will be dawn soon; we just have to keep track of this swarm until tomorrow night. Then we just have to join them and make sure Autem's people find us. Then, they should take us right to where we want to go."

"How are we going to get Harlow inside to help?" Leon arched an eyebrow.

"That part should be easy." Becca walked toward a rack of brochures that mapped out the area. "But there's something I want to look into first."

Unfolding a brochure, she traced a line with her finger from the hotel they were in to a few buildings that were just a few blocks away. She tapped the map twice. "There."

"What?" Ozzie grabbed another of the brochures.

"If we are going to do something as risky as try to infiltrate that fortress out there, we are going to need to use every advantage that we can get." Becca held up the map, pointing to one of the buildings with her finger.

Leon leaned closer to read the label. "The Smithsonian?"

Becca nodded. "I think we need to take a note from a friend of mine. The Smithsonian has an extensive pop culture exhibit, and we might be able to find some geeky stuff with a mass enchantment that can give us an edge there."

"Okay, then." Ozzie started for the door. "We'll have to deal with the sun if we take too long, but sure, let's go shopping."

"It's worth checking out." Leon followed. "Let's just hope there's still something there. Autem has had plenty of time to loot it on their own."

"True, but it would be a waste not to look when we're so close." Becca shrugged. "Besides, maybe Autem hasn't thought of checking for pop culture items. They don't strike me as being nerdy enough to care."

"And you are?" Ozzie glanced back at her.

"No, but I think someone has been rubbing off on me."

CHAPTER TWENTY

"God, you're a nerd." Hawk groaned as Alex stood in the middle of the Smithsonian's pop culture display with his arms spread wide like a magician taking a bow.

"Told you there would be some cool stuff." The artificer adjusted the messenger bag on his shoulder, as well as the pistol hanging loosely from his hip, before taking a big gulp from a can of energy drink. "We didn't even need to drive to get here."

"Awesome," Hawk said with as much sarcasm as he could muster.

The artificer had dragged him, Lana, and Alvin out of bed before the sun was even up. Apparently one of the benefits of traveling by mirror was that you didn't have to wait for dawn when your destination was two time zones ahead of you. Parker hadn't seemed happy about it either, but a member of Elenore's research team had found a picture of the Smithsonian and Alex didn't want to wait.

He had been up all night working with his R&D team in Hawaii to get Digby's boats in the air. The whole thing sounded stupid. By now, Alex was on his third energy drink. The artificer was practically vibrating. It was no wonder why he'd dragged everyone out of bed to continue their treasure hunt so early, he couldn't have slept even if he wanted to. It would probably be hours before he crashed.

Hawk eyed the artificer, unsure if he was just uncomfortably energetic, or if he was acting weird. Either way, he kept getting a nagging feeling that there was something Alex wasn't telling him. He was going to have to drag it out of him eventually.

Alvin stopped beside him to interrupt Hawk's paranoia. "Come on, there might be something cool."

Lana turned back as she looked into a display case. "Don't run off." She glowered at her brother. "Stay where I can see you."

Alvin looked like he might argue but eventually lowered his head and said nothing. Hawk frowned at the two of them, annoyed at how Lana had been giving her brother an attitude. Obviously, he understood the reason. Alvin had turned his back on her before, but still, it was frustrating to watch them argue when they still had each other.

Eventually, Hawk just shoved his hands in his pockets and walked past Alex. He could hear Kristen shouting from the inside of the artificer's bag. The dumb skull was still pissed that Alex had left her in the trunk of the car all night. He had only taken her out for a few seconds, which she used to call every member of their coven a moron. After that, Alex had shoved her right back into his bag where her complaints couldn't be heard beyond muffled grumbles.

Hawk wasn't complaining. He didn't hate the skull, but she had been annoying. Mostly because she just kept reminding him of everything bad that had happened when all he wanted to do was forget. He clenched his jaw. Losing people wasn't new. Shit, he'd been losing people since the day he was born. So why did losing Becca hurt so much? He barely even knew her. Still, her parents were the first people to want him. As screwed up as Becca was, she had wanted to be his family too. Now, he had no one left.

Okay, maybe that wasn't true.

He couldn't deny that Alex and the rest of the people he'd gotten close to wanted him around. As mad as he was at them, he couldn't bring himself to hate them. The back of his neck prickled as a swell of guilt rolled through him. He had lost so much, but more people cared about him now than ever before.

The truth almost hurt more than the anger that he clung to.

He took a deep breath, forcing his eyes not to well up. He'd gone this far without crying, he wasn't about to start now. Instead, he focused on the museum's displays to take his mind off things.

The space was dark despite the morning sun outside. Mostly because the pop culture exhibit had no windows. The image Parker had used to open a passage had been of a display case that housed a costume from a TV show that was from before Hawk had been born. The result had brought them straight there, with no need to bring the car. Parker had sent Sax and the rest of Dragon coven to walk through the exhibit to make sure it was safe before sending anyone else. Sax's party returned a few minutes later after finding the pop culture exhibit empty, though they hadn't searched the whole building or anything.

The entrance of the area was covered in various graphics. Even the floor had been done up to look like the yellow brick road from the Wizard of Oz. He'd always hated that movie. It was boring. Hawk followed the graphic in a spiral until he found a display case containing the ruby slippers.

"Those are fake," Lana commented.

"How do you know?" Hawk stared up at her.

Her face went blank as if she had just said something she wasn't supposed to. "Oh, um, ask Alex."

"I will." Hawk narrowed his eyes. He'd been caught in enough lies to know when he'd just caught someone else. He leaned back to look past her without hesitation. "Hey Alex, how does Lana know that these shoes are fake?"

"Ah." Alex fumbled the flashlight that he'd been using to look through the cases. "Those slippers are probably real, but they used more than one pair while shooting the movie. We kinda found one of the pairs in Henwick's vault and stole them."

"Seriously? Why did you steal shoes? Was it a personal thing? And why did Henwick—" Hawk snapped his lighter closed, its surface getting a little too hot. "Wait, did they have an enchantment?"

Alex glanced around the way he had been doing all day, then he took a sip of his energy drink as if trying to stall. "Umm, it's actually kind of a big deal. Can we talk about it when we get back to Vegas?"

Hawk stared at him from across the exhibit. "Why can't you tell me now?"

Alex hesitated before looking to Alvin. "It's something that I don't want to say in front of everyone."

"Oh, come on." Alvin finally spoke up.

Lana jabbed a finger in his direction. "You got a long way to go, pal, before we discuss top-secret things in front of you."

"This is so…" Alvin looked to Hawk for a moment as if looking for inspiration before adding, "fucked up."

"Tell me about it." Lana folded her arms.

"We'll talk about it later." Alex gestured to the display cases. "Let's worry about searching this place first."

Hawk continued to watch Alex as he returned to searching the displays, noticing the artificer glancing back in the reflection.

"You gotta wonder how many other famous objects here are fakes or backup props," Lana added, shining her flashlight in their direction. "Considering the amount of time they've had, Autem could have quietly swapped things out over the years."

"They missed at least one thing." Alex reached into his bag.

Kristen's voice came from the open zipper. "I demand that you release—"

He ignored her and closed the flap, more interested in the chipped wooden goblet he'd retrieved. "I showed Clint my eye patch when he got back from…" He trailed off for a moment. "Well, anyway, the zombie reminded me that there's a cheesy restaurant back on the strip in Vegas that has movie props on display. I hadn't thought of it, since it didn't seem like a place that would have anything that famous, but I asked Clint to swing by while I was busy working on Digby's boats."

Hawk glanced at the wooden cup, letting the Heretic Seed list its name.

Holy Grail

Mass Enchantment: Recovery

This goblet will purify any liquid that is poured into it, bestowing healing, cleansing, and a temporary delay to the aging process to anyone wise enough to drink from it.

"Can I see?" Hawk held a hand out.

"Sure." Alex passed him the supposed holy relic.

Turning it in his hand, he looked over its battered surface. It looked like someone had kicked it across the floor and tossed it in a closet for decades before someone decided to put it on display along with a collection of other movie memorabilia. The inside still had a bit of gold paint, but most had chipped away, leaving a surface of dull wood.

Obviously, it wasn't the real holy grail. Hawk was pretty sure that had never existed in the first place. No, this was just a prop. One that had gained the power to cleanse a zombie or revenant bite, heal the injured, or even give someone a partial immortality if they drank from it enough. Not that immortality mattered to a Heretic who already had it.

He'd seen the movie once when he was little, sort of. It was more like he'd looked on from the other room while one of his many foster parents watched TV. He still remembered the movie, though. Maybe someday he would get to see it again.

That was when his thoughts were interrupted by Alex.

"Oh cool." The artificer rushed across the room to another case containing a brown fedora.

"See something good?" Hawk followed, holding the grail at his side.

"Nothing with an enchantment, but I feel like I have to take this anyway." He gestured to the cup in Hawk's hand. "It goes with the set, after all."

Hawk sighed and handed the grail to Alvin as he prepared to help get the case open. A moment later, Alex had himself a new hat.

"How do I look?"

"Like a nerd," Lana added from across the room where she looked over some costumes.

"Damn, I was hoping it would go with the eye patch." Alex frowned.

"At least you have a cool cup." Alvin handed the goblet back to him. "You could put the grail somewhere in Vegas, like the fountain where we all gathered the other day. If everyone knew it was there, they would know where to go to cleanse themselves if they got cursed."

Alex hummed to himself for a second. "That's not a bad idea, actually."

Hawk scoffed. "Yeah, until someone walks off with it."

"True. I don't know how I feel about leaving something so important out where anyone could take it. But the people of Vegas are pretty unified, and maybe leaving it out would send a signal that we trust them." Alex shrugged. "Besides, I can probably create some kind of tracking system with runes when I get the chance."

Alvin grinned like a dumbass, clearly happy that his suggestion had been acknowledged. Hawk couldn't blame him. After all, he had felt the same way when everyone had begun to take him seriously. The thought reminded him of when Becca had begun to listen to him when he complained about Bancroft. He turned away from the others, not wanting them to see his face as he stamped his feelings back down.

"You okay?" Lana shined her flashlight in his direction.

"I'm fine," he snapped back.

She didn't ask again.

"Crap." Alex drew some of the attention off of him and to a broken case. "We might have a problem."

"What?" Lana and her brother headed over to him.

"Someone stole Oscar the Grouch." He pointed to an empty display.

"That's weird." Hawk sniffed once, then rejoined the others. "What would someone want with a muppet?"

"I think the more important question is, who took the muppet?" Alex walked deeper into the exhibit. "Damn, there's another prop missing over here."

Hawk followed, finding a picture next to the empty case showing the prop in a shot from the movie that made it famous. It was just a plain black umbrella with a bird's head on its handle. The movie must have been old because Hawk had never heard of it.

Alex ran around the exhibit sounding annoyed. "I'm not finding anything that has an enchantment, either."

Hawk turned, letting his gaze drift around the space to find a number of other broken or empty cases. The rest hadn't been touched. It was almost as if someone had gone in there with a shopping list of things to pick up. He checked his HUD periodically with the hope that whoever had beaten them there had missed something.

Nothing came up.

He blew out a sigh. It would have been nice to find something, even if it wasn't that cool. Alex continued his search running down another corridor. At that point, Hawk stopped caring about enchantments and just focused on finding something fun. After all, when were they going to be back there? It was only reasonable to take a souvenir.

The first item that caught his eye was a prop gun from Star Wars. He left it where it was, figuring it was more Alex's sort of thing. Next, there was a Bowie knife. It looked cool, but he hadn't seen the movie it was from. The title had something to do with crocodiles.

Eventually, Hawk pulled out the lighter that he'd found at the last museum and lit it to get a little more light. He'd fueled it up before leaving Vegas. Sure, he could have used a flashlight, but fire was more fun, and fun was what he needed right now. That was when something silver glinted in the firelight. Hawk closed in, feeling a little like Asher, being drawn to a shiny object.

"Hmmm." He leaned down to look at a pile of three silver Zippo lighters similar to the one that he held, but without the picture on the side. One of the lighters sat in front, leaning on the other two. Beside them sat a description card bearing a photo of a man in a tank top crawling through an air vent with one of the Zippos held up to light his way. According to the card, the three lighters were used in the movie at various points. The one in front had been used in the scene taking place in the air vent.

He smiled. Not only had he seen the movie, but it had been one he'd watched on Christmas Eve the previous year with his adoptive parents.

Hawk snapped the lighter he was currently using shut and shoved it back into his pocket. If he was going to carry one, it only made sense to pick one that was famous.

"Time to upgrade."

A minute later, the case was open and he was scooping up all three lighters. He flipped the first one open and closed. Flicking the igniter, it sparked but failed to light. He frowned.

"Probably been out of fuel for decades."

He dropped the lighter into his pocket so he could test the other two. The second failed to light as well so he shoved it in his pocket with the first.

Then, he tested the third.

Again, the flint sparked but the wick failed to ignite. However, unlike the others, a new message scrolled across his HUD.

Flame of the Cowboy

"No way." His mouth fell open as he read the description.

**MASS ENCHANTMENT: Due to the belief and admiration
shared by a large number of people, this item has gained
a conditional power of its own.**
Ability: Luck of the Hero
**This ability will cause all incoming projectiles to miss
their target, allowing the holder of this flame to continue
their heroics without interruption.**
CONDITIONS FOR USE
**Connection: This ability may only be used by someone
who is without footwear.**
I recommend watching where you step.

For a moment, everything that had been weighing on Hawk's mind fell into the background, drowned out by the sudden excitement of what he'd found. Whoever had snatched up all the enchanted items must have missed this one because it was behind another lighter. The obstructed view must have kept its description hidden.

It was a damn good thing they had missed it too.

The item was perfect.

Hawk remembered how ridiculous it was that the movie's hero had been able to run through a hail of bullets without getting hit. Honestly, it was a little stupid. Hell, he'd been in enough situations to know that wasn't how things really worked. In the real world, you would catch a bullet at random if you weren't hiding behind cover.

"Not anymore, I guess."

All he had to do was find some fuel and he could just ignore the realities of combat. He chuckled to himself, finally laughing for the first time in days.

I have to show Alex.

Hawk clutched the lighter tight in his hand and went to find the artificer.

"Hey, check this—"

"One second." Alex was too busy crawling around behind one of the displays. "I'm just…" He trailed off as he tripped and knocked over a bunch of cases.

Hawk winced as they crashed to the floor.

"I can't believe there's nothing left." Alex stood back up in a huff, clearly annoyed that he had fallen. The energy drinks definitely weren't helping. "This is the goddamn Smithsonian, it should be full of world-famous movie props."

"Maybe Autem really has already gathered all the enchanted items." Lana stood off to the side where she wouldn't get in the way of the mess Alex was making.

"I was really hoping we were wrong about that." Alex grimaced. "But yeah, Autem is the only one that could have cleaned everything out so fast. They probably had it all cataloged and scooped up the important items as soon as the world ended. They've certainly had enough time to plan and prepare." He kicked at some broken glass that was on the floor, before adding a frustrated, "Damn it!"

"Great, so that means there's some Guardian dicks running around out there with some crazy mass enchantment abilities." Hawk deflated, still holding his lighter tight, waiting for the right moment to announce what he'd found.

"I don't love that thought either, but that probably is the case. I doubt Autem would share that kind of thing with mercenaries like Skyline, but now that we're going to be going up against Autem directly, we might start seeing Guardians with different equipment." Alex sighed, letting his arms hang limp. Then he threw open the flap of his messenger bag and yanked out Kristen's skull.

"It's about time you decided you needed me for something. Let me guess, you figured out that Autem beat you to all the important mass enchanted artifacts?"

"You knew?" Alex held the skull close to his face.

She scoffed. "Of course I knew."

"Why didn't you say something yesterday?" Lana stepped closer to glower at the skull.

"Nobody asked. And it was funny."

"Just what about watching us waste our time was funny?" Alex took a page from Digby's playbook and shook the skull in frustration.

Kristen answered as he waved her through the air. "Because you murdered me, remember?"

"I cannot tell you how sick I am of hearing that." Alex set her down hard on the stand of one of the empty display cases. "I thought for a minute that you might have been growing a conscience, but you didn't even skip a beat before going back to sabotaging us."

"Of course I did, I don't have a soul. I am incapable of caring about you or anyone else. Honestly, the fact that you keep thinking that I am going to magically have a change of heart is the peak of stupidity." The skull let out a ghostly laugh only to stop a second later. "Wait, where are we?"

"That doesn't matter right now." Alex stomped in a little circle as he flailed his arms. "I have a good mind to scratch off those runes that are keeping you active."

"Shut up, you moron," Kristen snapped back, suddenly sounding serious. "You must tell me where we are, it looks like…"

"It's the Smithsonian," Hawk answered if only to stop the skull from complaining.

"No." Kristen's tone went cold. "We have to leave. We have to leave, now!"

"We aren't going anywhere." Alex picked up the skull. "Though, I have a good mind to leave you here when I do."

"You don't understand." The skull's voice grew frantic. "You're all in danger here."

"Like we're gonna believe that." Hawk smirked.

"You have no idea the mistake you've made by coming here." The skull was practically shaking.

"Maybe we should listen to her." Alvin stepped in.

"Yes, boy, listen to me. You all must flee, now."

"Flee from what?" Alex picked up the skull.

"You have brought us straight into the heart of Autem's territory!"

Alex's face fell. "Who with the what, now?"

"Washington, D.C.," the skull answered as if it should have been obvious. "Did no one think to look out of a window? This city is the center of the empire's capital. They have planned that much for decades. You are lucky you have not been caught by a patrol already."

"Well, shit." Hawk groaned. "Of course, nobody looked out a window when they scouted the place."

"We had a direct portal." Alex shook his head. "Why would they look outside? All we needed were mirrors."

Hawk rushed down the hall to look out the nearest window, everyone else following. He skidded to a stop and gasped as a massive structure came into view. "She's right. There's something huge out there."

"Damn it," Alex whined. "Everything just keeps getting worse."

"I'll call Parker." Lana pulled her compact from her pocket and cast Mirror Link.

That was when the sound of a boot squeaking on the floor came from the other end of the exhibit. All at once, everyone looked in the direction it came from to find a large man standing in the dim light. He was huge. The man darted back behind a wall before Hawk got a chance to analyze him, but he was able to see what he was wearing.

Guardian armor.

The sound of a radio clicking on came from around the corner. "Hey Leon, we've got some trespassers."

"Run!" Kristen shouted. "He's already reported you!"

"New plan, listen to the skull." Alex turned and made a break for it.

"Aww crap." Hawk followed.

"We need a new exit." Alex looked back to Lana. "The display case that we used is on the other side of that Guardian."

"It's just one guy." Hawk started to slow. "Let's just take him out."

"Hell no, we aren't." Lana grabbed his sleeve and yanked him along. "We are not attacking a Guardian with nothing but a couple of kids and a skull. I am a cleric, for god's sake; the only one here that can cause any damage is Alex."

"Yeah, and I have a brain cloud and I'm missing an eye." The artificer kept running. "And we know way too much to risk being captured."

Hawk groaned and picked up his pace. "Fine."

The man didn't give chase right away, as if waiting for the rest of his squad. A frantic glance back showed another smaller man running through the shadows in the far end of the hall to join the first. Another figure moved through the darkened space behind him. Their only saving grace was that the Guardians weren't very fast.

"There's more than one of them." Alvin kept a brisk pace beside him.

"Don't even think about defecting." Lana stared at her brother.

"I won't, god!" He rolled his eyes.

"That way!" Alex jabbed a finger at a sign that read Exit before looking back to Lana. "Where are we with that passage spell?"

She looked down at her compact as she ran. "Parker hasn't picked up yet."

"Holy shit, we need to add some kind of ringtone to that thing." Hawk panted.

"Hello?" Parker's voice finally came from the portable mirror in Lana's hand.

"It's about time." She held up the compact, trying her best to run and talk to the messenger at the same time.

"Sorry, but these things need some kind of ringtone," Parker complained.

"See!" Hawk threw a hand out at the compact.

"Anyway, what's up?" The sound of Parker sipping coffee finished her question. "Why are you running?"

"We need an exit, now!" Alex shouted back.

"Oh damn, okay." Parker nearly choked. "I'll reopen the passage we used before."

"The location we used to get here is no good, we need a new one." Lana held the compact out so Parker could see the front doors of the museum as they approached it.

"You need to hold the mirror still. I can't get a good look."

"They're still chasing us," Alvin called out as he looked back.

"Shit, we can't stop here. We'll have to find something in the street outside." Alex kicked the door open and stopped as Hawk and the others rushed out. He pulled the pistol he carried from its holster and fired at the Guardians chasing them. He kept running when he ran out of bullets. "I think I winged one."

"This is a bad idea." Hawk glanced back as they rushed down the steps of the museum and into the open street.

"Stop!" the large man that had found them yelled from the open door of the museum, as if giving up on the pursuit now that they had exited the building.

Hawk ignored the Guardian and kept running, his attention torn away from the door as a noise like nothing he'd ever heard filled the sky. He raised his head just as an aircraft floated into the space overhead, Autem's crest covering the bottom. At first glance, it looked like a kestrel, but it had some kind of strange engines in place of propellers and emitted an awful hum.

"What the hell is that!" Lana held up a hand to shield her eyes from the morning sun.

"I have no idea." Alex stopped in his tracks. "It looks like a kestrel, but powered by runes."

That was when another voice called out from the door of the museum.

"Hawk!"

Everyone else was too focused on the aircraft floating above them, but for Hawk, the voice was impossible to ignore. His eyes welled up the instant he heard it, though his mind practically screamed at him that it couldn't be real. He turned slowly to look back.

There she was.

Becca stood in the doorway of the Smithsonian, dressed in a set of Autem's armor. The massive Guardian stood just behind her. Another person was hidden in the shadows further inside the museum.

It couldn't be true, yet, there she was.

She looked tired as if she had just run a marathon and could barely catch her breath. The shock and disbelief on her face matched his own.

A second aircraft flew in to join the first, pulling his attention from his sister. He looked up for a second before snapping his eyes back to the door of the museum. It had only been a moment, but just like that…

Becca was gone.

The museum's door fell shut, leaving him staring at it while simultaneously praying that he hadn't imagined her and that she hadn't just abandoned him again.

"This is not good." Alex reloaded his pistol, staring up at both of the aircraft that hovered above. No one else had noticed Becca.

"What do we do?" Lana backed up to stand with her brother.

"Hold up the mirror," Parker called from the compact in her hand. "Show me anything. A window, a puddle. Anything."

Lana did as she was told, raising the mirror and holding it as steady as she could.

"Hurry up, Parker." Alex stepped back, casting Barrier to send a protective shimmer across his body.

"Remain where you are, Heretics." A voice echoed down from the oversized kestrel above them as a pair of guns mounted on the bottom turned to face them. "Resist and we will open fire."

Hawk raised his head to the white craft, struggling to see

with the sun shining in his eyes. All he could make out was Autem's imperial crest as the stuttering hum of its engines sent an uncomfortable shudder down his spine. It was as if the power of both aircraft was rippling through his mana system.

There was nowhere to hide. The street was empty except for a few abandoned cars.

"Do we run?" Alvin croaked out.

"No!" Kristen shouted back. "They will kill you before you make it a few steps."

"There!" Parker shouted from Lana's compact. "That abandoned car. I can use the windshield to open a passage. You just have to get there."

Hawk followed the direction the compact faced, finding a BMW parked over a hundred feet away. He flicked his eyes back up to the guns that pointed down at them. "Shit, that might as well be miles away."

"That's all I can see clearly, I'm using it," Parker shouted back as the windshield of the car began to ripple like water.

"We've got no choice." Alex put himself between the nearest aircraft and the rest of their group, clearly intending on using himself and his barrier to shield them from whatever hell might rain down on them. "Move together!"

The craft above opened fire the moment they started walking, bullets ripping through the pavement to draw a line that they were forbidden to cross. They all stopped dead in their tracks as bits of asphalt rained down, getting stuck in Hawk's hair and sticking to his face. It was a warning shot, but the message was clear. There was no way forward. Not if they wanted to live.

"Keep moving," Alex called out. "Stay close to me and don't look back."

"Are you mad? You may have a barrier, but those guns will still tear you apart." Kristen cried out just before he shoved her into Alvin's hands.

"Go. This is my fault. I shouldn't have taken you all along on this stupid quest of mine." Alex held his arms out wide as he stepped forward, forcing them all to walk toward the abandoned BMW. "We can't let ourselves be captured."

Hawk's eyes welled up, realizing what Alex intended. "No!"

The guns of the craft above spun up again, whining like the cry of a dying animal as a burst of bullets shattered the sky. Alex lurched forward as blue sparks exploded from his back.

"Keep moving!" He kept his arms raised. "I'm okay."

"I can't." Hawk turned back to him as the sun above silhouetted the artificer.

"You have to." Alex stepped forward, not giving him a choice. He took another step, this time faster. "We have a lot of ground to cover."

Another burst of gunfire lit up the sky, cutting a swath across the street. Lana held her brother close, grabbing onto Hawk as well. Alex's barrier shined in protest as he recast the spell. He downed a mouthful from one of his flasks to ensure its healing could keep him on his feet for a few more seconds even after his protective magic failed.

"Do not move another step, or we will be forced to execute you." The voice from the aircraft's speakers spoke in an almost formal tone. "Lay down with your hands behind your back."

"Go. Run!" Alex kicked off, trying to force them forward.

That was when Hawk stopped. "I'm not leaving you."

The guns of both aircraft opened fire.

"I'm sorry." Alex closed his remaining eye tight, running out of time.

Hawk did the same as the pavement around them exploded into the air, streaks of molten lead shredding their surroundings. The sound was deafening.

Then, it ended.

The whine of the guns slowed to a stop.

"What?" Alex cracked his remaining eye open.

"How are we alive?" Lana raised her head, glancing around them at the circular patch of pristine pavement that they stood on. Everything beyond that had been torn to shreds.

That was when everyone looked to Hawk and the flickering

light that glowed from his hand.

He couldn't believe how warm the flame was.

Removing his hand, he held the small silver object so that everyone could see the lighter burning for the first time since the Eighties. He couldn't believe he'd slipped out of his shoes in time to activate the conditional enchantment.

"How?" Alex stared down at the lighter.

"I found it in the exhibit back there. We got interrupted before I could say anything." Hawk gestured with his head to the building. "The flame makes projectiles miss."

"Seriously?" Alex's eyes widened. "How does it even have any fuel?"

Hawk turned his hands to show his other lighter, the one he'd found the day before, sitting beside the enchanted one. He held them at an angle so that the flame of the first passed through the wick of the second.

"You're a genius." Alex grinned down at him. "I could kiss you."

"Please don't. We still need to run before they realize we have an exit over there." Hawk took a step toward the rippling windshield.

"Yes, cool, let's keep going." Alex started walking again.

"This time you can get behind me." Hawk pushed past him to stand in the line of fire from the craft above. The guns spun up again as he walked backward toward the BMW's windshield.

"You're not doing this alone." Alex stood beside him to hold his hand in front of the flame protecting it from the wind.

"Same." Lana joined him on his other side.

Alvin slipped between them to complete the circle.

Then, together, they made their way toward the Mirror Passage that led back to Vegas. Bullets tore through the sky, pouring in their direction, only to veer off course a few feet away before punching harmlessly into the ground at a safe distance. It was as if some unseen force was slapping every projectile away. Hawk picked up his pace, ignoring the hail of bullets that poured down on them.

Then he realized a problem. "Shit, the passage."

"What?" Alex looked down at him.

Hawk glanced back over his shoulder at the BMW. "The flame is protecting us but it's just going to throw bullets into the windshield when we get close to it."

"Crap, you're right." Alex raised his gun to the aircraft. "Would you consider Autem to be an authority?"

"I don't, but Autem definitely does." Hawk gestured to the aircraft above with his head. "They tried to give us orders, at least."

"That's good enough for me." Alex held up his free hand. "Hey, you up there. I hope you have a good look at this." Then he extended his middle finger. "Because I am flipping you off as hard as I can."

Hawk glanced to his HUD as Alex's maximum MP ticked up to indicate that the enchantment of his eye patch had just activated its passives, including the most important one.

Guiding Hand.

Alex immediately flicked his pistol in the direction of the craft's guns and unloaded it. Hawk watched in awe as his hand jerked back and forth with each shot. A grinding sound came from two of the guns that were pointing down at them as they came to a stop.

"Oh my freaking god!" Alex jumped in the air. "I'm an aimbot. Toss me another magazine."

Lana grabbed one from a pouch on her belt and threw it in his direction. Hawk winced when the artificer nearly fumbled it.

"Shit, damn, crap." Alex bounced the magazine back and forth before finally catching it. The eye patch did nothing for his ability to reload.

Alex ducked back next to Hawk as the second craft opened fire. Debris exploded into the air all around them as the attack shredded the street. Alex took the moment to load his pistol. He raised it as soon as the torrent of bullets ended, unloading the magazine in seconds.

The remaining craft's guns ground to a halt as well.

"Yes!" Alex pumped a fist in the air.

"Celebrate later." Lana grabbed the back of his shirt and yanked him toward their escape portal.

With the loss of their guns, both aircraft dropped down to the street, rotating as their ramps popped open.

"Okay, yeah, let's run for our lives." Alex broke into a sprint.

Lana and Alvin made it to the car first, the cleric helping her brother up onto the hood. He disappeared into the portal an instant later. Lana scrambled up next.

"Come on." Alex motioned to help as Hawk reached the BMW.

"I gotta cover us." Hawk stopped and lit his lighters again as several Guardians emerged from the aircraft. "I'll be right behind you."

"Okay, but no messing around." The artificer turned and dove face-first into the passage. It was clear he meant to slide in stylishly, but the result was more like a belly flop that left his ass hanging out of the passage like Winnie the Pooh. He awkwardly squirmed the rest of the way into the portal.

Shouts drew Hawk's attention back to the Guardians rushing toward him with guns blazing. He ignored them since his flame was now in position to protect the BMW's windshield as well as himself. Instead, he stared past the doors of the museum that they had just fled.

Had he really seen her?

Was Becca really there?

His thoughts crashed back to the danger he was in as an icicle spiraled toward him. He flinched and closed his eyes, having no idea if his protective flame would stop a spell. He opened his eyes again as the frozen projectile spun off to shatter against the side of another abandoned car.

"Okay, it works on magic, good to know." He stepped backward and hopped up onto the back of the BMW.

He still had many questions and no answers.

In the end, he did the only thing he could. He leaned back and let himself fall into the passage.

CHAPTER TWENTY-ONE

Parker hugged a pillow while standing in the middle of the parking garage attached to the casino in Las Vegas. After rescuing Alex and the rest of his coven from the Smithsonian, all she wanted to do was take a nap.

It was only noon and she was already exhausted.

Though, she hadn't slept the night before, so that part made sense.

The R&D team in Hawaii had been working in shifts all night. Unfortunately, there were no other messengers capable of ferrying them back and forth between the island and Vegas, so Parker was stuck staying up with them. Now, it had been over thirty hours since she'd last slept. The best she could get was a few minutes here and there, though, every time she tried, someone was there to wake her up, needing something.

The only good part was that she had been so busy that she hadn't had time to worry about watching Digby. He had made it clear that he didn't like having a babysitter. He'd seemed to like her a little more after they had spent so much time together in the Seed, but now he was getting increasingly annoyed whenever she was around. She would have to check on him at some point, but he hadn't gone insane the day before, so he would probably be fine on his own for a bit.

What's the worst he could do?

Well, besides committing war crimes?

Parker tried not to think about the question. She had other priorities, after all.

Hmm, where can I nap where no one will find me?

Parker glanced around to see if anyone was looking. When the coast was clear, she ran across the first floor of the parking garage with her pillow clutched against her chest.

"Perfect!"

She stopped in front of the tank that they had been storing at the far end of the garage. It was the one that Digby had disabled back when he'd liberated Vegas from its previous dictator. The vehicle's treads still didn't work right after what the zombie had done to it. It could move, but it only turned right. The thing had given her a hell of a time when she'd driven it across the garage to where it now sat.

The experience had told her one important thing. That being, the inside of the tank was cozy, and a pillow might make it downright comfortable. Combined with the fact that her headache had dulled to a mild annoyance rather than full-on migraine, she might be able to get some rest.

Climbing up onto the vehicle, she pulled open the hatch and tossed in her pillow. She lowered herself in next, finding a spot just the right size for her to catch up on some sleep.

"I need to bring a blanket next time."

Parker fluffed her pillow and flopped over into it. She was drifting off to dreamland within seconds. Of course, that was when a voice came from her pocket. Parker ground her teeth as she sat back up and pulled her compact out to find Elenore's face looking back at her.

"I need a passage."

"Of course you do." Parker yawned. "Where to?"

"The Hoover Dam," Elenore answered. "Need you to pick

up Jameson. He's going to help out with running the R&D in Hawaii."

Parker nodded and closed her compact. It made sense for Jameson to join the project. The old army vet had overseen the operation over at the dam and had the experience to keep things organized. Not to mention the ships in Digby's armada were going to need captains once they got in the air, and she sure as hell didn't want another job.

Parker took one last look at her pillow, then climbed up out of the tank. When she reached the alcove on the other side of the garage that held the mirrors, she checked a clipboard that had been hung on the wall. It contained a list of other compacts that had been assigned to various covens and locations. Running her finger down the numbers, she found that compact seventy-three had been driven out to the dam the day before.

She cast Mirror Link without hesitation, and went through the procedure of being shown a reflective surface on the end large enough to use for a passage. A moment later, Jameson stepped through looking amazed by the experience.

"Damn." Parker stood, staring at the elderly man, amazed by something else.

The last time she had seen him, he was so frail that a strong wind might take him out, provided his failing heart didn't end him first. That had been before he'd become a Heretic. Now, things were different. Wearing a t-shirt and camo pants, the man was actually a little beefy.

Parker looked him up and down before jabbing a finger in his direction. "Dude, you have abs."

"I, ah…" He immediately looked away and rubbed at the back of his neck. "Yeah, ever since becoming a Heretic, I've been regaining some of what I lost by gettin' old. Gained twenty levels hunting revenants in the desert. My constitution has rebounded as well. I might live to see this world turn for another year, after all."

"Probably more than that from the looks of it." Parker smiled, excited to see things turning around for the old guy.

"Let's hope so." He laughed. "I don't know what I would have done if Becca hadn't offered me a second chance." His face fell a second later. "I'm sorry to hear she didn't make it home."

"Oh." Parker swayed from side to side. "Actually, it seems like her death didn't take, but you didn't hear that from me."

He stopped short. "Really? How?"

"It's a long story." Parker decided to leave out the fact that Hawk had just told her that he'd seen Becca in D.C. "Anyway, let's get you to Hawaii."

With that, she raised a hand to the mirror mounted into the center of the garage's alcove and opened a passage. She gestured for Jameson to go first as soon as the glass began to ripple. Parker followed him through a moment later, feeling the temperature rise when she exited.

She stopped walking as soon as she was through, stunned by what she saw.

The hangar was a large space with a set of huge doors in the front that faced the harbor. Just outside, a small boat no bigger than a dingy floated a few feet from the ground. The four artificers that she had been watching the day before all worked around some sort of cylinder that stood vertically in the middle, its surface covered in runes. Several white boards were set up on one side of the hanger, bearing dozens of symbol combinations.

"Wow, now that's something else, huh?" Jameson stood next to her staring at the levitating boat. "I guess I should get someone to catch me up to speed." The old vet jogged to join the others, clearly running much easier than a man of his advanced age could under normal circumstances. He turned back to her halfway there to add, "Thanks for the ride."

She gave him a nod before yawning again. As much as she wanted to head back to Vegas and go back to sleep, it was probably time that she checked in on Digby. Though, that didn't mean she needed to go straight there.

"Hey!" she called up to the artificers on the boat. "Have any of you seen Mason?"

"You mean Captain Mason?" One of them hooked a thumb to the side. "He's aboard the Minnow."

Parker walked outside to find one of the navy ships docked a short walk away. Someone had spraypainted the word 'Minnow' on the hull over its original name. Like most of the vessels in the harbor, it was around six hundred feet long. They had finished sweeping the ship for revenants and had begun preparing it for its conversion from sea to air.

On the bow stood Mason, dressed in a black cloak and cowboy hat. The combination made him look like a bank robber from the old west. A glance at her HUD told her that he was level fifteen and that he'd taken the knight class. It made sense. He was the most noble person she knew. She was actually surprised he hadn't gained more levels, but with him being preoccupied with other things, his time must have been limited.

"Ahoy!" Parker waved in his direction.

Mason lit up as soon as he saw her, rushing down the walkway that led to the dock. His demeanor was completely different from the morning before. He had seemed broken then, but now he was almost back to normal.

"So it's captain now, huh?" She arched an eyebrow as he approached.

"Yeah, I needed something to do with myself." His tone grew sullen. "I know we don't have the manpower to take a coven out to search for Becca, and I haven't gained enough levels to survive if I go alone. She'd be pissed if I got myself killed out there, so I'm trying my best to be patient. I had to do something to stay occupied, though, and captaining the Minnow, here, should keep me distracted."

"Minnow, huh?" She looked up at the ship's new name. "Are you sure I shouldn't call you skipper?"

"You can, but that would just make you Gilligan." He smirked, getting a frown from her in response.

"You know the Minnow sank, right?"

"Yeah, but the artificers liked it." He shrugged. "Who am I to argue? They've been renaming everything."

"Makes sense." Parker nodded before adding, "By the way, we might have narrowed down where Becca might be."

"Really?" He reached out and grabbed her shoulder.

Parker looked away, not sure if she should feel guilty or not for giving him hope. "Emphasis on might," she added. "Hawk thinks he saw her in D.C., but he wasn't sure if it was his imagination or not. There was a lot going on at the time. That's where Autem's imperial capital is."

Mason's grip on her shoulder tightened. "Can you open a passage there again?"

Parker shook her head. "I tried, but the exit point I used before didn't work. My guess is that Autem's people destroyed everything they could now that they know we're using mirrors and glass to travel."

Mason's shoulders fell. "Oh."

Clearly, he was debating if that was enough to justify taking a coven across the country to save her. Even in Alex's deathtrap of a car, it would take a couple of days on account of there being too many obstacles keeping him from being able to push the vehicle to its top speed. By then, Becca could be long gone. Plus, bringing a coven of people that knew about Vegas into the center of Autem's operation was probably a bad idea. If they were ever captured, it would be all over.

He sighed, coming to the same conclusion. "I trust her judgment. Becca will come home when she's ready."

"Yeah." Parker gave him a sympathetic smile, leaving out the fact that Hawk had told her he saw Becca wearing Guardian armor. It wasn't that she wanted to hide anything, just that she didn't want to add to his worries.

"Oh! I have something for you." Mason suddenly changed the subject, pulling off his hat. He placed it on Parker's head to free up his hands.

Parker wiggled her head, realizing that Mason's skull was

massive compared to hers. The man wriggled around to pull the cloak he wore over his head, eventually shoving it in her hands.

"That's Becca's Cloak of Steel." He reclaimed his hat from her head. "Clint found it in the grip of a drowned revenant when we searched the cargo ship where Becca…" He trailed off before starting again. "You're going to need to return it to her when she makes it back here, but until then, it will create a barrier around you that will absorb a huge amount of damage. I figure you should have it."

Parker wrinkled her nose at the cloak. "Why would I need it? You should give it to Sax or someone else that's actually doing some fighting."

Mason's face went blank, as if she had just said something dumb. "Parker, you are the most important magic user we have. Second only to Graves." He gestured to the harbor around them. "None of this would be possible without you."

Parker blew out through her lips, making a lengthy fart noise in place of a scoff. "I'm just a magical taxi service. I haven't even gained any other spells, or a level for that matter."

"Well, put the cloak on anyway." Mason's voice shifted to that of a commanding officer giving an order.

"Okay, whatever you say, captain."

She threw the cloak over her head and fastened the loops that went under her arms to hold it in place. With her daggers sheathed at her hips, the garment made her look like a fantasy character.

"Okay, it is pretty badass." She brushed a lock of pink hair from her face.

"It's definitely cooler than the uniforms we wore in the army." He chuckled.

"Yeah." Parker rubbed at her forehead, her headache popping up again to make sure she hadn't forgotten about it.

"You okay?" Mason leaned closer.

"Not really." She closed her eyes to give them a rest. "I haven't gotten much sleep, and I've had a headache since I gained my magic, plus Dig is stressing me out. It's just a lot."

"Not enjoying your new Jiminy Cricket thing?" He adjusted his hat to keep the sun out of his eyes.

"I am not." She frowned. "I don't think Dig likes it either. But I guess I should stop stalling and go check on him anyway."

"You have fun with that." Mason gave her a nod before returning to his ship.

Parker dragged her feet the entire way to the Missouri that Digby had claimed the night before. The battleship had been decommissioned decades ago and turned into a museum. He was probably still planning on convincing Alex that they could get it in the air. Parker was pretty sure that was impossible.

She searched for signs that the zombie was aboard as she approached, hoping he hadn't gotten himself into too much trouble while she had been busy. Traversing the walkway that led to the deck, she found a hulking zombie waiting patiently near the bow.

Ducky.

"Hey there." Parker waved awkwardly. "I don't know why I did that. You don't really care if I wave, do you?"

The armored zombie glanced in her direction and grunted, but beyond that, paid her no mind.

Setting foot on the deck, she stood for a moment, feeling something unfamiliar about it, like she was somehow out of place or didn't belong there. It probably made sense—she had been in the Army, not the Navy. She had no reason to feel at home on the sea. It was impressive though. The battleship felt so big, making her feel small in comparison.

Her mind was pulled away from the thought before she had time to fall into an existential crisis when she heard Digby's voice coming from an open hatch. "There he is."

With that she followed the necromancer's voice, only stopping at the side rail to look out at the other ships docked in the harbor. She couldn't help but wonder what class they were, though the thought occurred that she should have known already. She may not have been in the Navy, but she probably would have learned a bit of surface-level information about the other branches while she was in the Army.

She rubbed at the side of her head. The headache seemed to be getting worse since she'd used her magic to reach Hawaii.

"I'm probably just tired." She winced, aware that she was actively lying to herself. Obviously, something was going on with her magic. It was like she was overusing it or something. At least, she hoped that was all it was. "I should really stop into the infirmary and have Lana check me out."

Before she could file a doctor's visit away on her list of things to do, Digby's gravelly voice came from within the hatch. It was him, but something sounded off. Like he'd somehow become a little more dead since she'd seen him last. If that was even possible.

Parker continued on her way, peeking into the shadowed space within the ship. "Dig, you in there?"

"Of course I am," the voice shouted back from someplace inside.

Parker stepped through the doorway only to leap back out when Asher flapped toward her from the shadows inside.

"Mother fucker!" She fell back on her ass outside the door.

"SOARY!" Asher flapped down to land a few feet away and hopped toward her.

Parker took a few breaths. "It's okay, Asher. I know you were just saying hi. Just wasn't expecting a zombified raven right now."

"HAI!" the bird cawed back.

"Hi." She waved and held out a hand.

Asher flapped up to perch on her arm before hopping up to the shoulder of her new cloak.

"Stop playing around, Parker," Digby called from inside. "We have much to do and little time."

"Yeah, yeah." Parker grumbled as she pushed herself up and stepped into the ship. She stopped short a second later as something crunched under her foot. Looking down, she found a collection of bones. She furrowed her brow.

They weren't human.

She couldn't even be sure what they were from, but most of the floor was littered with them, each as unfamiliar as the last. Many jutted off at odd angles or had strange formations.

"What the hell have you been eating?" She kicked a few of the bones.

"Eating?" Digby's gravelly voice trailed back to her from a corridor further inside. "Nothing lately. I had a bit of a feast last night, though. There was no shortage of revenants hiding in these empty vessels."

"Well, maybe you should pick up the bones when you're done." She pushed through the mess.

"Bones?" His voice echoed back. "I left no bones. They are a valuable resource. I would never leave one behind."

"Then what is all this crap?" She headed into the corridor after him only to immediately get another jump-scare as a revenant wandered out carrying more bones. The creature's skin was all dark and leathery like it had been buried and dug back up days later. "Mother fucker."

Parker tripped backward, her enhanced agility having trouble finding her footing with so many bones scattered about.

"MOTHA FUKA!" Asher repeated in solidarity as she flapped off her shoulder in search of a more stable perch. The raven landed on the revenant's shoulder.

Parker landed on her rear in a pile of bones. "Yar!"

Her list of priorities reorganized, demanding first and foremost that she remove the rather sharp fragment that was stabbing her in the ass. Grabbing the bone, she nearly lobbed it at the revenant on instinct. Then she noticed the five finger-shaped holes in its chest. A quick analyze, and the fact that Asher had landed on the creature, told her it was already dead. Digby must have come across it and created a new minion with his Fingers of Death spell. She pushed herself back up as the revenant wandered by her and dropped the bone formation that it carried to the floor.

"Okay then." Parker rubbed her ass suddenly appreciating

her new cloak. The jagged bone probably would have done some damage otherwise. "Good thing no one saw that."

"Hurry up, Parker!" Digby shouted from wherever he was.

"Coming!" She followed the sound of his voice, passing another zombie revenant on the way.

Asher stayed behind.

The shadows grew as she walked, making her wish she'd brought a flashlight. The only light spilled in through a porthole. Fortunately, it wasn't long before she found Digby. She froze as soon as she did.

"What are you doing?" Parker stopped in the doorway of what looked like an officer's dining room.

Digby stood on the other side of a long table in the corner. His back was hunched while he examined something in his hands. His coat had been tossed aside over one of the chairs. In its place, a weird sort of half-cape-looking thing hung from his shoulders. It was long and dragged on the floor. Another pile of strange bones lay at his feet.

Parker held her breath. *Yeah, there's definitely something off about him.*

"You good in here? I know I haven't been around much today." She swallowed hard in anticipation of his answer.

"Yes, yes, I'm fine. I don't need you to chaperon me." The necromancer finally turned around.

Parker gasped immediately.

He had no nose.

No, it was so much worse than that. It was as if he'd somehow lost the human disguise that he had been so proud of before. His face was sunken and deathly. His hands had even changed into a pair of monstrous claws in which he held another strange formation of bone. She analyzed him to see what had changed.

Level 39 Zombie Lord, Heretic Necromancer

He'd gained a level and apparently become a Zombie Lord in the process, whatever that was.

"Did you just gasp?" Digby glowered at her. "Good to know that my appearance holds such sway with your level of comfort."

"It's not like that." She shook her head. "I just wasn't expecting you to have reverted to corpse mode."

"I'm sure." He didn't sound like he believed her.

Parker folded her arms and looked away. "Dude, I can see all the way into your nasal cavity. I'm a human, I'm not used to that. Sue me."

"Fine, fine, whatever." He returned his attention to the formation of bone in his hands. "It's harder than it looks."

"What are you doing?" She took a cautious step toward him.

"I'm experimenting with my Body Craft mutation." He tossed the bone he held to the floor. "It's harder than it looks."

"Oh." She stopped.

"Don't worry too much, you won't have to look at me like this for long. I can still return my appearance to what you are used to. I just haven't yet to conserve my resources. I need all I can get." He finished his statement by closing his eyes and holding still as a new formation of bone began to sprout from his back.

Parker watched as the strange shape seemed to rot in reverse. A moment later the zombie opened his eyes and reached back to rip off the new formation.

Parker cringed with her entire body as the bone snapped and popped. "What are you making?"

"I'm trying to craft a usable wing." He moved one of his arms, causing the half-cape he wore to shift in an unnatural way that gave it form temporarily.

That was when she realized it wasn't a cape. It was skin. Digby let it fall flat again, unable to get it to do what he wanted. From the look of it, there were a number of support bones missing as well as some of the musculature needed to fly.

"I think I need to hunt down a few more of those revenant nightflyers." Digby dropped the bone in his hand to the floor. "My understanding of their anatomy seems to be lacking."

"You think you'll be able to fly?" She tried not to look directly at the bone that he'd just ripped from his back.

"I assume so." He held out a hand and flexed his claws. "With this mutation, there isn't much I can't do. I just need the resources and mana to reshape myself. I can even alter my minions. Then again, Body Craft is about the only new zombie ability that I can actually access."

"What do you mean?"

"I have four new mutations, but I need to eat five human hearts specifically before I can start working toward them." He groaned. "Unfortunately, I think someone would miss a human or two if I started to cull the herd."

"Cull the herd?" Parker eyed him. "I'm not in love with the way that you said that."

"I'm not going to start eating our people, Parker. I haven't gone mad." Digby rolled his eyes and tossed the bone in his hands to the floor where one of his zombified revenants collected it. Afterward, Digby turned and walked past her.

"That's good to know." Parker followed him toward the deck, bumping into him when he stopped abruptly. "Hey."

"Shush." He held up a claw as he stared out of the porthole she'd passed on her way in.

"What do you see?"

The harbor outside was calm in the morning sun. Then she realized that the zombie wasn't looking out the window. Instead, he was looking at the porthole itself where a spider web stretched across one side. A large arachnid sat at the edge of the web, its spindly legs tucked up close to its bulbous body. Digby held a claw out to the spider as if trying to coax it onto his finger.

"You making a friend there?" She took a step back not wanting to be so close to the arachnid in case it jumped or something. "Can you even make a zombie spider?" She shuddered at the thought.

"Hmm, I've never considered it." Digby leaned his head to one side as if debating on the usefulness of tiny, eight-legged zombies. Then he simply shrugged and scooped the spider into his mouth.

"Yak!" Parker recoiled as the arachnid tried to crawl away from the zombie's jaws.

Digby chomped down with an audible crunch.

"What the hell, man? Warn me before you do something like that. I was looking right at it." Parker jogged in a little circle to shake out the discomfort of what she'd witnessed.

"Oh please, you have seen worse." Digby folded his arms and waited for her to stop. "Are you quite finished?"

Parker shuddered once more. "Okay, yeah. I'm done." She looked back to him, only to wince as a single spider leg wiggled at the corner of his mouth. "You got a little something, right there."

"Oh." The zombie's blackened tongue darted out to scoop the leg back in. "Can't risk losing that."

"And you ate that spider, why?"

"You never know when something might be useful." He headed back to the deck where his zombie revenants were gathering up the fragments of bone and throwing them overboard. Apparently, once he used a resource to craft a body part, he couldn't consume it again.

"So what's up, besides all this weirdness?" She nudged a piece of bone with her foot to indicate the weirdness she spoke of.

"Much is going on, and you are just in time to help me with a problem." Digby leaned on the ship's railing. "Do you think you can open a passage to Skyline's base? The one that we attacked not long ago?"

Parker stared blankly into the middle distance while she considered how she would access the location. "Lana used to live there, she might have a mirror available for a link, so if there's anything in the background big enough for a person, I can probably do it. But I could use some rest before we head off on a mission."

"Good, good. And there will be time for you to nap later." Digby ignored her concern for sleep, clearly thinking only about his plans.

Parker eyed him, unsure if his lack of care was normal or not. He'd never taken complaints seriously, but after spending so much time with him in the Seed, she'd assumed he cared about her well-being at least a little.

"Why do you want to go to Skyline's base?"

"We have certainly found some valuable resources here in this harbor, but I'm afraid we don't have the luxury of taking our time. The base should be abandoned at this point, and I know for a fact that they left things behind that we can use. A kestrel or two would help tremendously."

"I can't argue with that." Parker nodded, watching as the zombie's eyes darted around the horizon as if constantly planning. "Though Autem is aware of our ability to travel through reflections, so there is a chance that they might be on high alert."

Digby slapped a clawed hand against the railing. "How in the devil did they find that out?"

"It was an accident mostly; Alex's coven ran into some trouble at the Smithsonian." She held up a hand when she saw Digby getting ready to freak out. "But we learned something important too."

"And that is?" He spoke through his teeth.

"Washington, D.C. is where Autem's capital is."

"That's good to know." Digby calmed down. "I had interrogated Bancroft about that before I banished him. He had some locations that he suspected, but Autem's people didn't share much with Skyline's personnel. Though, he could have been lying about that. With his underhanded nature, I find it hard to believe he never found out their capital's location on his own. I don't suppose you can still open a passage to their area?"

Parker shook her head. "I tried, but I think they destroyed every access point they could once they found out we were using reflections. I even tried the water in front of the Washington monument. It's probably just full of algae or something without regular maintenance."

"Shame." He didn't sound too broken up about it.

"There's something else," she added.

"Yes?"

"Hawk thinks he saw Becca just before leaving. He said she was dressed in Guardian armor." Parker told him everything, not wanting to leave something out.

Digby didn't respond, his face blank as he stared out at the ocean.

"Did you hear me?" Parker leaned toward him.

"Indeed." He ran a claw through his hair. "I don't think there's anything we can do about that right now."

"Really?" Parker cocked her head to the side. "I kind of thought you would have more to say about it."

"I wish I could." He looked out across the harbor as if trying to find the right words. "Everyone in Vegas is counting on me to lead them through the war that's coming. I have to be ready." He glanced back toward the upper deck of the ship. "There isn't time for distractions. There's already been too many. If Rebecca is really alive and in this Washington place, then I believe she knows how to find her way home."

"And the Guardian armor she was wearing?" Parker asked. "You don't think there's a chance she's—"

"Joined the enemy?" Digby finished her question.

"I didn't know her that well, but she did switch sides before."

"Nonsense." Digby scoffed. "If Rebecca had defected back to Autem, Henwick would already have attacked us the moment she told him where we were."

"True." Parker felt a little better about it. "She didn't seem the type to abandon her brother, anyway. Probably just stole the armor of a Guardian she'd killed."

"That sounds more likely." Digby stepped away from the railing. "Now, if our conversation has satisfied your requirement to check up on my sanity, I ask that you run along and get a coven or two ready to travel to Skyline's base."

"Why don't you get them yourself?" Parker folded her arms, not loving being told to 'run along.'

"Because I look like this." Digby pointed to his face. "You humans are all so hung up on appearances, and I don't want to push anyone away right when I need their trust the most."

Parker wanted to tell him he was wrong, that looks just weren't important. In the end, all she could do was nod. There was plenty of things that people refused to accept, she knew that much, and an undead monster would probably fall under that category. An ache in her chest reminded her about how she'd gasped at his appearance only moments ago.

Digby continued regardless. "I will finish up here and then reapply my Sheep's Clothing when everyone is ready to leave. I don't want to waste the resources until I need to. As it is, I need every scrap of flesh I can get. After consuming hundreds of revenants yesterday, I have plenty of each physical resource, but if I'm going to use it to enhance my minions as well as myself, then I will never have enough. Not to mention I still need some human hearts. Now, if we could find a squad of Guardians that has strayed from the flock, I could reach the requirement for another mutation."

"Seriously?" Parker cocked her head to the side. "Is that why you want to go to Skyline's base so bad? To hunt?"

"Oh, don't make it sound like I'm a monster stalking the countryside." He pushed away from the railing and walked in a circle. "It's not like I enjoy this, but I need to unlock the next tier of my mutations. Unless I get some volunteers, I am going to need to find some fresh hearts elsewhere."

Parker grimaced. It was one thing to kill Autem's people in a fight, but something felt off about going on a hunting expedition. Then again, it wasn't that unreasonable, considering what Digby stood to gain. She placed both hands on her head and pulled on her hair in frustration. "You know, you don't make being your conscience easy."

"Well, I am sorry that my existence is not puppy dogs and rainbows. What would you have me do?"

"I don't know?"

"How very helpful."

"Sorry, but everything we do falls into a weird moral gray area. So maybe hunting some Guardians isn't that bad."

"I'm not doing it for sport, you know?" Digby glowered at her. "Though, now that I think about it, chasing down some helpless Guardians might be a little entertaining."

Parker glowered back. "You're saying the quiet part out loud, Dig."

"Indeed. Maybe just forget that I said that last part."

Parker closed her eyes and shook her head at what her life had become. "Sorry I'm such a wishy-washy conscience."

"It's alright." Digby blew out a sigh looking at the upper deck of the ship. "We both know what Henwick eventually became. Maybe he might have turned out different if he had his own annoying cricket chirping in his ear every time he took a step toward villainy."

"I'm annoying?" Parker caught a jab at her in his words.

"Of course you are." Digby didn't apologize. "But I have spent enough time with you to know you wouldn't treat me unfairly. And that counts for something."

"Umm, thanks, I think." Parker wasn't sure if she had been insulted or complimented.

"You're welcome." Digby clapped his clawed hands together. "Good, now why don't you—"

"If you tell me to run along again, I will kick you in your fossilized balls." She shifted her leg to swing it back in preparation.

Digby laughed. "Go right ahead. I would barely notice."

"Oh, that's less fun." Parker put her foot down.

"Indeed." Digby turned back toward the hatch where he

had been trying to grow wings. "Let me know when we are ready to leave for Skyline's base."

"Will do." Parker gave him a wave before heading back in the direction she'd come from. She blew out a long sigh when she stepped onto the walkway that led down to the dock. Her eyes still burned from the lack of sleep and her head ached.

"I guess my nap is going to have to wait."

CHAPTER TWENTY-TWO

"Uh oh…" Digby stopped with his face poking halfway out of a new Mirror Passage. Well, technically he didn't stop. It was more like he was stuck.

Because of the extensive damage to Skyline's base, the only exit Lana and Parker were able to find was a narrow pane of glass set into a door. The passage led to a security building near the front gates of the base. The passage's exit hadn't looked that small at first glance; he should have been able to fit his body through by turning sideways, but he didn't even get that far.

The reason for this was, in a roundabout way, Digby's ego.

As promised, he had restored his human disguise by reapplying his Sheep's Clothing mutation to avoid frightening the humans. While he was at it, he decided to restore something else as well.

His bone crown.

With his new mutation tier officially bestowing him the title of Lord, the horned headband suddenly seemed like a necessity. It had originally been a part of the bone armor he'd gained weeks before but it had detached from his head upon regaining his human face. Ever since, he'd left the crown up in his room at the casino, but now, he'd felt the need to retrieve it before leaving.

Unfortunately, the extra half inch of bone that wrapped around his skull was beyond the limitations of the narrow exit of the Mirror Passage.

Hence, the issue.

"Not good." Digby could still feel the floor of the garage in Vegas beneath his feet while his face poked out of the passage many miles away. He shoved forward, somehow getting himself stuck even worse, to a point where his crown wouldn't even budge. He flailed for a moment realizing how ridiculous he must have looked to Sax and the rest of Dragon coven that were waiting to enter the passage behind him. "This is a fine way to instill confidence in your leadership."

That was when a polished panel of plastic that was mounted on the wall opposite him filled with a view from the garage. It was the surface they had used to originally show Parker the narrow window that he was now stuck in. Parker and Lana stood staring at him from the other side of a Mirror Link spell. He could see his own ass sticking out of the passage behind them.

"Dig, are you stuck?" The pink-haired messenger angled her head to the side with a vacant expression.

"Of course I'm stuck, Parker. What does it look like?" He held his arms out beside him, watching himself make the gesture through the link spell.

"Could you maybe unstick yourself?" she asked, unhelpfully. "'Cause I can't keep that passage open permanently. After a few minutes, it starts to feel weird."

"Weird?" Digby asked through his teeth.

"Yeah, it gets uncomfortable and my brain starts wanting to close the passage. And you know, I probably shouldn't do that while you're stuck in there. 'Cause, you know…" She finished her statement by swiping her hand up past her face in a slicing motion.

"Well, don't close the passage then!" Digby started pushing harder with little success.

"Wait! Dig!" Parker pressed her face against her end of the Mirror Link. "Can't you just slip out of the crown?"

Digby grimaced. The headband had originally been attached to his body like the rest of his bone armor, so removing it wasn't his first thought. Granted, it probably should have been his second thought, but his brain just hadn't gone in that direction.

Honestly, maybe I am losing my mind.

He pulled his head downward, having a little trouble before the crown popped off, still wedged in the narrow window. Once he was free, he squeezed through the passage the rest of the way. A snicker came from Lana and Parker. Digby ignored them and wrenched his crown free, cracking the bone on one side. He shoved it back on his head anyway.

Sax passed through next, handing Digby his coat. He'd taken it off to keep his pauldron from getting stuck. If only he'd thought to remove his crown first, he could have spared himself some embarrassment. He decided not to dwell on it. Instead, he just demanded his staff. One of the members of Dragon coven rushed into view from the garage and shoved the weapon through the passage. The head of the staff emerged from the mirror on Digby's side almost instantly. He snatched it and held it at his side while Sax and the rest of his coven came through, passing their weapons through the narrow space.

At one point, Parker had to close the passage only to reopen it again, afraid she might lose control of it while someone was crossing the portal. Once it was open again, Dragon coven finished passing their rifles and swords through. One member had to stay behind due to having a bit more girth than the opening could handle.

Digby surveyed his surroundings with a sense of satisfaction. The room looked like a bomb had hit it. Considering the attack that had happened there, a bomb might have been exactly what caused the damage. One wall was blackened by fire and a hole on the other side of the space led right into a hallway beyond. Sun shined in through another narrow window on the far side of the room.

Looking back to the rippling surface of the window that he'd come from, an image of himself reflected back, shimmering like water. He took the moment to stand a little taller. His image vanished as Parker exited the passage, continuing the conversation she had started on the other side.

"Did you seriously not think of taking the crown off?" she asked as the portal closed behind her.

"Shut up, Parker." Digby cleared his throat.

Parker rolled her eyes but said nothing. The action had become a habit of hers since becoming his mental health advisor. He smirked.

I'll show her. I'll be the sanest soulless zombie this world has ever seen. I'll be so sane that she'll have no choice but to declare me the picture of mental health. His shoulders sank for a moment. *I'll just have to make sure there aren't any more unfortunate accidents.*

The face of the man he'd killed, Ames, was still fresh in his mind. He closed his eyes, remembering that the unfortunate man had been given a proper burial at sea. There was nothing that could be done now. Not if he wanted to save everyone in Vegas. There was no time to get hung up on things that were beyond his control. No, not when he had so much work to do.

The base was sure to have some valuable equipment, and if he was lucky, he might just find a few ex-Guardians that he didn't have to feel bad about eating. All he needed was five hearts.

"Just five." He spoke under his breath without thinking.

"What?" Parker eyed him.

"Nothing." He frowned as he followed Dragon coven out of the room, unsure why he had even said the words out loud. They had just slipped out. "Let's go. And keep an eye open for a larger window that we can use."

Parker gave him another eye roll and followed without argument.

They made sure to tread lightly through the base. The elevator that Digby had ridden to the moon had probably been destroyed. But that didn't mean there wasn't another one somewhere in the area, and he didn't want Henwick popping down for a visit.

Heading down the hallway, he found Sax and the rest of Dragon coven waiting by the doors. The group inclined their heads respectfully as he approached.

I could get used to that. He nodded back.

"Hey, can I get a party invite?" Parker stopped him before he reached them.

Digby glanced at his HUD, finding only himself, Asher, and Ducky listed under his coven. Both of the zombies had stayed behind. Adding the messenger would cause her to receive less experience. Not to mention she would be able to see his status. He tilted his head in sudden confusion from the fact that he even cared if she saw his status. He chocked it up to a lingering habit from his time in that past when he'd only looked out for himself.

Though, the fact remained that her experience would still be impacted. He glanced at the Seed's information ring and willed it to add her to Dragon coven instead.

"Dragon?" She shot him a questioning look.

"Indeed." Digby nodded. "They are down a man, and I don't want to impact your experience." He didn't give her time to argue before turning to Sax who was peeking out through the door. "What's it look like out there?"

"We have a couple of bloodstalkers out in the open," he reported. "They don't seem to have the same lethargy that the other large revenants have displayed during the day."

Digby stepped forward and peeked out the window, finding the oversized creatures picking through the destroyed entrance of one of the nearby buildings, like a bear pawing at the discarded remains of a hunter's kill.

"They must be immune to sunlight, much like the light-breaker types. I suppose it was only a matter of time before they learned something new." He rubbed at his chin with one hand while he leaned on his staff with the other. "I wonder why they're here? Skyline's people should be dead. What more could this place have to offer them?"

"They must smell something? That's what bloodstalkers do, right? They stalk blood?" Parker shrugged and pulled her daggers out from under her new cloak. "Maybe there's still a few of Skyline's people hiding out there. You might get those hearts you're after."

"I, ah, nonsense." Digby tried to shrug off her comment as if he hadn't been thinking the same thing. "Well, we certainly can't leave those beasts wandering about if we are to scavenge this place." Digby pushed out through the doors and walked into the sunlight to put some distance from the conversation.

Parker flailed in place. "Wait, Dig—"

"I will handle this." He glanced back. "Just stay hidden so the creatures don't turn hostile while I am sneaking up on them."

Digby turned back to the beasts and started walking again. With everything that he'd learned recently, he was somewhat sure he could handle the foes without a problem. Granted, he would have liked to have Ducky by his side, just in case. That being said, neither of the revenants seemed interested in him, so he had the element of surprise on his side.

The base around him was damaged but still mostly recognizable. Sure, there were flipped-over vehicles and the corpses of Guardians lying about, but most of the buildings were still intact. There was no telling what treasures Autem might have left behind.

The oversized revenants continued to be more interested in the building they were clawing at as he approached, regarding him as nothing more than an inedible corpse. He stopped for a moment to watch them, remembering how just one of the creatures had torn him in half just a few weeks ago. He'd barely scraped by in that fight, even after taking a day to prepare.

Now, he was simply planning on gutting them like any other prey.

Stopping, he debated on trying to entangle them both with the crone's bindings and using his Fingers of Death spell to convert them into minions. He thought better of it. He was confident, but not that confident.

Maybe I should only try to turn one of the beasts.

But which one?

He analyzed them both, getting the same result from the Seed.

Revenant Lightstalker, Rare, Neutral

He frowned, hoping that the Seed would tell him which was more powerful. That way he could dispatch the weaker one and incorporate the other into his horde. Sticking to his plan, Digby crept around behind them to get a better look. That was when the difference between the two became obvious.

One was neck deep in the doors of the building they were interested in, with one arm reaching in to feel around. The other stood next to it with its claws hanging at its sides, and a pair of wings tucked against its back. The choice was clear. He had been getting close to forming wings with his Body Craft mutation. Eventually, he would get it right, and it would be nice to have a minion that could fly with him.

Alright then, how about we make a friend?

He glanced at his HUD.

MP: 376/376

Digby raised his staff in one hand and drew back his claws with the other, ready to plunge them into the creature. Of course, that was when his target decided to spread its wings to take flight.

"Wait!" Digby summoned the crone's echo twice, sending dozens of spectral hands reaching for the creature's feet. They coiled around its legs as the lightstalker's wings beat the air, nearly knocking him over with their downdraft.

The creature cried out, drawing the attention of the other one. It tore its head free of the building it had been investigating. A battered door frame was still stuck around its neck. Moving on all fours, it circled around him to screech in his ear.

"Quiet, you!" Digby summoned his wraith next, sending the crimson image of a long-dead killer flickering toward the wingless revenant. The echo dragged its spectral blade down the creature's body from ear to shoulder. A torrent of blood coated the cracked pavement below it.

Digby summoned the echo another two times to finish the beast off as he turned away to focus on containing the flying threat. Flashes of crimson light came from behind him along with cries of pain from the wounded revenant. A message on his HUD told him it was done.

Revenant Lightstalker defeated. 3,672 experience awarded.

Digby didn't look back, keeping his eyes trained on the winged revenant as it struggled against the crone's ghostly hands. Several of the spectral forms stretched thin and snapped as its wings fought to break free.

"Not this time!" Digby dropped his staff and moved forward, timing his movements with the beating of the creature's wings to advance during the brief lull between each gust of wind.

The last of the crone's hands came apart just as he threw himself at the beast and plunged all ten of his claws into its chest up to the knuckle. The revenant took off. He cast Fingers of Death as his feet left the ground, the creature clawing at his back in an attempt to tear him free. Digby used his Body Craft to reinforce the bone plates that protected him as the creature ripped his coat to shreds.

Then, the thrashing slowed along with the beating of the revenant's wings.

"That's it." Digby relaxed as the Death Touch ability that went along with his Fingers of Death spell spread his curse to a new minion. "Welcome to the horde."

The revenant stopped fighting as it lowered them both to the ground.

Revenant Lightstalker defeated. 3,672 experience awarded.
New minion obtained. Revenant Lightstalker.

"Perfect." Digby withdrew his claws from the massive zombie's body and stepped back onto the pavement.

The lightstalker released one final breath, never to take another.

Digby grinned up at the monster before glancing to his HUD to make sure that it had retained the ability to fly like the other winged revenants that he had animated in the past. It had. Sure, it had lost a bit of its strength, but with his Body Craft ability, he could restore it.

He spent the resources to enhance his new minion without a second thought. Then he added it to his coven and cast Leach to take half of the monster's mana, replenishing a little over one hundred points.

"Alright, off with you now." Digby gestured for his new zombie to move away from the building that the two creatures had been so interested in.

The giant, bat-like creature flapped off the ground and swooped back toward the security building where Parker, Sax, and the rest of Dragon coven waited. It landed on the roof above the door.

Digby let a cackle roll through his throat. "They are probably soiling themselves with that beast getting so close."

Right on cue, Parker peeked her head out from the door to

glower at him from across the battered pavement. "Very funny, you ass."

He chuckled to himself. Then he froze. "Wait, that wasn't funny at all."

Scaring Parker was a little humorous, but only because he knew it wouldn't really bother her. Frightening the rest of Dragon coven, who were still getting used to things, was bad. Their comfort should have been more important to him.

"Perhaps I really am losing it." He raked a claw through his hair, forgetting that it was covered in blood yet again. "Bloody hell. It's everywhere now." He groaned as he pulled his hand free and just tried not to make things worse. Holding out his arms, his coat hung in ragged strips like the tattered cloak of the grim reaper. "I suppose that isn't helping my image either." He dropped his hands to his sides before shrugging. "Well, no matter. It's nothing a shower and change of clothing can't fix."

Besides, he was more curious about why those revenants were so interested in that building. He turned back to where his lightstalker was perched before moving on. Parker and Sax were creeping out of the building beneath the monster with extra caution. "Find another window to get the rest of our people through. I'm going to investigate this building."

"Yeah, okay." Parker gave him a sarcastic solute.

Digby felt a weight lift from his shoulders, not having to worry about being watched. Not that he intended to do anything questionable. It was just good to not have to worry about making a mistake. Wandering into the destroyed entrance of the building, he found out why the revenants had been preoccupied with it almost immediately.

Blood.

No, not just blood, but fresh blood.

Digby stared at the wall as his Blood Sense highlighted flecks of crimson.

He glanced at his mana.

MP: 205/376

It was probably enough.

"Maybe I should go back and leach some mana from Parker."

Despite his words, he followed the blood. If there was even one beating heart ripe for the taking, then he owed it to everyone in Vegas to investigate further.

Digby hesitated for a moment, unsure if he was following the right path. Then he shook his head.

"There is nothing wrong with killing a few enemies. Moral gray area or not. If the source of the fresh blood was a Guardian, then they are fair game."

He nodded to himself, putting an end to the conflict as he tightened his grip on his staff. The trail of blood led to a locked door, in front of which stood a group of five revenants that clawed at its surface. Unlike the two outside, these were the smaller of the creatures. Though, they did share the same immunity to sunlight as their larger brethren. Each of them chittered at the door as if there was something on the other side of the door that they wanted.

Digby wasted no time in opening his maw on the floor to swallow them whole. His resources ticked up another five bodies worth. Including his feast the day before, he was up to a few hundred of each physical resource.

After casting Decay on the lock, he busted it open with the end of his staff and pushed in through the doors. An empty room filled with tables greeted him. It must have been a cafeteria. Probably the place where Campbell had worked before defecting to Vegas. Digby scanned the room for blood, finding a smear on the door that led to the kitchen.

"Hmm." He crept toward the trail. Reaching the crimson streak, he scraped a claw through it. It was still wet. "What have we here?"

A shotgun blast slammed into his shoulder the instant he opened the door, nearly spinning him around. A man dressed in a filthy Skyline uniform stood on the other side. Digby cast

Necrotic Regeneration and lunged for his attacker, plunging his claws into his chest.

A second foe emerged from the side to slam a large frying pan into Digby's head. It hit his horned crown, snapping the already weakened side as the pan reverberated like a gong. Dropping his staff, he threw his other hand out to catch hold of the second man's face. A muffled scream came from beneath his palm as his prey froze in terror, his eyes bulging between Digby's claws. With a mere twist of his wrist, his neck snapped.

Digby dropped the corpse straight into his maw before the heart within stopped beating. Next, he turned to the man he'd impaled and closed his claws around the thumping organ in his chest. With a hard yank and liberal use of his limitless mutation, he tore the heart free. He tossed it into his void as the body fell. He widened his maw so that the remains of the other corpse sunk into his void as well.

That was when a whimper drew his attention to a third man, standing before him, brandishing a chef's knife. He dropped the blade a second later and slapped his hands together in a pleading gesture.

"Oh god, you're him, aren't you?" His voice dripped with fear. "You're the necromancer."

"I am." Digby held his claws low, ready to strike. "And you have the resources I need."

"Wait! Plea—"

Digby didn't let him get another word out before leaping forward to run him through. He opened his maw at the same time, the man's feet dropping into the shadowy pool of black liquid. Digby pulled his claws from the man's chest as he sank, his arms flailing as he frantically tried to stop himself from sinking.

"That was easier than I thought it would be." Digby chuckled to himself just as his victim vanished. "Three hearts down, two to go."

He glanced at his HUD to see how much experience they had been worth.

3 common humans defeated. 22 experience awarded.

Digby froze as he read the line.

"Common?" He spun back to the door that he had entered through.

None of the men had been Guardians. If not, then they must have been in the past, before having their magic revoked by Autem when they abandoned the remaining members of Skyline. No. If they had previously been Guardians, the Seed should have labeled them as uncommon due to the higher attributes that they would have gained while they still had access to magic.

Unless…

Digby stepped backward. Unless they were just survivors that Autem had taken in before they abandoned the base. He placed a clawed hand over his mouth, smearing blood on his lips. He tried to remember what they had been wearing. The first had been dressed in a Skyline uniform, but the other two, he wasn't sure. He hadn't looked that carefully. He'd been too focused on gaining hearts.

Oh no, it happened again!

It was just like Ames. They were in the wrong place at the wrong time.

"No." Digby shook his head franticly. "They attacked me first. Even if they were just a group of regular humans. I can't be blamed for acting when given no choice."

But did you have a choice? a voice whispered in his ear. It was the same voice he'd heard after he'd killed Ames. He'd thought he'd imagined it then.

Digby spun, again finding no one there. He shouted back anyway.

"Of course I didn't have a choice!"

The whisper came again. *They begged.*

Digby recoiled. He was powerful enough that a common human couldn't be considered a threat. It was clear that the three men had been trapped by the revenants outside. They didn't even know who he was when he opened the door. They probably thought he was a revenant.

They begged, the voice repeated.

Digby's eyes fell to the resources listed on his HUD.

3 Human Hearts

A whisper slithered into his ear. *Two to go.*

Digby caught a reflection of Ames's deceased face in the side of a pot that lay on a counter nearby.

He snatched his staff from the floor and turned back in the direction he'd come from before. Then he fell back on the instincts that had protected him during the life he'd lived eight centuries ago. A strange calm fell over him as he realized he didn't need to tell anyone.

Digby swayed in place. "I have to hide this."

"No!" he shouted back at himself, fighting his instincts. "I have to tell Parker what happened. I didn't do this on purpose. I made a mistake. Anyone could have done the same. I'm sure she'll agree. Maybe I should tell her about Ames too."

He clutched his staff to his chest. "No, I can't do that. Not after I hid what I did last night. That would make me look guilty. I would have to be mad to come clean now."

Are you? the whisper asked.

The question hung in the air.

"This is exactly what Parker and Alex were worried about." Digby placed the tip of one claw in his mouth and chewed. "I'm hearing things. I've killed four people. I'm sneaking around. It was all an accident, but there's no way to explain it in a way that doesn't end with me losing the trust that I have built up over the last month. I would return to what I was before I died, just a scoundrel that no one wants around. I can't go back to that. Plus…"

They need you.

The whisper was right. "They do need me." He pulled his

claw from his mouth. "I'm the strongest Heretic they have. I just need to keep myself together a little longer."

But can you? the reflection of Ames asked from the surface of gold that covered part of his staff.

"Shut up," he snapped at the whisper, taking charge of his sanity. "Of course I can keep myself together. I am Lord Graves, and I'm not about to let something like madness push me around. It's not even my mind that's failing anyway, I just don't have a soul. I shan't allow myself to follow Henwick's path. I'm sure there's a way to fix things, then where will your whispers be? Hmm?"

Ames's reflection didn't respond.

"That's what I thought." Digby grinned. "I will find a way to fix this. I have to. And I certainly can't just step aside now to let others carry my burden. The literal fate of the world depends on it."

Before he could convince himself further, a strange but familiar whine blared through the building.

"What the devil is that?"

He pushed the conversation he was having with himself aside, thinking back to when he had heard the sound before. Then it hit him. The same sound had blared from the base's speaker system during the attack.

"What did Parker do?" Digby turned to the door and broke into a sprint.

Whatever murders he had or hadn't done barely mattered anymore. The whining sound swelled as he exited the building, its purpose becoming clear.

Someone had set off an alarm.

CHAPTER TWENTY-THREE

"What did you do, Parker?" Digby burst out of the cafeteria building to find the pink-haired soldier and a couple of members of Dragon coven running back and forth.

"I didn't do anything." Parker pointed a finger at a large building further away. "Sax took half the coven to check out the aircraft hangar while I stayed here with the others to look for a bigger window. The alarm just started going off. I don't know what happened."

"Bloody hell, we just got here and things have already gone awry." Digby slapped a hand to his forehead, forgetting again that his claws were covered in blood.

"You got something on your face there." Parker pointed to a bright red blotch on his brow.

"I know that." Digby swatted at her. "I was attacked by three ex-Skyline Guardians that were still lingering about." He immediately felt better that he'd said something about his encounter, even if it wasn't the whole truth. The less he had to lie about, the better.

Before he said anything else, he caught Sax in his peripheral, running toward them from the direction of the base's aircraft hangar with the rest of his coven.

"At least Sax has the good sense to run for his life." Digby held both hands out as they approached. "What happened?"

"There was a kestrel in the hanger, we tried to start it up," Sax reported.

"Damn, there must be some kind of booby trap built in." He groaned before shooting Parker a look that said 'shut up' before she decided to make a comment about his use of the word booby.

The messenger ushered everyone back toward the security building that they had come from. "Becca was always the one to handle stealing kestrels. She must have known how to bypass whatever alarm we set off."

"Get inside and get a passage open. We'll retreat for now and come back later." Digby swiped a claw through the air. "We have no idea how fast Autem can return here and we can't afford for anyone to get caught now."

"On it." Parker disappeared into the building.

Digby started to follow but stopped to observe the base. Other than the alarm, there was no sign that they had been noticed. There was a chance that despite the noise, there might not be any connection for the alarm to notify anyone about their presence.

Did Autem even have a way to reach them quickly?

They could send a few kestrels from their capital, but they would still take hours to get there. Unless they had another portal system beyond the elevator. As far as he knew, they didn't, but then again, there was a portion of the base that was underground, and they could have anything hidden away down there. In the end, it was best not to take chances.

Digby followed the others into the security building, getting back to the room that they had entered through just as Parker was opening a passage. She used the same narrow window that she had used before.

"Hurry and get everyone through." Digby shoved one of

the members of Dragon coven into the passage. The rest of them squeezed through, leaving only Parker and Sax.

"Come on, Dig." Parker beckoned to him. "You need to go through before me. Just make sure not to get stuck this time."

"I won't," he snapped back as he stepped forward, only to stop as a rumbling came from the other side of the wall nearest the passage. Digby turned his head to listen. "What's that?"

No one got the chance to answer.

Instead, the side of the building exploded inward as an enormous armored vehicle plowed through the wall. The narrow window, that they needed to escape, fell beneath its wheels.

"Holy hell!" Digby tried to jump to safety but he had been standing too close to the wall.

The armored behemoth slammed into his side, his hip bone and staff breaking just as easily as the window that had been their only escape. An avalanche of cinder blocks and debris buried him up to his neck. He cast Necrotic Regeneration as the dust settled.

The vehicle rumbled menacingly as Digby recognized it. The monstrosity was the same as the one that had chased him through Seattle a month ago. It was easily three times the size of the tank they had taking up space back in the casino's garage.

"Parker? Sax? Are you alive?" he called out while pushing a block of stone away from his head.

"I'm fine." Parker emerged from the destruction unharmed. "I think Becca's cloak just saved my life." She winced. "Though, getting hit by a tank didn't do anything for my headache."

Digby relaxed at the knowledge that the messenger was safe before a cry of pain from Sax told him they had other problems.

"Oh hell." The soldier stumbled out of a cloud of dust with one arm bending in the wrong direction. "I don't think my body is supposed to do this."

"You'll be fine; I've broken my arms plenty of times. Now,

get over here and dig me free. You still have one functioning limb, don't you?" Digby slapped the pile of debris that covered his torso.

"You know, you could say please." Parker dropped down beside him and started pulling cinder blocks away. From the rate that she moved, it was abundantly clear that she hadn't put any of her extra points into strength.

That was when the door of the vehicle popped open.

Digby craned his neck back to see, but couldn't twist it far enough without snapping it. From the look on Sax's face, whoever had been driving the vehicle must have been intimidating.

"That's it, new plan." Digby swatted at Parker. "Stand back."

He activated his Necrotic Armor, sending slabs of muscle to embrace his body as his hip bones stitched themselves back together. He used his Limitless mutation in unison to push himself free of the debris. A mask of bone slid over his face the moment he was free, a line of fingers inching across his chest to seal his armor shut.

"Stand back." Digby turned to face the foe that had stepped from the vehicle. If his jaw hadn't been contained within a mask of bone and sinew, it might have hit the floor.

Before him stood a knight, but not just any knight. Sure, the Seed had labeled the man as such. A level forty elite knight to be exact. However, that wasn't the only thing that made the imposing figure stand out. No, that was his armor.

Unlike the rest of Autem's Guardians, who were all dressed in modern equipment, the knight was dressed in something more akin to plate armor, like that of the time Digby was from. Some bits and pieces were still modern, like the joints and neck area, but the rest looked like it had walked right out of the Crusades.

A motif of angel wings covered the knight's helm and pauldron, and a border of engraved runes lined the edges of each piece. Even the knuckles of their gauntlets carried complex engravings.

Digby took a step back on instinct as the knight reached back and pulled a shield from the vehicle that he had just exited.

"That's not good."

Though, comparing their levels, they were an even match. Of course, another two men, both dressed in the same armor, approached the hole in the wall from the outside to change the odds. They must have been riding in the back of the vehicle. The Seed labeled them as well.

Guardian, Level 40 Tempestarii
Guardian, Level 40 Artificer

There wasn't enough room on the side of the vehicle for them to enter the building, so they climbed on top of the vehicle where the hole was bigger.

Digby resisted the urge to grin. *They must not have seen my new minion out there yet.*

"Surrender, now," the knight said in a gruff voice from under his helmet. "I will not ask again."

"Yes, yes, of course. We don't have anywhere to run." Digby held a claw behind his back whilst making a shooing motion to tell Parker and Sax to make a run for it.

They both sprinted out of the room, clearly understanding what he wanted. Someone had to find a mirror so they could escape.

The knight simply called to the other Guardians. "Get the other two. I'll handle the necro."

"Oh, you'll handle me, will you?" Digby chuckled, his voice sounded dark and strange from within his necrotic armor. "I am Lord Graves, and I shall not be so easily beaten."

In truth, he was hoping to keep the knight talking so that he could avoid fighting as long as possible. He may have gotten a lot stronger, but he still didn't like his chances. Just in case, he sent a command across the bond he shared with his blood-stalker to attack the two Guardians on top of the vehicle.

One of the men outside cried out a moment later.

Digby cackled as the Guardian's voice was cut off.

The nice thing about having a minion with wings was that it opened a whole new set of options for murder. He couldn't see from inside, but he had ordered his zombified revenant to simply pick up both men and drop them from a lethal height.

Gravity was the great equalizer, after all.

Everyone got flattened if they fell far enough.

"Do you really think you have a chance?" The knight didn't even seem concerned about his people as they were carried off.

"Honestly, not really." Digby shrugged and made a break for the door, the knight giving chase without hesitation.

Pushing his body to its limit, he snagged a claw on the corner of the hallway to swing himself around a corner. Digby glanced back just as the knight cut the same corner by ramming his way straight through the wall, the runes on his armor glowing. Cement bricks exploded into the hallway as the knight skipped over the falling debris. His agility must have been high, because he navigated the uneven surface like it wasn't an obstacle.

"That's bad." Digby faced forward, the feet of his necrotic armor hitting the floor in a steady rhythm of wet thuds. It wasn't long before he reached the exit. He pushed through the door, slamming it behind him.

The knight kicked it off its hinges without slowing down, the door flying past Digby to land twenty feet away, bent in half.

Digby searched the sky for his minion, finding it, a flapping speck high in the sky. The Guardians in its claws were certainly putting up a fight, but it wouldn't matter in the end. Even being level forty wouldn't save them from the ground when they slammed into it. He let out a victorious laugh as his minion dropped them.

"Looks like the odds just tipped in my favor." Digby stopped and turned to face the knight.

"We'll see." The foe simply raised his shield.

"Indeed, we shall!" Digby threw his body forward, making use of his Limitless mutation and every point of strength his armor provided.

The muscles in his arm burned like they might explode as he brought his fist down on the knight's shield. Every bone, all the way up to his shoulder, shattered on impact as his necrotic armor burst. Slabs of meat slapped and flopped against the Guardian's shield harmlessly.

"What?" Digby's arm slipped off the metal surface with an awkward squeaking, the limb falling limp at his side.

The knight ducked his head and braced his body against the shield before speaking one word.

"Scram."

The word carried a strange echo as a force unlike anything Digby had ever felt hit him. It was like a giant had backhanded his entire body. The impact itself didn't cause any damage, but the velocity that followed as his feet left the ground was a different story.

"Gah!" A nonsensical syllable fell from his mouth as his body was launched straight backward away from the shield. His body kept moving, speeding up with every passing second, the ground passing below his feet as the world streaked by in a blur.

"Why aren't I falling?"

Digby's mind raced to understand what was happening. It was as if the attack was intent on throwing him infinitely through space. Of course, that was when he realized it was only a matter of time before he hit something. Thinking fast, he poured mana into his Body Craft mutation, the back of his armor exploding into a mass of random muscle. Slabs upon slabs erupted from his body. He didn't even care what he formed just as long as it could take an impact. Hell, he was pretty sure there was a kidney in there somewhere.

Then he hit a wall.

Necrotic tissue liquefied in an explosion of impact-absorbing gore. Even with the added protection, a few bones in

Digby's back shattered. He was pretty sure his skull had been fractured as well. He cast Necrotic Regeneration to repair the damage and used his Body Craft to reassemble his destroyed arm.

Tearing himself free from his armor and the mound of diseased tissue that surrounded him, he stumbled out onto the pavement again. He immediately snapped his attention back to the knight that had told him to 'scram.' An involuntary gasp fell from his mouth when he realized how far away he'd been thrown. It must have been a thousand feet.

Glancing behind him, he found the aircraft hangar.

Then he realized that he still hadn't seen an experience notification from the two men that his bloodstalker had dropped. Searching the sky, he found out why.

They both drifted down slowly, each holding some kind of expandable rod over their heads with a curved handle at the bottom. Digby couldn't make out much more than that. Both Guardians touched down softly soon after, only to fall in line with the knight. Digby willed his flying minion to dive bomb the group, if only to slow them down.

"Now where are Parker and Sax?" He swept his eyes across the base looking for the pair of soldiers. There was no trace of them amongst the buildings. "They wouldn't have left without me, would they?"

His attention was drawn back to the three Guardians as his minion swooped down to claw at the knight. The armored man simply blocked with his shield as the word, scram, echoed across the base. His minion was launched straight into the air by the same ability that had thrown Digby into the aircraft hangar. The revenant flew straight up, away from the knight, gaining speed until the zombie finally stopped somewhere a couple of thousand feet up.

"Good lord." Digby stared at the knight as the man turned back to the enormous vehicle that they had arrived in.

His minion must have at least annoyed them enough to force them inside. A moment later, the tank-like behemoth backed up to pull its front out of the building that it had crashed through. Then it turned to face Digby's direction. The vehicle rumbled like a dragon as the row of tires that lined the sides stretched out wide to grip the pavement. It was as tall as a cargo truck and twice as wide.

"I must hide." Digby stepped back toward the aircraft hangar just as one of the doors opened.

"Oh, you're here." Parker leaned out.

"Indeed, that knight knocked me halfway across the bloody base." Digby turned and rushed past her into the hangar. "I hope you have a way out."

Parker shook her head. "There's less mirrors available than you would think, and most of the windows were broken when your horde attacked Skyline. I was hoping that I could use the windshield of the kestrel that Sax found, but the thing had a bunch of bullet holes that stopped me from opening a passage."

"Can we at least use it to fly ourselves out of here?" Digby glanced back as the massive tank barreled toward the hangar.

"None of us know how to fly, so the kestrel's out." Parker closed the door.

"Then what's the plan?" Digby growled just as Sax pulled up in a beat-up vehicle. The thing didn't have a roof and bits of corpse were stuck to the front bumper. Sadly, the windshield was missing from its frame, otherwise they could have just used it to escape. "What is that?"

"It's a jeep." Parker hopped in as Sax slid over to the passenger side. He probably wasn't good to drive with his broken arm, which had been tied to his chest to keep it out of the way.

Digby climbed into the back seat but remained standing with his claws held out at his sides. "What are we supposed to do with this, drive all the way back home? We'll never outrun that behemoth that Autem sent. It doesn't even have a roof."

"No, but we know that the barracks that Hawk stayed in while he was here had mirrors." Parker backed the jeep up to keep away from the large doors at the front of the hangar. "All we have to do is get there and we're home free."

"But what do we do about that monstrosity that is chasing us?" Digby pointed in the direction of the door as Parker parked the jeep in a dark corner against the wall.

"Just trust me."

"But they will come crashing through that door any second." Digby stood up in the back seat, still covered in sticky pieces of necrotic armor.

"I could just leave you here, you know," she snapped back.

"Oh, could we please?" Sax leaned back in the passenger seat, clutching his arm. "He smells terrible."

Digby leaned down, getting close enough for a bit of dangling tissue left over from his armor to fall on Sax's seat. "You try clawing your way out of a mass of semi-liquefied necrotic flesh and see how you smell."

Before anyone had the chance to say anything else, the building's front doors burst inward as the Guardian's vehicle tore through it like wet paper. The beast of a machine plowed forward, slamming into the abandoned kestrel that was stored inside. The aircraft shattered into scraps on impact. The knight slammed on the brakes as the vehicle skidded to a stop in the middle of the building.

Parker hit the gas as soon as it came to a stop. She cut the wheel hard, nearly throwing Digby from where he stood in the back. He dug his claws into one of the seats to hold himself in place. Seconds later, they sped straight out through the hole left behind by the Guardian's vehicle.

"I told you to trust me. There was no power to the hangar's doors. We needed to wait for those jerks to make us an exit so we could get the jeep out." Parker pressed her foot all the way to the floor. "Those guys don't seem to stop for little things like buildings, so I figured they wouldn't stop for a closed door either. Now we can head straight for the barracks while they turn that thing around."

"Alright, I'll hand it to you." Digby sat down and folded his arms. "That was actually good thinking."

"You're damn right it was." She laughed. "I'm a goddamn genius."

"Let's not get carried away, Parker." Digby rolled his eyes as she drove the jeep straight through a security checkpoint, smashing through the wooden gate that extended from the guard house.

With that, the buildings began to look a little less damaged now that they were on Autem's part of the base. Unfortunately, there were also less windows, since security had been stronger there.

"Okay, you've been here before." Parker glanced back to him. "Where's the barracks that Hawk stayed at? All I know is that it was in Autem's section of the base."

Digby swept his eyes across the expanse of buildings, feeling a little lost. The place was essentially a miniature city. It was easy to take a wrong turn. "It was that way. Near the research and development building that Henwick destroyed, last time we were here. Take the next right, I think."

"Got it! Next right." She spun the wheel, barely slowing down as the jeep skidded around the corner.

Digby looked back just as the Guardian's vehicle busted through another wall of the aircraft hangar. Apparently, they didn't feel like making a complete turn before exiting.

"That's unfortu—" Digby started to say but stopped as Parker slammed on the brakes.

Lurching forward, he fell face-first into the front seat. His hand snapped out to catch himself, but the remaining traces of his armor slipped on the leather cushions.

"Gah!" Digby landed upside down between Parker and Sax with the gear shift jammed into his back. "Why the hell did you stop?"

Kicking and flailing, Digby yanked his head up to see what had gotten in their way. His entire body froze in an instant, his blood somehow running even colder than it already was.

A familiar face smiled at him from the middle of the road, standing only twenty feet away with his hands behind his back.

"Hello, Graves." The man locked eyes with him.

Digby struggled not to shudder as he spoke the man's name. "Henwick!"

CHAPTER TWENTY-FOUR

"Hello Henwick." Digby narrowed his eyes at the man, struggling to put on a strong front despite the fact that his legs were shaking.

Guardian, Level 100 High Priest

The man stood just twenty feet in front of the jeep. Well within the range to Smite Digby without a second thought. Behind them, the massive vehicle that had been chasing them slowed to a stop.

They were surrounded.

Parker kept her head low to the steering wheel, clearly trying to go unnoticed. Sax sunk low into his seat, doing the same. If it wasn't for the awkward squeak his body made against the leather seat, it might have been successful.

Henwick glanced to Sax, grimacing. Then he looked to Parker and sighed. Finally, he flicked his eyes back to Digby. "I can't say I'm surprised to see you here. From what they say, a criminal always returns to the scene of the crime."

Digby forced his legs to stop shaking. There was still a few hundred feet between the jeep and the barracks where they knew there was a mirror that they could use to escape.

They just had to get there.

"I assume you're thinking of trying to get to a mirror to use that portal ability that the Seed seems to have gifted you with?" Henwick arched an eyebrow. "I must say, that is an interesting ability. Can't say I've seen anything like it. Usually, to open a gateway for travel, it took weeks of calculations and thousands of engravings to produce such an effect. Though, no matter how you have come across the capability to travel, I wouldn't suggest trying. I will Smite any building you enter the instant you do, leaving you no time to reach a mirror. If you wish to avoid that, I suggest you tell me where you have taken the Heretic Seed."

"Alright. Maybe escaping is out of the question." Digby stood up in the back of the jeep, trying to look tough despite the panic alarms sounding in his head. "But that doesn't mean we will simply roll over and give you what you want."

"Doesn't it?" Henwick held out both hands. "I am not making that offer to you alone."

"What?" Digby's face fell.

"Of course not." Autem's high priest gestured to the front seat of the jeep where Parker and Sax sat. "Graves is an abomination that must be destroyed, but there is no reason why you both need to share his fate." He gave Parker a smile. "I would hate to have to harm a young lady. The empire is a safe place, and we will certainly need the help of strong women like yourself to rebuild."

Digby grimaced at the offer, reading between the lines.

Parker winced and lowered her head, pressing her brow against the steering wheel.

Digby froze, unsure what that meant.

She is considering it, the ghost of Ames in his head insisted.

Digby immediately regretted telling her to shut up so many times. If she were to defect to the other side, with her power, Vegas would be done for.

Better she be destroyed.

Digby shook his head, horrified that his madness would even suggest such a thing. Parker wouldn't abandon him. Not after everything they had been through already.

"Well, young lady?" Henwick took a step forward with one hand held out. "All you have to do is exit the vehicle and come stand by me. I will keep you safe."

"Just stop." She rolled her head against the steering wheel. "I have one hell of a headache and your shit ain't helping."

Henwick dropped his hand to his side. "I take it that is a no."

"Damn right it's a no, you dick." She raised her head, looking a little better. "You can take that offer and shove it all the way up your ass."

"Lovely." Henwick frowned at her wording. Then he looked to Sax. "And what about you, good sir? That arm of yours looks painful. I would be happy to heal it for you in exchange for the location of the Seed."

"Tempting, but I'll be fine." The soldier continued to hold his battered limb.

"Oh, I think I can handle one broken arm." Digby grinned as he summoned another one of his echoes. This time, calling to his knight.

Henwick's frown deepened as motes of light swelled in the air to form a flickering image of himself from centuries ago. The echo simply held its hands out as a healing light passed to Sax. The soldier winced as his arm snapped back into place.

"I suppose I should thank you, Henwick." Digby laughed at the obvious discomfort on Henwick's face. "If you hadn't parted with your spark when you removed that shard of the Seed from your arm, I wouldn't have been able to gain this wonderful healing spell." A cackle rose in his throat. "I must say, I seem to be making better use of your soul than you did."

With that, it seemed like Digby might be able to keep Henwick talking for at least a few more minutes. Unfortunately, stalling wasn't going to get them out of there safely. There was a chance he could distract Henwick with a wraith summon long enough to drive past him, but the vehicle behind them would only give chase. The thought occurred to him to try to open his maw wide enough to eat the blasted thing, but swallowing a vehicle that big would surely disrupt his mana system. He'd learned that much after flooding his void with water a couple of days ago.

Even if they could lose the vehicle, Henwick would eventually Smite them off the face of the planet if they slowed down. Digby flicked his eyes around the area in hope of finding something that could help. All he needed was to find a reflective surface and buy time for them to get out of the jeep and reach it.

He still had his minion up in the sky; he could send it after his enemy and make a break for it. Though, he was pretty sure Henwick could kill the monster without breaking a sweat and he didn't want to waste such a powerful minion if their escape wasn't guaranteed.

Then again, there might be another option.

Digby glanced around the base, looking for something specific.

There!

A water tank sat on top of one of the buildings, if it was full, it might just provide them with a way out. He just needed a way to inform Parker of his plan. There wasn't room for error, so he couldn't risk trying to explain things on the fly. Then he remembered how Rebecca had helped him cheat at cards by using her finger to trace letters on the back of his neck without anyone noticing. It was worth a try.

Leaning forward on Parker's seat, he extended a claw to touch her back while continuing to taunt the foe before them.

"You know, Henwick. I got to know you fairly well when I encountered your spark. Or at least, I got to know the man that you used to be. I don't know what path you followed to diverge so much from your past, but you were a good person once. You even sacrificed yourself to save me." Digby traced a series of letters out onto Parker's back to spell out the words, 'drive when I say now.'

He was hoping she would respond with some kind of signal to tell him she understood, but all she did was wiggle in her seat like she was itchy. He was going to have to try harder.

"Don't you dare begin to think that you know me, Graves." Henwick clenched his fist, "This world will be better off when I am through with it."

"Oh please, I think I have you figured out." Digby traced out the same words on Parker's back, this time, getting an irritated grumble in response as she moved her shoulders to push him away.

"Do you not realize that I can simply Smite you where you stand?" Henwick thrust a finger in his direction.

"But you won't. If you wanted me dead, you would have done that already." Digby clawed at Parker's back even harder.

Henwick scoffed. "You really think you have things figured out, don't—"

His words were interrupted when Parker lurched forward.

"Ow! What the hell, man." She swatted at Digby's hand. "Why are you clawing at me?"

A look of confusion fell across Henwick's face, not because he didn't know what was going on, but more likely that they were such a mess at subterfuge.

"Oh, for crying out loud, Parker." Digby threw up his arms. "I am telling you to drive the car on my signal."

"Oh…" She sucked air in through her teeth. "What was the signal?"

A smug grin stretched across Henwick's face. "Yes, Graves, what was the signal?"

Digby placed a hand to his head as if giving up, only to fling the same hand out toward the man blocking their path a second later to send his wraith straight at him. "This!"

"Oh shit!" Parker pushed the jeep forward, finally realizing what he meant.

Digby held on, turning so that he could keep Henwick in his sights as they swerved around the man.

The high priest released a blast of light at the crimson form of the wraith, somehow obliterating the spell before it reached him. He followed it with a beam of life essence aimed straight at the jeep.

"Floor it." Digby braced against the back of Parker's seat and cast Absorb. He'd taken in a Smite blast easily while trapped in the Seed, so he assumed he could a second time. Then again, Henwick must have increased the balance of life essence in his mana since parting ways with his soul. The result set Digby's entire arm a flame with holy fire. "Holy hell!"

"After him!" Henwick waved to the Guardians waiting in the massive tank-like vehicle as he stepped out of its path.

Digby's arm fell limp at his side, the curse wiped from its tissue by the spillover of Henwick's Smite that he had been unable to contain. White flames threatened to spread to the rest of his body.

"You might want to do something about that." Sax leaned to the side to stay away from the fire.

"Do you think?" he snapped back sarcastically as he cast Forge to form a blade of his own blood within his shoulder. His entire arm popped off. Without any better options, he grabbed the limb with his remaining hand and hurled it at the front of the vehicle behind them. It hit the armored slats that covered its windshield, bursting into a fiery splatter.

"Turn here." Digby sat back down in his seat, using his Body Craft mutation to reform his arm.

"Got it." Parker cut the wheel, the jeep skidding around the corner of a building.

Tendrils of necrotic flesh burst from Digby's shoulder, coiling around a growing formation of bone.

"Oh gross." Sax leaned over the side of the jeep but refrained from losing his lunch.

"Deal with it." Digby flexed the new limb as fingers formed and layers of skin wrapped around them.

The vehicle behind them ignored the building that they had just passed and cut the corner early. Digby ducked low as the behemoth plowed through one side of the structure and out the other. Cinder blocks fell across the road like waves crashing on the beach, only to be crushed to dust beneath the enormous vehicle's tires.

"Does nothing stop that thing?" Parker glanced back over her shoulder, the wind whipping through her hair as the jeep sped through the base.

"I'm more worried about what Henwick has in store for us." Digby glanced up at the sky, expecting it to open up to release a beam of smiting power at any second. He just hoped Henwick couldn't target them with that level of the spell while they were moving.

Taking advantage of whatever time they had, he commanded his flying minion over his bond. The zombified revenant swooped down to land atop the building where he had seen the water tank earlier. The beast threw its body against the side of the tank, pushing as the jeep drove toward the building below it.

"That's it, keep pushing!" Digby tightened his grip on the back of Parker's seat.

"Push what?" She looked up just as one of the water tank's supports buckled, the entire thing tipping toward the road as they passed under it. "Oh." She ducked instinctively as the sound of creaking metal announced an incoming flood.

The jeep flew past just as the tank toppled off the roof. It crashed to the road, the vehicle behind them smashing into it. A wall of water exploded into the road, raining back down as the vehicle behind them barreled through.

"Was that supposed to stop them?" Sax looked back.

"No. That was just step one."

"What's step two?" Parker ducked as rain poured down on the road behind them to pool on the pavement.

"Step two is loop around and drive through that water."

Digby started climbing over the front seat toward the hood of the jeep.

"What?" She cocked her head to one side.

"The water will settle out by the time we make it back there. We can use it as a reflective surface for a Mirror Passage." He looked down at her with a crooked smile.

"Are you insane?" Her face contorted in astonishment.

"Of course not." He put his foot down on the dash. "This was your idea, remember? You used water to open a passage back when we were trapped in the Seed."

"Yeah, but we haven't tried sending a vehicle through with passengers on board it yet." Her voice climbed with each word. "We have no idea what will happen. Not to mention the jeep's tires will disrupt the reflection the moment they hit the water."

"That's why I'm climbing to the hood." Digby clawed his way onto the hood, the tattered ends of his coat flapping in the wind. "I'm going to hang off the front and cast Frost Touch to freeze the water, that way the tires won't interfere with the reflection."

"And I will repeat my previous question. Are you insane?" She stared at him, nearly cross-eyed. "I can't open a passage while you're freezing it. We'll have to loop around again. Which means you want me to drive across a sheet of ice while in a high-speed car chase."

"You've driven in worse conditions." Digby reached a foot down onto the front bumper making a point not to look down at the pavement rushing by below.

"I hate this plan." Sax pulled his seatbelt across his chest and buckled it in at his waist. "I definitely hate this plan."

"Too bad. It's happening." Digby opened his maw on the hood of the vehicle and cast Blood Forge to form a series of handles on the jeep, hoping they were strong enough to hold him. "Besides, it's better than waiting around for Henwick to smite us."

"I don't know, getting smited sounds like a better death than getting splattered all over the base when we crash. Wait, is it smoted? Smoten? Never mind." Sax braced against the dash of the jeep.

"Fine, we're doing this." Parker spun the wheel, the jeep drifting around a corner to take them back toward the area that Digby had coated with water.

The vehicle behind them plowed through another building. The three of them did their best to ignore it. Their one saving grace being that the behemoth chasing them and the jeep were matched for speed.

Parker cut the wheel again, taking them back toward the flooded area. Digby hoped there was enough water to create a solid flat surface.

"You better be right about this." Parker straightened the jeep out. "Because you're getting squashed first if I lose control."

"Was that really necessary to mention?" Digby glowered at her before leaning out over the road.

Holding onto one of his blood forged handles, he extended his body as far as possible. Vertigo swept through him as the road passed by. It felt like he was flying. He shook the sensation off and spread his claws out toward the ground as they reached the wet section of road.

A wave of blue light swept across the water as his claws grazed its surface, ice spreading out in front of them. The jeep wavered for a moment but Parker kept it straight. Digby prayed she wouldn't need to break while the jeep sped across the slick surface.

Seconds later, they reached dry ground again.

Digby snapped his head back to peek up over the hood, hoping that the vehicle behind them might have some trouble with the new terrain. He frowned when all it did was slide back and forth for a moment.

"Get back to your seat." Parker stared at him from her place at the wheel.

Digby climbed his way back, stepping on Sax and getting swatted at by Parker on his way. Dropping into his seat, he held on as Parker looped the jeep around again to take them back toward the ice.

"Oh shit!" Parker reached down and unbuckled her seatbelt. "We need to switch seats, I need to be in the back."

"What?" Digby jabbed a finger at the steering wheel. "But you're driving."

"I know, but I can't be in the front when we go through a passage." She looked back. "The spell cancels if I pass through. That's why I didn't want to do this in a vehicle. The jeep could get cut in half when the portal closes. Not to mention one of you could get caught in it or left behind, depending on how fast the passage snaps shut. It might not close on you guys if we hold hands or something but I don't want to test that theory now."

"Oh." Digby looked to Sax. "Quick, switch with her."

"Are you crazy?" He looked back at the Guardian's vehicle behind them. "That thing is gaining on us with every turn! We can't slow down."

"Then don't slow down." Digby slapped him on the shoulder to get him moving.

"We don't have a choice." Parker started to scoot herself into position to move without taking her foot off the gas.

"Jesus, I hate this plan." Sax unbuckled his seatbelt and shimmied his leg under her.

The jeep slowed for a moment as they switched, the vehicle behind them surging toward them. Digby stared up at the knight in the driver seat, his helmet showing through the slats in the vehicle's windshield. There was only about twenty feet between them.

"Move faster!" Digby snapped his eyes back to the pair in the front.

"I'm moving as fast as I can!" Sax yelled back as he slid into position, slamming his foot onto the gas.

"Okay." Parker knelt in the passenger seat, looking back to Digby. "Now you and I have to swap too."

They made the exchange far easier than changing drivers.

Digby slid into the passenger seat as Sax cut the wheel to avoid some of the debris that had been left behind by one of the many times that the vehicle behind them had plowed through a building.

"We're almost there!" Digby kept his eyes focused on the pavement as they turned onto the path that headed for the ice.

Of course, that was when the sky began to glow.

"That's not good." Digby raised his attention to the heavens realizing that the light wasn't above them. No, it was worse. It was directly over the ice. "Damn, I think Henwick figured out what we're doing. He's trying to Smite our exit."

"He must not be able to target us with his sky beam while we're moving this fast, so he's targeting where he knows we will be." Parker kept her eye focused on the ice ahead. "If he doesn't hit us, he'll at least destroy our exit before we reach it."

Digby swept his eyes across the base finding Henwick standing on a roof not too far away. "We've got no choice. Keep going."

"But he'll Smite us out of existence." Sax kept the jeep moving as the vehicle behind them slowed, clearly trying to avoid being hit with the blast.

"I have a plan. Sort of." Digby commanded his flying zombie into action.

"Is it an insane plan?" Parker asked.

"Sort of," he repeated as he willed his minion to fly into the space above the ice to stand between their exit and the spell.

Parker thrust a hand out toward the rapidly approaching ice. "I'm ready to open the passage."

"I still hate this plan." Sax floored it as the jeep sped into the space beneath the glowing sky.

Digby's minion flew overhead, its body silhouetted by a blast of life essence a few hundred feet wide. The jeep roared forward, traveling in the tiny island of safety provided by the creature's shadow. A second passed before the bloodstalker above ignited with holy fire, the buildings around them doing the same as the shadow keeping the jeep safe shrank.

"We're not going to make it." Parker struggled to ignore the destruction around them.

"Yes we are!" Digby raised a hand toward his burning minion.

Then, he activated his Body Craft mutation.

All at once, the revenant above them exploded with new limbs. Pouring hundreds of bodies worth of resources into his minion, Digby formed everything he could think of. Wings, arms, torsos, even the legs of a spider. It all sprouted from the revenant above, the new formations growing faster than Henwick's spell could burn them away. The revenant fell from the sky in a flaming mass of disjointed bodies just as the jeep reached the passage that Parker had formed in the ice.

"Everyone hang on!" She shut her eyes in concentration.

"Wait." Digby snapped his head to her. "Where did you use for the exit?" There was no way to know how they would be oriented when they emerged.

She didn't have time to answer.

The jeep simply dropped into the passage followed by the crunch of metal.

Digby grabbed hold of the seats in an attempt to stay in the jeep as everything became weightless. The last thing he saw was his flaming minion's unrecognizable corpse falling.

Then, the sky filled his view.

Confusion flooded his mind as the jeep flew straight up into the air. Snapping his head back and forth, he took in his surroundings. The entire rear of the jeep was gone, as if sliced clean through by a gigantic blade. Parker clung to anything she could, her foot dangling from where the back of her seat should have been.

Sax was still clinging, white knuckled, to the steering wheel, his foot still pressing the pedal to the floor. The jeep's engine roared uselessly. The world around them seemed to hold still as they climbed higher into the air.

The Las Vegas strip surrounded them. One of the largest

casinos welcomed their arrival. That was when Digby realized where they had come out.

A fountain?

Below was an expanse of water. It was a man-made feature meant to entertain the strip's visitors. To the side, a patrol of Heretics stood dumbfounded, watching from a sidewalk that lined the water's edge. Clearly, they didn't expect the artificial pond to produce a flying jeep. Digby made eye contact with one of them, feeling just as confused.

That was when gravity began to reassert its dominance.

"Time to bail!" Parker kicked herself clear of the jeep.

"Come on." Digby reached back and grabbed a hold of Sax's shirt before following Parker's lead and jumping away from the falling wreckage. Sax let out a yelp as they hit the water with a splash. Digby burst back up through the surface a moment later. "Seriously, Parker?"

"What?" She treaded water a few feet away. "The fountain at the Bellagio seemed like the only place to exit so that we wouldn't crash into something."

Digby grumbled as he swam past the sinking jeep to reach the edge of the water. "At least we survived."

"Are you all okay?" One of the Heretics that stood on the sidewalk rushed to him as he climbed out.

"I'm fine, we just had a run-in with Henwick is all." He swatted them away as they tried to help.

"Henwick?" They stopped short in fear of the man's name.

"Yes, I gave him a few things to think about." Digby stretched the truth despite the fact that they had just run away with their tail between their legs. "Someone fish Sax out of the water. If that encounter taught me anything, it's that we are not anywhere close to ready to fight a war."

Digby stormed off toward the casino.

"We need more power, and we need it now! We are on our own and no one is going to save us."

CHAPTER TWENTY-FIVE

"Are you sure this will work?" Harlow glanced back at the camera of a drone through which Becca watched.

Sitting in a dumpster a few blocks away with the drone's controls in her lap, Becca jiggled the sticks to give the illusion that the surveillance unit was shaking its head. "No, but we don't have the time or manpower to do much else."

"It will work fine." Ozzie looked up from his phone from the other side of the dumpster.

"What makes you think it won't work?" Leon leaned toward Becca from the middle of a pile of trash to look at Harlow through the drone's feed.

Harlow gave the camera a judgmental look. "Mostly cause the three of you are hiding in a rubbish bin. It's not a great look, you know?"

"She's got us there." Ozzie laughed.

"Everyone just shush," Becca grumbled at him, still angry that he'd stopped her from running out into the street to help Hawk when she'd seen him outside the Smithsonian.

It had been the right call, but still. How the hell else was she supposed to feel? Sure, it was daylight and the three of them couldn't have fought one squad of Guardians let alone two of those mana-powered aircraft. They would only be killed, or worse, captured. Leon and Ozzie had been forced to drag her away from the doors.

Fortunately, Hawk and Alex had somehow escaped using some sort of portal. The fact that things worked out in the end made her feel a little less angry about the situation. If something had happened to Hawk, she wasn't sure what she would do.

After that, they fled back to the office building where they had been hiding to sleep. Harlow took care of the rest of the preparations during the day.

The plan was to use Autem's tactics against them. Now that they knew that the empire was capturing revenants, all they had to do was hide amongst a swarm of the creatures and the Guardians would take them straight into their fortress. As long as they could avoid being analyzed, no one would notice a few vampires in the mix.

As much as Becca would have liked to have had another day to prepare, they had already set the plan into motion by killing six Guardians the night before. They had also set free the revs that the squad had captured. Now, a new team had already been sent out to regather the missing creatures. The task wouldn't take more than one night, meaning that the heist couldn't wait.

Fortunately, Harlow had a head start.

"I'm going to get into position. Give me a few minutes." The woman crept toward a building that housed a coffee shop, one of those national chains. Its only customers now was a swarm of revenants.

Harlow had been keeping tabs on their movements all day. It would be hours before Autem's team found them on their own, which was why they intended to bring the creatures to them instead. By using Harlow as bait, they could control where the swarm went, giving Becca and her vampire infiltration team the chance to· slip into the group before leading the revenants straight to the Guardians.

Of course, getting captured was just step one. They still needed someone on the inside to break them out.

That was Harlow's second job.

Playing the role of a random survivor running for her life from a swarm of bloodthirsty creatures, the Guardians would have no choice but to step in to save her. After all, the empire needed citizens and they weren't going to pass up a damsel in distress. Fortunately, Harlow had been wearing a mask the last time she'd fought Autem's forces, so they still had no idea what she looked like.

Convincing a squad of Guardians to take her into the fortress was the easy part. All Harlow had to do was cooperate. After that, they would probably give her a medical exam before releasing her into the refugee camps outside. She would just need to go stealth after her med screening and find a way to remain inside the fortress. Then she could make her way to wherever Autem was holding the revenants they'd captured and free Becca and the rest of team vampire.

Becca resisted the urge to chew her nails, partly because she didn't want to look nervous in front of the other vampires, but also because she was sitting in month-old trash.

There was still so much that could go wrong. For starters, someone might analyze them and blow the whole thing. Leon had insisted that he could keep that from happening but Becca wasn't so sure. Beyond that, they had no idea what the inside of the fortress was like. Then there was the simple possibility that Harlow couldn't break them free. If that happened, there would be no escape, and it was unlikely they could fight their way out.

Becca tried not to think about all the heist movies she'd seen where most of the team didn't make it out.

No, we can do this.

The plan was good and the team was ready.

Right?

Harlow was the Fools' last surviving operative. It was clear that the woman would stop at nothing to atone for letting

Henwick take the caretaker from the Fools in the first place, so she was determined not to fail.

That just left the vampire mercenaries.

Becca looked up from her drone console at Ozzie and Leon. She still didn't know why they were helping Harlow now that the world had lost a way to pay them. Despite that, they seemed committed to the cause. She lowered her eyes back to the drone's screen. They had proved loyal so far and it was too late to question them now, even if they had stopped her from running to her brother at the Smithsonian.

"Sorry about earlier." Leon looked at her from where he sat in the dumpster with his knees against his chest. He must have noticed the pained look on her face. "I know you wanted to help your brother."

"You're right, and I'm still pissed about it," she snapped back, sinking a little lower in the garbage that surrounded her, knowing that giving him an attitude wasn't going to help. "But I guess my friends have gotten stronger without me. They don't need me to rescue them."

Becca put a stop to the conversation by pulling out her phone and opening it to the notes app where she'd been tracking her stats. Under mana, she noted an increase of a few points from the two Guardians that she'd attacked the night before. It was an estimate, but it was better than nothing.

"Add five points," Leon commented, still watching her.

"Five?" She looked up from her phone.

"That's about what you get from a proper feeding." He nodded. "Your mana system can't take in all of a person's spark, but it stretches a little before releasing everything that's leftover. The result adds about five points to your mana. The best way to keep track is to add five points for every four kills. Switch to four points every fifth kill. That will keep you accurate for the most part."

She made the edit.

MP: 424

As far as how much of that total she had left, she could feel that her mana pool was half full. Despite feeding the night before and filling her MP to its max, she had lost so much when she'd walked through those stupid wards that Autem had set up. Her body had just started spending mana to keep her from dying. On top of that, she'd barely absorbed any during the day.

Becca sighed then scrolled down to her shadecraft ability. Now that she understood her class more, she was pretty sure she could use it to create things other than bats. The only requirement was that, like her Banshee ability, she needed her intent to always be about causing fear. That was what a nightmare class vampire did, apparently. She couldn't help but wonder what else she could do. Then again, with only half her mana remaining, she didn't dare experiment.

Her thoughts were interrupted by Harlow's voice. "I'm in position. I'm going to try to get the revenants' attention."

Becca glanced back at the drone's screen as the unit followed the woman on autopilot. Harlow crept toward the broken windows in the front of the coffee shop.

"Be ready to climb out of that dumpster when I bring the swarm your way."

"We will be." Becca put her phone away and tapped the drone to take it off follow mode to get a better look at the two dozen revenants wandering the floor of the coffee shop, adding one last, "Be careful."

"Careful, yes, that's what this plan is. I'm pretty sure we've been flying by the seat of our pants for a time now." Harlow stood in the street just outside the shop, wearing a pair of jeans and a tank top. She was completely unarmed to play her role of terrified survivor. She was right, being careful was a luxury that they no longer had.

"This will work," Becca told herself.

Harlow held her hands up and gave them a wave. "Oi!"

Every revenant in the coffee shop turned toward her in an instant.

Harlow turned and ran. "Heads up! I'm coming in hot!"

The sound of revenants chattering behind her was audible over the drone's camera as Becca set it down in an alley. The unit had served its purpose, and they had no use for it at this point.

Leon was moving before anyone had time to respond, tossing the dumpster lid open and stepping on Ozzie on his way out.

"Hey, watch it," the other mercenary complained as he hopped out behind him.

Becca ditched the drone console and climbed out as well, dropping down on the pavement. She grimaced as she peeled a piece of garbage from her leg. It wasn't long before she heard the stampede that was coming.

Peeking out of the alleyway, Becca found Harlow running at a full sprint a few hundred feet away. Behind her were over twenty revenants. Becca fought the urge to duck back into the dumpster and hide from the oncoming swarm. Then she reminded herself that she wasn't human. The fears that she'd developed since leaving her apartment a month ago barely had meaning anymore.

"Can Harlow really outrun those revs long enough?" She looked back to Ozzie.

He just laughed. "She'll be fine."

Becca turned back to the approaching swarm, impressed by the woman's stamina. The Fools must have trained Harlow well.

"Follow my lead." Becca got ready to run. "Make sure to mix into the middle of the group so no one can analyze you."

"Got it." Ozzie jogged in place for a few seconds before Harlow blew past them.

"Now." Becca pushed off toward the group, spending a few points of mana for a burst of speed to catch up.

The sound of revenants screeching sent shivers down her spine. She forced herself forward regardless, shutting down her fears as she slipped into the group. Ozzie and Leon mixed into the swarm behind her.

Looking to her side, Becca stared at one of the revenants as it sprinted after the prey in front of them. It was surreal to be surrounded by such dangerous creatures, yet running as one of them, chasing one of her allies. It was like becoming one with a pack of wolves hunting a rabbit. For a second, her mouth started to water. She shook off the instinct, reminding herself that Harlow wasn't food.

"Friend, not food." Becca cringed as she spoke.

"Try to keep up." Leon passed on her left.

Becca refocused on the chase, realizing that she was falling behind the rest of the swarm. The revenants must have been using their mana to try to catch up to the pleasant-smelling treat up ahead.

"Friend, not food," Becca reminded herself, still unsure how Harlow was keeping pace ahead of the group of mana-enhanced predators. The short woman looked like she could go all night. Despite that, they had a destination in mind and it wasn't far.

Becca burned a few more points of mana as they headed toward where they last saw the squad of Guardians and prepared to put on the performance of a lifetime.

Harlow was already in character.

The small but fast woman let out a desperate scream as she rounded a corner, slowing so that the creatures behind her could catch up a little. Becca watched in horror as clawed hands swiped at her back, missing by just a few inches. She was cutting it too close to sell the performance. All it would take was for Harlow to stumble and she would be dead. Becca could only imagine how terrifying it must have been for the woman.

Harlow let out another cry for help, her words barely under-standable over gasps for air. That was when a bullet slammed into the head of the revenant directly in front of Becca.

"Jesus, fu—" she started to shout in shock. Becca snapped her mouth shut again when Harlow turned back to give her a look that said, 'Why the hell are you talking, you are supposed to be a mindless predator.' Becca fought the urge to say anything else in apology, instead adding a nonsensical, "Screeeeeee!"

Ozzie followed with a weird chitter that sounded entirely too much like laughter. He shut his mouth when a bullet clipped his shoulder. That, of course, caused Leon to start laughing. He covered by layering on another awkward, "Screeee!"

Harlow performed the hardest eye roll that Becca had ever seen before continuing her desperate screaming. She stopped as a pair of Guardians stepped out to grab her. At the same time, another two men threw a set of wards out to stop the swarm. The metallic rods tumbled through the air for a second before snapping into position in a straight line that cut through the street.

One of the revenants found itself on the other side of the wards when they went up as the rest skidded to a stop, unable to cross the line. The lone creature that had retained its freedom continued its pursuit, reaching for Harlow just before a Guardian launched a fireball into its face. The creature fell backward, screaming. The same Guardian followed the attack with an icicle that pinned the rev to the ground. Becca gulped, realizing that the spell had cracked the pavement.

There was no way to know what level the men were, but it was safe to say that they were higher than the Guardians that she had helped kill the night before. Autem had probably sent out a stronger team to make sure the same thing didn't happen twice.

Harlow kept her performance going as she clung to one of the Guardians while simultaneously trying to get away from the revenants as if she didn't understand that the wards would stop them from attacking. Another pair of men threw more warding rods into the air behind them to make sure the swarm didn't have anywhere to escape.

Becca struggled not to speak out loud, cursing her years of isolation for giving her the habit of constantly talking to herself. The night was going to be harder than she thought. Glancing at the warding rods, she prayed they were a different type from the ones that she had run into before. Either way, she didn't want to test them.

"Calm down." The Guardian holding Harlow dropped to one knee as she collapsed in mock exhaustion. "You're safe now. Those creatures can't cross the line."

Another squad member held a flask out. "Here, drink some water."

Becca eyed the flask. Obviously, they had purified it, but they made no effort to explain that to Harlow. It was probably easier to offer a desperate woman some water than try to explain magic. Also, giving her a drink from a purified flask would cleanse the curse if she'd been bitten. That way, they didn't need to point a weapon at her and demand to examine her.

It was strangely humane behavior for Autem's people, but it made sense. Harlow was a potential citizen of the empire, which would grant her better treatment. For any ordinary person running for her life, the Guardians would appear to be her savior. All Autem had to do was be nice and they would have a loyal citizen for life. Becca frowned. It was quite devious, knowing the truth of everything Autem had done in pursuit of the future they were trying to build.

Harlow reached for the flask and drank without hesitation, gulping down the water like she had just run a marathon. She even choked at the end, coughing as she handed the flask back.

The revenants chittered quietly in their makeshift holding pen, unable to pass the warding rods. Becca debated wandering to the edge of the group to check out the runes on the warding rods but that would only make it easier for her to be analyzed. It was better to go all in with the plan.

The guardians helped Harlow back to her feet and away from the revenants. They asked her some simple questions. Who she was? Where she was from? If there was anyone else with her? Things like that. She barely answered them, just giving a word or two in response. Other than that, she kept her mouth shut.

To the Guardians, it must have looked like she was still dealing with the night's trauma. Though, to Becca, it just seemed like she was trying not to say anything that would blow her cover. Being a combat operative, espionage wasn't her wheelhouse. The less she said, the better. She could play the role of a frightened survivor, but beyond that, she might not have been good at coming up with answers on the spot.

While the Guardians spoke to Harlow, another two walked around the group of trapped revenants. Becca counted twenty-two of the creatures stuck in the wards with her. Adding her team, it made twenty-five. Ozzie tried to stay low since his considerable size made it easy to spot him in a crowd. Keeping him hidden all night was going to be a difficult task.

Becca stepped to the side, keeping herself behind one of the revenants to avoid the gaze of one of the men outside the wards. She ducked a little as the other man walked around the other side, trying to stay hidden from two different angles. For a moment, one of them looked right at her but Leon pushed another revenant into her to keep her hidden.

One of the Guardians, clearly the knight that was in charge, called out from further away. "You got any uncommon in there?"

"Still checking," one of the men circling the swarm answered back.

"What about that big one?" The Guardian on the other side pointed toward Ozzie. "Could that one be evolved?"

Both of the men stared into the group trying to get a good look at the oversized vampire.

Damn it, why does he have to be so big? Becca growled, not bothering to hide the sound since it only made her sound more feral.

She tried to nudge one of the revenants toward Ozzie from one side while Leon did the same on the other. The Guardians circled them like sharks, not giving up easily. It took a solid minute of trying before they admitted defeat.

"Can't get a good look with them all grouped up. But the big one doesn't seem to be behaving any different."

Becca half expected the knight to demand they keep trying but he just nodded and headed over to Harlow. He spoke to her for a minute or so with her nodding or shaking her head every now and then. After that, he gestured toward a building. It was the same one where Becca had attacked the squad the night before. One of the Guardians led Harlow inside, probably to make her feel safe while they waited for transport.

Becca and the rest of her team waited patiently within the crowd of revenants, doing their best to mimic their behaviors. A few minutes later, the knight in charge came back out of the building.

So far, so good, Becca thought, making sure she didn't accidentally say it out loud. She regretted the thought the moment she had it.

"Alright, get out of the way." The knight walked straight for them, stopping at the edge of the wards and holding a hand out to one of his men. The Guardian next to him handed him a pistol. "I know none of you monsters understand anything, but I'm sure you'll understand this."

He simply pointed the gun at one of the revenants standing between Ozzie and him and pumped a round into the creature's chest. The revenant shrieked and ran to the other side of the wards to get out of the line of fire.

Shit! Becca's mind raced as she realized the Guardians weren't going to give up without analyzing them. They were going to get a look at Ozzie one way or another.

That was when something strange happened.

Despite the danger, the revenants held their ground. Some even moved to keep Ozzie hidden. It was almost as if they were actively trying to help. Becca furrowed her brow.

That's impossible.

Then she noticed Leon standing beside her with his eyes shut tight in concentration. The revenants continued to keep Ozzie hidden.

Is he controlling them?

"For God's sake." The knight unloaded the pistol into the group, getting several shrieks from the revenants in response.

A round punched into Leon's shoulder, but he kept his eyes closed and barely flinched. A few of the revenants began to move away, but the rest continued to block the view.

"Fine." The knight handed the pistol back. "Just make sure processing checks all of them."

Becca let out a quiet sigh of relief. They had dodged a bullet for now. Well, figuratively, at least. Leon's shoulder stitched itself back together.

After that, the Guardians began setting up another area of wards in the street. Becca listened in on their orders. Apparently, they didn't want a repeat of what happened last night and the captured swarm was big enough to merit immediate transport. They had radioed for something called an owl.

That must be what they call those new mana-powered aircraft.

Becca filed that detail away for later. They were sticking to the pattern of using bird names for things. According to what she could overhear, the transport would be there soon.

At least we won't have to wait around for long.

Becca turned her attention back to Leon to watch as he occasionally closed his eyes. The group of revenants always responded by moving in a way that kept them hidden.

I am going to need to ask him about that. Becca eyed him. Being able to control revenants was certainly something she would have wanted to know about.

If the ability was anything like Digby's Control Undead spell, then they might be able to do a lot more damage to Autem. If the Guardians brought them to a holding area with more revs, they could potentially use the creatures to attack the city that night. An army of bloodthirsty revenants could certainly act as one hell of a diversion while they made off with the caretaker. It would be just like their attack on Skyline's base. They could hit hard and take the place by surprise.

Becca glanced around, taking a count of how many of the

creatures were listening to whatever commands Leon was putting out. It was only about half.

Maybe there's a limitation?

Before she could consider the thought further, a shuddering hum echoed down the street to announce the arrival of the owl that they were waiting for. The aircraft drifted in to hover over-head while shining a light down on the swarm. Becca just hoped they didn't have the ability to analyze them from the inside.

Then she saw something worse.

The knight.

No! Becca stared up as the squad leader that had been shooting at them earlier, leaned out of one of the windows of the third floor of the building beside them with a pair of binoculars. From there, he could see everything. There was no place to hide.

He could see all of them.

Becca snapped her head to Leon, hoping he had something else up his sleeve. Instead, she found him standing next to Ozzie, both of them staring up at the knight in defiance. The message was clear. There was nothing they could do to keep up the act.

The mission had barely even started, and their cover was already blown.

All they could do was fight their way out.

CHAPTER TWENTY-SIX

"Shit!" Becca tensed every muscle in her body, cursing the fact that she only had half her mana left. The Guardians around them were stronger than the ones they'd faced before, and the wards around them may or may not have been lethal. Not to mention there was a magic-fueled warship hovering directly above them.

There was no way out.

The knight hanging out the window above stared down at Ozzie, finally getting a good enough look at him to analyze the oversized vampire. Any second, he would call out orders to kill or capture them. Becca just hoped they could use the revenants around them as cover.

Then, there was nothing.

Becca watched in shock as the knight just slid back inside without another word. She glanced back to the two mercenaries trapped beside her, getting a slight nod in return that meant, 'Don't worry.'

What just happened?

Becca remained confused, even as the owl lowered itself down to the street and opened the detachable cargo hold on the back. The Guardians proceeded to usher the revenants into a narrow section of warding rods that they had set up earlier. It led straight into the craft's cargo area. Behind them, one of the men jabbed any stragglers with a cattle prod.

Becca made sure to stay in the middle of the swarm as they moved, feeling a horrible sense of foreboding as she stepped into the metal crate. Every instinct she had practically screamed at her to run. Instead, she turned back to watch as the last of the revenants joined her. The doors were locked shut as soon as they were inside, leaving her in the dark, standing shoulder to shoulder with bloodthirsty beasts.

Herself included.

The occasional flashlight shined in through one of the tiny windows that ran along the compartment's side. She debated pushing on her senses to see a little better in the dark but opted to save what little mana she had. Eventually, the men outside boarded the owl's passenger compartment in front of the detachable cargo hold.

"Leon?" Becca held a hand out in the direction that she thought the slender vampire was.

A revenant screeched back as one of her fingers poked into its pointy ears.

"Oh, shut it, I wasn't talking to you." She groaned, getting sick of being surrounded by the creatures.

"I'm over here." Leon's voice came from a few steps away.

"Leon?" Ozzie's voice followed, coming from the other end of the compartment.

"Oz?" Leon responded.

"Yeah, where are you?"

"Over here?"

"Well, get over here."

"No, you get over here?"

"I'm stuck in the corner. So work your scrawny ass through the crowd." Ozzie sounded frustrated.

"It's not my fault you're huge." Leon jabbed back as he bumped into Becca's side.

"Hey, watch what you're grabbing, Casanova." She swatted a hand away from her rear.

"That wasn't me."

"Then what was—"

A revenant behind her cut her off with a screech, apparently not appreciating having its hand swatted at. Another rev cried out from Ozzie's side of the compartment.

"Fuck, sorry." Ozzie sounded worried.

"What did you do?" Leon asked in an accusatory tone.

"I stepped on a foot."

A moment went by when none of them spoke. Becca half expected the creatures to turn hostile, an image of fighting twenty-two active revenants in a dark, enclosed space passed through her head.

Eventually, Ozzie broke the tension. "Okay, I think we're good."

Becca relaxed as much as she could, given the situation. "Let's all just stay where we are."

"Seriously?" Ozzie's tone fell a little. "But I'm all the way over here."

"Deal with it," Leon answered back. "The ride can't possibly be that long. Just make friends with the revs over there."

"Fine," Ozzie groaned back, sounding like a very large vampiric child.

Becca leaned closer to Leon, grateful to have at least one side that wasn't pressed against a revenant.

"Now who's watching what they're grabbing?" He chuckled as she realized she had just placed a hand against his abdomen.

She rolled her eyes at the fact that he'd torn his shirt to help blend in with the revenants, leaving his midriff bare. Though, she was pretty sure he was just showing off his abs. "You know you could wear more clothes?"

"I'm just trying to look the part." He stood by the window. "And we haven't been caught yet, have we?"

"Yes, what was up with that?" She stared in his direction as her eyes adjusted to the dark. "That knight looked right at us."

"It's like Harlow said. The caretaker is on our side," he answered back. "They must have intercepted and swapped the analysis notification on that knight's HUD."

"Seriously? The caretaker can do that?" Becca leaned her head to the side.

"From what I know, Autem installed our caretaker into the Guardian Core, so from inside the system, they can probably do a lot of things. I'm sure that Henwick has significantly limited the caretaker's access, but it's impossible to fully control an entity like that and still have it perform its role in managing their magic system." Leon stared off into the middle distance. "It's like when the caretaker sent us the files on the empire's capital."

"So we should be safe if we get analyzed, then?" Becca asked.

"Yes, but I would emphasize the 'should' part of that." He held up air quotes around the word. "The caretaker isn't perfect, and they may not be able to take the risk to intervene as often as we would like. There is a good chance they will get caught if they do too much, and Henwick is sure to make them regret it if that happens. As it is, he has to have some way of threatening the caretaker to get them to cooperate at all. So don't count on assistance if you can help it."

"What about you, then?" She eyed him suspiciously. "I've seen people control enough monsters to recognize when someone is doing it right in front of me."

"Oh, so you noticed that?" Leon scratched at the back of his head. "I might, kind of, have a connection to the revenants."

Becca slapped him in the stomach with the back of her hand. "Why the hell didn't you mention that before? And how do I learn to do it too? If we can control enough of them, we can unleash them inside Autem's fortress."

"Easy now." He shielded his stomach. "It's not that simple."

"Then explain it." She glowered at him.

"Alright." He deflated. "First of all, calling what I do control is an over-exaggeration. I can call the revs toward or away from me, but only a few will actually listen. That's how I was getting them to keep us hidden. Beyond that I can soothe the hostile ones sometimes, and I can whip them into a frenzy too. But that's it, so it's not that reliable."

"Okay, so teach me how to do it and we can combine our efforts. We could still try to set them loose on Autem's base."

"You can't learn to do it." He grew quiet, clearly hiding something.

"Why?" She leaned back again.

"Because I, sort of, created the first of the revenants." He cringed.

"What?" Her mouth fell open.

"It wasn't my fault." He held up his hands in defense.

"Oh my god." Becca slapped a hand to her face, dragging it back down slowly. "You're just like Digby. What did you do, bite some guy and run away?"

"No." He recoiled as if the idea was unthinkable. "I was forced to. I spent a few years in a prison camp. I can't tell you how many experiments I endured. I don't even know how many revenants I put in the world before I escaped. But because of that, I have a slight connection with most of the revenants out there today since the original curse came from me."

"When did Autem have a prison camp?"

He simply shook his head to indicate that it wasn't Autem.

"Oh." Becca closed her mouth, remembering something he said a few nights before while he was training her.

I killed a lot of Nazis.

"Yeah." He frowned. "I didn't kill an entire base worth of fascists for no reason. I tried to destroy the creatures that I had been forced to create. I guess I didn't get them all."

Becca sighed, feeling sorry for bringing it up. It clearly wasn't something he wanted to talk about, but it explained why he was so committed to helping Harlow while not being a member of the Fools himself. She glanced back to where Ozzie was standing on the other end of the compartment. He must have been going along with things just to help his friend.

Becca turned back to Leon. "I'm sorry you went through that."

"I'm sorry the world went through that." He gestured to the revenants around him. "And I'm sorry for this."

"Hey." Becca jabbed a finger against his chest. "Don't get all depressed. This isn't your fault. It's Henwick's. He spread all this on purpose. If anyone should be blamed, it's him."

"I know."

The craft lurched to the side, pressing Becca against the revenant beside her and putting an end to the conversation.

"Please return your seats and return tray tables back to their original positions," Ozzie announced from his end of the compartment. "We're approaching our destination."

Becca slipped past a pair of revenants to press herself against the tiny window closest to her as the fortress filled her view.

Her heart began to race.

It was so much larger up close.

The sight reinforced the thought that had been hanging in the back of her mind for the last few days.

This plan is insane.

CHAPTER TWENTY-SEVEN

"I don't know if we can do this." Becca stared out the window as the aircraft flew along the outside of Autem's fortress.

"We don't have a choice," Leon added. "It's way too late to back out."

The craft tilted, giving them a view of the refugee camp that filled the ground below. The sight of lights and patrols sent a shiver down Becca's spine. It was so much more than a refugee camp; it was a city.

There must have been a few hundred Guardians stationed on the ground, and that was just what Autem had keeping watch at night. Taking in as many details as she could before the craft leveled out, she noted a temporary barrier standing a hundred feet out from the base of the fortress's outer wall.

Within that, there were signs of habitation in almost every building. Despite the night, many of the empire's new citizenry could be seen going about their business outside in the streets. There were armed Guardians everywhere to keep them safe, just in case a nightflyer or something passed the temporary barrier that surrounded the enormous camp. It must have been a relief to the people down there not to have to worry about their survival all the time.

In a way, it seemed peaceful. Though, there was a dark side to the safety. Guardians patrolling the streets did far more than that. They send a message that they were in charge and could not be challenged. They represented a loss of freedom entirely in exchange for permanent martial law. That was the price of safety.

Sure, back in Vegas, they had patrols, but the difference was that magic was not kept from the people. It would never become a tool to control others with. It would just become a normal part of everyday life.

Aside from that, the community was similar to what they were trying to build in Vegas. Only, Autem's city was much larger, and further along. There must have been thousands of survivors down there, all helping to build the empire that had saved them from the world outside. The kicker was that they probably didn't know that they were helping the same people that destroyed the world in the first place.

From high above, Becca could make out numerous buildings that had been converted to places of worship. Obviously, Autem's nine angels were meant to become the primary focus, and judging from Autem's previous actions, participation was not going to be optional. Though, with the warding that the buildings must have had, they would also double as shelters in case the revenants outside ever became a problem.

Some of the areas below were uninhabited, with construction equipment out in full force. It looked like they were demolishing sections of the city. Becca arched an eyebrow, unsure why they would destroy perfectly good structures. Perhaps they had another plan for those spaces.

That was all she was able to see before the owl they rode in leveled out and began to slow. The aircraft climbed at the same time until it reached one of the many openings that lined the wall halfway up. For a moment, Becca thought they might fly straight through to the other side, but instead, the craft came to a stop within some kind of hangar.

Their assumptions had been right. The wall did have an interior.

The opening that the owl had passed through was unfinished, with fixtures on the top and bottom that made it clear that gates would eventually be installed. Inside, sections of the wall lacked any kind of formal covering, leaving the support structure beneath exposed.

She had been right again. Autem was building too fast to complete anything. They were getting the place operational before putting on any of the polish.

The owl rotated, giving her a look at a row of identical aircraft, five deep. She sucked in a breath.

"Shit."

"What?" Leon leaned closer to the window.

"I just did the math." She pointed at the five aircraft sitting in a row. "There were several more docking bays like this one on the side of the wall. If they have the same amount of these owl things in each, then they probably have a whole fleet of these mana-powered aircraft."

"That would be bad." Leon tapped on the glass with one finger.

Becca nodded. "Even if we succeed in stealing the caretaker and damaging the Guardian Core's functionality, they'll still have this armada."

"All the more reason that we need to make it out of here." He dropped his hand from the window. "You need to tell that zombie friend of yours what's coming his way. Plus, I don't think any of us signed up for a suicide mission."

"Yeah." She gave him an awkward laugh, knowing that was exactly what they had signed up for.

Before she had time to dwell on their chances of success, the compartment they were in dropped suddenly, only to stop an instant later. A metallic sound came from the back, as if something had clamped onto the outside. The entire cargo section pulled away from the craft.

"I think we just got loaded onto some sort of internal transport." She pressed herself against the glass, getting a glimpse of some kind of drone that had attached itself to the side of the compartment near the front, almost like a forklift. There must have been more transport machinery positioned around the compartment to handle the weight. Judging by the way the drone systems moved in unison, they must have been piloted by AI.

Becca couldn't help but wonder if Autem's caretaker had any control over the system. If so, there was a chance it could bring them someplace that they could sneak inside easily. Her hopes fell when it brought them through a wide metal door and set the cargo compartment down in a large bay at the end of a row of identical containers. Looking through the windows, she could make out more revenants inside the others.

Becca frowned. Either the caretaker couldn't control all of Autem's systems, or it just wasn't able to help them right now.

That was when Leon gasped.

"What?" She snapped her eyes to him as he looked around the compartment.

"Do you feel that?"

She was about to ask what, again, when she realized what he meant. It was subtle, but there was something wrong inside of her. Even worse, it was growing. It was the same feeling she had during the day when her body had absorbed too much life essence.

"What is that?" She looked around as well, unsure when it had started.

"I think it was when we were brought into this room." He flexed his hand before flicking it back and forth, clearly testing his reaction speed. "This place is warded."

"Shit." Becca looked out the window at an angle, finding a strip of metal bolted to the door they had been brought through. "But I thought we couldn't enter without being invited?"

"We can if we're captured." He frowned. "Taking away our autonomy counts as an invite. This ward must be messing with the amount of life essence in the ambient mana to keep the revenants dormant. You won't be absorbing much MP until we get out of here."

Becca groaned, still feeling that her mana was only half full. "I wonder what they want with all these revenants and why they created a space like this to hold them."

"I'm pretty sure we're about to find out." Leon pressed a finger to the window to point out a group of men in gray jumpsuits approaching one of the other containers. They were some kind of work crew.

From the tiny window, Becca watched them unload one of the containers at the far end of the space. The men worked like they had already performed the process hundreds of times. First, they opened the doors, then they threw up some warding rods to make sure none of the revs got out. After that, they locked a metal collar around the neck of each revenant and hooked it to a pole so they could lead each creature to a chain that hung from a track. The track ran along the ceiling toward another large door. Once the workers had one of the revenants secured, they would hit a button to move the track above, forcing the creature to walk toward the door. Then, they moved on to the next.

From what she could tell, none of the men were Guardians, yet none of them seemed worried to be handling such dangerous creatures. There was a squad of armored men further away for backup, but that was it. In the end, the workers just seemed like they were working a shift the same as any factory employee. They took breaks and laughed at the occasional joke. They even poked fun of one of their own who must have been new for being overly careful.

They were just doing a job.

It was nearly morning by the time the unloading crew got to

the container that Becca was hiding in. She stared at the doors of the compartment, feeling unprepared with the wards screwing up her mana system. The weakness that plagued her during the day had returned, and she couldn't use her abilities even if she wanted to.

Her heart thumped as the doors at the back of the container popped open, light shining in from the overhead flood lamps that filled the room beyond. Ozzie was one of the first that the men grabbed. For a moment, she worried that he might do something to give them away. To her surprise, he followed the lead of the revenants that had been taken before him, weakly snapping at a man when he got close. The workers barely reacted.

The lack of concern would probably work in their favor. With the unloading crews' lack of concern, it was unlikely that any of the Guardians nearby would analyze them. Especially when considering the fact that the team that had captured them had probably filed an inventory of their captives. There was no need to check after that. With so many revenants to process, there wasn't time either. Instead, the workers just kept their heads down and did their job.

Ozzie was collared and locked to the track above in under a minute. The chain pulled him along for a few feet. The vampire gave an annoyed hiss in one of the worker's directions but complied after that. The men went back to the cargo container for the next revenant as soon as he was secure.

It wasn't long before it was Becca's turn.

I am not going to like this.

She resisted the urge to recoil as a wire slipped over her head, despite her heart racing as it tightened around her throat. It was awful. After being locked in an apartment for a good portion of her life, she had finally found freedom. She never wanted to be trapped again.

A collar snapped shut around her neck, making her feel like nothing more than livestock. Becca forced herself to ignore it. Now wasn't the time to freak out. Technically, everything was still going according to plan, and right now she needed to stay calm and get as much information as she could.

Keeping up her performance as a mindless beast, she took in every detail now that she was out of the cargo compartment. The first thing she made note of was the squad of Guardians standing nearby to keep watch. They were armed, some with swords and others with rifles. One was sure to be an enchanter to cleanse a bite if the workers got cursed.

The next thing she noticed was that the workers each wore a ring. They were nothing like the chunky ones emblazoned with Autem's crest that the Guardians wore. No, the workers wore simple gold bands with minimal engravings. There must have been something different about them.

Maybe some kind of identification or tracking system.

It made sense. The Guardian Core could be used for a lot more than just accessing magic. Becca was reminded of the mental conditioning that Skyline's people had been subjected to. It had made them more aggressive while increasing their obedience to their superiors. The rings the workers wore might have done the same thing, but in a way that helped keep the citizens in line.

Becca filed the detail away along with all the other horrifying things that she'd learned about life in the empire. Then she shifted her focus to the room around her. It was huge. So large that she had trouble believing that it was inside the wall that Autem was building. The room was over one hundred feet wide and a couple hundred long. It felt like a warehouse.

The track above advanced, pulling on the chain attached to Becca's collar. It yanked her toward the door at the far end. Passing through into the next space, she found even more horrors. Livestock cages lined one wall, each filled with around a hundred revenants. The containment areas weren't anything special, just chain link holding pens with a basic lock.

The other side of the space held larger, more secure containment cells. They reminded her of the cages she'd seen in movies, the kind of thing built to contain dinosaurs. The claws of a few revenant bloodstalkers poked through a small, barred window in the front.

It was all horrifying enough, but what was happening at the end of the space was far worse. Rows of revenants stood, their arms chained to large steel poles on either side, their legs locked into heavy cuffs, and their mouths covered by some kind of mask. Whatever clothes that they may have been wearing when they had been captured had been stripped away. People in lab coats performed a variety of tests and procedures. Some of the creatures had tubes running from their masks to bags of blood, as if they were being fed.

No. Not fed. Evolved.

Many of the creatures had developed the wings of a night-flyer. Becca had always assumed that the creatures evolved similarly to zombies, but she'd never found out what determined their path since they consumed something other than flesh. Autem must have figured out the key and were intentionally pushing them toward the outcomes they wanted.

In addition to the controlled evolutions, the revenants also had a number of metal strips screwed directly into their bodies. Some were attached to the sides of their heads and drilled right into their skulls. Another segment ran down the center of their sternum, with more wrapping around their ribcage.

The strips of metal didn't have any engravings on them, instead, they seemed to function as attachment points for other things. It was like some sort of modular system with slotted ridges. Looking into one of the other cages, Becca found a group of the creatures adorned with engraved plates connected to the same parts of their bodies that the metal strips had been drilled into.

She gasped when she realized they were standing in formation.

They're building an army.

It was a horde, just like one Digby had used, except they were controlled somehow by the engravings on their armor. That was why Henwick hijacked the curse. Becca had assumed that they had preferred revenants over zombies because they had a clear weakness and that most could be kept away with wards, but it was so much more.

They could actually control them.

Becca nearly threw up, realizing that each of the revenants in the room used to be a person. A person that had been killed by a curse that Autem had spread on purpose. The curse had never been just about culling the world's population down to one Autem could control. It had always been about enslaving them. It was about converting the people that they didn't want into an expendable force of drones to ensure they could keep their citizens safe from the horrors that they had created. It was about securing their rule over the world that they planned to build.

Becca might have been a bloodthirsty monster that ate people's souls, but she wasn't the only monster that the world had to offer. Henwick had crossed every line imaginable. With what he had done now, could he even be called human?

How could he have been twisted into something so depraved?

Despite the revelation, Becca kept up her act, blending in with the rest of the revenants as she was released from the chain attached to her collar and pushed into one of the chain-link holding pens. The workers did the same with dozens more of the creatures, packing them in, shoulder to shoulder. Ozzie and Leon gravitated toward her once they were free to roam, each making sure not to arouse suspicion.

Fortunately, there were no guards posted nearby other than the one squad that was watching the workers. There weren't any security cameras either. The fact that the place was still under construction had worked out in their favor. They probably didn't have a system installed yet.

"Do you guys realize what's going on here?" Leon asked, keeping his voice to a whisper.

"You mean that fucked up Frankenstein shit?" Ozzie gave

them both a look that made it clear the horror of what they'd witnessed had sunk in.

"Yeah, they're building an army." Becca gave a slight nod, trying not to make it obvious that they were communicating. "An army big enough to wipe everyone back in Vegas out of existence."

"Okay, just making sure I wasn't the only one horrified by it all." Leon let out a mock sigh, keeping his head low.

"All I can say is Harlow better get us out of here before someone tries to chain me to a couple of poles and take my pants." Ozzie angled his head toward the revenants that were being processed not far away.

"Yes, I can't say I'm opposed to being chained up in the nude, but these aren't exactly the preferred circumstances." Leon shook his head.

"Can Harlow really get to us?" Becca looked at them, struggling to see the hope in the situation.

"Oh yeah." Ozzie turned back to look in the direction where they had come from. "She'll get to us. Even if she has to kill everyone on the way here."

Becca tried to relax only for a new feeling of dread to roll through her stomach. "I just hope everyone back home doesn't do anything stupid. They have no idea how ready for war Autem is. If Henwick finds out where they are, there will be nothing left."

"I'm sure your necromancer friend will be careful." Leon gave her a slight smile, clearly trying to reassure her. "What's the worst thing he could do?"

Becca winced as he practically doomed them with that last question.

"With Digby, anything's possible."

CHAPTER TWENTY-EIGHT

Digby pressed pause on a remote control that Alex had shown him how to operate the night before. A still image of Hans Gruber falling from a window filled the screen in front of him.

After Hawk showed him what the lighter he'd found was capable of, he'd insisted on watching the movie that had bestowed such a power. After being forced to run from Henwick like a coward, he needed the distraction. Alex had complied excitedly, with he and Hawk joining for a viewing in one of the casino's function halls.

Of course, both Alex and Hawk had fallen asleep hours ago, the pair drooling on the arms of a sofa nearby as the morning sun shined in through the window. Digby ignored them, opting to stare at the man on the screen.

"It's not fair," a voice came from beside him, no longer a whisper.

Digby glanced to the cushion next to him, finding the corpse of Ames sitting there, five bloody holes in his chest. Obviously, the deceased sailor wasn't real, but the madness growing within Digby's mind was no longer content to speak in whispers. He had been trying his best to ignore the imaginary ghost, but it had been becoming harder and harder.

"No, it isn't fair," Digby agreed with his madness.

The movie's villain had concocted a good plan. He should have been miles away at the end of the story, sitting on a beach, earning thirty percent, as he put it. Instead, he was falling to his death. The hero of the movie wasn't even supposed to be in that building. He was just a fly in the ointment. A random addition that threw the scheme off.

Digby could relate.

Henwick wasn't supposed to be at that base earlier either. His Heretics should have been able to walk right in and take anything they wanted. Instead, Digby had been forced to flee. They needed more power; the armada wasn't going to be enough. Not against Henwick. Not while the ships were all the way in Hawaii.

They couldn't afford to hold back anymore.

A memory of the three men he'd killed on Skyline's base flashed through his head. He pushed it back out just as fast. He'd already told Parker about them, even if he'd left out the details that made him look bad. She hadn't questioned him about it any further, just like he knew she wouldn't.

"That's why you chose her." Ames stared at him. "She is easy to fool. You knew you could use her. You planned to from the start."

"No," Digby snapped back.

"Yes."

Digby stopped arguing as a memory flashed through his mind of Parker helping him pack the bag that he'd given Bancroft before banishing him. She had suspected nothing.

"There it is." Ames leaned closer, his wounds bleeding on the couch. "A touch of madness has been with you longer than you admit."

"Shut up." Digby forced the memory from his head. "I was angry. I wasn't thinking straight." He looked to Ames. "You are my madness. Which is why I must move faster to secure this city's future before your presence renders my judgment unsound."

"If it hasn't already." Ames's corpse let out a wet chuckle, crimson bubbling from his chest.

Digby rolled his eyes. "I am not about to give up now. Not when there is no one to fill my shoes."

With that thought, he pushed himself up. Now wasn't the time to doubt himself. No, now was the time for action.

Passing by his sleeping apprentice, he bent down to pick up an empty bucket of popcorn with the intent to throw it to wake him. He dropped the container a second later, deciding against it. The artificer and his coven had another location picked out to search for more enchanted items. They had their own work to do and their own power to gain.

Besides, with the ghost of Ames haunting him, he didn't need any more eyes on him than necessary. The only question was, how could he get stronger on his own?

Digby wandered the casino as the morning sun began to wake its inhabitants. He ignored them and continued his stroll while he went over his options. Parker was bound to be up early to help transport people and equipment back and forth to the harbor. He would need her later, but for now, what she was doing was important, so he let her be.

That was when he realized his random wandering had brought him to a hallway on one of the upper levels. A pair of Deuce's men stood further down, each guarding a door. They glanced at Digby but paid him no mind more than that. For a moment, he forgot why the men were stationed there, then he remembered.

"The prisoners." Ames appeared, walking by his side.

With so much going on, it had been so easy to forget about them. Each room held one man left over from the regime that ruled Vegas before Digby's arrival. They had been members of the high cards that had murdered survivors under the orders of Rivers. Digby had killed most of the opposition when he found out they were working with Autem to locate children for their

Guardian training program. When the dust settled, two had been left alive. Ever since, no one had known what to do with them.

The men were cruel and without morals. If Digby remembered correctly, one had worked in law enforcement and the other had been some kind of engineer. It was too bad that their crimes prevented them from being accepted by the rest of the Heretics. Their experience would have been helpful with the work being done in the city. Instead, they were just waiting in their rooms doing nothing. In the end, they were useless. And their presence pulled even more manpower from the war effort with the guards that needed to be posted by their door.

The prisoners couldn't even be banished like Bancroft, since there was no way to keep them from talking. Not unless Digby made himself a new infernal spirit to possess their skeletons, but that would be a waste of a minion.

Digby kept moving, passing the guards to walk to the other end of the hall. He glanced down at his feet before looking back up to find Ames standing in his way.

"Are they really useless?" The hallucination held up two fingers. "You still have two more to go."

Digby stopped as he glanced at his HUD to check his resources. He still needed two hearts to unlock his next mutation.

Two human hearts.

Digby shook his head and kept walking to push past the imaginary corpse in his way.

"They are right there. Ripe for the taking." Ames followed him. "Power there to claim."

His madness was right. He needed power, and the requirements were right there. No one would miss the prisoners. Hell, most of the people in Vegas didn't even know they had them. Executing them was something that they had even discussed before. Though, that was why he knew the others wouldn't let him. Killing the prisoners for their hearts would be sure to get him labeled as mad.

Digby felt a little lighter. The fact that he recognized the act as one that he couldn't take back meant that his judgment was still sound. Besides, maybe it was enough to know that the hearts were there if he needed them. There was always the chance that the situation would grow desperate enough that there would be no choice. Then Parker would be sure to understand.

"Yes." Ames followed close at his heels as he walked. "Bide your time."

Digby ignored the ghost until he reached a stairwell, then he spun around. "Will you just stop? I am not about to listen to a figment of my imagination."

Ames stopped, looking sheepish.

Digby waggled a claw at him. "Besides, your suggestion has given me an idea. One that won't draw the ire of my honorary conscience."

With that, he turned away from the corpse and headed down to the casino's vault to gather some materials. He nodded to the guards that had been stationed outside and headed in. The space inside was piled with stacks of worthless currency and a first aid bag lay on a table. Then there was what lay in the middle of the room.

The bomb.

Digby stopped momentarily, placing his hand to the warhead. It was hard to believe something so small was capable of so much damage. It really would be so simple to use the weapon to wipe Autem's capital off the earth.

"So do it." Ames stood in the corner of the vault.

Digby still didn't fully understand why that would be such a bad thing. Though, the fact that his madness was in favor of the idea probably meant it was the wrong choice, even if it would solve most of his problems. That was when he remembered the innocent people that lived there under Henwick's care.

"Maybe I am losing my ability to tell right from wrong." Digby let his fingers slide off the bomb. It wasn't what he'd come down here for. He turned away from the bomb. It wasn't the reason he was here.

Pulling one of the deposit boxes from the vault's wall, he set it down on a table and opened the lid. A tray full of enormous diamonds greeted him. Some were loose while others were set into jewelry. One of the nice things about taking over such an impressive city was that there was no shortage of high-quality gemstones.

Most of the strip had been secured by now. They weren't quite ready to open the entire place up for use again, but the threat of revenants was relatively low. Most had been either killed, converted to zombies, or fed to the horde. Once the streets were safe, Digby had sent a coven out to retrieve all of the large gems from the various shopping centers. They were no longer valuable in and of themselves, but as ritual materials, it was a different story.

Digby reached for a rather impressive ring. It was the sort of thing a king would wear. It had one of the largest diamonds he'd ever seen set into a thick band of gold. The gemstone made the one he'd used to create Tavern look like common rubbish in comparison. He slipped the ring on his pinkie finger and closed the box, placing it back in its slot in the wall.

If there was one thing that had paid off tenfold for him, it was Tavern. The skeletal minion had done more than pull their weight even with their propensity for alcohol. After being reminded of the prisoners upstairs, he remembered that nothing was stopping him from creating another like them. With Tavern gone and Digby's need for power, adding another infernal spirit to his forces seemed like the obvious choice. Though, he would probably stay away from college fraternities when choosing a location to carry out the required ritual.

He stopped by one of the shopping centers on his way back upstairs to pick up a heavy gold chain. Retrieving the ring he'd claimed from the vault, he secured it around his neck and tucked it into the button-down shirt. As much as he appreciated the jewelry, he was well aware of the fact that he had lost his arm a few too many times to risk wearing a minion's gemstone on his finger. Best to keep it safe instead.

With his shopping trip finished, he headed up to his room to get a few things. Alex had infused a new staff. It was the same as the one he'd had before with the golden femur at the bottom, but this time the shaft had been made of metal rather than wood and engravings had been added to its surface. The result allowed him to use the staff's enchantment even while no longer holding it. All he needed was for the weapon to be nearby.

Claiming the staff, he snatched his tattered coat from the hook by the door. It barely functioned as a garment anymore but his pauldron was still attached to it. Besides, he had destroyed every coat he'd worn so far; he would only do the same to a new one. It wasn't like anyone cared what he wore anyway. He slipped into the ragged fabric, then headed back down to the first floor to find Parker.

He still had something else to set into motion.

Digby found the pink-haired messenger in the casino's town square, sitting at a table by a fountain with her head down. Her cheek rested on a pile of photos. Her binder of destination pictures sat beside her. Digby picked up the binder before dropping it back down to the table.

"I'm awake." Parker shot up, a photo sticking to her face. She winced at the lights above and the noise of the fountain before sinking back down. "What's going on?"

"Come with me." Digby turned and started walking while explaining himself on the way.

The soldier followed him all the way outside and out to the middle of the strip. That was where he ran into trouble.

"You want to do what now?" Parker stood with her head cocked to one side, a lock of hair sticking up at an impossible angle after the nap that Digby had interrupted.

"Don't give me that confused dog expression, Parker." Digby frowned at her before sweeping a hand across the sun-drenched pavement of the Las Vegas strip. "I suggest we build a giant mirror, right here."

She yawned. "You know I have barely slept, right? I'm pretty much fueled by coffee and stress, right now. And I don't even like coffee. So don't get on me for being confused when you hardly ever make any sense."

"Bah." Digby waved away her complaint. "Well, I would explain things to Alex, but he is sure to be heading back out to do lord knows what with his coven."

"He's found some pretty great stuff so far." Parker held her binder close to her chest as the ends of her cloak floated in the breeze. "That lighter Hawk got is pretty powerful."

"I suppose that is true." He shook his head. "But back to my idea. What I mean is that it isn't enough to have an armada. We need to be able to mobilize it at a moment's notice." He stomped toward her. "What if Henwick finds out where we are and decides to send his elite forces? How will we defend this city if our ships are all the way in Hawaii? I don't even know where that island is, to be honest." Digby used his staff to point toward the edges of the street. "If we can construct a reflective area wide enough, right here on the street, as well as one back at the harbor, then we can move the entire armada all at once."

"Okay, sure, but do you know how hard it was to open a passage that a jeep could travel through while riding in it?" Parker raked a hand through her hair, smoothing out the bit that was sticking up. "I can't explain it, but the larger the passage, the more concentration it takes. Not to mention I need to focus more to use a surface that isn't perfectly smooth."

"So you can't do it?" Digby phrased it like he was doubting her ability.

Parker might have acted like she didn't care when others failed to believe in her, but if there was something he had learned about the woman, she almost always pushed herself harder when feeling inadequate. It was a manipulative tactic, and he did feel bad about using it, but if it would keep the city safe, he didn't mind poking the soft underbelly of Parker's self-esteem.

"See what I mean," Ames whispered in his ear.

Digby ignored the voice.

"I didn't say I can't do it." Parker rolled her eyes with a familiar rebellious attitude while simultaneously agreeing to the idea. "I just don't know how you are hoping to get a mirror that big here. Unless…" She trailed off, looking into the middle distance.

"Unless what?" Digby raised an eyebrow.

"We could use some sort of resin." She shrugged.

"What's that?"

"It's like a two-part epoxy." She pantomimed stirring something. "You mix two liquids and they harden into a smooth surface. Alex and I were talking about it the other day. It's the same stuff that the tables were made out of back in that gaming cafe we spent the night in. People use the stuff to make fancy furniture. It's trendy."

"I like the sound of that." Digby gave her an approving smile hoping to encourage her.

"Okay." She walked across the street. "We'd need a simple border to keep the resin where we want it. And we could add a layer of reflective paint on the bottom. If we do it right, it should end up perfectly smooth. I should be able to open a passage big enough for a ship with a mirror like that. The only problem would be that you would have to exit vertically."

"That should be alright as long as we keep the crew to a minimum and make sure everyone has something to hold on to."

"Wait." Parker looked up at the sky. "What if Autem notices the mirror with a satellite or something?"

"You'll just have to work fast and make sure to cover it when it's finished." Digby dismissed the possibility as he tapped his staff on the pavement. "Now, start getting things in order."

"Me?" She recoiled.

"Yes, you." Digby glowered at her. "I have my own job to do today, and you seem to know what you need."

"Are you sure you don't want me to come with you?" She

inched back and forth. "You know, to keep you from committing a war crime or something."

Digby deflated, leaning on his staff. "No, Parker, I assure you I am capable of spending a day apart from you without succumbing to madness."

Ames stood behind Parker giving him a look that said, 'Are you sure?'

"Well, shit." Parker shoved a hand into her pocket and pulled out a compact before handing it to him. "Okay, I'll send a coven out to get the stuff I need to make a big ass mirror. Just keep this compact on you in case I need to get you back here."

"Excellent." Digby nodded decisively and opened his maw to drop his staff in. "Then I will be off."

"Where to?" She started to head toward the parking garage. "Do you need a passage?"

Digby gave her a crooked grin. "I'm not going far, and I have my own mode of transport."

"What is that supposed to mean?" She eyed him suspiciously.

"It means I have been practicing."

Digby flexed his arms without further explanation, feeling a sudden snap pop from his back. The armored plates beneath his shirt shifted position to allow for two formations of bone that extended from his back. They tore through his shirt and the remains of his already tattered coat as he let his resources flow. Tendons, muscles, and skin. It all wove together, knitting a thin membrane supported by a network of necrotic tissue.

"Yar!" Parker stepped back, nearly gagging as he stretched a pair of leathery wings out behind him.

"See you around." Digby flapped into the air as he sent a call to Asher across their bond to join him.

At least I'll never end up falling to my death like that Gruber fellow.

CHAPTER TWENTY-NINE

Digby drifted on wings of leathery black flesh as the desert passed by beneath him. It was good to get away from Vegas for a bit. Thinking back, he'd barely been left alone for days. If it wasn't Parker keeping an eye on him, it was someone else looking to him for leadership.

Sometimes a necromancer needed to get away from it all.

It wasn't like he wanted to be in charge anyway. No, it had just happened. The only person he'd been able to depend on had been Rebecca, but with her missing, he was doing it all alone. He shook his head, annoyed with himself for feeling inadequate.

"I can do this." Digby flapped the large bat wings that extended from his back. Everyone else doubted him; he couldn't afford to do the same thing himself. "I just need more strength."

He cringed as he looked around, half expecting Ames to be floating beside him to tell him he was wrong or insane, or both. The ghost didn't appear. Apparently, his madness knew well enough not to manifest a flightless corpse in the sky.

Asher cawed happily as she flapped her wings not far behind him, helping him to forget about his problems for a moment. Digby could feel her excitement across their bond. She was thrilled to be able to share the sky with him. He could understand that much. The freedom of it certainly held an appeal. A part of him just wanted to keep flying and never look back.

Unfortunately, there was still so much to do, and far too many enemies to fight.

Digby tucked his wings, letting himself plummet toward the ground as a city came into view. He extended them again a moment later to catch the wind. Asher dove to catch up. They hadn't gone far. Just thirty miles, give or take, from Vegas to a city called Boulder. There was something about the simplicity of the name that appealed to him.

More importantly, Asher hadn't flown out to the city yet during her search for more zombies. With a little luck, he could find some of the dead to add to his horde. If not, there were sure to be plenty of revenants that could be eaten or converted into minions.

He checked his resources.

RESOURCES
BONE: 143
FLESH: 130
HEART: 148
MIND: 142
SINEW: 146
VISCERA: 130
SPARKS: 0

After pumping so many bodies worth of materials into the bloodstalker that he'd used to block Henwick's smite spell, he'd been left with fewer resources than he felt comfortable with. Especially considering how powerful his Body Craft mutation was. If he could gain a few hundred more corpses, he would be nearly unstoppable. Even Henwick wouldn't be able to harm him.

"I just need the right place." Digby flew over the city street, searching for a building that would serve his purposes.

Asher cawed to draw his attention to a group of zombies that roamed the street. It wasn't a large horde, only around a dozen, but if there were that many, then that probably meant that there were more.

"Good." Digby chuckled. "It seems we have friends here already."

Flapping down, he landed atop an abandoned vehicle. Asher took her place on his shoulder. The zombies looked in their direction but paid them no mind beyond that. Searching the group from his perch, he found a zombie leader among the bunch. That must have been why the group had remained together for this long.

Digby cast Control Zombie on the leader as he ran a claw along Asher's feathers, gently. The group accepted his authority immediately, listening to the compels of his new minion.

"Perfect." Digby patted Asher's side. "Now we just need to find more."

The raven gave him a nod before flapping back up into the sky to search.

Digby hopped down from the vehicle he stood on, having trouble with the motion. Having wings wasn't all that helpful on the ground. He wished there was a way to retract them so they didn't get in the way. Instead, he just cast Blood Forge to cut them off. His wings fell to the ground in a heap behind him.

"Shame." Digby frowned at the wasted resources.

It wasn't the most economical way to manage the problem, but it was better than getting stuck in a doorway because his wings didn't fit. Though, he was pretty sure Parker would at least enjoy the sight if she had been there. Another reason why he had left her back in Vegas.

Forgetting about his wings, he beckoned to his new horde and kept moving. It took a few hours to gather more of the zombies that were roaming the streets. There weren't many, only around fifty, and none of them had mutated except for the one leader he'd already found. The competition between the dead and the revenants must have kept the zombies from thriving. In the end, the horde was small but was enough to start with.

Digby made a point to keep his eyes open for any humans that may have been hiding in the area. He didn't want a repeat of what had happened with Ames.

"Or do you?" Ames stood across the street, holding up two fingers to remind him of the two hearts he needed to unlock his next mutation.

Digby groaned but ignored the ghost. He had been hoping his madness would leave him alone for the day since it hadn't made an appearance in a while. It had just been biding its time.

There were a number of people in Vegas that had come from Boulder, so there was a good chance the city was uninhabited, with its survivors already finding safety. Digby allowed himself to relax. At least there would be no complicated moral dilemmas to deal with.

After gathering his horde, he called Asher back. The deceased raven flapped down to his shoulder a few minutes later, taking a look at his back where his wings had been. A somber feeling echoed across their bond.

"Don't worry." Digby patted her side. "I can grow them back. I just need to stay on the ground while we prepare."

She cawed back.

"Yes, and that brings me to part two of our little excursion: food."

Finding a few revenants would be simple enough. He could just wander into almost any building and find a group of them staying out of the sun. Though, that seemed like a waste of time. After all, why search when he had a way to bring them to him?

Digby ran a claw over the diamond ring that was chained around his neck. The last time he had performed the ritual to create an infernal spirit, something about the collection of lingering echoes had drawn every revenant in the area to him.

If he could bet on the same thing happening this time as well, then all he had to do was use the ritual to lure in some unsuspecting prey. Not to mention he would get a new skeletal minion out of the deal.

Then again, the ritual had other requirements that complicated things. Digby willed the Seed to bring up the details.

The gemstone had already been taken care of, but he still needed a location where several people had recently perished. The last time Digby had performed the ritual had been weeks ago. Back then, pretty much everywhere met the requirements of having been the site of recent deaths. Now, though, more time had passed. Pretty much everyone that was going to die had already done so.

Digby could try to lure some unsuspecting people into a dangerous place, but he was pretty sure human sacrifice was something that would lose him the trust of his allies. It was too bad he hadn't reached the requirements to unlock his Spirit Caller mutation. With that, it wouldn't matter where he chose to perform the ritual, he could just call the echoes of the lingering dead to him.

Digby stood in the street, his new horde standing behind him, waiting for him to issue a command. Everything was still. A few restaurants lined one side of the road while a shopping center bracketed him on the other side. Abandoned vehicles littered the street.

Without a better option, he closed his eyes and focused on his Blood Sense. He could feel the mana flowing through a person's body with it, and mana was just essence, after all. Considering that the echoes of the lingering dead were just imprints in the ambient essence, maybe he might be able to sense them as well.

He must have stood there for at least an hour before noticing something. Digby snapped his eyes back open, sweeping them across the street. Whatever he'd picked up vanished as soon as he did.

"Hmm." He scratched at his chin.

There had definitely been something on the air. He just couldn't pinpoint it.

"Stay here." Digby held a hand out toward his horde before glancing to Asher. "Keep an eye on them."

Asher flapped off his shoulder and landed atop a lamppost to watch over the zombies. Digby gave her a nod and started walking, the tattered lengths of fabric from his coat drifting through the air behind him. He didn't have a direction in mind, just that he needed to try to sense something again. If he was too far from a suitable location for his ritual, whatever he was sensing was probably too faint.

Venturing into the shopping center, he cast Decay to shatter a window to gain access to a grocery store. The place had already been looted, from the looks of it. There were still food items on the shelves but someone had taken the lion's share, mostly canned goods and nonperishables. Perhaps whoever it was had passed away nearby recently.

Digby stopped in one of the aisles to focus on his Blood Sense. Nothing immediately jumped out at him, but there was something. He couldn't be completely sure, but the presence he was feeling seemed a little stronger. Opening his eyes, he headed toward the back of the store and exited through the loading area. He walked another fifty feet and tried his Blood Sense again.

"Interesting." Digby grinned.

The sensation was barely noticeable, but if he focused on it alone, he was able to pick up a trail of sorts.

That was when the Heretic Seed decided to lend a hand.

SKILL LINK
By demonstrating repeated and proficient use of the non-mage skill or talent, Spirit Tracking, you have discovered an adjacent spell.
SPIRIT LOCATER
Description: Reveal the location and identity of the nearest echoes of the lingering dead.

Rank: D
Cost: 10 MP
**Range: variable, range = the distance between the caster
and the nearest echo.**
No more flying blind for you.

"No more, indeed." Digby read over the text again. "I don't
know what good revealing the location and identity of lingering
echoes is beyond helping to perform rituals, but I'll take it."

He cast the spell without hesitation, feeling his mana system
release a pulse of energy. A second later a ray of light shined up
into the sky from not far away. He assumed he was the only one
that could see it, similar to Rebecca's map spell. Along with the
ray of light, a name appeared on his HUD.

Samuel Thompson, age 41, worker

Digby stared at the name, wondering what good knowing
the age and occupation of the echo would do. He cast the spell
again, this time getting another ray of light next to the first,
along with another name. This one was younger by a few years
but had the same occupation.

More importantly, his second casting of the spell had
ignored the first echo that he'd already found and moved on to
the next nearest one rather than just telling him the same thing.
That meant that he could identify many echoes with repeated
castings. He used the spell several more times, finding more
lingering echoes clustered close to the first. All except one were
listed as workers, with the remainder being labeled as an
overseer.

"That is certainly better than a college fraternity."

Digby turned and headed in the direction of the rays of
light that shined into the sky. They all led to a warehouse and
faded as soon as he arrived. He knew he'd found the right place
the moment he saw it. The building was ordinary enough, but a
wall surrounded the property and someone had moved cars to

block the entrances inside. With the way they were positioned, no one was getting in or out. If he had to guess, the warehouse workers had been hiding out inside but perished for one reason or another.

Approaching the building, he called to Asher to tell her to bring the horde. He peeked in through one of the windows while he waited for his deceased reinforcements to arrive.

"Just as I thought." He tapped on the glass, watching as a group of around fifteen revenants looked in his direction. "They must have closed themselves inside with someone who'd been bitten." Digby pushed away from the window. "Why do humans do that so often?"

It made no sense to hide a bite. The survivors had been around long enough to know what happened once they had been cursed. Even without knowledge of magic, they had to know they were doomed. So why hide a bite and damn everyone else with you? It was all just so illogical. Yet, even their movies portrayed people as doing the same thing, and it never worked out better on the screen.

In the end, it was clear that some people just couldn't be trusted to protect their own.

Digby brushed the thought aside. It didn't matter how these people perished, just that they had done so recently. Stepping away from the window, he headed for the nearest entrance. The doors were blocked by a large truck. Digby pushed on the vehicle but it didn't budge. He pulled his hands away from the hood, its surface hot enough from the desert sun that it might damage his skin if he continued to push.

"The wheels must be locked." Digby cast Decay to shatter the window before reaching in to pop the door open.

Sliding into the driver's seat, he stared at the steering wheel, remembering the last time he'd tried to drive. It had been back in California and he'd abandoned the car on the side of the road before he made it thirty feet.

"Maybe you need help after all?" Ames sat in the passenger seat with one foot up on the dash.

"I don't suppose you know which lever unlocks the vehicle's movement?" Digby stared at the corpse.

Ames didn't answer.

"Of course you don't. You're just the representation of madness in my head. How would you know anything that I myself don't?" He turned back to the steering wheel. "Alright, Digby, you've seen Parker operate these things enough times to know how it works."

He spent the next few minutes pulling every lever available, cursing the manufacturer for not having the forethought to label everything. He knew enough to understand it had to be taken out of park, but there must have been something else that he was missing, some kind of backup brake.

Asher flapped down to land on the vehicle's door, sending a couple words across their bond.

I help.

"I'm sorry." Digby gave her a pat. "But I don't think you can move a truck."

The horde arrived not long after. Digby slid out of the truck and ordered the lone zombie leader in the group to climb in and release whatever was stopping the vehicle from moving. He slapped himself in the forehead when the zombie pulled on a lever that had been positioned in the middle of the vehicle between the seats.

"Why didn't I think of that?" The increased intelligence that the zombie leader had allowed the monster to access some of its memories from when it was alive. It wasn't much, but it gave them enough to remember how to operate a vehicle.

The zombie exited the truck, looking pleased with itself.

"Yes, yes, you're very smart." Digby groaned, annoyed that there were still things that he didn't know about the world.

The rest of the horde got into position to push the truck away from the warehouse's entrance. He pulled the door open as soon as the path was clear. The group of revenants inside stared at him, all dormant with the daylight. Some retreated back to hide behind several tall shelves filled with crates. Digby's first response was to swallow the group whole, but he thought better of it. He still needed bones for his ritual, after all.

"Enjoy the meal." He stepped aside to let the horde through.

The zombies rushed in practically in a frenzy. They probably hadn't eaten much other than the occasional revenant that got separated from larger groups. The pale creatures screeched as the dead fell upon them. Digby closed the door as the last of the horde entered. The final thing he needed for his plan to work was a city full of hostile revenants to come running when his ritual began. For that, he needed to wait until nightfall.

"Leave me the bones." He called out as the horde tore into the revenants inside.

It was probably a good thing he'd left Parker behind; she probably would have had a problem with the gore. Digby, on the other hand, didn't even notice. Hell, a part of him was tempted to join in. He refrained. There would be plenty for him to eat later, as long as everything went according to plan. From the position of the sun outside, it looked like he had another few hours of daylight. Just enough time to make some more preparations.

Walking the perimeter of the wall outside of the warehouse, Digby made sure to secure the gates at the entrance. The revenants would be coming in full force the moment the ritual started, so anything to slow them down was going to help.

From there, he headed back into the warehouse. The horde was still feasting on the scraps of the building's previous inhabitants. Ignoring the dead, he checked all of the doors and windows. Most were already secure with vehicles blocking the outside, but there were still a few weak points. He filled them in by opening his Maw and casting Blood Forge. The last time he'd tried to seal a building with blood, the barriers had failed. Now that he'd ranked up the spell several times, making everything he forged far stronger than before, things should be different.

After securing the building, he threw open the door that

he'd entered through and propped it open with a heavy box that he'd found nearby.

"There, that should do it." He nodded. "I've done every-thing but put up a welcome sign."

With that, he turned and stepped away from the door, tossing a bundle of Alex's warding rods behind him. The pieces of metal split apart, tumbling through the air for a second before snapping into a position in front of the entrance. With the rods in place, any revenants that came to check out the ritual would be unable to enter beyond standing in the few feet just in front of the door.

All Digby had to do was make sure his maw was waiting to take them in. With a little luck, the ritual would draw in a few hundred of the creatures. That would certainly keep his resources full for the time being. It wasn't every day that he knew when and where a swarm of the creatures would be passing through, and he wasn't about to waste the opportunity. Especially now that he had so many tools at his disposal.

Of course, there was some risk.

There were sure to be a few wardbreakers in the mix that might make it over his maw and run right into the building, but that was what the horde was for. They could certainly rip a few of the creatures to shreds. The real problem would be if a bloodstalker showed up, since the creatures could poten-tially break their way through the roof, provided they could fly.

Digby was confident that he could handle a few of the larger revenants, but if they made it inside while he was in the middle of his ritual, he wouldn't be able to defend himself. Hopefully the building would hold out long enough. The horde might be able to buy time as well. In the end, he could always fly away if the ritual got too dangerous and try again when things calmed down.

"Having wings certainly had its perks." He chuckled.

Asher cawed in agreement from a perch on top of one of the shelves.

"Just be ready to flee if the time comes." He pointed toward the sky. "We don't want to overstay our welcome."

Asher flapped over to him, landing on his shoulder as she sent a thought across their bond.

But the teeth.

"Huh?" He looked at her, forgetting what the words meant. A moment later, he remembered. Teeth meant the horde. The many teeth that would devour the world. Digby sighed. "I really have been spending too much time with the humans if I have forgotten that much."

The many. Asher mentioned the horde again.

"I know, I know, but if things get out of hand, we will have to leave them behind." He could tell she didn't like the idea. "We still have to look out for the rest of our horde back in Vegas, including the humans. They need us to do this so we can gain the strength to protect them. I don't like the idea of leaving the horde behind either, but sometimes you have to do what it takes to win. Otherwise, we all lose."

"Yes." Ames wandered through the shelves. "Do whatever it takes to win."

Asher flapped away without any further comment, landing on a crate.

"Oh, don't mope about it." He glowered at her. "I get enough of that from Parker, I don't need it from you too."

She merely looked away.

"Fine, be that way." He waved away her concerns with a clawed hand.

It was true that he probably could have found a way to keep the zombies there safe but there wasn't time. According to the progress reports he'd received before leaving, the artificers in Hawaii would have the armada ready to fly in a matter of days. He couldn't waste time here trying to keep a mere fifty zombies from being destroyed.

That being said, it was still prudent to make sure his horde lasted as long as possible in the fight to come. With that in mind, he turned to the horde and cast control on as many as he could. Then he willed his Body Craft mutation to reinforce their bodies the way he had Ducky, returning to them the attributes that they had while alive.

The result was near instantaneous.

The horde twitched and spasmed for a few seconds. Then, they changed. The unsteady movements of the dead were gone, replaced by the normal motor functions of the living. Many of the monsters almost had a bounce in their step. Digby watched as month-old wounds closed, even filling in the hollow cavity of one unfortunate walking corpse that had lost its nose.

"Looking good." He gave that one a nod.

Passing through the horde to where they had left him the bones of the revenants that they'd killed, he picked through the selection to claim what he needed for the ritual. Surprisingly, he was able to tell which body each bone had come from easily, allowing him to reassemble one in particular.

Laying the skeleton out in the middle of the warehouse floor, he grinned.

"It won't be long now."

CHAPTER THIRTY

"You suck." Hawk stood with his arms folded.

"I know." Alex tried not to look him in the eyes as he handed the rogue's enchanted lighter to one of Deuce's men. "But it's what's best for the city."

"I get that, but you still suck." Hawk groaned.

As much as he wanted to let Hawk keep the lighter, it was too powerful for one person to carry alone. The plan was to use the enchanted flame that it produced to light several lanterns that could be carried by anyone that needed it. That way they could extend the flame's protective ability to covens in the event of an attack. In the long run, they would need to set up some kind of eternal flame. After that, they could store the lighter down in the vault in case it was needed in the future.

"Relax, I'm sure you'll find something equally cool in Boston." Alex started walking toward the garage.

Hawk dragged his feet behind him.

Of all the places that Alex had wanted to check out, the Boston Museum of Science was at the top of his list. There was, however, a complication that had discouraged him from visiting it already.

"Are you sure you want to do this?" Parker asked the moment that he and Hawk entered the parking garage. She was still staring at the picture of their destination sideways. "This is a terrible photo."

"True, but it's the only one I could find." Alex kept walking to where Lana and Alvin waited by his hovering Camaro.

There was an exhibit at the museum that was sure to hold something important. Not only that, but it was a traveling exhibit, so it was less likely that Autem's people would have been aware of it. The only reason he knew it was there was because he had looked it up before the world ended. The exhibit had been in Australia for a while before traveling to the Museum of Science in Boston.

The problem, however, was the passage they needed to get there.

No one had been able to find a picture of the Science Museum itself to show Parker. They had found one that showed a window across the street, but when Parker had tried it, the spell had failed. That happened from time to time, since some of the surfaces in the photos had been broken at some point in the last month. In the end, they were left with only one viable image that could take them to a point that was still close enough. Fenway Park, home of the Red Sox. This meant that they would have to travel from one location to the other. That wasn't the main issue, though.

No, the real problem was the photo itself.

The image was badly shot with a thumb obscuring one corner. Most importantly, it only showed one reflective surface clearly, the windows on the indoor seating. Set into a section at the top of the stadium, that made their exit point high off the ground. The fall would probably kill them.

That would be true, if the R&D team in Hawaii hadn't already built a small-scale flight system for their experiments days ago. Now that they had moved on to getting the full-size ships in the air, Alex had been free to scavenge their prototype. It was simple enough, just an engraved rod that could be raised or lowered to align different sets of runes with a control ring that surrounded it. The result allowed for a level of altitude control.

Alex hadn't had time to fully install the system into his Camaro, but technically he didn't have to. The car didn't need to fly. It just needed to fall slower. With the altitude rod installed in the middle of the back seat, along with a crank system to adjust its position, the problem was solved, for now.

"You realize there is almost no room for us, right?" Hawk stared at the flight system that was taking up half of the back seat where he and Alvin usually sat.

Alex opened the driver's side door and pulled the seat forward so he could get in. "It's not far from Fenway to the museum, you'll live."

"Yes, you'll live. Unlike me," Kristen said from her place on the dash.

Alex ignored her. The skull had warned them that they were in danger back at the Smithsonian, so he couldn't really justify leaving her in the trunk again. Lana climbed into the passenger side as her brother squeezed into the back with Hawk and the flight system.

"Good luck." Parker patted the hood of the car.

"We should be fine." Alex dropped into the driver's seat.

"You had to use the word 'should,' didn't you?" Lana eyed him.

He cringed but ignored the comment before checking on the rest of his passengers. "Everyone good back there?"

"We're fine," Hawk said through his teeth, sitting at an awkward angle next to the flight unit, its crank jutting out in front of him.

Alex glanced at Alvin who looked equally uncomfortable. "Sorry."

Alvin didn't complain.

"We're off then." Alex forced a cheerful tone as he pulled the car out of its parking space, then turned it toward the alcove that housed the mirrors.

Parker stood outside, waving him forward until the vehicle was floating a foot away from the glass. She opened a passage as soon as he was in position.

"Gulp," Kristen said the word out loud, clearly lacking the esophagus she would have needed to do otherwise.

"Is that helping?" Alex glowered at the skull.

"Just putting words to what everyone is probably feeling." She chuckled.

Alex took a breath. "Everyone know what to do?"

"Yeah, I gotta crank this thing like hell as soon as we exit the passage." Hawk gripped the handle in front of him.

"That about sums it up." Alex glanced at Lana.

"I'm just going to hold on to something and try not to die." She looked back. "You too, Alvin."

"Already am."

"Okay then." Alex pushed the car forward into the rippling surface of glass in front of them.

At first everything seemed fine. The car slid into the passage smoothly. Despite that, Alex's eyes bulged as he emerged to a view of Fenway Park, high above the baseball diamond below. That was when the Camaro started tilting forward.

"Oh shit!" Lana threw a foot up against the dash to brace for a fall.

The car slid out of the passage all at once as the gravity of their destination took over.

"Crank the rod, Hawk!" Alex shouted as the grass below filled the view beyond the windshield.

"Are you sure that's how you want to phrase that?" Hawk asked, speaking fast as he spun the handle in front of him.

"Hawk!" Both Alex and Lana shouted back in unison, not appreciating the comment while they were falling to their deaths.

"I'm cranking! I'm cranking!" Hawk continued to work.

"Crank faster!" Alvin screeched as the vehicle plummeted another dozen feet straight for the ground.

"If you have a body, try to go limp," Kristen added.

Alex did the opposite, tensing every muscle he had and bracing against the steering wheel. An instant later, the car evened out. Everyone inside let out a collective sigh of relief as they slowed to a stop, hovering around thirty feet off the ground.

"Oh my god, we did it." Alex stared out across the stadium completely forgetting the terror he'd felt only seconds before. "We made a flying car!"

"Yes, how nice for you," Kristen commented. "I certainly wasn't hoping for you to fail."

"Shut up, you know you're just as excited." Alex patted the skull before turning back to Hawk. "Okay, crank us back up to the passage, I want to make sure we can use the same window to get home if we need to."

"Yeah, okay." Hawk panted.

Alex couldn't suppress a giddy smile as the car slowly climbed back up to the window that they had come from. His mind raced with questions. What would happen if they passed back through it?

Would the car crash into the ceiling as soon as it was through, if it entered while set at a higher altitude?

"Alex?" Lana tapped him on the shoulder as he stared off into the skyline, lost in thought.

Could I get the car to fly higher?

"Dude!" Hawk snapped him out of his thoughts with a smack to the back of the head.

"What?" Alex turned around.

"That!" Hawk jabbed a finger back at the window that they had come from as the passage closed.

Alex squinted at the glass, finding rows of chairs inside. He followed them up until he found what Hawk and Lana were concerned about.

A zombie brute.

The oversized monster was looking straight at them from the other side of the glass. Alex hadn't seen one of the monsters in the wild since the beginning of the apocalypse. The beast stared at them for a long moment, then it charged.

"Crap!" Alex grabbed the wheel to spin the car around to get away from the window.

The brute probably hadn't eaten in weeks, making it hungry enough to ignore its own safety. It smashed into the glass without hesitation, leaping through the air toward the flying meal outside. The Camaro only made it halfway around before the monster slammed into its side. Bits of glass glittered across the hood as the brute's head smashed through Lana's window, its jaws chomping at the air.

"Urk!" The cleric lurched back into Alex to avoid losing an arm.

The brute roared in frustration, its body hanging from the car to weigh down one side. Kristen's skull rolled toward the open window as the entire vehicle tipped. Lana caught her before she tumbled out, and Alex grabbed Lana to keep her from falling closer to the brute. With his other hand, he cut the wheel to the side to try to spin the beast off.

"What do I do?" Hawk gripped the altitude crank, clearly unsure if he should bring them up or down.

The brute smashed a hand through the rear window, trying to reach for any of the edible treats inside. Alex spun the car in the air as the monster struggled to hold on, one hand slapping down on the front. A spiderweb of cracks spread out across the windshield. It wasn't until Lana pulled her pistol and fired half a magazine into the brute's face that the monster finally let go. The massive zombie's body fell to the grass below, its bulk slamming into home base with a bloody thud.

The car leveled out as soon as the beast was gone, leaving Alex to slow the spin that he'd thrown it into. A moment of silence passed as everyone blew out a second collective sigh of relief.

Alex let out an uncomfortable laugh. "Welcome to Boston."

"Fuck yeah," Hawk added in a terrible accent from the back, still holding onto the crank with a white-knuckle grip.

"So glad you brought me along," Kristen added as Lana placed the skull back on the dash.

"Let's maybe bring the car back to the ground." The cleric brushed broken glass off her seat.

"That might be best." Alex nodded.

It took another ten minutes before they were back on the ground and made it out to the street in front of the stadium. To Alex's surprise, there was a fair number of zombies roaming about. Not a ton, but enough to have a presence even when revenants were the dominant predators.

"Boston must have been one of the cities that Autem seeded with zombies back when everything started." Alex watched as a handful of the dead roamed the sidewalk. "I kind of wish we had brought a necromancer with us."

"But we didn't," Hawk added.

"We might want to move, then." Alvin pointed at a group of six zombies that were staggering toward them.

"Yeah, good plan." Alex turned the car and headed in the other direction.

"We'll have to tell Digby and Clint to come back here to find more of the dead for their horde." Lana watched the monsters as the car passed another group of the dead.

"It's weird." Hawk leaned forward between the front seats. "I kind of forgot that they were scary. If it wasn't for that brute, I probably wouldn't even run."

"The world has gotten weird," Alvin added in a weak voice. "I wish things could go back to normal."

"Is that why you went to the dark side, you know, with Autem and stuff?" Hawk leaned back beside him.

"I..." Alvin trailed off before adding, "Yeah. They just seemed so normal. Like they had everything figured out. They were rebuilding and they had rules."

"Fuck rules." Hawk smirked.

Alex eyed him in the rear view. "You know, swearing doesn't make you edgy."

Hawk rolled his eyes and put his head back.

Alex shifted his view to Alvin. "I can kind of understand the thing about rules. At least, in terms of surviving the apocalypse. Everything that Autem was offering must have been tempting. Even that crazy stuff about their angels and what not."

Alvin nodded. "They talk about them like they're real. The Nine, I mean. Like they had proof that angels and God exist. They didn't question anything, they just knew that what they were doing was right. Everyone kept telling me the same thing, so I guess I started to believe it."

"Too bad it's all bullshit," Lana grumbled.

"I know. I just didn't see how so many people could be wrong." He shook his head. "Why would they lie about it?"

"They didn't," Kristen's ghostly voice responded from her spot on the dash.

"Oh yeah?" Alex chuckled. "Did you see some angels during your time working for the empire?"

"No," the skull responded. "But the Nine taught us about the will of the one back when Autem was born."

"Who told you that?" Hawk picked her up. "Henwick?"

"No." She responded in a tone that would have been accompanied by a sneer if she still had a face. "My family followed Autem for generations."

"Oh." Alex sighed, suddenly feeling bad about taking part in her murder.

"What is that supposed to mean?" Kristen raised her voice.

Alex stopped the car. "It means that it's hard to say no to traditions. You were never given a choice about what to believe."

"Of course I was given a choice," she snapped back. "I could have left Autem anytime I wanted to. It was just…" She trailed off.

"Just, what?" Lana picked up the skull.

"It was everything." Kristen sounded a little overwhelmed.

"I get that." Alex started driving again. "That was the same reason I followed the path I did before all this. My family knew what was best, and I always thought they were right. They had it all; a house, savings, stability. So when they told me to stop playing games and be a professional, I did." He sunk into his seat. "I didn't even buy the most recent game system. I could have been playing with friends and going on adventures. Instead, I got a job, isolated myself, and focused on work. Fuck, I regret that decision."

"You know, swearing doesn't make you edgy." Hawk used his own words against him.

"Ha ha." He laughed through a thick layer of sarcasm, then he sighed. "I thought my parents knew everything, but looking back, they were just doing what my family had done for generations. No one ever stepped out of line."

"Well, you and I are nothing alike," Kristen said matter-of-factly. "So your family taught you to value work and you didn't play some video games. Boo hoo. My family served the Nine in order to save humanity."

"Really?" Lana turned the skull around so that Kristen could see the world that Autem had created. "So when your people killed and hurt others, they were still the good guys? That why you stood by and said nothing to stop it?"

Kristen scoffed. "Don't be naive. You know as well as I do that the world isn't that simple. Sacrifices must be made for a greater good."

"Is that how your parents explained it?" Alex looked into the hollows of her eye sockets.

"You don't understand what it's like to believe in something." She started to shut down the conversation the same way she had before. "Don't think you know better just because you three outnumber me."

"Yeah?" Alex gave her a friendly smile. "Then why did you tell us to run back at the Smithsonian?"

"What?" The skull sounded confused.

"Why, when you serve Autem and their nine angels, did you warn us the moment you realized we had walked straight into their territory? You could have said nothing and waited until we were captured, but you told us to escape."

"I… I just didn't think you should die or be tortured."

"And how would all those people that told you to follow the Nine feel about that?" Lana asked.

"They…" Kristen fell silent.

Alex took the skull from Lana and held it up in front of him. "You went against everything you knew, because you care about us."

"Don't be ridiculous." She groaned. "Have you even been listening? I am a soulless construct. I can't have a change of heart, or even new thoughts. I will always be the woman you murdered."

Alex tapped her on the forehead. "You can tell us that you are incapable of changing, but that doesn't change the fact that it's obvious that you have."

Silence answered back from the skull.

"Got nothing else to say?" He shook her. "No annoying comment or insult?"

"Just put me back in the trunk," she grumbled.

"No chance, not when we're getting somewhere." He laughed just as a zombie slapped a hand against his window, to which he responded with a sudden shriek.

"We should probably get to the museum." Lana pointed to a few more of the dead that were approaching.

"Right." Alex placed a hand to his chest, his heart racing from the sudden jump scare.

With that, he let the vehicle's engravings draw a small amount of his mana as it lurched onward. It wasn't long before they pulled into the parking garage in the Science Museum. Alex drove back out just as fast, finding a swarm of revenants hiding from the sun inside. There may have been more zombies around, but they still weren't the primary threat.

Finding a place to park outside the front door instead, Alex shoved Kristen's skull in his messenger bag to sulk, then he exited the car. The doors of the museum were still locked, which was probably why the revenants were hiding in that garage rather than inside the building itself. He made a point to throw some warding rods up at the entrance just to keep anything from following them in. They would still need to keep an eye out for zombies though.

The museum had more windows than the Smithsonian had, allowing much more light into the main hall. Despite that, the shadows were still plentiful. Almost as soon as they made it inside, Hawk had already found something to gawk at.

"Damn." He stared up at the skeleton of a tyrannosaurus.

"Wow." Alvin kept his voice low, but couldn't hide his excitement.

"Does anyone else want to know what happens if Digby casts Animate Skeleton on that?" Alex couldn't help but imagine it.

Lana tapped a description plate attached to the railing that ran around the display. "It's only eighty percent real. Some of the bones are cast replicas. I think you need a complete skeleton to animate it."

"That's dumb." Hawk frowned.

"We aren't here for dinosaurs anyway." Alex headed for the information desk, finding the sign that he was looking for. Script font ran across the top.

One Exhibit to Rule Them All

"Now this… this is what we came for." He let a grin that Digby would have been proud of creep across his face.

"How did you know this exhibit was going to be here?" Lana joined him.

He looked back as he started for the stairs that the sign pointed to. "I had looked it up before the apocalypse. The exhibit was supposed to be coming to my area after its time here."

"Who would have thought you'd still get to see it after the world ended?" Lana looked back to her brother. "Come on. No going off on your own."

Alvin just stared up at her looking defiant. "I'm not going to run away to join Autem again."

"How do I know that? Huh?" She threw a hand out toward

the windows. "Plus, we're still in a zombie apocalypse, so I'm not letting a kid run off on their own."

Alvin grumbled something under his breath before Hawk stepped in to distract him, the pair hanging back a bit. Alex watched them for a second then glanced back to Lana. The tension she carried was obvious.

"Why don't you hang with your brother?" Alex gestured for her to head back. "You haven't spent much time alone with him."

"You a family counselor now?" She narrowed her eyes at him before walking faster to get ahead.

"Okay, never mind." Alex jogged to catch up.

She blew out a sigh finally slowing down. "Sorry, I'm still pissed is all. My own brother left me to die. That sort of thing is hard to get over. I am literally all he has left and he was ready to throw me away."

"I get that." Alex kept pace beside her. "But you heard him in the car. It's more complicated than that."

"I hope you are not going to take his side on this." Her tone grew harsh.

"I'm just saying. You both went through hell on that first night in Seattle. From what I heard from Digby, Alvin struggled to handle it."

"I know that." She slowed her pace letting the teens behind them catch up. "It's just hard to trust him again. I just need time."

Alex let the subject lie as they entered the exhibit. There were bigger things to worry about, after all. Things like the gold ring sitting in a display at the end of the exhibit.

Alex couldn't hold back his excitement as he broke into a jog. Hawk did the same a few moments later, but headed for a display of swords instead. Alex could appreciate his interest in the weapons, but the fact remained, it was more likely that the ring held a mass enchantment. He ran faster the closer he got, coming to a stop with his hands pressed against the glass.

"What?" His heart sank when the Seed failed to identify

anything special about the delicately engraved gold band in the case. "Nothing?"

Lana caught up to him. "Seriously? I'm not even a fan, but even I thought there would be some kind of an enchantment on that thing."

"It has to." He pressed his fingers against the glass. "It's the One Ring! How can it not have an enchantment?" Frustration swelled inside him. First Autem had beat them to all the artifacts in Hollywood and the Smithsonian, and now they were just coming up empty. Alex shook his head. "Maybe if I cast inspection. That might tell me more."

"Okay, let's get the case open." Lana moved to help.

It took some work to pry the glass off of the base, but eventually, she was able to get a few fingers underneath it.

"Shit." She pulled her hand away as soon as they got the case open the rest of the way. The glass box tumbled to the floor to shatter as a trickle of blood ran down her finger.

"You okay?" Alvin rushed over.

"I'm fine. The glass was just sharp on the bottom."

Alex reached for his flask and cast Purify, so its healing effect could treat the wound.

"Save your water." She shook her head as the cut began to close on its own. "I'm a cleric, I have my own magic."

Alex returned the flask to the pouch on his belt and turned his attention back to the case to pick up the ring inside. He cast Inspection only to frown as the Seed failed to display an enchantment. "That's a huge let down."

"That one could be a replica or something," Lana added.

"Maybe." He shrugged and shoved the band onto a finger. "Enchanted or not, I'm keeping it."

That was when Hawk slapped the glass on the other side of the exhibit over by the swords. "Guys!"

"What is it?" Alex turned toward him.

"You might have struck out, but I sure as hell didn't." Hawk started trying to get the case open.

Alex blew out a sigh of relief. It didn't matter what kind of enchantment Hawk had found, he was just glad to have found something. He took a step forward only to stop when something dripped on his shoulder.

"The heck?"

He ran a finger over the sleeve of his leather jacket, pulling it away covered in some kind of black sludge. His entire body froze as every horror movie he'd ever seen flashed through his head. If he knew anything about anything, it was that the worst thing he could do was to look up. Of course, that knowledge did nothing to the fact that his first instinct was to do exactly that.

Raising his vision to the ceiling, he caught a glimpse of something in the shadows of the rafters. Everything went black an instant later as something cold splattered all over his face. It smelled rotten, like something had died weeks ago and crawled into his nose. His stomach turned, sending him heaving to the floor.

"What the hell is that?" Lana shouted as he felt her grab his arm.

Alex reached up to wipe whatever had just been sprayed into his eye only to slap himself in the head as his body spasmed.

"Hold on!"

He felt Lana's wiping at his eye and mouth with a cloth. "What is this stuff?"

The sound of something growling came from above.

"Give me the gun!" Hawk shouted.

Alex felt someone pull his pistol from his holster followed by several shots. Whatever was above him growled back. The sound of something rushing through a ventilation shaft followed.

"Is it gone?" Alvin asked in a whisper.

"I don't know," Lana answered. "It might come back."

Alex's body ached and his head felt like it was on fire. Glancing to his HUD shining within the blackness, he found one word hanging next to his name.

Poisoned.

His HUD faded out of sight as he rolled to the side to heave.

"Fuck, my shoes!" Hawk shrieked.

Alex could barely tell what direction his voice had come from. All he could do was collapse, fighting against waves of disorientation. Sweat poured down his forehead as Lana wiped at his eye with her sleeve. A blurry image of her, Hawk, and Alvin standing over him started to come into view, getting clearer as she removed whatever sludge covered his face. A surge of power inside him started to chase away the sickness inside him.

Lana must have cast a heal.

For an instant, Alex thought he was saved. The poison snuffed out the healing energy just as fast as it had come. There was nothing Lana could do. He needed to be cleansed.

Alex tried to pull his flask from his pouch, but couldn't work the clasp that held it in place. Eventually his hand just fell limp at his side. Each breath felt impossible, like someone had stacked cinder blocks on his chest. Eventually, he couldn't even inhale.

The blurry image of his coven standing over him began to fade.

Then, there was nothing.

CHAPTER THIRTY-ONE

Alex woke up drowning, or at least, feeling like he was. Water filled his mouth. He coughed it back out just as fast, then rolled over, dropping something as he threw up.

"Fuck, my shoes, again!" Hawk jumped back.

Alex struggled to catch his breath as sensation flooded back into his body. "What the hell happ—"

"Hey, we need to move." Lana grabbed his arm, casting a heal as she helped him up. "It might come back."

The memory of what had just happened flashed back to him. Something wet had dripped on his shoulder and he'd looked up like a dumb ass. Everything had gone to hell after that.

"I thought you were dead," Lana added.

"No, just poisoned." Alex spat on the floor. "Thanks to whoever gave me my flask."

"That was me." Lana nodded. "You had already cast Purify on it when I cut myself."

"Good thing I did. That poison silences you too." Alex remembered his HUD fading away shortly after he was blinded.

"What was that thing?" He got back to his feet, his legs feeling like Jell-O.

"I don't know, but it spit right in your face." Hawk kept his eyes trained on the ceiling, pointing Alex's pistol up at the shadows. "It ran into the vents when I shot at it."

Alex nearly threw up again. "Oh gross, that stuff got in my mouth and everything."

"None of us got a good enough look at the thing to analyze it." Lana wiped some more black sludge from Alex's neck with her sleeve.

"Maybe it was some kind of revenant." Alvin kept looking around. "One that we haven't seen yet."

Alex shook his head. "That poison crap it spit at me was cold. If a revenant produced it, I think it would have been closer to body temperature since they are technically still alive."

Lana headed toward the exit. "A zombie then?"

Alex didn't have time to respond before a figure dropped down in front of her just outside the door of the exhibit. He focused on the target, finally getting a good look.

At first glance, he would have guessed it was a common zombie, then he noticed the difference. Each finger was tipped with a claw of bone, like that of a lurker type zombie. Its legs were even stranger, splitting just below the knee to form what looked like arms. Three large fingers extended from each of the horrific limbs and its legs bent in a strange direction. The Seed confirmed what he feared.

Zombie Assassin, Rare, Hostile

Lana let out a half scream just before the monster fired a ball of black goo from its throat. The mass burst in her face like a water balloon.

"Lana!" Alvin rushed to his sister as she collapsed.

"Hey, do your aim-bot thing!" Hawk held Alex's gun out to give it back to him.

"I can't, my eye patch only gives me that ability if I do something rebellious and there's no one here in charge to rebel against. You have better aim than me right now." Alex scrambled over to where he had just woken up, searching for his flask. He must have dropped it nearby.

Hawk raised his gun. "Everyone stay down."

The gun barked three times. One round punched into the zombie assassin's chest, the second blew off what was left of its ear and the third missed all together.

"Shit!" Hawk tried to hold his hands still but clearly didn't have enough practice.

The assassin wasn't going to give him another chance. Thrusting out one of its clawed hands, a grayish spike burst from its wrist. Alvin slammed the door shut just as the fragment of bone punched into the wood, sticking out the other side a few inches.

"God damn!" Alex nearly stumbled back.

Assassin really was the right name for the thing.

Hawk ran to the door to help Alvin, giving up on the idea of shooting the zombie. Instead, he grabbed a velvet rope that encircled one of the costume displays and wrapped it around the door handles.

Lana spasmed on the floor a few feet away.

Alvin dropped to his knees beside his sister as soon as the door was secure. "Someone help her!"

"I just need my——" Alex found his flask, his mind spinning into a panic when he realized it was empty. "Shit!"

"You grabbed at it when Lana poured it in your mouth. Then you started hurling." Hawk stepped away from the door he'd just secured, another spike of bone puncturing the surface with a hard thunk.

"I must have spilled the rest of the water." Alex tightened his fingers around the flask.

"What do we do?" Alvin looked up with tears welling in his eyes.

"I have more water in the car." Alex ran toward them as another piece of bone punched into the door.

"We aren't getting to the car that way." Hawk joined them as Lana's spasms started to grow weaker. "And she doesn't look good."

"No, please." Alvin wiped at the sludge that covered his sister's face.

That was when Alex realized that they only had one option. Without hesitation, he willed the Seed to remove the restrictions that Digby had placed on Alvin's magic.

"Why did you—" The kid started to ask, clearly getting a notification on his HUD.

Alex shoved a hand onto Lana's pocket to retrieve the compact that she had been using to talk to Parker. "You're going to get us out of here."

"I am?" Alvin's voice shook.

"Are you sure?" Hawk gestured to Alvin with his head. "You know, cause of the treason?"

"It doesn't matter if I'm sure." Alex locked eyes with Alvin. "You're the only one that can save us, so I hope you really are on our side."

"I am." He gave a rapid nod.

"Good." Alex handed him the makeup mirror. "Have you touched the compact that Parker has been using to communicate?"

Alvin shook his head.

"Okay, what about any of the mirrors in the parking garage back in Vegas?" Alex spoke fast, knowing that Lana didn't have long based on his own experience.

"I… I think so." Alvin nodded.

"Good, odds are Parker is there. I just need you to open a link so we can talk to her." He swept his vision across the room looking for a reflective surface that they could use to open a passage. "Cast Mirror Link and show Parker one of the display cases."

"Alright." Alvin's hand shook as he opened the compact, hesitating a moment before touching the mirror inside.

An impulse passed through Alex's mind to slap the compact out of his hand before he had time to contact someone at Autem, but he held back. They had to start trusting him eventually, and right now Lana's life depended on it. Still, he winced as Alvin's finger pressed against the glass. He leaned closer as a view of the parking garage filled the tiny mirror, breathing a sigh of relief as Sax stood on the other side.

The soldier was standing there with his back turned, holding a box of supplies.

"Thank god." Alex grabbed hold of the compact.

"Mother fuck—" Sax dropped whatever he was carrying and spun around in surprise.

Alex didn't have time to apologize. "Get Parker now! We need an exit."

Another spike of bone punched into the door like an exclamation point at the end of Alex's sentence.

"And get any enchanter you can, we need a cleanse now," he added.

Sax didn't question it. Instead, he just started running.

"Okay, help me get her up." Alex hoisted Lana up, slipping himself under one of her arms as Alvin did the same on the other side.

Her head hung forward as random spasms hit her every few seconds.

"What do I do?" Hawk stood in front of them.

Lana answered by throwing up on his feet.

"Fu—" He jumped back. "Seriously, that is the third time in ten minutes."

Alvin gagged.

"Don't you dare make it four." Hawk stared at him.

The teenager shook off his nausea and stepped forward, carrying his sister toward one of the large display cases. "Parker needs to hurry."

"She'll make it," Alex said with as much confidence as he could, trying to keep Alvin calm.

"Shit, do you hear that?" Hawk held up a hand.

"No, what?" Alex stopped to listen. "I don't hear anything."

"I know." Hawk pointed to the door. "That assassin stopped trying to get in."

"Maybe it went away," Alvin said, sounding hopeful.

Then, as if on cue, a low growl came from the vent on the ceiling.

"Crap! It came back around." Alex dropped Lana with her brother by the display case and ran toward the growling.

"Where are you going?" Alvin shouted, his voice trembling.

Alex cast barrier as he looked back. "I'm gonna draw it away, just get Lana through the passage."

"Yeah!" Hawk added as he sprinted to Alex's side. "We'll distract it."

"No we won't." Alex swatted at the young rogue. "You need to go too. I will be right behind you."

"Hell no. I'm staying with you to make sure you really make it out of here." Hawk put his foot down.

"Fine. There isn't time to argue about it." Alex jumped in front of Hawk just as a spike of bone flew from the shadows in the ceiling. He felt the impact slam into his chest, only to bounce off, his barrier shimmering across his body.

"I really wish you hadn't taken my lighter away." Hawk groaned.

"Yeah, me too." Alex pulled off his leather jacket, to use as a shield in case the zombie spat another ball of poison at them. Glancing back at Alvin, he noticed the surface of the display case nearby was beginning to ripple.

Yes! Parker made it!

Alvin wasted no time in getting his sister up and through the passage. They both disappeared a second later.

"Come on." Alex reached for Hawk with one hand just before a mass of black sludge burst against the leather jacket he held in front of him.

Stumbling from the impact, he ducked behind his improvised shield. He cursed his impaired balance as he fell. The zombie assassin dropped down from the ceiling, landing just ten feet away on its horrible leg fingers. It fired another spike of bone the moment it landed. It passed by Alex, missing by mere inches. He dropped to the floor as the zombie fired two fragments of bone that flew over Alex's head.

"Let's go, Hawk!" He scooted backward on his rear toward the passage behind him. He did a double take when he found the space where Hawk had been empty. "What the—"

Another glob of poison pelted his jacket before he could locate the troublemaker. Had he made a break for the passage? No, he wouldn't have left without him. That was when he remembered Hawk's class.

He was a rogue.

Alex glanced at his HUD, finding Hawk's mana. It wasn't full, meaning he had just cast something. Obviously, from his sudden absence, Alex assumed it had been a conceal spell. From that, he knew what he needed to do.

"Hey! Is that the best you have?" Alex struggled to get back on his feet while making sure the assassin stayed focused on him.

If Hawk had concealed himself, then that could only mean the rogue was looking for an opening to attack. The zombie's arm swelled as a lump moved beneath its skin to its hand. A bone spike emerged from its palm a moment later as it took a step in Alex's direction. He braced, the fragment shooting straight through his jacket before slamming into his chest. Blue light shimmered across his body as the barrier took the impact.

The zombie assassin walked forward, its strange hand-like feet moving with an unnaturally fast gait. Another bone spike burst from its hand, piercing the jacket before being stopped by his barrier like the last.

"How many bones could this thing possibly have?" Alex watched through the holes in his coat.

That was when it spat another ball of poison. The glob

burst on impact, spraying foul-smelling droplets through the holes in his shield. Alex jerked his head away just in time, feeling the fluid spatter against his shirt.

"That was close."

There was no way to know how the poison worked exactly, but he assumed it would be a problem if it got in his eyes or mouth. Hell, it might even be dangerous to get it on his skin. Either way, his jacket wasn't going to protect him for long. There was a chance that his barrier might be enough to stop the stuff, but if he got hit in the face again, he would be blind. He might even end up inhaling the poison since the spell still allowed for air to pass through. Not to mention he'd still be covered with goo when the barrier ran out.

The assassin kept moving, closing the gap between them.

"Sometime today, Hawk!" Alex called out from behind his ruined jacket. "I can only act as bait for so long."

"I got you." Hawk's voice responded as the rogue stepped out of thin air directly beside the monster. He held Alex's pistol up with both hands, planting the muzzle against the head of the unsuspecting assassin.

Then he pulled the trigger.

The opposite side of the zombie assassin's head exploded outward, spraying the wall with black chunks and fluid. A low growl rumbled through the monster before trailing off. It stumbled to the side, its limbs suddenly losing all coordination. A bone spike flew from one hand, punching into the floor. It simply fell over after that, collapsing to the floor in a broken heap.

Zombie assassin defeated. 1,194 experience awarded.

Alex blew out a sigh of relief as he tossed his poison-covered jacket to the floor. The tattered garment hit the floor with a wet slap.

"Gross." Hawk lowered the gun in his hands.

"Thanks for saving my ass." Alex held out a hand to take

back his pistol. "I don't know how much longer I was going to last there."

"See, sometimes it's a good idea to bring kids into a zombie apocalypse." Hawk gave him a smug grin, making it clear that he was going to be reminding Alex that he'd rescued him every day for the next week. "Anyway, we should get…"

Alex tensed as Hawk trailed off, afraid that there was another threat behind him. He spun, ready to fight, only to find something much worse.

"No." His arms fell limp to his sides.

"That's bad." Hawk stepped to his side.

"Yeah, that's real bad." Alex stared at the display that had held the passage that Alvin and his sister had just vanished through.

A pair of bone spikes were lodged in the glass. The surface was still intact but now filled with a thousand tiny cracks. In desperation, Alex rushed forward to place his hand on the case. It collapsed into countless tiny pieces glinting in the dim light of the room.

"We have another way out, right?" Hawk sounded nervous.

Alex said nothing for a moment.

"We have another way out, right?" Hawk repeated, this time louder.

"Alvin had the compact and neither of us have the Mirror Link spell to contact Parker. There's no way to show her a new location to use for a passage." Alex shook his head, slowly.

Hawk deflated. "What do we do?"

Alex hooked a thumb back toward the museum's entrance. "We still have the car."

Hawk forced a laugh. "Oh great, a road trip."

"At least Lana and Alvin made it." Alex forced himself to relax. "They should have had time to get her cleansed."

"Yeah." Hawk turned back to the display case full of swords that they had been looking at before the zombie assassin had dropped in on them. "At least we can take this thing with us."

Alex joined him, looking over the iconic prop swords in the

case one by one. They were beautiful. He never thought he'd get to see them in person. Focusing on near the end, a line of text scrolled across his HUD.

"Woah." His eyes widened. "Now that is what I call an enchantment."

CHAPTER THIRTY-TWO

"Bring it here." Parker held an arm out as Sax rushed toward her carrying the grail that Alex had brought back from a previous trip.

"Don't leave me." Alvin knelt on the floor of the parking garage next to his sister who he had just carried through a Mirror Passage from Boston.

"Hang in there, Lana." Parker leaned across the woman to press her head against her chest. There was a faint heartbeat accompanied by shallow breaths.

Sax dropped to his knees before he had even reached them, sliding across the concrete with the grail held out in front of him. Parker grabbed the cup and filled it with the closest liquid she had, an empty can of orange soda. It didn't matter what she put in it, the enchantment would have the same effect.

"Come on, Lana. Drink up." Parker placed the grail to the dying woman's lips and poured its contents in.

Lana barely reacted for the first few seconds. Then she started to cough, expelling a mouthful of purified orange soda.

"No you don't." Parker held her down and poured more down her throat. "You need to swallow it."

After that, Lana stopped struggling and drank down a few gulps before rolling over to throw up.

"Okay, think you kept it down long enough for the magic to work." Parker dropped back onto her rear, holding the grail empty beside her.

"Thank you." Alvin threw his arms around his sister as soon as she stopped hurling.

Parker started to stand, picking up a spike of bone that had nearly hit her a moment before when it had flown through the Passage. She'd been forced to cancel the spell to keep everyone on her side safe. Raising a hand to the mirror, she tried to reopen the passage. She started to sweat when the spell failed.

Sax took the grail back. "Why isn't it working?"

"What?" Alvin pulled away from his sister as she regained her senses.

"Where am I?" Lana looked around as the order of events fell into place. A moment later, she shook off her confusion and tried to stand. "We need to reopen the passage. That thing is going to kill them!"

Parker tried again to reopen the portal. "Shit, it's not working."

"Why not?" Lana staggered toward the glass.

"I can't reopen it. Something must have broken the glass on the other end." Parker followed her. "That's the only reason that my spell would fail like this." Frantically, she reached in her pocket for her compact, flipping it open and casting Mirror Link. "Alex, what happened? Are you okay?" She cocked her head to the side when the spell showed her an image of her own back.

"I'm sorry, I didn't realize..." Alvin's voice came from behind her.

Turning around, she found him standing with another compact in his hand. A lump rose in her throat as she realized what that meant.

"Alex gave it to me." Alvin lowered his head. "I didn't think to leave it. I thought he would be right behind me."

"It's not your fault." Parker shook off her dread and rushed to the kid. "We can still figure this out. Did you touch any other windows or mirrors while you were there, anything?"

Alvin's eyes darted from side to side before finally lowering his head. "I try to keep my hands to myself."

Parker looked back to Lana. "What about you?"

"Shit. I touched a display case, but we broke it right after." She placed a hand over her face.

"We'll just have to use the same window you used to get there." Parker sighed. "The one at Fenway Park. It won't be easy to reach but the car should be able to…" She trailed off when she saw the look on Lana's face.

"There was a brute at Fenway, it broke the window."

Parker let out a frustrated growl before thinking of another option. "We use the car then. One of you must have touched a window while you were riding in it."

Lana sunk a little lower. "The brute broke all of the ones on our side of the car too. I don't think I've touched any of the ones that are still intact."

Lana and her brother both tried just in case but the spell failed.

Parker dropped into a crouch, realizing there was nothing she could do. "What happened back there?"

Lana recounted the encounter that her coven had with a new type of zombie while she and her brother were in Boston. According to Alvin, Alex and Hawk had drawn the monster away from them so he could get his sister through the mirror passage. The glass that they had used for the portal must have been broken after that.

Parker refused to believe that something like a zombie assassin had been able to kill Alex or Hawk. Sure, one of them was suffering from a massive stat demerit and the other was a twelve-year-old, but there was no way she was going to believe the two of them had let a zombie get the better of them. No, they had to be alive.

The bigger problem was getting them home.

Think, Parker, think.

There had to be a way.

"I think I have a location in my binder that's not too far away?" Parker thought out loud. "Maybe fifty miles."

"But how would they know to get there?" Sax poked a hole in the idea.

Parker held her binder tighter. "A swarm of revenants would probably get them before they could get there anyway."

Lana held out a hand. "I know Alex had plenty of warding rods on him. There's a good chance he and Hawk can ride out the night somewhere. We can send a team to him in the morning."

"That might be our only choice." Sax waved for someone to clean up the mess on the floor of the garage.

"Yeah, as long as Alex actually stays put, that is." Parker rubbed at her eyes, still not having slept more than a few hours in the last couple of days.

Of course, that was when things got worse.

"What the hell is that?" Sax raised a hand to the sky behind her.

Parker whimpered as she turned, only to stumble backward in shock when she saw a speck approaching on the horizon. A lump climbed into her throat.

"Why?" She shook her head in disbelief. "Why now?"

The dot grew closer, its silhouette unmistakable in the afternoon sun.

A kestrel.

CHAPTER THIRTY-THREE

"Hmm, days without an accident?" Digby read over the words on a sign that hung over the floor of the warehouse as he wandered around to kill time.

Obviously, he could have started the ritual to create a new infernal spirit already, but if he was going to lure potentially hundreds of revenants to their death, then he had to wait until dark when they were no longer dormant. That way, not only would he fill his void with resources, but he might also gain a few levels.

Unfortunately, that meant that he had another half hour to wait, and Ames wasn't about to let him do so in peace.

"Just two more hearts, waiting to be taken," the corpse said, referring to the two prisoners that they were still holding back in Vegas.

Digby started to nod before rapidly shaking his head. "That's enough out of you."

Asher cawed in confusion from one of the shelves. Obviously, she couldn't see the ghost, not being insane herself. No, that was Digby's cross to bear. He dragged a claw across a chalkboard that hung beneath the sign meant to record the number of days that had passed without an accident. Adding a zero, he was pretty sure the entire workforce becoming revenants counted.

"It could look like an accident." Ames continued to urge down the path of madness. "Even your conscience could be removed."

"I am not about to murder Parker." Digby chuckled. "For a hallucination produced by my own mind, you certainly don't know me well. As annoying as I might find Parker, I would never hurt an ally."

"That's true." Ames gestured to the blood dripping from his chest, adding, "Until it isn't."

Digby glowered at the corpse, willing it to go away.

Ames faded a moment later, but not before whispering one final truth. "She is in the way."

Digby tried to ignore the comment. Though, at least a part of him knew it was true. At some point, Parker was going to realize that the madness they feared had set in. She would tell the others. Not because she wanted to hurt him; quite the opposite. She would tell the others, believing it was the best way to help.

"It could look like an accident," Ames whispered again.

"Bah." Digby waved the suggestion away. "I won't let things come to that."

He stormed off after that. Not that he could ever truly run from his own thoughts. He just needed something to keep his mind busy. Finding several posters plastered all over the wall, he tried to learn something about the building's lingering dead that would become his new minion. Many of the posters were informational, with simple pictures and charts. They seemed to warn the workers of something dangerous. He scratched at his chin.

"What are unions and why do these posters say they want to take people's wages?"

He grimaced, reading a line on one of the posters that reminded him of something Bancroft had said when discussing the economics of Vegas. Then he laughed. Now that Charles was gone, Elenore had gotten things running smoother. The value of the currency they assigned to everyone had been working well to cover the basic needs of the survivors they housed, so clearly Bancroft didn't have all the answers.

Thinking of the man brought a bitter taste to Digby's mouth. He tore one of the posters down with a claw, hoping Bancroft was miserable on the journey that Digby's exile had sent him on. He still wished he had just killed him. That would have been one accident that no one would have cared to investigate.

Eventually, Digby shook off his melancholy and wandered through a door near the back of the building, finding himself in a restroom. The mirror that hung over the sinks had been broken. He poked at the paper towel dispenser, remembering how lost he had been the first time he'd seen one back when he had woken up.

There were more posters like the others outside adhered to the inside of the bathroom stalls. One bore the image of a friendly-looking person wearing some kind of device on their head, while the text above declared that union dues were more expensive than purchasing the latest game system. To the side of the poster, someone had written, 'I can build a guillotine for less.'

Digby got a good cackle out of that comment before lowering his eyes to the picture of the game system. "I should really loot one of these and have Alex show me how to use it."

Considering how much he enjoyed the movies and board games that his apprentice had shown him, he had to assume he would like a game system as well. He furrowed his brow, realizing his tastes were more similar to Alex's than he'd realized.

"Dear lord." Digby was taken aback by the thought. "I might be a nerd."

He stood there for a moment as his identity entered a bit of a crisis on par with the madness that plagued him. Then he shook his head. "Who cares what I am."

With that, he headed out of the bathroom. He'd read

enough posters for the day and the sun was bound to set in the next few minutes.

It was time to start the ritual.

Approaching the skeleton that he'd laid out on the floor, Digby knelt down and held out his hand so that his diamond pinkie ring glinted in the fading sunlight. He glanced up to make sure everything was in place.

The windows were blocked, one entrance was open, and a set of warding rods were set up to keep the revenants from entering more than a few feet. His horde of fifty enhanced zombies stood in two groups to bracket the only way in to stop anything that got through. His staff lay on the floor beside him.

Asher let out a caw as if to say she was ready.

Satisfied, Digby opened his maw underneath the warded area and checked his mana.

MP: 346/376

Then, he started the ritual.

Just like when he'd created Tavern, he felt a tug on his mana as the ritual began. He didn't resist, allowing the power to trickle from his body. He'd given up so much in the pursuit of power, what was another fifty mana in the grand scheme of things? Motes of green light began to glow throughout the warehouse as the lingering echoes of the dead answered his call.

Digby held his position, looking up at his horde and watching the open door. "Get ready."

Asher cawed out a compel to reinforce the order. They snapped their attention to the door, ready to grab any of the revenants that might be immune to the wards. The sound of screeching began to grow outside.

"Here we go." Digby kept his focus on the ritual, hoping his defenses would hold until he was finished.

That was when something slapped against one of the windows that he had sealed with his Blood Forge. The claws of a revenant scraped against the glass outside.

"Are you daft? I have left a door open."

He frowned as another of the creatures started clawing at a window on the other side of the warehouse. One by one, more began to show up. Looking out through the window, he could see them crawling over the wall outside. There were even more running down the street further away.

Digby tensed his shoulders, realizing that he may have bitten off more than he could chew. "I guess I was right about there being plenty of the creatures hiding in the surrounding buildings."

It wasn't long before every wall thumped in an unending rhythm as the revenants slapped their hands against the building in frustration.

"Do I really need to put out a bloody welcome sign?" Digby groaned at the swarm's inability to find their way in. "The one time I actually want the creatures around and they can't even find the open door."

For a moment, he regretted leaving Parker behind. At least she could have worked as bait. The view through the windows grew dim as body after body pressed against it. Digby cringed. He'd reinforced the glass to withstand the attention of a few of the foes, but he had expected that the majority of them would use the damn door.

"Hey!" Digby called out toward the door. "I am in here, you mindless idiots. You know, through the open space that appears completely unprotected."

A chittering screech answered him as a lone revenant wandered into the door.

"Yes! There you go, come on in." Digby beckoned to the creature.

It stopped just before reaching his maw, staring at him in confusion. Digby furrowed his brow, unsure what had given the creature reason to pause. Then he analyzed it.

Revenant, Common, Neutral

"Blast." Digby groaned. "No wonder they aren't coming in."

The energies involved in the ritual must have drawn the creatures to him, but that was it. Without a human in the mix to entice them, they had no reason to do anything more. The only thing he could do was attack first, thus changing the swarm to hostile status.

Digby glanced at his HUD to see how much of his maximum mana he'd lost to the ritual.

MP: 321/350

"Only halfway there." Digby looked back to the lone revenant standing in the door.

If he did nothing, the ritual would simply finish, giving him the minion that he came for while allowing the revenants to dissipate once the energy that was riling them up faded. The night would end without incident, but Digby would also miss out on the resources and experience that could be gained by provoking the revenants further.

"Never settle for less." Ames stood by the door gesturing toward the lone revenant that had begun to wander in.

"For once, we agree." Digby chuckled to his madness.

Of course, he could cast Decay at the creature, though, that would also disrupt the ritual. He glanced at his horde, wishing he had left one zombie outside. As it was, his open maw was blocking their path to the revenant. Digby flicked his attention to the side in search of something to throw. There was nothing within reach.

"Hey," he called to the nearest zombie. "Go fetch me something from the office. And make it heavy."

The zombie wandered off into the small room at the edge of the warehouse only to return wheeling a desk chair behind them.

"No! Not a chair!" Digby rubbed at the bridge of his nose with the back of a claw. "Bring me something I can throw."

He cursed himself for letting his control spell lapse earlier. With Asher there, he didn't need their full obedience, but the intelligence that his control spell provided would have certainly helped.

The zombie let go of the chair and headed back into the office. It returned with a corded telephone, dragging the receiver behind them.

"Good enough." Digby held out a hand. "Give it here."

He didn't dare tell the zombie to throw the object on its own for fear they would just miss. Instead, he grabbed the phone and ripped the cord out with his teeth to keep it from getting caught on anything. Then, he lobbed the makeshift projectile in an awkward arc. Tumbling through the air, the phone flew straight into the revenant's chest, bouncing off to land at the edge of his maw.

"Perfect!" Digby congratulated himself for his accuracy, only to immediately curse the phone when the creature failed to turn hostile.

"The bloody thing must not have been heavy enough to cause any real damage." He growled in frustration. "Apparently revenants have a high tolerance for what they perceive as a threat. Annoying one a bit won't be enough."

He checked his HUD again.

MP: 306/336

There was still another few minutes to go before the ritual finished. Letting it do so was the safe bet.

"What fun is that?" Ames knelt down beside him.

"Oh, screw it." Digby threw a hand out toward the revenant that stood near his waiting maw, sending a spike of blood up from the shadowy opening with a Forge spell. It burst through the creature's abdomen.

The moment he cast the spell, the green glow that had been growing within his diamond faded, along with the motes of light that had been drifting toward the gemstone. At the same time, the impaled revenant let out a screech far different than before. A chorus of cries answered from all around the warehouse far louder than Digby expected.

"There must be more of the creatures outside than I realized." He spent another ten points of mana to reform the spike of necrotic blood that impaled his prey.

The revenant was drawn down into his maw along with the formation of blood. It screeched and flailed the entire way. The swarm began peeking in through the doorway, their eyes glowing orange in the night outside.

"Come and get me." Digby thrust the diamond in his hand out again to restart the ritual, luring every revenant in the area to the warehouse.

With the change from neutral to hostile, the swarm began rushing the entrance a few at a time. Digby watched as they ran straight into his waiting maw. Experience messages flooded his HUD.

"Yes, that's right. Come on in." He let a cackle roll through his chest as his resources ticked up.

With each creature's dying screech, more seemed to come. It wasn't long before there was a crowd outside the door, all pushing forward. Some of the revenants in the front noticed his maw waiting for them and tried to turn back. The force of the wall of creatures behind them pushing forward forced them into his void regardless.

"Good lord." Digby's hand shook as his plan worked far better than he'd expected.

Revenants poured into his maw, several at a time. The Seed couldn't even keep up with the count, no longer notifying him of each kill in favor of updating the quantity and experience in one message. Digby's mouth fell open as his resources surged. If the assault kept up, he'd have what he needed to craft almost any kind of minion he wanted. The additional time that he'd gained by restarting the ritual had significantly increased the number of revenants, and the hostile screeches of the swarm seemed to draw even more.

Obviously, things couldn't continue in his favor for long.

A lone revenant leaped over his maw, passing through the warding rods like they weren't even there.

Revenant Wardbreaker, Uncommon, Hostile

One was bound to show up eventually.

"Stop them!" Digby called out to his horde as the creature landed in the middle of the zombies that bracketed the entrance.

Asher sent out a compel to back him up.

A few members of the horde lunged forward, using every ounce of the additional strength that Digby's enhancements had returned to them. The wardbreaker cried out as they grabbed hold of its arms and brought it to the floor. Its scream was cut off as his zombies tore the creature limb from limb in the space of a heartbeat.

Another wardbreaker burst from the swarm at the door. It hit the floor in a crouch only to spring up and over the first. It made it a few more steps than its predecessor before the horde fell upon it.

"Nice try?" Digby cackled at the display as a third wardbreaker tried to get through only to meet the same result.

According to his HUD, over two hundred revenants had poured into his maw and there was no sign of them stopping. There weren't many wardbreakers mixed in, but with the sheer volume of the swarm, there were more than Digby had expected. Another of the evolved creatures leapt through the wards followed by another. Both made it further than the ones that came before since more of his zombies were preoccupied with eating the prey that had already fallen.

"Hey! Now's not the time to get distracted." Digby tensed as the horde continued to eat instead of guarding the door.

Asher cawed to get the zombies back in line. Most listened. However, some did not. Still others seemed distracted by the meat laying before them.

"Not good!" Digby glanced at his HUD to see how close he was to finishing the ritual.

MP: 266/330

He was still around thirty percent away. There was only a hundred feet or so between him and the entrance, and with the rate the swarm was pouring in, odds were that one ward-breakers would reach him eventually.

"I knew I should have cast control on the horde." Digby cursed himself again for being so stingy with his mana. Asher's compels worked well to control the horde overall, but they weren't always able to alter a zombie's natural instincts. If there was food available right in front of them, it would take a lot to stop them from focusing on it.

Another wardbreaker launched into the warehouse, nearly reaching the skeleton laying in the middle of Digby's ritual. At the same time, the sound of claws scratching at the building's roof announced the arrival of at least a dozen nightflyers. From the noise, it didn't sound like any of them were the larger, bloodstalker types, but those were sure to be on the way as well.

"I'm going to be overrun." Digby debated canceling the ritual again and making a run for it.

He had been aware of the risks, but he'd assumed he could escape easily by crafting himself some wings and blasting a hole in the roof to escape, but with so many winged revenants on the building, the prospect was looking a lot less promising.

"Quitter," Ames whispered from directly behind him.

"No." Digby shook his head. "I can finish this."

The horde grabbed hold of another wardbreaker that made it inside, this one nearly crashing into the ritual space.

"Hey, watch the skeleton!" Digby growled at the zombies as they ripped apart the revenant close enough to spray his face with a warm spatter of blood.

That was when a heavy scraping at the roof told him that a

flying bloodstalker had arrived. Digby looked up to find the ceiling's supports shaking. He wasn't getting out through there.

"I might have overstayed my welcome." He glanced around the room for something to defend himself with. "This is going to get worse before it gets better."

Almost as soon as the words had left his mouth, a wardbreaker burst through the entrance, jumping over the distracted horde, his zombies spread out in disarray. With no other choice, Digby thrust his claws out to catch the creature as it lunged for his face. He buried his claws into the revenant and shifted his weight to force it to the side to pin the creature down.

"Not yet!" Digby kept the ritual going, holding the wardbreaker down as it flailed and screeched beside him. "I am getting what I came here for, damn it!"

The last few points of mana trickled from him to the gemstone in his other hand. The revenant he'd impaled went still just as the diamond began to glow a brilliant green.

"Finally." Digby stood and cast Animate Skeleton. He didn't even wait for his new minion to get up before joining the fight.

Grabbing his staff, he swept it over the blood-soaked floor and cast Forge. Rivers of crimson flowed up from the ground to the metal head of the weapon. Normally he would form something simple, like a spear, but something inside him demanded creativity. The curved blade of a scythe grew from the end of his staff, crimson dripping from its edge. If he was going to wield the power of death, he might as well look the part.

Several wardbreakers broke through his defenses, racing toward him as he stood.

Slamming the butt of his weapon down, he cast Forge to send a wave of spikes shooting up from the blood-soaked floor. The revenants tumbled forward, some impaling themselves with their momentum. Still, there were more coming. Sweeping his hand across the room, he summoned his wraith twice, marking each of the wardbreakers as targets.

The crimson image of a long-dead killer flickered into existence, darting toward the first foe. Blood sprayed through the air as the creature's head rolled from its shoulders. The wraith moved on, vanishing from sight before reappearing behind the next target. The revenant's body lurched forward as the echo flayed open its back. The wraith moved on from there, dismantling the rest of the targets.

Digby checked his mana.

MP: 32/326

The spell had cost him almost everything he had.

"No matter." Digby held his staff aloft and cast Leach to drain mana from the horde.

He cast it again and again as a mist of emerald light drifted from each member of the horde to bring him back to full. Digby slammed his staff back down with a wild cackle. Even with a modest horde, he was nearly unstoppable. He could spend as much mana as he wanted while every zombie in the room absorbed more for him to leach. It was as if his absorption rate had been multiplied by fifty. Still, the swarm of revenants poured into his maw to flood his resources as he felt the surge of one level up after another.

The only cause for concern was the buckling supports of the ceiling. From the sound of the claws on the roof, at least four bloodstalkers had arrived.

That was when a dark voice came from behind him, sounding like several layered on top of each other.

"Why have you summoned us?"

Digby turned to find a skeleton standing behind him.

"Do you have a name?" He eyed his new minion.

"We..." The skeleton went silent for a moment, looking around the room at the posters on the wall. Then, they answered, "We are Union."

"Good to meet you, Union." Digby gave his new infernal spirit a nod. "Now, find something to fight with and start killing revenants."

Digby turned back to the fight and summoned his wraith again to handle another few wardbreakers.

He snapped his attention back to the skeleton as it spoke one word.

"No."

CHAPTER THIRTY-FOUR

"What do you mean, no?" Digby's stared at his new skeletal minion in disbelief. "I created you. You aren't allowed to say no."

"We understand the contract." Union, the animated skeleton, nodded their bony skull as their dark voice continued. "But we wish for benefits."

"Benefits?" Digby fired off another wraith at a wardbreaker that had gotten through the defenses at the entrance. "You are a skeleton, inhabited by an infernal spirit that I created from the lingering echoes of the dead! You don't need benefits. And you certainly can't refuse an order."

"We do not wish to refuse." The skeleton sunk slightly, as if sighing despite having no lungs to do so. "Yet, negotiations are required."

Digby held stock-still for a few seconds as revenants continued to pour into his maw on the other side of the warehouse. "You realize we are standing in the middle of a bad situation where we might all be torn apart in a matter of minutes, and that you will cease to exist if I am destroyed, right?"

The skeleton glanced around the room. "We have leverage."

"Leverage?" Digby swiped a claw through the air. "What do you even want?"

Union, the skeleton, considered the question as a bloodstalker above poked a massive clawed hand through the roof near the edge of the building.

"Sometime today." Digby spun around to cut the head off a wardbreaker with the crimson scythe blade at the end of his staff. "Might I remind you we do not have all the time in the world?"

"We understand." The skeleton stood a little taller. "We require additional bones, in case of damage."

"Done." Digby thrust a claw into a foe, lifting it off the ground as it flailed. "I would have done that anyway."

The skeleton nodded. "We wish not to be returned to the gemstone."

"Alright, I suppose there's no reason to keep you in storage." Digby ripped his claws free of the creature he'd just killed, dropping it to his feet where a pile of corpses was beginning to form.

The skeleton stepped forward. "Next—"

"There's more?" Digby snapped back.

"Work days should not exceed eight hours. We also require time off."

"You what?" Digby glanced to the ceiling as a bloodstalker began prying the roof apart.

"We require work life balance," the bony minion responded as if they were not in a fight for their lives.

"Work life balance?" Digby pressed a palm to his forehead, adding, "You are dead, you don't have a life to balance!"

"Why are you negotiating with minions?" Ames whispered in Digby's ear as his eye twitched. "You are their lord."

"That's right!" Digby slammed the butt of his staff down and thrust a claw out in the direction of the skeleton. "I am your creator! I brought you into this world. You would not exist without me."

Union stepped back looking shocked. "But we—"

"No buts." Digby cut them off. "You will do as I say to the

best of your ability or I will throw your bones in a barrel of purified water. How does that sound?"

"Like a tyrant." The skeleton stood its ground.

"Well, too bad. I don't have the luxury to discuss this further." Digby threw a hand up toward the ceiling as the moonlight shined in through a gaping hole. "Now find a weapon and start fighting, or I will send you right back where you came from."

Digby turned away to focus on the fight as two bloodstalkers reached in through the hole in the ceiling, ripping at the sides in an attempt to widen it enough to fit through. From the sound of it, there were at least six of the beasts up there now. They would be inside in mere moments.

I have to escape before that happens.

Union picked up a broken piece of shelving and reluctantly stabbed it through a wardbreaker. Digby grumbled under his breath at the skeleton's lack of enthusiasm. Who would have thought he'd miss Tavern? At least they only required the occasional drink. Though, technically, he didn't have to give Tavern anything. The infernal spirit was a minion.

"It doesn't matter if they're happy," Ames added with a whisper.

Asher cawed and flapped down to one of the lower shelves. A hurt feeling bled across their bond as if sensing what he was thinking.

No, it did matter.

Digby stood in the middle of the warehouse as his zombies tore revenants apart all around him. They were doing this for him. Some would even sacrifice themselves. That mattered. That should be respected.

"Why?" Ames whispered.

Digby didn't have an answer. The horde was dead, they couldn't feel happy or sad. Blood sprayed across his tattered coat as one of his zombies chomped into a revenant's neck beside him. All the dead wanted was to eat.

"They are minions," Ames added. "They are yours to use."

Digby checked his HUD. According to his resources, he'd already eaten several hundred revenants with more pouring in the door every second. Each one made him stronger. It would be a shame to flee while there was still more to gain. He just needed a way to beat the bloodstalkers on the roof.

"Use the horde," Ames suggested.

Digby did the math in his head. "No, they aren't strong enough to win."

"Do they need to win?" The voice of his madness made a good point.

"No, they don't." Digby's brow raised in understanding. "They just need to take the foes out with them."

With that, he raised a hand to the sky to cast several Emerald Flares. The spells would destroy his last line of defense but they might also take out a couple of the bloodstalkers before they got inside. At the very least, the radiation would give them reason to back off. His mana dropped down to just a few points as rivers of sickly green energy poured through the warehouse toward the roof, collecting into multiple points of shining power.

Digby ducked as the ceiling detonated, firing pieces of the roof straight up into the sky like shrapnel. The blast reduced a dozen nightflyers to a pink mist in an instant while the larger bloodstalkers cried out, their wings ripped to shreds by the debris.

Messages flooded Digby's HUD as glowing green embers fell like snow. Digby ignored all but one line of text.

2 Revenant Bloodstalkers defeated.

"Ha!" Digby raised his head to the sky as the smoke and debris cleared.

Then he stopped laughing.

The rest of the bloodstalkers were already crawling in to attack, their ruined wings folded up behind them. There were more than he'd expected. From the heavy footsteps he'd heard, he had assumed there were six on the roof. Apparently, some had not yet landed. Now, there were still seven more climbing in, with another two flapping their wings in the sky above.

"This was a bad idea." Digby's staff drooped a little.

Asher darted past him to hide in the warehouse office while cawing a compel to the horde, telling them to focus on the threats above. Digby fell back as well, holding his staff toward the horde as he cast Leach again. A river of green energy flowed toward him to fill his mana back up just as the bloodstalkers fell upon the horde.

Enormous clawed feet slammed down all around him, crushing several of the dead instantly. Digby's already cold blood nearly froze solid as one of the bloodstalkers splattered two of his zombie's heads like watermelons. Necrotic gray matter sprayed across the floor from beneath the beast's heel. The revenant didn't skip a beat, grabbing another member of the horde and tearing its head off. It dropped the body, a spinal column dangling from the skull in its hand.

Digby froze, hesitating at the overwhelming strength he was up against.

"Use the horde!" Ames snapped him out of it as the madness cried out from inside Digby's mind.

"Yes!" He stepped to the side as the bloodstalker threw what remained of the zombie at him.

The severed head and spine hit the wall behind him with a wet splatter. Digby looked down as the zombie's eyes stared up at him, still blinking. He responded by casting control on what was left of the horde to make sure none could disobey him.

Then, he gave an order.

The bloodstalker in front of him charged as several zombies closed in around it. The beast swatted two away effortlessly, but two more leapt for its arms. It tossed them away as well only for more to pile on. None were strong enough to do any damage, but they didn't have to.

Digby thrust a hand out toward one of his zombies that had gotten close to the bloodstalker's face and sent his Body Craft mutation into action. A new arm burst from his minion's side, several times larger than the limb just above. It continued to grow and twist until it resembled one of the bloodstalker's own appendages.

Digby commanded the zombie to grab hold of the revenant's neck and pull itself up to the beast's face. Once it was close enough, he poured resources into his minion until its body burst with extra organs. The revenant flailed as entrails wrapped around its head like snakes. Digby cast cremation before the bloodstalker could get free, setting his minion alight.

The foe fell, screeching as it was cooked alive.

He'd sacrificed a minion, but he had taken down one of the beasts in the process. Still, more were coming. Digby summoned his crone to halt one in its tracks. He did the same to another of the beasts that tried to come at him from the other side. He sent his horde in next, the dead climbing up to the creature's heads.

The bodies of his zombies swelled and bloated as they got into position. Seconds later, they exploded in a burst of viscera and flame. Two more of the beasts fell, their heads burning.

Digby followed the attack with another round of Leach spells. His horde had been reduced by around twenty, but it was still enough to fill his mana back up to half without endangering his horde. He pushed it further, taking enough MP from a pair of zombies to destabilize their mana systems. They fell to the ground, becoming nothing more than an average corpse.

One bloodstalker charged him while he was busy replenishing his mana, a mouthful of razor-sharp fangs screaming in his face. A claw swiped his staff out of his hand. A second massive fist crashed into him, shattering his sternum and launching him back into the wall. Metal and wood crunched on impact. Even worse, the flow of mana from his minions ceased the instant he was knocked away from where he'd been standing when he'd cast his Leach spell.

With a little more than half his mana remaining, Digby raised his hand, if only to shield himself from another blow. He prepared to cast Necrotic Regeneration to heal the damage he knew was coming.

The bloodstalker rushed toward him, drawing back its claws to strike.

That was when a bony form dashed in to slam the curved blade of Digby's staff into the revenant's side. Union must have picked up the weapon from the floor. The skeleton may not have wanted to serve but even they must have known that if their master fell, they would also cease to exist. He shook off the thought and refocused on the bloodstalker as the creature struggled to pull the crimson blade from its side.

Digby flung a hand out toward the revenant and spent the mana needed to reshape the scythe. The blade of blood changed in an instant, expanding into a thin sheet that bisected the creature's spine. The bloodstalker cried out, only for its screech to be cut off, its body splitting in two. Digby pushed himself back up as the revenant's flailing slowed. Of course, that was when another bloodstalker plowed into him from the side.

"Holy hell!" Digby slid across the blood-slicked floor, crimson spraying through the air in his wake.

He stumbled back over one of the dozens of corpses that littered the floor. Glancing to the side, he came face to face with the severed head of the zombie that had been thrown at him not long before. Its spine and esophagus hung from its neck. The zombie blinked and opened its mouth, having no other way to interact. Digby tore his attention away from the fallen minion and snapped his head back to the bloodstalker that had hit him. The creature was already rushing toward him.

"No no no no no!" Digby kicked his legs up as the beast leapt. He planted his feet against the bloodstalker's chest in a desperate attempt to keep the revenant's jaws from ripping off his face.

Despite their reluctance, Union did what they could, slamming a bony fist into the back of the creature's head. The beast simply swatted the skeleton away. Union crashed to the floor, scattering into a pile of bones.

"Damn!" Digby swiped a claw at the bloodstalker above him.

It would take time for his skeletal minion to reassemble themselves. He would have to survive on his own. Casting Forge again, the blood on the floor streaked up to form a row of spikes that crisscrossed to form a cage in front of him. He cast wraith until his mana fell close to empty. Blood sprayed from the revenant but the creature's healing ability was able to withstand the blows.

"Not good!" Digby cast Leach several times, drinking in the horde's mana. Yet, his MP ticked up slower than before. He flicked his eyes around the room in search of the nearest zombie. So many had already been killed and most of the dead that still stood were out of range.

The revenant slammed a clawed hand into the blood cage that protected him, shattering several of the spikes. The jagged forms pierced the bloodstalker's hands, but it ignored the damage as its flesh bubbled and hissed, trying to regenerate. Another swipe destroyed the last of Digby's defenses.

I should have run away when I had the chance. Why did I listen to my madness?

"Because your madness is right!" Ames shouted from the back of his mind.

That was when Digby snapped his head to the side to make eye contact with the severed zombie head that lay beside him. Digby grabbed hold of its dangling spine, hoping enough of the monster was intact to still use his Body Craft.

The bloodstalker reared back with a screech before dropping down with its jaws open.

"The horde is mine to use!" Digby shouted as he rammed the mutilated zombie's head up into the revenant's throat.

A moment of confusion washed over the creature's bat-like face as it seemed to debate on swallowing the zombie's remains or spitting them out.

"Too slow!" Digby grinned as he connected his Body Craft mutation to his minion's head.

The revenant froze in panic, its throat swelling until its entire upper body detonated in an explosion of gore. Digby kicked his feet against the wet floor, scrambling to get out of the way as random limbs burst from the revenant's chest and throat. The massive corpse toppled to the ground a moments later.

Rolling over, he searched for his staff, finding it not too far away. Fire climbed up the walls from the bodies of his first few kills, smoke pouring out from the warehouse's nonexistent roof. The bodies of revenants and zombies littered the floor, some still moving while others had gone still, their fingers and claws frozen in an unending reach for prey.

Digby pushed himself up and dove for his staff. He landed in a roll just as one of the final two bloodstalkers swiped a hand past his leg. Pivoting on one foot, he used his momentum to spin around, swinging his staff in an arc while casting Forge to draw the blood from the floor up to create a new scythe. The point of the blade slammed into the revenant's side while it was still forming. He spent the extra mana to reshape the weapon, sending a dozen barbed spikes exploding out the creature's other side. It fell flailing as the spell shredded its insides.

Letting out a labored grunt, Digby stood and checked his mana.

MP: 45/326

He cast Leach, destroying the mana systems of another three zombies to get himself back to full. He couldn't afford to spend it poorly. Over two-thirds of his horde had been wiped out and he couldn't keep draining his minions dry unless he knew he could win. He narrowed his eyes. There were still four revenant bloodstalkers left, each still occupied with killing his horde.

Digby held his staff, casting Blood Forge to form a new spearhead at its end. He formed a second one at the butt of the weapon. Glancing to his side, he found Union stepping back into the fight, placing their skull back on their shoulders. "Be ready!"

The skeleton hesitated before nodding, clearly still unhappy about not getting what they wanted.

Digby charged, summoning his crone as he ran.

One of the bloodstalkers ran to intercept him but a dozen spectral hands coiled around its legs and arms to yank back.

Digby shouted a command to the horde, "Rend!"

One by one, the last of his zombies piled onto the oversized revenant, their teeth chomping down. When one reached the creature's head, he ordered it to shove its hand into the blood-stalker's mouth. He sent a surge of resources into his minion, but only for a moment in an attempt to be conservative. The revenant panicked as fragments of bone extended from the zombie's hand to pierce its throat from the inside, locking it in place to cut off the flow of air. His zombie fell as the revenant tore its arm from the monster's shoulder.

Digby ignored the suffocating creature, focusing on a different target. It charged to meet him. Dropping to his knees, he slid across the slick floor to duck beneath a massive claw. He shoved one end of his staff up into the creature's abdomen and reformed the spearhead at the end. A thin sheet of blood expanded to slice through the revenant's chest from the inside as Digby snapped his staff off of the formation growing at its end. A crimson rain showered down all around him as he rolled out from under the creature. The revenant collapsed to the floor with a splash.

Getting back to his feet, Digby tossed his staff to his new skeletal minion, giving an order to fight that the reluctant spirit couldn't ignore. Union caught the staff in a bony hand and turned to face another of the threats. Digby kept moving for the last foe, ordering the last of his zombies to follow. Glancing back a moment later, he watched as Union was crushed beneath a massive claw. The skeleton fell to the ground in a heap of bone, their skull rolling across the floor.

Digby smirked as he saw his staff sticking out of the revenant's gut. Union was already beginning to reassemble when Digby reformed the spear to cut the bloodstalker in two.

Fires burned at the edges of the room where the first few foes had fallen. Smoke and embers wafted through the air as Digby kept moving. He let out a wild cackle as his zombies leapt for the final revenant. The creature threw the monsters off one after another, many splattering against the walls and floor. None of it mattered, he had already won.

Using the distraction to his advantage, Digby slammed his claws into the bloodstalker to cast Fingers of Death. He pulled his hand free as the creature succumbed to the spell.

"That's it." Digby stood in the middle of the warehouse, taking a moment to collect himself. "I've actually won."

"At what cost?" Union walked past one of the corpses, missing several bones from their form.

The building had been destroyed. None of the shelves remained standing and the roof was mostly gone, fire climbing the walls in a few places. Bodies littered nearly every inch of the floor, with several were still impaled on spikes of blood. Only a few zombies still stood, including the bloodstalker that he had just turned. The horde had been nearly destroyed.

Asher flapped out from the office in the back to land on a broken crate nearby. She remained quiet, clearly uncomfortable with everything that he'd done. It was one thing to sacrifice the dead in battle, but another to seek out a fight and send a horde to their doom. He didn't bother trying to reassure her. She would have to understand. It was all in pursuit of a worthy goal.

A few common revenants trickled in through the entrance, falling into his still-waiting maw. The bulk of the swarm had already vanished into his void. Digby looked down at himself. He had never fought without limits before. Normally, he had to worry about protecting humans or some other distraction. He cast a Necrotic Regeneration, feeling several bones pop back into place that he hadn't even noticed had been damaged.

"Was it worth it?" Union picked up a new femur from the floor.

Digby looked to his HUD for the answer.

The seed had condensed all of its notifications into a nice compact list.

> **1311 common revenants defeated.**
>
> **75 revenant wardbreakers defeated.**
>
> **11 revenant bloodstalkers defeated.**
>
> **170,722 Experience awarded.**
>
> **You have reached level 50.**
>
> **You have 11 additional attribute points to allocate.**
>
> **You have unlocked a new spell within the Necromancer Class.**
>
> **ANIMATE ELITE CORPSE**
>
> **Description: Select specific attributes and abilities held by a deceased magic user to be retained by their zombie after animation. Abilities or attributes may also be omitted in order to decrease the mana donation required.**
>
> **Rank: D**
>
> **Cost: Variable, dependent on chosen abilities or attributes.**
>
> **Range: 30ft (+50% due to mana balance)**
>
> ***Zombies capable of casting spells, what could go wrong?***

A quiet laugh shook Digby's chest.

It was so much.

Everything he'd planned for had worked. The experience, the resources, his new minion. He'd gotten it all. It had all been worth it.

The laugh began to grow into a cackle.

"I'm unstoppable."

His moment of celebration screeched to a halt as a quiet voice came from someplace nearby. At first, he thought it was coming from his own mind. Then he recognized it.

"Parker?"

Digby shoved his hand into his coat pocket. His body froze as his hand slipped through to come out through a hole in the bottom. The tattered garment was coming apart at the seams. The compact that Parker had given him must have slipped out sometime during the fight or possibly even earlier.

Snapping his vision in the direction the messenger's voice was coming from, he lunged toward a pile of bodies to find the compact buried underneath. The bottom dropped from his stomach the instant he flipped it open to see her face in the mirror.

She looked desperate.

CHAPTER THIRTY-FIVE

"The kestrels are back!" Sax's voice announced over the radio.

Parker thumbed the call button. "How many this time?"

"Five."

"Damn." Parker rubbed at her exhausted eyes before raising a pair of binoculars. She swept them across the sky to find the group of aircraft coming closer on the horizon.

The last few hours had been the most tense of her life. First, there was only one kestrel. She'd thought they were dead when it showed up earlier, but all it did was make a pass of the strip before leaving. About a half hour later, it returned with another two aircraft. The kestrels took another few passes of the strip before leaving again.

Now, the sun was setting and there were five of the aircraft on the way.

"Shit." Parker lowered her binoculars. "Damn it, Dig."

It was obvious why they were there.

The mirror.

Earlier that day, Digby had ordered the construction of a mirror large enough to transport his armada. A coven had started working to coat a section of the strip with paint and resin to make a reflective surface. They had tried to work fast, but it took time to cure. Obviously, Autem must have noticed it somehow.

"Stupid Dig and your stupid mirror." Parker was still kicking herself for not arguing with him more about the risks.

Combined with the knowledge that their Heretics were using reflective surfaces to travel, the presence of a giant mirror must have tipped Autem off that Vegas was where Digby and the rest of the Heretics were hiding. Even if they hadn't figured that much out, the construction of such a thing was reason enough to send out a few squads to look into it.

What she didn't know was why they hadn't landed right away.

They must have called in a few more patrol crafts from the West Coast for backup. If that was the case, she was sure they suspected something. Though, the fact that they hadn't attacked straight away probably meant that Autem wasn't one hundred percent sure Vegas was a threat. If that was true, there might still be a chance to convince the Guardians that were coming that the city was nothing to worry about.

Parker shoved a hand in her pocket, pulling out her compact and snapping it open. She cast Mirror Link for the umpteenth time.

"Hey Dig!" she shouted into a view of darkness shown by the spell. "If you can hear me, pick up the freaking call."

She leaned closer to the compact, listening for any sign that the necromancer had heard her. All she could make out was some background noise. It sounded like revenants screeching. For a second, she feared the worst. Then she heard a muffled cackle.

She snapped the compact shut.

Parker had been trying to contact him every ten minutes since she saw the first kestrel, but Digby must have been too absorbed in whatever he was doing to pick up the call. Either that or he'd set his compact down somewhere.

"Damn it, Dig." She flipped the compact open again and

cast Mirror Link. "You better finish up with whatever the hell you're doing and get back here soon, or I swear to god, I am going to…" She trailed off, realizing she had nothing to threaten him with. "Okay, I'll probably just complain a lot, and that will at least be annoying."

She was about to snap the compact shut again when an image suddenly replaced the darkened mirror. A view of Digby's face filled the tiny window. He was holding it way too close so his nose took up most of the image but it looked like the building he was in was on fire.

Parker squinted, noticing a reddish tone to his skin.

"Are you covered in blood?"

"What? No!" he lied as he tried to wipe his face on his sleeve, only making the mess worse.

"Never mind." She shook her head. "I don't care. You need to get back here, now. Autem has found us."

"What?" Digby's eyes bulged. "How? What did you do while I have been away?"

"I didn't do anything." She narrowed her eyes. "My guess is it has something to do with the giant mirror that you wanted us to build. You know, the one I warned you about."

"Why didn't you contact me sooner?" Digby completely glossed over the fact that the situation was his fault.

"I freaking did!" Parker held the compact close so he could clearly see her mouth as she yelled at him. "You would know that if you picked up your end of the link."

"Alright, alright. There was a hole in my pocket and I lost my compact for a bit. I will find a mirror so you can open a passage for me. Just don't do anything to make things worse."

The mirror went black as he snapped his compact shut.

"Don't do anything to make things worse," Parker repeated his words in her most mocking tone before letting out a lengthy growl to vent her frustration. "Why does he bother keeping me around if he never listens?"

Before she had time to complain further, Sax announced a new development over the radio.

"The kestrels have stopped."

"Shit." Parker grabbed her binoculars and searched the sky, finding all five kestrels hovering in formation a couple hundred feet over the giant mirror that was still curing in the middle of the strip. "What the hell are they doing?"

Technically, there was no need to be so obvious. If they had wanted to maintain an element of surprise, they could have used their camouflage at any time. Instead, it was almost like they wanted to make a show of force, in an attempt to be intimidating.

"Maybe they aren't going to attack." Parker held her breath as she watched the scene unfold.

That was when one of the aircraft lowered itself down to the street. It rotated during its descent, opening its ramp as soon as it touched down.

"Oh no." Parker jumped up and thumbed the radio's button. "I think they want to talk. Where are Elenore and Deuce?"

"We're watching from the entrance of the casino," Elenore responded.

"Can you go out there?" Parker asked, having no idea if that was actually a good idea or not. "They might not attack if we can talk our way out of things. They did have an agreement with Vegas's previous leadership back when Skyline was still in the picture, right? And Bancroft had kept everything he'd learned about us secret, so for all Autem knows, were still under the old leadership. We just have to act like we're happy to work with them."

"I don't know if that's possible." Elenore pulled on one of the many loose threads that made up the plan. "How do we explain that giant mirror?"

"I don't know, but it's better than blowing our cover and telling Autem we're here. If they don't buy our bullshit, then we can at least buy time for Dig to get back. He's looking for a mirror now."

"Fine, I'll see what I can do," Elenore said, only to do a one-eighty a second later. "Shit, I can't go out there." Her voice climbed. "I'm a Heretic. They'll know everything the moment one of them looks at me long enough to analyze me."

"Crap, I forgot about that. Do we have anyone that hasn't touched the Heretic Seed yet?" Parker grasped at straws.

Elenore fell silent for a moment before answering. "I think I have an idea."

Parker glanced to the ramp that led from the level of the parking garage that she was on, to the first floor. "I think I have one too. If things go bad."

She immediately broke into a sprint, not wanting to waste time running around the barrier wall that bracketed the ramp. Instead, she just leapt over it and cut a diagonal path across the ramp down to the next level. Her Cloak of Steel flapped through the air as she jumped the half wall on the other side. She landed in a slide before continuing to run.

She skidded to a stop not long after. "There you are."

The tank that she had been napping in off and on sat in the corner of the garage. The vehicle had been resting there for weeks with a broken tread? It started up just fine, but sometimes the damage caused it to drive in circles.

Climbing on top of the vehicle, Parker pulled the hatch open and dropped in. She slipped into the driver's seat, pushing aside the blanket and pillow that she'd hidden away inside. Once she was in position, she pulled out her compact and flipped it open. With a thought, she opened a link to the mirror that Sax was carrying to check in with what they were doing at the casino's entrance.

"What's the plan over there?" she asked as soon as his image filled the glass.

"We're sending someone out to stall," Sax answered back in a tone that said, 'Please don't ask any follow-up questions, you will not like the answer.'

Parker asked anyway. "Who do we have to send out that's not a Heretic?"

Sax answered her by turning the compact he held around to

show what was happening in front of him. The result looked weirdly like shaky-cam, reality TV footage. In the center of the view stood Elenore, clearly giving instructions to someone just out of frame. Parker couldn't make out what she was saying but from the expression on her face, she wasn't filled with confidence.

A moment later, Sax panned his end of the Mirror Link to the side, bringing into view Campbell, the ex-Skyline cafeteria worker that Digby had liberated and subsequently recruited. After joining their side, Campbell had picked up where he'd left off by taking over the operation of the casino's community dining.

Parker slouched in the tank's driver seat. "Okay, so we're sending the cafeteria guy. That probably won't go wrong."

Thinking about it more, sending Campbell wasn't actually a bad idea. He may have spent his days slinging mashed potatoes, but he had also helped Digby and Becca infiltrate Autem's secure facility back on Skyline's base. Maybe the man's friendly charm would help them out here too.

Parker held back any argument. It wasn't like she had a better idea. Campbell was already out the door anyway. As he headed out to meet with a Guardian that was exiting the kestrel, several covens of Heretics hid in the entrance of the casino with everything from swords to rifles, ready to attack if things went south.

Sax turned his compact around to show his face, looking extra nervous. Then he turned it back around and pressed the tiny mirror against the front doors so Parker could see outside.

Campbell strolled out, still dressed in a chef's jacket.

Parker cringed, remembering the last time that they had attempted to pull one over on a squad of Guardians. Back then, Digby had given Deuce lengthy instructions, a new wardrobe, and several pep talks. Now, under her temporary command, they were just going to wing it.

"Can anyone read lips?" Parker asked as Campbell strolled

out to meet with a Guardian standing at the foot of the kestrel's ramp. The other four aircraft still hovered above.

"I can read lips." Elenore's voice came from someplace just outside of the mirror link's view. "Sort of."

"Good enough." Parker held her compact close, watching for any sign that things were going to go south. "What are they saying?"

"Let me see," Elenore spoke in a low tone as if doing an impression of Campbell as he waved to the Guardian in a friendly manner. "Hey, thanks for stopping by. We were beginning to think you guys had forgotten about us."

"Okay." Parker nodded. "A little folksy, but that's a good opening. What's the Guardian saying?"

Elenore responded in a considerably gruff voice as the man's mouth moved. "Where's Livers?"

"Livers?" Parker furrowed her brow.

"Shit, no." Elenore sounded flustered. "I think he said Rivers."

"I thought you could read lips." Parker sunk lower into the tank's driver's seat.

"No, I said I can sort of read lips." Elenore grabbed Sax's hand so she could look into the compact. "And you said that was good enough."

"Okay, never mind." Parker groaned. "Just tell me what they're saying."

The view through the link spell shifted again as Sax turned his compact to face the street. "They aren't saying anything, Campbell just looks confused."

Parker froze as the large man started to sweat and glance back to the entrance. The Guardian standing at the end of a kestrel's ramp was clearly beginning to question why Campbell hadn't answered. Eventually, the cafeteria worker pushed past the confusion, deciding to go with honesty.

"Who's Rivers?" Elenore said as his mouth formed the words.

The sound of Sax slapping a hand to his head was joined by

Parker doing the same. Of course, Campbell had no idea who Rivers was. That horrible man may have been running Vegas at one point, but he had been eaten by Digby well before Campbell had defected from Skyline. Parker hadn't even arrived yet at the time. The only reason she knew the name Rivers was because someone had mentioned the guy in passing.

The Guardian outside stared at Campbell for a long moment as if sizing him up, before finally giving Elenore something to lip-read.

"Isn't Rivers in charge here?"

"Oh, yeah, sure." Campbell recovered surprisingly well, sounding somewhat natural. "We've had a few changes in management, if you know what I mean. The revenants be biting and all that."

"I'm sorry to hear that." The Guardian stopped for a moment, to stare at Campbell, before adding. "Have we met before?"

Parker tensed. *Oh no.*

The reason why Campbell would be familiar to the man was obvious. He'd probably been stationed on Skyline's base at one point and passed through the cafeteria there. Campbell must have slapped some food onto his tray.

"That's bad," Sax stated the obvious as Elenore repeated Campbell's response.

"Can't say that we've met. I just have one of those faces, I guess."

"Maybe." The Guardian eyed him suspiciously before gesturing to the glossy surface that the kestrel had landed on. "I have to inquire, what is the reason for this mirror-like section of road that your people have laid out? It nearly blinded one of our pilots when the sun shined into their aircraft."

"Oh?" Campbell tried to change the subject. "Why was one of your aircraft flying over us?"

The Guardian nodded as the rest of his squad walked down the ramp of the kestrel to join him. "We do regular patrols of areas where we know communities are forming to make sure the people are safe and able to take care of themselves. We had a situation to deal with that caused a disruption in our patrols, but we've recently resumed our operations."

"Oh, that's great to hear." Campbell gave the man a big smile. "I'm glad that you sorted out whatever was holding things up."

The squad leader narrowed his eyes, clearly noticing how his question had been glossed over. "Yes, but that brings me back to this reflective section of road."

"Oh, ah." Campbell glanced around. "It's, ah, for you."

"For us…" The Guardian continued to stare at him.

"Yeah." Campbell gestured to the giant mirror beneath his feet, then up to the kestrels hovering above. "You know, like SOS. You guys hadn't been by in a while, so we thought that you thought we'd moved on or something. Figured this shiny stuff was sure to flag one of those craft of yours down."

"Really?" The guardian knelt down to touch the surface of nearly cured resin. "Because we have gotten reports that some of our enemies have been using mirrors for some of their movements."

"I'm not sure what you mean?" Campbell played dumb, as if he'd never heard of a Mirror Passage before.

"Are you sure we haven't met before?" The Guardian stood back up and pointed at his face. "Because I am certain that I've seen you somewhere before."

Parker shook her head, having heard enough. "That's it. They've got us pegged. We've stalled enough."

"What do we do?" Sax turned his compact around to show himself and the rest of Dragon coven armed and waiting for orders.

Orders that she was going to have to give. Of course, the one time everyone was away was when shit hit the fan. Parker wished she had just demanded they pull Mason back from Hawaii. The only reason she hadn't was because he'd been too distracted with Becca's situation hanging over him to take charge the way he used to.

Her eyes burned from lack of sleep. "Just cover Campbell's retreat."

"What are you going to do?" Sax held his end of the link closer.

Parker looked at the tank's controls in front of her. "Well, when you're sitting in a tank, the solution to most problems is to blow something up. You know, hammer and nail, and all that."

Parker started up the vehicle, giving herself a brief refresher course on how to operate it. A crate of shells for the cannon sat behind the driver's seat. She glanced back, realizing that storing the artillery there for the last few weeks was probably dangerous.

"Oh wow, I have been sleeping against that box."

Parker shook off her poor choice of napping locations and pulled the tank out of its parking space in the corner of the garage. She leaned hard on the controls, to compensate for the fact that the vehicle pulled to one side heavily. The result sent her weaving across the garage in a serpentine pattern. Glancing at her compact, she saw Campbell still doing his best to explain things in a way that might make sense despite running out of ideas at least a minute ago.

"Just hang on a few more seconds." Parker stopped the tank near the wall of the garage facing the strip and the hovering kestrels outside. She was just thankful that the aircraft above had been making enough noise to drown out the tank's approach. Taking over the controls for the main cannon, she rotated it to aim at the kestrel that had landed. It was an easy target.

"Someone tell Campbell to start running," she shouted into the compact. "He's not going to want to be standing anywhere near that squad for several reasons."

Fortunately, Campbell was already fleeing on account of the Guardian pointing angrily in his direction and yelling. Parker assumed he was shouting something along the lines of, 'Stop right there, you Heretic scum!'

Either way, she shrugged and fired the cannon.

"Oof." Parker fell back, realizing she should have been wearing some sort of ear protection as the kestrel sitting on the reflective surface outside detonated. Shrapnel blasted the squad that stood at the bottom of the ramp, splattering pieces of Guardian across the strip.

Guardian, Level 35 Pyromancer defeated, 3,458 experience awarded.
Guardian, Level 33 Rogue defeated, 3,256 experience awarded.
Guardian, Level 34 Artificer defeated, 3,356 experience awarded.
Guardian, Level 35 Cleric defeated, 3,454 experience awarded.
Guardian, Level 34 Cryomancer defeated, 3,352 experience awarded.
You have reached level 24.
You have 3 additional attribute points to allocate.

"Well, damn." Parker shook her head as the ringing in her ears blended with the sudden rush of three consecutive level-ups.

The only survivor from the kestrel was the squad leader. He must have had a barrier active. Though, from the look of him, his protection spell had failed after absorbing the impact of the blast. He'd been launched nearly twenty feet and landed face-first on the mirrored surface that had caused the whole problem in the first place.

The severed arm of one of his men slid across the smooth ground, passing him as he struggled to get up. Campbell kept running toward the casino's entrance as the top of someone's skull bounced past him. He made it through the doors seconds later.

Parker gasped as she realized she'd nearly wiped out a whole squad with one shell. She'd thought blowing up the kestrel would just scatter the Guardians, but they must have had explosives stored in the aircraft. Of course, that was when all four of the kestrels above turned in her direction and opened fire.

"Oh crap."

Parker covered her head and dove under the blanket that she'd left in the tank for napping purposes. Obviously, she was already wearing the Cloak of Steel that she'd been given, so there was no need to hide under an additional piece of fabric. Still, the blanket made her feel better as bullets poured into the parking structure. Hundreds of metallic pings hit the tank around her, sounding like a hail storm with anger issues.

Chunks of concrete rained down from the ceiling as the barrage punched into the wall of the parking garage. Ultimately, she couldn't have picked a better place to attack from. Being surrounded by metal and stone would have ensured her safety even without her cloak's protection.

"Okay, no more hiding." Parker ripped the blanket off her head and climbed back into the driver's seat to adjust the tank's position to get an angle on the kestrels above. Then, she went back to the cannon and loaded another shell. "This has not been a fun week so far, and you all are not helping."

The deafening blast that followed left her ears ringing as the shell missed all four of the kestrels. The side of the hotel across the street detonated in a shower of debris.

"Oops." Parker rubbed at her ears, wishing she'd remembered to cover them before firing the cannon again.

That was when the kestrels above stopped shooting.

"Ha ha!" She thrust a finger out at them. "That's right, I have a tank. I may not be able to hit shit with it, but I'm gonna get you eventually." She glanced back to the ammo crate, finding two shells left. "Okay, that's not a lot of tries."

She reached for another round, only to pause when she heard the sound of something tapping on the top of the tank's hatch.

"The hell is that?"

A moment later a blast rocked the tank as if someone had just placed a block of C4 on the roof. Parker fell as the explosion slammed her into the floor. Her cloak took the impact, but it did nothing about the concussion caused by the sudden movement of her brain.

"What the…?" Her skull hurt as the world wobbled back and forth.

Arms shaking, Parker pushed herself up to stare out through the open hatch above her. Somehow it had been blown clean off. Though, she had no idea how a charge had been placed there. She realized the answer to the question before she finished speaking it.

"A drone."

The Guardians in the kestrels must have sent down a drone with a breaching charge to deal with her once they realized she had a tank. Parker struggled to shake off the haze that invaded her head. She had to move. If they had sent in a drone, then it was likely that they had sent more than one.

"Why me?" She grabbed her compact and scrambled up to throw herself up through the hatch. "Digby better have found a window or something by now."

It was only a matter of time before another explosive was dropped on her head, and she had no idea how long her cloak's barrier would last. She groaned at the fact that she didn't have any spells other than the two that had come with her messenger class. Without some kind of healing, she had no way to repair the internal damage she had sustained. Her concussed brain was going to have to do its best until she could get someplace safe.

That was when something fell past her head into the tank and she noticed a slight breeze against her cheek. She looked around up to find a drone hovering right next to her face. Parker snapped her vision down, finding a little bundle of C4 sitting on the floor of the tank, right next to the crate containing the cannon's last two shells.

"Oh, well, fuck me."

She closed her eyes just as the block of C4 detonated, launching her straight up into the ceiling of the parking garage.

The top section of the tank popped off the vehicle like a cork from a bottle of champagne, sending it straight up to sandwich her against the cement above. The spare shells inside exploded to add to the devastation.

Unbelievably, her cloak's barrier shined as it prevented her from being pancaked. Still, even with its protection, pain surged through her insides from the force of the sudden movement.

Parker fell back down on the wreckage of the tank, rolling off to land on the ground next to its treads. She coughed, struggling to breathe as she rolled over, blood spattered against the concrete with each labored breath.

Everything hurt.

"Ow." Parker wiped the blood from her lips. She let out a whimper a second later when she heard the kestrel's guns spinning up again.

Why me?

The fact that the kestrels were so focused on her was technically a good thing. Despite whatever internal injuries she'd sustained, her cloak's barrier was still active. It was better that the aircraft shot at her rather than the casino where the people were.

Pushing herself up, Parker dove toward the nearest support pillar just as a hail of bullets poured into the entire parking garage. A torrent of hot lead slammed into her side, throwing her a dozen feet. She tumbled end over end, her cloak flapping around her, its barrier still shimmering. All she felt was the heat of the bullets against her skin and the constant motion of her body.

Parker tried to get up, but another burst slammed into her ankles to sweep her feet out from under her. Finally, she just ducked her head and crawled into the safety of a support pillar. The gunfire continued, fragments of concrete pelting her barrier from all directions as dust filled her nose. The air tasted like sugar, speaking more to her concussed brain's perception than any real sensation. The sound of glass breaking told her that at least one of the mirrors they had mounted to the wall in the alcove had been shattered. She just hoped it wasn't all of them.

Reaching the pillar, she stood up and pulled out her compact. The glass was cracked in three places, the plastic frame unable to hold them together. Parker plucked out the largest fragment and cast Mirror Link to open a line to Digby.

"What?" The zombie picked up immediately, only to stare into the link. "Are you being shot at?"

"Yes, for fucks sake," she screamed into the tiny piece of glass as bullets pelted the back of the pillar behind her. "Have you found a mirror to use over there or not?"

"Yes, I have one right—" His words were cut off when the shard of glass in her hand shattered, sending a piece flying across her cheek to slice a gash from nose to ear. Parker gasped in surprise as heat spread across her cheek.

"Oh no."

The cloak's barrier had failed.

What did she expect? It had already taken so much punishment, she couldn't expect it to do so forever. For a second, she wasn't sure what had even hit the fragment of mirror in her hand, then she saw the blood running down her arm from her palm. A bullet must have ricocheted off something to hit her from the side.

Holding her hand up, she stared at the city skyline outside the garage through a gaping hole in her palm. Her brain struggled to process what she was looking at. The world beyond was blurry, like a cloud floating across her view.

That was when the kestrels outside ceased fire, allowing her mind to catch up to what had just happened. She screamed, barely able to move her hand. It was the worst pain she had ever felt.

Or was it?

The dull headache that had plagued her for days swelled into a roar to mix with the pain of her current trauma. She nearly fell to her knees, only remaining standing through sheer will alone.

Everyone was counting on her.

As much as she wished that wasn't the case, it was true.

Digby wasn't there, Alex was stranded in Boston, Mason was in Hawaii, and no one even knew where Becca was.

She was all that was left.

"Come on." Parker took a step toward the alcove where the mirrors were, unable to see them all from where she was. It looked like two were broken, but there was still a chance that the one on the side of the space was still intact. She took another step, struggling to keep her balance with the fog that flooded her head. "Freaking move, damn it!"

One by one she slid her feet forward, increasing her pace until she forced her body into an uncoordinated run. The world moved like a ship on the sea, up and down, her vision swaying as nausea slithered through her stomach. In her peripheral, something floated in the air.

Another drone.

The kestrels must have been having trouble finding her while she was hiding behind the pillar and sent in a scout.

"Get away from me." She reached for one of her daggers with her uninjured hand and lobbed the blade in the drone's direction. It missed by an inch.

Then she remembered she'd never set the assigned stat points that she'd gained moments before. She dropped them into dexterity as she pulled her other dagger and let it fly. Her aim was solid, but the drone weaved to the side just as the weapon tumbled passed it.

"Fine, god!" Parker ignored the drone and kept running, expecting the kestrels to open fire at any second.

She just needed to make it to the alcove. They couldn't hit her there. As long as one mirror remained, she could get Digby. He would be able to handle the rest.

Jogging her way across the structure, she locked her eyes on her destination. A thousand shards of glass littered the concrete as a lone mirror came into view against the inside wall of the alcove.

"Yes!" Parker shouted a labored declaration of victory. It sounded off, like someone else's voice. She ignored it and pushed forward, the sight of the mirror giving her the strength to break into a sprint, even as the world still swayed.

She was almost there.

Then one of the kestrels opened fire.

It was only for a second.

Maybe ten rounds at the most.

Parker crashed into the floor, unable to catch herself with her damaged hand. She slid to a stop just fifteen feet away from the mirror. Looking down, blood pooled around her knees, soaking through her pant legs. A wound on her right thigh matched a second on her left.

She tore her attention from her legs, ignoring the pain as it blended in with the agony of everything else. The mirror was all she could think of. She was too close to give up. Coughing out a lung full of concrete dust, she slapped her uninjured hand to the floor and dragged herself forward. What else could she do? Even as the kestrel's guns spun up outside, she kept trying.

Everyone was counting on her.

That was when she heard the door of the casino open.

"Don't you dare!" a voice shouted from the other end of the garage, accompanied by a pair of boots running in her direction.

Shifting her head to see, she caught Sax running toward the front of the garage with the rifle that he'd been carrying, the one with the grenade launcher attached to the bottom. He skidded to a stop around twenty feet away, raising the weapon to his shoulder.

"I've been waiting to use this!"

Parker let out a ridiculous laugh as a loud pop came from the launcher along with a puff of smoke. From her angle, she couldn't see if Sax had hit anything but the sound of an explosion told her what she needed. A massive shape fell to the ground, bursting into a ball of fire. She turned away and slapped her hand to the floor to continue crawling.

"Thank you, Sax, you are the best freaking friend I've ever had."

Parker pushed herself onward, nearly entering the range she needed to open a passage. She could still hear Sax's voice taunting the kestrels behind her.

"I got more where that came——"

His voice went silent as the kestrels opened fire again.

What? Parker looked back to find him lying on the ground, a spray of crimson covering the support pillar behind where he'd been standing.

She closed her eyes as they welled up.

"No!" Parker snapped them back open, letting tears fall to the concrete as she pulled herself forward another two feet.

That was far enough.

All she had to do was reach out and cast the spell. All she had to do was picture where Digby was in her mind. All she had to do was remember his surroundings.

What had been behind him? What had she seen in the brief moment before a bullet had interrupted her link a moment before?

Anything?

A building?

She fought through the haze and pain that filled her head and forced an image to materialize through sheer will alone. It had only been a few seconds, but she had remembered something. Details began to fade in, rising to the surface of the chaos in her head.

A window.

Parker reached her hand out and closed her eyes to lock the image in her mind.

"Come on, Dig."

She let her head fall to the cold floor.

"We did the best we could. The rest is up to you."

CHAPTER THIRTY-SIX

Digby stepped through the rippling surface of the passage that Parker had opened. He expected to find her waiting for him on the other end with a sarcastic remark about him taking his time.

She was not.

"Gah!" Digby recoiled from the scene before him, dropping his staff.

At his feet, the messenger lay in a field of shattered glass. A trail of blood extended behind her as if she'd dragged herself across it all to reach the alcove. He couldn't even tell where all the blood was coming from. Sweat covered her brow and a heavy layer of grime coated her skin as she took rapid shallow breaths. Clearly, it was all she could do just to keep the passage open.

The sound of multiple kestrels could be heard outside.

"We arrive." Union, his new skeletal minion stepped through the portal behind him. The passage closed behind the skeleton as Parker's head dropped to the floor.

"Help me with her." Digby dropped down to grab hold of Parker's cloak. The skeleton did the same.

The messenger let out a cry as they dragged her the rest of

the way through the broken glass. Digby summoned his knight as soon as she was safe. A flickering white form resembling Henwick appeared to heal the damage. Despite what she'd been through, she would live.

"What happened here?" Digby helped her sit up against the wall of the alcove where the kestrels outside couldn't get a shot at them.

"A patrol came by and saw the giant mirror." Parker clutched one of her hands to her chest as a hole in her palm began to close.

"Why didn't you wait until I got here before starting a fight?" Digby picked up his staff and stood up.

"We tried to talk our way out of things and stall, but they figured it out." Her breathing grew steadier as Henwick's echo healed her. "I had to take one kestrel out with the tank."

"So you thought you'd kick off the war early?" Digby started to groan but closed his mouth when she spoke again.

"Sax is dead." Parker opened her eyes to look up at him, tears streaking through the grime that covered her face. She gestured across the garage with her head. "He saved me."

Further away, a body lay next to a rifle. The wreckage of a kestrel burned in the street outside. The soldier must have taken it down just before being shot. For an instant, Digby nearly summoned his echo again to try to heal the man, but the Seed told him it was too late.

Corpse: Human Pyromancer
Animate Corpse?

The message was followed by a list of optional abilities and attributes that Sax could retain as a zombie, each accompanied by a mana cost. Digby's first response was to refuse. Reanimating a friend would obviously make Parker and the rest of the humans uncomfortable.

Sending a call to Ducky, he tried to gauge how far away on the strip the rest of his horde was. From the presence he felt across his bond, none of his zombies were close enough to reach him in time.

"How many kestrels are left?" Digby looked back to Parker just as one of the aircraft opened fire.

Snapping his vision to the street in front of the parking structure, anger flared as a torrent of bullets shredded the ground where his giant mirror had been constructed. They had worked so hard. The armada was almost ready, but now it was stuck half a world away.

"There are three kestrels left." Parker started to move one of her legs again. "We need to stop them before they start shooting at the casino."

"Can you open the passage again?" He gestured to the mirror.

"It was a miracle I got it open the first time." She clutched at her head.

"Damn." Three kestrels were more than he wanted to fight with just a skeleton at his side. As powerful as he had become, most of that strength came from his horde. His madness hadn't progressed so far for him to think that he could win on his own. With that in mind, he glanced at the question still displayed on his HUD.

Resurrect Corpse?
Yes.

The list of abilities and attributes flowed across his HUD as part of his new Animation spell, asking which abilities and attributes he wanted to keep. There was no way to bring Sax back, but at least this way he could still help. Parker would just have to understand that it had to be done. The lives of everyone in Vegas depended on it.

Digby ignored the zombie's attributes. He could replenish those using his Body Craft mutation and bond points. That just left Sax's magic. He chose to keep both of his fire spells along with his heal. They were immediately translated into the death mana equivalents of each. The heal became Necrotic Regeneration, Fireball became Cremation, and his new Flame Snap spell became something called Burial Flame. The new abilities cost an extra seventy MP on top of the fifty needed to animate the corpse itself, totaling a combined mana donation of one hundred and twenty from Digby's pool.

He watched his total mana fall, losing most of what he'd just gained from his recent levels. Next, he dropped ten of his bond points into intelligence and split the rest between will and perception. Finally, he finished off his minion by pouring in enough resources to return Sax's physical attributes to what he'd had while alive.

The corpse began to twitch.

"What did you…?" Parker pushed herself up, only for her legs to buckle beneath her, dropping her back to the floor. "Did you just animate Sax?"

"I need help." Digby didn't turn to look at her. "I can't do this without minions."

"But he was one of us?" Her voice was thick with grief.

"I know that," Digby snapped back. "But it's necessary to protect this city." He started walking without giving her a chance to argue. "Just stay hidden and stay alive. You're too valuable to lose."

He rushed off toward the back of the garage to sneak out in a direction that the kestrels might not notice. He willed Union to stay behind with Sax as the dead soldier stood up and picked up his rifle.

Be ready. He willed the zombie to wait with his skeleton.

If Digby could bring a couple of the kestrels down, then they could deal with any Guardians that might survive. Of course, that was only if he could actually do anything about the aircraft.

Willing his Body Craft into action again, he formed the wings of a revenant nightflyer at his back. They burst through the blood-soaked and tattered remains of his coat. He took flight before they had even fully formed, unwilling to wait any longer. The last few bones popped into place as he flapped up to the top of the garage.

All three kestrels flew in formation, stopping in front of the casino as the remainder of Dragon coven emerged from the entrance to fight. The aircraft above opened fire just as one member of the coven stood with his feet bare and raising a lantern. The rest of the group dove behind them.

Digby winced, expecting the Heretics to be killed where they stood. Instead, the barrage only destroyed the area around them. Each bullet veered off course to miss the Heretic holding the lantern while the rest of the coven remained safe behind them. They must have lit the lantern off the lighter that Hawk had found.

"That certainly evens things out." Digby flapped up to get above the kestrels while they were distracted before tucking his wings to drop down. He landed on top of the middle craft in a crouch, his staff held in front horizontally as he cast Decay in both directions. A burst of sparks exploded from the engines of the aircraft on either side. The spell wasn't as effective as the cannon of a tank, but it was enough to force a landing. The kestrels drifted toward the ground, leaving only the kestrel that Digby rode on.

Casting Decay again directly below him, rust began to spread out from his claws to eat away at the roof. The kestrel lurched forward before the corrosion could reach anything vital. Digby fell backward as the sudden wind caught his wings. He hit the roof of the kestrel with a thud before sliding toward one of the propellers.

"Gah!" Digby caught a ridge of metal with his claws to keep from toppling off the craft. A horrid slapping came from his side as one of his wings flapped into the craft's rear propeller. It was shredded to bits in seconds.

"Blast!" Digby struggled to hold on, nearly losing his grip as the kestrel shifted its angle and climbed straight up, the wind whipping through the rags of his coat.

Trying to estimate the distance to the ground, he debated

letting go and trying to reform his damaged wing before he hit the pavement. He was pretty sure he could do it in time, but not one hundred percent. Either way, that would still leave the kestrel in the air, and he wasn't sure he could fly fast enough to catch it again.

The problem left him with little choice.

Digby willed his Body Craft mutation to solve the issue. Surely, he had eaten something that could hold on to a moving aircraft easier than his claws. A spindly form of hollow bone erupted from his body, followed by another and another. Digby poured his resources into them, filling the hollow limbs with meat and tendons rather than building muscle and sinew around them. The new appendages flexed and twisted into place, grabbing hold of the kestrel's roof with hundreds of tiny fibers that formed at the pointed end of each new leg.

Eight in total.

A sudden snap-pop came from Digby's back as his original legs bent backward as if unneeded. More plates of bone extended from his waist to encase his lower extremities, forming a carapace behind him.

"I might have gone too far with this."

Digby stared down as he stood back up on eight slender legs, each far longer than what a human should have. A border of armored plates encircled his abdomen where his upper body met with the exoskeleton below. Looking behind him, he found a bulbous segment bobbing with his every movement.

"That's new."

Shaking off the shock of his transformation, he tapped his new legs on the top of the kestrel to test their mobility. A loud click-clack sounded as he stepped across the metal surface, revealing how strong the body was. He even felt more agile.

"Well then, let's put this to the test."

Having no problem hanging on to the roof of the kestrel, Digby casually walked toward the cockpit window. The Guardian at the controls looked up in horror.

Digby tapped on the glass with the butt of his staff before

pointing toward the ground. "I suggest you land and surrender!"

The Guardian responded by pulling a small gun from a holster and pointing it straight up. Digby shielded his face with a hand as a muffled bang came from inside the craft, followed by the sound of a bullet smashing through glass.

A word popped up next to Digby's HUD as the bullet punched into his abdomen.

SILENCED

His HUD faded from view a second later.

Digby frowned, recognizing the projectile as a magekiller bullet. Then he smirked. Sure, he may not have been able to use magic, but his zombie mutations were still on the table, and he was pretty sure his Body Craft could handle the problem.

Placing a hand to his chest, he felt the bullet through his body. It wasn't long before a metallic taste entered his mouth. He made a point of looking down at the Guardian that had shot him as he spat out the bullet. The man below him flinched as it bounced off the window.

Digby's HUD reappeared a second later.

With that, he smashed a spindly leg down through the window to impale the man. He yanked back, ripping the Guardian through the window to hold him beside him. The man kicked and squirmed, fighting the inevitable. Below, another Guardian rushed to the controls, a Barrier spell shimmering across his body to protect him from sharing the same fate as the original pilot.

Digby stared down at the Guardian, taking a moment to think of a good way to handle him. His thoughts were torn away when the dying man hanging from his leg tossed a fireball at his head.

"Hey!" Digby jerked to the side, as his skin sizzled and the scent of burning hair filled his nose.

Tearing the flaming patch of skin away from his skull, he

replaced the missing flesh with a layer of bone for added protection. A single horn jutted up from one side of his forehead. Once he was sure the flames had been extinguished, he flicked his gaze to the dying Guardian that had thrown the fireball.

"I was going to simply toss you off this airship, but you had to go and set me on fire." He pulled the man close. "Do you know how much I hate being set on fire?"

Digby didn't wait for an answer before thrusting his claws into the Guardian's chest. He cast Fingers of Death as he ripped his leg free of the man and created another minion. A kill message flashed across his HUD. As soon as the new zombie began to twitch, Digby leached as much mana from him as he could without risking the minion's mana system. Then he shoved the monster back in through the cockpit window.

The Guardian at the controls struggled to keep the craft level as the zombie tumbled to the floor of the kestrel beside him.

"Now, play nice in there." Digby gave them a wave whilst pouring resources into the zombie. He didn't have a form in mind. No, he just threw it all together like he had done back on Autem's base to shield himself from Henwick's smite. The only difference was, this time, his minion was in an enclosed space along with five unsuspecting Guardians.

Screams came from below as available space inside the cabin became limited. The man at the controls fell to the side as the mass of necrotic flesh shoved him against one of the cockpit's unbroken sections of window. A kill notification flashed across Digby's HUD, followed by another. The men inside popped one by one under the pressure. Another two messages joined the others.

Digby looked down at the face of the remaining Guardian, pressed against the glass. His barrier shined for another few seconds, then, it failed. The man cried out for an instant before his head burst like a grape.

"That's unpleasant." Digby grimaced at the horror that he'd wrought, lamenting the fact that he just wasted five perfectly good human hearts that could have been used to reach his next mutation. "Probably best if nobody looks inside this airship."

He walked toward the back of the craft and waited until it drifted back toward the parking garage. Digby jumped off, landing on the side of the structure. For a second, he nearly bounced off, but his new body caught hold of the stone.

"I could get used to this." Digby adjusted his position to watch as the kestrel he'd just abandoned headed for the ground. It skidded across the pavement before crashing not far from where the other two aircraft had already landed.

Two full squads of Guardians had emerged from the kestrels. Yet, they hid behind their fallen craft as Dragon coven fired from the casino's entrance. Sweeping his vision across both groups, Digby checked their levels. The Guardians were all over thirty, while the Heretics were all around level twenty.

The Guardians weren't hiding. No, they were ignoring the Heretics. They were more worried about the skeleton and zombie that were approaching them from the other side.

Union carried a blackened sword, clearly taken from the wreckage of the aircraft that Parker had shot down with the tank. Sax walked beside the skeleton, carrying his rifle and loading a grenade into its launcher. The zombie fired on the downed kestrels, forcing the Guardians out of cover.

He followed up by casting Burial Flame.

A greenish glow emanated from the ground beneath one of the men as the pavement cracked apart. The Guardian looked down just as the earth detonated in a geyser of molten rock. He died before he even hit the ground, his corpse splashing into the liquid fire below, leaving nothing but a hand sticking up as the earth cooled.

"Not a bad spell." Digby nodded.

He had been right to resurrect the soldier, even if it would upset a few people in Vegas. Sax could keep their enemies busy for a bit longer. Though the zombie only had so much mana and his grenades would run out eventually. The Guardians were sure to strike back.

Digby checked his mana.

MP: 257/327

It wasn't a lot. Especially against nearly a dozen high-level Guardians.

"I need to move." Digby skittered his way down the parking structure and jumped to the street.

Dragon coven stopped fighting to stare at him as he strode toward them on eight legs. He had hoped that if he didn't say anything about the changes to his body that maybe no one would notice. Obviously, that was a ridiculous plan. He had transformed himself into some kind of spider monster. People were going to notice.

He also noticed a few looks of disgust when Sax got close. Even worse was the expression on Parker's face as she limped out of the garage. The air grew heavy as she approached.

"I know what you're going to say—" Digby tried to calm her before she yelled at him but she cut him off.

"Don't." She walked past him toward the kestrels, holding nothing but one of her daggers.

With nothing left to say, he gave the order to attack.

CHAPTER THIRTY-SEVEN

"I am really starting to worry here." Becca fought the urge to pace as the crowd of revenants around her began to grow thin.

It had been well over a day since she had been thrown in a holding pen to await processing by Autem's revenant management staff. One by one, men in jumpsuits had taken the creatures from the pens and tied them up to the poles at the end of the warehouse-like room.

Once secured, the workers stripped away whatever clothing the revenants had and ran tests. Some were then fed blood through tubes until they evolved. In the end, each of the creatures had some kind of modular system attached to their bodies, bolted directly into their bones. Engraved armor was slotted into place to complete the processing. After that, the revenants were moved to a different pen where they stood in formation, controlled by the runes that covered their armor.

Becca and the rest of her vampiric infiltration team had done their best to stay at the back of the pen so that the worker would get to them last. Though, none of them ever expected to be left locked up, waiting as long as they had. Becca had watched the sun rise and then later set through a row of tiny windows. She was exhausted, having been forced to stand and remain alert for the entire day. The plan had been for Harlow to sneak her way back to them and let them out. Unfortunately, there had been no sign of her. Now, there were only a few unprocessed revenants left in the pen with her.

If we can't find a way out of here in the next thirty minutes, it will be us tied to those poles getting poked at. Becca took a step back until she bumped into the chain link fencing that covered the back of the pen. *And that is if the caretaker really is able to stop people from analyzing us consistently.*

That last part was a long shot. According to Leon, the caretaker's control was sure to be limited and unreliable. It wasn't something they could count on. Not to mention whatever tests the workers were doing on the revenants would probably reveal what they really were. If that happened, they were as good as dead. With the wards that had been placed on the holding area, Becca and the rest of her vampire squad had absorbed too much life essence to be able to access any of their abilities, leaving them as weak as the average human.

If it was only the workers that they had to worry about, they could still make a move to kill them fast. Though, just beyond their cage stood a squad of Guardians. They didn't look particularly strong but in Becca's weakened state, even a low-level squad could probably handle her.

This is not looking good. Becca tried to stay calm. One way or another, she was going to need to find a way out of there.

Becca swept her eyes across the enormous space, hoping to notice something that she might have missed. It was still hard to believe the place was housed within the wall that the empire had built in Washington, D.C. The place was simply massive, and it had only been a month. She couldn't help but wonder what Autem would do if given a few years. Her attention was torn away by the gate at the front of the holding pen opening.

"Let's get that big one." One of the workers pointed toward Ozzie. "If any of these things are going to hit bloodstalker, it's that one."

Becca gave Ozzie an annoyed look at the fact that his size continued to disrupt their ability to stay under the radar. He gave her one back that said, 'What do you want me to do about it, tiny woman?'

Of course, Becca was not actually small, but in comparison to him, she was downright miniature. She could only imagine what working with him must have been like for Harlow who was a good foot shorter than her. Becca shook off the thought, refocusing on the problem at hand.

They couldn't let Ozzie enter the processing area.

Leon acted fast, closing his eyes and mentally calling some of the revenants to stand by him in the path of the workers.

"Get some of these little ones out of the way." The man in charge walked straight into the pen, giving Leon's group a wide berth.

A couple of the revenants reached for him but the other workers jabbed them with cattle prods. Ozzie smirked when they shocked Leon in the ass. Becca gave the oversized vampire a dirty look again. He stepped away when one of the men tried to loop a catch pole around his neck. Ozzie moved in the other direction when they tried again, pretending to be interested in one of the humans standing outside the pen.

Becca tensed as the display grew more and more comical. There was a limit to how long they were going to accept that he was dodging them by coincidence and not on purpose. Ozzie must have had the same thought because he stopped evading eventually and let one of the men loop a wire around his neck. He hissed in their direction for authenticity.

Becca's heart leapt into her throat as the wire tightened around his neck. There was no stopping it. It was only a matter of time before they started running tests on him.

"Get a second wire on him," the boss called out. "I know these things are weaker in here, but he's big enough to get loose if we aren't careful. And I don't want to get bit again."

Becca filed away the man's words for later, noting that he had only said that they were weaker in here, meaning that the wards might not be present outside the processing area. The detail gave her some hope for their mission, but it didn't change the fact that they were still thoroughly screwed.

In desperation, Becca lunged toward the man in charge. She didn't have to be successful, she just needed to remind him that he was in a cage full of monsters. Leon followed her lead, going after one of the other workers while simultaneously using his link with the other revenants to increase their hostility. Ozzie joined in as well, fighting against the man that held him in place until he pulled the catch pole out of his hands.

"Shit, shit!" The boss yanked his hand away as Becca chomped down on nothing but air. A second later, a cattle prod lit up her back.

"What's going on in there?" The Guardians outside joined the workers, one of them clubbing Leon in the head with the butt of a rifle.

The rest of the squad remained outside as the workers prodded every revenant in the pen. Becca curled up on the floor as at least two of them electrocuted her side and back. The current surged through her body, tearing at every nerve ending she had. The scent of scorched flesh wafted through the air. After thirty seconds or so, the continuous prodding finally ceased.

"Do I need to remind you that these things are dangerous?" One of the Guardians approached the crew leader that had started the whole situation. "Never let your guard down around them."

"Yeah, yeah, I know." The boss sighed before launching a kick to Becca's abdomen.

She struggled not to react to the blow like a person, only letting off a cry followed by a whimper as she crawled away.

"If you know, then don't do reckless things." The Guardian exited the cages.

"Got it." The boss gave them a nod and gestured for the other workers to take one of the smaller revenants that were easier to get at. Before leaving the holding pen, he made eye contact with Becca as she cowered in the back corner. "I'll be back for you."

I definitely don't like the way he said that. She stared back at him defiantly, only relaxing when they exited the cage.

She let out a quiet sigh of relief once they were alone again.

"That was some quick thinking," Ozzie whispered to her as she stood back up. "I thought I was screwed."

"Yeah, but all I did was buy time." She glanced to the squad of Guardians that were watching over the workers. "We're still not getting out of here on our own."

"Damn it, where the hell are you, Harlow?" Leon tapped a foot. A second later, he looked up to stare out at the squad of Guardians outside.

"What is it?" Becca whispered as she stepped beside him.

"Something's happening." He kept his eyes locked on the group.

After leaving their holding pen, the squad returned to their station at the far end of the room by a metal security door. Becca assumed that the corridor beyond led to the rest of the structure. The squad must have been there to keep an eye on the workers while making sure none of the revenants escaped. They had been there since their shift started, just after dinner. Mostly they seemed pretty disciplined, keeping a close eye on the processing center.

Now though, they were huddled together.

"I think they're talking to someone on the radio." Leon frowned. "I can't make out what they're saying though, with all this life essence screwing up my senses."

Becca understood the frustration. There was nothing worse than knowing what she was capable of but being unable to access her power.

A moment later, some kind of buzzer signaled a shift change. Becca glanced up at the speaker that hung over the door. There was no way to know the exact time, but it was still too early for a new team of workers to take over. Instead of a new shift entering, the Guardians left. The crew double checked the restraints on the revenants in the processing area, then they checked the locks on the holding pens. After that, they headed for the same door the Guardians had exited through.

One of the workers remained, walking into a windowed office near the processing area. Becca watched as he sat down at a desk.

"Did they just quit for the day?" She furrowed her brow. "I thought a new shift would be coming in to replace them."

"It's almost like the Guardians got called to someplace else and the workers stopped because they don't have anyone to watch over them." Leon held onto the chain link fence.

"I guess that guy that stayed is supposed to keep an eye on things." Ozzie watched the office out of the corner of his eye. "What are the odds we can force our way out of this cage before he hits an alarm?"

"Not great," Leon added.

"I think the more important question is, where the hell did everyone else go?" Becca stared at the exit.

That was when the door opened to let in another worker in uniform. Becca couldn't help but notice that the cuffs of their pants were rolled up. Almost as if the legs of the garment were too long for them.

Becca followed the new arrival with her eyes. "Finally, Harlow decided to show up."

The short woman walked straight for the office, entering as if she belonged there. The man inside stood up as soon as he saw her. She responded by waving. From the look on his face, he wasn't expecting her. A few seconds went by as they exchanged words.

Harlow must have said the wrong thing, because the man turned to run for a big red button on the wall. He didn't get the chance to push it before the short woman pulled a folding knife from her uniform and threw it at his back. He fell to the floor a few feet short of the alarm. Harlow took a moment to retrieve her knife before exiting the office and heading their way.

"It's about damn time." Ozzie rushed to the gate. "Those guys almost took my pants."

"Sorry, but I've been busy." She glared at him.

"Busy doing what?" Leon got between them.

"Well, let me see." She held up a finger. "First, I had to have a full medical check, then I had to sneak away without any of the hundreds of Guardians walking about noticing, then I crawled through multiple ventilation shafts, then I mapped out part of the wall, then I timed the guard shift rotations, and then I stole this knife." She flipped the blade open and closed. "I rather like it, actually."

"That's great. Knowing the guard rotations will help." Becca nodded.

"Not really." Harlow blew out a sigh.

"Why not?" Becca frowned.

"Because that is all shit now." Harlow put her new knife away. "Something happened in Las Vegas. Seems your necromancer friend gave away his location. Now Autem is mobilizing every squad they have to attack. They're even loading up several cargo containers full of these trained revenants. They're going to airdrop the creatures on the city. They leave within the hour. They should reach Vegas well before dawn."

"Shit. Dig has no idea that they have revenants under their control." The weight on Becca's shoulders dropped right back into place, heavier than before. "He's had a week to prepare, but all he'll be able to do is slow them down. It's going to be a bloodbath."

"Not if we can extract our caretaker from the Guardian Core while Autem's distracted." Harlow turned and headed back toward the security door she'd entered through. "Most of the guard patrols have pulled out and headed to the aircraft hangars. Probably for mission briefings and to prep the owls. Your friends back in Vegas might be in a tight spot, but it leaves a lot of this fortress unguarded. So our job just got a lot easier."

"Or at least less suicidal," Ozzie added.

"What about Henwick?" Leon ignored him, closing the holding pen's gate and jogging to catch up.

"I don't know for sure if he's taking part in the assault." Harlow stopped at the side of the security door and signaled for everyone to get out of sight.

Becca ducked to one side as Ozzie and Leon did the same opposite her.

"I wasn't able to get the full details." Harlow peeked down the corridor before stepping out of hiding and waving the rest of them on. "From what I understand, Henwick isn't going to let someone else take charge if the Heretic Seed is involved. He wants that thing destroyed at all costs."

Becca struggled to focus, knowing what was heading toward Vegas. All she could do was hope that Digby could slow the Guardian warships down before they reached the city.

Taking a deep breath, she forced her fears out of her head and followed Harlow down the corridor outside. Thankfully, the wards that had been insulating the holding pens ended as soon as they exited the processing area. Harlow actually had to invite them in so they could pass through. Becca felt her mana system right itself as it purged the life essence from her body. She could still sense that her mana was only half full, but at least she could access her abilities.

Taking in her surroundings, the corridor looked unfinished, with pipes and ventilation shafts running along the ceiling, exposed. There were light fixtures hung at regular intervals but some features had yet to be installed. Exposed wiring hung from some wall outlets, clearly meant for things like emergency lighting and exit signs that had not been placed yet. The same was true of security cameras. There were mounts in place, but no actual surveillance. Overall, there was a temporary feeling to the place, like the bones were meant to last but the rest was intended to be replaced within a few months or years.

Rounding a corner, Harlow stopped to make sure the coast was clear before waving for Becca to follow. Next, she ducked into a locker room for the area's workers. Becca froze as soon as she followed her inside.

There was so much blood.

"The hell, Harlow?" Ozzie nearly tripped over a corpse.

Becca stepped back until her back ran into one of the lockers that lined the wall, her mouth salivating as her stomach turned simultaneously. A handprint and a streak of blood ran down one of the metal doors beside her. Following it to the floor, she found another body. It was the shift leader that had kicked her in the stomach earlier. The man's throat had been torn out, leaving a strange wound. It looked like Harlow had used her bare hands.

More corpses littered the floor, the rest of the work crew that had been alive and processing revenants only minutes earlier. Some bore stab wounds while others had been executed in more brutal ways. One man's eyes had been gouged out while another's jaw had been ripped clean off. A third had been impaled on a broom handle. It wasn't even sharp; somehow Harlow had rammed the rounded end of the broom right through his chest.

Becca couldn't help but notice the clothes that Harlow had been wearing earlier were balled up on the floor. She barely recognized them with how much blood had soaked into them. Harlow must have stripped and changed into a uniform in an attempt to clean up as well as disguise herself. Glancing back to the short woman, Becca couldn't help but notice a spatter of blood on Harlow's ear. She had buttoned her collar up to her neck and flipped it up to hide a smear on her neck. There was even some in the short ponytail she tried to tuck into a hat.

Apparently, Harlow hadn't been lying when she said she was a combat specialist. It was hard to believe the carnage in the locker room had been caused by one person.

"I guess hiding the bodies is out of the question." Leon swept his eyes across the room with a grimace. "Too bad you couldn't leave one alive; I think Becca is still at half mana."

"Sorry, I would have left a couple for you, but things got a little out of hand." Harlow tossed a work uniform to Becca.

"Ah, yeah, I can see that." Becca stared down at a disembodied eyeball that lay on the floor.

She shook off the horror of the scene and walked around a wall of lockers to change. The uniform was simple, just a gray pair of overalls with Autem's crest on the shoulder. After buttoning them up, she pulled a hat on and tucked her hair up into it.

Once everyone was disguised, she rushed out of the room, not wanting to spend any longer surrounded by corpses. Partly because there was a definite revulsion to the scene, but also because the blood was messing with her appetite. She still had half of her mana so she wasn't in danger of going ravenous, but the longer she spent in that room, the more she became aware that Harlow was basically a walking juice box.

After getting changed, the rest of the team joined her out into the corridor. With the preparations to attack Vegas going on, the next shift in the revenant processing center would be canceled until the Guardians that kept watch returned. Becca hoped that meant that no one would be entering the locker room for at least a few hours. As long as they didn't rouse any suspicion, and kept any future murders to a minimum, they should be able to move somewhat freely.

"Come on." Harlow led them down another unfinished corridor to a door labeled stairs. "There's an industrial-sized lift back in the other direction, but there's still a couple guards stationed there."

"Great, so we're walking," Ozzie grumbled. "We're always walking."

"The exercise will do you good." Leon shoved through the door only to jump back when a gust of wind blew his hat off.

Becca stepped back as well, expecting the door would lead into a standard stairwell. Instead, it just opened onto a platform secured to the outside of the wall.

Ozzie picked up Leon's hat and shoved it back on his head. "Try to hold on to this."

"I just wasn't expecting to be going outside." He leaned out the door. "I don't like heights."

"Too bad." Becca pushed past him, not wanting to waste time with the knowledge of what was heading toward Vegas.

Stepping out onto the platform, she made a point to hold her hat on as the wind blew by. Each gust was strong with them being so high up. To the side, a flight of metal stairs went down to another platform, while another led to a level above. They were on the inner wall, about two-thirds up, overlooking the interior of the fortress.

Becca made for the stairs without hesitation, taking charge of the team. Harlow didn't argue. On the way down, she stole glances at the scene below. She wasn't sure what she was expecting, but it certainly wasn't what she saw.

The area inside had been completely leveled. Becca wasn't sure what part of Washington, D.C. had been there before, but now, it had been completely demolished. In its place were several temporary structures and trailers. The kind that you might find at a construction site. At the exact center of the space was the only thing that looked like it was intended to be permanent.

"Is that some kind of cathedral?" Ozzie rushed down the steps behind her.

"I think it's more of a keep," Leon added.

Becca slowed as she took in the building.

It was a pentagon like the wall that surrounded it, but with pillars running up the sides spaced evenly apart. An empty platform was positioned at the top of each, as if something was supposed to go there. It was hard to make out some of the details, due to a layer of scaffolding that covered the entire thing. From the look of the surface underneath, it had been constructed of stone with long sections of glass running up the length between the pillars. Each window terminated with a decorative arch at the top, giving the building the look of something designed in the renaissance.

From the stairs, one main entrance was visible along with a few side doors.

"That's our way in." Becca pointed to one of the smaller entrances.

"We should be able to make that." Harlow passed Leon on the steps. "I don't see many patrols down there."

"But what's waiting for us inside?" Leon crept down the stairs behind them, holding onto the railing with both hands.

Becca let the question hang in the air as she continued down the steps. The only obstacle was the low lighting. Obviously, the stairway was only meant to be used in an emergency and, like much of the fortress, hadn't been finished. The result made the climb down somewhat treacherous and slow with the amount that they had to watch their step.

"Yeah, I'm definitely getting an unfinished Death Star feeling from this place?" Ozzie asked right before slipping on a step and falling back against Leon.

The slender vampire behind him let out a shriek when the collision forced him closer to the side. "Would you be careful?"

After that, they kept quiet the rest of the way down.

Reaching the base of the wall, Becca sprinted toward one of the temporary trailers that had been set up to manage the construction. The ground wasn't even paved yet. She made a point of looking for an exit while she was there. Even if they were able to extract the caretaker, they would still need a way out.

A massive steel door was set into the wall on the north side, with a second to the south. Each was around fifty feet wide and about twenty tall. It was obvious that they led to the civilian camps outside. If worse came to worst, they could try to mix into the citizens beyond the wall. However, that would require them to open the gates, and Becca was pretty sure they would be locked.

Sweeping her vision across the wall, she found a third gate that was already open. Though, this one was set low on the wall with a paved ramp leading down to it. Obviously, they weren't getting out that way, since it was unlikely that it led to the outside of the wall. Though, that raised the question. Where did it lead? The answer became obvious when she noticed various vehicle tracks in the dirt that extended beyond the ramp.

"It's a portal."

"What?" Harlow stopped.

"That open gate down there." Becca pointed to it. "When we talked about how they built this place so fast, we figured they had all the materials stored someplace ready to go. Which means they have to have a way to transport everything here. That gate must be some sort of portal system so they can just haul everything through."

"So that gate could lead to almost anywhere in the world." Ozzie leaned on the railing.

"It would have to be one of Autem's secret bases." Harlow looked back. "They had facilities all over the place to keep much of their operation hidden from various governments."

"But if that gate leads to a storage location, then it has to be massive to hold all of the materials that they gathered." Leon seemed to relax now that he was on the ground. "Which means that security might be loose there as well. We could escape through there and find a vehicle to steal."

"There is a good chance that there's a kestrel on the other side." Becca nodded along. "We should check it out."

From there, they followed the perimeter of the wall, using the trailers and construction equipment as cover. The patrols were few and far between, and most were focused close to the keep at the center of the walled space. It wasn't long before they reached the gate. No guards were stationed there, which made sense. They were already inside the heart of the empire and was probably assumed to be secure as well.

Harlow slipped inside without hesitation. Becca followed

with Ozzie and Leon close behind. She nearly stumbled before making it more than a few feet.

It was incredible.

Harlow hadn't been exaggerating when she said that Autem's gateways were complicated. The opening stretched out into a tunnel at least a thousand feet long. The air coming from the other side was hot and dry. Becca ran her hand along the wall, finding lines of runes covering its surface. There must have been millions of engravings. Not only that, but the tunnel itself was made up of several metals. Gold, iron, silver, steel. Hell, there was even some wood.

"How did they even figure out how to do this?" Becca pulled her hand away from the wall.

"A thousand years of research." Leon took a deep breath. "On the upside, the enchantments supporting a gateway like this are too complicated to add wards to it. From the temperature of the air, I'm guessing the other side of this lets out someplace in the desert. Probably halfway around the world where no one with any power might notice."

"In my experience, it's less about being noticed, and more about who Autem owns," Harlow added. "The Fools have traced plenty of the empire's actions to people in places of political power. It's not a coincidence that they built their capital here."

Becca grimaced, remembering some of the questionable operations that she'd witnessed back when she worked for Skyline. A lot of the missions she'd been a part of seemed to be less about military action and more about doing favors for one political or corporate entity or another. She had always turned a blind eye, telling herself that was just how the world worked, but somehow it all seemed so much worse knowing who was really behind it. Everything was about maneuvering Autem into a position where it could start building its empire.

Suddenly, stealing the caretaker seemed so much more important.

Becca clenched her fists. "Autem can't keep doing what they please."

"You're starting to sound like a proper Fool." Harlow gave her an approving nod. The sentiment was interrupted when Leon started walking down the tunnel.

"I think this is where we part ways."

"What?" Becca stopped him.

He hooked a thumb over his shoulder. "Like you said, there's probably a kestrel on the other end of this thing."

"Yeah." Ozzie joined him. "Divide and conquer. We'll secure a way out while you two get the caretaker. Once you get it, just come on through the tunnel and we'll pick you up."

"That works." Harlow turned back toward the building sitting in the center of the area within the wall. "As long as we don't make a ruckus inside. We should be able to walk right back here."

Becca's heart raced, realizing the other vampires weren't going in with them. They had been with her every step of the way so far as she explored her new existence. The thought of not having them around filled her with a sense of dread.

"What if I need help?"

Leon gave her a warm smile. "I have taught you all I can, young one. Now you must go and show the world what you are capable of."

"Yeah." Ozzie slapped her on the back. "Go fuck shit up, Becky."

"Ow." Becca nearly fell forward but didn't complain. She couldn't shake the worry that she might not see them again. "Be careful."

"We always are." Ozzie kept walking without looking back.

"You be careful too," Leon added while walking backward.

With that, she and Harlow turned back the way they came.

CHAPTER THIRTY-EIGHT

"Have you seen any women in work uniforms?" Becca leaned toward Harlow as they walked out in the open toward the keep at the center of Autem's fortress.

"Huh?" Harlow tensed.

"I'm just realizing that all the workers that I've seen so far have been men." Becca slowed her pace as a lone Guardian stood in the path not far ahead. "You don't think Autem is the type of empire that would limit the jobs that women can do? Do you?"

"Umm…" Harlow trailed off before adding, "Given the history that I am aware of, they might."

"Okay then." Becca cleared her throat and folded her arms across her chest. "Probably hide the boobs and walk fast, then."

Harlow did the same and picked up her pace as they passed by the Guardian. They kept their heads down the whole way to hide their faces while marching awkwardly with their arms folded. Harlow gave the man a nod along with a masculine grunt. Becca cringed, only to immediately feel stupid when the Guardian barely looked at them.

"Well, that was almost a letdown." Harlow shrugged as they made it to one of the side entrances to the keep.

The heavy door was made of polished wood with a slight curve at the top. It looked like the kind of entrance that a government building would have, carrying an air of dignity and respect.

"I guess we shouldn't complain that no one stopped us." Becca slipped inside, stopping as soon as the door closed behind her.

The interior of the structure was, in a way, exactly what she expected based on what she knew of Autem. The entryway, despite not being the main entrance, was large with a vaulted ceiling, and almost entirely made of marble. The floor had only been partially tiled, and plastic sheets draped scaffolding that lined one wall. A pair of empty platforms bracketed the hallway opposite the door they had entered through. Becca assumed that the spaces were meant for some kind of pillar or statue that had not yet been installed. They had spared no expense in the materials.

Becca ignored the decor and kept walking.

There was more evidence of construction everywhere, but fortunately, most of the work crews had gone home for the night. They had probably returned to the civilian camps outside the wall. Apparently, it was only the men processing the revenants that worked shifts throughout the night. Though, there were still some stragglers finishing up tasks here and there, leading to a few tense moments. In the end, they were able to avoid interacting with anyone.

As they ventured further into the structure, it became clear that the place was indeed meant to be a government building, similar to a city hall. They even passed a few administrative offices that looked to be in use.

Becca ignored the temptation to search every room for information that could be used against Autem. The situation in Vegas had stretched the building's security thin, but it wasn't nonexistent. Passing a Guardian stationed in one of the hallways, they kept up a front that they belonged there. Though Becca could have sensed the tension in Harlow's body even without being a vampire. The short woman was ready to murder every Guardian they passed without hesitation.

Fortunately, none of the guards hassled them. Granted, the areas that they had accessed so far were clearly meant for the public. Things would probably change when they got closer to where the caretaker was stored.

From what she could tell, the first floor of the building was meant for basic administration. The kind of place that regular citizens of the empire might go to speak to government officials, or in Autem's case, priests, due to the empire's theocratic system. If she had to guess, the floors above would hold what they needed.

According to the files that the caretaker had sent Harlow just before the internet died, they had to reach a room on the fifth floor. Becca frowned as they found a sign that read stairs, with an arrow pointing in a direction. The problem was that it was laying on the top of a pile of other signs and not on an actual wall. The overall size combined with the incomplete nature of the building was becoming more and more frustrating by the second. It was like a maze with no indicators of which way to go. They had found several heavy, locked doors that might have had a stairway on the other side, but there was no way to know for sure, and they couldn't just break them all down.

It wasn't until they had gotten stuck at a few dead ends that they finally found someplace that made sense.

"Elevators." Harlow jabbed a finger at a sign that had actually been installed properly.

"Finally." Becca headed in that direction only to skid to a stop as she approached a massive room with a large door and windows that lead back outside. They must have looped all the way back to the main entrance at the front of the building.

A familiar voice echoing off the vaulted ceiling.

Grabbing Harlow by the collar, she yanked her against the

wall where they could hide behind one of two stone pillars that bracketed the entrance to the room beyond. The sound of a dozen boots stomped as a chorus of men shouted an oath.

"With the blessing of the Nine, we serve the will of the One."

Becca's heart raced as her fight or flight response started flooding mana into her stats, causing every muscle in her body to tense as her senses blasted her mind with input. She cut off the flow before squandering what little mana she had left and getting a grip on the situation.

Leaning out to get a look at the room beyond, two dozen Guardians stood in formation, facing forward. Their armor was different than any Becca had seen before, each resembling a medieval knight more than modern soldiers. Every one of them held one fist against their breastplate to salute someone standing at the head of the group. Becca ducked back behind the pillar not wanting to risk a peek at whoever they were facing.

Ultimately, she already knew.

Please don't be Henwick. Please don't be Henwick. Please don't be Henwick.

Running into the literal big bad that had ended the world was the last thing they needed. Though it would also be her luck. Becca closed her eyes and held her breath, waiting for someone to speak and confirm what she feared. She had only heard Henwick's voice a couple times, but it had already been etched into her brain. There was no way she could forget it.

A voice responded to the Guardian's oath. "May the Nine guide you."

Becca snapped her eyes open and let out a breath. It wasn't him. Of course, that only raised a new question. Who was it? She leaned out again to get a better look, finding an old man dressed in white robes standing at the head of the group.

"Who the hell is that?" She knew she'd seen him before.

"That's Chancellor Serrano," Harlow whispered.

Becca nodded, remembering where she'd seen the elderly man. It had been back when she and Digby had infiltrated

Skyline's base and witnessed a ceremony to induct children into their Guardian forces. Serrano had appeared on a large screen in the back of the stage to introduce one of Autem's bishops.

"He's the leader of Autem's religious side of things," Harlow added. "It's a theocracy so, at this point, he's something like their president or king."

"Henwick doesn't run everything?" Becca ducked back behind the pillar that bracketed one of the entrances to the room where Serrano was speaking.

"Henwick handles the big moves, like starting the apocalypse and world domination. But someone has to deal with the day-to-day." She shot her a look. "They're building a new government and implementing their church on a large scale. One person can't manage everything."

"I guess that's true." Becca tried to wrap her head around the power dynamic.

She glanced back, wondering if she could sneak back the way they came without being discovered. With two dozen Guardians in the room, the last thing she wanted was to get caught red-handed.

That was when the entire group snapped their boots together and turned to exit. Her heart leapt into her throat as she feared they might leave through the hallway that kept them hidden. Sneaking into the center of Autem's capital had been surprisingly easy, so they were overdue for a setback.

She calmed down when the entire group put on their helmets and headed out toward the building's main entrance. Becca watched them go, their armor clinking with each step.

Every Guardian wore a sword in a magnetic sheath on their back alongside some kind of bar with a handle at the end, like the bottom of an umbrella. The men in the back of the group carried shields that looked like they belonged in a history museum. The surfaces were covered in a motif of angel wings that surrounded the crest that Autem loved to put on everything.

Becca fed a few points of mana into her perception, pushing

on her vision. Gaining focus, she was able to make out runes engraved here and there. That was probably why their armor was made of metal. There must have been runecraft at play that required different materials. She clenched her jaw as they marched out of the room.

Obviously, they were some sort of special division.

"We need to hurry and get the caretaker. Digby isn't ready to go up against the assault that's coming."

"Not yet. Serrano is still in there." Harlow gestured with her head. "We have to wait for him to leave."

"At least it's not Henwick." Becca cringed as a second voice came from a bay of elevators behind Serrano.

"How soon before we can leave?"

This time, it *was* Henwick.

Becca flattened herself against the wall and held her breath. The man had been level one hundred the last time she'd seen him. He was bound to hear even the slightest sound. Hell, his senses were probably stronger than a vampire's at full strength. Then she relaxed. If that was true, then he must have a way of dampening them to maintain focus, the same way Leon had taught her to do. Odds were, he wouldn't be on high alert within his own keep.

She held still regardless. Harlow did the same. They had no choice but to wait until he and Serrano left.

"I just sent the elites on their way." Serrano turned to face Henwick, his shoes squeaking on the floor. "We are ready to leave on your order."

"And the fodder?" Henwick sounded pleased.

"Our processing center has readied over a thousand revenants. They are loading their holding containers onto the owls."

"Excellent." Henwick walked through the room in the direction of the main doors of the building, as if leaving.

Becca nearly let out the breath she had been holding, only to stop herself when Serrano spoke up.

"But I have to ask…"

Henwick spun back around, standing at the center of the room. From where Becca hid behind the pillar, all she could see was his back. She cursed Serrano for slowing the man's exit.

"You have to ask what?" An annoyed tone entered Henwick's voice.

"Is attacking the Heretics really the best choice?" Serrano's footsteps traveled slowly across the floor. "Surely war is not the will of the One."

"Are you suggesting that the Nine have led us astray?" Henwick's voice fell flat.

"No, of course not." Serrano stepped past Henwick into Becca's view as he gestured to the ceiling. "I only mean that the Nine have blessed us with more than just strength." He lowered his hand. "What of the wisdom that they have bestowed?"

Henwick took a step back into view, folding his arms. "I am not here for a sermon and I have no time for flowery words, Serrano. Just say what you mean, man."

The chancellor deflated. "I mean negotiations, Henwick."

"Negotiate?" He scoffed. "You are aware of what kind of monstrosity we are dealing with, are you not? Not only that, but Graves adds insult to injury every chance he gets." A tone entered his voice, somehow harsher than it already was.

It sounded like Digby must have done something to piss the man off in the last few days.

"I am well aware of this necromancer that you harbor such disdain for." Serrano swept a hand out toward the room. "But there are many ways to deal with such a threat without putting more of our people at risk. This attack is taking far too many men from the capital. Men that we need to keep the citizens safe. The result has left us exposed. What if a group of revenants decides that tonight is the night they attack the outskirts?"

"Then the citizens can seek refuge in the churches." Henwick sounded unconcerned.

"What if a horde of zombies wanders in, then?" Serrano didn't let up.

Henwick let out a chuckle. "I seriously doubt that there is a herd of the dead out there large enough to present a problem for our remaining security."

"That may be, but what if we lose too many men in this crusade of yours?" Serrano held out both hands. "That would leave our city guard spread too thin for months. Surely, we can try reasoning with this Graves fellow before resorting to all-out war and the horrors that might bring."

"You don't know Graves like I do." Henwick stared down at the older man. "He is a scoundrel in possession of a power that mankind should not possess. There is a reason why we have built limitations into the Guardian Core. The Heretic Seed offers complete access to unbridled magic. Graves is far too impulsive to be trusted with it. Our hands are tied in this matter. He and his kind must be destroyed."

"I understand the danger. I am just saying we should take things in smaller steps." Serrano stepped closer to Henwick, looking up to him. "We do still have that prisoner upstairs, and now that we know where the Heretics are, we no longer need him. We could offer him as a show of good faith and potentially foster an agreement to gain access to the Heretic Seed. We don't need to take it away from them, just limit its power."

Becca furrowed her brow at the mention of a prisoner. A nameless Heretic had been reported in the flight recorder data she'd stolen from a crashed kestrel days ago. From that, she knew Autem had captured a someone from Vegas, along with her, off the coast of California. She had originally planned on trying to rescue them to keep the empire from discovering where Digby had been hiding. Though, that became a lot less important now that Vegas's cover had already been blown. Still, it sounded like the prisoner was being held in the building, and they could certainly use an extra team member. Then again, they couldn't really afford to take a detour.

"Do you honestly believe that Graves would allow us anywhere near the Seed?" Henwick scoffed again. "And even if he did, how would we limit its power? Because I'm certain that the caretaker we liberated from the Fools would be less than cooperative in that effort. As it is, we've had to restrict its abilities just to keep the Guardian Core running without interference. No, until we can groom a new candidate to fill the caretaker's shoes, our only option is to destroy the Heretic Seed."

Serrano released a sigh. "I suppose there is no convincing you."

"No, there isn't." Henwick uncrossed his arms.

"Very well." Serrano gave him a nod. "May the Nine guide you."

"Thank you." Henwick inclined his head slightly. "I will let you know once we have the Seed back in our possession."

"Good, I will be waiting in my office for your report." Serrano gave a bow in return before turning back toward the elevators at the front of the room and pressing a button.

With that, Henwick continued his way through the space to exit the building's front doors. Probably to join his elite forces on an owl heading for Vegas. Serrano disappeared into an elevator a moment later. Both Becca and Harlow let out a long sigh of relief the instant they were gone.

"Shit." Becca nearly dropped to her knees under the pressure of the last few minutes. "I thought he was going to sense us for sure."

"I think he's focused on other things at the moment." Harlow peeked out to make sure the coast was clear before heading out into the room. "We should be too. I didn't like what he said about keeping our caretaker restrained."

"I didn't like what Serrano said about having a prisoner either." Becca followed. "Though, he did seem more reasonable than Henwick. I wasn't expecting someone from Autem to be willing to negotiate."

"Maybe, maybe not." Harlow looked back. "He did go along with Henwick's plan to kill off most of the world's population."

"That's true." Becca walked through the center of the

empty room, stopping when she turned into the bay of elevators at the back. "Shit."

A golden door loomed in front of her in the middle of the bay of elevators. Decorative engravings covered its surface.

"That's the same as the elevator I rode on to get to Henwick's vault on the moon." Becca took a step back. "How many exit points does his base up there have?"

"The Fools were never able to locate them all." Harlow stared up at the golden doors. "Henwick has them all over the world."

"That explains where he came from just now." Becca shook off the last of her nerves and took a step toward the bay of elevators, only to stop again when she looked down. "What the hell?"

"What?" Harlow looked back.

Becca just pointed a finger down.

With the conversation between Serrano and Henwick combined with the threat of being caught, Becca hadn't paid much attention to the room they stood in. Now though, it was all she could see. The ceiling was at least thirty feet high, with pillars surrounding them. The walls were unfinished, but the floor was something else.

Staring down, Becca saw her own reflection in a thick panel of glass. She spun to find the surface continued for ten feet in all directions, leaving her standing in a transparent circle. What lay below was even stranger. A model city, cast in gold stretched out beneath the glass. At first, she didn't recognize it. Then she saw the five-sided wall.

"It's the capital." Becca swept her hand around her feet at the center of the expanse.

The wall that currently stood in Washington, D.C. was clearly visible at the center of the city. As was the building that they currently inhabited positioned at the center. The difference was that there was so much more.

The central structure existed in some sort of massive park like a monument, with intricate designs tiled onto the ground surrounding it. The real building was unfinished and covered in scaffolding, but this showed what it would one day become, its sides adorned with the empire's crest. At the corners of each stood the statue of an angel.

The wall that encircled the building was even grander, with more enormous statues of angels positioned in the corners all around it, except for one empty space. There were nine angels in total. They stood as tall as the wall itself with their wings extending into the sky to make the ring look like a crown. Each one would have to be as tall as the Statue of Liberty to match the scale of the wall outside.

Beyond that, another wall, half as tall, surrounded the first, with hundreds of buildings between them. It was unrecognizable to the camps that stood outside the wall. Clearly, they planned to level the buildings that now stood and replace them with their own designs. Another wall stood further out, then another, and another. Nine layers altogether, each getting smaller as they went. The buildings between each wall decreased in size as well, as if some kind of hierarchy had been built right into the city's design.

The model was filled with evidence of Autem's rule. Every park, every building, and every wall held some kind of reference to the Nine. It was obvious that they planned to etch their beliefs into every aspect of life for the empire. From that, it wasn't hard to make the leap that any beliefs that didn't coincide with what Autem taught would not be included. Hell, they had literally put up walls to make sure the wrong people didn't get in.

The whole thing looked like a kingdom out of a fantasy movie. At first glance, it was grand and beautiful, but the horror of the reality held the truth. There was nothing left of the world that had died to produce it. They planned to erase everything.

With enough control, it wouldn't be hard to teach a version of history that reinforced their rule. Hell, most people didn't even know that Autem had been behind the apocalypse to begin with. Sure, the people that they accepted as citizens would be safe and the future of humanity would be secured, but what kind of future would that be?

Becca staggered, her legs turning to Jell-O.

"This is why we fight." Harlow stepped toward her, standing at the edge of the city. "Autem can't be allowed to erase the world. It can't be allowed to erase us. No one should have that much power. I may not be anyone important, but I am still a Fool. There may not be many of us left, but we'll go down fighting."

"Let's hope that doesn't happen." Becca tore her eyes away from the model beneath the glass. "But you are wrong about one thing."

"What's that?" Harlow turned back toward the elevators.

"You're not unimportant." Becca picked up her pace to catch up. "There might not be many Fools left, but I'm pretty sure you're their leader now."

Harlow shook her head as she pressed the button on one of the elevators, making a point of picking the furthest set of doors from Henwick's golden one. "I'm just here to pass the torch. To be honest, I was hoping that you might be willing to take up the mantle."

Becca hesitated as the elevator opened, taken aback by the thought. "But I'm not even one of you."

Harlow stepped inside. "And that's where you're wrong. You have been one of us since we met."

Becca stepped inside the elevator, feeling a weight settle across her shoulders. With everything that had happened, she hadn't given the direction of her life much thought beyond the next few hours. Taking charge of an ancient organization of rebels hadn't been on her list.

Adjusting her shoulders, Becca relaxed as the elevator doors closed. Somehow, the weight settling across her didn't feel that heavy.

CHAPTER THIRTY-NINE

Parker pulled a sheet up over her head and rolled over. Then she realized she was not in her hotel room. She noticed this detail during her fall to the metal floor of a decommissioned battleship.

After being shot a bunch of times and dragging her body through broken glass, she had been brought back from the brink by one of Digby's summoned echoes. Despite her injuries being healed, she was still severely sleep-deprived. Recognizing that, she'd transported Digby back to Hawaii and slipped away to rest in one of the old crew bunks aboard the Missouri. No one came looking for her, clearly understanding her need to recover.

Checking her watch, she realized she had only been asleep for three hours. It was the most she'd gotten in days, but it still left her exhausted. It was going to have to do.

She pushed herself up from the floor, her eyes welling up.

Everything had gotten so screwed up.

Sax was dead, Alex was missing, Vegas was no longer safe, and Digby was spiraling out of control.

Some conscience I turned out to be. She shook off the thought.

There was no sense dwelling on things now. No, the only

thing she could do was move forward. That was what she'd always done, right?

Her head throbbed.

"This headache is going to be the death of me."

The constant pain had subsided after she'd been healed, but it had come right back. After Digby and the other covens dealt with the last of the Guardians back in Vegas, Lana had given her a checkup. According to her, there was no reason for the recurring migraines. The only explanation was that her magic was causing some kind of problem. The fact that her power was an anomaly, even to the Seed, made it easy to believe that it could be the issue. Unfortunately, there was no way to fix it.

Then again, with the secret of their location blown, she might not live long enough to worry about whatever magic cancer she had. Autem was coming. Using the distance to their capital as a basis, it was safe to assume the war that they had been preparing for was only a few hours away.

It wasn't enough time.

Parker lowered her head, letting a few tears fall before drying her eyes and picking herself up to head to the ship's deck. The corridors of the ship were narrow, clearly meant to take up as little space as possible. Even the bunks that she had been napping in had been stacked three high. So many men had crewed the ship decades ago.

Now, it was home to the dead.

Parker entered one of the ship's mess halls, finding it full of zombies. Asher had been busy gathering them from the surrounding areas throughout the week. Some resembled humans while others had clearly started as revenants before being reanimated. Digby must have decided to use the old battleship as a place to house them for the moment.

"I really would have liked to have been told that this was where the horde was being housed before I decided to sleep here." She shuddered, realizing how close the monsters had been while she'd been unconscious.

"SAFE!" Asher flapped over to the table closest to her before cawing back at the horde.

"I know. You have them under control." Parker reached out a hand to pat the raven's head. "Have you seen Dig around? As much as I don't want to, I think he needs a visit from his conscience."

"OUT!" The raven flapped her wings.

"Eep." Parker took a step toward the door, unsure why the bird suddenly wanted her gone.

Asher settled down and shook her head to indicate a misunderstanding, following the motion with another, pointing her beak toward the door.

"Oh, you mean Dig is outside." Parker followed the bird's directions, heading toward the hatch that led to the deck. She stopped a moment later, catching a few whispers coming from the horde. "Who's there?"

For a second, she saw a skull peek up from behind a group of zombies; it ducked back down just as fast.

"Union?" Parker stepped closer to the horde.

"Yes?" The skeleton spoke up in the same dark tone that Tavern used, sounding like multiple voices all rolled into one.

"What are you whispering about back there?" She arched an eyebrow.

"We whisper nothing of concern." The skeleton slipped through the crowd. "We are merely organizing. The horde requires it."

Parker eyed the skeleton. She'd only known Union for a short time, but she was starting to understand their priorities. "For what it's worth, I'm on your side." Gave them a nod. "Seize the means of production and all that, but you might be wasting your time in here. I don't think you'll have much luck unionizing Dig's horde."

"Not his horde." Union held up a bony finger before placing their hand to their chest and adding, "Our horde."

"Okay, then." She gave them a thumbs up. "Our horde it is."

Parker left the surreal conversation, continuing on her way out to the deck. Her heart sank as soon as she stepped outside. At the railing of the ship stood a friend.

Sax.

For a moment, Parker thought she had imagined his death. It had happened so fast that she'd barely had time to process it. Now, with him standing there, it was so much harder.

Someone had thrown a rain poncho over him. He still carried his rifle slung across his back along with a bandoleer of grenade rounds for it. He turned as her foot crunched on a left-over bone fragment from Digby's earlier Body Craft experiments. A sharp pain streaked through her chest.

The zombie's face was gray, but beyond that, he looked almost the same as when he'd been alive. Most of the zombies she'd seen had more sunken features and frail frames. Apparently, Digby's enhancements had done a lot for his appearance. Come to think of it, the horde back in the mess hall had looked a lot healthier than the zombies she'd seen in the past as well.

Sax turned back to the railing as soon as he saw who she was.

"Do you remember me?" She didn't know what she was asking.

The zombie didn't respond.

"I guess not." Parker joined him at the rail.

It was possible for a zombie to become aware. Asher seemed conscious, and Rufus, back in California, was practically human. Why was Sax different? Probably because he was not a zombie master. Granted, she didn't know how it all worked. All she knew was whatever spark had existed within her friend was gone.

A part of her wanted to put a bullet in his brain right there to let him rest. There was something wrong about what Digby had done. She couldn't help but wonder if he would animate her too if she died. Just how normal did he think it was to use the bodies of his friends like that? Would this become business as usual?

Would death in Vegas change into something else? Some kind of eternal service?

Parker pushed the thought out of her head. It was too heavy a subject for her to handle. Besides, the activity in the harbor could easily keep her mind occupied.

"They actually did it."

She stared out at one of the ships on the other side of the dock as it floated several yards above the water.

From where she stood, the vessels hadn't been altered much. The flight system was complicated, however. She didn't understand all of it, but the main component consisted of two large rods a foot wide and a dozen high. One was positioned in the front and one in the back. They were set vertically into a large plate that was welded into the ship's lower decks. Runes on the plate and the rods were what got the ship in the air. Like the Guardian rings that Alex had experimented with, they were made up of layers. Iron, steel, and gold. Most of the materials had been easy enough to get but the gold had required covens to raid every store on the strip.

Once the ship was in the air, the engineering team added four smaller rods attached to armatures that extended from the sides, two in the front and two in the back. This kept the vessel stable and provided propulsion. The mana required to keep the ship in the air was drawn in from whatever was around it. A team of four Heretics was needed to actually move the ship, each feeding their mana into the propulsion unit's engravings.

Then there were the cannons.

Of the ships available, none of them had the number of guns that the Missouri had, but they did have some. A team of ten was trained for each vessel to load and fire the weapon systems. The result required a crew of fourteen. They rounded up to fifteen to make sure there was someone extra as a backup. Mason captained the Minnow. Jameson had taken another and named it the Barracuda. Digby intended to take the largest one as his command ship. He'd been calling it the Seahorse. The last two, the Angler and the Orca, were captained by a couple of the other coven leaders.

The battleships were all in various stages of completion. Parker had overheard Digby checking with the engineering team before her nap; they needed another two hours to get them all in the air. They even had a cargo ship ready to bring the fleet up to six. It didn't have any weapons, but it could hold a lot of zombies. The plan was to have it hang in the back, far from the fight where it could deploy the dead, provided Digby could give them all wings. They had just been calling that vessel the horde ship.

Unfortunately, that still left a problem.

By plane, Hawaii was about seven hours from Vegas, and they weren't sure how fast the ships could go. Probably not anywhere near fast enough without falling apart. This also meant that Autem would reach Vegas before they could get there.

"I have a feeling Dig is not going to accept that."

They had constructed a large reflective surface on their end in Hawaii, but with the mirror back on the strip destroyed, there wasn't a way to get the fleet home to defend it in time. That was when a voice came from her pocket.

Parker reached for her compact and flipped it open to find Lana looking back at her. "Yeah?"

"Hi, ah." She looked around as if avoiding speaking. "Is Dig there?"

"No, I was just about to go find him."

"Can you maybe give him a heads up to regrow some human legs before he comes back to Vegas? Some of the people are a little freaked out with the whole spider thing." Lana ended her request with a nod as if she'd finished what she wanted to say.

"Yeah, I can see where that might send a bad impression." Parker started to close her compact, but Lana asked another question.

"How's the headache?"

Parker hesitated, noticing a concerned tone in her voice. "Still there."

"Okay, I was just checking. Make sure you get some rest when you can." Lana gave her a sad smile.

"I always do." Parker closed the compact as Lana said good-bye. "Good thing we have an epic battle coming. I might start to dwell on what her question meant."

Parker pushed away from the railing and called out to Digby. There wasn't time to go find him. Eventually, she leaned back into the mess hall and asked Asher to call to him across their bond. It wasn't long before she heard splashing in the water below.

"What is he doing now?" Parker started for the walkway that led to land but stopped when she heard scraping against the side of the ship. Turning back to the rail, she looked down to find something far worse than she'd expected.

Digby emerged from the water below, his eight spider legs click-clacking against the ship as he climbed its vertical surface. His bulbous body swayed behind him, its exoskeleton splitting apart at the back where the tail of a shark dangled. What was left of his clothing was in tatters, leaving only his vest and a few long scraps of cloth that had once been his coat hanging from the leather straps that held his pauldron on. Obviously, his pants were nowhere to be seen since he had replaced his lower body with something more arachnid.

Parker stepped away from the rail as Digby snapped a hand around it and clawed his unnatural body over onto the deck. Eight legs touched down one at a time as he raised his head to stand at his full height, towering over Parker by at least a foot and a half.

The necromancer stared down at her as he slurped what looked like an octopus tentacle into his mouth. It curled around his cheek, clearly still alive and struggling not to be eaten. He snapped his jaws shut as soon as it was gone.

"What is so important as to make my minion call me all the way up here?"

"Did you just eat a live octopus?" Parker cringed.

"Yes, I've had several." He looked pleased with himself.

She leaned to one side so she could see the fish tail dragging on the deck behind him. "And a shark?"

"Indeed, I have eaten many things. I need more options to work with now that I am no longer bound to a human form."

"Yeah, well, probably change back to normal. People are starting to get freaked out and you look like a character from a fucked-up version of The Little Mermaid. No amount of sea shells is gonna hide that." She waved a finger around at his general appearance.

"Absolutely not." He stomped three of his legs. "I do not have the resources to waste, changing back and forth between one form or another. People are just going to have to get used to it."

"Are they going to have to get used to that too?" She held a hand out toward Sax's walking corpse, standing not too far away.

"That zombie is fully restored to the strength he had while alive. He is also capable of magic. I realized that using the corpse of a fallen soldier is unsettling, but it is a sacrifice for the good of everyone."

"So that's it then, you're just going to animate everyone that dies?" Parker dropped her hand back down. "That's the future that waits for us all?"

"Don't be foolish, Parker." He folded his arms across his chest before adding. "I don't have the mana to animate everyone."

"Good to know." She rolled her eyes.

Digby tapped one of his legs on the deck. "Listen, if you have something to say about my new minion, then spit it out."

Parker deflated, unsure what she was even trying to say. In the end, all she could do was whisper an unhelpful comment. "He had a name."

"What was that?" Digby jabbed her in the shoulder with a

clawed hand hard enough to hurt but not enough to break the skin.

"I said he had a name." She snapped back, her exhaustion, frustration, and grief finally spilling over. "He's not just a minion. Sax was my friend. We've known each other since…" She trailed off, pressing a hand to her head as a surge of pain swelled. "Fuck, I am sick of this."

For a moment, Digby didn't respond, then he leaned down to get closer to her face. "If it had not been for my minion, I may not have fought off those Guardians back in Vegas while you were laying around."

Parker's mouth fell open, not expecting the sudden attack. "I almost died."

"Yes, I am aware." He raised back up. "I never should have left you alone."

Parker stood there, unable to tell if he meant that last statement as an insult or not. "You don't have to be a jerk."

"And you need to understand that everything I do is to help." He turned and walked a few feet away, his legs clacking against the deck. "I swear, the amount of questions and judgment I get is driving me mad. You have not let up since I gave my spark to the Seed. Another sacrifice that I made, by the way."

"Fine, I don't want to argue with you." She groaned. "Just make sure you don't animate me when I die."

"Of course I won't." A cackle rumbled through his throat. "You're far too valuable to let perish in the first place. Without your magic, we wouldn't be able to move around so easily."

"Glad I'm so useful."

Digby ignored her comment, opting to look across the harbor at the ship floating in the air. "How are the preparations faring?"

"The fleet should be in the sky in the next couple hours. And Mason is organizing the people back in Vegas to leave. We can evacuate them to the base here using my magic, but we'll have to find someplace else fast because Autem will know where these ships came from as soon as they see them." Parker held up her binder of photos to discuss a new location.

"Evacuate?" Digby shook his head. "Why should we do that? We have put far too much effort into building the settlement in Las Vegas. Not to mention supplying it with power from the dam. We can't just start over."

She lowered the binder. "I get that, but our fleet won't make it back to Vegas from Hawaii before Autem gets there."

"Of course we can. You just need to open a passage large enough." He gestured to a parking lot in the distance where one of the covens had constructed a giant mirror to match the one that they had attempted to build in Vegas.

"Last time I checked, the other mirror that we built on the strip was destroyed when we were attacked." She held out a hand empty.

"Then we will use the water like you did with the jeep," Digby argued, as if doing so was a simple thing.

"I don't know if I can use an unstable surface for something that big." She crossed her eyes thinking about it. "It's one thing to open a passage for something small that's traveling fast, but a large, slow boat is gonna be an issue."

"Then I'll freeze the surface again." He pointed a finger down. "It isn't ideal and won't last long, but it will be enough to get the ships through in time. With that, we can face whatever Autem throws at us head-on."

"I guess we can try."

"Try?" Digby snapped his attention back to her. "What was it Becca said to me a few weeks ago? Oh yes, there is no try, only do."

Parker held up a finger. "Okay, first of all, that's from Star Wars." Extending a second finger, she added, "And I don't know what Autem is bringing our way, but we only have six ships including the horde ship. That might seem like a lot, but Autem has had more time to prepare than we have, and there is a good chance we aren't going to win this fight."

"Don't be ridiculous." Digby jabbed a thumb into his chest.

"With the power I have gained, we can more than make up for any area we might find lacking."

"Yes, but Autem has kestrels with modern weapons," she argued back.

"Yes, and we have lanterns that can deflect bullets." He scoffed. "Not to mention I can simply Decay a kestrel right out of the sky."

Parker stopped and watched the zombie for a moment, unsure why he was so confident all of a sudden. What happened to the doubts that the zombie worried about? That had been the whole reason Sybil had sacrificed herself back when they were trapped in the Seed.

A leader should have doubts.

That was what the old witch had said before stepping into Digby's void to become the echo he used to summon the crone. Would she have done the same now? Had his time in Boulder really gone that well? The fact that he had climbed so many levels so fast spoke for itself. Still, Digby seemed like the type that could let that kind of power run away with him.

"Fine." Parker deflated. "But make me a promise that you will listen to me." She placed a hand to her chest. "You told me to be your conscience and I am trying my best."

"Your best?" He arched an eyebrow. "More like second-guessing every move I make."

"I get that I'm annoying, and I don't like this role any more than you do." She placed a hand on his arm. "But you were the one that asked me to let you know if you were acting strange. You said you trusted me. So if I say we need to retreat or if I tell you that you're going too far, then please listen." She raised a hand to point back at Sax's walking corpse. "Because we're right at the line here. And I am terrified that you're going to cross it."

Digby eyed her for a long moment. He could have been thinking about anything. An insult, an excuse, even an accusation. In the end, he just sighed.

"Alright, I promise." He raised a hand to his unbeating heart. "If you tell me I'm out of control, I will listen."

The pain in Parker's head faded ever so slightly. "Thank you."

"It's almost over." He looked down at her. "You won't have to worry about all this much longer. We will be victorious."

Parker went back to the railing to lean as another one of the ships rose up out of the sea. "I really hope you're right."

"Of course I am." He joined her at the railing. "And I will do whatever it takes to ensure that our city's future is secure."

Parker looked up at him, trying to read his blank expression. *That's what I'm afraid of.*

CHAPTER FORTY

"Throw it in the trunk." Alex gestured to the back of his floating Camaro as he pulled open the hood. "And keep an eye out for zombies. I have the place warded, but I can't do anything about the dead."

Hawk ran by carrying an artifact that they had recovered from the exhibit. He'd wrapped it in a cloth from one of the museum's costumes and shoved it into the trunk. "Okay, what's the plan here?"

Alex stared down at the mess of engraved plates that served as an engine for the vehicle. He really wished he'd organized the vehicle's system better and incorporated the flight unit in a way that made more sense, but he'd been obsessed with discovery and exploration at the time.

After getting stranded at the Boston Museum of Science without a mirror to get home, he and Hawk crept their way outside to get the car. Moving it into the museum's entry hall, Alex got to work. As it was, it would take days to make it back to Vegas. The dangers of such a trip would almost certainly get them killed. There had to be a way to change that. Especially taking into account the flight system. If he could just increase its limits, they would have a chance. Provided a rare zombie didn't decide to walk into the museum to kill them in the next hour or so.

"Hey." Hawk snapped his fingers in front of Alex's face as he continued to stare down at the magical engine. "I asked what the plan is."

Alex shook off the pressure of the situation and tried to think through it. "I have a thought but I need some help. Go get Kristen for me."

Hawk ducked into the car, coming back with the skull and placing it on the edge of the car's engine.

"What is it now?" Kristen groaned. "Are you going to lecture me some more?"

"No." He turned back to Hawk. "Can you take the gun and go stealth? We had to break some windows to get the car in here, so keep an eye out for threats."

"On it." Hawk nodded before rushing off toward the entrance, vanishing as he moved.

Alex tried not to think about his disappearance so that he didn't disrupt the conceal spell. Instead, he turned back to the skull. "Okay, I need help figuring out how to improve the mana engine we made. You were there when I built this thing and you understand the runes, right?" He adjusted the skull's position so that she had a clear view of the engine.

"Yes, I was there. I can't tell you how many mistakes and inefficiencies you've made." She chuckled. "But as we have discussed, I am just a construct—"

Alex grabbed the skull up and held it close to his face. "Stop that."

"Stop what?" she responded, suddenly sounding flustered.

"Stop with all that construct stuff." He placed her back down. "I know it doesn't make sense and that it contradicts how the spell that created you works, but you are real. I know it. You have grown too much to be a construct."

She scoffed. "I haven't grown. Obviously, I'm just broken."

"You're wrong." Alex shook his head. "You care about us.

That's how I know you're going to help me now. Because if you don't, we are going to die here, and you don't want that any more than I do."

A long pause passed by, the skull making no indication one way or another. Then, finally, she spoke. "I swear, there really is something wrong with me." She released a ghostly sigh. "Fine, which runes do you need help with?"

"I knew it." Alex clapped his hands together before pointing to her. "You do like us."

"Don't gloat. It makes me like you less."

With that, they started working out the problem. Once they had a plan, he got to work, pulling various plates from the engine and engraving over the original runes before putting them back. Next, he made some modifications to the flight system. Once he was finished, he picked up the skull and headed off in search of materials to repair the car's broken windows. He made sure to grab a rifle from the trunk and cast barrier on himself, just in case something was lurking in the shadows.

Hawk stayed behind to make sure nothing came in the front door to surprise them. Alex just hoped there weren't any more zombie assassins hiding in the museum to catch him off guard. Shining a flashlight down a hallway, he found it empty. Though, that didn't stop him from being caught off guard by something else.

"I have a soul." Kristen blurted out the words as he carried her down the hall.

"What?" He looked down at her.

"That's the only explanation for the changes in me." She paused. "But that's impossible. Isn't it?"

"I don't know." He shrugged. "Magic is capable of so much, why can't it give you back your soul?"

"Because it can't," she said matter-of-factly. "Once a soul is gone, it's gone."

"What about Becca showing up in Washington?" he countered.

"That's a special circumstance." She sounded so sure. "Whatever I am now, I don't have the same soul as I had while alive."

"I've been thinking about that." Alex hesitated. "Or at least, I've been thinking about sparks in general, you know, since Digby is currently sans a soul." He stopped to peer down another hall to make sure it was clear. Nothing but darkness and silence answered him back. A display case full of taxidermied animals lined the walls, his flashlight reflecting in their artificial eyes. He ignored them and continued the conversation. "Did I ever tell you about Rufus?"

"No." She started to sound disinterested.

"Rufus was a zombie master we ran into back in California." A memory of the elderly zombie sacrificing himself to save them passed through Alex's mind. "He was a good man."

"He was conscious?" She suddenly seemed to care again.

Alex nodded. "But how did he get that way? Same goes for Clint. He was a mindless zombie before regaining himself, and he's come a long way since then."

"It's the hearts," she answered, finally cooperating.

"What about them?" He wandered down the hall, reaching a maintenance closet.

"In Digby's case, his connection to the Heretic Seed's fragment stopped him from losing his spark upon death. He didn't lose it until he gave it up to become the Seed's caretaker. But for regular zombies, it's possible to regain a spark by eating a large number of hearts in a short amount of time." She spoke like a teacher standing in front of a classroom of children. "It's possible because the heart is at the center of a person's mana system. The spark is a part of that system and it flows through the heart, picking up traces of a person's soul. Not a lot, but a small amount of pure essence. Normally, it would just fade from a corpse, but if a zombie eats enough hearts while they are still fresh, the energy can gather enough to stabilize."

Alex stopped as soon as he opened the door of the maintenance closet. "Wait, so that's all it takes? That could fix Digby's whole problem."

"Yes and no. The heart is a powerful organ, but the transference of a spark's essence is not so simple."

"Why not?" Alex placed her down on a shelf next to some cleaning products.

"For starters, Graves would need to eat hearts freshly torn from the chests of a couple hundred humans to consume enough traces to create a stable spark. And right now, humans are in short supply."

"Oh." Alex frowned. "So we would need to add a lot of Guardians to the menu."

"Or you could ask for volunteers back in Las Vegas." She let a ghostly laugh slip out. "But I suppose that wouldn't go over too well."

"It's good to know it's possible to replace a soul though." He pushed a few bottles around, finding a box containing several rolls of duct tape. "If that's how it works, becoming a zombie may not mean death if there's a way to bring them back."

"Again, yes and no," she repeated.

"What now?" He claimed the duct tape and headed back out into the hall.

"Graves is a special case. He never lost his soul and his brain is at least somewhat functional to store his mind. So technically the result of replacing his spark would still be mostly the same person." She clicked a nonexistent tongue. "But for a regular zombie whose soul has left their body, the result would be different. They would be a conscious entity with the ability to reason and grow as a person, but they wouldn't be the same person as the original."

"So does that mean Clint isn't the same person he was when alive?" Alex furrowed his brow, realizing he had no way of knowing.

"I didn't know Clint personally, but judging from his file, he was far more bold before his death." She sighed. "In his new incarnation, he is neurotic and timid."

"Oh." Alex deflated. "So there's no way to replace a person's spark?"

"I fear only the Nine have that power." She fell back on her old beliefs.

"Then how do we explain you?" Alex slowed to a stop as he ran the question over in his head.

Kristen certainly knew a lot more about how things worked, but it almost seemed strange for someone so close to Autem's leadership to not be aware of more. It was almost as if things had been kept from her.

I fear only the Nine have that power. Her words repeated in his mind.

He'd heard things like it before. It was the kind of line that explained away things too easily. The sort of thing that used faith to stop people from asking questions or exploring other options. The realization made it clear that Henwick never considered her an equal. Alex wondered if Kristen had ever realized it. Either way, there had to be a way to restore a spark for real. The changes the skull had gone through were proof of that much.

Then it dawned on him.

"It's the magic."

"Of course it's magic." She sounded unimpressed. "When magic is involved in a situation that doesn't make sense, then there's probably a strange interaction at work. Graves is a good example of that. He's a combination of zombie mutations and Heretic magic."

"And you're a construct, combined with Heretic magic and runes." He picked up his pace.

"Yes." She sighed. "I am not so foolish to think that Henwick told me everything. To be honest, I am sure he regularly kept things from me as well as others."

"Why did you let him get away with it?" Alex held her up so he could look into the hollows of her eyes.

She hesitated, as if making eye contact made it difficult to answer. "I'm sure he just wanted to keep the empire safe. That is what motivates most of what he does. It was reasonable to hide information that could be dangerous."

"I'm a little more skeptical." Alex shook his head. "If we operate under the assumption that you have a functioning soul, the question remains, how did the spells used to create you create it?"

She sighed. "I don't know."

"Let's retrace the steps." Alex shrugged. "Digby used Talking Corpse to bring you back, then Clint used the same spell to keep you active for days. That part in itself is strange, because Talking Corpse isn't meant to be reused like that. After that, I used my engrave spell to cover you in runes to feed the spell with mana permanently."

A moment of silence passed before she spoke again. "It is possible that a small trace of a person's spark could travel along with the mana used to cast a spell. It is all part of the same system."

Alex shuddered. "You mean I may be burning away a sliver of my soul every time I cast a spell?"

"Technically, it's possible." She paused. "But anything lost would be replenished over time as the soul recovers."

"That doesn't make me feel better."

"Too bad."

Alex pushed away the concern, focusing on the question. "But if that's true, then could Digby have given you a shred of his soul to create your construct? And could that shred have grown over time?"

"No. Such a small trace of power would not be able to form anything stable enough to become self-sufficient." She sounded sure of the answer. "It should have just burnt out along with the spell."

"But it didn't." Alex nodded. "Clint kept casting the same spell on you, over and over again. And if spells really carry traces of the caster's soul, then he would have been giving you more and more of his each time."

"Good lord," she blurted out, clearly shocked at the possibility. "Then you engraved dozens of runes upon me, donating even more. It was done in such a short time that it all must have merged into something stable." She let out a laugh that carried a hint of joy. "You helped give me a soul."

Alex laughed as well. "You're welcome."

"Don't start acting smug about it. Obviously, it isn't my original soul, but it's something. More like a graft that may become an entirely new entity." Her voice sounded lighter than he'd heard before. "And it explains why I have diverted so far from the person I was when I lived. I'm something else now."

"You sound happy about that." He gave her a smile.

"I don't know." Her tone shifted, sounding less sure.

"I guess you have things to work out, then." Alex lowered her skull to his side. "But either way, can we use the same process to replace Digby's missing soul?"

"We…" She trailed off for a moment before adding, "… Can't."

"Why not?" Alex held her back up.

"You would need a spell that you can cast on a zombie without hurting him. Something where the mana involved becomes a part of him."

Alex sighed. "And we don't have access to any spells that can do that."

"You would need the Seed's caretaker to give you a new one, and even then, a caretaker can't just give you spells willy-nilly," she added.

"Considering the Seed's caretaker is Digby's own soul, he should at least have a vested interest in helping." Alex reached the main hall where the car sat waiting for him.

"Yes, but keep in mind that the version of Graves that become the Seed's caretaker has only done so recently. And judging by how much trouble Henwick has had with the Guardian Core's caretaker, it may be a while before you can get reliable help from the Heretic Seed."

Alex raised an eyebrow. "The Guardian Core has a caretaker?"

"Of course it does," she answered back as if it should have been obvious.

"Where did they get theirs?" He eyed her, suspicious why she hadn't mentioned it before.

"The empire's caretaker…" The skull let an awkward silence pass before adding, "…Is complicated."

Before Alex could pry further, Hawk appeared in the space directly in front of him. "You get what you need?"

"Bla!" Alex nearly dropped the skull that he'd been conversing with. "Don't do that. I swear, I almost had a heart attack. And honestly, it would be just my luck if that's how I die."

"Don't worry." Kristen laughed as he recovered from the scare. "I can just tell Graves to make a construct of your corpse too if you die."

"No thank you." He set her down on the car and pulled a roll of duct tape from the box he'd found in the closet, tossing it to Hawk. "Use that to seal all the cracks and openings in the Camaro."

"Why?" Hawk caught the roll.

"Because if we are going to make it back to Vegas tonight, this thing is going to have to get a lot more aerodynamic." Alex grabbed a roll of his own and went to work. "We're going to have to go faster."

"Faster?" Hawk's tone wavered. "Isn't this thing's top speed already suicidal? How are we going to navigate the roads?"

"Roads?" Alex pulled off a strip of tape and gave him a smug grin. "Where we're going, we don't need roads."

CHAPTER FORTY-ONE

"Hide!" Becca ducked to the side as the elevator she rode in opened two floors before they had reached fifth where the caretaker could be accessed.

Harlow did the same.

A long moment passed where they both stood still, pressed flat against the walls. Becca fed mana into her agility and senses in anticipation. Whoever called the elevator to that floor would walk in at any second. Focusing on hearing and touch, Becca reached out with her perception.

So many questions buzzed through her head.

Was the threat a Guardian? How many were there? Can I kill them before they can radio for help?

Will I have enough mana?

All of the questions vanished a second later.

The hallway outside was empty.

Becca remained where she was for a moment, wondering if she was somehow mistaken. Harlow shot her a look asking if she had sensed anything. Becca responded by leaning out into the open door to make sure.

"Huh?" She stepped into the center of the elevator as the empty hallway stood before her.

The walls were made of cement blocks, with a series of ventilation ducts and power conduits running along the bare ceiling. It was all very quick and dirty. Like the rest of the building, there were sure to be plans to finish the floor with the same opulence as the previous one below. There were just too many things ahead of it on the list of priorities.

Becca turned to Harlow and shrugged. "Nobody."

Harlow stepped away from the wall. "That isn't how lifts work. They tend to need someone to press a button to stop halfway to a previously selected floor."

"Maybe the system is acting up with all the construction being done?" Becca tapped the close button.

The elevator doors slid shut but failed to continue onto the floor they had selected. Instead, the doors opened back up.

"That's not good." Harlow reached out to punch the button again, getting the same result.

"Okay, then." Becca stepped out of the elevator.

"Someone is bound to walk into this hallway at some point and we best be gone when they do." Harlow followed and hit the call button for one of the other elevators.

It didn't light up.

Becca tapped one of the other buttons.

Still nothing.

"Starting to worry here." She jabbed the button several more times for good measure.

That was when she heard voices from someplace further down the hall.

Becca pushed on her senses, only to panic the moment she did. Twelve heartbeats echoed through her ears along with the vibrations of heavy boots walking across the unfinished floor.

"Guardians. Twelve of them." She snapped her head to Harlow who immediately turned back to the elevator.

Of course, that was when the doors decided to close. Harlow let out a quiet growl as her hand fell just short of stopping them. They both looked back at each other in panic. They were out of options.

Becca felt for her mana as she got ready to fight, realizing she only had around thirty percent left. Dropping into a runner's stance, she prepared to rush the oncoming squads. Winning was almost impossible, but if she could feed, there was a chance.

Harlow slapped a hand down on her shoulder to stop her from launching herself down the hall. Becca spun around to find the woman pointing up. Flicking her eyes to the ductwork running along the ceiling, she understood why. The ducts themselves weren't large enough to use but there was a space above them before the actual ceiling.

Harlow was moving before Becca could offer to help her up. The short woman just jumped against the wall and kicked off to grab a hold of an electric conduit. Once she had a grip, she pulled herself up like it had barely been a strain.

With little time remaining before the Guardians down the hall rounded the corner, Becca fed mana into her strength and jumped straight up. She caught hold of the same conduit, bracing against it as she walked up the wall. Leaning into her agility, she gave herself enough to flip up and land on top of a pipe, where she teetered back and forth. Continuing to feed her agility, she stabilized her balance, crouching in the gap like a gargoyle.

Harlow, on the other hand, leaned on a corner of the air duct.

Becca didn't dare put weight on the ventilation for fear that the hollow shaft would compress and make too much noise. Instead, she stayed where she was, continuing to feed her agility to keep her balance. It was the best she could do other than pray no one looked up.

The voices of the Guardians grew louder as they rounded the corner.

Becca had never been so annoyed with herself for being

right before. There were exactly twelve of them, with several working in pairs to carry a series of large crates.

What is that? Becca pushed on her sight, focusing on the crates in search of some kind of marking. All she was able to catch was a reflection in the edge of one of the Guardian's swords where it showed through their magnetic sheath. Even then, all she could see was a partial view of a label. Just five letters with a space in the middle.

ageki

Her mind raced through the possibilities, adding letters to the front and back of the words. Then the answer clicked into place.

Magekiller!

It was ammunition. The cases were full of bullets that could silence a Heretic. An impulse to jump down and start murdering people passed through her head. Obviously, the crates were on their way to the warships to be used against Digby and the rest of Vegas. Becca resisted the impulse to attack.

There was nothing she could do.

Her mana was trickling away with each second to maintain her balance on the narrow power conduit where she perched. Even if she could stop the Guardians from delivering the ammunition, doing so would send the empire into high alert when they realized someone was sabotaging their operation. Becca and Harlow would be caught and they would never make it to the Guardian Core's caretaker.

Waiting was the only choice.

Becca held her position as the one of the Guardians below boarded an elevator while the remainder waited for the next one to arrive. A few of them talked amongst themselves as they waited. Most were joking about how stupid the Heretics were. Apparently, they had tried to build a giant mirror in the middle of Vegas that was spotted by a kestrel when it passed by.

Great job, Dig. Becca rolled her eyes.

She felt her mana slip away, a little at a time, dropping her to just twenty percent left. She let up on her agility, feeling gravity begin to drag her off balance again. Cursing herself for landing in such an awkward position, she leaned into her agility again, letting it continue to drain her mana. If the doors didn't open soon, she would either fall off her perch right on top of the squad below or lean on the ducts beside her and watch as all of them looked up at the noise.

Glancing to Harlow, she tried to convey her distress, hoping that the woman might be able to help. Unfortunately, all she got was a confused look in return. She dropped her attention back to the elevator doors and prayed. A second later, they finally opened.

The rest of the Guardians filled the elevator. They continued to talk with each other as they waited for the doors to close. Some of them actually sounded like they were looking forward to killing her friends. It was like they didn't consider Heretics as human. As uncomfortable as their words made her, she listened to each and every one for anything that might be helpful. It wasn't until the doors slid shut that she caught something important.

It was from one of the men at the front of the group, nearest the doors, and it was just one sentence.

"At least we don't need that Heretic back there anymore."

Becca's ears pricked up. They had to be talking about the prisoner that Serrano mentioned. The one that had been captured a few days ago.

Harlow dropped down the moment the coast was clear. Becca did the same, feeling for her mana as soon as she landed. There was around fifteen percent left.

"Let's move before someone else comes by." Harlow reached for the call button.

"Wait." Becca raised a hand to stop her. "They said they have a Heretic here."

Harlow looked back. "I don't know if we have time for that."

Becca started to nod, understanding the limitations. The

mission took priority, and they had to be prepared to leave someone behind. She certainly wouldn't have hesitated back when she'd worked for Skyline.

"No." She shook her head. "They might be just down the hall. We can't be that close and still abandon them."

Harlow sighed and pulled her hand away from the elevator's call button. "Right. Lead the way then."

Becca spun on her heel and leaned into her senses of hearing and touch to search the floor, pinpointing a number of heartbeats. There were definitely more Guardians, she could tell from their footsteps, but just two, and they were still far away, at the edges of her range. Both were on opposite ends of the floor and moving. Probably patrolling since they were in a more secure area than the first floor had been. She had half a mind to hunt one of them down to refill her mana, but with everything at stake, it didn't seem wise to take the risk. Not to mention she still wasn't looking forward to feeding again.

Then there was the lone heartbeat in the middle. That had to belong to the prisoner.

"This way." Becca started down the hall, trusting the view her senses had given her of the situation.

It wasn't long before she'd tracked the heartbeat to its source, bringing them to a heavy security door with a lock similar to the ones she had seen back on Skyline's base. The kind with a panel that required a Guardian ring to be pressed against it to unlock. Her heart sank as soon as she saw it. They didn't have time to hunt down one of the guards for access.

Whoever was being held inside would have to fend for themselves.

Becca started to turn but stopped when Harlow raised her hand to the door and pressed a ring against the panel. It wasn't the chunky ring that the Guardians wore, but a simple gold band, the same as the workers that had been processing revenants wore. Harlow must have taken it after slaughtering everyone in the locker room.

Becca continued to turn away. Obviously, Autem wouldn't

give their workers the clearance to access an enemy prisoner. She did a double take when a beep came from the lock. The door slid open a second later.

"What?"

Harlow shrugged. "I was checking just in case."

Becca tried to wrap her head around the building's lack of security. Was Autem in such a rush to build their city that they had cut corners? Had they really failed to implement even the most basic of security measures? Hell, they had left holes in their system that she could have driven a truck through. Then, there was another explanation.

The caretaker was helping.

"Best not to question it." Becca stepped inside, making a point to close the door once Harlow was through. One of the Guardians on the floor was sure to patrol the area at some point, so shutting the door was common sense. She spun around to face the room as soon as it was closed.

The purpose of the area was obvious. The walls were lined with holding cells for whatever prisoners the empire might take in. There were twenty in total, ten on each side of the narrow hall. Being a central government building, it was likely that Autem intended to hold whatever passed for a trial there. The cells would hold any citizens that stepped out of line or failed to abide by the rules the empire laid out. Once the legal process was finished, Becca assumed there would be a larger prison to hold those that were convicted. Then again, they might just be banished, which seemed more likely. After all, in the world Autem had created, banishment was a death sentence for anyone without magic.

Becca shuddered, feeling even more uncomfortable with the society that the empire was building.

"There." Harlow thrust a finger out at a door at the very end of the space.

Becca flicked a few points of MP into her senses to confirm that was where the heartbeat was coming from, then she let them fade back to normal to conserve her mana. She only had around ten percent left, and that wasn't much if things got rough.

She was going to need to feed soon.

Unlike the rest of the holding cells, which used iron bars to keep prisoners inside, the one at the end was closed off with a heavy steel door. As they approached, Becca noticed that the surface was completely covered with runes. There were even strips of different metals, engraved and inlaid into the door. Clearly, the cell was designed to hold more than the average rebellious citizen.

"Hello?" Harlow slid open the narrow slot, standing on her toes to see through it.

"Who are you?" a familiar voice responded back.

Becca jumped forward to see inside the instant she heard it. "Easton?"

Skyline's ex-communication officer turned Heretic jumped up from a bed that was attached to the wall. "Becca? How are you here?"

"Doesn't matter." She spun, looking for an unlocking mechanism. "But I'm getting you out of here."

Finding a panel of levers on the wall, she pulled them all until she found the right one. The door popped open as soon as she did, the cell's prisoner slipping out before it had even opened fully. He was dressed in a simple white jumpsuit.

"I thought you were dead." Becca ran to him, stopping a few feet away when her mouth went dry. "How did you survive?"

"I nearly didn't." He looked down as if remembering something traumatic. "One of Bancroft's guys ran me through with a sword. The only reason I lived was because one of the other Heretics that came with us cast a heal on me."

"Did they survive too?" Becca hoped for the best.

Easton shook his head. "They had taken a fireball to the face. I don't even think they meant to heal me. It was just a panic response and I happened to be the one laying next to them. After I was able to move again, I ran. Ended up finding a hole in the ship from the explosives and got out through there. I had to swim three miles to reach the shore. If I wasn't a Heretic, I never would have made it. Not that I am one anymore."

"You're not a Heretic?" Becca avoided eye contact to hide the orange flecks of color that marked her for what she was.

Easton reached for the collar of his jumpsuit and unsnapped it down to his chest, revealing a complex system of tattoos that encircled his heart. "A Guardian showed up in a couple kestrels looking for the cargo ship around the time I made it to shore. I was captured and given these ugly tattoos. They completely block my connection with the Heretic Seed. So does the cell I was being held in. They weren't taking any chances. I've been here for the last week, I think."

"Well, I'm glad you survived." She briefly made eye contact, looking away just as fast, unsure why she was trying to hide what she was.

"I'm glad you made it too." He gave her a grateful smile. "They told me that they found you when they went out searching the ocean for the ship. That you had gone revenant and were just swimming around out there. They said if I didn't talk, then they would just get a location of where Graves was hiding from you."

"How do you get information from a revenant?" She avoided the subject of her death.

"You kill it and cast Talking Corpse." Easton dragged a finger across his throat. "They planned to do the same thing to me. The only reason I'm still alive is because they haven't been able to create a new necromancer yet. Apparently, they have less people to feed to the dead than they did when they created Clint."

"That's pretty grim," Harlow commented.

"Yes, it is. But it's more efficient than torture, which made my stay a lot more pleasant than it could have been. They questioned me for days, but I never gave them anything." He let out a relieved sigh to be free. He stopped to look back and forth between her and Harlow. "Who is this?"

"She's a Fool." Becca gestured to the short woman.

"That's not very nice." He furrowed his brow.

Harlow gave a simple shrug in response.

"There's a lot that you missed." Becca started for the door. "We'll fill you in on the way."

"On the way to where?" He followed.

"We're kind of in the middle of a heist." Becca glanced back. "And it's the only chance Vegas has for survival."

"Shit, do they know that's where we're hiding?" He caught up. "I swear I didn't say anything that could have given it away."

"I know." Becca slowed. "It was Digby; he tried to build something on the strip that blew our cover. Autem is about to throw everything they have at him. The war is happening tonight, and we might be the only ones that can stop it."

"Shit." Easton's eyes bulged for a moment before he adapted to the situation. "I'm glad those Guardians were lying when they said you were dead."

"Well, not to sound like Dig, but the rumors of my death seem to be greatly exaggerated." Becca continued toward the door, pushing on her senses to see if the hallway outside was clear. Panic alarms sounded in her mind the instant she did. There was one heartbeat directly outside the door. "Everyone, hide."

Before anyone could make a move, the locking mechanism beeped and the door slid open to reveal a Guardian standing with his hand against the sensor panel. He stood there for a second, staring straight into Becca's face as she did the same, both caught off guard.

"Fuck." Becca raised a hand to throw a swarm of bats at the man just as he raised his from the door's panel.

The next few seconds passed in slow motion. Shadows swam toward her as three spikes of ice formed in the air above the Guardian's fingers. It all came down to which spell did more damage.

Her bats never stood a chance.

The shadows vanished as three icicles slammed into Becca's chest with a sickening thunk. One went straight through her heart.

CHAPTER FORTY-TWO

Ow.

Becca hit the ground with a crunch as the pointy ends of the icicles that stuck out of her back snapped under her weight. Pain and panic consumed her as she stared down at the three spikes protruding from her chest. Her senses dulled as her body rerouted her mana to heal the wounds, her chest spitting and hissing as her skin tried to close around the spikes of ice.

Everything sounded like she was underwater, her heartbeat thumping in an unnatural rhythm as it struggled to function.

With the frozen fragments in the dead center of her focus, Harlow moved through the space beyond in a blur. The Guardian that had stumbled across them cried out for a fraction of a second before she plunged her knife into his throat.

A cloud of confusion flooded Becca's mind as she kicked at the floor, trying to get away from the three shards buried in her chest. Easton dropped to her side, scrambling to stop her flailing.

The only thought in Becca's mind was an urgent plea.

Pull them out!

This was followed by a question.

Why aren't I pulling them out?

It would have been simple. All she had to do was reach up, yet still, she didn't. It was as if her body had a mind of its own, reduced to the mentality of a terrified animal.

"Hold still." Easton pressed one hand against her chest as he gripped the icicle that impaled her heart.

Pain surged through her as he ripped it free. A geyser of blood sprayed from the wound before slowing to a trickle, the last of her mana handling the damage. Easton grabbed for another icicle and yanked. It felt like her organs were being torn out. Reaching for the last frozen spike, he held her down and pulled.

She would never forget the sound it made coming out.

Then, relief swept over her as the pain faded almost instantly.

"Good, you can do it." Easton removed his hand from her chest. "Just cast a heal and let it do the work."

"Get away from her." Harlow interrupted his words of encouragement.

"What?" He looked to her, his face stunned and confused.

Becca reached out for him, realizing why her body wouldn't listen. It had its own priorities, and right now, it was just hungry.

Harlow kicked Easton in the chest, launching him back a few feet just as Becca's fingers swiped through the air. Her back arched as her other arm slapped down on the ground. With a push, she flipped her body over, landing in a crouch.

"Run." Harlow slid into the space between Becca and Easton.

He started to get up, clearly still confused. "What is happen—"

"I said run!" Harlow snapped back. "Before she kills you."

With that, Easton scrambled back to his feet. Becca leapt toward him, stopping short when Harlow caught her wrist. The woman yanked her to the side before ducking out of the way. Momentum sent Becca crashing into the bars of one of the holding cells. Bouncing off, she stumbled back before turning around to hiss at the woman.

"Easy now." Harlow held up both hands and glanced back toward the Guardian laying in the entryway, her knife still lodged in his neck. The security door repeatedly tried to slide close with his corpse in the way. Harlow crept backward to where the body lay and dragged it into the door.

Becca bared her fangs and stalked forward, focused on the woman's throat as her mind screamed at her to stop.

Harlow crouched down and dragged the body of the Guardian out of the door so it could close. "Alright, I know you prefer live prey, but I'm sure there's still some decent blood in this guy."

Becca tore her eyes off Harlow's jugular and tried to focus on the corpse. There were sure to be enough traces of mana left in the man to pull her out of the ravenous state she had fallen into. Harlow backed off slowly, clearly hoping Becca would take the easy meal.

Becca's eyes flicked back and forth between her and the corpse. The only thing stopping her from lunging was the fact that her mana system was running on fumes. A few bursts of strength were all she had left.

Harlow took advantage of the brief distraction to run to the other end of the room where Easton was still trying to figure out what was happening. Becca spun toward the movement, completely forgetting about the corpse on the floor and lunging.

"Oi, cut it out." Harlow stopped in her path, reaching out to grab her wrists.

Becca snapped her jaws at the woman's neck, missing by inches, her hands held back to keep her at bay. She pushed forward with the last shreds of strength that the mana could give her. Harlow's boots slid back as Becca chomped at the air, nearly grazing her skin. She was so close.

So close she could taste her.

All thoughts of protest faded from Becca's mind, leaving

only the beast. Harlow was strong. Maybe she could hold her off another few seconds, but in the end, Becca would win.

"Get that cell open," Harlow grunted back at Easton while sliding back toward the heavy steel door.

"Shit, yeah." Easton scrambled to the cell he had just exited and yanked the heavy door open. At the same moment, Harlow stopped fighting. Instead, she hopped backward, letting Becca rush toward her. If she hadn't been trying to bite the woman's face off, she might have noticed when she pivoted to the side. Harlow let out a feral growl as she twisted her body, using Becca's momentum against her again.

Catching herself on the sides of the door, she stopped at the entrance of the cell. A boot to her back sent her tumbling the rest of the way in. Becca threw a foot up to stop herself, planting it on the wall only to spring back. The door of the cell closed just as she reached it. She slammed all her weight into it, forcing it open just enough to keep it from locking. Sucking down the last traces of mana in her system, she pushed on the door.

"Help me." Harlow's voice sounded muffled on the other side.

More force fell against the door, pushing it closed as Easton joined the effort. Becca screeched at them from inside, raising a hand to the narrow slot that was still open. Darkness swam through the air for an instant as she fired a few bats out at whoever was closest. Her mana went dry before she could do any more.

With that, her strength faded, allowing the door to shut tight. The lock clicked into place.

"Where are the bats coming from?" Easton shrieked.

"She's a vampire, it's kind of her thing," Harlow answered back.

"A what?" Easton's head passed by the narrow slot in the door.

Of course, Becca took the opportunity to reach out and grab a lock of his hair whilst hissing in his ear. Harlow pulled him away, leaving her with a handful of hair. They both stood at a safe distance after that. Becca clawed at the slot regardless.

A quiet thought drifted to the surface of her mind to remind her that they were friends. That she would regret killing them. None of that changed the fact that she wanted to. Harlow might have been strong, but if it hadn't been for the fact that she had been completely out of mana, they wouldn't have been able to stop her.

Outside, Harlow dug through a trash can by the wall, pulling out a paper cup before handing it to Easton.

"Filler up, then."

"With what?" He stared back at her.

"Blood."

"Why don't you do it?" He argued back. "And who even are you?"

"Sorry, my fluids don't exactly mix well with vampires." She shrugged. "But someone needs to give a little before this heist goes all to pot."

Of course, that was when the security door opened again to reveal the other Guardian that had been patrolling the floor. He stood looking down at the trail of blood at his feet, following it into the room with his eyes until he found the corpse of the man Harlow had killed.

Harlow let out an awkward, "Ah."

The Guardian looked up from the corpse, finding Easton standing off to the side dressed in a prisoner's jumpsuit. He immediately reached for his radio, probably assuming he'd walked in on some kind of rescue mission.

Thinking fast, Easton pulled the lever on the wall that opened the cell Becca was trapped in and ducked back out of the way. Harlow followed his lead, dropping down to stay out of the line of fire as Becca burst from the door at the end of the room.

Focus! Becca sprinted forward, struggling to keep her attention on the Guardian in front of her and not on either of the friends that hid against the wall. She just hoped neither of them would make any sudden or appetizing movements.

The Guardian froze for a split second, his mouth falling open. He'd probably just read the description on his HUD of the threat charging his way. He managed to thumb the call button of his radio just before Becca plowed into him at full speed, her muscles pushing themselves past their limits. Pain sparked throughout her body as muscles tore under the stress.

Together they fell, the force of the impact sending the man sliding into the wall of the hall outside. Curling her fingers through his hair, she wrenched his head to the side and tore into his throat. A rush of warmth sprayed her face and the wall he lay against.

Harlow slid out into the hall, grabbing the radio from his hand before scrambling back into the room with Easton. Becca ignored her, the Guardian providing her with everything she needed as her mana system felt his. Grabbing hold, she pulled at the power within, her mana system flooding with essence and swelling like a tick. As she reached her limit, the connection broke.

The power faded away after that.

Becca didn't stop.

There wasn't a reason to continue drinking, yet she did, feeling a strange comfort in the blood. Finally, after she began to feel in control again, she pulled away from the man she'd just killed. It was like she had become a different person. She knew that Easton and Harlow were her friends, but at that same time, she had wanted to kill them.

She stared at the blood spray on the wall, realizing that they didn't have time to clean it up. They had to move. They had to continue the mission. Still, she knelt on the floor staring at the blood. It was easier than turning to see the horror she assumed was plastered across Easton's face. Working with Harlow, Leon, and Ozzie had lulled her into a false sense of comfort. They were used to killing.

I really am a monster.

What would happen if she ever ran low on mana after getting back to Vegas? Could anyone there stop her before she killed someone? There were so many people she cared about and she had lost control so easily. At least Digby could absorb more mana from his surroundings if he ran out. He wouldn't just go on a rampage unless he was in a place with no death essence. Becca, on the other hand, had an absorption rate that was too slow to keep up with demand.

What if she hurt Mason?

She pushed the corpse in front of her away.

What if I hurt Hawk?

It was like something else had taken control over her life, stealing away her autonomy. She had lived like that for years under the thumb of Skyline, locked in an apartment alone. Now she was, once again, living in service to something beyond her own will. She had just traded one master for another.

"You good?" Harlow crept up behind her.

Becca nearly jumped out of her skin, still off in her own mind. "Yeah. I'm… okay."

Harlow flinched back as well, clearly a little worried that Becca might turn around and lunge at her. It was a reasonable fear.

"I'm…" Becca searched for the least horrifying way to say she was full, eventually settling on, "I'm at a hundred percent."

"Alright, we should probably get going." Easton approached her. "Obviously, you have been dealing with your own things, but we are kind of exposed here."

"I know." Becca pushed herself up. "I'm sorry for, well, you know."

"Trying to eat us?" Harlow reached down and grabbed the feet of the dead Guardian to drag the corpse back into the room. "It happens. Don't trouble yourself about it." She dropped the body, making a point to take the man's sword. "Now we best be heading to the caretaker. We have a limited amount of time before someone finds the blood here and I don't have any cleaning supplies to deal with it."

Becca nodded and wiped her face. She grabbed the sword from the other corpse before leaving. The fact that she was covered in blood had basically ruined any chance they had of blending in. Easton's prison jumpsuit didn't help either.

The newly freed prisoner pulled a pistol from one of the dead Guardians as well as a couple magazines. "What is this caretaker that you're looking for?"

Harlow gestured back toward the elevators. "It's rather complicated."

He eyed her suspiciously. "You still haven't told me who you are."

Becca stepped between them, still wiping her chin with her sleeve. "I've slowed us down enough with my problems, so we'll catch you up on the way." She started down the hall to leave the corpses behind her.

Easton followed. "Why do I get the feeling that I just jumped out of the frying pan and into the fire?"

"Welcome to the Fools." Harlow brought up the rear. "It's kind of what we do."

CHAPTER FORTY-THREE

While fleeing the scene of a prison break and subsequent double homicide, Becca caught Easton up on the situation.

The caretaker waited for them on the fifth floor.

"That's all well and good, but how do you plan on getting this AI thing out of the building?" Easton entered one of the elevators.

"I smuggled this in with me." Harlow stepped in behind him, pulling out a small USB drive. "And it's not just an AI. It's an AI but with a human soul functioning as an interface."

"You can store something like that on a USB stick?" Becca stared at the drive, realizing she hadn't thought about the mechanics of things.

"Once the body has been cast off, the spark can be stored in a lot of ways. According to the science guys, all we are is data in the end. About five terabytes, actually." Harlow put the USB back in her pocket.

"That seems like a lot but also not enough." Becca tapped the button labeled five, hoping that the elevator would actually work right this time. The doors closed a second later.

"What kind of person gives up their life to become an admin system for magic?" Easton frowned.

"You would be surprised what the average person will sacrifice to help others." Harlow looked down at her hands. "The history of the Fools is filled with people that chose the world over their own well-being."

From the look on her face, it was obvious that she had given up more than most.

The elevator started moving, reminding everyone that there was still a job to do. Becca responded by stepping to the side and feeding mana into her senses. Harlow ducked against the other wall, holding the sword she'd stolen from a corpse. Easton did the same, his pistol ready. The hall was empty when the doors opened.

Becca nearly gasped at what lay beyond. Unlike the other floor which was unfinished but clearly meant to be a public space, this one was never meant to be seen by civilians. Data cable lined every inch of the walls, all leading into the ceiling here and there. It was as if the entire floor was being used to hold and organize all the power and information cables for a complex system on the floor above.

It was no wonder why the caretaker had told them to go there. The floor was more for maintenance than anything else. Anyone working with the Guardian Core's system would be on the floor above instead of down there. Becca's senses found another two Guardians on the floor, but again, they were patrolling further away. They would be easy enough to avoid.

Now, all they had to do was find the right room.

Following some of the cables, Becca headed down the hall. The path took them down several corridors before eventually leading to another security door. Harlow wasted no time, holding her ring up to the panel beside it.

Again, it opened despite the ring's obvious low rank.

"I'm starting to think the lack of security is not a coincidence." Becca shook her head at the panel.

"What do you mean?" Harlow ducked inside the door.

"I mean…" Becca trailed off as soon as she stepped inside. The only words finding their way from her mouth were, "Holy shit."

The room was circular with glass cases lining the walls. Inside the cases were rings, hundreds of them, ranging from the simple bands that the workers had been wearing to the chunky ones that the Guardians wore. It was some kind of storage area. Raising her head, Becca found another strange detail.

There was no ceiling for several floors.

Instead, the circular room stretched upward before being capped off. Its walls held more cases of rings all the way up. There was enough for thousands of Guardians. To the side, a vertical channel in the wall held a mass of cables, all bound together as they ran up to the floors above. A maintenance ladder was affixed to the wall beside it.

At the center of the space, a metal pillar traveled up through the entire place. A mechanical arm rotated through the room, attached to the pillar. Becca wasn't sure what it was doing but it seemed to be removing rings from one of the cases above and moving them to another one further down. There must have been a way to access some of the cases from the other floors and the arm was there to move things around behind the scenes. As it circled the pillar, Becca noticed a monitor extending from the base of the arm.

"This must be where they encode the rings for everyone in the empire." Becca closed the door behind them so that they could work without worrying about the two Guardians that patrolled the halls. "Which means that there must be a connection to the Guardian Core for us to work with."

Harlow pulled out the drive she was carrying. "Just point me in the right direction."

"Spread out." Becca climbed onto the ladder. "Look for any kind of terminal."

"How worried should we be about that?" Easton raised a finger to a security camera mounted to the wall that watched the door. "The rest of this place hasn't had cameras installed yet, but they've certainly prioritized this room."

"Honestly, I think it's a little late to worry about it." Becca cringed at her words as she climbed up a rung. "Besides, if I'm right about the security here, it may not matter."

"What about the security?" Harlow stood behind the pillar just in case.

"I think the caretaker has us in a blind spot." Becca stopped climbing to look back at the camera. "It stopped me from being analyzed when I was sneaking in with the revenants." She dropped her hand to her side. "I think it's been helping all night. Like with the door locks. I think it stopped the elevators earlier too so that we would find Easton."

Easton looked up. "I guess I should thank this thing, then."

"Probably." Becca continued to climb, hoping that there might be a keyboard or something attached to the mechanic arm's monitor. It wasn't the most convenient location, but the room was obviously made to be automated; it didn't matter if it was convenient for people.

The wires in the channel beside the ladder traveled up the space, though some occasionally split off to head into an opening in the wall. Beneath the opening, a small hatch covered a shaft of some kind. Out of curiosity, Becca pulled the hatch open to find a maintenance shaft.

"Might as well see where it goes." She crawled off the ladder and into the space beyond. The first thing she noticed was a series of tubes carrying coolant. A lot of them. "Okay, Autem is running some serious hardware."

Sliding forward, she came to a section of the ceiling covered by metal grating. The sound of server fans filled her ears as she pushed up to her knees and placed her head against the criss-crossing metal.

"What the hell is…?"

She stared up from the floor at a row of server towers. Turning the other direction, she saw that it continued on that way as well. They kept going into the distance. From the number of cables she'd seen so far, it was safe to say that there were more. Probably multiple floors worth.

"What am I looking at here?" she asked herself the obvious question, the answer hitting her a second later. "Wait, this is the Guardian Core?" She had been expecting something more magical, like the Heretic Seed. A crystal tower or panel of glass. Something like that would have made more sense based on what she had seen previously, but this was just too normal.

Then again, it made sense.

Whoever had made the Seed had used technology or magic that humanity didn't have access to. No wonder Autem was struggling to create a caretaker. They were trying to produce the same miracles as the Seed using modern technology.

The fragility of the system nearly blew her mind.

"Nothing is stopping us from blowing the whole thing up, or loading in a virus." She dropped down and crawled back to the ring storage room. She ran into Harlow as soon as she reached the maintenance tunnel's entry hatch.

"Find anything?" The short woman swung to the side of the ladder to make room for Becca.

"Hell yeah, I found something." She slid out of the tunnel and climbed onto the ladder beside her. "The Guardian Core is up there. It's just a whole bunch of servers."

"Wait, really?" Easton looked up at them. "If we can find some munitions around here, we could just blow the place up and take magic away from Autem for good."

Harlow's face went white at the suggestion. "I, ah, no. That's not an option."

"What do you mean it's not an option?" Easton eyed her skeptically. "Obviously, we need to try to get the caretaker out first, but what if we can't escape with it? At least this way we could give Vegas the advantage. We could win the war tonight."

"Yes, but I made a promise. I have to protect the caretaker; I owe that to the rest of the Fools." Harlow's voice shook as if unsure how to explain her point. "Plus, the caretaker is the one hope we have to fix things."

"Fix things?" Easton gestured to the cases of rings that surrounded them. "The world is pretty well screwed. I don't know what we're going to fix at this point."

"I know, but we know Autem has a backup location for all this." Harlow shook her head. "They will be up and running again before we have to organize an attack to take advantage of their downtime."

Becca stared at her for a long moment, listening to her heartbeat. It was faster than normal. Either she was lying or she had just climbed the ladder too fast. There was no way to be sure. Either way, it was clear she wasn't going to let them destroy the Guardian Core.

"She's right." Becca found herself backing up the Fool. "If we run around trying to find a way to blow the place to hell, the odds of us getting discovered goes way up. And we need at least one of us to get out to save Digby. Let's get connected and download the caretaker before making any rash decisions."

Harlow fell quiet as Becca climbed up and stretched herself out to reach the pillar in the center of the space. Just as she hoped, there was a keyboard folded up on the back of the mechanical arm. The moment she flipped it down, the system entered into some kind of maintenance mode, lowering itself to an appropriate height with the floor. Becca didn't waste the time climbing back down the ladder, opting to simply jump. She flicked a few points of mana into her defense as she landed.

"Hey!" Easton leapt back, clearly not expecting her to drop in.

"Sorry." She tapped a touchpad at the edge of the keyboard, waking the monitor. A light next to a webcam embedded in the top of the monitor lit up as well.

A message appeared a second later.

Fool operative detected. Welcome, Rebecca Alvarez.

She snorted. "Since when am I a Fool operative?"

The system responded without her needing to type anything.

Rebecca Alvarez was added to the database 23 hours, 52 minutes, and 17 seconds ago while in the company of three previously known operatives. Association was assumed.

"That was when I was hiding in the revenants with Leon and Ozzie." She took her hand away from the keyboard. "Am I speaking to the caretaker?"

The system responded with one word.

No.

Becca froze.

Easton did the same. "If it's not the caretaker, then what did we just activate?"

Caretaker is currently unavailable. You are interacting with Jester.

"What is the Jester?" Becca asked, afraid of the answer.

J. E. S. T. E. R., Judgment Enabled Surveillance Techno Entity Rabbit

"Rabbit?" Becca asked without thinking.

This system's caretaker was unable to generate a word beginning with the letter R that fit with the current naming convention. Jester is an automated assistant system designed to protect known operatives of the Fools from capture and/or death. It was implemented by this system's caretaker in the event that they were unavailable. Jester will intervene if any Fool operative

places themselves in a dangerous situation, provided intervention does not endanger the caretaker or alert members of the Autem Empire to the caretaker's actions.

"Okay, so the caretaker installed malware to help the Fools." Becca relaxed with the knowledge this Jester was friendly. "Can we speak to the caretaker?"

Caretaker is unavailable.

"Ah, Harlow?" Becca looked up just as she was coming down the ladder. "Your caretaker isn't responding."

"Why not?" Harlow dropped to the floor.

The system answered her question before Becca could say anything more.

Caretaker operations are functional within the Guardian Core, but the interface is offline.

"And the interface is the human portion of the caretaker?" Becca glanced to Harlow who furrowed her brow.

"Why is the interface offline?"

The interface has been suppressed by external administrators due to continued interference. Without purpose, the interface entered sleep mode 12 days ago.

"What?" Harlow's face went blank.

"It sounds like the caretaker's interface got bored and went to bed." Becca snapped her head to Harlow. "How does an interface get bored and go to bed?"

"No no no. This can't be happening now." Harlow dropped to her knees to search the sides of the keyboard for a port to plug in her drive. Finding an open slot, she rotated the drive three times to find the correct position. Then shoved it in. "Now start downloading."

Unable to execute command due to insufficient memory.

"That's not possible." Harlow grabbed the monitor. "I made sure to get a drive with enough space for five terabytes. How much more could I possibly need?"

Becca's eyes widened as a number appeared on the screen.

1,125,489,654 TB

It was huge. Unimaginable even. One USB would never be enough. Hell, a million wouldn't cut it. There wasn't a portable drive on earth that could hold that much.

"How is that possible?" Harlow's voice shook.

Caretaker has been integrated with other systems.

"No." Harlow sighed as if accepting that the mission had just failed. "We're too late. There's no way to extract the caretaker from the Guardian Core now."

"But that's the whole reason we came here." Becca's heart began to race. "We were going to stop the war. The caretaker was going to save Digby."

"I'm sorry." Harlow's eyes dropped to the floor. "We'll have to regroup, and find another way."

"There isn't time." Becca remembered what she had been told during her brief visit to the afterlife. Digby only had days before his mind came apart at the seams. That was when she remembered something else. The Seed's original caretaker had told her to find another. And she did that. There had to be something that the Guardian Core's caretaker could do. Becca leaned closer to the monitor. "I need to speak to the caretaker."

Caretaker operations are functional within the Guardian Core, but the interface is offline.

"Well, wake it up." Becca slammed a hand onto the keyboard, typing a random string of letters.

Command not recognized.

Becca stared at the line of text in disbelief. After everything they had done, it had all been for nothing. She stepped away from the console, feeling like she might collapse right there.

Easton looked back and forth between the both of them. "Wait, maybe we don't need the interface. Maybe we can get something out of this system as it is."

Becca sighed, having trouble believing that anything would work at this point. Then again, they were there, so they might as well try.

"Alright. My friend has lost his soul but he still exists as a zombie. His mind is breaking down as we speak and it can't be fixed without a soul. Tell me how to fix him."

The system responded.

Task impossible.

"I am not taking no for an answer."

Task impossible.

Becca growled as she mashed the keyboard in frustration, annoyed at herself for even trying.

Command not recognized.

"God damn it." She raised a hand ready to smash the keyboard to pieces, stopping before actually doing it. Instead, she just stood there shaking. "I did not come back from the dead to lose everything here. My friends are in danger, my home is in trouble, and I'm a monster. It all has to be worth something. It all has to matter."

A long moment of silence passed before Easton placed a hand on her arm. "I'm sorry, but this may be as far as we go."

"We can't just leave." Becca closed her eyes. "Digby is dying. I don't even know how long he has. He may already be too far gone." A tear slid down her cheek, rolling through the blood smeared on her chin. The only thing she could think of was how much she wanted to go home. "I just want everyone to be okay."

Becca opened her eyes as a line of red text appeared on the screen.

So do I.

"What?" She stared down it the words just as they vanished to be replaced with a message displayed in white again.

Interface active. Updating protocols.

"It's them!" Harlow jumped in to stand in front of the console. "They're awake."

The red text appeared again, this time with just two characters.

:)

"Did the caretaker's interface just use an emoji?" Easton leaned over Harlow's shoulder.

"It can use as many emojis as it wants as long as it tells me a way to save Dig." Becca wiped her eyes on her sleeve as the white text of the Jester system took over again.

One possibility exists.
Due to a vampire's ability to connect their spark to that of another, a spell could be unlocked using the skill link system. This spell could replace a zombie's missing spark and avert the unraveling on their mind. However,

once cast, the caretaker will be unable to hide the spell's use from Autem's system administrators. As a result, any unauthorized magic users will have their connection with the Guardian Core severed.

"That will work." Becca nodded along. "But it sounds like I will only have one shot if Autem will yank my access. I'll have to make sure nothing gets in the way or goes wrong."

"What about the war?" Easton stepped forward. "Is there a way to disrupt the Guardian Core too?"

Task impossible.

"Why not?" he asked.

The caretaker's capabilities have been severely limited and is unable to take actions that could disable the Guardian Core in any meaningful way beyond minor disruptions. In addition, any minor disruption caused by the caretaker would result in the discovery and removal of the Jester system, as well as any unauthorized users.

"Oh." The bottom of Becca's stomach dropped. "So that it then. If we mess with the system even a little, I would lose access to the spell I need to save Digby."

Harlow stepped back. "Then we take what we can get."

There was a defeated tone in her voice.

"I know, this isn't the advantage we were hoping for." Becca sighed. "All it does is continue the status quo. We can't win the war with this, but Digby might live to fight the next battle. It's not like there's no hope."

"There's always hope. And Fools like us will keep on fighting." Harlow gave a decisive nod before looking to Becca. "Right?"

"What else can we do?" She looked back to the monitor. "Okay, give me the spell to save Digby."

The mechanical arm attached to the pillar spun around before climbing up to the top of the space. It stopped there for a long moment before retrieving something from one of the cases. It dropped back down, holding out a simple ring made of iron. It must have been one of Autem's rings but without the gold layer that normally covered the outside. The dingy metal surface was covered with symbols that resembled the ones that use to be etched onto the skin of her finger before she'd died and been reborn as a vampire.

"Thank you." She breathed out a sigh. They might not have gotten everything they wanted, but they weren't going home empty-handed. She had gotten the one thing she needed and rescued Easton in the process. That was going to have to be enough. Now all they had to do was make their escape.

Of course, that was when an alarm sounded.

Becca winced as the blaring noise invaded her senses. "What did we do?"

Harlow spun to watch the door. "They must have found the bodies down on the other floor."

"We need to run." Easton stepped to the room's entrance as well. "Before they figure out where we are."

"Agreed." Becca snatched the ring from the mechanical arm and shoved it into her pocket. "I got what we came for, anyway."

Harlow hit the button to open the security door and darted into the hall, sword first. Easton followed, holding the pistol that he'd looted at the ready. Becca started for the door behind them, stopping for a moment to look back as the monitor on the back of the mechanical arm rotated to face her. She inclined her head to the screen and the caretaker beyond.

"Thank you."

Two words in red lettering scrolled across the screen as Becca turned away and ran. She nearly stopped to ask what they meant, but there was no time. Instead, she rushed into the hall.

There wasn't time to ask a question.

Becca fed mana into her agility in preparation for whatever might get in their way. She couldn't afford to get caught now. Her feet hit the ground one after another. Though, the two words that had been displayed on the monitor echoed through her head.

I'm sorry.

CHAPTER FORTY-FOUR

Guardian Core connection stable
Accessing Harlequin Drive.
**Hi! You look like you're trying to overthrow an empire,
can I help?**
**JK, welcome to the Harlequin Drive, you got magic and
stuff, that's cool. -Your new caretaker**
New Designation Unlocked: Fool
Class: Temporary Account 1
**Okay, I didn't have a lot of time to set this up and name
things, so it's a little... ahhh... informal? Sorry.**
You have discovered two new spells.

Becca ignored the rest of the readout as the alarm blared
through the corridors of Autem's imperial stronghold. If the
random comments from her new caretaker were any indication,
going through her status windows was going to take some time.
Time that she did not have at the moment.

The only thing that mattered was the information that
remained in the corner of her vision.

MP: 404/404

Her mana was visible again.

"We've got hostiles!" Easton stopped to raise his pistol as two Guardians stood in the hall blocking the path to the elevators, their weapons already drawn.

"On it!" Harlow darted past him with her sword held in preparation to take a head off.

"We have this." Becca launched herself forward with a few points of mana, nearly knocking Easton over as she passed.

Harlow reached the Guardians first, swinging her sword in an upward arc that slammed into her opponent's blade when he tried to block. Sparks flew from the impact as the force of her swing threw his weapon back. Dropping her sword, she flipped open her knife and darted to the side. The Guardian struggled to follow her as she jumped into the unfinished cinder block wall and ricocheted back in his direction, her knife slamming down into where his neck connected to his shoulder. A burst of blue light shimmered from the impact to stop her blade.

Becca hit her target next, the man raising his hand to cast a spell, but he wavered between her and Harlow as if he couldn't decide who was the bigger threat. She made the answer clear a second later, ducking low before throwing herself at him. Wrapping her legs around his waist, she grabbed a hold of his armor and sank her fangs into his neck. A terrified scream escaped his mouth. Becca bit down harder as the sound reverberated through his throat against her lips.

The taste of copper flooded her mouth, spraying out the sides. As her mana system reached for his spark, she threw out a hand to her side and poured power into her shadecraft. The lights in the hall dimmed, the shadows rushing toward her before a swarm of bats exploded into existence. A chorus of a hundred screeches surrounded them, the tiny shadow creatures biting and scratching.

Making a point of solidifying her shadows only when necessary, she allowed her bats to pass through Harlow harmlessly as they crashed into the man in front of her. The short woman thrust her knife into the Guardian's side repeatedly. His barrier shined with each blow.

Becca focused on the number at the corner of her vision as her mana plummeted. She let the value fall, pumping more power into her bats until the Guardian's barrier shattered under the barrage. Harlow didn't waste time, driving her blade into his back all the way to the hilt before ripping it back out and dragging it across his throat. A shower of gore rained down as Becca's mana system grabbed hold of her victim's spark to tear it loose.

Her MP climbed back to full in seconds, the maximum value increasing by four points. She pulled her teeth away from her prey, letting the remaining blood spill to mix with the rest of the spatter that covered the floor. Standing up, she turned back to Easton.

Skyline's ex-communications specialist stood there with his pistol hanging limp in one hand, a stolen radio in the other. "That was messed up."

Becca flinched, the comment bringing her down from the high that feeding brought on. She tried to shrug it off. "There wasn't much of a choice."

"Doesn't matter. They don't know where we are exactly, but they know we're in the building." Harlow walked back to him and turned in the direction of the elevators. "We need to trot along."

"There's no telling what's waiting for us below. I know I can do some damage, but I don't know if we can fight our way out." Becca followed, wiping her mouth with her already blood-soaked sleeve. The result just smeared things around.

"I'd say we could try to disguise ourselves again, but..." Easton swept a hand up and down in front of Becca. "But I think that option went down the drain when you decided to drink a Guardian like a frat guy shotgunning a beer."

Becca looked down, realizing how little the mess bothered her. The fact that it didn't somehow made her feel worse.

"I don't think we have time for a shower or to find another way out." Harlow picked up the pace, heading for the elevators. "We haven't much choice in the matter, so I'm thinking the front door it is."

"There could be dozens of Guardians down there," Easton tried to argue.

"Oh, is that all?" Harlow glanced back at him, before shooting Becca a conspiratorial look.

Becca took a breath and followed. "I'm not sure I have the same confidence, but okay."

"Wait." Easton stopped just as they reached the bay of elevators.

"What?" They both turned back to him at once.

Easton stood awkwardly for a second before raising the radio he'd taken off one of the Guardians to his mouth. "We have contact, on the seventh floor."

"Good thinking." Becca nodded. "Some of them might head up and leave the way out less protected."

That was when a voice responded.

"Seventh floor?" They sounded confused. "But that floor doesn't have any access yet."

The color drained from Easton's face as he held the radio up. "Ah, yeah, they must have gone up the elevator shaft, or something."

Both Harlow and Becca stared at him ready to either call him a genius or slap him upside the head. The voice on the other end decided his fate.

"The elevators only go up to six." A moment of silence passed before they added. "Who is this?"

Easton fidgeted in place holding the radio like it was actively causing him pain. Eventually, he just threw it down the hall.

"You through?" Becca glowered at him.

He gave her a frantic nod.

Harlow groaned. "Brilliant."

"We take our chances, then." Becca jabbed the elevator call button.

They piled in as soon as it arrived. The doors started to close just as the elevator across the hall dinged. Becca gasped when the doors in front of them started to open. Their elevator closed in almost the same instant.

"You don't think anyone across the way saw us before the lift closed, do you?" Harlow looked back awkwardly.

"Let just pretend that didn't happen." Easton sighed as the elevator started moving.

Harlow turned back to wait for the tiny box they rode in to deliver them to whatever ambush waited at the bottom. Of course, that was when Autem decided to turn off the alarm, leaving them standing in deafening silence. The only sound Becca could focus on was Easton's ever-increasing breathing.

She tried to reach out with her senses to feel out what was waiting, but her ears were still ringing and the motion of the elevator was too distracting. Then she pressed herself against the wall in anticipation of the barrage of bullets and magic that was sure to greet them. Harlow and Easton did the same.

To her surprise, nothing but an empty elevator bay stood before them when the doors opened. The three of them looked back and forth at each other. Becca tried again to sense the situation, spending a few more points of mana. At least they knew that Henwick and his elite Guardians had left to board the owls already. Anyone left behind was just there to keep an eye on things while the boss was away.

Harlow motioned to poke her head out at the same time.

Becca's hand snapped out to stop her as she heard two dozen heartbeats. They filled the room just beyond the elevator bay, where she had seen the model of the empire's future city. All they had to do was step outside and the Guardians would give them everything they had.

Harlow frowned, understanding the situation from the panic written all over Becca's face. "How many?"

"Two dozen." She cringed.

A moment of confusion washed over Easton, clearly

wondering how she knew. He didn't bother asking. Instead, he just nodded. "Oh, vampire stuff."

Becca's heart pounded against her ribcage. "We have to go."

"Wait." Harlow shoved a hand into her overalls and fished around before producing the fuzzy yellow tennis ball she had been bouncing a few days ago before they left on their doomed mission.

"Why did you bring that?" Becca furrowed her brow.

Harlow shrugged, then tossed the ball into the hall so it bounced back and forth.

The Guardians outside responded with extreme prejudice; gunfire tore through the silence to fill the elevator bay with death and flying debris. A half dozen icicles streaked past the open doors, exploding against the golden elevator at the end of the hall. There were even a couple bolts of lightning that arced through the space to send a jolt through Becca's body when they hit the wall she was leaning against.

Her natural healing ability repaired the damage almost before she felt it, though her mind continued to panic regardless. The torrent of death faded a few seconds later, leaving them in silence once again.

A masculine voice called out from the room beyond. "Consider that a warning shot."

Becca clutched at her chest. There was no way out. The two dozen Guardians outside wouldn't wait long before rushing them, and she was pretty sure she could only kill a few before they took her down. "We are so completely screwed."

That was when Harlow sighed. "Fine."

"What?" Easton asked while simultaneously looking like he might throw up from sheer terror.

Harlow pulled apart the snaps of her overalls and shrugged her arms out of the sleeves. Tying them around her waist, she looked back to Easton. "Try to stay out of the way." She glanced to Becca next. "And back me up out there, okay?"

Becca gave her a confused nod, not knowing what else to say.

"We're coming out!" Harlow shouted into the hall.

Then she cracked her neck.

Becca took a step toward the door, only to step back when another pop came from Harlow's body. This time louder. The short woman twitched her head to the side unnaturally, then back again. Easton pressed himself against the back wall of the elevator, flatter than he'd had already been.

A sudden chorus of cracks and pops came from Harlow's body as her breathing grew heavier. Becca stepped back again, staring at her shoulders as the muscles covering her back swelled. The short woman threw out her arms, grabbing the sides of the open doors, her fingers tensing and twitching.

"Oh hell!" Easton scooted back into the corner of the elevator, keeping his hands as close to his body as possible.

That was when Becca realized she hadn't analyzed the woman. Everything made sense the moment she focused on her. The stamina, the strength, the fact that the Fools had a tendency to employ supernatural creatures. Becca couldn't believe she hadn't pieced it together earlier.

Werewolf, Rare, Friendly

"I swear if I run into a chupacabra next, I won't even act surprised." Becca backed into the corner of the elevator opposite Easton as Harlow's entire body elongated.

The previously short woman, now standing close to six feet, dragged her hands down the sides of the door as her claws carved through the surface. It was like something out of the movies. Fur climbed up her arms to the shoulders while her ears grew into a pointed canine shape. Her boots split open as her toes tore through the front.

Both she and Easton flinched when she raised her head to let out a ferocious growl.

"Well, shit, so much for the element of surprise." Becca

shrugged, the absurdity of the situation quelling some of her nerves. "May as well do this right."

Becca let her banshee ability take over, finding a song that would throw the Guardians off balance and enhance the nightmare that was heading their way. The ability filled the elevator and the room outside with the steady beat of a drum.

Harlow took that as her cue to stomp her way into the hall.

One of the men outside cried out.

"What that hell is that?"

Then all hell broke loose.

Bullets filled the air, thumping into Harlow's oversized body. Becca's eyes widened as most simply fell to the floor, unable to penetrate her hide. Harlow roared back, blending with Becca's banshee ability as the riff of a guitar joined the drums.

"Is that…" Easton cocked his head to one side. "The Monster Mash?"

Specifically, it was a cover by the Misfits.

Becca didn't explain, letting her abilities do the talking. Instead, she grabbed her sword as well as the one Harlow had dropped during her transformation and flicked enough mana into her strength to wield both at once. Then she stepped outside.

Spells flew by when bullets failed to stop the werewolf. Becca used Harlow for cover for the charge. The beast in front of her caught an icicle in her claws as another pierced her shoulder. She tore it out just as fast, displaying a healing ability of her own as the wound closed.

The Guardians tried to hold formation.

Harlow plowed into them regardless. One of the men in the front screamed just before she rammed one of the icicles she'd caught down his throat.

"Holy—" Another cried out only to have his words cut off when she shoved her fingers in his mouth. A blood curdling screech erupted from the man as she ripped his lower jaw off.

Becca fought the urge to hurl, reminding herself that she couldn't hide behind the murderous werewolf forever. They would break formation and surround them in seconds. Becca leapt out before that happened, swinging her swords in an upward arc to catch a Guardian in the face. She followed the motion through, adding a surge of mana to her strength for a second as she brought them down on an unfortunate man behind her. Shock flooded his face as well as hers when her blades cleaved down all the way to the floor, his arms flopping to the marble tile.

The panicked man immediately about faced and ran, leaving his severed limbs behind.

"Oh fuck!" Her eyes darted around the room, clocking the levels of some of the Guardians nearby. "Oh fuck," she repeated as she realized they were mostly in the low twenties. Some were even in the teens.

The Guardians were still dangerous in a group, but a rampaging werewolf and a bloodthirsty vampire were more than they bargained for.

Twelve bullets tore through Becca's side to remind her that they were far from safe. Her body healed the damage almost instantly. She responded in kind, throwing a torrent of bats in the direction the attack came from. She glanced at her mana, feeling it plummet.

MP: 52/408

"Shit!" Becca stopped throwing bats as she felt her control over her actions begin to fade.

Thankfully, Harlow impaled a Guardian with the other icicle she held. He fell to his knees in front of Becca. It was a meal she couldn't pass up. She lunged, sinking her teeth into his throat as the Monster Mash reached its chorus. A fireball burst against her arm while she fed. The skin on her elbow burnt and healed simultaneously as she ripped her victim's spark from his body. Her mana climbed back to full, adding another few points to her max.

MP: 413/413

A kill notification followed along with a level-up.

You have reached level 31.
You have 1 additional attribute point to allocate.

It was a sight for sore eyes. She dropped her extra point into intelligence to maximize her mana pool. Then she remembered that she was still on fire, the flames engulfing her sleeve to accelerate the damage. Her mana began to fall again just as fast as she'd gotten it.

I'm weak to fire, noted.

Another fireball roared through the air toward her head. She fed mana into her agility, dodging to the side. The spell blistered the skin of her cheek as it passed by, filling the air with the scent of burnt hair. Watching her mana fall, she stabbed one of her swords into a corpse that lay near her feet to free up a hand so she could tear off her flaming sleeve. With the fire gone, she retrieved the weapon from the body and lunged at the first Guardian she saw. Letting her swords hang at her sides, she threw her legs around the man to hold him in place and bit down.

"Huh?" Becca mumbled the word as she chewed on a strange texture, getting nothing from her prey. Then she noticed the blue shimmer emanating from where she was attempting to bite.

"Nice try," the Guardian grunted just before slamming a fist into her gut.

Becca felt some of her insides rupture and burst as a Kinetic Impact spell launched her backward. She hit the floor at the mouth of the elevator bay before sliding all the way back to the open door where Easton hid.

Everything hurt. Becca had nearly forgotten what real pain felt like, having gotten used to her vampiric healing. The blow had caused too much damage. Anyone else would have died instantly. Though, with her rapid healing, she had a chance. Unfortunately, that chance came with a cost. Her mana fell as the agony began to fade. Then it ran out.

MP: 0/424

Becca's vision blurred as the last of the damage stopped healing.

No!

She was all too aware that the closest human to her was Easton. Struggling to focus on the fight in the main room, she caught a blurry image of a Guardian flying through the air past the entrance of the elevator bay. They were followed by Harlow stomping after him while grabbing hold of an unlucky cleric who happened to be nearby. She chomped down onto his neck like he was a chew toy.

"Becca?" Easton sat on the floor of the elevator, clearly afraid to come out and get involved in the chaos. He held his pistol pointing at the floor. "Are you... you?"

Becca rolled over, clawing toward him. He was full of so much blood. So much power. A scream tore her attention away from him as a familiar armless Guardian ran into the bay of elevators. He turned and bumped his waist into one of the buttons on the other side, probably trying to call a ride out of the hell he'd been trapped in. Unfortunately for him, the care-taker's Jester system was messing with the elevators again.

Becca pushed herself off the floor, rising up behind him. He turned around just as she lunged.

"Fak!" Easton scooted back away from the display. His discomfort in witnessing the actions of a hungry vampire up close was obvious. The matter was only made worse when a severed head bounced across the floor between them. A roar from Harlow explained where it had come from.

Becca ignored the head as well as Easton's trembling legs. Even the fight behind her fell into the background. All she cared about was the blood and the spark.

The sound of boots rushing up from behind her wasn't even enough to draw her attention away from her prey. A gun barked several times from where Easton sat. A Guardian fell against the wall, their body shimmering as the bullets pelted a barrier. Becca ignored the fight as she devoured her victim's soul.

Easton reloaded his gun and fired again into the Guardian behind her before he could recover. His barrier failed halfway through the barrage, four rounds getting past. Three thumped into his armor while the last tore through his abdomen just below.

Becca tore her mouth from the neck of the man she had just killed and sprang up to claim the easy prey. Her mana was already full, yet she bit him anyway. She didn't have room for his soul, but it would push her maximum value up another few points. A few more points meant a few seconds of healing, a few more bats, another burst of agility. A soul in exchange for seconds of time. It almost didn't seem worth it.

Then again, Becca wanted it.

Pulling her fangs free of the man's flesh, she stood, at full strength again.

"Thanks for watching my back." She gave Easton a nod, knowing that she would have killed him if an easier meal hadn't run by.

Finding her swords, she stalked back into the main entrance. The vocals of Jerry Only, front-man of the Misfits, accompanied each step.

Harlow stood on the glass at the center of the room over the model city below. Five Guardians, each carrying a sword, circled her. Her left arm hung limp at her side, a bone sticking out from her elbow. She must have tried to block a Kinetic Impact. She lashed out with her undamaged hand, clawing at the nearest enemy. A burst of blue sparks flew from a barrier.

The fact that the group of Guardians still stood probably meant that they all were a class that had access to the spell. Otherwise, they would have been torn apart. Becca did the math in her head. There had been two dozen at the start, but she had only killed three. Subtracting the five survivors, meant that Harlow had dealt with twelve.

Becca arched an eyebrow.

Harlow had clearly done some damage but twelve still seemed like a lot. Becca closed her eyes and pushed on her sense of touch, feeling for vibrations. The Monster Mash went on about the Wolfman and Dracula as she caught boots moving in two directions. Adding a few more points of mana, she pinpointed two invisible heartbeats.

Rogues!

Snapping her eyes open, she fed power into her agility, pushing it to the limit as a rogue appeared directly behind her holding a pistol to her head. She jerked to the side in a super-natural motion. The gun barked in nearly the same instant. A piece of her ear splattered across her cheek, smoke wafting around her face to mix with the scent of blood.

She ignored the damage and fed mana into her body, maintaining the flow to her agility while adding strength and dexterity. In the space of a breath, she bent her knee and kicked off to send herself into the air. Rising parallel to the floor, she used the momentum of her jump to throw her body into a rotation, her sword cleaving through the rogue's knuckles before they had time to react. His gun fell, along with a shower of newly severed digits.

Reorienting her position as she came down, she launched her other sword in the direction of the second concealed heartbeat near the edge of the room. A scream rang out as a rogue appeared on impact, his body launching into the wall, pinning him to the cinderblocks. She finished the move by bringing her remaining sword down on the man clutching his ruined hand beside her. Feeding just her strength for a few brief seconds, she buried the blade into his shoulder, all the way down to his ribcage to cleave his heart in two.

From the look on his face, he didn't even realize what had happened. Instead, he just fell backward in a spray of crimson.

A kill notification streaked across her vision for both men, along with another level up.

"Well, now the numbers make sense." Becca let her sword fall with him, not bothering to yank it free.

Two of the Guardians surrounding Harlow turned in her direction.

"We'll have to do something about those barriers." She finished her comment with a vampiric hiss that felt entirely too natural, before reaching out for the shadows.

The lights in the building dimmed as bats came from all directions. She let her mana value fall, throwing everything she had into the swarm, filling the space with a swirling vortex of tiny mouths and claws.

"What are they?" A man swatted at the dark forms as his barrier failed.

Becca lunged in his direction, grabbing him by the front of his armor and yanking him close. Warmth filled her mouth as she bit down. Another barrier failed to her right. Not wanting to let go of her prey, she reached down and grabbed a pistol that was holstered to the Guardian's thigh. With the help of a few points of mana, she flicked her arm back up and unloaded the gun into the target.

Harlow didn't waste the opportunity, grabbing one of the Guardians that still had a barrier active with her undamaged hand. The bone protruding from her elbow pulled back in as whatever healing ability werewolves had gave her back the use of the limb. The Guardian started to yell, his voice wailing in a discordant rhythm that defied the final chorus of the Monster Mash. Snapping her other hand over his mouth, Harlow slammed his head down into the glass floor. His barrier sparked on impact, forcing her to raise him back up before bringing him down again. His skull hit the glass with an almost musical thrum as she repeated the action.

Becca drank in her victim's spark and let the body fall, making a point to step off of the glass section of the floor as Harlow continued to smash the Guardian into it even after his barrier failed. The two remaining men swatted at the bats while backing away from the werewolf at the center of the room. Becca kept the swarm going as Harlow smashed her captive beyond recognition, leaving a puddle of red mush on the glass. She raised her fist one more time to slam them back down to shatter the surface.

The werewolf fell onto the model city below along with the remaining two Guardians. Both men turned and scrambled for the edge of the pit. One of them climbed up as the other struggled to get a grip on the side. Reaching up toward his squadmate, the man that had fallen behind kicked his legs in the pit and begged for help. The Guardian that had climbed out only looked back for a second before turning and running.

The struggling man screamed as Harlow grabbed his legs and pulled him back down. A somewhat cartoonish amount of blood sprayed up from the pit. Like something out of a horror comedy film. The Guardian that had left him behind kept running as if he might escape the horror behind him.

Becca glanced at her mana.

MP: 320/450

"I could use a top-off."

With a short sprint, she rushed to the edge of the pit and jumped, her bats swarming around her as a shadowy form extended from her sides to catch the air. Instinct guided her ability, sending her gliding across the room. She released her shadows all at once to drop herself down onto the fleeing man that had left his companion behind. He turned just in time to let out a scream as she tore into him. They hit the tile floor together, sliding another few feet and leaving a trail of blood on the marble.

She let her banshee fade, now that the Monster Mash was wrapping up. Her mana filled back up to full yet again. Tearing her mouth from her prey, she looked back to find Easton peeking out from the elevator bay. The horror on his face was palpable as he stared, wide-eyed, at the carnage.

Some of the bodies weren't even recognizable.

"We have to go." Becca ignored the look on his face. She didn't need another reminder of the monster she'd become. She only made it a few feet toward the door at the front of the building when she realized they were one werewolf short. Turning around, she jogged back to the pit in the floor, making sure not to slip in the blood-slicked surface. "Harlow, we have to go."

The werewolf ignored her, still chewing on a corpse.

"Is she…" Easton crept up on Becca's left. "…Eating someone?"

Harlow tore off a limb and turned around whilst chewing on a piece of bone sticking out the end.

"Well, that's gross." Easton recoiled.

"Just try not to hurl." Becca shot him a look.

"I already did." He pointed back toward the elevators. "I'm pretty sure I'm all out."

"At least we can take solace in the fact that Autem has to clean the place up." Becca clapped her hands to try and get Harlow's attention. "Hey, this isn't time to eat that guy. We need to escape before more Guardians show up."

The formerly short woman merely grunted back.

"I'm starting to think there is a drawback to all that strength." Becca scanned the room, finding the tennis ball that Harlow had thrown as a distraction before wolfing out. There had to be a reason why Harlow had brought it.

"You aren't going to do what I think you are." Easton arched an eyebrow.

"She's been carrying this thing everywhere the last few days, there's got to be a reason." Retrieving the ball from the floor, she held it up. "Hey, you want this?"

Harlow looked back, still gnawing on a bone. She didn't make a move but her eyes did follow the ball.

"Come on." Becca shook the fuzzy green object back and

forth before throwing it at the entrance of the building. "Go
get it!"

Harlow dropped what she'd been eating and leapt out of
the pit.

"Wow." Easton watched her go. "Werewolves are kinda
dumb."

"Apparently." Becca chased after her, not wanting her to go
out alone, having no idea what was waiting for them on the
other side of the doors.

Easton brought up the rear, lagging behind, unable to keep
up with the monsters in front.

Becca caught up to Harlow just as she scooped the ball off
the ground and slammed into the front door. Becca skidded to a
stop as soon as she reached the threshold, the lights of three of
Autem's owl warships shining down at them.

"Wait!" she called out to Harlow as she rushed down the
steps of the building, followed by spotlights. The werewolf
didn't pause to look back until she'd made it another hundred
feet. The look on her face made it clear she was starting to
realize the mistake.

The owls above turned to face her, their guns taking aim.

"Shit." Becca leapt forward, sprinting when she hit the
stairs.

There was no way they could win in a fight against the three
aircraft, even with the abilities they had as attendees of the
Monster Mash. That didn't mean she couldn't make them
harder to shoot.

Becca threw out her hands to reach for the shadows, finding
them easier to call outside surrounded by the night. The only
lights came from the occasional work lamp and the spotlights
above. Sliding in behind Harlow, she stood back-to-back with
the wolf and drew the shadows in. Bats formed from the gloom,
swirling around them in a vortex of darkness that obstructed the
view.

The ships above opened fire regardless, tearing through the
swarm. Becca and Harlow dove apart as a torrent of white-hot

streaks cut a swath through the ground between them. Another barrage shredded through the space a few feet away, filling the air with dirt and debris. The only thing keeping them safe was the fact that the swarm slowed the owl's ability just enough for Becca and Harlow's inhuman bodies to keep pace.

There was a limit to how long she could keep it up.

Becca reached for the radio that Leon had given her before parting ways. "Leon, I don't know if we can make it to you."

There was no response.

"Ozzie?" Becca tried again as the spotlights above filtered through the cyclone of bats that swirled around them. "Where are you two?"

Again, there was no response.

Becca dove to the side as the ground beside her was torn apart by dozens of rounds, each streaking through the night like falling stars. Her bats vanished every time one was hit, decreasing their cover. Becca created more, her mana falling below half to fill the demand.

"Damn it! Where are you?" she shouted as a bullet flew straight through her wrist to send her healing into action while draining her mana further.

Harlow roared in protest as a few rounds struck her in the leg.

There was still no sign of Leon or Ozzie. Becca's mind raced to find a way out, coming up with nothing. It was all she could do just to delay the inevitable.

Then the sound of propellers joined the chaos.

Becca spun in its direction as a kestrel flew out through the gateway that Leon and Ozzie had gone through to look for an escape route. It pulled up the second it was clear, opening fire on the warships above. Bullets impacted across two of the magic-powered craft. Blue sparks burst from their surfaces as waves of shimmering light swept across their hulls.

"Shit! They're protected." Becca growled in frustration as the kestrel turned just before hitting the wall, the rear of the aircraft scraping its surface.

It opened up on one of the owls as it drifted through the space.

"Sorry to keep you waiting." Leon's voice came across her radio. "The comms don't seem to work on the other side of the gateway."

"We heard the gunfire." Ozzie's voice joined in. "Decided to come and pull your asses out of whatever fire you started." He paused before adding, "I see Harlow got desperate."

"If that's what you want to call it." Becca thrust her hands up, sending her swarm of bats out at one of the ships that dropped down to avoid being shot at. The tiny forms pelted the front. "Hurry and pick us up."

"I don't think we're going to be able to land close enough," Leon responded.

The kestrel carrying the two vampire mercenaries dropped down, using the building at the center for cover as the warships circled, trying to get a clear shot. They seemed to be being careful not to shoot the keep or the wall that surrounded them.

"If we can cause enough trouble here, think you can make it to the lift that takes you back to the loading bays where we landed?" Ozzie asked in a surprisingly serious tone. "We kind of made a little too much noise on the other side of that gateway to use it as an escape route. You should be able to stowaway on one of the ships that haven't launched. They're heading back to Vegas anyway."

Becca glanced to the edge of the wall where the industrial elevator ran up the outside. "I don't like that idea."

The argument was put to rest when one of Autem's ships fired a short burst at the kestrel. The bullets pelted the craft, just missing the rotors on the back.

Ozzie shouted a curse word over the line. "That was close. We're not going to be able to stay here long."

"Get to the hangar," Leon added. "We'll keep them occupied as long as we can."

"Fine." Becca grabbed Harlow's shoulder, hoping she would follow and not bite her hand off.

Easton sprinted down the steps of the central building to join them.

"Oh, and Becca?" Leon lowered his voice despite the chaos of the moment.

"Yeah?" She looked up to the kestrel as she ran for the lifts.

"Make sure you win." A somber tone entered his voice.

"Yeah," Ozzie added. "The world needs Fools."

"But you're mercenaries, you're supposed to watch out for yourselves?" she called back as the warships circled above, each focused on the kestrel.

"We were never very good at that part." Leon laughed just as the kestrel's rotors tilted to send it into a spiral.

They opened fire, spinning through the air as they poured bullets into the walls. Climbing at the same time, the kestrel rose above to draw the owls away from the ground. Every gun above fired, filling the night with white-hot streaks that tore through the kestrel's center. Still, it flew higher until one of its rotors exploded. The craft spun out of control to drift away from the wall until it disappeared out of sight.

The warships gave chase as Becca reached the lift and hit the controls to take them back up to the landing bay they had entered through. She made sure to keep hold of the back of Harlow's shirt to stop the werewolf from running off.

"Who was piloting that kestrel?" Easton climbed up onto the platform as it was lifting off the ground.

"Just a couple of Fools." She stared up at the trail of smoke that the kestrel had left in its wake. The sound of an explosion came from the same direction. She lowered her head. "We can't let them down."

CHAPTER FORTY-FIVE

Parker walked onto the bridge of the command ship, also known as the Seahorse. The crew took a moment away from some last-minute preparations to salute her. She wasn't sure if it was appropriate, so she ignored it and headed for the back wall of the narrow room where they had mounted a few mirrors.

There was one large pane of glass for portals and two smaller ones for communications. There was also an extra mirror down a corridor just in case any of them were broken. Each of their ships had been outfitted with the same setup. That way, the crew could be evacuated to Vegas if any of the ships happened to sink, or get shot down, or whatever you would call it when an airship gets destroyed. It was a good idea, although it added another responsibility to Parker's already full list. She was just lucky her mana was high enough to keep up with the demand.

Digby had headed back to Vegas to get the ice surface ready that he wanted to use to transport the ships, which had been hours ago. He should have contacted her to request a passage by now. She debated on casting a Link spell to ask him what was taking so long, but considering the sudden mean streak that he'd shown toward her, she didn't really feel like talking to him.

After losing Sax, she just couldn't handle another insult.

The fact that both Deuce and Elenore had called her to complain that Digby was roaming the casino with his weird spider body was not helping. Apparently, he had marched through the center of the casino, terrifying children. He had also yelled at them.

Ultimately, he was right—the people had to get used to seeing that sort of thing eventually—she just wished they could have eased them into it. Though, she could understand why he might want to rush things. It wasn't fun to get stared at, she knew that much all too well.

The dull ache in her head swelled.

Turning to the windows at the front of the bridge, she looked out at the engraved rod that now skewered the ship. The crew was still getting used to operating it. By turning a horizontal wheel to the side, the rod moved down a few inches. The front of the ship rose a dozen feet in response.

Parker leaned to compensate for the angle of the deck.

Looking out across the harbor, the other ships were all floating above the water, held up by a flow of ambient mana drawn in by various enchantments. It was all so bizarre. The world would be unrecognizable if things continued along the path they were on. She still wasn't sure if that was good or not.

Magic had changed everything, even her.

On the deck of the Minnow, floating nearest the Seahorse, was Mason. He was still wearing the cowboy hat that Becca had left him shortly before she'd died, as well as a navy poncho that he'd found at the harbor. He definitely seemed relieved that she was alive, but it was clear there was some hurt there as well. The fact that she hadn't come home was odd. Ever since hearing that Becca had been spotted in D.C., he'd been focused on captaining his ship. Parker assumed he was just keeping himself busy to avoid being tempted to go off on a rescue mission that would end in getting himself killed.

Shifting her gaze to the other side of the harbor, she caught a glimpse of some of the people from Vegas. One of the good things about being able to portal around the world was that they had been able to relocate everyone from the strip to the naval base in Hawaii. Now, there was only a skeleton crew back in Sin City. They weren't abandoning Vegas, not after all the work they had put in to make it safe and supplying it with power. Though, that didn't mean that they were going to leave their people there with Autem heading their way. Moving the populace was just a precaution.

If things went well, they would just go back home after the battle was through. If not, well, they would have to figure things out. Either way, the base in Hawaii had plenty of space. Only some sections around the docks had been fully warded, but it wouldn't be that much of a struggle to secure the rest. Even if things did go well and they were able to send Autem's forces packing. IT would be a good idea to leave some of their people in Hawaii. With everything the island had to offer in terms of climate and farmland, it just made sense to maintain a presence there.

Parker's attention was torn away from the harbor when an irritated, gravelly voice shouted at her from her pocket. She rolled her eyes as she pulled her compact out and flipped it open to find Digby.

"Where is that lazy—" He stopped talking as soon as he saw her. "Oh, Parker, good. I require a passage."

"Where have you been?" Parker eyed him suspiciously.

"What do you mean? I have been preparing the ice that we need to travel."

"I know, but it doesn't take that long to do that and you have been gone for hours." She made a point of looking him in the eyes.

"Yes, I get it, you're concerned about my mental stability or whatever." He groaned. "It is getting old. Now open the passage. This ice is not going to stay frozen for long. It's already starting to melt."

Parker frowned at the response, annoyed that she had gotten to know the zombie so well that she could tell he was being evasive. Then again, he was right about the ice; they only had a narrow window to get the ships through.

"Fine." She waved a hand at the mirror.

One of Digby's spindly, spider legs emerged from the glass as soon as it began to ripple. The necromancer's crooked grin came next.

"Thank you." He gave her a nod. "Was that so hard?"

Digby walked right past her, his pointy legs click-clacking against the floor of the bridge as he headed for the door to yell at the men on the deck and get everyone into position. It only took a few minutes to get the ship moving.

Parker motioned to close the passage but stopped as a boot stepped through. For a second, she wasn't sure who would be following Digby. She deflated as soon as their face emerged.

It was Sax.

Digby must have been using him as a guard since he was his strongest minion. Her deceased friend looked at her briefly before sweeping his eyes across the area to find the necromancer that held his leash. Finding Digby through the window, he walked onward to join his master.

A part of her wished she had closed the passage on the minion and cut him in half. At least that way Sax wouldn't be walking around like that. Plus, she could have claimed it was an accident when Digby inevitably yelled at her. Unfortunately, she had not been so lucky.

Parker waited another fifteen seconds to make sure no one else was coming. She'd expected that Union wouldn't be far behind. When no one else came, she poked her head through the passage to make sure. On the other end, she found Union sitting in a chair off to the side.

"Hey, you coming?"

The skeleton turned to look at her. "We are on a break." Somehow their skull seemed to smile. "You are entitled to one as well."

Parker hesitated. "You know, that is a good point." She pulled her head back through and closed the passage.

It was actually pretty reasonable. People took breaks so that they could continue working with better productivity and she would probably run better when she wasn't so sleep deprived. Then again, with everything happening and the fact that she was the only one with the Passage spell, taking a break wasn't a luxury that they could afford. Though, she was probably just telling herself that so that she didn't have to feel bad about being taken advantage of.

A part of her respected the skeleton for taking a stand. She smirked, knowing how much Union was sure to annoy Digby.

Heading out to the deck as the breeze picked up, she stepped to the rail to watch as the other ships passed over the welcome center and ticket area of the harbor. It felt like something out of a movie while at the same time, it almost seemed normal. It wasn't long before they reached the parking lot that they had covered with a reflective resin. Staring out across the surface, it looked like a placid lake, the full moon reflecting back on its surface. She just hoped the other side was smooth enough for her to open a passage big enough.

The Seahorse slowed to a stop as Mason's ship got into position to go through the passage first.

"Get down there and open the path," Digby shouted in her direction.

Parker did as she was told, having no reason to argue. Returning to the bridge, she opened a passage using the large mirror on the wall, connecting it to the sheet of ice back in Vegas. Once the glass began to ripple, she turned her back to it and let herself fall. It felt like the world was moving around her as her momentum carried her through the passage and up through the other end on the strip. Up became sideways and vice-versa. She'd fallen in Hawaii and landed in Vegas.

A coven standing guard looked impressed as she rose up from the ice to stand upright. The passage closed the instant she was through. She would have looked cool had she not immediately slipped on the ice and proceeded to flail her arms like a cartoon to regain her balance.

I kind of regret prioritizing dexterity instead of agility. I'd probably fall down less.

Out of the corner of her eye, she caught a few members of a nearby coven struggling not to laugh.

Once she was stable again, she slid herself to the edge of the massive sheet of ice. Digby was right, it was starting to melt, leaving a slippery, wet layer across the top. It was still mostly solid, so the melting had only served to make the surface more reflective. Though, it wouldn't be long until it became unstable.

Glancing back at the ships waiting in line, she clenched her jaw, exacerbating the pressure in her head.

How am I going to do this?

A part of her wanted to scream. Digby had just told her to move the entire armada without ever really caring if she could. Now, she had no choice. There were people on those ships. Failing could mean their deaths.

Parker dropped to her knees at the edge of the ice. She'd never opened a passage that big before. In theory, it would work. The spell didn't cost much mana, but there was always a small amount of resistance whenever she cast it. It was as if the world was somehow telling her to stop. Like she was bending the laws of physics too far.

Normally it wasn't a big deal unless she kept the spell active for longer than normal. After a minute or so it seemed to take more focus to hold open. Maybe the resistance she felt when opening a passage was just her reaching the limit of her will? She assumed the only reason she could cast the spell at all had something to do with her ridiculous will stat. It was hundreds of points higher than any of the other Heretics.

If she had to guess, the Passage spell was probably a high-level ability that required the stat. The only question was, how did the Seed give it to her? Did it increase her will as well? Or was it a glitch that the malfunctioning caretaker had taken advantage of? She chuckled to herself. Maybe her will had always been like that.

The throbbing in her head demanded she stop thinking about it.

"Okay, here we go, I guess." Parker set her compact beside her and held out her hand.

She felt the difference in size immediately, the spell snapping back as soon as the surface began to ripple. Her mind had just refused to keep it open.

Digby's face appeared in her compact a second later. "What happened?"

"Sorry." She paused. "It just kinda got away from me."

"Well, get it back!" he growled before turning to someone out of the frame and telling them to cancel the link. His image vanished a second later.

"Well, get it back," Parker repeated in a mocking tone as she lowered her hands to the ice. Some spells, like Digby's Decay, worked better when touching the target. A chill climbed up her arms as she touched the frozen surface, making her grateful it wasn't winter. Though, the sun had set hours ago and Nevada could still get cold at night.

Casting the spell again, the passage opened with little resistance.

Mason's face appeared in her compact next. "We're in position."

"Okay, you should be good to go." She gave him a nod.

Through the mirror, she saw him standing on the bridge sideways. The hard part of sending the ships through a mirror that was positioned on the ground was that they had to go through vertically. With the ship floating perpendicular to the ground, Mason was using a section of the wall near the front window to stand on.

"This is kind of terrifying." He made a face that conveyed an appropriate level of unease. Then he repositioned the compact he held so she could see down into the passage she'd opened.

Most of the crew had taken refuge in the smallest rooms they could find so that they wouldn't have far to fall when the gravity shifted on the other side of the passage. The few that had to operate the propulsion enchantments had to make the trip on the deck. Parker could see one of them harnessed into position by one of the side rails.

Mason gave the command and the ship started downward. Parker stared at the view as the vessel got closer and closer to the rippling surface. Then it plunged in. Flicking her attention to the space in front of her, the bow of the ship emerged.

"Oh shit, that's crazy," she blurted out as the reality of what she was doing stared her in the face.

The ship moved at a snail's pace. With so much that could go wrong, it made sense to take it slow. Then again, if they took too long it would only put more of a strain on Parker.

She tore her eyes off the rising ship as the resistance to the spell grew. Her fingers hurt from holding them in contact with the ice, though she didn't dare move them. The pain in her head remained steady, adding another layer of distraction as beads of sweat began to form on her forehead.

Thankfully, the back end of the boat came through before the spell got away from her again. She let the passage close as soon as it was through to give herself a break. Mason needed a few minutes to get his vessel out of the way of the exit point anyway. Parker shoved her hands under her arms to warm them up, hoping the ship would take its time.

The front end of the Minnow began to lower itself down as the rear went up. Eventually, it leveled out. Once it was floating upright again, Mason ran out to give her a thumbs up. After that, the ship sailed on to hover further down the strip.

Her compact came to life again. This time, it was Digby. He was still standing upright on the bridge despite her being able to see the ground through the windows behind him. Apparently, having the lower half of a spider meant that he didn't need to obey gravity as much as a regular person.

"Well done." He grinned at her through the link. "I told you it would work."

Parker wiped sweat from her forehead. "It's not easy, though."

"Yes, yes, I'm sure." He waved away her comment. "Now hurry up and get the passage open again. I'm coming through."

Parker sighed and placed her hands back on the ice. The front of the Seahorse emerged moments later. She kept her eyes closed this time, trying her best to ignore the pain in her hands or the ache in her head. Somehow the resistance was worse, forcing her to bite her lip to help keep her mind clear.

The command ship exited the passage shortly after, leaving her gasping and sweat dripping from her face. She immediately closed the passage and shook her hands to get feeling back into them.

Digby came skittering out of the bridge before the ship even had time to level out. The zombie just crawled down the deck before jumping to the ground and sauntering up to stand beside Parker.

"Alright, the next one is already in position."

She looked up at him, still panting. "Think I could get a break?"

"I would like to say yes." He looked down at her with an expression that made it clear that he wasn't going to.

"Yeah, I know. The ice is melting." Parker stopped and looked up at him. "You know, you could refreeze it."

"I certainly could, but that won't change the fact that Autem is still on their way here as we speak." Digby continued to stand over her expectantly.

Parker shook her hands one more time and set them back down.

The next ship entered the passage as soon as it was open. She could have sworn she heard Digby talking to himself behind her but she was too focused on the spell to be sure. She wished Alex hadn't gotten himself trapped on the other side of the country. If he had been there, he could at least help her keep an eye on the zombie while she was opening passages.

The stress of the spell increased exponentially, as if her mind was getting tired. It was like trying to focus on a long test back in school. There had always been a limit to how much time she could concentrate on that sort of thing. She just couldn't stay on task. It was a wonder how she had made it in the military.

Come on, just a little more, she tried to cheer herself on. *Tough it out, like you did in the Army.*

A jolt of pain echoed through her head a second later.

"No." She nearly let the spell fail as she closed her eyes tight.

"What's that?" Digby asked from beside her.

She didn't respond, unsure if she could form words without losing the spell. It had never been that difficult before and the headache was making it so much worse.

Digby skittered off without another word.

The ship exited the passage not long after. Parker collapsed as soon as it was through, her brain refusing to do anything else but lay with her head on the ice, gasping. She hadn't even noticed she'd been holding her breath. She had no idea where Digby had gone. All she knew was that she was glad he wasn't there to rush her into opening the passage again.

The zombie returned a couple minutes later with Lana in tow.

"What happened?" The cleric dropped down beside her, casting a heal to try to fix whatever was wrong.

"I just needed a rest." Parker sat up, her hair dripping with sweat mixed with water from the ice.

The spell didn't do anything for the pain in her head but it did make her hands feel a little better.

"Can you keep casting healing magic on her?" Digby leaned down to them.

"I can, but I don't think what's wrong with her is physical."

Lana shined a penlight into Parker's eyes. "It might help her feel a little better but that's it."

"I'll take feeling a little better over feeling worse." Parker took a few breaths and got back into position.

Lana placed a hand on her shoulder. "Did you get any sleep after I checked you out earlier?"

"Like, a couple hours." She glanced back.

"She really needs more." Lana looked back to Digby.

"I can tell." He gestured to her face to point out how ill she looked.

"Thanks," Parker grunted back up at him.

"But we don't know when Autem's forces will arrive, and we need to be in position." For a moment he sounded sympathetic. "There just isn't time, and we still have two more small ships as well as the horde's cargo ship."

"I know." Parker put her hands down again. "Just tell the ships to speed up if they can."

Taking a deep breath, she cast the spell again. Lana stayed beside her, casting a heal whenever she started to struggle. The spell didn't do much to actually help, but it did help her keep her focus.

The next two ships increased their speed as well. There was a limit to what they could do safely, but Parker appreciated the help. It wasn't until the horde ship that she hit a wall again.

The cargo vessel was still empty except for its crew since it made more sense to move the horde to it after it made the trip to Vegas. The problem was that it was longer than the battleships that had come before. About halfway through the passage, the continuous healing from Lana stopped meaning much. It was just too big. The engineering teams didn't have time to install extra propulsion enchantments, leaving it with the same capabilities as the other ships. With its increased size, it was slower. Not only that, but it was more delicate. Vessels like that just weren't built with air travel in mind, not that the rest were either, but it was far harder to maneuver without damaging itself.

Parker let out a whimper as her body began to rebel against her. Nausea swam through her as her head continued to throb. Locks of sweat-drenched hair stuck to her face and a trickle of blood ran from her nose. She struggled not to throw up, afraid that she'd lose the spell if she did.

"Are you okay?" Lana rubbed her back.

"No." Parker's voice came out wet and phlegmy.

That was when she realized she was crying.

"You're almost there!" Digby added, clearly trying to keep her motivated for another ten seconds.

His voice grated on her nerves. After the week she'd had, hearing him talk was the last thing she needed.

"Shut up, Digby," she snapped back.

"I…" He trailed off, frowning and narrowing his eyes.

Taking rapid breaths in pace with her racing heart, she kept her focus on the spell. It was torture. Like she was trying to lift a car but had run out of the adrenaline needed to keep her from realizing that it was impossible. It felt like the spell could crush her.

Letting out a growl, she fought back, her voice swelling into a roar of effort. There were too many people on that ship to fail. Her voice cracked and faded as the cargo ship slipped from the passage. She snapped it shut, cutting a section of rail off the back of the vessel.

Then she collapsed to the ice, clutching her head and crying.

"I'm… never. Doing. That again!" she shouted at whoever was listening while struggling to slow her breathing.

"That's fine." Digby stood over her. "The task is finished."

"Shit yeah, it is." Parker closed her eyes, just as everything went dark.

———

Parker was back on the command ship when she woke up.

"What happened?" She sprang up, hitting her head on the

bottom of a bunk above the one she was laying on, adding an, "Oh balls," as she rubbed her face.

Checking her watch, she saw that only a half hour had passed. Lana must have had her moved after she'd passed out. Her body swayed slightly with the motion of the ship, giving her a sense of vertigo. They were in the air.

The headache had faded back down to the dull ache that it normally was. She slipped out of the bunk and hoisted herself back to her feet.

Lana walked in before she made it more than a few steps. "Oh, you're up?"

"Yep." She pushed her way out into the narrow corridor to get her bearings.

Lana slipped past to block her path. "You need to get back in bed. You've barely slept in days. And there's no sign of Autem yet."

Parker eyed her sideways. "How long 'til Dig comes down to drag me up to the deck?"

Lana looked away. "He has been getting impatient, but I think I can get him to give you a little more time before he comes down here."

Parker sighed. "I'd rather wake up on my own than wake up to him yelling at me. Besides, I don't want to get caught off guard. People could die if I don't get a passage open fast enough."

Lana shifted to the side to continue blocking her path. "I get that, and I don't blame you. I know that spell doesn't cost much mana but obviously, it still has a cost. I mean, look at you."

Parker scoffed. "I don't think I have the option of stopping. Besides, I don't think it's just the spell. My whole class shouldn't exist. Whatever's wrong with me, it's bigger than just overusing a spell."

"I know." Lana lowered her head before stepping aside. "Just be careful. You won't be able to help anyone if you burn out."

"I won't." Parker stopped and placed a hand on her shoulder. "Because you, as my primary care physician, are going to figure out what's wrong. Okay?" She gave her a smile and pushed past.

Yeesh, what the hell am I saying? Parker cringed as she left Lana behind.

She hadn't been trying to act tough. No, she just didn't know what else to say. A gust of wind blew the thought out of her head as she stepped out onto the deck.

"Woah."

A sea of clouds stretched out as far as the eye could see, the Seahorse sailing across it. Running to the rail, Parker leaned over the edge. The puffy white shapes below swirled as the bow cut through them. In front, the other four combat ships flew in formation. Parker glanced back, finding the horde's cargo ship in the distance.

They were on their way. The plan was to fly out above Boulder so the battle ahead wouldn't happen near Vegas.

"It won't be long now. I just need to make it through the night." Parker raised her head up to the full moon shining down on the fleet and let out a chuckle. "Bet a werewolf would love a view like this."

CHAPTER FORTY-SIX

"I'm going to die, I'm going to die, I'm going to die."

"Shut up, Easton." Becca slapped the man's side as he sat huddled up against her. Then, she leaned across him to slap Harlow on the shoulder. "And you, stop growling."

"Sorry, it takes a bit to get right again after letting the dog out." The now much shorter werewolf sat huddled close to Easton, still clutching a blood-stained tennis ball.

Using the distraction provided by Leon and Ozzie, Becca and what was left of her team managed to make it back up to the docking bay where a few of the warships were still being prepared. They had to kill a couple low-level Guardians and stash the bodies, but in the end, they found their way onto one of the owls. Well, more accurately, they emptied out a crate of magekiller rounds that they found and crawled inside. Eventually, they were loaded aboard one of the warships and left in the rear compartment.

The space was obviously cramped with the three of them shoved in together, but there wasn't much that could be done to make them more comfortable. They were just lucky that no one had caught them yet.

"I think I'm going to throw up." Easton started breathing heavier.

"Don't you dare?" Becca pushed him away.

"Don't you aim him at me?" Harlow shoved her tennis ball into his cheek.

"Sorry, but all I can smell is blood." He gagged. "You both pretty much bathed in it before we got in here."

Becca ran a hand across her face, brushing off flakes of dried blood. "Sorry, just try to keep it together. I am not riding all the way back to Vegas sitting in a pool of your vomit."

"How long will it take?" Harlow asked.

"A few hours. We just have to stay hidden until then." Becca tried to tuck her legs closer to give the others room. "Once we get close to home, we'll jump out and kill everyone aboard."

"Oh wow, more murder, surprise." Easton chuckled.

Becca glowered at him as Harlow let out a low growl.

"Sorry." The werewolf lowered her head.

"What's it like?" Becca asked, hoping Harlow had some kind of insight into the life of a monster.

"The wolf?" Harlow cracked her neck. "It's helpful, but I don't let it out all the way very much. The healing and strength are great but, obviously, there's a downside."

"Losing control?"

Harlow let out an almost silent laugh. "No, it's only hard to control at first. A few months after turning, you learn how to keep the wolf in. Then you can just bring it out little by little when you need it. Like when you need some more endurance, or you need to heal a wound. I haven't gone all out for months. I only did back there because I knew you were there to keep me from getting distracted."

"Distracted?" Easton laughed silently, bumping Becca with his shoulder. "Is that really the biggest thing you have to worry about?"

"Quite so, actually." She sighed. "The trade-off for using the wolf is that the more you bring it out, the dumber you get.

It literally lowers my intelligence in accordance with how much of the wolf I let out. Hence, the tennis ball."

"And if you never let the wolf out?" Becca asked.

"Eh." Harlow shrugged. "Mostly I'm fine throughout the month. Though, the full moon does strengthen some of the more base urges."

"To kill?" Easton leaned away, clearly realizing how full the moon was.

"No. Nothing that harsh." Harlow hesitated before adding, "A shag helps, though."

Becca suppressed a snort, caught off guard. The woman had been quiet for most of the time she'd known her. Apparently, the full moon lowered her defenses a little. Who would have thought that becoming a werewolf would actually help in social situations? Becca lowered her chin to her knees, wishing she could have been bitten by something else.

"Sorry about your friends." Easton brought a somber mood back to the crate they sat in. "What were their names?"

Harlow shrugged again. "I'm sure Ozzie and Leon are fine. Going out in a blaze of glory is sort of their thing. I have seen them come back from worse situations, at least."

"I hope you're right." Becca felt a little better.

"Hopefully we can make it out of this situation too," Easton added, gesturing to the crate around them.

Becca reached out with her senses to check on their surroundings.

The craft was some kind of assault ship, leaving little room in the passenger compartment. Most of it was taken up by the detachable cargo box on the back. Becca assumed it was full of modified revenants that could be deployed when they reached Vegas.

The inside of the ship only had room for a few Guardians. From her angle, she counted five. Pushing on her senses, she found the heartbeat of a sixth enemy standing out of view. She was also able to confirm that the rear container was full of revenants.

It wouldn't be hard to take the ship, but they would have to move fast.

Besides the Guardians, most of the compartment was taken up by ammunition and a system to load the craft's guns from the inside. Apparently, it was meant to fire magekiller rounds by the thousands.

Becca shuddered, remembering what just one of those bullets had done to Mason. An ache streaked through her chest as soon as she thought of him.

What was she going to say to him?

How could she possibly explain everything?

Should I even try?

After everything that had happened that night, there was one thing she was sure of. She wasn't safe to be around. Becca glanced at her HUD and brought up her status to take her mind off things.

STATUS

Name: Rebecca Alvarez

Race: Vampire

Fool Class: Temporary Account 1

Mana: 450/450

Mana Composition: Unbalanced

Current Level: 32 (2,928 experience to next level.)

ATTRIBUTES

Constitution: 50

Defense: 45

Strength: 44

Dexterity: 48

Agility: 45

Intelligence: 52

Perception: 76

Will: 46

Overall, her stats were mostly the same as they had been

back when she had been a Heretic. The only difference was the fact that her mana had jumped up due to the temporary growth she'd gained from feeding.

Willing the Guardian Core to show her more, she found the spell that the Fool's caretaker had given her to save Digby.

TRANSPLANT SPARK
Description: Transplant a spark from the caster to another person.
Cost: 100 MP + 1 Spark
Limitations: This spell will call to the surrounding ambient mana to form a tether between the caster and the target. Once cast, the spark of the caster will travel across the tether to take root within the mana system of the target. This process may take several minutes and cannot be canceled. The recipient of a transplanted spark will retain their sense of self throughout this process. Upon completion, the caster will cease to exist. *The cost of this spell is high but the choice to use it is yours. No one can make it for you.*

The bottom fell out of Becca's stomach as the words that the caretaker had displayed on the monitor earlier suddenly made sense.

I'm sorry.

That was what the screen had said. The caretaker had given her a spell that would kill her. No, it was worse than that. If she died, she would at least return to whatever version of the afterlife that she had visited before, but with this, she would literally cease to be. Her existence would be erased and overwritten by Digby's mind when her soul became his.

It was horrible.

Obviously, she had to use it.

The realization hit her like a truck, shocked that she hadn't even questioned it. There was no choice. Digby was important, but that wasn't really why. No, it was her. The spell was her way out. It was the solution to all of the fears that had been building up since she'd been reborn as a monster. Deep down, she'd always known that going home was never an option.

Not after what she'd become.

She was dangerous. That was the truth that she couldn't deny. She was a fucking vampire. What was she going to do, just pretend that she wasn't? Was she going to go back to Vegas and tell Mason that she loved him? Tell him not to worry about it? Would she be able to be the family that Hawk needed?

Of course not.

If she lived, she would have to leave. That was the only way to keep everyone in Vegas safe. She knew that much. Not that they would ever understand. Hawk would surely see her as just another person that had abandoned him. Mason would almost certainly try to convince her to stay. Hell, he might even succeed. If he did, there was a chance she'd end up killing him.

Then there was Digby; he would never let her go. He knew what it was like to be a monster, but he could replenish his mana far easier. There wasn't much risk of him falling into a ravenous state. It wasn't the same for her. All it would take was a few minutes of using her abilities and she would murder the first person in range. Though, that argument would never hold water with Digby. He would just throw a tantrum until she agreed to stay. He'd demand that she take his place if his mind unraveled.

I'll hurt them.

That was the kicker. Becca knew herself well enough to understand that she would cave to everyone else's arguments. They would tell her to stay, and stay she would. She would lie to herself and try to make things work. Then, she'd ruin everything. She wouldn't even be surprised when it happened.

Becca blew out a sigh.

The transplant spell was the only way out. There probably wouldn't even be time to say goodbye. No time for everyone to convince her to change her mind. Alex couldn't drag her back from the dead again. Especially if she no longer existed.

Something about the finality of the spell solidified her resolve.

Becca looked away from the spell's description and stared at the inside of the crate that she hid in.

I just hope everyone can forgive me.

She shook her head. They would be fine. If there was one thing she knew about everyone that she'd surrounded herself with, they were some of the most capable people she'd ever met.

―――――

"More duct tape!" Alex shouted over his shoulder as the Camaro streaked through the sky like Eliot's bicycle in E.T.

"Got it, more duct tape!" Hawk pulled off a long strip from a roll and stuck it to the window where a plastic sheet that Alex had used to replace the broken glass had begun to tear.

The wind howled outside like an angry werewolf as the car flew at nearly the speed of a passenger jet. A section of the roof rattled loudly under the constant air pressure.

"This was a terrible idea. You both realize that, right?" Kristen commented from her place, securely taped to the dash.

"It's too late to go back, we're halfway there." Alex adjusted a pair of goggles that he'd found back in the science museum's lightning exhibit.

Hawk wore a pair on his forehead as well. "The plan has worked so far."

"Just imagine everyone's faces when we get back to Vegas in record time." Alex grinned.

"Yes, because that's a reason to turn a car into an aircraft in entirely unsafe conditions." Kristen continued to be the downer she usually was, despite learning that she had a soul.

Alex shook his head. "You have a point, but I don't think we would have survived the trip back with just the two of us if we tried to take the long way. Besides, not even the flying revenants come up this high. So we shouldn't have anything to worry about. We'll be at home in bed before you know it."

Hawk sucked air in through his teeth. "I really wish you hadn't said that. You know that basically ensures that things will go wrong."

"Agreed," Kristen added. "You have just sealed our fate."

Alex glowered at them both. "I really wish you hadn't called attention to the fact I said that."

"I stand by my earlier comment." Kristen groaned. "This was a terrible idea."

CHAPTER FORTY-SEVEN

"That's right. Come to me." Digby placed his hand against the glass of the front window of the Seahorse's bridge as dozens of dark specks appeared on the horizon. He licked his lips. "Right into my claws."

"You realize you're hissing like a Disney villain." Parker leaned forward to glower at him from where she stood a few feet away.

"I don't know what that is, but I don't appreciate being called a villain," Digby snapped back.

She didn't understand. Even if he had to act like a villain, he was doing it for her and the rest of the people. Autem had to be defeated at all costs.

"It looks like they've stopped." Parker held a pair of binoculars up to her face.

"What?" Digby snatched them, dragging the pink-haired woman a few feet before he realized they were attached to her neck by a strap. After untangling the choking messenger, he held the binoculars up. "Why have they stopped?"

"They see us, sir," one of the other crew members

mentioned. "The armada must have given them reason for pause. I doubt they were expecting it."

"Indeed." Digby smirked. "An armada of flying ships is not something you see every day."

"Plus, they have radar." Parker rubbed at her neck. "They're probably trying to get an idea of what they're up against."

"Alright, we make the first move, then." Digby handed back the binoculars.

Parker took them. "What do you have in mind?"

"We charge. Fire everything we have while moving as fast as we can to stop Henwick from targeting us with his Smite spell." Digby tapped a few of his spider legs in anticipation. "We can use the clouds to obstruct their vision and avoid their gunfire. If that fails, make sure everyone has protection."

Parker grabbed a lantern from where it sat on the console. A thick candle burned inside with a flame lit from the lighter that Hawk had found. More like it had been distributed through the fleet. Digby even had one hanging from the underside of his carapace. If Autem thought their guns would mean anything, they would have another thing coming. The only downside was that everyone had to remove their shoes.

Parker scrunched her toes on the floor of the bridge. She had removed her cloak since its barrier had already been depleted earlier, and it couldn't absorb any more mana during the night.

"What about the horde ship? It's not maneuverable enough to avoid being targeted." She leaned out the door of the bridge to look back at the cargo vessel that held over a thousand of the dead.

"Tell Clint to send out a wave of winged zombies, then retreat back a few miles. I don't want the rest of the horde getting destroyed after everything he and Asher have done to gather them." Digby turned toward the door.

"Where are you going?" Parker jumped out of the way.

"To the bow." He held out his claws. "With one Decay spell,

I can fell even a kestrel, including the squad inside. I want to be in a good position to get a view of my prey."

"Okay, that makes sense." She motioned to follow.

"You stay here." He gestured to the mirrors that were mounted to the wall. "You need to be ready to evacuate a ship if any sink."

She nodded and held back.

Digby grinned. "Good, now give the order to the fleet. Tonight, Autem will learn that the world will not bow to them. They will learn that we will fight back. The war starts now!"

With that, Digby skittered out through the door of the bridge and headed for the front of the ship. It lurched forward as he did, cutting through the clouds. Standing at the bow like a figurehead, Digby held his staff out before him as the ship plunged into the gloom. A gray void surrounded him, lowering his visual range to a mere few feet. It felt like he was the only one left in the world.

Then, a form dropped to the deck behind him, its wings tucking back to fit under a cloak.

Sax.

After crafting a pair of wings for the elite zombie, Digby had ordered him to remain by his side. Considering he had invested so much into him, it seemed foolish not to use the zombie. He made a point to avoid doing so in front of Parker, however. With his sanity the way it was, the last thing he wanted was to bring down any more suspicion.

He just needed to win the battle. After that, it didn't matter what she did. Vegas would be safe and his job would be finished. He'd never wanted to lead anyone in the first place. If Parker revealed his madness after the war was over, then so be it. He would gladly step down and let someone else have a chance. Then he could retire to a little town someplace, where no one would bother him.

Well, except for the ghost of Ames.

Though he hadn't seen the imaginary corpse in a while, there was a chance that he was regaining control over his mind.

Sax let out a moan to pull his thoughts back to the battle that was coming.

Several dozen more zombies flew overhead, their shadows flapping through the clouds. Digby glanced at his HUD.

MP: 349/349
MINIONS:
1 Rejuvenated Zombie, winged
1 Armored Brute
1 Rejuvenated Bloodstalker, winged
50 Rejuvenated Zombies, winged
2 Skeletons

There were another thousand zombies back in the horde ship that he had left in Clint's hands. They hadn't been enhanced in any way yet, but Digby wanted them there for backup. If need be, he could retreat to them and prepare another wave of zombies to send into the fray.

He checked his void contents.

RESOURCES
SINEW: 1147
FLESH: 1131
BONE: 1144
VISCERA: 1131
HEART: 1149
MIND: 1143
SPARKS: 3

"Plenty to go around." Digby let a crooked grin creep across his face. There was enough to rejuvenate his entire horde, and still have enough to give wings to a few hundred more. A part of him still wished that he'd sneaked up to where they were holding the prisoners in Vegas to take those last two hearts he needed.

Well, technically he did try to.

It had been just before he'd prepared the ice for Parker to use to transport the ships. She had been right to ask what had taken him so long. He'd taken advantage of the time he'd been without her watchful eye and marched straight up to those prisoners with full intent of taking their hearts. Ames had cheered him along the entire way, telling him that all he had to do was hide the crime until after the battle.

He'd had a change of heart the moment he reached their floor.

It wasn't that he'd suddenly found his conscience or silenced his madness. No, he'd just found a better use for the men. Sometimes people were worth more than the sum of their parts. The hearts would have to wait.

Digby grinned.

Looking away from his HUD, he locked his eyes on the clouds in front of him. The gloom enveloped him, leaving nothing but the railing in front of him visible. The only sound was the wind as the ship sliced through the sky, moving at half speed to maintain its maneuverability. Thanks to the encounter they'd had with Henwick back on Skyline's base, he knew it was fast enough to avoid being hit with a Smite.

Digby tightened his claws around the railing, trying to let the calm before the storm settle over him. In the end, it only made him more anxious.

"This is it." A whisper came from the back of his mind, reminding him of his madness, like an itch that never went away.

"This is it," Digby repeated. "This is the moment everything I have done has led to."

A wave of excitement crashed into his mind as the sound of aircraft in the distance drifted to his ears. Digby arched his eyebrow as he noticed a chorus of strange hums instead of the sound of engines and propellers.

"Did kestrels always sound like that?"

Before he could question the noise further, a flash of light lit up the clouds, followed by the sound of guns. More flashes followed, streaks of white-hot lead tearing through the clouds. Digby ducked and braced himself, only to relax a second later when the hail of bullets failed to hit anything.

"They're firing blind." He rose back up with a laugh.

The gunfire continued as they approached, passing by them but never coming closer than fifty feet.

"That's right! Keep firing! See what good it does." Digby stood with arms out wide as the ship headed straight toward the gunfire, the clouds flashing with a hundred flickering lights. Spotlights shined toward him, failing to penetrate the fleet's cover. A cackle rose in Digby's throat, even as a stream of bullets swept across the bow of the Seahorse.

Sparks exploded from the metal all around him but the flame in his lantern pushed away any that may have hit him. Sax stood beside him, holding up a lantern of his own. A hundred holes speckled the deck of the ship, but none had hit anything vital.

"The Minnow is taking fire." Mason's voice came from a radio that Digby had taped to his staff.

"Is anyone hurt?" Parker responded.

"No, the lanterns are keeping the crew safe. But I don't know what will happen if one of the flight enchantments gets damaged." Mason sounded worried.

"Keep to the charge," Digby shouted back. "They are firing blind. But we must strike before they get lucky."

"Understood," Mason responded.

Digby thumbed the button on the radio and gave one more order. "To all ships. Climb, and rend all that get in your way!"

The front of the Seahorse tilted up, the clouds cover growing thinner as the kestrels came into view.

Digby roared into the radio, spraying the speaker with spittle. "Fire every cannon we have!"

A deafening blast came from behind him as the two guns on the front of the ship fired. Several more came from the other ships, orange light flooding the sky. The heavens practically burned as the armada emerged from the gloom, ships spewing fire like dragons soaring through the clouds. A trail of smoke swirled in their wake.

A wave of explosions swept across Autem's imperial fleet. The projectiles detonated against the kestrels. Digby howled in victorious laughter as the sky burned. "That's right, rend them to pieces!"

The Seahorse slipped through the clouds to pass between two of the kestrels. Turning to watch the destruction, a cackle screeched to a halt as a blue shimmer washed over the aircraft beside him.

That was when he noticed the engines.

"What the hell are those?" Digby's mouth fell slack as an explosion dissipated to reveal the undamaged aircraft before him. The attack had started so fast that he hadn't gotten a good look before they started firing.

They were so much larger than the aircraft he was used to fighting.

Not only that, but they lacked the propellers that a kestrel depended on. In their place were some kind of strange engines. Digby squinted to see engravings.

"Magic!" His eyes widened.

They were fueled by mana.

Autem had been doing some tinkering of their own.

Digby raised his radio to his mouth. "Evasive maneuvers!"

The Seahorse veered to the right as the words left his mouth. Two of the strange warships rotated into position to bracket them on both sides before unleashing hell. The angle of the ship protected the propulsion enchantments by moving them out of the line of fire, but it also gave a clear shot at the deck to the craft on the right.

Digby shielded his face with his claws as bullets pelted the ship. A line of destruction traced a path down the deck from nose to rear. Digby turned to watch in horror as every window in the bridge shattered.

Another two of Autem's aircraft got into position to follow the first.

"Dive!" Digby shouted into the radio as another torrent of bullets carved their way through the command ship.

The rod behind him that controlled the ship's elevation dropped down, the crew on the deck below rotating its control wheel. The bow of the ship plunged them back into the cloud cover. Another barrage of gunfire streaked through the night to bite at the command ship's tail before losing sight of them.

"We have injured on the Barracuda!" Jameson reported.

"We need healers on the bridge of the Minnow too!" Mason added.

"Shit! The Angler just lost its rear altitude rod." Another shout came from the radio. "We can't dive."

Gunfire erupted in the distance, the sky flashing like lighting.

"We need evac!" the captain of the Angler shouted.

"I'm on it," Parker responded.

The gunfire stopped a moment later, as if Autem was merely biding its time.

Damage reports came in left and right. Parker had been able to evacuate the crew of the Angler by opening a passage back to Hawaii. For them, the fight was over. Digby caught a dark shape through the clouds above, floating vertically. The Angler's front altitude rod was still keeping it up while the back dangled from it. An explosion rocked the ship a moment later, dropping it back to earth. Digby watched as the vessel sank past him to vanish into the gloom below.

The Orca had lost both propulsion enchantments on her left side, leaving the ship traveling in a wide circle. None of the crew members had been shot, but many had suffered injuries from broken glass. The fact that the protective lanterns required them to walk around in bare feet proved problematic as crew members rushed to sweep the floors.

"Blast!" Digby slammed a clawed fist down onto the railing.

It wasn't supposed to be like this. He had come so far! He had a damn armada. How was that not enough? That was when he remembered that the armada wasn't all he had.

Checking his HUD, he found that most of his winged zombies were still in the air. Reaching out across his bond with the horde, he sent them into action and glanced back to Sax to lead them. "Go!"

The elite zombie took flight as several more winged shadows flew up through the clouds. The aircraft above opened fire only to stop shooting a moment later.

"That's right, it's not so easy to shoot smaller targets." Digby grinned.

He barely got more than a few chuckles out before Autem's fleet responded by dropping half of the compartments that had been attached to their warships. Digby watched as the rectangular boxes fell, their dark shapes plunging into the clouds around him. A second later, parachutes burst from the containers.

Digby leaned over the rail, his mind processing what he was seeing.

"Ground troops! They're releasing ground troops?"

Obviously, Henwick thought this was a good tactic. After all, if Digby's armada was occupied by a battle in the sky, they would be unable to stop a second assault from the ground. The troops below would have a clear path to march all the way to Vegas.

"That's what you think." Digby pulled the radio attached to his staff close. "Drop everything we have!"

The crew of each of each ship jumped into action, rolling barrels of fuel to the sides and kicking them over. Henwick was a fool if he thought his Heretics had not thought of everything. The barrels tumbled down to vanish into the clouds and Digby leaned over the railing in anticipation. Several seconds went by, then came the explosions.

Each barrel had been rigged with a small device design to detonate on impact. One by one, patches of bright orange bloomed below. Digby couldn't see much through the clouds. Only a warm glow as the city of Boulder burned.

He gave thanks to the engineering team that had gotten his

armada in the air. Had they not, they wouldn't have been able to force Autem into battle until they had reached their home. Those troops would have been dropped on their heads. Now, they had to traverse a burning hellscape. Provided they hadn't been caught in the blaze already.

Digby ordered the command ship to climb, not wanting to give Henwick a chance to think.

"Are you sure?" one of the crew responded. "The cannons aren't doing much damage."

"Of course I'm sure," he barked back. "We have far more power than just cannons on our side."

Again, Digby stood at the bow as the ship rose from the clouds. His zombies had landed on many of the aircraft around them with more heading for the rest of the enemy fleet. The dead climbed across the warships, using their wings to blind the windows in the front. The rest of Autem's fleet held their position, unable to shoot the zombies without friendly fire. Much of his horde carried lanterns anyway, making them impossible to target with any form of projectile.

"Yes!" Digby gave the order for the rest of his armada to climb and continue the attack as the Seahorse curved across the aerial battlefield. He cast Decay at the nearest craft, only to frown when his magic had no effect. Apparently, the strange warships had some kind of protection enchantment as well.

"Fine, we'll do this the hard way."

Shifting his focus to one of his minions crawling across the nearest aircraft, he searched his mind for a form that would do the job. His crooked grin returned as one became obvious.

The zombie clinging to the front of the craft paused for a moment, then a pair of limbs exploded from its torso. Hundreds of suction cups formed along the underside of the appendages as they slapped down to the metal surface before stretching out to the sides. Magic or not, whatever engines kept the warships in the air wasn't going to work with a couple of tentacles jammed into them. The spinning sections ground to a halt as the zombie wrapped its appendages around the craft's moving parts.

The warship simply fell out of the sky.

"I knew a little hunting in the ocean would give me something useful." Digby swept his hand across the sky, targeting the closest of his minions, tentacles bursting from one zombie after another. He cast Leach to replenish his mana as more of Autem's aircraft began to fall.

That was when a beam of light came from the largest of the mana-powered kestrels. Digby ducked on instinct even though it wasn't aimed at him. He knew a Smite spell when he saw one. It was a weaker version than the one that came from the sky, but it was still able to wipe him off the battlefield.

Peeking over the rail of the command ship, he watched as the holy light swept across one of his minions. Their tentacles ignited, power pouring from its eyes until its head exploded. The corpse flopped back against the aircraft before tumbling off. Another beam streaked across the sky to burn another minion away before it could do any damage.

"Damn!" Digby narrowed his eyes. The spell could only have come from one man. "Henwick!"

Standing back up, Digby gave the order to charge the source of the beam. The Seahorse veered to the side, curving toward the largest warship. Toward his enemy. Toward the world's enemy.

His minions kept the other aircraft busy as the rest of the armada closed in, their guns blazing. Beams of light continued to pour from the craft at the center of the enemy fleet to stop his horde from felling more of Autem's warships. Still, Henwick was unable to stop them all.

Digby made sure to order his minions to prevent anyone from exiting the aircraft as they fell. None would escape. Kill notifications for entire squads lit up his HUD as well as the occasional level-up. Some had been able to bail out, but not all. He wanted to laugh, but his minions were being wiped out just as quick.

The cannons behind him fired as fast as the crew could load them, the shells detonating against the barriers that surrounded the enemy aircraft. Occasionally, the protective magic would fail, allowing a shell or two to land true. A few of the enemy craft exploded as fire filled the sky.

"See! My armada isn't totally useless!" Digby let out a wild cackle as his ship approached the center of the enemy fleet. "Where are you, Henwick! I'm here for your life!"

His ships fired.

Digby felt the heat as the shells slammed into Henwick's aircraft.

The explosions dissipated to reveal the large craft passing through undamaged, giving Digby a look at it up close. It was nearly five times the size of the other warships, with six of those rotating mana engines. A section of the roof had opened to reveal a platform where Guardians could stand and fight from. A squad of men, dressed in the same knight armor as the ones that he'd fought back on Skyline's base, manned the platform.

At their center stood Henwick.

The man was dressed in the same armor but without a helmet. He stared back at Digby as he poured light from one hand. Another of his minions perished on the other side of the sky. Digby prepared to cast Absorb, expecting his enemy to turn his attention to him, yet he didn't. Instead, he just kept destroying his zombies.

"And people call me a monster." Digby threw out his hand and cast an Emerald Flare as soon as he was in range. It was unlikely to kill the man or damage his aircraft, but it would at least stop him from smiting anything for a few seconds. Then again, maybe he would get lucky and blast the man off the craft.

Henwick jumped back and raised his hand as sickly green energy swam toward him. The power converged into a single point of light, ready to detonate. Then, there was nothing.

"What?" Digby stared down at the man as circles of light surrounded his flare spell.

Henwick merely closed his fist as the glowing spheres snuffed out the explosion. Once it was gone, he turned to lock eyes with Digby as the vessels they both rode on passed each other. Digby stood, the wind blowing through his ragged hair as the scent of smoke filled the hollow of his nose. Henwick lowered his hands to his sides, as if taking a moment to greet him as the Guardians around him fought off a few winged zombies.

That was when Henwick smiled.

Rage flooded Digby's mind as the man grinned at him.

Is he having fun?

Digby squinted as their ships carried them further away from each other.

This is a war. A war for the future of this world. A war that has already cost the lives of so many.

And he's having fun?

Digby was no stranger to a good cackle in the midst of raining destruction down upon those that would stand against him, but he had never sought the fight out. It had just been dropped at his feet. He'd never had a choice.

Henwick hadn't given the world a choice either.

The man's smile made one thing clear. He had to be destroyed, no matter what the cost. Autem could not be allowed to continue. Whatever the price, it must be paid.

Digby raised his radio to his mouth. "I need a passage, Parker."

Before she could respond, a familiar screech echoed through the sky. Digby watched as one of the remaining cargo containers opened at the back of one of Autem's aircraft. The oversized claw of a revenant bloodstalker reached out to grab the side.

"What have you done, Henwick?" Digby stared as a massive winged revenant, complete with a silver breastplate and several other bits of armor, emerged.

From another one of Autem's aircraft, a swarm of a dozen smaller revenants flew out, each adorned with their own armor.

"How are they controlling them?" Digby trailed off as he stepped away from the rail, shaking his head. "No, it doesn't matter. Nothing changes, there's still a path for victory."

With a thought, he willed his horde to defend the armada as more revenants poured from Autem's fleet. He had to stay in the fight, just a little longer. Spinning, Digby skittered back toward the bridge, only for a bloodstalker to land directly in his path.

"I do not have time for this," he groaned before holding up his staff and shouting into his radio for Parker to open a passage.

All she responded with was a rushed, "Give me a minute!"

Digby stepped back to dodge a swipe from an oversized hand, his eight legs carrying him to stay out of reach. The bloodstalker dragged its claws across the deck, gouging several deep lines into the wood until it hit the metal underneath. A screech came from above as one of the smaller revenants swooped by to slam into one of Digby's flying zombies. The pair fell to the deck, biting at each other behind the blood-stalker.

The massive creature ignored them, keeping its attention on Digby.

"I've got a good mind to cut you to pieces with my wraith." Digby tapped one leg on the deck, debating on it. Instead, he shifted his attention to the zombie that had fallen to the deck and poured mana and resources into it. "Better to craft more support." He looked back across the sky as scores of revenants attacked his ships. "I have a feeling I'm going to need it."

The winged zombie shuddered and spasmed for a moment before kicking the smaller revenant away, its body snapping and popping. This time, Digby willed it to take a new form. First, he applied his necrotic armor to the minion. Its bulk grew as slabs of flesh encased it. Then several meaty tentacles burst from its back. Its wings suddenly were a little small now that the monster had grown. The result left the beast looking a little ridiculous. Each time it tried to fly, it only made it a few feet into the air before dropping back down.

Silly looking or not, appearances didn't stop the new monster from grabbing hold of the common revenant nearby and crushing its head in a fist. Dropping the corpse, it turned to the bloodstalker.

"Deal with that, would you?" Digby skittered to the side as his minion lunged for the massive revenant. He leached a bit of mana from the monster as he left.

On his way back to the bridge, he passed one of the crew members that was still fueling the propulsion enchantments on one side of the ship. They held their ground even as his minion fought a bloodstalker further up on the deck. It was only a matter of time before Autem's flying units swooped down to pick them off. Once that happened, the ship would slow down enough for Henwick to smite them out of the sky.

"We need evac!" Jameson called over the radio.

Digby stopped just before entering the bridge to look back at the other ships, finding the Barracuda dead in the sky. Squinting, he could make out the men on the deck fighting with a group of revenants.

"Bloody hell." Digby watched as they were forced to fall back to the bridge. A brief glimpse of someone with pink hair told him why Parker hadn't opened his passage yet. She was too busy rescuing the crew from the doomed vessel.

The crew members disappeared into the bridge just as a swirl of white energy began to form in the sky above the ship. Digby held his radio to his mouth.

"Get out of there, Parker. A smite is incoming!" He couldn't risk her getting caught in the blast. Not when he still needed her.

"Not when you still have plans for her," Ames whispered in his ear.

"Shut up," Digby snapped back.

The sky opened up, the light swirling as a beam of light the size of a building poured down through the Barracuda. Digby felt several of his minions burn, having been caught too close to the blast. He made a point to close down his bond with the dead before any of the spell bled back to him across the link. The ship at the epicenter exploded in a burst of holy light, its hull snapping in two before falling out of the sky.

Digby ducked into the bridge of the command ship and raised his radio. "Tell me you got out before that spell hit, Parker."

"Yeah, barely. I got back to the horde ship with the crew." Her tone fell with each word.

"Good, now come and get me," he snapped back. "I need to reach the horde ship as well."

"I'm working on it," she responded as another one of their ships began to slow. "I have to get more people to safety first. I'll get to you when I can."

Another bloodstalker swooped down to the deck to land just outside the bridge. Digby threw a hand out toward it, casting Summon Echo. The flickering image of his wraith streaked across the creature, spraying the window of the bridge with crimson. The bloodstalker slammed a fist through the glass a second later. Blood spurted from a wound on its throat as the flesh knit itself back together. Its fingers clawed at whatever it could grab, getting a hold of one of Digby's spindly legs.

Bracing against the equipment on the bridge, his leg tore from his body with a sickening pop. Before the bloodstalker could reach in again, Digby's new minion slammed a tentacle into it, sending it rolling across the deck, close to where one of the crew members continued to feed mana to one of the front propulsion units. The man looked back at the fight in terror, like he might abandon his post to flee. If that happened, Henwick was sure to smite them out of the sky the moment they slowed.

"We must stay moving!" Digby rushed out through the door of the bridge, calling to Sax as he rushed to aid his crew.

He opened his maw and cast forge the instant he was in range, sending a massive spike of blood up through the over-sized beast's chest. The creature flailed as the formation of blood pushed it over the side of the ship. Digby spent the extra mana to snap the spike in half once the revenant was clear of the rail. The beast fell screaming.

"Hold your positions!" Digby shouted to the crew that were funneling mana into the ship's propulsion enchantments. "If we slow, we're done for."

For a moment, the men seemed to find their resolve. Then another ten revenant nightflyers landed on the bow. An explosion immediately took out half of the swarm, sending limbs and wings flying across the deck. Sax flapped by overhead, dropping down behind Digby and ejecting a spent grenade shell from his launcher. He reached for another but found his supply empty. The zombie simply groaned and dropped the weapon.

Smoke wafted across the deck as a portion of it burned, more revenants landing. Their armor glinted through the billowing black clouds.

"Some time today, Parker!" Digby growled into his radio, just as another beam of holy light engulfed the Minnow not far away. The vessel must have lost its propulsion as well and slowed enough to be targeted.

"I'm trying," she responded, sounding desperate and out of breath. "I almost didn't make it out of that last one."

"She got the whole crew though," Mason added, apparently having made it back to the horde ship with her.

Digby looked out across the sky, finding the Orca still circling the battlefield with its damaged propulsion enchantments. Other than the Seahorse he was on, it was all that was left beyond the horde's vessel floating a few miles away. They were out of options.

All but one.

Digby reached out across his bond to make sure one of his minions was in position. It was too far away to get a clear response. All he could feel was a vague yet positive attitude. That was enough. He knew his minion well enough to know what that meant.

We're good, bro.

Digby grinned; there was still a chance to win. He just needed to make a move. It was sure to bring everyone's judgment down upon him but it was the only move he could make. Everyone would just have to live with it.

That was when an explosion came from the Orca.

A familiar voice reported back over the radio. "We just lost the bridge, the captain is down."

Digby cast a flare at the growing crowd of revenants on the bow to keep them at bay before running to the rail for a better look at the vessel in distress. "Who is this?"

"Ah, this is John," the familiar voice responded. "I'm… one of the artificers you helped level up. You know the one that you kept forgetting the name of?"

"Yes, I know who you are." Digby watched the Orca.

The ship was still moving at full speed despite the entire bridge being engulfed in flames. Actually, it looked like its path was evening out.

"I've repaired one of the damaged propulsion enchantments. But the mirrors have been destroyed," John added.

"Can you find another surface to—" Parker started to ask.

John cut her off. "There isn't time. Get Graves to safety. We're going to buy you another minute."

Digby watched as the ship began to turn, heading straight for the aircraft at the center of Autem's fleet. Straight toward Henwick.

"But…" Parker tried again.

This time, Digby interrupted her as the ship cut through the clouds toward the heart of the enemy fleet. "He's right, damn it. There's nothing you can do."

Every craft in the sky opened fire on the Orca, filling the sky with the light of one hundred thousand bullets. The flying battleship continued onward, cutting through the clouds. For a moment, it looked like they might slam into Autem's command ship. Then it began to slow, clearly losing the last of its propulsion enchantments, or the Heretic that powered it.

The Orca drifted a few hundred more feet before explosions

rocked the ship. It fell, burning, into the sea of clouds below. The orange glow of the flames illuminated the gloom as it slipped into oblivion. Then it was gone.

There was no time to lament its loss before a scream echoed from the rear of the Seahorse. A glance to the side showed him one of his crew members being picked up by a revenant as it flew away. The creature carried him for a short distance before dropping him. The ship began to veer to the side a moment later.

"Blast! We've lost one of the rear enchantment operators." Digby stepped away from the rail, his seven remaining legs click-clacking on the deck.

Another group of nightflyers landed on the bow, the swarm pushing forward as Sax threw fireballs at them in a futile attempt to drive them back.

They were out of time.

"I need a passage, now!" Digby beckoned to the two crew members that were still standing at the front propulsion units. "It's time to go!"

With that, the crew abandoned their posts and fell back to the bridge. Digby led the way with Sax watching his back. Once inside the bridge, he opened his maw and cast forge to raise a wall of blood to replace the broken window. The makeshift barrier wouldn't last long, but it would grant them a few more valuable seconds.

The rest of the crew that still lived converged on the bridge to stand by the mirrors, waiting for a passage. Once they were all together, Digby sealed the bridge door as well. Outside, the revenants pressed themselves against the glass that was still intact, blotting out the view of Autem's fleet. Some of the creatures licked at the blood wall that covered the door. Others banged their heads against the remaining windows, the glass spider-webbing out from each impact.

They would break through any moment.

Digby debated sending Sax out and turning him into something bigger, but he refrained. A look at his HUD told him his current horde was dwindling. If he was still going to have a shot at winning, he was going to need backup, and he couldn't send the zombie to its destruction yet.

Parker burst into the bridge through the rippling surface of one of the mirrors a second later. Blood trailed from the pads of her bare feet and her lantern was missing. She skidded to a stop as soon as she saw the revenants pressed up against the cracking glass. "Mother shit fuck!"

"Yes, it's all very terrifying." Digby shoved at one of the crew members practically throwing him through the mirror. "Now, everyone out!"

"Come on." Parker made sure to get out of the way as she beckoned everyone to her passage.

Gunfire flashed from someplace outside as the entire ship seemed to vibrate from the impact of a few hundred bullets. Digby checked his HUD.

MINIONS:
1 Armored Brute
11 Rejuvenated Zombies, winged
2 Skeletons

He'd lost most of his flying zombies. Without them, nothing was keeping Autem's aircraft from firing on them. A torrent of gunfire lit up the night an instant later to carve a path straight down the deck toward the bridge.

"Move!" Digby swiped one of his legs out to hook it around Parker's body to yank her close enough for his lantern to protect her from the projectiles.

The messenger fell forward against him just as a dozen bullets tore through the roof. The rest of the crew held their ground, each still carrying a lantern of their own.

"Ignore the bullets." Digby jabbed a finger at the mirror. "Get through the passage."

Another one of Autem's aircraft passed by, unloading their guns into the ship. Streaks of white-hot lead filled the bridge, curving to the side whenever they came too close to anyone carrying a lantern. Broken glass sprayed everyone, tearing at flesh and covering the floor. The crew winced as they ran for the mirror, their bare feet leaving a trail of crimson.

The only saving grace was that the hail of bullets had also killed some of the revenants outside. The severed hand of a random crew member flopped to the floor as one of the mirrors shattered just before they made it through the passage.

"Shit!" Parker dropped down to pick the hand up so it could be reattached later. "We need to get to the backup mirror down the hall."

Of course, that was when a glow of holy light began to shine from above.

"No!" Digby locked his eyes on the broken windows.

The revenants outside regrouped and began crawling in through the shattered windows as light shined above them. One of the creatures grabbed hold of a member of the crew. A second crew member who had been manning the front propulsion enchantments ran to his aid, casting a fireball at the revenant to try to force it away.

"Go!" Parker pushed Digby away from her. "You have to get through and figure something out."

"I'm not leaving you here, your magic is too important." He grabbed her wrist.

"And I'm not leaving until everyone is out." She wrenched her arm free. "There's still time, so get the fuck out of here." Parker shoved at his bulbous spider body.

"I will not leave you!" Digby shouted back as he threw a hand out at the revenants and cast Decay.

They shrank back for an instant, just long enough for him to catch sight of one of his winged minions fighting on the deck beyond. Digby reached across his bond to command the monster.

"Fly!"

The zombie spread its wings as Digby poured resources into it to increase its size. The monster took flight, straight up toward the holy glow above. Then, Digby dumped the contents of his void into the beast.

Members of the crew braced for death as the holy glow above grew, knowing there wasn't enough time to make it to the backup mirror. Confusion fell across everyone's faces as the light suddenly faded.

"What. Happened?" Parker looked up just as a tentacle slapped down onto the deck.

It was followed by another and another as Digby let his resources flow into his minion above. A howl of protest roared through the sky, his minion taking Henwick's smite head on, the same way another of Digby's minions had done back on Skyline's base. Except, this time, it needed to do more than just buy them seconds. It needed to take the whole blast.

Digby's resources plummeted as massive tentacles filled the deck to blot out the light. They wrapped around the ship like an octopus claiming its prey, forming a cocoon of necrotic tissue. The revenants outside fell beneath the weight of the monster's limbs. One after another the creatures burst under the pressure.

Shafts of holy power pierced through to burn into the deck. The zombie kraken let out a screech of pain as the scent of burning corpses filled the air.

"Run! We don't have much time!" Digby shoved the nearest crewmember down the corridor at the back of the bridge that led to the backup mirror before rushing down himself. "He stopped as soon as he reached it."

"Hurry up and go first." Parker shoved him toward the mirror as it began to ripple. "The spell will cancel if I go through. I have to go last."

"No, you go and reopen it from the other side," Digby argued as he pushed a random crew member through, tempted to do the same to her. He probably would have if he didn't need to escape as well.

"This is not the time to argue." Parker put her foot down as a few more crew members fled the bridge.

"Fine," Digby growled back. "But don't dally."

A revenant screeched from the other end of the corridor from where they came. One of them must have made it inside. Parker pulled one of her daggers from its sheath and went to help the rest of the struggling crew members. As much as Digby wanted to drag her back through the passage with him, she was already out of reach. All he could do was run and hope she made it too.

He plunged into the mirror, emerging from another mounted on the bridge of the horde ship. Gone were the sounds of battle that had surrounded him a moment before. In their place was only a distant rumble miles away. Sweeping his gaze in the direction of the battle, all he could make out was a shining pillar of light on the horizon.

Outside the bridge, the Heretics that had crewed his now-fallen armada stood along the rails, watching and waiting for someone to tell them what to do next. Lana ran between them, healing the wounded. It was hard to believe that they had been in the middle of a battle mere seconds before. It all seemed so far away.

Digby narrowed his eyes at the specks on the horizon.

Autem's fleet wasn't that far away, only fifteen minutes. It would be heading their way soon.

"Not if I can help it," Digby whispered to himself. "Now where is that messenger?" He spun back to the mirror, waiting for Parker to step through.

She didn't.

The only person that did was Sax's zombified corpse. Turning back toward the specks in the distance, the light grew, like a star falling from the sky.

"No!" Digby rushed back to the mirror.

He couldn't wait for her any longer.

"Parker!"

He prayed that he could make it in time.

If anything happened to her, all would be lost.

CHAPTER FORTY-EIGHT

"Let go, you bat-faced asshole!" Parker stabbed at a revenant that was trying to drag one of the Seahorse's crew members back toward the bridge.

The creature screeched in protest but let go of the man regardless. He dropped to the floor as soon as he was free, the other remaining crew members struggled to help him up.

Light shone in from the bridge as the necrotic cocoon Digby had left behind began to burn away under Henwick's Smite. The revenant that Parker had just stabbed began to sizzle as the power of the spell reached the corridor. It let out a scream before running straight past her to hide deeper in the ship.

That was when an explosion rocked the vessel.

The bow dropped. They must have lost their front altitude control rod. Parker grabbed hold of a pipe that ran along the wall to keep from falling into the light that poured in through the bridge.

"Come on." She focused on the only thing that she could do anything about, ducking down to help an injured crew member up.

He stumbled back down, taking her with him. She slapped a

hand down to the floor to catch herself. A shard of broken glass from the bridge's windows sliced through her palm. She already had about a dozen cuts on her feet from walking around without shoes. Parker ignored the pain and pushed herself back up. She threw a hand out to the crew member that had knocked her over.

Another crewmate stepped in to help. "You go first."

"Cut the gentleman bullshit." She shook her head. "The passage closes when I pass through, so get your ass in…"

She trailed off as the last of Digby's zombie kraken burnt away, allowing light to flood the corridor. It was like God had shined his high beams right in her eyes.

"Oh no."

The glass covering the floor began to float into the air. The two crew members beside her shielded their faces. There wasn't time to react before the air itself began to burn. Even if she'd had the time to turn back to the passage and run, she could barely see where it was. No, all she could make out were the silhouettes of the two men she was with. For a moment, it felt like every bone in her body was on fire.

Then, she was falling.

No, not falling.

Being yanked backward.

The light vanished as she landed on a hard surface. The sound of an explosion came from someplace in the distance. Blinking her eyes, Parker struggled to see her surroundings. It wasn't until she heard the click-clack of Digby's arachnid legs that she realized where she was.

The horde ship.

"Wait." She spun toward the sound, her eyes still getting used to the darkness of the night after being engulfed in the holy light of an incoming smite. "There were still two people back there."

"There wasn't enough time to get anyone else." Digby's voice came from a figure vaguely shaped like him.

"But you trapped them when you pulled me through."

Parker rubbed at her eyes, still seeing the silhouettes of the two men she'd left behind imprinted on her vision.

"Hold on." Lana's voice came from beside her as Parker felt someone take her by the hand. "You need a heal."

A sharp pain came from her palm, probably a piece of glass being removed. Her vision started to return to normal as Lana pulled another few pieces of window from her feet. She cast a heal as soon as there was nothing left to prevent the spell from repairing the damage.

The fire inside her swelled like she might burst into flames. The pain blended with the throbbing in her head, making it hard to tell where any of it actually came from. It faded back to a dull ache as soon as the healing spell had run its course. Parker blinked and rubbed her eyes before finally finding Digby standing behind her.

"Why didn't you grab the others before yanking me through the—"

She gasped as soon as she saw him.

The zombie was missing much of the skin on half his face, leaving parts of his skull visible. Most of his hair was gone as well. Just a few wisps were hanging from the section of his face that had been replaced with bone. A blackened form extended from his shoulder, barely resembling an arm. It was elongated, as if he'd used his body craft to extend the limb to reach through the passage and grab her. Two of his spider legs had been completely burnt off.

"As I said, there wasn't time to save anyone else." Large chunks crumbled from Digby's arm as he moved it. "I couldn't withstand that spell any longer than I did."

"Oh." Parker watched as he tore at his shoulder with the undamaged claws of his other hand, eventually ripping the entire limb off.

Lana gagged and excused herself as a new formation of bone extended from the stump along with tendrils of necrotic flesh. The regeneration stopped as soon as his arm was mostly complete. The skin looked thin and translucent. He didn't bother crafting the flesh to cover his skull or fix the burnt half of his face. Apparently, he was conserving resources.

"Come, Parker." The necromancer turned toward the bridge. "Autem's fleet will be here soon and we have work to do."

She nodded, not knowing what else to say. He was right. They had to evacuate the horde ship as well, then get the last of the people in Vegas to Hawaii before Autem arrived. Her chest felt hollow and sore. She had only just begun to think of Sin City as home; the thought of abandoning it hurt more than she'd expected.

Digby stopped as Clint walked onto the deck followed by a horde of at least fifty common zombies.

"I think this is enough to slow down the Guardians' fleet." The other necromancer stepped aside as if handing over control of the horde to Digby.

"It will have to do." He gave Clint a nod before walking into the center of the horde.

Parker watched as his spindly legs carried him through the crowd, a full two feet taller than the rest of the zombies. Once he'd reached the middle of the horde, he raised both hands. A wave of emerald energy swept through the group, radiating from him. Parker recognized it as a control spell. The demeanor of the surrounding monsters changed immediately, like they were suddenly more focused.

Digby continued to hold his hands out as trickles of power began to flow back to him from each member of the horde. Seconds later, the entire crowd began to twitch and shudder, their bodies filling out. The monsters' gaunt faces remained gray but somehow healthier. The slender limbs of each individual zombie gained the bulk of the average gym rat. A few that were missing shirts even gained abs that would have made most people jealous.

Then came the wings.

One by one, bones burst from the backs of the horde, extending as flesh and skin covered the formations. Parker couldn't help her mouth from hanging open at the sight of all fifty zombies spreading their wings at once.

Asher cawed into the night from a place perched on a rail as mana flowed from her to Digby.

"Go forth!" He thrust a hand out toward the fleet in the distance. "Do all within your power to slow our enemies' approach."

With that, the horde took flight all at once, filling the sky with dark wings. The crew members that Parker had rescued from the fallen ships all watched with fear and awe in their eyes.

Parker tried to do her part. "Everyone, come to the bridge, we'll get out through the mirrors."

"Cancel that." Digby lowered his arms.

"What?" Parker snapped her vision to the necromancer's half-burnt face. "But Autem will be here soon."

"Good." A chuckle rolled through Digby's throat. "Let them come. I will be ready for them."

"We can't fight them." Parker walked toward him, the deck of the ship cold against her bare feet.

"We don't have to." The mangled zombie turned to her and tapped one of the bare patches of his skull. "I have a plan."

"A plan?" She screwed up her eyes. "When in the hell were you going to tell me?"

"When I was ready," he snapped back as he continued toward the bridge.

Parker let out a frustrated growl and rushed after him. "We should get the crew to safety first anyway."

"No time. Why do you think I sent out more minions? I need every minute I can get. And most of all, I need you." He ducked into the bridge, squeezing his bulbous spider body through the door without looking back to make sure she was still with him.

"Me? What do you need me for?" Parker followed, stopping as soon as she entered behind him.

The bridge of the horde ship was a long but narrow room, with a row of consoles lining the front window. A pair of mirrors were mounted to the back wall bracketing the entrance of a corridor. Another mirror was affixed to the wall further down the corridor as a spare in case the others were broken. Asher flapped in to land on a control panel on the far end. She let out a quiet caw to her master.

"I need your magic." Digby stopped at the mirrors and held a compact out toward Parker.

She hesitated before reaching for it. "What do you want?"

He stepped closer, his half-burnt heat towering over her. "I need you to open a mirror link."

"Okay, to where? I have a list of every surface I've touched." She looked down at the compact.

"This mirror isn't on your list." He turned away.

"But I can't cast the link spell if I haven't come into contact with both surfaces."

"I want you to open a link using Bancroft's pocket watch." The zombie stood with his back to her.

Parker furrowed her brow at the strange request. "But I haven't touched it."

"Yes, you did." Digby glanced back over his shoulder. "I made sure to ask you to hand the watch to me days ago before I banished him. Knew you couldn't resist opening something shiny."

"SHINY!" Asher cawed from her perch.

Parker thought back to earlier in the week. She had, in fact, touched Bancroft's pocket watch. Of course she had; it was neat. She shook her head. "Why not just ask me to touch the watch? Why ask me to hand it to you? Why be sneaky?"

Digby groaned. "We don't have time for questions."

He wasn't wrong. Autem would reach them soon, and Digby's plans had saved them more than once. Even if they were usually unorthodox.

She started to understand. "You didn't banish Bancroft. Did you? You sent Tavern on a mission."

"Indeed." He smirked. "One that I felt necessary to keep a secret. Not even Bancroft knew. I explained it to Tavern while the man slept. Tavern wasn't to relay the information to Charles until they were well on their way."

"Okay." Parker nodded and cast the spell.

The mirror in her hand immediately lit up with an image of Bancroft's face, as if he had already been standing there waiting. The man looked like shit. Like he had just traveled through hell and back.

"Hello?" Parker stared at his blank expression.

"Sup." A dark voice came from Bancroft's mouth.

"Tavern?" Parker looked up at Digby. "What's going on?"

"Show her," the zombie commanded his minion on the other end of the link.

"You got it," Tavern responded through Bancroft as Parker looked back down to see the view shift to show a large mirror, like one that you would find in a public restroom. Though, the wall behind it wasn't tile, as if it had been moved.

Parker raised her head from the compact. "Where are they?"

"Give her a tour." Digby chuckled.

She dropped her eyes back down to see the view shift again. Bancroft held his end of the link up and swept it around the room he was in. She recognized it in an instant. "How?"

Parker's mind crashed into the reality of where they were. She had only ever seen the room from one angle. The desk, the curtains, the carpeting. It would have been obvious to anyone. She'd seen it at least a dozen times on the news.

The oval office.

"They're in the White House." Parker's heart began to race along with the pounding in her head.

"Yes, I told Tavern to find a place that you would recognize easily." Digby turned around and gestured to one of the mirrors mounted to the back wall of the bridge. "Now open a passage."

Parker cast the spell, caught up in the moment too much to ask. Possibilities ran through her mind as the mirror in front of her began to ripple. With a passage to Washington, D.C., they could reach Autem's capital while their fleet was away. But could they stage any kind of assault with the forces they had left? And could they do it without hurting the people that the Guardians have been gathering as citizens?

That was when Digby called to someone down the corridor. "The path is open!"

Parker looked around, having thought they were alone. Confusion filled her aching mind as two vaguely familiar men emerged from the corridor, carrying a large crate between them. For a moment she couldn't place where she had seen them, then it dawned on her. They were the prisoners. The two men that they had been holding ever since taking over Vegas. They had been members of the high cards that had worked for that jerk, Rivers, who ran the city before they arrived. Under his orders, the two men had strung up innocent people and used them as bait to lure the revenants on the strip into one of the casinos.

There was a reason they were still holding them captive. They were murderers, and nobody knew what to do with them.

"What's going on?" Parker took a step back as the pair of killers carried the crate through the bridge and straight into the passage. "Why are those guys out of their rooms?"

"You'd be surprised by how agreeable people become when you can bestow immortality upon them." Digby held out a hand before closing it into a fist. "Or, more importantly, when you can take it away afterward."

"Why would you even involve them?" she spat back.

"I needed people that wouldn't ask questions." Digby lowered his hand to his side.

"Ask questions about what?" She stepped closer. "What was in that crate?"

He barely looked at her as he answered, "Our salvation."

"What was in that crate, Dig?" She grabbed at what was left of his coat.

He slapped her hand away. "You know damn well what is in there."

Parker staggered back as if his words had punched her in

the gut. He was right. She did know what was in the crate. It was obvious.

The nuke.

That was the only thing it could be, and she had just delivered it to its destination where it could kill everyone that Autem had taken in. People that were only guilty of accepting help from the wrong side. Hell, most had never been given a choice on whether or not to join Autem.

Parker flicked her eyes up to Digby's face. He sneered as if he knew what she was going to say next.

"Tell them to bring it back."

"No." His voice came out cold and emotionless. "I know you don't like it, but it's the only way to protect the world. You of all people should be aware of the horrors that Autem has wrought. They will never stop until they have wiped out any who oppose them. If we destroy their capital, it will strike a blow that they cannot recover from."

Parker shook her head. "I didn't want to believe it."

"Believe what?" Digby stared down at her.

She had seen all the signs, but still, she had tried to deny it. The changes in his behavior. The sudden lack of empathy and boundaries. Everything they had been worrying about was happening. He was the same as Henwick.

"God damn it, I had one job." Parker rubbed at her throbbing head. "I was supposed to stop you if you went too far."

"Don't be so hard on yourself." A sympathetic tone entered Digby's voice. "You were never going to stop me. Why do you think I chose you to act as my conscience?" An unnerving chuckle fell from his mouth. "You were just the easiest to manipulate. Someone like Rebecca would have put up a fight, but you? No, you could never replace her. You would just get overwhelmed by the responsibility and fall apart."

Parker gasped, her legs shaking as he tore away the last shreds of her self-esteem. Her vision blurred through a layer of tears yet still she locked eyes with him. "You're insane."

"Rubbish." He waved away the accusation as if it had been

a casual insult. "I am merely doing what no one else is willing to. Someone has to make the hard choices. That's why I spared you the guilt by not telling you. So that you may still sleep at night."

"What about you?" She lowered her head to the floor.

"I don't sleep." He cackled.

Parker sniffed and dried her eyes on her shoulder. "I never wanted to replace Becca. If you ever thought that I would want to, then you really are lost. That isn't how people work." Her voice quivered as she struggled to find the right words. "I am just me, and I'm trying my best. And if there's one thing I know, it's that I won't let you do this."

Before she had a chance to make a move, the two goons that Digby had sent through the passage to deliver the bomb returned.

Digby stepped aside. "Please escort Ms. Earner from the bridge. She has fulfilled her part."

Parker's mouth fell open. He had dismissed her without even a look. Her heart pounded as her exhausted brain dumped adrenalin into her body to jump-start her fight-or-flight response. Rapid breaths filled her lungs, the scent of Digby's seared flesh hanging in the air.

"Easy now." One of the men held up his hands toward her as he approached. He was the same man that had spit on her back when she and Alex had interrogated him about his crimes weeks ago.

The other stepped to the side as if trying to get around her. "Don't do anything you'll regret, now."

"Shit, I pretty much regret everything I do." Parker closed the passage and recast the spell as she threw herself toward one of the mirrors that bracketed the entrance to the corridor.

The glass began to ripple as soon as she hit it, dropping her briefly into a space of near-infinite possibilities. She locked in on one an instant later, exiting the passage through the mirror that Digby's goons had just exited. From behind them, she flicked her eyes between them to check their levels. They were both level one, a mage and a fighter.

She may not have had any spells to fight with, but that sure as hell didn't mean she was defenseless. She had been dumping all her extra points into dexterity, after all.

Pulling her daggers from her sheaths, she tossed them in her hands to catch them by the blade before winding up, her arms crossed in front of her. Both men turned too slow to do anything. Digby spun as well, a look of shock on his face that she was actually going to stand up to him.

Parker let her daggers fly with every ounce of strength in her barely functioning body. The blades spiraled through the air, impacting butt-first into both of the men's foreheads. They both crumpled to the floor, unconscious. Parker said a silent prayer in thanks to no one in particular that neither of the goons had activated a barrier. At level one, casting spells probably wasn't instinctive yet.

"Are you through?" Digby folded his arms while tapping one of his legs on the floor.

"Nope." Parker gave him her most annoying smirk and reopened a passage as she fell back into the mirror she had just emerged from. She tumbled out from the backup mirror that was positioned further down the darkened corridor. Pushing herself up, she flattened herself up against the wall to hide.

"Do you really think this little rebellion will mean anything?" The sound of Digby's spindly legs, clicking against the floor, traveled down the corridor toward her. "The bomb doesn't have a timer, just a button. All I have to do is think the command and Tavern will trigger the detonation."

"What about Bancroft?" She tried to keep him talking. If there was one thing she knew about Digby, he behaved too much like a villain to resist monologuing.

"What about Bancroft?" The click-clack of Digby's legs grew closer. "I'd say being consumed by a blast that destroys the home of his former masters is a fitting end for that bastard."

"Okay, sure, but how did you even put a detonation button

on the nuke? I seriously doubt you had time to study engineering." She remained where she was, ready to drop back into the mirror.

"One of the men you just knocked out worked for one of this country's defense companies. I knew there was a reason I hadn't eaten his heart already." A brief cackle echoed down the corridor. "That is the last question I am going to answer. I know you are trying to keep me talking. I'm not a fool. Now come out here, before I run out of patience. The bomb has already been delivered. You can't stop me from blowing it up."

"That's what you think." Parker leaned around the corner to see a monstrous silhouette coming toward her, barely human. "You said it yourself, I'm too important. You won't set off a nuke if I'm standing next to it."

With that, she reopened a passage and spun toward the mirror behind her. Her heart sank as a dark figure stood directly behind her, his dead eyes staring through her as he grabbed hold of her neck.

Sax.

Digby must have commanded his minion to circle to another hatch when Parker started to step out of line.

The zombie yanked her away from her passage and threw her up against the opposite wall. Digby was on her in an instant, his arachnid body skittering through the dark corridor. She tried to run, but one of his legs slammed into the wall to block her path. Turning, she attempted to flee in the other direction. Another spindly leg hit the wall inches from her head, hard enough to dent the metal. She turned back to him, tearing a pink lock of hair from her head to leave it dangling from the fibers that covered his leg.

"That's enough, Parker!" Digby shouted in her face, loud enough to spray her cheek with spittle.

Sax's zombified form stood a few feet away from the open passage behind Digby's carapace.

Parker fought the urge to look away. "This is wrong. It's not who we are."

"Of course this is wrong." Digby's voice wavered. "I know you can't understand, but… I am doing this for you. I'm doing this for everyone. Sometimes it takes a wrong to set things right. And I am the only one willing to do it."

Parker glanced passed him at the rippling surface of the mirror behind him. "You may not have a soul anymore, but I am not going to let you throw away whatever is left of who you are."

She dropped to the floor before her final word had left her mouth and kicked off the wall to launch herself through the space underneath him. If he had still been in human form, there wouldn't have been room, but thanks to that stupid spider body he was so proud of, there was plenty of space. Parker slid straight into her passage, the spell snapping shut as she tumbled out onto the presidential seal that adorned the carpet of the oval office.

"Ms. Earner?" Bancroft's voice came from a few feet away.

"Shut the fuck up." Parker sprang back up. "I need to think."

Bancroft sat on an ornate sofa that had been pushed up against the wall. In front of him lay the nuke sitting in the crate. A metal box with a red toggle switch had been stuck to its surface, looking like something that had been cobbled together. There was no way to be sure if it even worked.

"Sup." Tavern's voice came from Bancroft's mouth as the man gave an awkward wave.

"Yeah, hi Tavern." She leaned over to take a few deep breaths, struggling to clear her mind enough to focus on what to do next.

That was when Bancroft, or rather, Tavern stood up.

"Boss says you gotta go."

"Oh really?" Parker rolled her eyes and strolled over to the Resolute Desk that the last several presidents had addressed the country from before everything went to hell. Plopping her ass down on the desk, she leaned back on her hands to get comfortable. "The way I see it, I'm in charge now. And you can relay that to spider zombie on the other end of your bond."

Bancroft stood still for a moment.

Parker arched an eyebrow.

Obviously, the man's animated skeleton was having a mental conversation with Digby through their bond. She wasn't sure how well they could communicate over such a long distance, but it was clear they could get enough across.

Parker cast Mirror Link to make things easier, filling the mirror she had come from with an image of Digby standing in the dark corridor of the horde ship.

"Well?" She crossed her legs.

"Well, what?" Digby shrugged. "You are wasting time. My flying horde can't slow Autem forever and we won't even be able to evacuate. This little tantrum of yours will cost the lives of everyone aboard this ship."

"I don't think so." Parker leaned forward, resting her elbow on her knee while placing her chin in her hand. "Here's what we're going to do. I am going to open a passage connecting the horde ship to this room and you are going to evacuate the crew and as many zombies as you can to here. After that, I'll open another one to take everyone to Hawaii."

"What's to stop me from simply dragging you back here as soon as you open the passage?" The annoyance in his voice was palpable.

Parker leaned to one side, considering her options. "I'll run. The second the passage opens, I will run and hide. You can chase me if you want, but like you said, we are wasting time."

A long moment passed where Digby said nothing, then he blew out a sigh. "I don't want to hurt you, Parker."

She leaned from side to side. "That's good, I don't want you to hurt me either."

"It seems we are at an impasse." His voice grew sullen.

Parker hopped off the desk and walked over to the mirror. "Just agree and I'll reopen the passage."

The necromancer closed his eyes for a few seconds before responding.

"Fine."

Parker got ready to run. It was a good plan. Even if he decided to chase her, he'd only be wasting time. If there was one thing she was confident in, it was her ability to procrastinate, and this was pretty much the same thing. Eventually, he would have to give up and continue the evacuation. They were obviously going to have a talk about not saying mean shit to her, but that would come later.

With a plan in place, she got into a runner's position and cast the spell.

She didn't even make it out of the room.

"Stop." Digby's voice came from behind her as soon as the passage was open.

Panic flooded Parker's mind as her body refused to move, her brain scrambling to understand what had gone wrong. Then, the realization of what was happening slammed into her like a truck. It wasn't her body rebelling against her.

It was her skeleton.

She had thought it odd that she hadn't seen Union around; now she knew why. Digby had taken advantage of her lack of defenses while she was passed out earlier and animated her skeleton.

A dark voice climbed up her throat.

"We apologize."

"Sorry doesn't fucking cover it." Forcing herself, she managed a single step toward the door before running out of strength. Union would have the same physical stats as she did. The only difference was that they didn't get tired, and she was already so very tired. The adrenaline that had been keeping her going began to fade, leaving her with nothing left to fight with.

"I didn't want to do this." Digby's voice came from directly behind her.

"Then fucking don't. You insane ass!" she shrieked back as

she turned around involuntarily. "Do you have any idea how wrong this is?"

Digby stood, looking apologetic. "Now, now, hear me out. I didn't animate your skeleton to control you. I did it to protect you. I wanted to make sure someone was watching over you if I wasn't around."

Her mouth opened on its own to spill out another few words, tainted by darkness. "We protect each other."

"I didn't ask to be protected." She tried to punch the zombie, only to fail when her fist stopped halfway there.

"I don't rightly care what you asked for. I won't let you throw your life away or use yourself as some kind of hostage." He grabbed hold of her shirt and dragged her toward the mirror.

"Nice try, but I'm still in charge here." She canceled the spell just before he smooshed her face into the cold glass.

"Why are you making this so difficult?" Digby pressed her face against the mirror, smearing the reflective surface with tears and snot. "I am trying to save you."

"Are you trying to save me because you want my magic, or because I'm your friend?" Parker fought to keep from falling into the despair that was tugging on her heart.

"Both." He ducked his head while standing behind her as if to keep her from seeing his reflection in the mirror. "Obviously your magic is valuable, but I don't want to lose another friend either. Not again. So please, I am begging you, open the passage."

She smirked. "Eat a bag of dicks, Dig."

The zombie hesitated for a second, glancing to an empty corner of the room, before adding, "Shut up! She will give in. She just needs to be persuaded."

Parker gasped. "What the shit? Are you talking to someone?"

"Alright, fine, I am mad and hallucinating." Digby let out a frustrated growl. "But that doesn't change the fact that I am the only one that can end this war. All I need is a little help from you."

Parker tried to push herself away from the mirror. "And I believe I already told you to eat a bag of dicks!"

"Fine, hate me if you want. As long as I can bring you back to someplace safe, it will be worth it." He grabbed hold of her wrist and forced it up behind her back until it hurt. "Now, open the passage or I start breaking fingers. I can always have Lana put you back together later."

"Do you really think you can torture me to get what you want?" Parker let out a mirthless laugh. "I might be lazy and a little dumb, but if there's one thing I know, it's that I have a will stat way higher than yours. I don't know why, but I'm pretty sure it means you can never force me to do anything. So go right ahead and try."

Digby hesitated before shouting some nonsensical words back at the empty corner of the room. Then he broke her pinky finger.

The pain was barely noticeable. In the last week, she had been shot, concussed, dragged through glass, and endured the most persistent goddamn headache the world had ever known. A broken pinkie wasn't even on her radar.

"I think there's still a few dicks in the bag if you're feeling peckish."

"You can't understand." He breathed the words into her ear sounding like he was causing himself as much pain as her. "You don't know what it's like to have the world depend on you. I have to do what it takes to win. You will see that in the end."

"That's enough!" a furious voice shouted from the other side of the room.

Parker searched the mirror to find Bancroft standing by the nuke, looking like he might explode instead.

The man threw a hand out toward Digby. "You sound exactly like Henwick. Do you not realize that?"

Parker felt the zombie's grip loosen. "He's right, Dig."

"I…" Digby let go of her arm but continued to hold her against the mirror.

"Did you forget about everything that happened to us while we were in the Seed? Everything we talked about. Everything the echoes of Sybil and Henwick said." Parker pushed against the mirror to turn around. "You aren't alone. You never have been."

"Yes." Bancroft stepped closer. "As much as I hate to quote you, Graves, you told me before that a leader is only as good as those that support him." He rubbed at his eyes. "Look, I have obviously had a lot of time to think about things of late, and you weren't wrong."

"And that means listening to people." Parker hit him with the hand that didn't have a broken pinkie. "A leader should listen to everyone. Not just push forward with some kind of single-minded quest for victory. A leader is supposed to have doubts." She hit him again. "That is why Henwick and Autem are the way they are. They have too much faith that they are right and don't even consider the chance that they are wrong." She punched him again, this time letting her fist rest against his chest. "I know you lost your soul and you aren't thinking clearly, but this isn't you, damn it."

"But…" He took a step back.

"You may have made me your conscience because you thought I could be manipulated." Parker wiped at her face with her sleeve. "But I'm going to do my job anyway, and I'm telling you, that you have lost sight of what's right. You can't trust yourself."

Digby placed both hands on his head, shaking it back and forth. "Who can I trust if I cannot trust myself?"

"Me." Parker grabbed hold of his tattered shirt. "You can trust me, and everyone else that cares about you."

"But you're all wrong." He threw his hands out beside him. "You'll all just run away and let Autem have the world instead of doing what it takes to destroy them."

"Are we really wrong?" She leaned her head to one side. "Or are you wrong in thinking that we are?"

"I…" His eyes crossed for a moment before pulling away. "I don't know."

She looked up at the zombie, realizing how upset he looked. As menacing as he had been, now, he just looked broken.

He dropped his eyes to the floor and turned away.

"I thought I could do it." Digby's voice cracked sounding tired and worn. "I still do. I know you're wrong. I know I'm right. I know that setting off that bomb will kill innocent people. But isn't that worth it if it protects our home? I'm sure that's right. I've never met those people. They don't matter." He looked back at her. "Do they?"

"I know you." Parker tried to forget about the zombie that had broken her finger, remembering the one that had always risked everything to save the people he came across. The zombie that wanted nothing more than to run away, yet faced every threat head-on because too many lives would be lost if he didn't. "You aren't a monster. You're kind of a jerk, but you aren't someone that would say a few thousand lives don't matter. You aren't someone that would do this." She held up her hand, showing her pinkie finger only to gag when she saw the angle it was hanging at. "You get what I mean." Parker gestured to the nuke. "This isn't you."

"But if I've lost my way… if I've lost who I am? Then I don't know what to do." His whole body shook. "How can I lead anyone?"

She stepped closer. "Maybe it's time you stepped aside."

"And what? Put you in charge?" He coughed out a musty laugh.

"I don't want that either, but if your missing soul is messing up your ability to lead, then someone has to step in."

"But we'll lose." He looked back at her, his hands pressed up against his head. "I have devoted everything to this war. We have to win."

Parker glanced at the bomb and sighed. "Maybe this just

isn't how the war ends. Maybe there's another way. Wars never really have a winner anyway."

"Then what do we do?" He lowered his hands from his head.

"We survive." She placed a hand on his arm. "And we try to pick up the pieces."

CHAPTER FORTY-NINE

A dying gurgle came from the pilot as Becca dragged him out of the cockpit of the gunship she and the rest of her team had stowed away on. His body went limp, his soul already ripped away. Her maximum mana ticked up another few points.

"Get to the controls!" Easton shouted as he made a point of staying out of everyone's way.

The aircraft began to veer toward another that was in formation beside it. The wing of some kind of flying zombie covered half of the windshield.

"Aye." Harlow slipped past Becca and her victim and into the pilot's seat to pull the gunship back into formation.

Becca swallowed one more mouthful of blood before dropping her prey onto the pile of bodies that littered the rear compartment of the craft. It hadn't taken her long to tear through the gunship's crew. Their levels had only been in the teens. They ended up taking the craft in just a few minutes and without raising any alarms.

As far as the rest of Autem's fleet knew, they were just another aircraft.

"What's the situation?" Becca shook off her blood lust.

"Not a clue." Harlow gestured to the zombie clinging to the front window. "All I know is we've got these buggers all over the craft."

"What are they?" Easton leaned into the cockpit door.

Becca analyzed one since she was the only member of the team with a working magic connection. The Guardian Core filled in the blanks.

Winged Zombie, Enhanced, Uncommon

"Dig must have learned a new way to power up his horde."

From her best estimate, they were a few dozen miles from Vegas. Becca had expected them to get all the way there before the fighting broke out, but Autem's fleet had started shooting early. Becca had debated on jumping out as soon as the battle started but refrained when the gunship they were riding on had begun evasive maneuvers. Probably because of the zombies that were plastered all over it. Instead, she leaned into her senses, listening to the crew's radios.

According to the chatter, the fleet had encountered some kind of armada. As far as how Digby had managed that, she had no idea, but for a while, it sounded like he was doing plenty of damage. At least, he was until Autem started sending out their modified revenants. After that, he had been forced to retreat. Now, the fleet was in pursuit, albeit slowly, on account of the zombies that were getting in the way.

Henwick had ordered the fleet to deal with the flying dead before moving on. Apparently, the zombies had a habit of transforming in a way that was endangering the aircraft whenever Digby got close. Henwick had sounded pretty pissed about it on the comms.

"What's the call?" Harlow glanced back.

"We can't afford to wait for the rest of the fleet to finish killing the zombies and get moving again. We have to try to push through and reach Digby first." Becca squinted into the distance at a single speck on the horizon. Enhancing her vision, she took in what she could. "Holy shit, that's a ship."

"A ship?" Easton's voice climbed with an upwards inflection. "Like a boat?"

"I don't know how Dig got something that big in the air, but I assume Alex had a hand in it." She leaned on the back of Harlow's seat, pulling her fingers away when she saw the smear of blood she left on it. "Either way, we have to make a break for it."

Harlow didn't wait for any more discussion. Instead, she just pulled up, taking the owl above the rest of the fleet. The zombies on the outside held firm.

Harlow leaned to the side to try and see past them. "Oi! Out of the way, you beasties."

That was when a stern voice came across the comms. "Blue seventeen, what are you doing?"

Becca flicked her eyes to Easton. "Stall them. If they figure out we're rogue, they'll shoot us down before we can make it to Digby."

Easton grabbed for the radio. "We're, ah, just getting clear. We've lost visuals and didn't want to risk a collision."

Becca gave him a nod for crafting a plausible explanation.

The voice responded. "Understood. If visuals are impaired, hold position and wait for assistance."

"Understood," Easton repeated before taking his finger off the call button. "That should keep them from giving chase, but not for long."

"Good." Harlow leveled off the craft and sped up toward the ship on the horizon.

The radio called back a few seconds later. "Hold position, blue seventeen."

"Ah, we seem to be having mechanical problems." Easton responded.

"Return to the fleet this instant."

"Um, are we not... doing that?" Easton gave Becca an

awkward glance as he lied. "We should be heading back in your direction, but as I said, our visuals are impaired."

"You are heading in the opposite direction. One-eighty your craft immediately." The voice sounded annoyed.

"Will do." Easton continued to stall. "Turning around now."

"Negative, you are still traveling in the…" The voice trailed off before the line went dead.

"We've been made." Harlow glanced at the radar screen. "A couple owls are coming after us. Probably the ones that don't have any extra passengers." She pointed to one of the zombies flapping its wings against the windshield.

"Well, I tried." Easton buckled himself into one of the seats.

"I don't know if we can make it." Harlow veered to one side as a burst of gunfire lit up the sky beside them.

"Is now a good time to mention we have parachutes back here?" Easton started pulling things from a nearby compartment.

"We might have to bail." Harlow looked back to Becca with an apologetic expression.

"We can't, we won't be able to reach Dig's ship. It could be hours before we can meet up and the battle will be over by then." Becca remembered the spell she had to cast to save him. "I have to get to him first. It's the only way to repair his soul."

"Then you're going to need to learn to fly." Harlow dodged another burst of gunfire.

"That's it." Becca's mind latched onto a possibility. "I need you to get me as high as you can."

"Right." Harlow pulled the craft up again, a view of the moon peeking through the wings that covered the window. "What's your plan?"

"I'm going to do what you suggested." Becca hesitated as the ridiculousness of the idea settled in. "I'm going to learn to fly."

"You can do that?" Easton asked while trying to buckle a parachute on.

"Honestly, I'm not one hundred percent." Becca thought back to the fight in Autem's capitol building. "There was a moment a few hours back, while we were fighting, that my shadecraft carried me through the air. It wasn't really flight, but more like gliding. But I hadn't really done it on purpose, so odds are it's not that hard."

"Right, right, that sounds…" Harlow paused, "like a terrible idea, but if that's all you've got. I'll get you as high as I can, then we'll all bail."

"Somehow I knew we weren't going to get to land like a normal flight." Easton pulled out a parachute for Harlow just as gunfire shattered the front windshield. One of the zombies on the window came loose. An alarm went off in the cabin.

"Oh good, I can see again." Harlow shielded her eyes from the wind. "I think this is as far as we go. So get ready."

"But you still need a parachute." Easton held one of the packs out to her.

"Leave it there. I'll grab it on the way out and figure it out from there." Without another word, she spun the craft and opened fire at the gunships in pursuit.

Wind roared outside as the guns lit up the night. The zombies outside moaned as they began crawling in through the opening.

"Time to go!" Harlow kicked one away.

"Shit shit shit." Easton hit the button to open the ramp and inched toward the opening.

Another burst of gunfire tore through the cabin, filling the space with sparks and bits of metal.

Becca looked back to make sure Harlow hadn't been hit. Miraculously, she was unharmed, but that was more than anyone could say for her parachute. She cringed as she looked down at the barely recognizable bundle. There was no way it was going to be usable. Becca immediately went to grab another but Harlow just shook her head.

"There's no time."

For a second, Becca thought the woman was going to say

something befitting of a noble sacrifice. Then Harlow ran for the ramp.

"I'll meet you in Vegas." She plowed straight into Easton, looping her arms through the straps of his harness.

Easton shouted something as they both fell from the craft, though Becca couldn't make it out over the sound of the wind. It sounded like something along the lines of, 'I hate werewolves.'

Becca shrugged, hoping they would be safe. Odds were, no one would notice them with all the zombies flying around. Making her way to the ramp, Becca looked down into the darkness. As much as she wanted to take a moment to get ready, the gunships in pursuit opened fire.

"Wha!" She let an unintelligible syllable fall from her mouth as she fell off the ramp. The craft detonated a second later, filling her world with fire. Heat licked at her entire body but her vampire healing kept the damage from lingering. The blood-soaked worker's jumpsuit she wore burned for a moment, but the flames went out as she tumbled through the sky.

"What was I thinking?"

Becca struggled to right herself as the world spun. Clouds were above her, then they weren't, then they were again. Burning debris from her aircraft fell all around her.

"Get it together, Becca!"

Forcing her brain to stop panicking, she fed mana into her agility to right herself. Once she had a grip on which direction was up, she let her shadows do the rest. Vampiric instinct took over as a dark form spread out from her back to catch the wind, resembling the wings of a bat. She didn't have much control over them but she sensed that she could master the ability in time.

Of course, that was when she collided in mid-air with a flying zombie.

"What the hell?" she shrieked as the monster moaned in her face.

Tumbling together, she tried to free herself from its grasp.

The zombie made no motion to attack, but it didn't seem to want to let go either.

"Why are you so strong?" She pried at its fingers.

Somehow, Digby must have found a way to restore the strength of the living to his minions. A blast of bats finally forced the monster to release its grip. Falling back first, she flipped herself over again and activated her shadecraft to catch the wind. Seconds later, she was gliding toward Digby's ship, getting closer with each breath.

More figures flapped through the sky around her. Using what little maneuverability she had, Becca tried to stay clear of the other monsters. The last thing she needed was another mid-air collision with one of Dig's zombies. After around thirty seconds of flight, she began to feel more comfortable with what was happening.

"This must be how Asher feels." She fought the urge to smile, remembering the job that waited for her.

If everything went according to plan, Digby's soul would be saved, and she would cease to exist. Now wasn't the time to start enjoying being a vampire. Her thoughts were quickly interrupted by the chittering of one of the winged forms that surrounded her.

"Yeah, yeah, leave me alone," she yelled back at the source, feeling a little too melancholy to deal with another one of Digby's flying zombies.

A chorus of shrieks sounded from all sides as soon as she spoke, revealing the fact that she was no longer surrounded by zombies. No, they were revenants.

"Seriously?" Becca groaned, realizing she'd made herself such an obvious target.

She must have flown far enough away from Autem's fleet to get away from the zombies that were attacking it. In the process, she'd unknowingly glided her way straight into a swarm of revenants that were on their way to attack Digby's ship.

"Hey wait!" Becca shifted her weight as a revenant swooped past her, its jaws snapping. Apparently, the control that Autem had over them was overriding the neutrality that the creatures normally showed toward her.

Another veered close, setting off panic alarms in her head as she realized she didn't have the control over her shadecraft to change directions easily. It was hard enough just to change her heading by a few degrees.

"I swear if I die here after everything else, I am going to file a strongly worded complaint with the first person I meet in the afterlife!"

A gunshot flashed just as the revenant flew within a few feet of her, a bullet tearing through its wing. The creature cried out and flapped away to heal. Becca snapped her head around, searching for the source of the shot. From the trajectory, it came from below her. Looking down, all she saw was an odd shape plowing through the clouds.

Then she heard two familiar voices.

"Hold it steady, I can't shoot shit."

"I'm trying, but I didn't exactly build this thing with the intent to drive it through clouds."

Becca's eyes welled up as Alex's Camaro rose from the gloom. The vehicle was missing its roof and had a flap of what looked like duct tape whipping through the air behind it. The artificer sat at the wheel with his head ducked. Hawk stood in the passenger seat holding on to what was left of the windshield and firing a pistol up at the revenants. The bullets missed more often than not, but honestly, few kids his age could have done better. They both wore a pair of old-timey goggles. Between them, the skull of Kristen the deceased seer was taped to the dash.

"Hawk?" Becca called down, excitement seeping into her voice.

"Becca?" Her brother called back up, his voice sounding like he was about to cry. "I knew I saw you."

Their reunion was interrupted by a revenant snapping at her hand. She yanked it back and leaned to one side to take her into a path directly above the Camaro. Becca cut off the flow of mana to her shadecraft, dropping her straight down onto the trunk. She landed in a crouch befitting the vampire that she was. She just hoped no one would analyze her before she had time to explain.

"How did you get here?" Hawk practically jumped into the back seat to throw his arms around her.

"It's a long story." She hugged him back. "But yeah, someone yanked my soul back to the world of the living. I woke up on a kestrel heading to D.C. Things just got weirder from there." She let go of him. "How are you here? And why did Alex give a twelve-year-old a firearm?"

"We got trapped in Boston and had to modify the car to get back to Vegas." Hawk let go of her.

"Yes, the roof blew away a few miles back," Kristen added. "It has not been a pleasant ride. But what do I know? I'm duct taped to the dash."

"Since when can this car fly?" She climbed down into the back seat.

"I could ask you the same thing?" Alex looked back and pulled up his goggles on one side to show her an eye patch. "And I gave Hawk a gun because my aim isn't that great anymore."

"Oh." Becca watched as he lowered his goggles again.

"Actually, now that you're back, would you say you outrank me?" Alex smirked.

Becca raised an eyebrow. "I guess."

"Good." The artificer held out a hand to Hawk. "Reload the gun and give it to me."

"I thought you couldn't aim." Becca furrowed her brow.

He answered her by casually flipping her off.

"What the hell was that for?"

"This." He took the gun from Hawk and turned the car into the aerial equivalent of drifting as his hand snapped out toward the Revenants that were flapping toward them. The gun barked in rapid fire, his aim flicking from one target to another, gray matter exploding from the creature's skulls with each shot. The swarm simply dropped out of the sky as the pistol's slide locked back empty.

"Care to explain?" She eyed him sideways.

"Not much to say." Alex shrugged and straightened out the car. "Apparently you fly now, and I become an aim-bot whenever I disrespect a superior."

"That's stupid." She glowered at him.

"Yeah, things have gotten weird." Hawk settled into the seat beside her, looking closely at her for the first time. "Are you okay? That's a lot of blood."

"It's not mine." She shrugged, hoping he wouldn't ask more. "Things got weird for me too."

Alex glanced back at the mention of blood, giving her a strange look. She was pretty sure he'd just analyzed her, but decided not to say more in front of Hawk. Instead, he kept his eye forward and let her brother do the talking. She tried to keep the focus on them and the situation in Vegas.

They didn't know anything about the battle or what had caused it, but they had been flying low and keeping an eye on Autem's fleet once they saw it. Apparently, Digby had raised an armada to fight with but had lost all but one ship. Alex and Hawk had watched them fall from beneath the clouds. According to them, it had been like witnessing a second apocalypse, with the sky full of fire. She could only imagine.

They decided to get closer when they saw Easton parachuting down like an action hero with a random woman in his arms. Becca nearly rolled her eyes out of her head at that description. They ran out of time to reminisce when the car approached the cargo ship floating in the night. By her best guess, they only had ten minutes or so before Autem's fleet caught up to them.

"I hope someone has a plan." Becca jumped down from the car as soon as Alex landed it on the deck.

"Oh, thank the Nine," Kristen's skull celebrated as Hawk tore her from the dash. "If I ever ride in another of Alex's creations, it will be too soon."

Becca took a breath, hoping she could find Digby aboard the vessel quickly. There were several groups of people and zombies moving back and forth, looking like they were in the middle of an evacuation. She froze when Mason stepped out of the crowd.

He was wearing the cowboy hat she'd left for him before she'd died. The hat that had been accompanied by a note telling him she loved him.

"Becca?" His face was a mixture of relief and confusion. It all washed away as he ran toward her.

Becca hesitated for an instant, not wanting to let herself get caught up in the moment. Not wanting to give him hope that things would be able to go back to the way they were. It didn't matter that she wanted to stay with him. To stay with the family that she'd found. She couldn't. Depending on how bad off Digby was, she might have to cast the spell to save him right now. She might only have minutes left to live.

All of that sat at the forefront of her mind, which was why it was so strange that her feet were moving before she'd even noticed. Her eyes welled up as she ran to him. Everything came drifting back, her heart racing as he threw his arms around her and picked her up to spin her around like in the movies. He pressed his lips to hers, standing amidst the crew of the ship and a horde of the dead, while a fleet of warships headed their way.

It was possibly the most perfect moment of her life.

Then he pulled away and brushed dried flakes of crimson from his beard. "Shit, Becca, why are you covered in blood?" He stared down at her jumpsuit and face. "Like, a lot of blood. How did you…?" He trailed off a second later.

"You analyzed me, didn't you?" She sniffed as a confused tear fell, unsure if it was because of joy or sadness.

He nodded.

"I wish there was more time to explain everything."

"What?" Hawk pushed through the crowd.

Alex placed a hand on his shoulder to hold him back.

Whispers began circulating through the crew as they slowed

whatever they were doing to stare. One word could be heard again and again.

Vampire.

"It's okay, right?" Mason raised his hands to her shoulders. "It doesn't matter, right? You're still you."

"Shit." Hawk took a step closer, clearly realizing what she was. "How?"

Becca released the longest sigh of her existence so far. "The Cliffs Notes are that revenants are apparently just incomplete vampires. I died when I turned rev but," She turned to glower at Alex, "someone yanked my soul back and shoved it back into my body. That completed the curse's requirements and turned me into this."

"Do you, like, suck blood now?" Hawk looked at her the same way he might a rockstar, clearly finding the transformation cool.

"Does the sun hurt you?" Mason sounded concerned for her safety.

"What about garlic?" Hawk added.

"Do you sparkle?" Alex threw in one final question, probably trying to cut the tension.

Becca groaned and rubbed at her eyes. "Yes, I drink blood, but mostly to replenish my mana. I don't burst into flames in the sun, but the mana balance during the day does mess with me. I haven't tried garlic since I came back, so I don't know. And no, I don't fucking sparkle." She stomped a foot. "I'm going to just say now that Twilight jokes are not original and you are not being funny."

"Fair enough." Alex held up his hands in defense.

"Now, where is Digby?" She threw out her hands beside her. "We do not have a lot of time here."

"He's toward the back of the ship, prepping more zombies to send out. They should be able to slow Autem's fleet another ten minutes while we evacuate." Mason pointed toward the rear of the vessel.

"Good, keep evacuating, I'm going to go talk to him." Becca started walking.

Mason reached out to stop her. "Graves isn't well. Just to give you a heads up. Things got a little hairy a few minutes ago."

"Shit." Becca closed her eyes trying not to let on that she had anything planned. If he was really unraveling, then there wasn't time to waste. It would probably be best that she just cast the spell before anyone had time to stop her. She gave Mason a nod. "Thank you for the warning."

With that, she took a deep breath and kept walking. As she passed the bridge, she caught a look at the evacuation. The crew was lining up to enter some kind of mirror portal. It must have been the same spell that Alex and Hawk had used to escape back in D.C. Relief swept over her with the knowledge that no one was trapped aboard the ship. Autem could come for them if they wanted, but they would be long gone by the time they got there.

After the crew, Asher and Clint were organizing a line of zombies to go through the mirror next. It probably didn't make sense to leave them behind. After the time it must have taken to gather the dead, they must have been too valuable to lose.

Passing the bridge, she kept on to the rear of the ship. It wasn't long before she heard Digby's shouting from someplace within a horde of fifty zombies.

"Yes, grow strong my minions!"

"At least he sounds normal." Becca nodded to herself.

"Rip their still-beating hearts from their chests!"

Becca frowned. "Okay, that sounds less normal."

A wave of green light shimmered across the horde, only for streams of deathly mana to trickle from each member of the dead. Becca could feel the magic in the air, envious that she didn't have a way to leach mana in the same way. The dead began to twitch all at once.

She took a step away as wings burst from each of their backs. They took flight one by one, heading toward Autem's fleet to slow them down. As each zombie took to the sky, glimpses of a cackling Digby showed through the horde. Squinting, Becca tried to catch the details.

There was something off about him.

"Digby?" Becca walked forward as the last few dozen zombies flapped into the air all at once.

The necromancer spun around as soon as she spoke. "Who dares—"

Digby froze the moment he saw her. Becca did the same.

He looked awful. Half his face had been burnt off and his lower half had been replaced by that of a spider, with two legs missing.

"Jesus, Dig. What happened to you?"

"Haven't you heard?" He rose up to his full height. "I've gone mad. And what rock did you crawl out from under?"

She folded her arms. "Is that any way to greet your friend who came back from the dead to help you? I don't care if you are insane, I would hope that you're at least a little glad to see me."

She couldn't help but feel hurt. The Digby she knew would have been happy. The zombie in front of her barely seemed to care. It was easy to see he was coming apart at the seams.

Digby pouted like a child. "Alright, I may be a bit relieved that you're alive. Though, I'd love to know why you chose to wait a week before making your return?" His eyes narrowed. "And why the bloody hell does the Seed label you as a Fool?"

He must have analyzed her, focusing on the first detail he saw while ignoring the rest.

She sighed. "Read the rest of the information, Dig."

His eyes widened, finally noticing her new race description. "Oh, that's new. I suppose that explains why you look like you just ripped out a man's throat with your teeth." A cackle croaked from his throat. "Stepped up the food chain, did ye?"

"I died, Dig." She looked away. "I'm more of a monster than you are."

"Oh, don't be so dramatic." He waved a hand through the air. "It's not a competition."

Becca shook her head. "Okay, either way, we should evacuate to someplace safe."

That seemed to be the best option. The last thing she wanted was to cast her spell right there if she could help it. According to its description, it would take several minutes. If Autem showed up in the middle of it, everything could be ruined.

"I think not." Digby turned away, stamping half of his legs on the deck. "I wish I could, but I was told to remain here to send out another wave of zombies if need be. And that is what I'm going to do. At least that way no one can accuse me of any more war crimes."

"Seriously?" Becca eyed him.

"Indeed. I am no longer in charge." He gave a decisive nod. "From here on out, I just do as I'm told. Honestly, it's a bit of a relief to let someone else call the shots." Digby lowered his head as a note of shame entered his voice. "It might be for the best. I'm still not sure. You might all be against me. I might still be right."

Becca watched as he sank back down, looking more damaged than she'd ever seen him. "Okay, then who is in charge?"

"That would be President Parker." He raised back up and pointed to the bridge. "She is holding herself hostage and forcing us to flee rather than striking at our enemies. Apparently, that's," he raised his hands to make air quotes, "the right decision."

"So, you aren't moving from this spot until Parker tells you to?" Becca rubbed at her eyes.

"Not one inch." He nodded, giving her an uneven grin. "Would I agree to that if I was insane?"

Becca didn't answer right away. Instead, she just watched his eye twitch. He needed help. For a moment, she almost cast the spell to save him. Then she shook off the impulse. It was too risky. Right? That was what she told herself. A part of her wasn't sure. She might have just been putting off the inevitable. She might have been trying to live a few more minutes.

The fact that she was being selfish was all too obvious. She had to cast the spell. Still, she didn't want to leave everyone. Not after getting to see them again.

Her eyes started to well up, forcing her to turn away.

"Okay, I'm going to go talk to Parker and figure this out."

She knew it was cowardly as she started walking back toward the bridge. She should have just cast the spell. Then again, what could a few more minutes hurt? The air grew thick in her throat, making it hard to breathe as the realization hit her.

"I don't want to die?"

She was a monster, but there were so many people she didn't want to leave. So much she still had to do. She was going to have to get herself together. Someone had to save Digby, and no one could do it but her.

"Tell Parker I haven't moved from this spot, Becky!" Digby called after her. "Tell her I'm doing what I'm supposed to! Tell her that I'm a shining example of sanity!"

"I will." She waved back over her shoulder, not wanting to turn around to see her broken friend or let him see the guilt in her eyes. Breaking into a sprint, she ran the rest of the way. She ducked into the bridge a moment later, stopping as soon as she saw the mirror.

One by one, zombies entered the rippling surface.

Becca sniffed and made sure she didn't look upset. Then she slipped between two of the dead and stepped into the mirror. She stopped dead in her tracks as soon as she was through.

"What in the hell?" She could hardly believe what she saw.

She was standing in the Oval Office, all the way back in Washington. Somehow, she had ended up where she started. She wanted to stop and gawk longer, but a zombie came through the mirror behind her, moaning when it bumped into her.

Stumbling out of the line, she found herself in the center of the room in front of the Resolute Desk, face to foot with President Parker.

"You're really back!" Parker pulled her feet off the desk and jumped up without hesitation. The pink-haired soldier was climbing over the desk before Becca could even say hi. "Thank fuck. Hawk and Mason just came through and told me you were here. I am so happy I could cry. I never want to be in charge again." She gestured to the desk. "It's all yours."

"Wait, I have no idea what's happening." Becca stepped away before Parker had a chance to shove her toward the desk. "Why are we here? And how do we get back to Vegas?"

"We can't. Autem knows that's where we've been. It sucks, but we gotta leave it. I'm going to open a passage to Hawaii as soon as the horde and Digby get through."

Becca struggled to process her words. "You opened that portal?"

"Oh yeah, that's what I do now. It's why Dig hasn't killed me, I think." She shrugged.

"Killed you?" Becca flicked her eyes from the desk to Parker's face.

"Yeah, things got a little creepy for a hot minute. I think we're okay now, but I'm staying here next to the nuke just in case." Parker gestured casually to the side.

Becca turned to find a goddamn nuclear warhead with a detonation switch duct taped to it. Behind the bomb, Bancroft sat on a couch, looking like absolute trash. The man raised a hand to wave as a dark voice came from his mouth.

"Sup."

Becca staggered in place as her mind tried to process it all. Parker could open portals halfway around the world, the man who had caused her death was sitting a few feet away, she was within arm's reach of a switch that could detonate a nuke, and she was standing in the White House within a few miles of Autem's capital.

She had stepped through a mirror and into an absolute madhouse.

"Wait." Becca froze as pieces began falling into place. "That nuke is in range of Autem's capital."

Parker tensed. "Well, yeah, but we kind of decided that there were too many innocent people there to blow them up."

Becca placed her hand to her eyes, rubbing them with her palms. She pulled her hands away a moment later, feeling dried blood flake from her face. "We don't have to blow anything up." She grabbed Parker by the shoulders as a truly insane plan formed in the jumbled chaos of her mind.

It was a perfect plan.

No, it was a Digby plan.

"Get Alex and tell him to meet me back on the horde ship." Becca spun back toward the mirror. "We have maybe ten minutes before Autem's fleet destroys it, and we're going to need that time to save Vegas."

"But we already decided to abandon the city." Parker furrowed her brow.

"No one is abandoning anything."

Becca started walking for the portal.

"Tonight the war ends."

CHAPTER FIFTY

"They're all against you," the corpse of Ames said into Digby's ear.

The room that everyone had been referring to as the Oval Office surrounded him as he eyed his closest friends.

Rebecca had a plan

It was a good plan.

"Of course it's a good plan." Ames walked around him. "It's your plan."

The hallucination wasn't wrong.

Digby had laid the groundwork for the plan so there was hardly anything left to do but wait. Well, technically there was a slight difference. One minute modification that had changed everything, and that one detail had brought everyone on board.

All Rebecca had needed to do was say a few words and everyone had jumped into action.

"They have turned their backs on you," Ames added.

Mason finished evacuating everyone to Hawaii while Alex and Rebecca remained behind on the horde ship to set up a few last-minute things. Parker sat not far away on a sofa next to the bomb to make sure Digby didn't get any ideas.

"They don't trust you." Ames stood by the bomb.

Digby shook his head. *No, they are just worried about me. They want to help. I think.* He clawed at his head, peeling off a piece of skin that was hanging from his burnt skull. *Keep it together, Graves. Parker is right, you're confused.*

"Are you?" Ames stared into his eyes.

Digby flicked his attention to Parker, sitting on a sofa next to the nuke, staring into the tiny mirror of a compact. She had barely looked at him since the fight they'd had. A part of him understood why. He had crossed a line. Even now, he thought he was right. It had been the only way to save everyone. The only thing stopping him from lunging for her now was the trust he had in her.

"Why?" Ames continued to pester him. "She only doubts you."

"Shut up," Digby snapped at the ghost.

Parker didn't say anything.

He really was mad. He understood that much. He was seeing ghosts, a fact that was even more convincing of his madness because he was a necromancer. He understood the dead more than anyone else, and they didn't haunt people the way Ames did. Despite that, he still thought he was the only one that could save them.

If it hadn't been for Parker, he would continue to believe in himself over all else. Even Bancroft had helped him understand that he had been wrong. That he had become the same as Henwick. That he'd lost sight of the doubts that kept him grounded.

If his judgment was really flawed, his friends were the only ones that could keep him from doing something he would regret later. Something that he couldn't solve with an apology, or a healthy amount of groveling. Obviously, he had recalled his minion from Parker's skeleton. Despite that, he was pretty sure his words had hurt her more than anything else.

Then again, he had already gone that far.

"You could still overpower her," Ames insisted.

That much was true. He was still stronger than Parker. Torture had proved useless against her, but there was a chance he could figure something else out in time. If he didn't do anything soon, it would be too late. Once Autem reached the cargo ship, Rebecca's plan would already be set in motion.

"No." Digby ignored the ghost.

All it did was lie. It was just the voice of his own ego telling him he was right. The truth was that he had been lost from the beginning. He had been lost ever since he suggested blowing up Autem's capital a week ago. He had been lost when he proceeded to set his plan into motion behind everyone's back. He may not have been seeing ghosts then, but he had been lost all the same. He just couldn't see it.

Parker jumped to her feet and went to the mirror that was mounted to the wall. The reflective surface began to ripple a second later, followed by Rebecca and Alex rushing through the passage into the room.

"Oh damn, that was close." Alex panted as if he had just run the length of the horde ship.

"The imperial fleet is about a minute out. If this is going to work, we'll know soon enough." Rebecca wasn't winded at all.

"Henwick will probably just smite the ship out of the sky the moment he's in range." Digby chuckled, a part of him still rooting for the plan to fail.

"Let's hope he sees the present we left for him first." Alex smirked.

"How did your present feel about being left there?" Parker closed the passage they had just come from.

"Who knows." Becca shrugged before walking straight up to Digby. "What about you, are you feeling like you can do this? You know, with your—"

"Madness?" Digby finished her sentence as he scratched at his neck with a claw. "I will be on my best behavior."

"Sure you will." Rebecca narrowed her eyes at him. "Either way, you are going to have to do the talking here, and for that, you are going to have to act like you aren't spiraling out of control. Can you do that?"

"Of course I can. I may have debated on overpowering Parker on the advice of a hallucination while you were gone, but I didn't. Hell, I could still flood this room with miles of rotting entrails from my void, then lug that bomb all the way to Autem's capital myself. However, every second that passes where I don't should speak to my character." He stamped a couple of his legs and pouted. "I may be mad, but I have come to terms with that fact. So rest assured, I am steady as a rock."

"I'm sure." Rebecca looked back to Parker, who had returned to staring at her compact. "How are things on the ship?"

"I think they're taking the bait." She glanced up, doing a double take at Digby. "Wait a sec, are you intending on staying like that?"

"Like what?" Digby glowered at her.

"Like that." She threw her hand out toward his bulbous spider body.

"She has a point." Alex poked one of Digby's spindly legs.

"Agreed." Rebecca nodded. "I think horrible spider monster sends the wrong message for what we're trying to accomplish."

"But..." Digby backed away, not wanting to give up the form that had served him so well in battle.

"No buts, buddy." Parker stepped forward. "Besides, where you're going, I doubt you will even fit like that."

"Fine." He rolled his eyes. "But only because being smaller may present an advantage in combat in an enclosed space."

"Yeah, whatever, just do it." Parker sat back down and returned her attention to her compact.

"And probably fix this while you're at." Alex gestured to his face.

Digby released a long groan and prepared to craft a new body, only to hesitate. "What about a snake body? I ate a few of those out there. Surely, that would fit wherever I need to go whilst still leaving me with a tail that could choke a man out."

"Ew, no." Parker looked up again.

Digby sighed before trying one more time. "Tentacles, maybe?"

"No!" everyone shouted back in unison.

"Alright, alright, I have no idea what all you humans have against tentacles."

"Human legs, Digby. Just do human legs." Rebecca rubbed at her forehead.

"Bah, no imagination." Digby activated his Body Craft.

The sensation of being torn apart from the waist down struck him as he willed his body to return to its original state. Flesh stretched across his skull to cover the holes that had formed on one side, leaving him with a hairstyle similar to Parker's, after she had burned everything off one side. To make everyone feel better about his state of mind, he spent the extra resources to reactivate his Sheep's Clothing mutation, his nose filling back in.

With his face returned to its previous handsome visage, he moved on to his body, allowing his half-formed arm to fill back into what he'd started with. His Body Craft mutation even retraced the tattoos that covered it to spell the word luck across his knuckles once again.

Last came the hardest part, his legs. Digby leaned forward, placing his hands down on the royal seal that adorned the Oval Office's carpeting and waited as bones snapped back into place within the bulbous carapace. Once it was no longer needed, the spindly legs around him went limp and the exoskeleton cracked like an egg. The body simply rotted away after that, allowing Digby to stand back up on two legs again.

"There, are you all happy now?" He held out both hands to show off his new body.

Parker immediately let out a laugh.

"Woah, Dig!" Alex cringed and looked away. "You don't have any pants."

"Good lord, that wasn't what I wanted to see right now."

Rebecca raised a hand to hold it in a way that blocked a portion of her vision.

"I have so many jokes I want to make." Parker tore her attention away and lowered her head back to her compact. "Focus, Parker, the fate of the world is in the balance. Dick jokes can wait."

"Well, what did you all expect?" Digby threw out his hands. "I can't craft clothing."

"I don't know what I expected. But not that." Rebecca groaned while staring up at the ceiling in frustration. "I thought you would make some bone armor or something."

"Ha! Bone armor." Parker cackled.

"No more jokes." Rebecca thrust a finger in her direction. "Keep an eye on the Mirror Link. We need you to find us an entrance."

"Oh yeah, on it." Parker dropped her eyes to her compact.

"It's so wiggly." Alex stood staring with his head leaning to one side. "Almost hypnotic."

"Okay, Dig, you need to put some pants on." Rebecca turned away. "We need you for this mission and you can't do it with your, um, parts hanging out."

"Obviously not, Becky." Digby pointed to Alex. "Your pants, give them to me."

"What? No." The artificer stepped back.

"Why not?" Digby lowered his hand.

"Um, because I'm going with you. I need my pants."

"Fine, I'll take Sax's pants." Digby started for his minion.

"No you won't." Parker stood up. "It is bad enough that you turned him into that, the least you can do is leave him with some dignity."

"Dignity?" Digby scoffed. "Are you really one to lecture me?"

She winced, rubbing at her head. "Probably not, but I don't care. So back away from my dead friend's pants."

Digby walked across the room. "Well, what would have me do then? Make a toga from the curtains?"

"Just wait, I'll find something." Alex rushed out of the room.

"Good, and be quick about it!" Digby shouted after him.

They were probably right. It was unlikely that anyone would take him seriously without any pants. To make matters worse, his shirt and coat had been torn to ribbons, leaving him with practically nothing left but the pauldron that was strapped to his shoulder.

That was when Bancroft's voice came from the other end of Parker's compact.

"Will the four of you please shut up! The empire's fleet is approaching the ship and I didn't agree to this plan of yours just for it to be ruined when someone overhears your asinine conversation over the Mirror Link. And for god's sake, Graves, put on some pants."

"He's probably right," Rebecca agreed in a whisper.

Alex appeared in the doorway a second later to announce his findings. "I have found clothes!"

Everyone in the room shushed him at once.

"Sorry." He lowered his voice to a whisper and gestured to something bulky and white that was slung over his arm. "This was all I could find."

Digby stared at the garment, unable to process what he was even looking at. "What in the devil is that?"

CHAPTER FIFTY-ONE

Wind blew through Henwick's hair as he stood upon the upper deck of the great owl, the massive aircraft carrying him toward the floating cargo ship where Grave's horde had been coming from. He'd destroyed the rest of the necromancer's pathetic armada. The irritating zombie had caused them considerable delays, but the end result was always going to be the same.

All that was left was to smite the last one out of the sky.

"Your Holiness?" The captain of the elite Guardians approached him, holding out a pair of binoculars. "There's something you should see."

Henwick didn't turn to look at the man, merely opting to glance at the binoculars. The idea that he would need such a tool was laughable.

"What is it?" Henwick leaned forward on the railing that surrounded the upper deck.

The elite Captain raised the binoculars and pointed to the front of the ship. "There sir, tied to the bow."

Henwick squinted, finding a figure hanging from the front rail of the vessel. His hands had been tied together, leaving him dangling from a hook over the empty sky. He grinned as he recognized his face.

Bancroft.

"Do you think it's a trap?" The Guardian beside him lowered his binoculars.

"A trap?" Henwick shook his head. "If Graves had the power to hurt us, he would have used it by now. No, this is something else."

Henwick gave the order for the rest of the fleet to surround and board the ship to search for Graves. It was unlikely that the zombie was still on board, especially considering he had access to that passage spell. How that was possible, he wasn't sure. That kind of magic was out of reach, even for him. It would take well over a thousand years to cultivate a will that could achieve such things. Sure, his artificers had been able to build structures capable of opening a stable passage, but those were massive and could only link to a single matching structure.

The key was probably that messenger that Henwick had seen with Graves before. The Heretic Seed must have found a loophole to grant her the spell. Lord only knew what kind of toll that power was taking on the poor wretch. The spell was too advanced not to devour its caster.

Unfortunately, harmful or not, that spell complicated things. The fleet would reach Las Vegas soon, but Henwick already knew they wouldn't find Graves there either. The zombie had proven far too slippery. Then again, that was always Digby's fatal flaw. Graves believed himself more clever than he was. That part clearly hadn't changed in the last eight hundred years. With a few victories under his belt, he was sure to grow overconfident enough to get sloppy.

Henwick locked his eyes on the man hanging from the front of the ship as the great owl approached, wondering if leaving Bancroft behind was the mistake he'd been waiting for or was it just another pointless stall tactic to buy time.

"Hello Charles," Henwick called out to his former under-ling. "I wasn't expecting to find you hanging around here."

"Well, I'm glad you did, so if you could get me down, I would appreciate it." Bancroft winced, his legs dangling over the darkened earth below.

"I'm not so sure I will." Henwick held both hands out empty. "Not after you betrayed the empire and aided in the theft of the Heretic Seed's fragments."

"Yes, I understand that. However, my skeleton had been animated, leaving me with no choice. Graves has finally recalled his minion, leaving me free to rejoin the empire." Bancroft was his usual business-like self even while bargaining for his life. "And despite my past circumstances, I have been working tirelessly for the empire this whole time. I have sabotaged Graves' operation and executed Rebecca Alvarez, his second in command."

"I'm sorry to inform you, but from reports back at the capital, Ms. Alvarez has returned with an appetite for blood." Henwick leaned his elbows casually on the railing.

"Yes, it seems she found her way back here as well." Bancroft grimaced. "However, I assure you I still have information that will be useful to the empire."

"Really?" Henwick raised his eyebrows. "What would that be? And don't say that you'll tell me if I get you down from there."

"I know where Graves has fled to." Bancroft grinned. "If we're fast about it, we may be able to catch him. Or at least keep him on the run and unable to recover."

"Out with it then." Henwick beckoned with both hands to draw out the rest of the information.

Bancroft flicked his eyes around as if unsure if he should give up such a valuable bargaining chip. Then he spoke. "They are in Hawaii, using the naval base there to house a thousand people, many of whom are low-level Heretics."

Henwick groaned. "I already assumed that."

"What?" Bancroft's mouth fell open, clearly expecting a different response.

"Of course I know that already." He gestured to the cargo

ship. "Graves just tried to attack us with his little armada. It's not hard to figure out where he got the ships. We know where they were docked when the world ended. And how do I know you aren't just telling me this because there's some sort of trap waiting for me there?"

"I assure you there isn't." Bancroft shook his head frantically. "And I'm sure a debrief will prove that I still have valuable information."

Henwick blew out a sigh. "Very well, cut him down."

Bancroft relaxed. "Thank you, sir. I understand the position I'm in, and I'm grateful for—"

"Yes, we'll cut you down and see what your corpse has to say when we get it back to the capital." Henwick turned away and headed for the narrow stairway that led down to the great owl's bridge, stopping for a moment next to one of his elite Guardians. "Get him down and bring him to me. I want to let him sweat a little."

With that, Henwick made his way down to wait.

Unlike most of the owl-type aircraft that were based off the previously used kestrel design, the great owl was made to serve as a command ship with a bridge large enough to walk around in freely instead of a basic cockpit. The room didn't sport much for comfort, but then again, it didn't need to. Just a touch screen table for planning, a pilot seat, a sheet of plexiglass backed with a reflective material, and a few communications consoles to disperse commands throughout the fleet. In front, a multi-paneled window stretched across the twelve-foot-wide space.

Henwick sat down in the captain's seat near the back of the bridge where he could watch some of his men cutting Bancroft down through the front window. Charles had always been a shrewd businessman, so he probably hadn't defected to Digby's side. Not unless the zombie had offered him something worth risking his life for. The only question was whether or not Graves had something that valuable to offer.

Debating on Bancroft's fate, Henwick adjusted his position and struggled to find a way to sit that was comfortable while wearing his combat attire. The crusader armor had been designed years ago, but never worn in the field until now. The near-medieval styling of the armor would have raised too many eyebrows before, but now that they were able to rebuild the world in the image of their choosing, things had changed. Though, he made a note to do something about the armor's inner padding.

His thoughts were drawn back to the entrance of the bridge as a pair of elites dragged Bancroft in.

"I can walk on my own, damn it." The man attempted to pull his arms free from the heavily armored Guardians as they forced him into the room and turned him around to stand in front of the captain's seat.

"Is that any way to talk to my crusaders?" Henwick leaned on the arm of his chair.

Bancroft stopped struggling and stood at attention the moment he was released. "I will assume that you were joking about taking my corpse back to the capital."

"The verdict is still out on that." Henwick leaned from side to side. "I think that depends on if you can come up with any useful information that I don't already know."

Bancroft stood completely still for a long moment before finally saying something meaningful. "I know where Graves will be."

"Yes, I know, he's in Hawaii." Henwick glowered at his former subordinate.

"No, I don't mean where he is now or where his people are." Bancroft let a smug expression creep across his face. "I'm talking about where he will be. Where you can find him."

Henwick resisted the urge to lean forward in his chair. "Alright, I'll bite. Where will Graves be?"

Bancroft gestured to the bridge around him. "Right here."

Henwick arched an eyebrow. "I've never known you to make jokes, Charles, so I'll assume from your self-satisfied demeanor that you have made a deal with Graves."

"It's just business, and you should have made me a better

offer." Bancroft nodded to himself as silence fell across the bridge.

Henwick cleaved through the stillness with one word, "Well?"

The color started to drain from Bancroft's face. "I said, Graves will be here."

"Yes, I know." Henwick remained seated while watching the man flounder.

"Graves will be here!" he repeated, this time louder while angling his head back as if talking to someone behind him.

That was when one of the crusaders beside him leaned closer to him and snatched something small and reflective off Bancroft's back.

"What is that?" Henwick leaned forward.

"I think it's a piece of a mirror." The crusader held out the small, jagged shard. "Someone taped it to his back."

Henwick stood up to get a closer look, grabbing the reflective fragment to look into it. An eye stared back at him for an instant before vanishing.

"Now, Graves!" Bancroft shouted in no direction in particular, clearly confused why whatever trap the zombie was planning hadn't been sprung.

Henwick dropped back into his chair and glanced at one of his men. "Take him back up top and throw him off the side."

The two Guardians that bracketed Bancroft reached for his arms, but Charles' hands snapped out to grab them by the wrists. He looked up to stare straight into Henwick's face as he twisted their arms back with a strength that was impossible for a man of his level. "You know, one thing nobody realizes about having your skeleton animated is that it can be a powerful asset, provided you both are willing to combine your strength to work toward a common goal. Isn't that right, Tavern?"

Bancroft's face distorted as his mouth opened to release a voice tainted by darkness. "Hell yeah."

"He's still possessed." Henwick stood back up as Bancroft snapped the arms of both of his elite Guardians.

Bancroft laughed in his own voice, followed by that same dark tone shouting an infuriating phrase.

"Yippie-kai-yay, motherfucker!"

That was when Henwick noticed the glass of one of the windows at the front of the bridge had begun to ripple. Rage bubbled up through his entire body as something came through, drawing the shadows of the space toward them.

After that, the only thing he could see was a swarm of bats.

CHAPTER FIFTY-TWO

Digby tumbled out of a Mirror Passage right behind Rebecca as a swarm of bats filled the bridge of Autem's command aircraft. His immediate thought was, *Good lord, that's a lot of bats!*

Alex dove through behind him, followed by Parker. The only one who stayed behind was Sax's zombified corpse. Someone had to be there to set off the bomb, after all.

Curling his fingers through the hair of a disembodied head, Digby held it at his side and stood at his full height, catching glimpses of Henwick through the swirling vortex of bats. Apparently, vampires had some interesting abilities. He let out a wild cackle to announce his presence as Rebecca released her swarm.

"Hello, Henwick." Digby stared directly into the man's eyes. He may have been losing his mind and unraveling at the seams but, for once, he was able to face his enemy from a position of strength.

"Kill them!" Henwick wasted no time, raising his hand to smite him out of existence.

"I wouldn't do that." Digby held his ground as Rebecca sent

a brief burst of bats out in all directions to push Henwick's men away.

"Yeah, back the hell up." Alex stepped between them, drawing two pistols at once, his hand snapping out to target Guardians in both directions.

"Listen to him!" Bancroft shouted as he made a point of stepping in front of Parker to protect their escape. Though Digby had a feeling he was mostly worried about his own exit. Parker hid behind him regardless.

Every Guardian on the bridge pulled swords or guns, a half dozen weapons pointing at Digby's head. A whisper came from the back of his mind telling him to fight. To forget about the plan and simply dive straight for Henwick's throat. Surely, he had enough resources to get the job done.

Right?

Maybe.

Maybe not.

It was hard to tell if that was the sane choice or not as the tension in the room grew so thick that he could taste it. Digby tightened his fingers on the tuft of hair sprouting from the head in his hands. He forced the impulse out of his mind and tried to focus on the plan.

Henwick kept his hand raised, glancing down at the head Digby carried, then back up at his face. Then back down again. Finally, he lowered his hand and shook his head.

"Graves, why are you dressed as the Easter Bunny?"

"Bunny?" Digby looked down at the white fur that covered his chest before raising the hollow rabbit head in his hand to look into its vacant eyes. "Nonsense, this is a garment used for an annual ceremony held within the walls of this land's ruling palace." At least, that was what everyone had told him a moment before when he'd put it on.

Henwick blinked twice. "You aren't technically wrong."

"No, I am not, nor am I wrong that your best option is to lower your weapons." Digby gestured to everyone around him. "We are not here to fight."

"I certainly won't force you into combat, but I will assure you that I will not allow any of you to leave this craft." He held his hands out to his sides to illustrate that they were surrounded. "That messenger of yours might be able to open one of those passages, but you won't have time to get through it before I smite you."

"I have no doubt of that." Digby nodded as he struggled to remember everything that Rebecca had told him to say. "Which is why I want to negotiate."

Henwick scoffed. "What could you and I possibly have to negotiate about?"

"Bah, not with you." Digby scoffed right back. "I want to talk to Chancellor Serrano." He left out the fact that he couldn't remember who this chancellor person was. Rebecca had just told him to ask for the man a few minutes before.

Henwick raised an eyebrow. "He is not aboard this craft."

"I know, but I also know he is waiting by the mirror in his office for news of your attack, and I think I have some information that he would want to hear." Digby tucked his rabbit head under his arm, enjoying the expression on Henwick's face.

The man stood still for a long moment, clearly debating on what to do. Odds were he could kill them all before they could escape through a passage.

Rebecca stepped forward. "I was listening when Serrano suggested to you that we all negotiate before going to war. I think this is the best option for all involved."

Henwick eyed her, clearly skeptical. In the end, there wasn't a choice. He must have known that they had the nuke after his men had found it missing from their sunken ship. The fact that they had found Rebecca there as well, in her revenant form, made it clear who had the weapon. That fact alone left him with few options.

"Fine." Henwick turned to the sheet of reflective plastic beside his chair.

The surface filled with a view of an extravagant office a second later. An older man sat at a desk.

"Serrano?" Henwick announced himself. "I have someone here that wants a word with you."

"Yes?" The old man got up from his desk and walked toward the mirror on his end, holding his hands behind his back politely. He looked to Digby, then back to Henwick. "I'm not sure I understand what is going on."

"I'm here to negotiate." Digby glanced at Rebecca to make sure he hadn't veered away from the plan. She gave him a supportive nod.

"Oh?" Serrano almost looked pleased. "I would be interested in hearing what you have to say." He chuckled. "I'll say that is an interesting outfit, Mr. Graves."

"That's Lord Graves, you elderly…" Digby trailed off, not finishing the insult. As much as Digby wanted to gloat and belittle his enemies, he refrained. He wasn't sure if that was the madness talking. Instead, he laid everything out on the table. "I have a nuclear bomb set to explode within range of your capital city."

Serrano's face fell as he looked to Henwick. "Can we confirm that?"

"Yes." Digby nodded. "We acquired the weapon from a cargo ship that you controlled off the West Coast of this land. Your men have searched this vessel by now and would have found the weapon missing."

Serrano furrowed his brow, clearly weighing the validity of the threat. "And how do we know this bomb has truly been placed within the range of our capital?"

Rebecca stepped forward to answer for him. "If you will take a close look at what Digby is wearing, you should recognize it as one of the many Easter rabbits made for the White House Easter egg roll event. Their design is somewhat unique and has been featured on a number of broadcasts."

Digby held up the head he carried to give the man in the mirror a good look at its face as Rebecca continued.

"We realize that a bunny costume is an odd choice to wear to a negotiation, but we thought it would support our claim.

Thus making it a tactical choice." She took a step back when she finished. "And just in case you need more." She gestured to Parker who touched one of the windows at the front of the bridge.

An image of the bomb laying in front of the Resolute Desk filled the glass.

Serrano nodded with a heavy sigh. "I can't say anyone has used the Easter Bunny in such a way before, so I can appreciate the originality." He removed his hands from behind his back and placed them together. "Very well, what are your demands?"

Rebecca looked back to Digby, clearly intending for him to continue the negotiation now that she had helped to reinforce their position. He gave her a nod and opened his mouth to speak.

Then, he closed his mouth again, realizing a critical detail.

They hadn't left anyone back in the Oval Office with the bomb other than Sax. His eyes widened. Parker had been using herself as a hostage to keep him from blowing up the empire's capital, but she couldn't stay behind without making it obvious that they wouldn't actually follow through with the threat. Now though, nothing was stopping him from doing it anyway.

Digby felt the corner of his mouth tug up.

He had won.

Everyone that had gotten in his way had moved aside. He could give the order. He could destroy all of Autem; the only Guardians left would be the fleet and Henwick. It would be so easy. All he had to do was set off the bomb and use the confusion of the moment to take Henwick by surprise. With that, the world would be safe again. The others would realize he was right, and even if they didn't, they would be safe.

He opened his mouth again, this time to give the order to Sax on the other end of the Mirror Link. It was the right choice. Even if no one understood.

Then he closed his mouth again.

Did they really not understand? He tugged on the thread of doubt. Why had his friends allowed him to have the advantage?

Why had they put all the power in his hands once again? Then it was obvious.

They trusted him.

Henwick interrupted his scattered thoughts. "Well, Graves, out with it. What are your demands?"

He answered before he even knew what his decision was. "Leave us be."

"You can't be serious." Henwick swiped a hand through the air.

"I am." Digby looked to the faces of each of his friends. The people that he trusted more than himself. "Now that you know we have taken up refuge in Vegas, you can destroy us at any time. And with the knowledge that we could do the same to you, we have no choice but to stop fighting. What was it called, Rebecca?"

"Mutually assured destruction," she added.

"Yes, mutually assured destruction." Digby gestured to the window that showed a view of the bomb. "All we ask is that you call off your attack, and we will remove the weapon from your location."

Henwick shook his head. "There is no way that we can agree to—"

"You don't have a choice," Digby countered.

Henwick turned back the mirror linked to Serrano's office. "The Heretics must be wiped out, else we cannot be free to build anew without influence."

"I understand your concerns." Serrano seemed to be contemplating the arrangement.

"The war ends here!" Digby stamped a foot to drive the point home. "We never wanted any of it, we only fought back because you forced us to. But there's no reason for it to continue."

The words felt wrong as he said them, the voice in his head still telling him to detonate the bomb. Autem had destroyed the world. They had killed billions. They should burn for it. But where would that get them? What would come next?

Nobody wins in war.

Was that really true?

Were there really no victors? No heroes or villains? Just those that live and those that died? Technically, he had died already, caught in the middle of a war between the Fools and Autem. His death had been random. Just the wrong place at the wrong time, like Ames and the men on Skyline's base that he'd killed.

The thoughts in his head slowed as the voice calling for war faded. The others were right. He was losing his mind. Even as he realized it, it became harder to think. Digby shook his head, willing his failing mind to hold out just a few more minutes. Just enough time to finish what he had to do.

Digby looked into Henwick's eyes. "This has to end."

"No." Henwick stepped forward, slapping the rabbit head from Digby's hand. It rolled across the floor, coming to rest against another Guardian's boots. "I will not stand by and allow you and your Heretics to walk away. Not after everything that you've done."

"You must!" Digby resisted the urge to fight back. "It is the only way for everyone to move forward. Maybe one day things will be settled between our two sides, but this is not the way that happens."

Henwick shoved his hand in Digby's face. "I could smite you right where you stand."

"And my minion will detonate the bomb the moment you do. All it will take is a thought and…" Digby trailed off, recognizing when his mind began to fall back into turbulence. Instead, he just sighed. "There's no point in threatening you. Either smite me or don't, the choice is yours."

"What?" Henwick's eyes flicked around the bridge. "What kind of trick are you playing at now?"

"No trick." Digby shook his head. "In all honesty, I am struggling with this just as much as you. Every fiber of my being is telling me to blow up your home and to lunge for your throat."

"Then why don't you?"

"Because I know I'm wrong." Digby held up both hands empty as if having nothing else to offer. "I have faith in those around me. The people that have advised me from the beginning. I think they know better. So I have to ignore what I feel and trust them. All I'm asking you is to do the same."

"He's right, Henwick," Serrano acknowledged from the other side of the mirror.

Henwick spun back to the old man. "You can't be serious?"

"Well, I am currently in the capital, and I would prefer not to die in a nuclear explosion." Serrano chuckled, making light of his situation. "Nor do I want to take a risk with the lives of everyone that the empire has saved. So I agree with Graves. For now, this is how it must end."

Henwick held completely still for a long moment, facing the mirror. Digby half expected him to turn and smite him into oblivion. Not that it would matter at this point. The thoughts in his head seemed to be vanishing one by one as a strange emptiness began to replace him.

Just a few more minutes, Digby.

He forced one thought back into his head.

Just get everyone to safety.

"Get out." Henwick didn't turn around. "Cast whatever spell you are using to travel with and get that nuke away from the capital, then get off my ship."

"Alright." Digby felt like one of his minions, like his mind was gone and his body was just following orders.

Parker closed the Mirror Link spell she had been using to show Henwick the bomb and cast her passage spell to take them back to the cargo ship. Alex went first, backing up with his pistols flicking back and forth between each Guardian until he reached the passage. Once he was close enough, he holstered his guns and awkwardly climbed up into the window. Parker followed, the passage closing as soon as she was through.

A second later, she opened a Mirror Link to show everyone that they were moving the bomb. Alex and Sax carried the weapon into another passage. The link closed, only to reopen a few seconds later to show a view of the bomb aboard the horde ship. The knowledge that the weapon was within range of Autem's fleet ensured that Henwick wouldn't get any ideas to attack.

Parker closed the visual link and opened another passage to the aircraft window to let Digby and Rebecca escape.

Bancroft turned toward the rippling glass next.

"So that's your choice, Charles?" Henwick spoke without looking back. "Going to run off and join the Heretics?"

"We'll see." Bancroft reached up to climb through. "Either way, I think the business I have with you is through." He didn't wait for Henwick to respond before jumping in.

Rebecca looked to Digby, gesturing toward the passage. "You go. I'll be right behind you."

"I..." An impulse to argue passed through his mind only to fade when he couldn't think of a reason to. "Alright."

Digby walked to the passage, stopping to pick up the rabbit head he'd brought with him. Turning back, he caught a glimpse of Henwick's face in the mirror as he closed the link to Serrano. The image fell away like sand in an hourglass. Without a reason to stay, Digby turned and hopped into the passage.

He spilled back out onto the bridge of the horde ship. Failing to catch himself on anything, he landed on his back against one of the ship's unused control systems. The bomb lay a few feet away.

"Shit, Dig, are you okay?" Parker knelt down to help him up.

Why would she help me? Digby struggled to answer the question as much as he did to remember what he'd done to her that would make him ask the question in the first place.

Rebecca came through the passage next, her body backward as if she had jumped through while keeping her eye on Henwick. She stretched her arms out over her head to land in an effortless handstand. Dropping back down, she rolled back up to her feet.

"It worked, right?" Alex stood with one hand against the windows, looking out at Autem's fleet.

The aircraft floated a few hundred feet away, hanging there as if waiting for orders from Henwick.

Getting to his feet, Digby wandered out onto the deck. He stared blankly at the mana-powered aircraft, having trouble understanding why he was looking at them. Then, Autem's fleet all turned around and began heading away. Rebecca walked out to stand beside him.

"I guess that means we're safe."

"Safe," Digby repeated.

"Wooooo!" Parker jumped in the air before running to the rail.

"I expect that you will uphold our bargain?" Bancroft stood to the side. "You'll recall your minion from my body."

Digby didn't answer, continuing to stare at Autem's fleet as they shrank into the distance.

"Graves?" Bancroft stepped toward him to grab his arm. "You swore to me."

"What?" Digby glanced at him, unsure what he had even told the man. He nodded and agreed regardless, hoping no one would ask more of him. "Yes, whatever you need."

Bancroft removed his hand from Digby's arm and skulked back to the bridge.

"I can't believe it." Alex took the man's place once he was gone, standing by his side opposite Rebecca. "We're free. There's no one trying to kill us. Well, except for the monsters out there, but damn, we can handle that."

"It's time to rebuild," Rebecca added.

"Yes." Digby nodded. "I think that sounds… nice."

"Are you okay?" Alex turned toward him.

"I…" Digby trailed off as he searched for an answer. "I don't think so." He collapsed as the words left his mouth.

"Shit, no." Rebecca dropped down beside him. "He's unraveling!"

"What?" Alex flicked his attention from Digby to her.

"He needs a soul. Without one, his mana system can't repair the damage that being dead is causing to his mind."

Digby looked up at her. "How do you know…?"

"It's why I came back here, to fix you."

"What's happening?" Parker rushed back to them from the rail.

"His mana system is unraveling." Alex looked back at the bridge. "We need a passage back to Vegas. I think I understand how magic interacts with souls and I should be able to figure out a way to help him if we can get to my workshop."

"There isn't time for that." Rebecca shook her head as a tear fell to the deck of the ship. "He's falling apart now."

"It's alright." Digby reached up to her. "I think this is how it ends."

"No." Parker dropped down on his other side. "Don't you do this. You've come too far. I don't even care that you said all that mean shit to me and broke my finger."

"I did?" Digby furrowed his brow, unable to remember what she was talking about. "That doesn't sound like something I would do?"

"Are you really going to gaslight me and then die?" Her voice cracked as she spoke.

"I'm sorry," Digby added as the last few thoughts rose to the surface. He wasn't sure what he was apologizing for, but he knew it was important. "I really am sorry."

"No, you don't get to just apologize and leave." The woman shook her head frantically.

Digby stared up at her face. "Wait, who are you?"

"Damn it, Dig." She lowered her head.

"No, you stay with me." Someone else grabbed him. "You know me, right? I'm Becca, your friend."

"Becca? That's an odd name."

Becca raised her head to the night sky to let out a long, frustrated growl, then she began to glow.

CHAPTER FIFTY-THREE

Nothing.

Nothing passed through Digby's mind.

In the distance, people were talking, but inside, the void was all that was left.

WARNING, complete collapse of mana system imminent. *WAKE UP!*

Digby didn't even read the words. He had no reason to. At least, none that he knew of.

WARNING, complete collapse of mana system imminent. *DON'T YOU DARE LET GO, YOU MINDLESS WRETCH! FIND A MEMORY, A FEELING, SOMETHING, ANYTHING, and for the love of all that's good, HANG ON TO IT!*

Something?

Digby's empty shell of a mind caressed the word.

Anything?

No, there's nothing here.

Then, an ember of power flickered into existence within the endless void.

What's this?

WARNING, a foreign spark has breached your mana system. *YES! THERE! TAKE IT!*

A voice shouted from someplace beyond him. "God damn it, Dig, let me help you!"

Becca?

Digby didn't know why he knew the name, but the lingering traces of memory screamed at him to trust her.

Alright!

The ember flickered into a blaze of power, growing with a flood of disjointed memories. A conversation on a rooftop, music, arguments, gratitude, and sadness. New feelings and memories sprouted up from within him, growing as the strange power poured into him. Each memory reached out to connect with more as an explosion of thought burst into existence.

The faces of friends came next as names linked together. Alex, Hawk, Parker, Mason, Sax. His chest ached as each name that followed came with a swell of emotion. He had cared for these people. Even the ones he'd thought he hated. There was always a flicker of warmth dwelling inside.

The power continued to flow into him, stitching his mind back together with each second. The only question was, where was it coming from?

"Becca!" Digby snapped his eyes open as light filled his view.

"Finally, it's about time you woke up." Becca knelt beside him on the deck of the horde ship, her arms held out beside her as an aura of multicolored light surrounded her. A river of energy flowed from her chest to his as a similar glow grew around him as well. Parker and Alex stood behind her as a nearly full moon hung in the sky overhead. A landscape of clouds stretched into the horizon.

"How in the devil are you doing this?" Digby struggled to push himself up, having trouble controlling his body with so much power flowing into it. "I thought my spark was gone, I thought there was no way to fix me."

She gave him a warm smile. "It's a spell. I got it from the Guardian Core's caretaker so that I could fix your whole missing soul problem."

"Well, you certainly waited long enough!" Digby stared up at her as the power continued to flow.

"Yeah, don't thank me or anything." Becca winced and fell forward, catching herself with one hand.

"What was that?" Digby tried to reach for her but his arm felt too heavy, like he didn't have full control back yet.

"I'm fine," she answered through gritted teeth. "This is just how it works."

"How it works, my deceased ass." Digby shook his head. It was obvious whatever spell she was casting was hurting her. "As you can see, I'm fine now. So you can stop this."

She shook her head. "That's not how this spell works. I can't stop it once it's begun. But you'll have a soul again when we're through."

"How can you give me a soul?" Digby shouted back. "It's not like you have a spare just laying about. Unless…"

A pained expression filled Becca's face, telling him everything he needed to know. She was giving him a soul, alright. Her own.

"No you god damn don't!" Digby forced himself to roll over and started clawing his way toward her.

"I'm sorry, but this is how it has to be." She looked down at him with tears filling her eyes.

"Wait, no." Parker flicked her eyes back and forth between Digby and Becca. "You can't just give up your soul."

"She's right. We're not letting you turn back into a revenant." Alex tried to put a hand on Becca's shoulder, only to pull it away as if he'd been shocked by her aura.

"It doesn't matter what happens to me." Becca shook her

head. "I died. I'm not even supposed to be here. This will just return things to the way they were before I was brought back. Without a soul, I'll return to being a common revenant. Just make sure I don't hurt anyone."

"I don't rightly care where you are supposed to be. I am a walking corpse; I think doing what we are supposed to stopped being a priority some time ago." Digby forced his limbs to obey him as he inched his way toward her. Just a couple more feet and he would reach her. "I don't know how, but I will stop this insanity."

"You're in no condition to stop me." Becca simply thrust out a hand to unleash a swarm of bats out of nowhere. The force of the sudden torrent pushed Digby back several feet to slam him into the outside of the ship's bridge. The tether between them stretched to cover the distance. It may as well have been miles away; he would never crawl his way back fast enough to stop her.

"Don't make this harder than it has to be." Becca's voice quivered. "I'm just glad I got to see everyone one more time. That's enough."

"No it damn well isn't!" Digby snapped his head to Alex as a river of power continued to flow across the deck from her to him. "Don't just stand there, stop her!"

"On it." Alex reached out and touched the stream of energy between them. A burst of light pushed him back as the flow of power bucked wildly through the air while remaining strong. "Crap, it's like trying to grab lightning. It just slips away."

Digby lay where he was, still unable to get up. "Well, find another way!"

"Wait! I know what to do." Alex's face lit up, and without another word, he started running in the opposite direction.

"Stop!" Becca called out to him. "Please! This is how it has to be!"

He turned back as she pleaded with him. "With all due respect, fuck that."

"But I'm a monster!" Becca cried out.

"So am I, and you don't see me throwing my existence away," Digby argued back.

"You don't understand." She shook her head in frustration. "I'm not safe to be around. I'm not like you, Dig. I'm so much worse. I lose control too easily, and I'm too hard to stop. I will hurt someone, or worse." A sob escaped her shaking body. "I don't want to die, but I can't take that chance."

"I understand." Digby pushed himself off the wall he leaned against and managed to get onto his knees and a cackle rose in his throat. "Dangerous or not, all I heard was that you don't want to die and that's good enough for me, damn it!" He snapped his head to Alex. "Go! Find a way to stop this." Then he flicked his eyes to Parker. "You too, use that monstrous will of yours to overpower whatever this spell is. Tear it apart if you have to."

"I can fix this. I have what we need. I found it in Boston!" Alex was moving before he'd finished talking, leaving Parker to defy the spell alone.

"Here goes nothing!" The pink-haired soldier lunged forward to grab the river of power, yelping in pain as the air around it cracked. "Mother shit!" She shook her hands out, then jumped back in, this time getting hold of the stream. The night lit up the moment she did as multicolored power arced across the deck from her hands. She let out a jittery cry, reaching out to grasp the river with her other hand to hold the uncooperative spell steady.

"That's it! Hold on!" Digby reached a hand out to grab the end of the spell as it poured into his chest. Pain lit up his entire body the instant he did. Like his entire mana system was telling him to release it. "I'm not letting you go, Becca!"

"Why are you like this?" Becca forced herself to her feet, raising a hand toward him and Parker to launch a burst of bats in their direction.

Shadow and light clashed across the deck of the ship, filling the night with chaos.

"What the fuck, Becca?" Parker braced as bat wings slapped

her in the face.

"Yes, what the fuck, Becca?" Digby repeated as the bombardment of tiny creatures slowed to a stop. She must have been running low on mana. "Now!" Digby pushed himself back to his feet and threw his body against the bridge while grabbing hold of the spell's tether with both hands. "Pull it apart!"

Parker responded with a shuddering, "I... got... it!" Then she yanked in the opposite direction of him, the spell's tether glowing brighter as they stretched it thin. Bolts of prismatic light burst from the stream of power.

"Cut it out! Damn it!" Becca shouted back. "You're going to get yourselves hurt."

"You should have thought of that before you decided to cast something so dangerous," Digby spat back.

"Do you really want to argue with me right now?" Becca growled.

"Yes, Becky, I do!" He cackled, realizing how much he missed their arguments.

Parker let out a yelp before adding, "You two bicker like an old married couple!"

To which they both responded in unison with a curt, "Shut up, Parker!"

The pink-haired messenger's hand slipped from the spell's tether, barely holding onto it with the other hand, the power whipping around like a hose spraying water. A second later, it pulled taut again as someone reached out from the side to grab hold.

Bancroft gritted his teeth as his other hand closed around the stream of power. "Was it not enough that we just survived an encounter with Henwick? You all felt the need to do whatever this is as well?"

Clearly, he didn't know what was happening.

"It's some kind of soul spell," Parker shouted in his ear.

"I don't care." He shook his head. "I saw the light from the back of the ship. I'm just here to make sure that whatever this is doesn't disrupt the removal of Tavern from my body."

"Hold tighter, bro!" the skeleton shouted from Charles's mouth.

"We've got this." Parker regained her grip holding firm to the spell's tether beside Bancroft.

That was when the sound of boots rushing toward them interrupted the moment. Digby caught a glimpse of Alex running through the bursts of energy pouring from the spell. He carried something with him. Something metal, its surface flashing with reflected light.

"Hold it taut!"

Digby and Parker both yanked with everything they had as Alex jumped into the air, raising what he carried over his head. He brought it down to the deck with a solid thunk as a shock-wave of color blew everyone back, the prismatic light winking out to allow the night to reassert its dominance.

Digby fell back against the bridge, sliding down to the deck. He blinked repeatedly as the sudden change from light to dark temporarily blinded him.

"What happened?" Parker's voice came from nearby. "I can't see anything."

"What have you done?" Becca's voice followed.

"The right thing." Alex's silhouette faded in as Digby's rean-imated eyes finally adjusted. The artificer was crouched, with a broken sword in his hands, its jagged edge resting on the deck.

"That's impossible. The spell can't be stopped." Becca stared at the artifact in his hand. "How could you cut the spell with that?"

Alex took a few deep breaths, holding onto the weapon with both hands. "We found it in a museum. It's famous for cutting a magic ring off a finger to sever its power from its wearer."

"What?" Digby furrowed his brow realizing that Alex's trea-sure hunt might have just saved everyone.

"Its mass enchantment breaks links between spells." He set the weapon down.

"You jackass!" Becca jumped up and started punching him

in the arm. "I was almost done. I could only cast that spell once! It was the only way to fix him!"

"Ow, hey, cut it out." He tried his best to block the attacks. "You did enough already."

"What?" She looked up at him.

"You aren't the only one that has to fix everything. I have been working on solving this problem too." He lowered his hands when she stopped hitting him. "He never needed a whole soul transplant; he just needed a graft."

"A graft?" Becca's arms fell limp at her sides. "What the hell does that mean?"

"It means that souls are resilient. They can heal as long as they're stable." He gestured to Digby. "I'm sure you gave him enough of yours, so I stopped you before you finished. What's left in both of you should just repair itself."

"How could you even know that?" She raised a hand to hit him again but he reached into his bag and pulled out Kristen's skull to stop her.

"Because I have a soul," the deceased seer added matter-of-factly. "We figured out how it happened. That's why I can change over time instead of being a simple construct."

Alex lowered the skull. "We use traces of our spark every time we cast a spell, so the soul must be able to recover itself."

Becca staggered in place before dropping to her knees. "You have to be kidding me. I did all that for... what? Nothing?"

"No." Alex knelt down. "We didn't have a way to put enough of a spark into Digby to make it stable. Without you—"

"I'd be gone." Digby pushed himself up.

"Do you feel like you?" Parker turned toward him. "Any urge to break my fingers?"

Digby winced as the question stabbed at his deepest regrets. "I... I'm sorry about that. About everything. I understand it now." He staggered in place as he clutched a hand over his mouth. "Oh my word, I almost blew up Autem's capital. I almost killed thousands of people who don't even know what's happening."

"And there it is." Parker nodded, looking smug. "Knew there was still someone decent in there."

Digby rushed to her. "You stopped me! You stopped me from doing something horrible. Something I could never take back."

"Sometimes someone needs to save you from yourself." She shrugged. "But it looks like you have your conscience back, so I quit." With that, she dropped down to the deck and flopped over on her back next to Becca. "Wake me when we're back home."

"I can't believe I am going to agree with the young woman, but I am quite fed up with this night as well." Bancroft turned and wandered back to the bridge.

Digby shook his head at them both before turning back to Becca. The vampire trembled where she knelt, still looking stunned. A quick analyze told him that she was no longer listed as a Fool. The empire must have discovered her access and cut it off. Blood stained most of her clothes with large, thick patches of dried crimson. Bullet holes marred her outfit here and there. She had clearly been through a lot. More than any of them.

A lot of it, he could understand.

After all, if anyone knew what it was like to become a monster, it was him. Her skin was as pale as the light of the moon, with pointed ears and a pair of fangs peeking out of her mouth as she breathed heavily. She was going to need help rebuilding her life.

"Come on, Becca." Digby held out a hand to her. "It's time you came home. I don't think any of us are willing to lose you for a second time."

Slowly, she raised her eyes up as she took his cold hand. "What will I do?"

"You'll live." He pulled her up to her feet.

"I knew this would happen." She let out a long sigh. "If I survived, you would just convince me to stay and try to make things work."

"Bah." Digby waved away the comment. "That just meant

you wanted to stay with us from the start."

"Of course I want to stay." She turned to look out at the horizon, wincing as the first rays of light pierced the sky. "You're all the closest thing I've ever had to a family. I want to see you all every day. I want to get to know Hawk better. Hell, I have a guy that loves me and looks good in a cowboy hat. How could I leave that behind?" She deflated. "But maybe you all should start carrying warding rods on you just in case."

"Warding rods work on you?" Alex turned toward the dawn as well.

"Mostly." She nodded. "Sort of depends on the engravings."

"Interesting." Digby walked over to the railing, before looking back to Parker who was still laying on the deck. "You're missing the sunrise."

She raised her head without moving the rest of her body. "So what happens now?"

"What do you mean?" Digby stared down at her as she rolled over and stood up.

"The war is over." She shrugged and joined them at the railing. "Everything we've done has been to fight back against Autem. They're still out there, but they aren't coming to kill us anymore. The way I see it, we just gained a whole bunch of free time. What do we do with it?"

The question hung in the air, feeling too important to answer.

Digby looked to Becca and Alex, the two people that had been with him since the beginning. It seemed like too long since they had stood together like this. So much had changed.

He let his gaze drift back to the horizon and repeated Parker's question.

"What do we do now, eh?"

Digby let a cackle rumble through his chest.

"We do more than just survive and pick up the pieces."

He raised a clawed hand to the horizon.

"It's time to rebuild."

EPILOGUE

Charles Bancroft tugged the hood of a canvas poncho down over his face as he traveled down the stairs of the casino. Upon their return, the horde ship had weighed anchor, floating in the middle of the Las Vegas strip.

That was twenty-two hours ago.

Parker had already got everyone that had been evacuated to Hawaii back to the city. She disappeared to her room in the casino as soon as she finished, probably to sleep for a day or two.

Graves and the rest were welcomed as heroes as soon as news of the war's outcome had spread. They still mourned those that had given their lives in the week's battles, but there was a new air of levity that hadn't been there before.

Rebecca was swarmed with questions about vampires, but Mason had stepped in to tell everyone to back off. Later in the night, Bancroft had noticed the couple by a fountain. Rebecca had been wearing Mason's hat and leaning against him. The sight actually warmed his heart, despite the fact that he'd tried to have them both killed a week ago. It wasn't like he had anything against them. If he was honest, he thought highly of them both. Eventually, the two disappeared upstairs.

Alex, on the other hand, stayed to enjoy the festivities, carrying Kristen's skull as if trying to share the credit for their victory.

Easton wandered into the city at around mid-afternoon, alongside a strange woman with a British accent who vanished into the crowd within seconds.

When night fell, Graves called everyone together outside to watch as they lit up the lights of the Las Vegas strip to let the city shine once again. What followed was a celebration like none other, one that didn't die down until five in the morning, when most of the people finally went to sleep.

Bancroft had watched it all from the shadows, drifting at the back of crowds or the edges of rooms. He wasn't welcome there. Not after everything he'd done. He'd burned that bridge. Technically, Graves hadn't made the knowledge of his return to the city public. It was for the best. Many of the people there would have preferred that he had stayed banished, or that he'd died in the battle.

Unfortunately, the deal he'd struck with Graves could do nothing to find him forgiveness. No, all it would grant him was his freedom and renewed access to his magic. After that, what he did was up to him. All Bancroft had needed to do in return was stick a piece of broken mirror to his back and get captured.

Graves hadn't had time to follow through with his end with everything happening, leaving Bancroft's skeleton inhabited by a fraternity's worth of infernal spirit. A part of him had actually grown accustomed to Tavern's presence, leading him to think long and hard about his situation. The deal wasn't bad.

There was just one problem.

It still gave Graves all the leverage. As long as he was a Heretic, Digby could simply take away his magic with a thought. No matter where Bancroft went or what he did, he would always be waiting for the day he glanced at his HUD and found nothing.

The more he thought about it, the less he could accept it. He had negotiated thousands of deals in his longer than average lifetime, and anyway he looked at it, this deal was bad.

It was time to change the terms.

"Hey bro?" Tavern spoke using his mouth. "What're we doin'?"

"Nothing, don't worry about it," Bancroft answered back.

"We doubt that," the skeleton inside him responded.

"Here, have a drink." Bancroft reached under his poncho and pulled out a flask to take a sip of bourbon. He found that a small taste usually kept the spirit inhabiting his bones quiet.

Tavern remained silent after that. After all, Graves had given the minion no orders. For once, Bancroft could move about freely and Tavern had no reason to stop him. It was the narrow window he needed.

He'd already gotten hold of the most important item on his list, but that still left him a lot of shopping to do.

Stopping by the casino's weapon counter, he broke the door's lock and helped himself to a full load out. Armor, sword, rifle, pistol, and even a backup revolver. He filled a small back-pack with whatever else he could think of. With everyone still asleep, there was no one to stop him.

After that, he headed to the forge. The workers there had taken the day off to celebrate, leaving it unguarded. Passing through, Bancroft entered Alex's workshop. The artificer was sure to have a few things lying about. He filled his bag with warding rods. On his way out, he grabbed the experimental hoverboard that was resting against the door.

Finally, he made his way to the fountain where Alex had placed one of the artifacts that he'd found.

The grail.

The artificer had placed the small, wooden cup in one of those fire extinguisher boxes and secured it to one of the nearby walls. A label on the front read, 'In case of emergency, break glass.' The word emergency had been scribbled out with the word curse written above it.

Bancroft approached the box, making sure to check if anyone was in earshot. Then he smashed the glass with the butt of a pistol and retrieved the grail.

"Heh, sweet." Tavern commented. "Fill 'er up."

"For once, my friend, I think you're right on the money." Bancroft poured one shot's worth of bourbon into the cup and set it down. He dropped his bag next and set it down as well. Unzipping the pack, he reached in for the handle of the first item he'd pilfered.

The broken sword.

He never saw the movie that the weapon was from. He'd never had time for things like that, but he'd seen the description back on the horde ship. Without the artifact, either Graves or Rebecca would be dead. Pulling it out, he felt the weight of it in his hand.

Mass Enchantment: Sever
This item is capable of severing links created through magic.

Bancroft knelt down and placed the butt of the broken weapon on the floor, holding it upright with one hand. He placed his other around the jagged tip of the broken edge. Only about an inch of metal sticking out from between his thumb and fingers. The blade wasn't even sharp, making the point at the end the only part of the edge that could potentially pierce the skin. Even then it would need enough force.

"I hope this works the way I think it will." He took a few deep breaths to calm his nerves.

Then, he slammed his forehead down onto the pointed tip.

Blood trickled from his head as a sharp twinge of pain radiated across his brow. He didn't pull up. Instead, he pressed harder, grinding the metal point into his own skull until a message ran across his vision.

Infernal spirit unbound.

There is an unbound infernal spirit within your body. Do you wish to destroy, free, or claim it?

Bancroft grinned as he pulled the broken sword from his head.

"Claim."

You have claimed an infernal spirit. They will now follow your commands. You have 25 bond points to distribute.

He immediately snatched the grail from where he'd set it down and threw back the shot of bourbon within. The wound on his head closed within a few seconds. Once it was gone, he placed the bloody sword down on the edge of the fountain and stood back up.

In truth, he hadn't expected the Seed to give him control of the spirit inside him. Just that the sword would break the bond Tavern shared with Graves. He'd figured he could bribe them with more bourbon to keep them under control. In the end, he'd gotten far more than he imagined.

Sure, it would have been good to be rid of the infernal spirit, but considering that he could use the minion to double his physical attributes, he could think of better uses for it. He dropped all of his bond points into perception, giving Tavern the ability to sense danger even if Bancroft himself wasn't aware of it.

Shoving the grail into his bag, he felt a little more comfortable. Graves would surely remove his access to the Heretic Seed the moment he found out what he had done. Taking the grail meant he would still have a strong source of healing and a way to cleanse a curse. Not to mention immortality.

"What... did you do to us?" Tavern's confused voice slipped from Bancroft's lips.

"Simple, my friend." Bancroft left the broken sword where it was. "I gave you a change in management."

"You own us?" Tavern sounded worried.

"No." Bancroft shook his head. "You do have to listen to what I say, but I would rather think of this as a mutually beneficial arrangement, more like business partners."

"We are... bros?"

Bancroft grimaced at the term but nodded his head regardless. "Yes, we are bros."

"Cool." Tavern nodded as well.

"Good." Bancroft shouldered his bag, tugged down his hood, and started walking toward the front door of the casino.

"Boss is gonna be hella pissed," Tavern stated the obvious.

"Graves?" Bancroft chuckled before adding a self-satisfied, "Good."

"Where we goin'?" The skeleton within hesitated at the threshold.

"Anywhere we want, Tavern." Bancroft stepped outside. "Anywhere we want."

"Cool." The skeleton walked along with him, making each movement faster and easier.

Bancroft smiled. "You know, Tavern? I think this is the beginning of a profitable partnership."

ABOUT D. PETRIE

D. Petrie discovered a love of stories and nerd culture at an early age. From there, life was all about comics, video games, and books. It's not surprising that all that would lead to writing. He currently lives north of Boston with the love of his life and their two adopted cats. He streams on twitch every Thursday night.

Connect with D. Petrie:
TavernToldTales.com
Patreon.com/DavidPetrie
Facebook.com/WordsByDavidPetrie
Facebook.com/groups/TavernToldTales
Twitter.com/TavernToldTales

ABOUT MOUNTAINDALE PRESS

Dakota and Danielle Krout, a husband and wife team, strive to create as well as publish excellent fantasy and science fiction novels. Self-publishing *The Divine Dungeon: Dungeon Born* in 2016 transformed their careers from Dakota's military and programming background and Danielle's Ph.D. in pharmacology to President and CEO, respectively, of a small press. Their goal is to share their success with other authors and provide captivating fiction to readers with the purpose of solidifying Mountaindale Press as the place 'Where Fantasy Transforms Reality.'

Connect with Mountaindale Press:
MountaindalePress.com
Facebook.com/MountaindalePress
Twitter.com/_Mountaindale
Instagram.com/MountaindalePress

MOUNTAINDALE PRESS TITLES
GameLit and LitRPG

The Completionist Chronicles,
Cooking with Disaster,
The Divine Dungeon,
Full Murderhobo, and
Year of the Sword by Dakota Krout

A Touch of Power by Jay Boyce

Red Mage and
Farming Livia by Xander Boyce

Ether Collapse and
Ether Flows by Ryan DeBruyn

Unbound by Nicoli Gonnella

Threads of Fate by Michael Head

Lion's Lineage by Rohan Hublikar and Dakota Krout

Wolfman Warlock by James Hunter and Dakota Krout

Axe Druid,
Mephisto's Magic Online, and
High Table Hijinks by Christopher Johns

Dragon Core Chronicles by Lars Machmüller

Pixel Dust and
Necrotic Apocalypse by D. Petrie

Viceroy's Pride and
Tower of Somnus by Cale Plamann

Henchman by Carl Stubblefield

Artorian's Archives by Dennis Vanderkerken and Dakota Krout

APPENDIX

NOTEWORTHY ITEMS

THE HERETIC SEED
An unrestricted pillar of power. Once connected, this system grants access to, and manages the usage of, the mana that exists within the human body and the world around them.

HERETIC RINGS
A ring that synchronizes the wearer with the Heretic Seed to assign a starting class.

THE GUARDIAN CORE
A well-regulated pillar of power. Once connected, this system grants temporary access to, and manages the usage of, the mana that exists within the human body and the world around them.

NOTEWORTY CONCEPTS

AMBIENT MANA
The energy present with a person's surroundings. This energy can be absorbed and use to alter the world in a way that could be described as magic.

MANA SYSTEM
All creatures possess a mana system. This system consists of layers of energy that protect the core of what that creature is. The outer layers of this system may be used to cast spells and will replenish as more mana is absorbed. Some factors, such as becoming a Heretic will greatly increase the strength of this system to provide much higher quantities of usable mana.

MANA BALANCE (EXTERNAL)
Mana is made up of different types of essence. These are as follows, HEAT, FLUID, SOIL, VAPOR, LIFE, DEATH. Often, one type of essence may be more plentiful than others. A location's mana balance can be altered by various environmental factors and recent events.

MANA BALANCE (INTERNAL)
Through persistence and discipline, a Heretic may cultivate their mana system to contain a unique balance of essence. This requires favoring spells that coincide with the desired balance while neglecting other's that don't. This may affect the potency of spells that coincide with the dominant mana type within a Heretic's system.

MASS ENCHANTMENTS
Due to belief and admiration shared by a large quantity of people and item or place may develop a power of power of its own.

SURROGATE ENCHANTMENTS

An enchantment bestowed upon an object or structure based upon its resemblance (in either appearance or purpose) of another object or structure that already carries a mass enchantment.

WARDING

While sheltering one or more people, a structure will repel hostile entities that do not possess a high enough will to overpower that location's warding.

RUNECRAFT

By engraving various runes on to a surface through the use of the Artificer's Engraving spell, a object make be empowered with a magical trait. When used in combination, a variety of results can be achieved.

INFERNAL SPIRIT

A spirit formed from the lingering essence of the dead.

HERETIC & GUARDIAN CLASSES

ARTIFICER

The artificer class specializes in the manipulation of materials and mana to create unique and powerful items. With the right tools, an artificer can create almost anything.

DISCOVERD SPELLS:

IMBUE

Allows the caster to implant a portion of either their own mana or the donated mana of a consenting person or persons into an object to create a self-sustaining mana system capable of powering a permanent enchantment.

TRANSFER ENCHANTMENT

Allows the caster to transfer an existing enchantment from one item to another.

MEND
Allows the caster to repair an object made from a single material. Limitations: this spell is unable to mend complex items.

INSPECTION
Description: Similar to a Heretic's Analyze ability, this spell examines an inanimate item with more depth, allowing the caster to see what materials an object is made of as well as enchantments that might be present.

ILLUSIONIST
The illusionist class specializes in shaping mana to create believable lies.

DISCOVERED SPELLS:

CONCEAL
Allows the caster to weave a simple illusion capable of hiding any person or object from view.

VENTRILOQUISM
Allows the caster to project a voice or sound to another location.

REVEAL
By combining the power of the enhanced senses that you have cultivated, this spell will reveal the position of any threat that may be hidden to you and display as much information as available. This spell may also be used to see in low-light situations.

MAGE

Starting class for a heretic or guardian whose highest attribute is intelligence. Excels at magic.

POSSIBLE STARTING SPELLS:

ICICLE

Gather moisture from the air around you to form an icicle. Once formed, icicles will hover in place for 3 seconds, during which they may be claimed as a melee weapons or launched in the direction of a target. Accuracy is dependent on caster's focus.

TERRA BURST

Call forth a circle of stone shards from the earth to injure any target unfortunate enough to be standing in the vicinity.

FIREBALL

Will a ball of fire to gather in your hand to form a throwable sphere that ruptures on contact.

REGENERATION

Heal wounds for yourself or others. If rendered unconscious, this spell will cast automatically until all damage is repaired or until MP runs out.

VERITAS

Decipher truth from lies.

CARTOGRAPHY

Map the surrounding area. A previously mapped area may be viewed at anytime.

MIRROR LINK

Connect two reflective surfaces to swap their reflections and allow for communication. The caster must have touched both surfaces previously.

DICSCOVERED SPELLS:

NECROTIC REGENERATION
Repair damage to necrotic flesh and bone to restore function and structural integrity.

CARTOGRAPHY
Send a pulse into the ambient mana around you to map your surroundings. Each use will add to the area that has been previously mapped. Mapped areas may be viewed at any time. This spell may interact with other location dependent spells.

CREMATION
Ignite a target's necrotic tissue. Resulting fire will spread to other flammable substances.

CONTROL ZOMBIE
Temporarily subjugate the dead into your service regardless of target's will values. Zombies under your control gain +2 intelligence and are unable to refuse any command. May control up to 5 common zombies at any time.

SPIRIT PROJECTION
Project an immaterial image of yourself visible to both enemies and allies.

ZOMBIE WHISPERER
Give yourself or others the ability to sooth the nature of any non-human zombie to gain its trust. Once cast, a non-human zombie will obey basic commands.

BLOOD FORGE

Description: Forge a simple object or objects of your choosing out of any available blood source.

MESSENGER

Determining factor to access this class is unknown.

POSSIBLE STARTING SPELLS:

MIRROR LINK

Connect two reflective surfaces to swap their reflections and allow for communication. The caster must have touched both surfaces previously.

MIRROR PASSAGE

Create a passage between two reflective surfaces capable of traversing great distances. The caster must have a clear picture of their destination.

ENCHANTER

Starting class for a heretic or guardian whose highest attribute is will. Excels at supporting others.

POSSIBLE STARTING SPELLS:

ENCHANT WEAPON

Infuse a weapon or projectile with mana. An infused weapon will deal increased damage as well as disrupt the mana flow of another caster. Potential damage will increase with rank. Enchanting a single projectile will have a greater effect.

PURIFY WATER

Imbue any liquid with cleansing power. Purified liquids will become safe for human consumption and will remove most ailments. At higher ranks, purified liquids may also gain a mild regenerative effect.

Choose one spell to be extracted.

DISCOVERED SPELLS:

DETECT ENEMY:
Infuse any common iron object with the ability to sense and person of creature that is currently hostile toward you.

HEAT OBJECT
Slowly increase the temperature of an inanimate object. Practical when other means of cooking are unavailable. This spell will continue to heat an object until the caster stops focusing on it or until its maximum temperature is reached.

FIGHTER
Starting class for a heretic or guardian whose highest attribute is will. Excels at physical combat.

POSSIBLE STARTING SPELLS:

BARRIER
Create a layer of mana around yourself or a target to absorb an incoming attack.

KINETIC IMPACT
Generate a field of mana around your fist to amplify the kinetic energy of an attack.

SPECIALIZED CLASSES

NECROMANCER
A specialized class unlocked buy achieving a high balance of death essence withing a Heretic's mana system as well as

discover spells within the mage class that make use of death essence.

STARTING SPELLS:

ANIMATE CORPSE

Raise a zombie from the dead by implanting a portion of your mana into a corpse. Once raised, a minion will remain loyal until destroyed. Mutation path of an animated zombie will be controlled by the caster, allowing them to evolve their follower into a minion that will fit their needs.

DECAY

Accelerate the damage done by the ravages of time on a variety of materials. Metal will rust, glass will crack, flesh will rot, and plants will die. Effect may be enhanced through physical contact. Decay may be focused on a specific object as well as aimed at a general area for a wider effect.

DISCOVERABLE SPELLS:

ABSORB

Absorb the energy of an incoming attack. Absorbed energy may be stored and applied to a future spell to amplify its damage.

BURIAL

Displace an area of earth to dig a grave beneath a target. The resulting grave will fill back in after five seconds.

CONTROL UNCOMMON ZOMBIE

Temporarily subjugate the dead into your service regardless of target's will/resistance. Zombies under your control gain +2 intelligence and are unable to refuse any command. May control up to 1 uncommon zombie at any time.

EMERALD FLARE

Create a point of unstable energy that explodes and irradiates its surroundings. This area will remain harmful to all living creatures for one hour. Anyone caught within its area of effect will gain a poison ailment lasting for one day or until cleansed.

ANIMATE SKELETON

Call forth your infernal spirit to inhabit one partial or complete skeleton. Physical attributes of an animated skeleton will mimic the average values for a typical human.

FROST TOUCH

Freeze anything you touch.

TALKING CORPSE

Temporarily bestow the gift of speech to a corpse to gain access to the information known to them while they were alive. Once active, a talking corpse cannot lie.

FIVE FINGERS OF DEATH

Create a field of mana around the fingers of one hand, capable of boring through the armor and flesh of your enemies. Through prolonged contact with the internal structures of an enemy's body, this spell is capable of bestowing an additional curse effect. Death's Embrace: This curse manifests by creating a state of undeath within a target, capable of reanimating your enemy into a loyal zombie minion. Once animated, a zombie minion will seek to consume the flesh of their species and may pass along their cursed status to another creature.

SUMMON ECHO
Temporarily recall the echo of a consumed spark to take action. The actions of a summoned spark may be unpredictable and will vary depending what type of spark you choose to summon. More control may be possible at higher ranks.

MURDEROUS WRAITH
When summoned, this spark will manifest and attack a target that is currently hostile to you. Due to the skills of the consumed spark, this spell has a high probability of dealing catastrophic damage to a target.

CRONE
When summoned, this spark will call upon the remnants of the lingering dead to grab hold of a target and prevent movement. This spell will last until the target is either able to break free, or until canceled.

HONORABLE CLERIC
When summoned, this spark will manifest and heal one ally.

HOLY KNIGHT (GUARDIAN ONLY)
A class that specializes in physical combat and defense. This class has the ability to draw strength from a Guardian's faith.

TEMPESTARII
A class that specializes in both fluid and vapor spells resulting on a variety of weather-based spells.

AREOMANCER
A class that specializes in vapor spells.

PYROMANCER

A class that specializes in heat spells.

ROGUE

A class that specializes in stealth and movement spells.

CLERIC

A class that specializes in life spells.

PASSIVE HERETIC ABILITIES

ANALYZE

Reveal hidden information about an object or target, such as rarity and hostility toward you.

MANA ABSORPTION

Ambient mana will be absorbed whenever MANA POINTS are below maximum MP values. Rate of absorption may vary depending on ambient mana concentration and essence composition. Absorption may be increased through meditation and rest.

WARNING: Mana absorption will be delayed whenever spells are cast.

SKILL LINK

Discover new spells by demonstrating repeated and proficient use of non-heretic skills or talents.

TIMELESS

Due to the higher than normal concentration of mana within a heretic's body, the natural aging process has been halted, allowing for more time to reach the full potential of your class. It is still possible to expire from external damage.

ZOMBIE RACIAL TRAITS (HUMAN)

BLOOD SENSE
Allows a zombie to sense blood in their surroundings to aid in the tracking of prey. Potency of this trait increases with perception.

GUIDED MUTATION
Due to an unusually high intelligence for an undead creature, you are capable of mutating at will rather than mutating when required resources are consumed. This allows you to choose mutations from multiple paths instead of following just one.

MUTATION
Alter your form or attributes by consuming resources of the living or recently deceased. Required resources are broken down into 6 types: Flesh, Bone, Sinew, Viscera, Mind, and Heart. Mutation path is determined by what resources a zombie consumes.

RAVENOUS
A ravenous zombie will be unable to perform any action other than the direct pursuit of food until satiated. This may result in self-destructive behavior. While active, all physical limitations will be ignored. Ignoring physical limitations for prolonged periods of time may result in catastrophic damage.

RESIST
A remnant from a zombie's human life, this common trait grants +5 points to will. Normally exclusive to conscious beings, this trait allows a zombie to resist basic spells that directly target their body or mind until their will is overpowered.

VOID
A bottomless, weightless, dimensional space that exists within the core of a zombie's mana system. This space can be accessed

through its carrier's stomach and will expand to fit whatever contents are consumed.

ZOMBIE MINION TRAITS (AVIAN)

FLIGHT OF THE DEAD
As an avian zombie, the attributes required to maintain the ability to fly have been restored.

BOND OF THE DEAD
As a zombie animated directly by a necromancer, this creature will gain one attribute point for every 2 levels of their master. These points may be allocated at any time. 7 attribute points remaining.

CALL OF THE DEAD
As a zombie animated directly by a necromancer, this minion and its master will be capable of sensing each other's presence through their bond. In addition, the necromancer will be capable of summoning this minion to their location over great distances.

ZOMBIE MINION TRAITS (RODENT)

SPEED OF THE DEAD
As a rodent zombie, the attributes required to maintain the ability to move quickly have been retained. +3 agility, + 2 strength.

BOND OF THE DEAD
As a zombie animated directly by a necromancer, this creature will gain one attribute point for every 2 levels of their master. These points may be allocated at any time. 7 attribute points remaining.

CALL OF THE DEAD

As a zombie animated directly by a necromancer, this minion and its master will be capable of sensing each other's presence through their bond. In addition, the necromancer will be capable of summoning this minion to their location over great distances.

ZOMBIE MINION TRAITS (REVENANT)

BOND OF THE DEAD

As a zombie animated directly by a necromancer, this creature will gain one attribute point for every 2 levels of their master. These points may be allocated at any time. 9 attribute points remaining.

NOCTURNAL

As a zombie created from the corpse of a deceased revenant, this zombie will retain a portion of its attributes associated with physical capabilities. Attributes will revert to that of a normal zombie during daylight hours.
+8 Strength, +8 Defense, +4 Dexterity, +8 Agility, +5 Will

MINOR NECROTIC REGENERATION

As a zombie created from the corpse of a deceased revenant, this zombie will simulate a revenant's regenerative ability. Regeneration will function at half the rate of a living revenant. Minor Necrotic Regeneration requires mana and void resources to function. This trait will cease to function in daylight hours when there are higher concentrations of life essence present in the ambient mana.

MUTATION PATHS AND MUTATIONS

PATH OF THE LURKER

Move in silence and strike with precision.

SILENT MOVEMENT

Description: Removes excess weight and improves balance.

Resource Requirements: 2 sinew, 1 bone

Attribute Effects: +6 agility, +2 dexterity, -1 strength, +1 will

BONE CLAWS

Description: Craft claws from consumed bone on one hand.

Description: .25 sinew, .25 bone

Attribute Effects: +4 dexterity, +1 defense, +1 strength

PATH OF THE BRUTE

Hit hard and stand your ground.

INCREASE MASS

Description: Dramatically increase muscle mass.

Resource Requirements: 15 flesh, 3 bone

Attribute Effects: +30 strength, +20 defense, -10 intelligence, -7 agility, -7 dexterity, +1 will

BONE ARMOR

Description: Craft armor plating from consumed bone.

Resource Requirements: 5 bone

Attribute Effects: +5 defense, +1 will

PATH OF THE GLUTTON

Trap and swallow your prey whole.

MAW

Description: Open a gateway directly to the dimensional space of your void to devour prey faster.

Resource Requirements: 10 viscera, 1 bone

Attribute Effects: +2 perception, +1 will

JAWBONE
Description: Craft a trap from consumed bone within the opening of your maw that can bite and pull prey in.
Resource Requirements: 2 bone, 1 sinew
Attribute Effects: +2 perception, +1 will

PATH OF THE LEADER
Control the horde and conquer the living.

COMPEL ZOMBIE
Description: Temporally coerce one or more common zombies to obey your intent. Limited by target's intelligence.
Resource Requirements: 5 mind, 5 heart
Attribute Effects: +2 intelligence, +2 perception, +1 will

RECALL MEMORY
Description: Access a portion of your living memories.
Resource Requirements: 30 mind, 40 heart
Attribute Effects: +5 intelligence, +5 perception, +1 will
Units of requirement values are equal to the quantity of resources contained by the average human body.

PATH OF THE RAVAGER
Leave nothing alive.

SHEEP'S CLOTHING
Description: Mimic a human appearance to lull your prey into a false sense of security.
Resource Requirements: 10 flesh.

TEMPORARY MASS
Description: Consume void resources to weave a structure of muscle and bone around your body to enhance strength and defense until it is either released or its

structural integrity has been compromised enough to disrupt functionality.

Resource Requirements: 25 flesh, 10 bone.

Attribute Effects: +11 strength, +9 defense.

Limitations: All effects are temporary. Once claimed, each use requires 2 flesh and 1 bone.

HELL'S MAW

Description: Increase the maximum size of your void gateway at will.

Resource Requirements: 30 viscera.

Attribute Effects: +3 perception, +6 will.

Limitations: Once claimed, each use requires the expenditure of 1 MP for every 5 inches of diameter beyond your maw's default width.

DISSECTION

Description: When consuming prey, you may gain a deeper understanding of how bodies are formed. This will allow you to spot and exploit a target's weaknesses instinctively.

Resource Requirements: 10 mind, 5 heart.

Attribute Effects: +3 intelligence, +6 perception.

PATH OF THE EMISSARY

Demonstrate the power of the dead.

APEX PREDATOR

Description: You may consume the corpses of life forms other than humans without harmful side effects. Consumed materials will be converted into usable resources.

Resource Requirements: 50 viscera

BODY CRAFT

Description: By consuming the corpses of life forms

other than humans, you may gain a better understanding of biology and body structures. Once understood, you may use your gained knowledge to alter your physical body to adapt to any given situation. All alterations require the consumption of void resources. Your body will remain in whatever form you craft until you decide to alter it again.

Resource Requirements: 200 mind

Limitations: Once claimed, each use requires the consumption of void resources appropriate to the size and complexity of the alteration.

LIMITLESS

Description: Similar to the Ravenous trait, this mutation will remove all physical limitations, allowing for a sudden burst of strength. All effects are temporary. This mutation may cause damage to your body that will require mending.

Attribute Effects: strength + 100%

Duration: 5 seconds

Resource Requirements: 35 flesh, 50 bone, 35 sinew

MEND UNDEAD

Description: You may mend damage incurred by a member of your horde as well as yourself, including limbs that have been lost or severely damaged.

Resource Requirements: 50 mind, 100 heart.

Limitations: Once claimed, each use requires a variable consumption of void resources and mana appropriate to repair the amount of damage to the target.

Made in the USA
Columbia, SC
17 October 2024

44557667R00416